Jack DeNova is the most feared and respected "no-holds-barred" prize fighter the world has ever seen. No man can match his strength and determination in, or out, of the caged ring. Anger and lost love fuel his rage, his ultimate weapon in any fight.

But even his strength in battle cannot stop the unraveling of his world when he is targeted by a dangerous Russian mob family. When tragedy strikes his personal world, he is thrust into the shadows of the Federal witness protection program, but the darkness of his violent past won't give him up that easily.

On the run from a powerful crime lord bent on vengeance, Jack risks blowing his cover to protect a beautiful and mysterious woman. Together, the two find comfort and safety in each other as they struggle to survive…and with their emerging feelings for each other. Leaving one life behind and struggling to begin another is now the greatest battle Jack will ever fight.

Full of adventure, love, plot twists and desperate struggles for survival, *Undefeated In Love and War* is the story of every person's struggle to leave the past behind and turn to the only one who can make the future worth living for.

UNDEFEATED
IN LOVE AND WAR

UNDEFEATED
IN LOVE AND WAR

By
Carman

Destiny Image₀ Fiction, Inc.

P.O. Box 310
Shippensburg, PA 17257-0310

ISBN 0-7684-2221-3

For Worldwide Distribution
Printed in the U.S.A.

1 2 3 4 5 6 7 8 9 / 09 08 07 06 05 04

This book and all other Destiny Image, Revival Press, MercyPlace, Fresh Bread, Destiny Image Fiction, and Treasure House books are available at Christian bookstores and distributors worldwide.

For a U.S. bookstore nearest you, call
1-800-722-6774.
For more information on foreign distributors, call
717-532-3040.

Or reach us on the Internet:
www.destinyimage.com

Table of Contents

Introduction

It was about ten years ago that I was introduced to a world I will not soon forget—a world that is not a work of fiction and really does exist as does its participants. Being a boxing fan all my life, I have always been intrigued with these modern-day gladiators—a man-to-man sport, two guys, no excuses, no one to pass the ball to, or should I say "to pass the gloves to," and all done under the most grueling of physical tests. It has always appealed to the weekend warrior in me.

That is, until I was watching TV while on tour and saw an ad for a whole new brand of competition that would be as outside of the box as anything can be. The ad said "Coming this Saturday to pay-per-view...The Ultimate Fighting Championship...No rules, No rounds, No judges, No weight limit, No time limit...judo verses karate, kung fu verses boxing, wrestling verses jiu jitsu...watch and see who is the best real-life fighter in the world!" I couldn't believe my ears. It sounded so barbaric, so vicious, so crazy...I had to see this!

What I saw changed my perspective on adrenaline-pumping sport competition forever. The best of the best were there, but the sport was dominated by a family of brothers lead by their father, all from Brazil. They were the Gracie Family. Undefeated in 75 years of no-holds-barred competition. Could this be true? And amazingly, they all were little guys...no more than 180 pounds, squaring off with 280-pound, muscled-up human assassins. But they won. They beat them all.

I had to talk with these men. After discovering that they had an academy in Torrance, California, I made contact. They were the most respectful and nicest people I'd ever met. We became fast friends. Their objective was to prove to the world that they could teach "the little guy" not to be pushed around by the giants of life. So I watched and learned and trained with them and heard their inner voices.

What you are about to read is a series of several true stories that are woven together to make one—things I saw, experienced, and was taught, just by observing. Many thanks to my good friend, creator of the U.F.C. and head of the clan, Rorion Gracie.

Some creative license has been taken to make this book into a novel, but little is fiction. The characters are real people with heart, huge families, determination, great pride and an unusual respect for their parents. They have experienced the greatest victories and the worst of human tragedies. From an American's point of view and a novelist as well, join me as I take you on a journey of love and war you won't soon forget. Names have been changed to protect the dangerous.

Chapter 1

The Roller Coaster Ride Starts Here

The office had the look of money—big dirty money trying to look legit, like a street punk in a too slick Armani suit. Floor to ceiling, the walls were dark mahogany with smooth dark columns spaced every five feet, their tops carved like a Greek temple and painted gold. An immense plate-glass window took the place of one wall, almost running the length of the room except for a sitting area at the far end. There, grouped in front of a giant screen TV, were sleek couches and armchairs. Outside and below the window spread the Miami skyline and its high-rises along the beach, sprawling into the ocean. The window curved slightly inward, as if the room itself surrounded the entire city. The walls arrogantly jutted forward, spreading to engulf the entire town, almost symbolic of the frame of mind of its owner occupant.

Between the columns on the opposite wall hung paintings, masterpieces of art, paling in the bright sun blazing through the window, suggesting the owner didn't know the damage the light would do—or simply didn't care. The paintings were vulgar scenes of death and power: a suffering matador gored by a dying bull, condemned gladiators pausing before the imperial thumbs-down, a blood-thirsty mob cheering an uncaring Caesar. Between the paintings hung far more lurid posters, red and black images of men throwing punches. The posters were advertisements for boxing matches, each emblazoned with the phrase: "The Colvack Group Presents…" touting bouts between household names like "Holyfield," "Tyson," "De La Hoya"—fights with big hype and bigger money. Rivers of cold cash that flowed into one faceless source: the Colvack brothers.

Yet neither window, paintings nor posters attracted the gaze of the man seated at a large marble table at the head of the room. The infamous head of the clan, Johnny Colvack, stared at papers on the table ignoring the room with the air of a man with little genuine respect for the priceless treasures he owns, vainly caring that they were his. The art, the posters, even the room itself were simply trophies to him, signs of power and ownership, nothing more.

Johnny Colvack was fifty-one, his dark hair streaked only at the edges with gray. His rigid body filled his tailored, blue pinstriped suit. He was obviously very fit and not given to indulgences of the flesh. His face was harder still, cold and calculating—deeply lined, yet ruthlessly handsome. He mumbled to himself as he counted numbers. His accent was obviously Russian, but his English was clear and distinct. He'd come to America on a mission. But something about his face and features suggested it was a dark one. Scanning papers without a twitch, his eyes were keen and his movements quick and sure as he flipped through the stack.

Double doors burst open into the office with an explosion of sound. Two burly men spilled through the door at the same time, laughing and shouting. Only family could get away with this type of entrance into Johnny's domain without getting destroyed. In came his two younger brothers. One bigger than the other.

First came Bruce. His athletic and cocky six-foot, 185 well-toned pounds were neatly outlined by an expensive designer jogging suit.

Bruce was followed by his big brother Mike. Mike looked like a force to be reckoned with, and he was. He stood at an imposing six-foot four-inches, and a steely 240 pounds. Dressed in a black leather jacket, tee shirt, jeans and handmade cowboy boots, he was a killing machine if there ever was one.

Neither one carried the elitist European air that Johnny displayed. They were pure East Coast thugs, with New Jersey accents that were obviously out of place in Miami. They were first-generation Americans who were trying too hard to fit in. Still, their chief goal in life was to impress their older brother Johnny.

"We killed em, Johnny! We killed em!" Bruce, the youngest, shouted as a third man entered the room behind them whose movements were more controlled, but his enthusiasm no less evident.

This was Hal. Second-in-line to the family dynasty and Johnny's generationally "juiced in" second banana. He was slick and well dressed too, but in a more sporting way than

Johnny. His custom-made burgundy silk shirt and pants matched perfectly with his custom-made burgundy suede shoes. Hal's Russian accent was equally impossible to hide, but less pronounced than Johnny's. He also was a bit more American in thought and action than his highly disciplined older brother of five years.

Bruce waved a videotape about like a trophy. All three younger siblings resembled Johnny in look, though definitely not in manner.

Johnny looked up, his stern face betraying only a slight wave of irritation.

"Brothers, brothers, please," he said with the tone of someone used to controlling the unruly. "I am trying to concentrate." His voice was crisp, with his thick but raspy Russian accent. "I have a promotional meeting with a Sam Bentley. I am *trying* to put something together for *us all...* Hal?"

He appealed to the third and eldest member of the clamoring trio.

"Sorry, Johnny, they're just excited." Hal shrugged his shoulders and spread out his hands as if to say *What cha gonna do?*

When he spoke to his older brother, his Russian accent thickened noticeably.

"Mike's got this video of his U.F.C. win from Mexico City."

"His what?" Johnny snapped back, irritated that something had occurred outside his approval.

"The U.F.C.!" called out Mike, the largest of the three intruders. "The Ultimate Fighting Championship!"

He slapped both fists down on the marble tabletop and leaned towards his brother.

"Johnny, I'm gonna make you a boatload of money. This is the future, Bro."

Unlike Johnny and Hal, Mike had yet to really prove himself and in his Jersey tough-guy way was trying to show Johnny he could come up with something new, something even Johnny didn't know about.

Johnny doubted that Mike would earn him much of anything, and his expression showed it. In Johnny's eyes, Mike was the one in the family with more muscles than brains. His disdain was painfully obvious.

An actual moneymaking idea? Johnny was quietly amused, but like a dutiful parent figure he gave his brother a slice of his attention. *Maybe, for once, he had something to contribute to the business.* He stared at Mike with controlled annoyance as he righted a penholder that had fallen over when Mike hit the table. Instinctively Johnny liked order.

"C'mon Johnny, my big brother is the U.F.C. Champ," yelled out Bruce from in front of the television. Bruce waved the videotape. "You got to see this!" Bruce jammed the tape into the VCR below the screen.

Sighing, Johnny lifted himself from his chair. Mike leapt over the back of the sofa in the viewing area and landed with a thud in the thick leather seat. Hal pressed a button on the wall, and vertical blinds slid silently across the window. The screen glowed and came to life. Johnny moved across the room, positioning himself behind the sofa, arms crossed, face impassive.

An announcer's voice boomed from the speakers.

"Here we have it, Jeff, the final showdown between Mike *the Monster* Colvack and Stan *Slam* Summers."

The severe faces of two sportscasters appeared on the screen. Behind and below them was an arena filled with screaming spectators surrounded by a large octagon, a cage of metal and cyclone fencing. Then the scene changed showing two men in Speedo-type athletic shorts, hands covered by black, lightly padded, sparring gloves, the type with the fingers and thumbs showing. The fighters' ankles were wrapped with tape. They stood facing one another at opposite ends of the cage fidgeting, loosening their muscles. One of the men was Mike Colvack.

"Mike *the Monster* is volatile and dangerous, six-foot, four-inches and 240 pounds of fighting nitro," the second announcer called out excitedly. The camera cut to a close-up of Mike, his eyes narrowed and focused. His expression was deadly.

"He'll have his hands full with *Slam,* four-time World Greco-Roman Wrestling Champion, two-time Sambo Champ of all Europe and undefeated in the Octagon," added the excited second announcer.

Stan was a hulking brute, the same size as Mike but not as defined in his muscularity. Thick and hairy, his over-confident air filled the screen.

Youngest brother Bruce snickered.

"We're about to see a massive train wreck," the announcer continued.

Bruce's snicker turned into a snort.

The television screen switched to a wide-shot of the two fighters mentally preparing to snap on the other. A referee in the center of the octagon shouted, "Let's get it on!" He danced quickly out of the way as the two men moved toward each other.

"Here they go, and it's…"

The announcer's sentence trailed off in astonishment as Mike exploded onto his opponent, snapping out a blur of four front kicks that landed into Stan's chest. Six punches followed like machine gunfire, hammering each side of his head. It all happened in less than twelve seconds. This stunningly quick attack sent Stan reeling backwards, arms flailing, striking nothing but air.

Stan's back slammed into the fencing as Mike moved in for the kill.

While Stan was still positioned against the fence, Mike loaded up and nailed him with two devastating rights to the temple.

Stan was failing, falling to his side, and the referee rushed in to halt the carnage. Mike's killer instinct was quicker than both gravity and the ref.

A fountain of blood gushed from above Stan's eye. In seconds, dark purple welts swelled on his face as internal bleeding formed great pools of blood under the skin. Stan slid to his right and flopped facedown on the mat as the paramedics rushed in, even before the ref could break up the action.

Mike Colvack, drunk with victory, spun around throwing his two fists up in the air in total dominance. Mayhem broke out around and behind him.

"Oh, my God!" the announcer gasped.

The train wreck was over in less than thirty seconds. Stan lay on the mat, blood streaked across his face. He breathed shallow, rapid breaths while his foot twitched involuntarily. But that was his only movement.

Mike's jubilant face filled the screen as he paraded around the cage, arms high in triumph. The crowd screamed.

The Mike that sat on the sofa reached his arms behind his head in satisfaction. Bruce stopped the tape.

"That is unbelievable," breathed Hal, frozen in his place by a window.

"Unbelievable?" cried Bruce. "My brother is a monster! An absolute freak of nature!"

Johnny said nothing. He stared at the darkened screen, expression unchanged, as if the event he had just witnessed was merely a line in a contract, something to be considered and kept if useful or removed if not.

The three brothers looked at him expectantly…

Johnny finally broke the silence. "This is what we do to guys who don't pay what they owe. As far as making money on it, I'll stick with a solid Roy Jones, Jr. fight. Gentlemen, please stop thinking like thugs and start thinking like businessmen. Hal, we need to talk…"

It would take much more than a show of brutality to impress Johnny. Though no stranger to the bloodthirsty fighting style, he didn't consider it a moneymaker. That is, not as yet…

The Bentley Meeting

A sharp knock broke the uncomfortable silence. Johnny turned towards the sound, and the question of the fight vanished with his movement. Johnny and the brothers looked to the already open door. She stood poised with the confidence of a woman who understands her own power—and knows that others lack the same quality. She was strikingly beautiful, her skin a rich tan, her hair long, thick, and black. A simple black business suit was perfectly tailored to show off her figure, while clearly sending a message that she was there solely on business. A chocolate-brown, leather file folder jutted crisply from her folded arm to accentuate the point. She could have stepped out of *Vogue* magazine, were it not for the calculating, determined look that marked her as far more than a fashion model.

Her dark eyes took in the room at a glance, surveying and analyzing everything and everyone in an instant. Bruce let out a low appreciative groan that Mike cut off with a quick elbow to the shoulder. The woman ignored both the groan and the elbow and focused her attention only on Johnny.

"What can I do for you?" asked Johnny, his intimidating tone slightly more demanding than his words.

"I think it's more like, *What I can do for you*," replied the woman, not in the least moved by Johnny's manner. She stuck out her hand, "I'm Samantha Bentley, promoter for the Fun Side of Miami."

"You're Sam? Sam Bentley?" Johnny replied in a tone of disbelief.

The woman flashed a mildly sardonic smile.

19

"Are you really gonna make me endure the never-ending testosterone dribble about my being a woman, or are we gonna do some business?"

The brothers stared at Johnny as if they half expected him to throw her out. The silence lasted just long enough that the same thought seemed to flicker in the woman's eyes. Then Johnny shrugged and gestured to a chair at the table.

"Have a seat," he said, dismissing the tension with a wave of his hand. "Let's do some business."

Samantha took the chair opposite Johnny's, as the others moved to their typical places around the table. Mike and Bruce sat at the ends of the table. Hal moved to a chair near Johnny's right. Johnny returned to his chair, easing into it like a board chairman taking his place.

"Ms. Bentley, I'm Johnny Colvack."

She nodded.

"These are my brothers, Hal, Mike, and Bruce. As you know, I own several hotels in Atlantic City and Miami. I'm looking for some new and fresh entertainment to keep my elite clientele satisfied."

"Mr. Colvack, I'm well aware of who you are," Samantha said, implying with her tone that she knew Johnny was far more than a hotel owner. "I wouldn't be here if I wasn't. I know the eight hotels and casinos you own and operate. And I know how you got them."

Hal glanced at Johnny sharply, but Johnny just listened impassively.

Samantha continued. "I also know what you need to keep the customers coming back for more. I've been in promotions since I was fourteen."

Hal looked unimpressed.

"I started running modeling shows with my mother, graduated to concerts, and ultimately moved into the entertainment business of the casino world."

Hal interrupted, his tone smug, "Hey, Miss, how do we know you understand *our* game?"

Samantha ignored Hal and looked at Johnny. "Johnny, who's in charge here? You or him?"

Johnny shrugged off the challenge. "Hal is my assistant. He runs things here for me in Miami. But…"

She cut him off. "But you run the whole carnival, so let's not waste time. I talk to you and you alone. Deal?"

Bruce and Mike stiffened at the retort, while Hal's expression changed from smugness into an angry glower.

A mixture of hardness and interest crossed Johnny's face. He nodded at Samantha. "Deal."

At the statement, Hal's glare seemed to refocus on Johnny, though he said nothing.

"I realize there's big money in the boxing game," she continued. "I've promoted everybody in the fight world from Sugar Ray Leonard to Mike Tyson to Oscar De La Hoya to Roy Jones, Jr. And they do bring in the high rollers—but nothing pulls down the big dollars from the mega-money people like the underground no-holds-barred fighting scene."

Johnny nodded his interest, "I think I am a bit familiar with this whole scene."

Mike and Bruce grinned towards each other. Only Hal continued to look unhappy.

Samantha pulled a paper from her folder and slid it across the table in front of Johnny. It was a printout from a spreadsheet, with a long list of figures.

Johnny glanced towards it without picking it up—but his glance said that he had scanned it for what he needed.

Hal bent over and stared at the page as if concentrating to follow its meaning.

Samantha did not wait for him to look up. "You're thinking of the Ultimate Fighting Championship…that it's now a legitimate sport. They call it Mixed Marshall Arts Competition. It has rules, rounds, time limits, judges, weight classes, and a governing organization. I'm talking about something entirely different. Something that will draw the hard-core partygoer and spender to you and you alone. What I do is create an event that is the grandfather, so to speak, of the U.F.C. But this type of fight has no rules, rounds, judges, time limits, or weight classes. In Brazil, where this type of event originated, they call it "Vale Tudo," pronounced *val-lay-two-doe.* It means "anything"—and I do mean *anything,*—"goes." It's purely underground and illegal in the States. But…we make millions every weekend from these events."

She nodded towards the paper.

"We'll make more in bookmaking, betting, and gambling off these cage fights than eight major boxing matches make in a year—mainly because these fighters are like the old Mafia dons. Not known to the mass public, but the most dangerous things walking. And compared to what you'd pay for a DeLahoya, they cost next to nothing."

Mike's expression soured. "Hey, wait a minute. I take that as an insult."

Johnny raised his hand gently. "Mike, I'll take it from here."

Mike quieted and sank deeper into his chair.

"Sam, my brothers are fighters," Johnny explained calmly.

Samantha didn't react.

"Cage fighters, as you say," he continued. "Mike here just won the Ultimate Fighting Championship—the pay-per-view event."

Mike's look indicated she ought to be impressed.

Samantha returned it with a cool expression that said she wasn't, even in the slightest.

Johnny ignored the war of glances. Suddenly he was reassessing his previous opinion of Mike's newfound fame.

"And my youngest brother, Bruce, is right behind him. They could be players in our business…"

Samantha's eyebrows raised slightly at this.

"But I won't bore you with their credentials. Just be aware of your surroundings."

She nodded.

Johnny gestured to the spreadsheet page. "But please, do go on."

Samantha looked Johnny directly in the eyes. "Please understand, Mr. Colvack, that I am not talking about the Ultimate Fighting Championship or any such sanctioned event. Anyone can do these and be limited to the comparatively minor profits they raise. They might as well do professional wrestling. I am talking about true no-holds-barred fights. No rules, rounds, time limit, weight limit, judges. The referee really is only there to pull someone off of an opponent when he no longer can defend himself—mainly to protect someone from death. It's the closest thing to two Roman gladiators fighting to the finish you will ever see. These men are an entirely different breed. They walk in that octagon knowing they could die. That's what makes it so attractive to the money people. Because anything can happen and anything goes. Only the most ruthless, meanest, best-trained, fistic assassins even consider entering such an arena. It's breathtaking."

"Fine by me," Mike interrupted. "Get rid of the referee, and I can take 'em out that much quicker."

Samantha ignored him, her concentration remaining on Johnny. "Mr. Colvack, we are talking entertainment for the rich and famous," she said. "Something that is exciting and something they can't get anywhere else—and they'll pay for it."

She glanced briefly towards Mike.

"But mind you, they know their fighters. They follow them like they're basketball or baseball stars. Name fighters draw in big spenders. I can put the names together that will bring in the money."

Johnny tapped his hand on the spreadsheet page. "What's in it for you?"

Samantha seemed to be working to hide a subtle grin. She had Johnny hooked, and she knew it. "I get fifteen percent of the gross. With the right fights, we'll do ten to twelve million. If it goes well here in Miami, we'll take it to all eight of your hotels, Mr. Colvack."

She could see the numbers adding up in Johnny's mind. She knew the deal was all but done.

Hal snorted derisively interrupting everyone's thoughts. "But it's illegal in the U.S.," he said dismissively. "The better fighters won't come here."

Samantha stared calmly at Hal, but spoke across the table.

"Johnny, I've taken care of the local authorities. We *must* keep it illegal. That's what makes it enticing."

She turned back to face Johnny. "My job is to bring the right fighters in and out of the country safely—and then we're all loving life."

Hal glowered again, but backed down.

"I'm ready," said Mike.

Johnny and Samantha looked at him. "I just won the U.F.C." He grinned with confidence.

Samantha shook her head gently. This time she spoke with respect. "Someday maybe, but not now. You're not enough of a name yet," she explained. "The most popular names are people the public at large never heard of. And they are spread all over the world. Only other fighters know them, at least they know their reputations. And they are not necessarily the biggest guys you ever saw. They just win fights— real fights to the finish."

"Great! I'm in!" Bruce almost yelled it. "I'm ready to roll. I'm a second-degree black belt in Kung Fu. I got two A.A.U. Tournament Championships."

Samantha raised her hand. "Hold it, we're not talking resume. We're talking box office." She turned back to Johnny. "There are two fighters you want to open your series, and I can get them both."

Johnny held his hand up to quiet Bruce's response. "Why should I let you be the matchmaker?" His tone suggested the question was as much a reminder of who he was as it was an inquiry.

"My first husband was an underground fighter. He was killed in a no-holds-barred fight in Bolivia. So I really do feel like this world of warriors owes me something," she replied with a renewed confidence. "I know them all. I promoted fights in Japan, China, the Philippines, the fateful one in Bolivia and here in the U.S., but mostly in Brazil where it originated. Nobody will do a better job for you than I."

She pulled more papers out of her folder—two glossy, black-and-white photos clipped to lists of stats and fight names. She didn't wait for Johnny to acknowledge his acceptance of her role before pushing the first photo across the desk.

Choose Your Weapons

"Now there are two names that will push an immediate button in this underworld community." She tapped the first photo. "Number one is Yamo Zakura."

Johnny glanced at the picture. A thickset oriental man wearing only a pair of waist-to-knee spandex pants stared out of the photo. He was crouched in a Judo stance, arms ready, reaching for action. His glaring expression seemed almost as formidable as his oversized body.

"He's a legend in Japan," Samantha continued. "They treat him like he's a god in his country. They have comic books and video games on him. He's big, flamboyant, and dangerous—the Dennis Rodman of the no-holds-barred world. Best yet, he's never been stopped. His only two recorded losses involved controversial decisions. And they were in legitimate national competitions. He's had over two hundred underground wins."

Bruce looked on with interest, while Mike was nodding his head as if he recognized the name.

"I know his manager real well," Samantha said. "I can get him for $40,000 plus entourage and expenses."

Johnny commented as if thinking out loud, "As compared to De La Hoya, who costs $15 million."

Samantha added, "Plus, he just won the Vale Tudo Tournament. Only Brazilians win that one; he's the first non-Brazilian to win."

Mike couldn't contain himself. "Zakura is the man!" he agreed with excitement. "I'd fight him any day, anytime, anywhere!" He looked ready to try.

Lighting the Fuse

Samantha's grin surfaced widely across her face. The meeting was going very much her way. She slid the second photo across the table.

"The second fighter is a little touchy, cause he doesn't have a manager. I'll have to deal with him directly."

"Who is it?" Bruce was leaning in for a better view of the photos. Mike's excitement was infectious, and Bruce was obviously very impressed.

"Jack DeNova."

Bruce had heard the name. "Jack DeNova? I can destroy him myself! He…"

Johnny cut off his exuberance. "Hold it, Bruce. Sam, tell me about this guy."

"He was born in Buffalo, New York. His parents are missionaries in Brazil, so he's a transplant. When his parents chose to stay in Brazil, Jack decided to study jiu jitsu so he wouldn't get his butt kicked every day. He's actually closer to his trainer than he is his own father. DeNova is legendary in South America. The man to beat. U.F.C. has been trying to get him for years, but he won't go because of all the rules and limitations. He is a purest. Trained as a child to destroy. A fight to him is like a cup of coffee to us."

"Yeah…" Mike interjected, "The no-holds-barred scene is like baseball down there in Brazil."

Samantha nodded slowly. "Well, obviously he strayed from the faith of his mommy and daddy—maybe out of rebellion, or self-preservation—whatever."

Clearly DeNova's motivations meant little to her.

"He started training in a jiu jitsu academy at age seven under the legendary champ Marco Brudel. By sixteen he was fighting in competitions for money. Brazilians see him as one of their own, a true countryman, but he cross-trains…"

"What's that mean?" Again Hal was reasserting his presence.

Mike took up the explanation. "He doesn't just study jiu jitsu, which is basically like deadly wrestling. They get a hold of you like an anaconda around a zebra. Then it's all over. DeNova's unusual in that he also trains in the kicking and punching arts, like Tae Kwon Do, Hapkido, and Muay Thai. He combines them all into his own thing. Because Brazil is along the Amazon jungle, they nicknamed him 'King of the Jungle' in a Japanese tournament. Nevertheless, his main discipline remains Brazilian jiu jitsu. It's there he is the ultimate artist—trains ten hours a day, six days a week…every fighter knows this guy."

Bruce stood up and slammed his hand on the table. "I can still beat him. I want him for me!"

Johnny rubbed his forehead. "Bruce, shut up." The command was icy.

Bruce sat down and said nothing.

"DeNova's never fought in the States." Taking Johnny's cue, Samantha steered the discussion back to the numbers. "It will cost $50,000. He is used to getting $10,000 to $20,000 a pop. Plus, he is undefeated in three hundred and two bare-knuckled fights. He doesn't do it for the money anymore; he does it for the honor of his fighting style. So he has to have a good reason to fight now. And we have one. The Brazilians are funny about things like this. They believe that since they started this phenomenon that the most prestigious title of 'Vale Tudo Champion' belongs to one of their own. Jack would bite on this. He'd love to reclaim the Vale Tudo title for his country and bring it back home. Plus, he's a legend. When you say the 'King of the Jungle' is coming, it's big—and I mean *big box office*."

Johnny leaned back into his chair, resting his elbows on the armrests, fingers intertwined, considering. "Would you safely say a fight between DeNova and Zakura would bring in what we need?"

Samantha's grin turned into a brilliant smile. "Give me the money and the OK, and I'll give you an event that will make you a very happy and an even wealthier hotel owner."

Johnny nodded and returned her smile. "Get me Jack DeNova, and you've got a deal." He rose and shook Samantha's hand.

From his chair, Bruce threw out an attempt at the final word. "I can still beat him on my worst day."

Mike laughed. "You can't beat *me* on your best day."

Samantha said nothing; she didn't care who beat whom as long as there was money in it for her. And this deal promised her a lot of money. They all nodded at each other, and Samantha disappeared into her world of money and motion. It was a new day in Miami. Business was about to change for the Colvacks forever.

Chapter 2

A Visit to the Lions' Den

A black luxury car rolled through the back streets of Rio de Janeiro. Kids in ragged, ill-fitted clothes watched the car, their eyes as hungry and suspicious as alley cats. Cars like this did not enter their neighborhood unless the driver was thoroughly lost, extremely confident, or very dangerous. The car entered a street where a small cluster of young men—barely older than boys—lounged beside an empty storefront. As the shiny vehicle slowed nearby, they rose from their languor and moved towards it. A handful of dirty children following the car saw the men and scattered.

The car rolled to a stop in front of a run-down warehouse sandwiched between a vegetable market and a shoe repair shop. The men eyed the building and the sign over the door: Brudel Jiu Jitsu. Without a word, the group broke apart, some returning to their lounging spot, others melting into side streets. No one approached the car.

The driver's door of the luxury car opened, and the black stockinged, shapely leg of Samantha Bentley stepped out of the car. She ignored the men and the children, barely glancing at the poverty-stricken surroundings. She had been here many times and displayed neither fear nor compassion for the neighborhood and its people. They meant nothing to her; her face was focused on the building directly in front of her. With the same confidence she had shown entering Johnny Colvack's office, she walked through the doors of the jiu jitsu academy.

The interior belied the shabby appearance of the building and its neighborhood. Samantha Bentley entered a large area filled primarily by a sizable gymnasium, clean and well lit. Thick padding that covered the floor continued up the walls to a height of about five feet. Sunlight streamed through skylights in the roof, forming squares of light on the padded floor. The room smelled of sweat, rich and thick like incense. Men and boys stood around the room, some stopping in the midst of grappling sessions. No one's head turned towards Samantha; for everyone's attention was drawn to a lone figure in the center of the room. Samantha's attention was fixed there as well.

The man from the second photo stood in a square of sunlight. She was now in the presence of the famed Jack DeNova. He seemed to exude a sense of calm and peace. His dark eyes almost betrayed a glint of humor. He was not at all the fierce killing machine she expected. He was six-foot tall and wore a white gi, the loose fitting traditional garb. A band of three stripes crossed the ends of a black belt that surrounded his body. Yet, Samantha's attention seemed sharply drawn to the well-defined contours of his steely muscles, still visible as he moved. He could have been mistaken for a fitness trainer, except that his thick neck marked him as an athlete ready for combat.

DeNova looked to be in his mid- to late-thirties, his hair black and thick. He wore it cut close to his head so an opponent's hand couldn't find anything to grab. His ruggedly handsome face seemed surprisingly unmarked for a man who made a living in extremely physical confrontations. His lean body was deeply tanned a golden copper, baked in by years in the hot Brazilian sun. Still, he did not have the look of a native of Rio. Through the years, he somehow remained noticeably American. His stance was loose and comfortable, his expression neutral. Except to breathe, he did not move.

An older man wearing a similar gi and belt walked around him. He was unquestionably Brazilian, his black hair heavily grayed, his face weathered and lean. "Marco Brudel Jiu Jitsu Academy" arched cross the back of his gi. He eyed the fighter with a sly smile, and stepped towards a CD player sitting on the floor.

The old man punched a button, and the sound of drums, congas, and deep percussion music filled the sweaty room. The music pulsated with a steady rhythm, the sound of a jungle, of a creature wild and dangerous and about to attack. The shadow of a grin briefly touched the face of the fighter; clearly the music was as familiar to him as a sacred ritual would be to a priest. The old instructor turned with steely determination and spoke in Portuguese.

"Jack, come on. Let's get going. You've been here long enough to know what this music means. Let's turn up the heat."

The man, drenched in sunlight and glistening sweat, laughed and spoke back in the native language. *"I hear you, Marco; you're the boss. I've been hearing you yak about turning up the heat for over twenty-five years. What have you got for me today?"* The tone of both men was jovial and familiar, their conversation part of a ritual as old as their friendship.

"Just a little music for you to dance to," Marco grinned back. *"C'mon, show me some technique!"*

Samantha, watching on intently, could not understand the exchange, but she followed what happened next. Marco nodded, and all the students rose from their positions of entanglement on the floor to quickly scramble with uncharacteristic chatter to line the walls of the dojo. Today was a once-a-month occurrence that all the students anticipated with eagerness. Some had joined the dojo solely based upon a desire to be present when this day arrived.

In Portuguese, it was loosely referred to as "the challenge day." This was when Marco would allow any fighters, from any discipline, to line up and take on the legendary Jack DeNova. The contenders could do anything they wanted. Any tactics were permissible to try to bring as much to their individual wars as they were capable of.

Marco was a tough trainer who understood that the best way to prepare a warrior for a war was to bring him real wars. Warriors from all four corners of the fighting world now came to lay their best offerings of brutality on the altar of the King of the Jungle's private little ceremony. Fighters and martial art experts were eager to fly in from other countries just to test their skill against the one they called "the man."

Now Marco motioned towards a small group of bystanders. These were the challengers of the day. Unlike the students, they were not dressed in traditional jiu jitsu gis. Some wore gis of other colors and other styles, some were bare-chested in shorts with their ankles and wrists taped, two were in one-piece wrestling suits, and another in the silk shorts of professional boxing. Their garb and manner distinguished them as outsiders, instructors of karate, hapkido, kung fu, kenpo, greco-roman wrestling, and western boxing.

Samantha's practiced eye read their features and stances, and she knew them to be true masters of their styles—men with the nerve to enter this dojo and challenge the man at the center of the room. Like a young gunslinger in an old western, each hoped to make his name by fighting the greatest of them all—and the greatest of them all looked more than ready. Samantha also was a student of the game. She could see the art that went beyond the madness and violence of the event. And she respected the vocation. Her husband had been a brutal fighter who taught her every nuance of the profession. Underneath her crisp, clinical exterior, Samantha Bentley was a huge fan at heart. She knew fighters as a doctor knows anatomy.

The first challenger stepped forward and nodded, signaling he was ready to begin. *Hmmm...fourth-degree black belt in kung fu,* Samantha thought to herself, reading his garb as another might read a racehorse.

35

The challenger formed his stance.

Yes, Argentinean style, she thought... *very interesting.*

Human Fireworks

The men faced each other, Jack's eyes focusing on his opponent. The challenger eyed Jack warily, moving around, looking for an opening. Jack barely moved except to shift his body, tracking the circling opponent like a gun turret on a battleship. Suddenly Jack's opponent darted in, throwing two lightning kicks at Jack's chest. Jack stepped easily backwards and the kicks fell short, striking only air. The man plunged forward again, snatching at Jack's gi with his hands—but Jack had already made his move.

In an instant, Jack dove under his opponent's grasping arms, seizing him around the waist in an unbreakable bear hug. The challenger kicked and chopped frantically, but he was helpless to find a target. Jack was glued to the man's waist, too far inside the blows for them to cause any harm. Jack wrapped his legs around the opponent, whose arms were starting to flail in panic. With a violent spin of his torso, Jack slammed his challenger onto the floor. As the contender seemed barely to be comprehending what had just happened to him, Jack spun his body around again. In a flash, Jack was positioned in a sitting position on his chest. From atop his challenger, he began to rain down punches into his face.

Stunned and about to lose consciousness, the man rapidly slapped the floor with his other hand, five, six times, signaling surrender. He admitted defeat.

Jack acknowledged his opponent's submission, pushed himself off his opponent by pressing into his chest and stood up. The challenger rose unsteadily. Graciously, Jack offered him his hands, and they shook vigorously.

The bystanders applauded their delighted approval.

Samantha watched briefly as the shaken man moved off. *Nothing like a Bruce Lee movie, is it? No shouts, no high-flying kicks to dazzle the audience,* she thought wryly of the man. *It's more like what happens when...animals attack.* She pictured an alligator latching onto a startled deer, pulling it off its feet and helplessly into the water. *Yes, that's exactly what it's like. Another world entirely.*

Her glance returned to Jack. A sparkle of admiration reflected quickly in her eyes. Marco had already selected another opponent, a 5th-degree karate master from a dojo in Sao Paulo, Brazil. The name of his dojo was emblazoned in gaudy orange script across a black gi. The new challenger started with a high kick.

Didn't you watch the last guy? thought Samantha.

Again, DeNova slipped under the kick and grabbed the supporting leg. Jack lifted the karate master off the mat and slammed him back down to the ground face-down. Again, Jack was on him, spinning him around, hooking his legs around his opponent's back, twisting until he faced away from the mat—a dangerous place to be...Jack quickly wrapped his arm around the man's neck, like a child holding on to his dad in the deep end of a pool, and yanked him backward. It was a perfect display of the devastating and deadly classic chokehold.

Samantha smiled at the sight of the classic choke. It was the Ali shuffle of the mixed martial arts world. *Fight's over, pal. I wonder if you know it yet?*

Jack tightened his grip, closing the man's carotid arteries.

He's stopping the blood flow to your brain, friend, thought Smantha. *You have about six seconds to tap out or it's night-night time.*

As if on cue, the man tapped Jack on the side of his leg. Marco quickly pulled Jack off.

Good thing. That little move can have permanent results. Mr. Fancy Gi must have ticked DeNova off. Samantha nodded to herself.

Challenging a man in his own dojo was best handled with decorum. The flashy black gi suggested that decorum was not in the man's character—and he had nearly paid dearly for his indiscretion.

Nothing flashy about DeNova, she mused. This is definitely not Hollywood. It's so simple, yet so animalistic. But the skill, the balance, the technique—they're mesmerizing to watch. DeNova knows the deadly art of his craft like no one else in the world.

Samantha watched with satisfaction as one by one Marco selected an opponent and one by one Jack defeated them. Jack finished off each challenger differently, each of his moves unique. His attackers experienced side chokes, front chokes, rear chokes, ankle locks.

Double Jeopardy

And then, suddenly, Marco did something that no one expected. He selected two opponents to go against Jack at the same time. Two against one. A murmur buzzed through the group of watching students as if a trapeze artist were about to attempt a triple flip and asked for the net to be dropped.

The selected men, two Japanese kenpo senseis, stepped up to the mat. They approached in traditional karate stances, throwing strikes and kicks, which Jack blocked with superb skill by simply backing up and slapping what was left of the force of the blows away with his hands. Then Jack suddenly stepped between them, and with a surprise double-kick of the same foot, dropped them both with kicks that landed squarely in the center of their torsos.

The first sensei, caught in the solar plexus, collapsed. His breath gone, he rolled on the mat gasping for air. The second managed to jump back up, looking very unsure about what to expect next.

Samantha grinned. *You weren't expecting him to do any kicking, were you?*

Jack didn't continue kicking. Instead, he went after the kenpo master like a boxer on crack, throwing punches so fast the man couldn't see them, let alone block them. A punch to the jaw, to the side, three more to the face, four to the torso—Jack drove the man backwards. The sensei lost his senses and his balance. He fell back hard, bouncing off the wall and slumping to his side.

Samantha eyed the fallen men. *I could have told you that these **two** against that **one** wouldn't be fair.*

The wrestler and boxer next in line looked at the two fallen men, then each other.

Samantha could read their expressions easily—*We don't need any of this!*

Both men stepped quickly away from Jack, bowing out of the impromptu competition.

The students in the dojo applauded, yelling cheers and shouting Jack's name. Marco waved them back to their sessions, and the students began training again with a new fervor—each one imagining he was Jack DeNova, able to take on anybody, anywhere, anytime.

Marco tapped the stereo and the music stopped. *"OK, Jack, that's enough for today!"*

The opponents all looked as if they agreed.

The old man frowned at Jack. *"Maybe tomorrow you'll do something to impress me."*

Jack laughed again. *"The day I impress you is the day the building belongs to me."*

Marco smiled and joined in the laughter, slapping his star pupil on the back.

Samantha studied the two with interest, waiting. Jack turned his head to spot her, raising an arched eyebrow in a surprised look. He grabbed a towel and walked towards her wiping trickles of sweat off his face.

"[You're] Samantha Bentley," he said to her, his tone as much a question as a statement.

"I don't speak Portuguese," Samantha replied calmly.

Jack grinned. "I'm so sorry," he said in English. His voice had no more accent than a man from Ohio. "I'm so used to this place, eight to ten hours a day, I almost forget I speak English. Can we go in my office and talk?"

He motioned to a low side structure that jutted into the gym. Samantha followed his direction towards the open door into the side room.

Jack turned towards Marco and spoke, again in Portuguese, *"Marco, come with me. I want your impressions."* The old man nodded and followed them in.

The office was small and bright, lit by fluorescent lamps clamped to a white particleboard ceiling. One wall had a plateglass window looking into the dojo. The other walls were lined with cheap paneling, covered with newspaper clippings and shelves of trophies and medals. Most of them featured Jack, although one clipping seemed completely out of place. It was a small article from a stateside paper picturing an older couple in front of an old mission-style church. The headline read, "Arthur and Julia DeNova Celebrate 25 Years in the Amazon."

A small desk sat next to the window, a strictly industrial piece, gray painted metal with a Formica top. A framed copy of the picture from the article stood on the desk next to a state-of-the-art computer.

Samantha was impressed, because a computer was a very rare thing in this neighborhood. The fact that it still sat on the desk was a testament to the respect—or fear—the neighborhood had for the dojo.

Two well-worn office chairs sat on either side of the desk. Samantha slipped into one and eyed the clippings and trophies. Her glance fell on the article about the couple, but she quickly dismissed it and moved on to a cover photo of Jack on a martial arts magazine. Jack's white gi broke her gaze as he moved around her. He picked a gold medallion and chain off the desk and slipped it around his neck. When he sat, the chair settled under him with a raspy squeak. Behind her, Samantha glimpsed Marco as he placed a dented folding chair by the door as if he were a spectator.

Jack grinned at her. "Obviously, Miss Bentley, our Brazilian sunshine loves you." He waved towards the beams streaming through the skylights. "As you can see, it has come out to greet you today." His smile was very winning.

"Well, thank you, sir. That's very flattering." Samantha returned the smile with a polite one of her own, though still pleasant. Her eye fell on Jack's medallion. "I'm curious about that medal you have hanging around your neck. What does it mean?"

Jack held up the medal as if he had forgotten its presence. "Oh this? It was given to me when I won the finals in the Battle Cage Tournament in Japan. It says, 'King of the Jungle.' I don't know about the king part, but I am from the jungle." He dropped the medal back on his chest and grinned widely at her again. "Speaking of the jungle, what brings someone as beautiful as you to this part of the world?"

Samantha flashed back her own smile; if there was a hint of the shark about it, Jack didn't look as if he minded.

"Jack, we have figured out a way where you can fight in the U.S. and make $50,000 guaranteed, with no troubles from the law."

Jack gave a nod as if he was pleased by the amount she'd mentioned. "Sam, that sounds like a beautiful deal— appropriately so, if you're here. And since you're here, I'm sure it must be true. So who would I be fighting?"

"Zakura," she replied, watching for his reaction.

Jack sat back in his chair. The hinged squeaked in low protest. "Good fighter. Be nice to bring the Vale Tudo title back home." His tone was low, almost to himself. He looked back at Samantha. "And for whom would I be fighting?"

"The Colvack brothers."

Samantha heard a low grunt from Marco. Jack's eyes darted to his mentor.

He spoke casually in Portuguese. *"Boss, I know what you are thinking. Let me finish with her, then we'll talk."* He turned back to Samantha, his smile gone. "You know they're dirty. I want all my bases covered."

"Jack, please." Her tone was soothing and unconcerned. "I have this totally under control. You have nothing to worry about. Besides, this will really bring mixed martial arts competition into the U.S. The Colvacks want this to go right." She gestured to the magazine cover. "And for that to happen, we need you, Jack. We need your name."

Jack glanced at the cover, then back to Samantha. She could see him thinking her offer over. He absentmindedly placed his hands on the arms of the chair, tapping the metal with his fingertips in a rapid staccato beat. She could see that tattooed across his knuckles were the letters V-A-L-E on his right hand and T-U-D-O on his left.

43

"I'll talk it over with my trainer…" he began, then shrugged as if to say *why not?* "He'll give me a hard time, but when's the date?"

Samantha smiled. She knew the play on his pride would work. "June eleventh. Can you be ready by then?"

Jack grinned. "Miss Bentley, I'm ready right now. I'll need plane tickets for myself and three people, and security three days before and two days after. You know the routine."

She nodded with confidence. "I've got it all; just say 'yes.' "

"It's not fair that you're a woman," Jack laughed. "I haven't learned to say no to beauty yet." He leaned across the desk and held out his hand. "You're on. I'll be there."

Samantha shook the hand with pleasure. "Thanks, Jack. I'll treat you right. This is the first of many."

Jack held her hand with both of his, and said in an exaggerated stage whisper, "If I win, as a bonus I want a kiss."

She slipped her hand gently out from between his. "If you win, I'll kiss you and Marco."

Marco looked at them curiously at the sound of his name. Jack laughed. "I'll keep that secret to myself."

Chapter 3

The DeNova Ritual

The next day found Jack driving his sturdy-but-solid, forest green jeep down a dirt road in northern Brazil. The road was barely wider than one lane, heavily rutted, and deeply pitted. On one side of the road was a wall of lush, green growth towering high above and hanging over the road like a thick canopy. On the other side stretched the wide waters of the Amazon River.

Jack's sleeveless tee-shirt exposed his dark tanned torso to the Brazilian sun. On each bicep was a tattoo; the green, yellow, and blue Brazilian flag rippled on his left, and the navy-blue N.Y. of the Yankees boldly on his right. He hummed to himself, unaware that he did so, the soft, melodic murmur hinting at a voice both rich and pleasant.

On the seat beside him, bouncing along with the jeep, sat a small box wrapped in bright pink paper. A shimmering pink bow sat perched on top. The package seemed completely out of place on the dusty, dark vinyl, with the murky river rushing past. As always, bumping along the primitive road, raising the customary giant cloud of dust behind him on the way to his mom and dad's house gave Jack plenty of time to reflect.

At least once every week or two he made the same journey. The ride took nearly an hour, time enough for Jack's mind to file through the same series of emotions and memories. It became a ritual that prepared him to enter a world that was completely opposite of his own.

Many times he would try to turn on the radio and play some music or pop in a favorite C.D. But eventually the ritual would take over. He would end up shutting off the music to allow himself to mentally detox, to rewire his brain, re-traveling the journey from his present life of controlled brutality to the simple mission started thirty years prior. Over the years, Jack had learned to accept this little mental ritual, realizing his need to ramp up emotionally for each of these controlled encounters. So much unfinished history remained between Jack and his parents that the ritual nearly resembled what others go through when a close loved one is near death and their own life scrolls before their eyes. Jack was far from any near-death experience. But he did have to die to his current life, even if only but for a few hours, in order to reenter the world of his parents.

Unconsciously as he approached the mission, his mind began to rehearse the steps that led to him to the life he now knew. His decisions, how he got to where he was, and the hurtful events of the past began to play over in his head. Still, he never doubted that it was well worth undergoing the ritual to see his parents. He loved and respected them a great deal.

So...as he drove along with the wind blasting in spurts through the open windows, the jeep bumping along on the dirt road, his suntanned face reflected his deep, faraway thoughts, smiling, frowning, or scowling depending on the memory.

It has always been the same succession of events that has flashed before his mind, and he has even found himself speeding up or slowing down as a particular memory affects him.

First he recalls the friends he had in Buffalo, New York, and the security of relationships he had with other kids who would run out and play at a moment's notice. They were the good buddies he walked with to school every day. Then there was the excited anticipation of returning home to play in his big backyard. That grassy yard had two great apple trees, which he climbed every day like a set of stairs that had to be ascended first before he could even think of entering the house.

Mom and Dad were the epicenter of that childhood world, and they provided a warmth and comfort that made him completely unaffected by the dangers and difficulties of the adult world. Dad was always there to wrestle with or teach him how to play football. Art DeNova was quite a physical force to be reckoned with before he got saved—an ex-marine who made his name as "the Punisher" in boxing clubs on the barracks. He was famous for the damage he would cause to other soldiers with just a few blows of his naturally oversized hands. Even in a simple sparring match, Arthur DeNova, aggressive by nature, was much stronger than even he realized.

But Art had a soft side. This tenderness was no more evident than when he drifted into one of the small civic centers on a lazy weekend to watch the musical *Cabaret* produced by a local theater company with talent supplied by a nearby Assembly of God church. Art thought it was a laugh, a bunch of church kids trying to turn up the heat on a play like *Cabaret*. He had nothing else to do, so he decided he would take it in, if only for a few laughs. Art was due for release from the Marine Core in two months and he had built up some extra "weekend leave" that he was now cashing in before he left.

The cast was really pretty tame, as he thought it would be, even changing a few story lines to accommodate their church background and moral ground rules. What he hadn't anticipated was the lead character, Sally Bowles. This girl was gorgeous. She obviously was a trained dancer and singer and had such a presence that Art was mesmerized by her. She had long, beautiful legs like a dancer, and her face was pretty and almost sweet. She also had high cheekbones, short black hair, pale green eyes, and a smile that would make any mother insist her son marry this woman today.

Art waited around after the performance until the crowd of about 120 cleared the theater that sat about 400. He made up his mind that he wanted to meet this girl. Maneuvering his way backstage, he walked by a young girl with long, curly auburn hair and a yellow sundress who seemed totally out of place.

"Say, kid, where's the chick who played Sally Bowles?" rapped the thick marine.

Sheepishly, she looked up at the hulking man with black hair and flashing eyes. Well over six-foot, two-inches tall and thickly muscled, not to mention the Marine uniform, he would have been an impressive figure to any woman.

She uttered in barely a whisper, "Oh, that was me."

Art was in shock and in love at the same time. The young woman had the sweetness of somebody you'd take home to meet Mom and the fiery adventurous spirit of somebody you'd take home to meet Dad. From that day on, Art DeNova was at the Assembly of God church every time the doors opened.

Julia Martina

Though he was trying to get close to this unusual combination of fire and ice named Julia Martina, something else started to happen that Art didn't plan on. He also was getting closer and closer to the Lord. When Art accepted Christ at a Sunday night service, Julia's heart finally came out from hiding. Three months later they were married by the pastor of the church and now that Art was out of the military service, they were off to the northern part of the state—Buffalo to be exact, to start a new life together.

DeNova had a few relatives on his father's side who lived there. Going back would allow him to provide a sense of extended family and home, he reasoned. And should they start their own family, the children would have cousins to play with. For some quick work, Art became a bouncer at the local pub and picked up a few easy bucks, but soon realized that life wasn't for him anymore. He had come to despise his old way of life; a lifestyle built around intimidation had lost its appeal.

Art found another job making home deliveries for a furniture store, and eventually Julia joined him as receptionist. Over an extended period of time they continued in faithful service to the church and hard work at the job. Eventually they were promoted to a management level and became a team in the business. This was when their one and only son was born. They named him after two Bible characters: John and David.

John David DeNova. For a while his dad called him J.D. But that all changed the day that Julia was singing to her two-year-old son an old classic ballad, "I Don't Know Why I Love You Like I Do." He looked into her face with his giant, dark eyes and started to try and sing it back to her. It just stole her heart right there on the spot.

She decided that her little prince was born with her own natural love for the arts. From that moment on, she started to call him by a name that played off the nicknames Art and Julia had for each other. Art was the king of hearts, and Julia was the queen of hearts. That left the jack of hearts. She would call him Jack.

From that moment on, John David was "Jack." The name stuck. And since Julia was always an admirer of John

Kennedy whose nickname was Jack, that sealed it. Jack DeNova was his moniker from that moment on.

Art was a forceful, war-like sort of man, where Julia was the sensitive, artistic one. Art's fearlessness in the world became resolute boldness in the ministry. He often held small evangelistic meetings in the roughest sections of the city. Just one look at him and local thugs thought twice about giving him a hard time.

Jack, a more sensitive soul, was often found at his mother's side. She would sing to him and watch movies with him. Every drama was an adventure, as Julia carefully explained to her son the story lines and what makes a movie good or boring. Both loved mysteries and would play games trying to figure out the plot before each movie was over. Eventually, Jack could unravel even the most complicated movie after about twenty minutes. He enjoyed a beautiful, active relationship with both his parents, but he was the joy of his mother's life.

Then, on one otherwise uneventful Sunday morning, a couple came into church with five children in tow simply known as "The Wilson Family" to talk about a two-week annual mission's trip they were taking from their home in Tampa, Florida, in order to help the poor and needy children in Brazil. Art and Julia were so moved that they decided to take one of these two-week excursions with Jack. Two months later, after school left out for vacation, they got to Rio de Janeiro, and saw the needs firsthand. Art, in his aggressive and fearless way, decided right there on the spot they should leave Buffalo and move to Brazil. Jack didn't realize what it all meant, and Julia was naturally hesitant, but both soon would find out the consequences this decision would make on their behalf.

As Jack drives on, his hands tense against the wheel and his grip tightened as thoughts of his first year in Brazil are resurrected in his mind.

He sees himself in a new school not understanding the language. He hears the laughter and feels the humiliation as local toughs mock him in Portuguese using profanity and laughing because he can't understand. He relives getting beat up almost every other day by these unusually proficient fighting juveniles.

Jack was always returning home, lunch money stolen, bruises around his face. He would lay on his bed at night and cry for hours, begging his parents to take him home. He hated Brazil. Art provided little comfort. He despised weakness, but refused to teach his son how to defend himself. Something inside of Art just couldn't put his mind back into that zone. As a minister now, Art considered that his religious trappings forbade him from helping his son learn to fight. Perhaps he was afraid of what he would teach Jack. Perhaps he saw some of himself in Jack and didn't want to feed it.

But Julia was always there to comfort Jack. He was her heart. She would hold him, sing to him, and make him laugh and ultimately feel better. Inside, however, Jack began to resent his father. Art brought them into this new painful life.

Jack began to stop listening during the church services, staring blankly instead as his father spoke.

Julia could see the changes in her son. As the months rolled on, Jack developed a certain hardness and a distance from his father. That distance would eventually include the church and its activities. By the end of that first year, Jack stopped coming home bruised and broken. The side of his father that Jack inherited by nature began to surface, and Jack learned how to strike back at his aggressors. But it wasn't long before Jack's self-defense tactics started to go over the top. Every time he faced a tormentor on the streets, he lashed out at him as if he were responsible for everything that went wrong in Jack's life. All of Jack's angst would come out when he fought. Deep in his heart he was his mother's son…but in order to survive the rough streets of Rio de Janeiro, he became his father's evil twin.

Jack bumped along the dusty road and glanced at his watch. Another twenty minutes. Jack would need to decelerate his adrenaline, and the one thought that always worked was the memory of the first time he saw Marco Brudel. It was outside of a local restaurant that he first watched a towering man begin to shout and scream profanities at a smaller man for taking his parking space. He'd better move his car or get the beating of his life, the red-faced giant of a man threatened. The smaller man remained perfectly cool and unaffected in the face of what appeared to be certain destruction. Then Jack, along with the crowd of people who had gathered, gasped as the huge man took a vicious swing at the smaller one. But the little guy ducked under the blow and tackled the big man in a most unusual way.

Inexplicably, the big guy went flying backwards, smacking down his back on the hard pavement. The smaller man seemed like a magician. He crawled up the fallen torso of this man and did something to his arm that made the big man actually cry out in pain like he was being electrocuted. Jack was in awe. The people around him started to cheer like it was a soccer game. Finally, the little guy casually got up off the sobbing bully and straightened out his clothes.

Jack rushed over to the man, and in his newly-learned, fractured Portuguese, said, *"That was amazing! I've never seen anything like it. How did you do that to him so quickly?"*

The man looked at Jack and smiled. He was a little bigger than he appeared from a distance. The larger man made him look smaller. At five foot ten inches and 190 pounds, he looked at Jack and said, *"He could hear the birds singing but he didn't know where."* It was an obvious traditional mock to the fallen foe.

Then with a warm smile he reached out his hand to shake Jack's hand and said, *"My name is Marco Brudel. I teach jiu jitsu at the Brudel academy around the block."*

An instant bond was made between them. Jack blurted out, *"Can you teach me how to do that?"*

Marco smiled and said, *"Son, that's what I do for a living."*

That was it for Jack. He was sold. Down to the bone, Jack wanted to *be* Marco Brudel. He knew his parents would never pay for him to take jiu jitsu lessons, so he went to Marco's school and begged him for a cleaning job, washing gis, scrubbing mats, anything…if he would only be able to take lessons there. Marco respected Jack's rare determination and took him under his wing. Jack and Marco became inseparable. The faster Jack learned, the more attention Marco gave him. Within five years, Jack earned a black belt and a steady job as an instructor at the academy. While the chasm between Jack and his dad grew deeper, his father's responsibilities at the mission increased. Jack drew ever closer to Marco. They were often mistaken for father and son.

Julia knew what Jack was doing. Eventually events came to a head when the Wilsons, who brought the DeNovas to Brazil in the first place, came to visit with their five children. In the mission playground, Jack demonstrated how to escape headlocks to the oldest sons while the two daughters watched in fascination. Art noticed and blew a fuss as never before. It became a point of separation for Jack and his father.

Soon Jack needed an outlet for his built-up aggressions beyond the sportsman-like competitions at the academy. Young Jack wanted to taste the blood of real-life war. That's when Marco introduced him to the small money world of underground no-holds-barred fighting. Jack jumped at the opportunity and began fighting for money at the age of sixteen.

Beating men twice his age, Jack was making Marco proud. But when Art learned about the new lifestyle, he forbade Jack from living at home anymore, and Jack had to move out. So he moved in with Marco.

Despite the escalating tensions, Julia did a masterful and charming job at keeping the family together. After a couple years of stubborn polarization passed, Art and Jack began to accept each other's choices in life. They decided at one of Julia's forced sit-down meetings to reconcile as father and son. Underneath it all they really did respect and love each other deeply. They were just so much alike. Both were aggressive and forceful, both willing to risk it all for the sake of honor. And neither one was willing to budge an inch to give the other the satisfaction of winning an argument or making a point. So they *agreed* to disagree—agreeably. The new lifestyle choices stayed the same, but the love came back.

As Jack was pondering this final thought about that day of reconciliation, a smile came on his face, and an inner warmth of belonging soon followed.

It's been a tough going for all of us, he whispered softly to himself.

Then, almost as if on cue, Jack's jeep rounded the final turn and the mission appeared ahead in his view. The worst of the family drama was over, the boundaries had been drawn years ago. There remained the mutual respect of two completely different men—very different but very alike—living out their separately forged lives to the best of their ability. They could live with the truce, respect one another's choices, and, despite the obvious rub, continue to admire each other for standing his ground.

Not Just Another Day

The road opened into a long, wide clearing that sloped towards the river. The old mission stood beside the road facing the water like an aged sentinel. A low wall of whitewashed stone surrounded the building. Despite its age, the mission was well kept, the bushes along the wall trimmed and neat, the grass throughout the clearing mowed. Had Samantha Bentley been there, she would have recognized the building from the photo on Jack's desk.

The road continued past the mission turning towards the river and a cluster of buildings, a mixture of simple wood and tin huts, all clean and in good repair. A pier near the buildings jutted out into the river surrounded by small flat-bottomed boats and an occasional canoe. At the end of the pier, a small floatplane bobbed gently up and down with the river's motion. The place had a peaceful air about it, a haven in the midst of the jungle.

Jack pulled up to the front of the mission and stopped quickly, causing the gift to slide forward on the seat. Jack caught it deftly and slid it backwards. Hearing conversation in Portuguese, he looked up to see a large man balancing on the steeply sloped terra-cotta roof, while above him two young Brazilian boys were laying terra-cotta shingles into place. The man balanced against the roof with one hand while pointing directions to the boys with the other. He was older than Jack, in his sixties or so, with white hair that had thinned considerably.

"Hey Pops, what's up?" Jack yelled up to him. "Where's Mom?"

Art DeNova turned to look down at him. "Never mind 'where's Mom,' " he yelled good-naturedly. "Why don't you get up here and do the work of the Lord?"

Jack laughed. "How come whenever you do the work of the Lord, it's preaching in an air-conditioned sanctuary, but when I do the work of the Lord, I'm carrying bricks and rocks and laying shingles?"

"It's because I outrank you," his father yelled back with jovial good humor. "Let's see what those muscles are good for. Get your lazy behind up here!"

Jack shook his head with amusement. "Can't. I gotta get ready to fly to Miami for five days and do some business."

Art frowned. "Your kind of business is illegal in Miami. I'm telling you, you're gonna get your tail in trouble. And I don't have to study Scripture to figure that one out." He suddenly stopped in mid-thought. "Wait, you can't go," he said. "It's your mother's birthday on Saturday!"

Jack nodded. "I know. That's why I want to see her." He held up the pink box. "I got a present."

Jack's father shook his head, and a wry smile spread over his face. "You're gonna have to turn on some serious charm to get out of this one, Slick."

"Tell me about it," Jack grinned back. "Where's she at?"

"She's by the river with her ladies' meeting." Art nodded his head in the direction of the pier. "You know where the benches are."

"I'm gone—see you next Wednesday!" Jack put the jeep in gear.

"Be careful up there. I hope you're saving your money," called his father. "Speaking of which, where's my tithe check?"

Jack waved the bright pink package in the air as he sped down the road towards the river... "It's in the mail."

I Don't Know Why...

A few seconds later, Jack stopped the jeep in the middle of the road. About twenty yards below him a large cinchona tree spread its branches over a small collection of benches, the river flowing silently in the background. A group of women of all ages, their features revealing them as descended from the native tribes of the area, sat along the benches singing a hymn. The music would have been at home in any sleepy southern church in America, but the words were Portuguese.

" 'Tis so sweet to trust in Jesus..."

A slender woman with thick salt-and-pepper hair, which appeared once to have been as auburn as Jack's own, stood in front of the women. Her back was towards him, and she swayed slightly as she led the singing. Behind her two men strummed guitars.

Jack slipped quietly out of the jeep, scooping up the pink box and hiding it behind his back. He crept up behind the guitar players and whispered to them. They smiled and nodded at his instructions but continued to play. The ladies on the benches began to giggle. The song leader frowned slightly, unaware of Jack's presence, but continued to direct the singers. Suddenly, in perfect unison, the guitar players changed their chords, starting a completely different pattern of music. She turned to admonish them and saw Jack. A wide smile, as broad as Jack's own, slid across her face. The women began to applaud, their giggles growing. Jack stepped forward and grabbed his mother around the waist with his free hand, leaning in to kiss her cheek.

"Ah, the prodigal prince, my Jack of Hearts," she said softly to him.

Jack turned to address the women on the benches. "Ladies, as you know this Saturday is my mother's birthday, but I'll be gone on business."

Julia DeNova gave him a playful, reproachful slap on the shoulder. "What do you mean 'gone'? I'm your mother—your only mother. You're supposed to adore me!"

Jack nodded to the guitar players who began the new song in earnest, shifting into key.

Jack grinned, "Mom, I not only adore you, but..." and Jack picked up the melody of the song, the same one he'd been humming on the road, his voice rich and full, "I don't know why I love you like I do. I don't know why, I just do..."

Julia laughed and turned her head towards the women. "This is my favorite...and he is such a brat!"

"I don't know why you thrill me like you do," Jack continued. "I don't know why, you just do."

"He gets his talent from my side..."

Jack took his mother's hand, starting to dance. She protested slightly, but gave in as the ladies increased their giggles.

"You never seem to want my romancing," he sang. "The only time you hold me, is when we're dancing." He spun her gently, and she responded with obvious grace.

"He gets his brutality from his father," she said.

Jack ignored the jibe, continuing to sing—and Julia joined in with gentle mockery. "I don't know why I love you like I do. I don't know why, I don't know why, I don't know why, I just do."

The music ended and the ladies applauded and cheered. A few stood up excitedly, and then sat down quickly as if they'd committed a social faux pas. Jack dipped Julia with an exaggerated sweep, then kissed her gently on the cheek when she was standing again.

She turned to the ladies and spoke in Portuguese, *"This is not a song we learned in church."*

The ladies smiled and shook their heads towards each other in amused agreement.

Jack laughed and hugged his mother. "Mom, give 'em a break. You've been teaching them English for twenty years..." He turned to the ladies and bowed slightly. "Ladies..." He nodded to the guitar players. "...and gentlemen, I'm here to wish my beautiful and charming..."

"Now I know he wants something," interrupted his mother.

"...mother, a happy birthday."

And Jack handed her the pink box. The women applauded, as Julia unwrapped the gift and opened it. She pulled out a gold heart on a long gold chain. Opening the locket, she read the inscription. "From the Prodigal Prince to the Ultimate Queen of Hearts, Happy Birthday—your Jack of Hearts."

She pulled her son into a hug and kissed his cheek. "You are forgiven. You are so spoiled."

Jack laughed as the ladies gathered around to admire his mother's new necklace.

Chapter 4

V-a-l-e T-u-d-o

Three days later, Jack sat on a plane watching the sunrise over Miami. Marco slept beside him, stirring slightly as the sunlight slipped through the window and across his eyelids. Seeing the city below, Jack reached for his wallet and pulled out a laminated card. The plastic was worn and scratched with years of handling. A picture filled one side of the card, but Jack flipped it over without looking at the photo. On the other side, a small silver cross bulged slightly through the plastic.

With an unusual sense of concentration, Jack began to rub his thumb gently on the cross. While going through this ritual he performed as often as he fought, he looked down at his hands with an eerie chill that crawled slowly up his arms. More than any other time before, Jack caught a revelation that froze his thoughts for a minute.

In his hand was a symbol of something he'd lost along the way, yet on the outside of his hands were the markings indicating where he'd been and who he'd become. He lifted his hands a little and stared at the tattoos on his knuckles. V-A-L-E on the right and T-U-D-O was carefully emblazoned across the left. The infamous phrase defined Jack DeNova to his entire country. *Vale Tudo. Anything goes...* It was innocent enough looking.

The Vale Tudo Tournament was held in Rio de Janeiro every year where the baddest of the bad fought each other, and nothing was forbidden to use to defeat your opponent. Marco won this most prestigious title when he was young, and, as a Brazilian, was fiercely proud that the no-holds-barred fighting scene originated there. Only those with fire in their blood and a mind trained for physical destruction could even hope to win it.

Two years prior, Jack had taken the coveted title home easily. Marco had bonded to Jack in almost a spiritual way after that. It seemed especially significant because by heritage Jack wasn't born a Brazilian. He'd won the title strictly with the skills Marco taught him. Marco was proud that his teachings gave an American-born Brazilian the title. In fact, he might as well have taken the trophy home himself.

Yet, in this brief, shining moment, Jack experienced an overwhelming surge of feeling, a sense of not belonging anywhere. His relationship with the Lord was short-circuited by all the hard feelings that had grown between himself and his dad. No longer could Jack pray audibly. So after years of training, fighting, and bonding with Marco, by the time Jack was a fighting teenager prodigy he came to a resolution in his mind.

As a teenager Jack had made a self endued spiritual compromise.

He would not utter another word of prayer to a God who wouldn't hear any of his cries to take him out of this strange country and bring him back to where he belonged, where family, home, cousins, and true friends lived.

The day came when Jack just couldn't address God anymore with his own lips. It was useless to try. The little laminated card he now held between his fingers was Jack's only remaining feeble line of communication with his Maker. And though it might not be much, it was the only place of spiritual comfort he could find.

But those tattoos…they defined where his life really was. Jack remembered the day he got them with Marco by his side. He was so proud of winning the title that he chose to do something once and for all that separated him from his father's covering.

Art DeNova was known all over the country for his mission along the Amazon River, and now his son would be known all over the country for becoming an icon of the most violent sport on the planet. What a dichotomy.

Jack's thoughts flashed back to the day when his dad first saw the tattoos. He didn't yell, throw a fit, or scream at Jack.

He looked down at Jack's hands, having heard on the news of Jack's latest accomplishment. In almost a whisper, he said, "Congratulations, my son." Then he dropped his eyes and slowly walked out of the room, disappearing for the entire evening. Jack learned later from his mother, that for the first time ever, she saw her big tower of faith and strength go into his bedroom, lay across the bed, and cry like a lost three year old. Art cried until 5:30 the next morning. Julia hadn't known he was capable of feeling that deeply about anything.

He kept repeating, "I lost my son. I lost my son. I've won thousands of people in this country to Christ, and I couldn't win my own flesh and blood to the Lord. I have failed as a father."

"In" and "On" Jack's Destiny

A simple glance at what was "in" Jack's hands and what was "on" Jack's hands told the whole story. But maybe the symbolism went a step further. What was in Jack's hands represented what was deep in Jack's heart, and what was on Jack's hands represented what was branded to Jack's life. Only a miracle could bridge the gap—a miracle Jack didn't have the faith for or the power to contemplate right now. Abruptly, Jack shifted in his seat to reach for his wallet to shove the card back in.

Jarred slightly, Marco stirred in his sleep and awoke. He did not sit up, but simply turned to look at Jack's hands. *"Why do you do that little ritual before every fight?"* he asked, his voice a bare murmur over the gentle mechanical hum of the plane's cabin. *"Is it a superstition?"*

Jack continued to concentrate on the card. *"No boss, it's much more than that,"* he replied, almost struggling to get the words out to explain himself. *"You know my parents are missionaries. I obviously haven't followed their faith. But this is very personal. It's my way of...well, of...praying. And hoping."*

"Hoping for what?"

Jack dropped the card in his lap and grinned. *"Hoping you will mind your own business before I choke you out right here!"*

Jack crossed his arms and grasped Marco's lapels as if to pull them into a classic choke, but the old instructor instinctively blocked the move. The two friends laughed quietly together as the plane descended towards Miami.

Chapter 5

A Gladiator's Day at the Office

The ballroom of the exclusive Tropics Hotel in Miami's South Beach was packed with hundreds of people representing a blend of nationalities and backgrounds and all bearing the look of money. Tuxedos mingled with designer suits and casual dance shirts, thousand-dollar gowns with spaghetti straps and miniskirts. Here and there, faces as familiar as the covers of a supermarket tabloid appeared in the crowd, hiding behind thick, dark sunglasses.

Loud, driving music pounded the room, as a gaudy light-show flashed the beat across bodies of dancing women clad in outfits that would have made a Hawaiian Tropic's girl blush. The occasion might have looked like a premiere in Hollywood or an exclusive party in Atlantic City if not for the cage at the center of the room.

A six-foot-high wall of black cyclone fencing ringed a large, padded octagon. The posts and upper rims of the cage were covered in thick, black padding. A crowd sat in bleachers that pushed up to the octagon on all sides, except for the narrow aisles to the doors of the ballroom. Two wider aisles connected with gates at opposite sides of the octagon, leading back to curtains hiding doorways at either end of the hall.

Mixed with the music rose the burble of the crowd straining to talk with each other above the pulsating rhythm. The air was thick with excitement—a mixture of anticipation and tension—the feeling that something both primal and forbidden was in the offing, and every human soul wanted a taste. A brand new and exciting sin could be found here, and the crowd craved it.

Samantha Bentley and the four Colvack brothers stood beside one of the open gates to the octagon, surrounded by the spectacle. Samantha watched it all with the confident air of someone who's proven herself beyond all doubt. Johnny's eyes scanned the crowd, ticking off each guest like a number in a ledger, totaling the columns with greedy satisfaction. Hal's look alternated between pride and jealousy. A glint of fear flickered through his self-satisfied smirk, possibly concern that he'd be found out by Johnny or the financial family backers back in Russia as a less capable dealmaker than how he'd sold himself. Mike's eyes were glued on the cage and filled with the hunger of an athlete longing to be in the field and not the stands. Bruce eyed the dancers with a hunger of a different kind.

The music ended, and a deafening crash filled the room as a shower of pyrotechnic sparks poured around the octagon. Samantha smiled and stepped into the center of the cage. A lone spotlight surrounded her as she grabbed the microphone dangling over her head.

"Ladies and gentlemen of the world, welcome to the wild side of Miami!"

The crowd yelled and applauded.

Samantha continued. "Tonight you are going to witness a fighting scenario like you have never seen before. Tonight there are no rules, no rounds, no judges, no weight limits, and no time limits! Tonight, absolutely anything goes!"

The crowd exploded into noise, the room echoing with their cheers. Samantha paused to soak in the roar. The sound did not abate, the crowd unable to hold its eagerness. With perfect timing, Samantha began to tease the bloodthirsty spectators.

"I want to introduce to you now one of the greatest fighters ever to walk into the steel cage. He is the three-time Japanese Judo champion, two-time Intercontinental Full-Contact Karate champion, 1998 Olympic bronze medallist in tae kwon do, and the only Asian ever to hold the coveted no-holds-barred, Vale Tudo Tournament championship belt. Tonight he puts that belt on the line. From Osaka Japan, I introduce to you the ferocious Yamo Zakura!"

The curtain at one end of the hall swept aside and a shower of golden sparks lit up the aisle from pyrotechnics mounted on the floor. Yamo Zakura walked into the spotlight, his body thick and heavily muscled, though he did not have the defined tone of a body builder. His skin was slightly paler than that of most Japanese men, although every other feature revealed his Asian ancestry. His hair was cut in short bristles like a scrub brush and dyed a brilliant orange, as were his eyebrows. A sparse mustache still held its natural dark color, creating an even more exotic effect than if it had been the same shade as his hair.

Zakura's eyes were little more than narrow slits, giving nothing away and revealing no emotion. It was impossible to tell if he was afraid or confident about the coming fight. The bright shade of his hair was matched by the equally vibrant orange-colored spandex pants that hugged his body from his waist down over his thighs to his knees. His knee pads were strapped on with tape in the same shade of orange, while his feet were bare. Only his hands broke the orange theme, his wrists wrapped in white tape.

Spotlights now revealed a large entourage that had followed Zakura into the cage: trainers, assistants, even two young women in matching orange spandex halter tops and boy-cut shorts. Zakura stood before them like a warlord approaching battle. When he entered the center of the cage he turned to the audience on either side, raising his arms straight in the air to receive the grateful adulation. The crowd cheered in response. Like an alligator on a riverbank, he eyed everything, weighing what was prey and what was not.

"Now, ladies and gentlemen," Samantha called out above the noise. "I am proud to introduce to you, fighting in the United States for the very first time..." She was interrupted by even louder cheering. "...the four-time Brazilian jiu jitsu light heavyweight champion, the winner of the Battle Cage Tournament in Osaka, Japan, for five straight years, and former three-time Vale Tudo champion. He is here to reclaim that title and bring it back to his homeland. He is undefeated in 302 no-holds-barred fighting events. Would you please welcome, from Rio de Janeiro, the King of the Jungle, Jack DeNova!"

The noise was unlike anything before. Shouting, screaming cheers—even the most staid faces could not hold back. Now the opposite aisle lit up with sparks, and Jack DeNova stepped through the curtain. He wore the traditional white jiu jitsu gi he had sparred in at the dojo, his black belt wrapped tightly about the waist. Behind him followed Marco and two Brazilian assistants, dressed in simple tee-shirts and "Brudel" gym pants. The small group could have been headed for a workout at the gym; there was neither flash nor pretense in their appearance.

Jack walked casually towards the cage like a man headed to work. He barely seemed to notice the crowd. Even Marco and the assistants acted as if the lights, noise, and fireworks were no more unusual than the streetlights outside their dojo. Jack was a man walking into his own customized world of the bizarre.

Jack entered the ring without acknowledging the crowd. Carefully, he removed his gi as easily as if preparing for a shower. Underneath he wore a simple pair of black swim trunks with white bands around the thigh. On the back of the trunks were printed two white eyes, fierce and narrow as a predator's. His dark tan contrasted sharply with Zakura's pale skin, like a jungle panther facing off against a large African lion.

Jack nodded to the referee as Samantha left the ring. Jack and Zakura faced each other at opposite ends of the octagon, neither saying a word.

Let's Get It On!

"Let's get it on!" the referee shouted and retreated quickly to the side of the cage away from the fighters.

Jack extended his left hand, holding the right near his chin. The stance looked as if he were telling someone to calm down, but his eyes held no promise of peace. It was Jack's traditional way of measuring his distance. Zakura began to dance around the octagon, circling Jack, bouncing up and down, first to one side, then the other. Jack barely moved, rotating his body to follow Zakura. His expression seemed bland, but his eyes burned holes of concentration into Zakura's moving form.

Suddenly Zakura snapped his leg forward, striking out first with a strong and forceful front kick. Jack's response was equally quick, his foot catching Zakura's thigh, keeping the kick from rising, and causing Zakura pain from the stiff-legged block. Zakura spun around, throwing his other leg upwards in a back kick towards Jack's head. But he hesitated just long enough for Jack to slip underneath the kick before it was even extended. Grabbing Zakura's other leg left for balance, he lifted it up sharply and swept Zakura off both his feet. The burly Asian's back slammed into the floor as the crowd cheered with surprise.

Before Zakura could move, Jack had scrambled into a sitting position on his chest using the same textbook moves he displayed in the dojo back in Rio. Instinctively, Zakura, while lying on his back in a panic, punched at Jack's jaw. Jack simply tilted his face back and out of danger and then grabbed one of Zakura's fists with both hands. Jack tucked Zakura's clenched fist against his chest, and with a swift move, fell to his side. At the same time, he draped his left leg across Zakura's face and draped his right leg over Zakura's chest. Zakura's arm was still locked tightly into Jack's chest and between his legs. Now Jack began to arch his hips up, leaning backwards, pushing the elbow further and further up towards the ceiling, trying to snap it back the wrong way. The muscles in Zakura's arm tried to resist, attempting to pull out of this fatal position. But Jack was too much a technician to let him escape. It wasn't about strength now. It was simple physics. The elbow would pop backwards in a few more seconds, damaging Zakura's arm for life. It was basic jiu jitsu 101, executed by a master.

Zakura's face grimaced in pain. He could no more fight the leverage Jack was asserting than fight gravity and fly. It was a matter of time—seconds—that he would give up or his elbow would pop back the wrong way. Zakura screamed, slapping his left palm against the mat. Three…four…five times.

Jack released the arm and while lying on his back, he pushed Zakura away with his feet and stood up. Ever the gentleman sportsman, he bent over to help his opponent rise. Zakura nodded his head in defeat. Jack honored Zakura with a handshake and a respectful hug. Then Zakura moved towards his stunned entourage as the nearly useless referee lifted Jack's hand in triumph. The ringside clock read thirty-two seconds.

Crowds Just Wanna Have Fun

The room that had been filled with cheers suddenly echoed with boos. This was no fight, no show. The crowd wanted blows and blood, not pulled arms and a humbled giant. Yet the true fight enthusiasts cheered at the proficiency of Jack's flawless technique. But they were the minority tonight.

Johnny frowned at the boos, while Hal and Mike looked around at the angry crowd in confusion. This was not what they expected either. The enterprise that promised vast money was beginning to look questionable. The Colvacks had promised entertainment; the crowd, many new to this type of real-life combat, was denied the pleasure they had been hyped into expecting.

Soon these high-roller money people were shouting accusations and threats. Only Bruce seemed oblivious to the potential financial disaster facing his brothers. His own boos joined the chorus of the crowd.

Jack seemed no more moved by the boos than he had been by the cheers. For him the fight clearly was over. Like a workman at the end of his shift, he'd done his job and he was ready to be paid and leave. Marco and the two assistants moved into the cage, carrying Jack's gi, bringing a towel and water, though he needed neither. They were no more surprised by the outcome than Jack, and equally unconcerned about the fickle crowd.

Suddenly the gate to the cage swung open. Before the other Colvacks could react, Bruce jumped into the octagon, screaming at Jack with all the frustration of the crowd.

"That's it? That's no kind of rumble! Is that how the little girls fight in Brazil? Come on Jungle Thing, try one of your little chiropractic tricks with me. I'll split your head wide open!"

Jack glanced at Bruce. Dismissing him with barely a shrug, he turned to leave.

"You can't beat a real fighter like me," Bruce screamed. "Don't turn your back on me, you coward!"

The word was a touchstone for Jack. He spun to face Bruce, his eyes narrow with anger. Stepping forward, Marco's arm wrapped around Jack's chest. The beloved trainer shook his head no, blocking Jack's anger and turning him away towards the gate and the aisle back to the changing room.

Marco had known Jack since he was a scared little boy who entered his dojo crying because local thugs had beaten him up for his bicycle. Marco had trained Jack never to fight in anger. An angry fighter is one out of control. Jiu jitsu was about being able to walk away from a fight with dignity, knowing the damage you could bring to someone. One look from Marco reminded Jack of all this, and instantly he cooled down.

But Bruce roared on with anger. "I said don't turn your chicken back on me! You're afraid! You're scared—you and your whole greaseball family!"

The crowd jeered along with Bruce, but Jack and his group kept walking away with their backs toward Bruce.

Then with sudden fury Bruce charged the group throwing a vicious right hook. His fist slammed into Marco's jaw from behind. The old man fell to the floor, bleeding and barely conscious. Immediately Jack and the assistants dropped down to his aid, lifting him from the floor.

Bruce continued to scream. "You haven't fought anyone tonight until you have fought me!"

Jack stood erect; without Marco to monitor his behavior, the controlled Brazillian tactition had submerged and the

American New York street fighter had come screaming to the surface. Gone from his face was the nonchalance he had before the fight. Rage filled his eyes, and his jaw was set with hatred. The sight of his mentor and father figure lying on the ground, semiconscious and bleeding was more than Jack could bare. Marco was the only person alive who could control that side of Jack, and he was unable to respond. It was all New York Jack now.

Defending the honor of his mentor, he shouted back to Bruce and the crowd. "If you want entertainment, I'll give you entertainment. Let's go right now."

The mood of the crowd changed as instantly as a gust in a storm. They could not only hear Jack's words, but now they could see his fury. This was what they had imagined the King of the Jungle would act like. His stance and manner were clear; the fighting was not over tonight.

Samantha could see it too, and in this frantic, unrehearsed moment she hoped she could salvage the evening. Grabbing the microphone, she trotted back to the center of the cage.

"Well, it seems like y'all want to keep on going tonight!"

The crowd roared its approval.

"Is anybody up for a little on-the-spot grudge match?"

The cheers rebounded against the walls.

"How would you like to see Jack and Bruce Colvack go at it right now?"

The two men stared at each other, motionless, ignoring the cries of the crowd. Outside the cage, Johnny Colvack frowned. His eyes narrowed as he watched the events in the octagon unfold. He sized up the opponents with a look that said he knew the outcome, but he did nothing. The sound of the crowd echoed in his ears, the memory of their anger was fresh in his mind. This was about money, and money trumped all.

Next to him, Hal cheered for his brother and jeered at Jack. Mike knew better. Worry filled his eyes. Bruce was out of his league, and as a fighter Mike knew it. But the heat of the moment was beyond his control. He could only hope to coach Bruce from the sidelines and believe that one of Bruce's kicks would find a home on Jack's head. It was a long shot, but Mike could do little else than watch with the rest of the crowd.

The wave of anger had swept them in as well, all of it pouring into the octagon, as if their shouts and screams could wash Jack into the sea.

"OK, ladies and gentlemen, we're going at it one more time!" Samantha had turned back into the master showman, leading the audience where she wanted them to go.

Bruce quickly began to take off his shirt and shoes. Always one to wear pants that had stretch to them, Bruce threw his excess clothing over the fence and stepped into his place in the sun. He desperately wanted to prove himself to his brothers, especially to Johnny. This was his moment.

Samantha shouted into the mic, "He's a second-degree black belt in five animal kung fu events, and a two-time American AAU Tae Kwon Do Tournament Champion. He calls himself the Beast from the East. From Camden, New Jersey—Bruce Colvack!"

The crowd bellowed for their new champion. The chant, "Colvack, Colvack, Colvack" swelled through the room. Not a voice lifted Jack's name in praise.

"OK boys, let the good times roll!" Samantha dropped the microphone and signaled to the referee.

The referee looked at both men. "Let's get it on!" he shouted and then backed away.

Jack sprang towards Bruce; gone was the casual poise of his earlier approach. His leg lashed out in low kick after low kick, slamming into Bruce's legs with vicious thuds. Bruce attempted to dance backwards, but Jack was too quick, chasing Bruce around the octagon with violent speed.

Bruce tried a kick, but Jack slapped it aside with a sharp, brutal foot block. Bruce threw punches, first to Jack's head, then to his chest, but none of the blows landed.

Jack was elusive, his hands firmly slapping aside Bruce's fists. Jack continued to kick—one, two, three—left, right, left, right. Twelve kicks in all struck Bruce's legs, calves, and thighs with brutal fury. Jack's feet pounded into Bruce, striking inside his left knee, then inside the right knee, then to the sides of his thighs again.

Bruce's face twisted with pain, and cold fear rose in his eyes. Bruce could feel the blood vessels breaking in his legs, the muscles beginning to spasm and the swelling actually making his pant legs tighten.

The pulsating chant of "Colvack, Colvack" had ended. "Jack, Jack, Jack" was now the cry.

Mike lunged for the cage, but Johnny and Hal grabbed him, pulling him back between them.

Jack closed in on Bruce, his hands no longer open, but locked tightly into fists. Jack began to pound Bruce like a machine gone out of control. Blows pummeled Bruce in the stomach, kidneys, chest, and across the neck.

Bruce's blocks were feeble, his return punches wild and unfocused, striking only air.

Eighteen machine-gun cracks from Jack's fists slammed into Bruce's body; not one from Bruce so much as grazed Jack's hair. With vicious accuracy, Jack threw his fists into Bruce's head like he was working out on a heavy bag at the gym with no thought of a returned punch—once, twice, four times—snapping the head back with each crack.

Bruce's face emerged as little more than a glaze of spattered blood, his expression vacant and lost. He slumped against the walls of the cage, the fencing was all that held him upright.

The referee moved forward to stop the fight, but Jack was already in motion. His body spun around, his foot whirling upwards in a blur to connect with Bruce's neck. A muffled crack filled the air, and Bruce toppled to the ground with a sickening thud.

"You want a show?" Jack screamed at the crowd. "Here's your show!"

The thundering cry of "Jack, Jack, Jack!" roared through the room, and the audience surged into the cage, surrounding Jack and ignoring Bruce where he lay against the fence.

Johnny, Hal, and Mike screaming for the paramedic team fought their way through the crowd to reach their brother.

Bruce did not move. The paramedics reached him and checked his pulse. One began CPR, pumping Bruce's chest, breathing into his mouth. The other charged a defibrillator, and the two alternated between the paddles and CPR.

Hal and Mike crouched beside them, their eyes focused on their younger brother, but Johnny stood and moved away. He walked with resignation to salvage the situation and move on.

Bruce died right there on the mat. His internal bleeding was beyond repair. But ultimately it was a broken neck that put him down like an old horse. He most likely was dead before he hit the floor, but he had brought the fatal conclusion upon himself.

For Johnny, his brother's death was another item to calculate later on the ledger, a factor whose impact on the total was not yet known.

Rage in the Cage

The other brothers were not so stoic. The realization came slowly to them, but with it came in a rush of emotion. Mike bellowed in rage and grief. Hal knocked aside the now useless paramedics, grabbing Bruce's body, shaking it, and yelling in Bruce's face as if he could order his brother back to life.

Cued by their cries, police officers appeared in the ballroom. Minutes before they were nowhere to be found. But now they got a cell phone signal from Samantha that they needed to get involved. They rushed for the octagon. The sight of the dark blue uniforms parted the crowd, and tuxedos, suits, gowns, and miniskirts headed for the exits. The officers ignored the crowd, except to guide the dignitaries discreetly through the back doors.

Jack and his entourage were not so lucky. They owned neither power nor prestige in Samantha's world. Within seconds Jack was handcuffed, watching officers carry off Marco and the assistants in cuffs as well. Across the octagon, Mike screamed incoherently, pouring his rage at Jack. Five policemen pressed him against the mesh walls of the cage to hold him back. Two more officers pulled Jack out of the room.

As he left he heard Hal yelling, "You're dead, DeNova, dead! I'll destroy every bit of DNA in your family! You're a dead man!"

Samantha Bentley watched from the hotel lobby as the police pushed Jack into a squad car. All around her, patrons murmured excitedly about the fight. She moved across the lobby and grasped the shoulder of her assistant who stared at the flashing police lights with an expression of shock.

"Relax," she said softly. "The people got exactly what they wanted. And in this business, whenever my clientele hear that I'm throwing another event, the audience will double—and so will the money."

Even though Jack—whom she secretly admired—had to take the fall, business was business. A satisfied smile spread across her face. "And I can certainly live with that."

Chapter 6

Visitors From Another World

The room had gray walls, a gray floor, a gray ceiling, a gray metal table and three gray metal chairs. A one-way mirrored window reflected all the gray back at Jack, who sat with his cuffed hands resting on the table. The door to the room opened and two men wearing suits walked in. One was a tall, young black man, and the other a thickly built white man in his late forties.

The two men said nothing, though the thin edge of a smile lifted the corner of the black man's mouth. Jack couldn't decide if that was a good thing or not. Their silence made the room seem grayer. Both men took off their jackets, revealing shoulder holsters under their arms. Jack noticed that both holsters still held their guns. He couldn't decide if this meant the men trusted him or not. The black man draped his jacket over a chair at the opposite side of the table and sat down, his back to the mirror.

The other man stepped behind Jack and leaned against the corner of the room.

"Jack, I'm Agent Watkins," the black man said. "This is Agent Phillips." He gestured towards the man in the corner.

Jack glanced at him, but the man made no sign of acknowledgement.

"Agent?" said Jack, his eyebrow rising slightly. "Are you guys local or federal?"

"Federal," said Watkins. "We're the FBI."

Jack shook his head. "Oh, man, I can already tell you're gonna ask me to go somewhere I got no business going."

The man behind him spoke. His voice was firm, almost threatening. "Jack, you're in a very deep well. Illegal pit fighting, manslaughter—a good prosecutor could turn that into murder one."

Watkins nodded. "Not to mention an accessory to illegal gambling, bookmaking, underground betting…"

"Let me guess," interrupted Jack. "You want me to do something really stupid, so you can bust somebody who'll make my life an inferno till the day I die, right?"

Watkins leaned forward looking Jack in the eyes. "We want the Colvacks. All of them. We can put them away longer than you can live on this planet."

Phillips spoke up again from the corner. "Johnny is connected to the Russian mob, has been for decades. Where do you think he made the money to own eight hotels in Atlantic City and Miami?"

"He's a murderer nine times over," Watkins continued. "Johnny Colvack made his mark as a button man for the Russian drug cartel."

"And he's training his hotheaded brothers Hal and Mike to take over his operation in Miami," added Phillips. "They're both killers for hire."

Jack leaned back in his seat holding his hands up in front of him. "Guys, I understand this deadly safari you're on. You want to bag an elephant, a rhino, and a gorilla. And you want me to load your guns. But if I do, a lot of other people will go down while you're claiming your trophies."

Watkins sat back as well, spreading his arms like a man presenting the inevitable. "Jack, you're not gonna survive the pen. Fight or not, self-defense or accident, you killed their brother, and you're going to get whacked in there. You're a dead man."

Phillips moved forward, his hands on the edge of the table, his body leaning in towards Jack. "Look, we've been working on these guys for two years. We're not crying over the loss of Bruce Colvack. He had blood on his hands before he ever saw you. As far as I'm concerned, you did us a favor. And you can finish that favor by helping us take down his brothers. Go state's evidence, Jack. Give up your contacts. With what we've got so far and your testimony, we'll have an airtight case. All we need is somebody who can testify that they've been hired by their organization or somebody legally connected to it. The whole house of cards will fall."

Jack shook his head again. "Gentlemen, I have my own money to hire my own attorney. I know enough to understand this was not premeditated murder and I was defending myself. I do a year or two of real time, and I'm out. I'll do what time I got comin' and take my chances. I can handle myself." He shrugged. "My father was right. I should have never brought my business to the States." He looked at Watkins, ignoring Phillips. "Is that all?"

Phillips stepped away from the table, grabbing his jacket and opening the door. Watkins eyed Jack for a moment. "For now, but we'll be talking again." He rose, pulling on his jacket to follow Phillips. As he stepped out, he turned back to Jack.

"By the way, you have a couple of visitors." He left Jack to wonder who else in Miami would want to see him.

The visitors' area was a long room with a single table stretching down the center. The table was divided into partitions separated in three-foot intervals that spread the groups of people apart. An armed guard led Jack into the room. Jack looked around as the guard removed the handcuffs.

"Booth number seven, DeNova," the guard growled, nodding towards the far end of the table.

At the name, two figures stood up on the opposite side of the far booth. Jack nearly shouted in surprise at the sight of his parents. He walked to them and reached across the table to hug them. The embraces were long and heartfelt, as if letting go would somehow be final. Julia began to cry quietly. Jack said nothing, unsure of his words. They sat silently as Julia wiped her eyes with a tissue.

Julia was the first to speak. "Jack, are you all right? What happened? We've been praying for you the whole way here."

"When did you get here? Who told you?" Jack asked in disbelief.

His father had an almost wistful smile on his face. "Art heard about the fight from the students at the academy," Jack's mother said quietly.

Jack looked at his father in surprise.

"He watches over you like a hawk, Jack. Whenever you're gone, he always finds out where and even whom you're fighting, as well as learning the outcome. I never realized until today how much he knew about what you did," she continued softly.

Art spoke up, " It's not exactly the life I would have chosen for you, but I was always proud of your courage and abilities. Every time you left to fight, I would always go to the church nightly and pray for your safety till you came home. Sometimes I would even come and watch you when you fought in Sao Paulo," Art said. "Can't fault a father for watching his son compete." There was a sad hint of pride in his eyes, though his voice turned somber. "When I heard what happened, we took the seaplane to Rio and caught the first flight here." He looked Jack in the eye. "They said you killed that man. Jack, my son, is that true?"

Jack nodded, dropping his head down. "Yes, Dad. It's true." He looked up again. "But we were in a normal competition. That thug jumped in and tried to start trouble; he attacked Marco and nearly broke his jaw. We fought and...well...you heard what happened. I didn't try to kill him. I was angry that he took a cheap shot at Marco and wanted to teach him a lesson. You know the rest." He looked down at his hands as if expecting to see the cuffs still there.

His mother reached across the table and touched his hands. "Now what happens, Jack? Are you going to be here long? Don't they know you were trying to protect yourself?"

Jack glanced at his father. Art shook his head, *No, she doesn't really understand it all.*

"That's up to the attorneys, Ma," Jack replied squeezing her hands. "It'll all work out. Where are you staying in the States?"

"With the Wilson family," Art said, sounding relieved at the change of subject. "You remember them, don't you?"

"How could I forget," said Jack, his voice almost gruff. "They're the missionaries that brought you down to Brazil on a two-week mission trip thirty years ago." He looked at his father; it was Art's turn to look at his own hands.

Julia didn't seem to notice the underlying intensity of the exchange. "They're having a family reunion this week, so we'll be staying with them. Remember how our families used to get together all the time?"

Jack continued to look at his father. "Every year. Then they would check up on us in Brazil, give us their blessing, and leave." His voice turned cold with the sound of an old, unhealed emotional wound.

Art spoke softly, "Jack, I know you never really understood, but that was our calling from God."

"Your call, Dad, not my call. I just got beat up every day 'cause I couldn't speak Portuguese." The accusation came out in a burst of pain. "Why do you think I made the career choice I made? 'Cause I like to get kicked in the head?"

Julia reached for Jack's shoulder, a move to calm him and to break the wall rising up between them. "Boys, please…"

her voice held the pain of this moment and many others. "Not now."

Art looked Jack in the eye and touched his hand. "I'm sorry, Son…" The apology seemed to take in the true gravity of the past and the present. "I…I…" He had no words.

"It's all right, Pop." Already Jack regretted the outburst and false blame. "We'll make it through. We've had tougher times." He pulled his father's hand into his grip, and they sat there, the three of them bonded together, all holding each other's hands, unwilling to let go.

Julia spoke quietly, earnestly. "Jack, do you have your Bible with you?"

Jack laughed softly, shaking his head with wry amusement. "You mean the one you gave me when I was ten? No, I think I left it at home." Even if he had been at home, he probably could not have found it.

Julia looked at Art. They nodded to each other as if to say they knew, and to signal a decision that had already been made. Art reached below the table and brought out an old leather Bible. The edges were tattered, the dark brown cover worn to a creamy tan in spots, the spine creased and faded to the color of toffee. The book was large and rested easily in Art's large hands. A cloth zipper wrapped around the edge, but bulged open at the top where worn pieces of paper stuck out from between the pages, covered with tiny, cramped pen marks in faded blues and blacks. Art laid the book into Jack's hands. "Well then, here Jack. Take mine."

Jack held the book in stunned silence for a moment. "Dad, I can't take your Bible. This has been yours for forty years. It has all your notes in it. I can't…"

Julia interrupted, her voice gentle but firm. "Jack, your father needs to give this to you. Take it."

Art gave a wry smile, "Yeah, you'll have plenty of time to read it now."

The laughter that came from Jack and his parents was bittersweet, tinged with both love and regret.

"Thanks, Dad. I'll cherish this." Jack gripped the Bible tightly, feeling the warmth of the old leather between his hands. "It means a lot…more than you know."

The guard stepped forward. "Time's up, DeNova." With a swift, practiced move, he pulled the Bible from Jack's hand. Jack bristled, but his father quickly grabbed his son's hands, squeezing them as if to signal patience. The guard unzipped the book, fanning the pages and thumbing the notes to dislodge any contraband. Satisfied, he handed the Bible back to Jack. He tilted his head towards the door, and Jack got up.

As they rose, Julia leaned across the table and hugged her son again. "We'll be staying at the Wilson's. Their number is written inside the cover." She whispered softly, "Along with a note from your father."

The guard pulled Jack away, prodding him to stick out his hands. Jack complied, and the cuffs snapped on his wrists again. Jack glanced at his father and saw a thin tear cloud his eye. He held the Bible up as if to say, *It's all right, Dad—I'm on the right track now,* then walked through the door, back towards his cell and the long days ahead.

The waiting room outside the visiting area was as drab as the rest of the jail. The walls were dull gray, the lower portions streaked with the marks where people had leaned against them, propped up a foot, or simply idly kicked, tapping out the minutes before a visit. A low, thinly padded vinyl bench rested against one wall, along with a handful of chairs. Mike and Hal sat on the sofa, away from the door into the visiting room. Mike's muscles were visibly tense through his body shirt, his legs bouncing rapidly as he sat. His eyes jerked around the room, as if looking for a target for the tightly clenched fists that he kept drumming against his leg. He rose abruptly, walked across the room, turned and marched back to the bench, and sat beside Hal again. All the while he grumbled in low, angry tones, his words barely audible.

Hal seemed unaffected or unaware of Mike's behavior. He sat on the bench almost perfectly still, his eyes staring at the far wall, cold and fixed like a predator eyeing his prey. Suddenly his glare snapped to the right as the door to the visitor's area opened into the waiting room. Mike followed his stare, watching as Art and Julia stepped through the doorway. Mike's eyes narrowed and his body became instantly still, only his head followed Art and Julia as they left the waiting room.

"Is that them?" he asked, his voice cold.

"Yes," said Hal coldly. "That's his mommy and daddy. How touching." The words were bitter, thick with hate.

The guard who had opened the door for Art and Julia called to the brothers. "OK, Colvack, we're ready for you."

Hal glanced at Mike who nodded a grim, determined nod. Hal followed the guard into the visiting area, leaving Mike on the bench. Mike stopped fidgeting and leaned against the back of the bench, folding his hands behind his head. A look of dark satisfaction crossed his face, as if he expected an evil wish would soon come true.

The guard closed the door behind Hal and nodded towards a booth.

"Number five, Colvack."

Hal sat in the booth, his eyes on the door leading to the prisoners' cells. The door opened, and a man in a sleeveless orange prison jumpsuit walked through. He held up his cuffed hands, but the guard just snorted at him.

"Number five, Moon."

The prisoner shrugged and moved towards Hal's booth. He was a large man, well over six feet five inches tall. His head was clean-shaven, and a swastika was tattooed across the top of it. From shoulder to wrists, his arms writhed with tattoos—a jungle of snakes, skulls, and daggers mixed with racist slogans and obscenities. Raymond Moon was a notorious leader of a southern faction of the skinheads. He was a suspect in dozens of murders and hate crimes, but the D.A. never had enough evidence to convict him. He was doing ten to twelve years on a manslaughter conviction, one he couldn't escape because he stomped a black man to death in a roadside bar for entering an all-white hangout. Lots of witnesses watched the bloody spectacle.

He lumbered toward Hal, his movements methodical, almost calculating. His expression betrayed a mocking smile. The guard watched him intently, eyeing his every move with suspicion. The prisoner sat down and leaned back, cocking the chair on its rear legs.

"Hello, Hal." The grin was cocky and evil. "It's been a long time."

"Raymond," replied Hal, his voice casual. "It's a long trip up here."

"Longer for some than others," Raymond replied, his tone curious.

"The trip made me hungry. I need something to eat." Hal's manner was casual, but his eyes narrowed.

"What, you want me to get you some McDonald's?" snorted Raymond. He looked around the room. "Maybe some Wendy's? Burger King? How about fries and a shake?"

"No. I want some Jack in the Box," Hal's voice was colder, grimmer.

Raymond raised an eyebrow. "Oh really? You want some…Jack?"

Hal nodded, staring into the skinhead's eyes. "In a box."

Raymond lowered the chair back onto all fours, returning the stare. "Sounds like a big order. Can you afford it?"

Hal smiled, lips parting like a shark's. "Oh, yeah."

Raymond nodded. "Guess you'll get your dinner, then."

Hal stood up. "I'm looking forward to it. The sooner the better."

"It's on the grill." Raymond rose as well. "See ya, Hal." He walked back to the door, not even looking at Hal.

Hal turned to join Mike, feeling satisfied for the first time in days.

Chapter 7

Death Trap Within a Death Trap

Were it not for the fifteen-foot-high, chain-link fence topped with razor wire and the armed guards outside the fence, the exercise yard might have been mistaken for muscle beach. Inside the fence, Jack stood next to a worn weight bench, doing curls with a set of dumbbells. A mix of other prisoners, almost all Blacks or Latinos, stood loosely around Jack; some were using the weights, while others watched Jack with obvious admiration. His name, victories, opponents—all were the subject of the jailhouse banter.

For the first time since the fight, Jack felt at ease. He could survive this; he had lost his freedom for a time, but he could bear it. He could spend his days working out, his nights sleeping—how would that be any different from his previous life? A survival plan formed in his mind: stay quiet, plead manslaughter if necessary, do the time, and go back to Brazil and the dojo when it was all over. And, oh yeah, never again fight in the States.

In the midst of his daydream he heard the din of voices turn quiet. Glancing up, he saw an oversized prisoner approaching from about ten yards away. The man's arms were tattooed, his head shaved bald with a large swastika tattooed across the top. Three other men, heads shaved and bodies tattooed also, moved around Jack, one on his left and two on the right. The other prisoners backed away from the area. Jack realized at a glance that they hated the skinheads, but also feared them. Jack's face slid into a calm expression of certainty and purpose, the face he wore in the arena. Jack had the ability to shift into fight mode in an instant.

Raymond Moon moved quickly, but Jack was faster. Two 30-pound dumbbells left his hands in a forceful thrust, smashing into the skinhead's shins. Raymond screamed with pain and dropped to the ground. The skinhead on Jack's left charged forward, but Jack grabbed two 5-pound plates off the bench, ducking under a wild punch. Jack came back up and slammed the plates against this man's head like cymbals; the skinhead grabbed his skull and collapsed into a heap. As the two other men attacked from his right, Jack double-snap kicked his right leg into the stomach of one, then the other; the kicks sent both sprawling, just like on challenge day at the dojo. This time the move toppled Jack's attackers into a weight rack with a crash of metal plates and cries of pain. Raymond rose, howling with rage, and Jack hurled another five-pound weight like a discus straight into Raymond's forehead. There was an audible crack. Raymond fell backwards, his body bouncing twice as it hit the ground, fracturing his skull and putting him in a coma for two weeks.

Casually, Jack picked up two 25-five pound plates and turned to face the skinheads who were scrambling up from the tangle of barbells. Jack eyed them calmly. "Boys, are you ready to die today?" he asked as casually as if he were asking their names.

They looked at him, their two fallen comrades, the blood, and the crowd. The two remaining skinheads fled as the guards burst into the compound, grabbing Jack and tending to the two thugs on the ground. The murder-for-hire attempt had lasted less than a minute. Inside the building, near a window overlooking the yard, a guard frantically dialed into a small black cell phone.

The houseboat floated in an upscale marina, nestled amongst other luxury yachts, with the wide blue waters of Miami Bay stretching out before it. Mike Colvack lay on a foldout bench on the open deck, soaking in the warm Miami sun. Hal sat nearby under an awning, sipping a drink and watching pelicans swoop and dive into the bay. A cell phone rang on a nearby table. Hal flipped it open, his face twisted in a satisfied smirk, and he lifted the phone to his ear. He said nothing, but as he listened the smirk dissolved into an angry grimace.

"Thanks," he said flatly. "I'll take it from here." He snapped the phone shut with a furious clapping sound.

Mike looked over at the sound. "What happened? How bad did he get hit?"

"He didn't," replied Hal, barely able to control his rage. "He took 'em all out. Every one of those idiot skinheads." He hurled his glass at a pelican; the bird dodged out of the way, and the glass struck the water with a splash, vanishing instantly.

Mike sat up abruptly. "We can't let this one go! We gotta call Johnny and…"

Hal cut him off brusquely, his face determined and set. "No. We don't call Johnny. I can handle this. I need to handle this. Somebody's gonna learn a harsh lesson."

Mike looked at Hal, curiously. "Hal, what are we gonna do?"

Hal gave Mike a grim, evil smile.

Out over the water a thunderhead was forming, drifting slowly towards the city as the afternoon slipped away.

The storm broke after sunset. Rain poured across the streets of Miami, turning the air into a thick curtain of driving water. A stream rolled over a highway at the edge of town, flowing past a convenience market whose neon lights cut invitingly through the watery haze. Rain streamed down the windows of the store in sheets, blurring the sights inside and making even the posters on the windows indistinct. A pale blue sedan with rental plates pulled to a stop in front of the store, its wipers beating futilely against the driving downpour. Inside the car, Julia peered through the rain, trying to read the street sign at the corner and then read a road map at the same time.

"I know the Wilsons live right around here somewhere. It's been so long that everything looks different."

A dark gray Mercedes pulled in next to the sedan, the doors opening almost as soon as it stopped.

Art squinted and tried to read the map as well. He shook his head. "I'll go in and ask for directions."

The occupants of the Mercedes got out in the pouring rain and positioned themselves in front of the sedan. Slowly, up from their sides, they drew guns, one in each hand. Four 45-caliber pistols with magnum loaded bullets. Though they were only six feet away, they aimed as if in a shooting gallery. In a flash, Art and Julia looked up at the soaked, shadowy figures standing before them in the downpour. Just as Art squeaked out a barely audible "Oh Jesus, no," the guns began to fire in rapid succession. The windshield of the sedan shattered into tiny bits of glass, the roaring of the rain broken by the staccato pop of gunfire.

After eighteen overkill shots were fired into the front windshield of the small sedan, Art, struck by four bullets in the chest and three to the face, fell back against his seat. Julia, with six bullet holes punctured through her soft pink sweater in the upper torso area slumped sideways against Art. They lay together in a position symbolic of the "till death do we part" vow they made to one another forty years earlier. Her head dangled over Art's chest, held up by the shoulder belt taut against her body. The rain washed in on the shards of broken glass, the heavy drops cleansing red streaks off tiny glass fragments that salted the seats and dash and floorboards.

Outside, Mike and Hal Colvack turned at the sound of an engine roaring behind the sedan. They shot at a retreating car and heard the crash and smack of bullets hitting glass and metal. The car continued to speed off.

"Did you see the driver? Did you hit them?" Hal yelled over the pounding torrents.

"Yeah, I think so, but the rain is strong. I can't tell for sure!" Mike yelled back.

Hal cursed. "There are people in the store! We can't let them see our faces. Let's shoot out the windows, scare 'em good, and then get in the car and get outta here!"

Mike pumped several bullets into the glass, and it crashed down around the walls. Inside, vague forms ducked and fell to the floor in horror. Hal jumped into the passenger side of the Mercedes, while Mike, the car still moving, raced backwards into the rain before his door was fully closed.

There was no movement in the sedan, only the lifeless forms of two loving missionaries from Brazil who had dedicated their lives to helping people. They lay silently as the rain soaked their lifeless forms, mixing water with blood. They were added to the numbers of innocent victims tragically sacrificed because of the Colvacks' hunger for money and power. So tragic. So pointless. So final.

Agent Phillips fell backwards as the metal table crashed over towards him. Jack was screaming, leaping across the fallen table, grabbing Phillips and slamming him into the mirrored glass of the interrogation room.

"You're lying! You're lying!" he yelled, over and over, his hands grasping the agent's throat.

Watkins jumped backwards, pulling his pistol and bracing his feet, both hands on the gun. "Jack, Jack, pull it in!" he shouted. "Pull it in! Let him go *now*. I'll have to shoot you, Jack! Stop! I'll have to shoot!"

A guard burst through the door, his gun drawn and leveled at Jack. Jack spun around, tossing Phillips into the guard, knocking his arms so the gun pointed upwards at the ceiling. Phillips and the guard were sprawled on the floor.

"Jack! *Pull it in!*" roared Watkins.

Jack turned away from Watkins, slamming his fists into the wall. His screams faded into sobs of grief as he slumped down into a heap of helpless despair on the floor.

"It's not true; it's not true." His voice grew fainter, as if he weren't talking to anyone in the room at all. "You're lying; you're lying." On the floor, leaning against the wall, he looked like just another lost child of the streets.

Watkins holstered his pistol, his eyes remaining cautiously on Jack. Phillips rose and helped the guard up. He caught the edge of Watkins' eye, nodded *I'm okay,* and motioned the guard out of the room.

Jack's breathing came in gasps, and Watkins stepped over the table to crouch beside him. Behind them, Phillips slowly righted the table and chairs. Jack looked up at Watkins, as if seeing him for the first time.

"Why? Why them?" he asked, his voice soft and broken. "What kind of animals would do that? It wasn't their fight, it was mine..." A gasp of breath broke his sentence. "Come after *me,* not them..." His voice broke again, falling into sobs.

This dangerous man was just a momma's boy after all. His dad was his hero. They were all the family he had. His big body was now shaking and weak.

Watkins placed a hand gently on Jack's shoulder. He spoke softly with all the comfort he could offer.

"What can we do, Jack?"

Jack grasped the hand and shifted his body, righting himself and trying to steady the sobs.

"I need time to think. I just need some time."

Phillips stepped to the other side of Jack and bent to help him up. "We'll give you all the time you need," he said gently. "But we need to move you to another cell. The Colvacks aren't about to stop with this. They still want you dead. We've got to put you under high security."

Jack nodded weakly. All his energy was gone.

A guard entered to take Jack back to his cell. He held a pair of handcuffs. Jack barely noticed as Watkins pushed away the cuffs, shaking his head no to the guard. The men walked slowly from the room saying nothing. It was a pitiful sight to see.

It was night in New York City, and the city lights glowed outside Johnny Colvack's penthouse office. The room was even more opulent than the office in Miami, with marbled walls and inlaid furniture. Johnny and Samantha sat across from each other at a desk, papers spread in front of them, promotional plans for another fight. An office phone on the edge of the desk blinked with a faint white light. Johnny and Samantha ignored it.

A faint tap sounded on the door. Johnny frowned and spoke firmly towards it. "I told you I didn't want to be disturbed."

The door jarred open slightly, and Johnny's secretary peeked into the room. "I'm sorry, sir, but it's Hal from Miami. He says it's an emergency. Very, very important." She closed the door swiftly, retreating from sight.

Johnny stared at Samantha. "What could this possibly be?" he growled.

Samantha shrugged. "I don't know what you have him in charge of," she replied. "I don't have a clue."

Johnny grunted and picked up the phone. "What is it?" he spoke brusquely. His eyes widened in surprise, then glowered with anger.

"What? What? What's going on?" asked Samantha, both curious and concerned.

Johnny was seething, his expression growing darker, angrier. He burst through the silence with rage. "You *what?!* You *whacked them?* You stupid, stupid, asinine fools! You wasted two people and you didn't even think to consult me? Did anybody see you?"

105

Somewhere inside Samantha came the uncomfortable thought that she should not be hearing this. She ignored it.

"What were you *thinking*?" Johnny's voice rose with anger. He turned towards her, though he seemed as if he'd forgotten she was even there. She could hear Hal at the other end, talking excitedly and rapidly.

"No! I tried to have him put away in the can by the skinheads, but they blew it," Hal protested on the line.

Johnny pressed his hand against his temple in frustration. "The skinheads? They're grunts. They knock over liquor stores. Who gave you the authority to have *anybody* whacked? This is an extremely volatile, high-profile hit. Did you go over my head for the OK?"

"No, Johnny, no." The plea was high and tinny, but the fear was evident.

"So you went *through* my head," said Johnny coldly. "You killed his parents."

Samantha's eyebrows shot up in surprise.

"I can't believe how *stupid* you have the capability of being!"

I can, thought Samantha.

"But Johnny, he killed Bruce!" Hal's voice yelled from the phone. "What did you want me to do, just let it go?"

Johnny's voice was like ice. "Bruce killed himself. He went where he wasn't ordered to go. He didn't ask for permission, just like you didn't ask for permission. He got *himself* killed, and now you're gonna get us all nailed to the wall."

Samantha could hear Hal's confusion. "What do you mean? All we gotta do is…"

Johnny cut him off angrily, "Never mind, 'all we gotta do is—'; I can't believe what an utter *imbecile* I have for an underboss. Jack would have done his time. One, two years max and been out and gone. He doesn't want heat from us. But you two utter *morons*.... When you kill a guy's parents, he's got nothing left to lose. Now his soul lives and breathes with payback. Now he goes to the FBI, who's been on us for two years. He cuts a deal, goes state's evidence and brings us all down!"

Hal's reply was feeble. "Nah...you think?"

"You *idiot!*" Johnny roared. "Yeah, I think! You'll never get him now. He'll be under such high security that sunlight won't be able to touch him!"

The voice on the other end of the phone was in total collapse. "Johnny, I'm sorry. I just thought..."

"Stop thinking, stop doing, stop planning, stop talking!" yelled Johnny. "You and our other *genius* brother just sit in the hotel room and wait for me to fly in from New York. Don't talk to *anybody*. Don't even talk to each other. *Idiots!*" Johnny slammed the phone down.

"This guy DeNova has gotta go. If I have to bury him myself, he has to go." He turned to Samantha and pointed at her. "He knows you and me. We've got signed contracts." He turned away, his hands pressed against his temples. "I've got idiots for brothers, and on top of that I've now got a pit fighter with revenge in his eyes breathing down my neck like a panther." He slapped a hand against his desk chair, spinning it in a violent whirl that sent it slamming into a nearby credenza. With his hands on his hips, Johnny glared out the window in fuming fury.

Samantha looked from Johnny to the chair. The nagging doubt returned to her mind, along with a certainty that the Colvacks and Jack weren't the only ones on dangerous ground; now she had a lot to lose as well.

Chapter 8

A Decision With Precision

Jack was back in the gray room again. There was no sign of his earlier rampage, either in the room or on the faces of the men sitting there. The gray walls, the gray table, the gray chairs all looked the same, as if they never changed, as if the room were a portion of limbo on earth, a place where nothing happened, a place waiting for a decision. Watkins and Phillips sat on one side of the table, their hands folded, watching Jack, waiting like the room for a decision.

Jack sat across from the agents, his face stern and cold. His right hand was on the table, his forefinger tapping slowly. Jack was staring down at his finger, concentrating on it as if he were counting out in his mind what he wanted to say, point by point. Except for the faint tapping, the room was silent.

The tapping stopped. Jack looked up firmly at Watkins and Phillips. When he spoke, the words came out almost in monotone, like a man reading a death sentence. "OK, here's the deal," he said. "It's nonnegotiable. It has to be this way or I'm completely out and I'll take my chances on the inside."

Watkins looked at Phillips, but neither spoke or nodded.

Jack continued. "You want the Colvacks, and I don't fear death. So, are we talking?"

"Go on," Watkins replied, his tone neutral but interested.

Jack nodded, and clasped his hands together. "If I stay in prison till I testify, I die." His voice was matter of fact, logical, and emotionless. "There's too much time. They tank me, you lose your case. So I move, and I move tomorrow. I'll do the witness protection thing, but I pick the location. I don't trust anybody right now, so hear me out. There's a vacation spot I used to go to in central Florida with my parents' friends, the Wilsons. It's a small amusement park surrounded by a sleepy little town. Mid-South Amusement Park, ever hear of it?"

"No," Phillips said.

Jack rephrased the question, "Ever hear of Summerville?"

"No," Watkins said, looking at Phillips. Phillips shook his head with a shrug.

"Exactly," said Jack. "It's so small it doesn't even show up on the map. It's just an exit sign. *That's* where I'll go and the only place I'll feel safe till I testify."

Watkins looked at Phillips. His partner nodded.

"We'll check it out," said Watkins. "We'll have to find someone to shadow you for us. An FBI operative might be around there somewhere. We'll try, Jack." He looked at Jack; his voice was sincere.

Jack nodded. "One more thing. Before I disappear, I need to go and bury my parents at the mission in Brazil."

Phillips looked at Watkins.

Jack could see the concern on their faces. He shrugged. "Talk it out, boys. You pull off those two things, and I'm in." He stood and walked to the door, knocking on it. When the guard opened it, Jack stuck out his hands for the cuffs and walked through. The door closed after him, leaving Phillips and Watkins behind in the gray room to make their own decision.

Choices and Losses

The walk back to his cell was quiet for Jack. Something had gone out of him; the confidence and surety of action were missing from his gait.

The drab prison walls looked different now, as if he saw them—and his whole life—truly for the first time. He remembered the bright green, vibrant foliage around the old mission, and the wide, deep waters of the Amazon teeming with both life and danger. He recalled the taunts of the Brazilian boys, the fights, and the beatings. He reflected back on how he had blamed his father for those fights, how he had turned away from his father, the mission, and Christianity for the promise of the temporal power he saw in the dojo. And he considered the promise of safety he thought he saw in the strong, fearless face of Marco Brudel.

He remembered his first fights under Marco's teaching, how he had poured all his pent-up young rage on his opponents, as if they were responsible for denying him his life in Buffalo, for taking him to the jungle and away from school and baseball and video games and all the other things he

111

thought should be his. He remembered how Marco challenged his anger, using it to fuel his progress on the mat, until he learned to control it. Marco taught him to force it below the surface—but never far enough.

He saw again the sad look on his father's face when he told him about his first tournament, the look he now understood as a bittersweet mixture of pride as a father and loss as a minister. He considered how he had turned more and more to Marco in those days, and at long last he felt the pain he knew his father felt then.

He remembered the struggle his mother made to heal the rift, a memory that called more recent days to his mind—the dance by the river, the locket, the last sad meeting in the visiting area.

And, amidst it all, again and again he saw the frightened, lost image of Bruce Colvack's face just before his own foot caught his neck and ended it all. The slam of the cell door behind Jack had echoed that fatal crack.

Jack sat down on a chair facing his bunk. He leaned back, his eyes drifting around the room, not seeing the walls but Marco, Bruce, his mother, and his father. His eyes fell on the familiar, worn, leather Bible that lay on his bunk. Jack moved from the chair to the bunk, picking up the Bible and clutching it to his chest, clinging to it as if he could feel his father in it, as if those tattered pages contained the answers to everything his life had been and was supposed to be. A faint, bittersweet laugh rose from inside of him, and he lay the Bible on his lap.

"Well Dad, I guess you were right," he said quietly. "Now I've got time to read this thing."

Suddenly he remembered what his mother had said about the note inside, and he opened the book. Inside the cover, in the same precise, tiny handwriting that covered the bits of paper sticking out of the book, was his father's note. He read it quietly, saying the words aloud as if his own voice could be his father's.

"My dearest son Jack," he read, and tears came into his eyes. "I pray the words of this book will bring you the life and relationship with Christ they have brought me."

Jack bowed his head, all the memories of his life flooded back again. The words his father had said to him throughout the years—the loving advice he had shoved aside not wanting his father to be right, not wanting the move to Brazil to have been the right decision.

Suddenly he saw how empty his own life had been, how the fighting and the tournaments and the glory amounted to nothing, nothing but a jail cell and a family lost. A sob shook his body. He choked it back and finished the note.

"He came to this world not to save the righteous, but the sinner. You've given the world your best—now give Jesus the rest. Your loving father, Reverend Art—Daddy."

Facing the Music

The book fell closed in his lap. His body heaved with sorrow and loss, shame and regret. His face dropped into his hands, his breath gasping, sobbing, all the pain and anger and sorrow and shame welling up inside of him, pouring out. There was no way to push it down, no way to control it, no one to fight in that cell except himself. He slid off the bunk, collapsing to his knees, the words flowing from him in a desperate torrent. "I'm so sorry, Dad. I'm sorry, Mom. Lord, forgive me, change me. Can You make Your way into my heart? I need You now, Jesus; give me a new life. I'm ready. I'm ready now."

He stayed down on the bunk, his face in his hands as the sobs faded. He didn't know how long he had been there—maybe an hour or so—or how he knew it was time to rise. But he rolled back in the bunk and lay with his head propped up against the steely backboard. Throwing a pillow behind him, he opened the Bible again. He turned to a page marked with a ribbon. *Hmm...the Gospel of John.* Jack started to read and continued without pause into the deep dark hours of the next morning.

A song filtered through the open doors of the mission, reaching out into the clearing and the bright green jungle, down towards the river and past the benches where the ladies had sung just a week earlier. Now the voices were tinged with sadness, the Portuguese words adding a lyrical melancholy to the music. A few late arrivals wandered up from the riverside towards the church—a small flotilla of boats of all descriptions rocked and bumped against each other along the pier, and more kept arriving. Other mourners stood on benches outside to peer through the open mission windows. The native visitors eyed with curiosity the white man in a black suit and dark sunglasses who stood by the mission door. Even as he looked them over, his face remained impassive. On the road in front of the church two more men, similarly dressed, stood next to a large black SUV with tinted windows.

The church was packed with mourners, all natives of the Amazon region, many crying, some joining in to sing with the ladies' choir. In front of the church, two coffins lay end to end, lids open, covered with flowers that spilled extravagantly onto the floor, creating a carpet in the same vibrant colors of the forest.

Amidst the flowers lay Art and Julia, their faces barely visible above the generous tide of blossoms. Behind them, a simple wooden pulpit stood facing the crowd. As the song ended, a middle-aged native man stepped forward. He began to speak in Portuguese, his voice gentle and strong. The mourners listened and nodded, murmuring agreement, the tears on their faces glinting in the sunlight that poured warmly through the windows.

In the front row sat Jack, face down, whether listening to the eulogy or praying, his companions could not tell. Watkins sat on his right, Phillips on his left. They understood neither the eulogy nor the song, but waited patiently through both, occasionally glancing discreetly around the room with cautious eyes.

The eulogy ended, and the pastor spoke in cultured English. "Ashes to ashes. Dust to dust. From the ground we came, and to the ground we will return. We live to die, and die only to live again."

He walked forward to Jack, leaning over to whisper in soft tones. "Jack, it's time to close the coffins and say good-bye. If you don't want to do it, I'll do it for you."

Jack looked up at him. "No, I need to do this myself."

The Last Farewell

Jack stood up, steadied himself, and walked to his father's casket. He stared quietly at the body for a moment, remembering times bad and good. Jack reached under his own collar and lifted a gold chain and medallion from his neck. The medallion slipped off the chain and into his hand. He looked at it one last time, reading the inscription, then he bent over the casket to place the medallion in his father's coat pocket.

He spoke softly, "Dad, I was never the king of anything— you were. They called me the 'King of the Jungle,' but you...you brought the King to the jungle...I love you Daddy and...I'll miss you every day."

Jack gently closed the lid of the coffin, and a tear trickled down one cheek. Slowly he walked to the other casket, his body now shaking a little, his grief rising as he approached it. He put his left hand on the coffin to steady himself.

Straightening up, he looked in the casket at his mother. His hand slipped under her left, holding it among the flowers. Slowly he slipped Julia's gold wedding band off her hand. He threaded the gold chain through the ring, and hung the chain back around his neck, a new medallion to replace the old.

"I will always keep you close to my heart, Mom," he whispered softly. "And someday, someday I will make you proud of me. I promise...I'll always love my Queen of Hearts."

He closed the coffin lid and turned to follow Watkins and Phillips out of the church to the waiting car and a future he could not predict.

Chapter 9

The Shadowlands

Once again, Jack sat in an airplane looking out the window and watching the sunset west of Florida. This time the jet was smaller, an FBI plane, and the only passengers were Jack, Phillips, and Watkins. As on his last flight, Jack pulled out the small laminated card with the faded picture on the front, and, as he had done so often, he turned it over and began rubbing the little silver cross on the back.

Phillips sat across from Jack watching him rub the card. If he was curious about the odd little ritual, he didn't show it.

Watkins was out of his seat, walking back towards the pair and holding two cups of coffee. He offered one to Phillips, then sat down facing Jack.

"Hey, Jack," he said. "We did find somebody to be our operative that you'll be accountable to in this Summerville place."

Jack looked up from the card. "Oh, yeah? Who is he?"

Phillips smirked and gave a knowing chuckle. "You want the good news first or the bad news?"

Jack looked at him with curiosity. "I think I can use some good news right about now."

Watkins sat back and sipped his coffee. "His name is Frank McQue. He's an ex-FBI man. He's worked with us several times before in witness protection situations. When we have a tough case that needs to be eyeballed real close, often we bring Frank in. But this is the first time we're actually sending one to him…as you will see for obvious reasons. But this is where you want to go sooo…"

Phillips leaned over to Jack. "His specialty during his FBI years was undercover disguise. He loved the challenge of going under the criminal radar screen. He could make himself look like anyone. But he's retired now and has some pretty firm ideas on how to rehabilitate somebody."

"What do you mean?" asked Jack.

Watkins laughed lightly. "Well Jack, my boy, that's what we figure to be the downside for a guy like you and why we never sent somebody to him. You see, at one time Frank considered becoming a chaplain within the FBI system. But he liked workin' the streets so much he decided he would wait till he retired. Now he's a pastor."

Jack sat up slightly. "A what?"

Phillips chuckled again. "Figured that would freak you out."

Jack settled back into his seat, smiling to himself. "No, I'm cool. A pastor? How funny. Art must be up there cuttin' some deals with somebody."

"Are you gonna have a problem with that?" Watkins asked.

Jack looked over to him, grinning. "No, I obviously need it."

Watkins laughed again. "Comin' from where you've been, that's an understatement."

Throughout the discussion, Jack held the card in his hand rubbing the cross.

"What are you doing with that little card, Jack?" asked Watkins, eyeing the motion of Jack's thumb.

Jack smiled again, looking at the cross on the card as if for the first time. "Just a tradition I have before I face a big challenge."

The plane banked to the west, and a last ray of sunlight streamed through the window gleaming off the card and the tiny metal cross.

It was Saturday evening when they drove into the town of Summerville. Just as Jack had said, it was little more than an exit, a side stop for summer tourists on their way to somewhere else. They passed a run-down gas station outside of town, its lights off as if the owner expected no one else to pull in, though it was barely 9:30 p.m.

The town itself consisted largely of small, mom & pop tourist restaurants and a small long-outdated amusement park, the kind of place only locals go—or vacationers without the funds for more famous places. Looking at it, Jack remembered peering out the car window with longing as a young boy as his family drove past the signs for Disney World, Epcot, and SeaWorld and instead pulled in here.

For years it had been the last place he wanted to go; now, strangely, he had the feeling it was the only place he felt good about.

Phillips turned the car into an unusually crowded parking lot in front of a brick and corrugated metal building, which was set back at the end of a row of small shops and businesses. A large wooden sign in front of the building declared the establishment to be "His House."

To Jack's eyes it looked more like a warehouse than a church. A flash of memory of the dojo in Rio raced through his mind. A small illuminated sign with black push-on letters sat out front. The sign read, "KIRK FRANKLIN TONIGHT 8 PM".

"Who's that?" Phillips asked. "Ain't never heard of him."

Watkins grinned. "Oh yeah. I got his records."

"Is he like a musician or something?" asked Jack.

Watkins grinned even bigger. "Oh, you'll see. You'll really dig this guy."

As they walked through the doors of the church, noise hit them like a sudden wave crashing off the beach. The room vibrated with heavy, pounding bass rhythm, the sound of hip-hop and funk music. Jack and Phillips looked at each other in stunned surprise, but Watkins could barely keep from dancing himself. Almost unconsciously, his head and shoulders began to weave to the music.

On the stage a young black man was dancing back and forth, singing, shouting, rapping. Behind him, a choir in hip-hop clothing sang along, dancing in moves choreographed to the hard funk beats of the music. From the front of the stage back to the doors, the place was filled with young people—teenagers, college kids, men and women in their twenties and early thirties—a mass of humanity, all grooving and dancing to the music.

Jack grinned and turned to Phillips, shouting over the music, "If they had music like this in my church when I was growing up, I probably would never have gotten involved in jiu jitsu!" Like Watkins, he started moving with the rhythm.

Watkins nudged Jack and pointed towards the left side of the stage. "Yo Jack, that's McQue. That's Frank."

Jack looked and saw a large, muscular black man clapping his hands, dancing, and shouting with the music. The man wore a short beard and had a light blue bandanna tied on his head "dew rag" style. He was wearing a long, loose sports jersey and jeans. A thick gold ring glinted on one hand.

"He looks like somebody I faced in a tournament one time in Japan," he shouted back.

"As soon as the concert is over, probably another fifteen minutes or so, I'll introduce you to Frank in the back office. You'll like him," Watkins yelled.

Jack nodded, watching Frank as the man danced on stage with the singer. The words of the song echoed in his mind, words about change and hope and the promises of God. Suddenly, against all the raw pain of his memories he felt like something new was happening.

The eyes that had been dulled by grief and guilt seemed to brighten in a glimmer of hope, as if in the music he could hear the possibility of a new life, like a dream forming in his heart. As if looking at a new home, he scanned the room watching the others dancing, totally oblivious to his presence. His eyes fell on an attractive young woman in the back row clapping her hands to the music, the dim light from the stage just barely revealing her features.

This time it was Jack's turn to nudge Watkins and point. "Now if they'd had babes like that in my church when I was a kid, I definitely would have stayed!"

He and Watkins both laughed and began to both jam to the music. Phillips looked at them in amusement, but even he was nodding his head with the beat. It was definitely a different kind of church.

Frank McQue's office was oddly peaceful after the celebration of the concert. A large bay window looked out over woods that ran behind the church and away from the town. The bookshelves and walls were decorated with a mixture of mementos, from photos of Frank at youth events and church activities, to newspaper clippings and plaques from his years in the FBI.

One series of photos in particular caught Jack's eye; it was a framed group of twelve pictures, each apparently of a different person. Yet something in each picture reminded Jack of

Frank. He looked under the photos and read a small inscription at the bottom of the frame: "Frank McQue—Master of Disguise! From the boys downtown."

Jack studied Frank out of the corner of his eye, mentally comparing him to the pictures. He was an older man, maybe fifty-ish, but still very fit. He looked like a fighter.

Frank removed the bandana, revealing a smooth bald head. As he wiped off a thin layer of perspiration from his scalp, Jack noticed that the gold ring Frank wore was engraved with a small cross.

Frank sank into a simple, padded, wood and leather chair behind a desk constructed of warm maple. Photos of Frank and children, from infants to teenagers, encircled the workspace. Sermon notes, study books, and a worn leather Bible also lay open on the desk. The Bible reminded Jack of the one his father had given him; the sight of it gave him a sense of familiar comfort.

Watkins and Phillips sat in two chairs near the window, and Jack slid into a third opposite Frank, setting his small backpack on the floor beside him.

Frank grinned as Jack sat down. "So, Mr. DeNova, you're a pretty interesting character. It's gonna be fun havin' you around."

Jack looked at him, surprised. "How do you mean?"

"Well, now I'll have somebody I can watch all those pay-per-view fights on TV with." When Jack looked at him with even greater surprise, Frank laughed. "I used to be a self-defense instructor. I trained the new FBI recruits."

Phillips gave an exaggerated groan as if in memory. Obviously one of Frank's former pupils.

Jack's interest perked up. "Oh really? What was your main discipline?"

"Well, it was a combination of things." Frank said in the tone of someone warming up about a favorite hobby. "Some Russian Sambo, several judo throws, and of course jiu jitsu for the finishing holds."

Jack nodded. "I kind of figured that was what you guys would use. How'd you feel about boxing? I felt it was an essential for me."

Frank grinned. "Every day I'd make 'em all go at least of couple of rounds, slippin,' duckin,' counterin'—nothing prepares you better for the streets than taking a real shot and firing one back."

Watkins looked at Phillips with a grin.

Jack laughed. "You and I are gonna get along just fine."

"Maybe someday we can spar or roll on the mats," Frank suggested with equal good humor.

"As long as you don't wear your collar," joked Jack. "I don't want to lose my concentration."

Frank joined in laughing with Jack, and the two banged their fists together like fighters starting a match.

Watkins spoke up from his chair, "Well, Frank, we didn't realize you guys would have as much in common as you do."

"I think I understand a bit about who and what Jack is," replied Frank, nodding in reply, but still looking mostly at Jack. "And I certainly understand the world where he comes from." His eyes fell on Jack's backpack. The old brown Bible was sticking out from an outside pouch. Frank pointed to the Bible. "Is that yours, Jack?"

Jack glanced down at the book. "It's my father's. He gave it to me." He looked at Frank, feeling the need to go on. "I'm just starting to read it—I mean, really read it."

Frank smiled, the soft, gentle smile of a friend. "I hear you, player. Maybe I can help with that too."

Jack smiled back as if to say, *Thanks—I could use it.*

Phillips leaned forward. "Frank, we'll need to know the specifics about jobs, living quarters, work routines, and general daily operational patterns until the trial."

Frank sat back. "Well, Jack, you can live in the basement of the church. It's a totally finished studio apartment; I started out in it myself."

Jack nodded his acceptance.

"You will be put to work immediately, " continued Frank. "Ushering, cleanup, or volunteering as needed—but I expect you to find a small job in Summerville to fill out the rest of the time. We'll meet every day, and guys, the rest is business as usual for us."

"There are some pretty ferocious characters after Jack," said Watkins, "and we want a daily report on who he runs with, walks with, and sits with."

"I'm aware," replied Frank looking at Jack. Jack shrugged his OK; he expected to have to put up with some nurse aiding.

"Jack, you're gonna need a new identity for protection," added Phillips.

Frank glanced at Jack's hands. "What's that across your knuckles, Jack?"

Jack splayed out his hands, holding them up. "It says 'vale tudo.' " He pronounced the phrase "val-lay-two-doe."

"Anything goes, eh?" Frank shook his head in amusement. "Well, since there are no Brazilians around here, there's only one way to explain that—that's now your new identity. Frank pronounced the name, "Vail Too-doo."

Jack grinned. "At least it'll be easy to remember."

The men laughed.

Frank stood up and stuck out his hand to shake Jack's. "Comin' from where you've been son, it looks like you've done the full 180. So I guess all that's left to say is, it's good to meet you, Vail. Welcome to 'His House.' "

Jack stood and accepted Frank's hand.

"Come on, Jack. I'll show you your new digs," Frank said, opening the door to the office.

Watkins and Phillips rose to follow them.

"The stairs are at the front of the building, so we'll cut across the stage." He led them down a short corridor and through a door that opened behind a curtain at the back of the stage. On the stage, volunteers were busy loading out the concert equipment through a large side door, leaving only the church piano behind. Frank wove through the busy workers, clapping people on the back and thanking them. Suddenly they heard a cry from the back of the sanctuary.

Jack looked out to see a figure in a hooded starter jacket running out the front doors.

"He just grabbed the offering!" yelled a man sprawled on the floor.

Without thinking, Jack jumped off the stage, racing after the thief.

"Wait, Jack, no! I'll take care of this...no!" Frank yelled after him, but Jack was already bursting through the doors.

Outside the church, Jack's face took on the same focused expression as in the ring. He ran after the thief, his arms moving like pistons, his stride paced and calculated like a decathlete in a competition. The thief saw Jack behind him and started running as fast and frantically. Suddenly he darted to the left, crossing the street, barely dodging a station wagon. Jack lept over the hood of a parked car and crossed the street at an angle, closing the distance. The thief ducked into a narrow parking lot in front of a single-story apartment complex. The lot was barely more than an alley surrounded by a high wood fence. Trapped, the young thief started grabbing doorknobs, trying to get into the apartments. The doors were locked. He was trying the last door when Jack rounded the corner. Jack slowed to a walk, not even winded, and moved towards the thief like a predator stalking its prey.

In the lights from the parking lot, Jack could see that the thief was young, a teenager no more than 17. The boy's eyes were angry and nervous. He screamed at Jack, "OK, here it is! You want it? It's yours!" and tossed the heavy plastic deposit bag at Jack's head. Jack slipped to the right as if dodging a punch, and the bag whizzed over his shoulder. Jack heard it hit and skid along the ground behind him, but he ignored the bag and continued to approach the thief.

"Get off me, man!" The boy yelled. "I don't have it! It's yours now; I don't want it. I'm done. Leave me alone!" He backed away, hands out as if to fend off Jack.

Jack's eyes narrowed, and he shook his head with anger. "Nobody steals God's money. You're gonna pay punk."

The kid's eyes grew wild with fear. With a snarl he rushed at Jack, his right hand swinging wildly. Jack easily ducked under the punch and swung his left foot out in a swift, low arc, sweeping behind and through the boy's legs. The boy fell backwards, his feet in the air, his back slamming to the pavement.

The wind and the fight were out of the boy, but Jack was on top of him in a flash, his knee on the boy's shoulder, his left hand grabbing the boy's shirt, pulling him up as the right hand smashed into his face. Once...the boy was groaning. Twice...blood flowed from a cut. Three times....

On the third swing, a huge black arm wrapped around Jack's neck, yanking him up and off the boy like a massive noose. The teenager lay whimpering, feebly trying to shield his face from another blow. Frank's left hand shoved Jack's head further into the chokehold he had with his right arm. Spinning Jack around, he then slammed him, face first, into the brick wall of the apartments.

At that moment Watkins, Phillips, and several church members rounded the corner. Phillips scooped the bank bag off the ground.

"Frank, I've got the money!" he yelled. "It's right here."

Frank continued to press Jack into the wall, preventing Jack from moving or breaking the hold.

130

"OK man, cool down." Frank said firmly. "And I mean right now. You've gone over the top, and if you don't let your temperature drop, I'm going to put you to sleep right here. We understand each other?"

Jack was breathing heavy, the adrenaline slowly fading. He could feel the hold tightening around his neck, just like a thousand chokes he had used on his opponents in the octagon. There was no way out but to submit. His anger cooled; he reached back with his left hand and tapped Frank on the hip four times. Frank acknowledged the signal, loosening his grip and stepping back, giving himself distance in case Jack made a move. Jack stepped away from the wall.

"Nice choke," Jack said to Frank as he rubbed his neck. "Couldn't have done it better myself." He nodded towards Phillips. "In case you are wondering, I got the money back."

Frank's tone remained firm and hard. "Yeah, but we may never see this kid around here again. You and me need to have a serious talk tomorrow. I want you in my office at 9 a.m. Don't be late, or I'll hunt you down. Are we cool?"

Jack looked at him, unsure of what was going on. "We're cool."

Frank bent down to help the boy up. He clung to Frank's arm, groaning softly. Frank gently dabbed a handkerchief against the boy's face.

A police car, lights flashing, pulled into the parking lot. Faces peered out of a few of the apartment windows, watching what was going on.

The policeman stepped out of the car and called out, "What happened, Frank?"

Frank walked with the boy towards the car. "The boy just got in a little scrape. Can you take him down to the county clinic and have him checked out?"

The officer nodded. "Sure thing, Frank. Put him in the back. I'll take it from here."

Like a father tending to a wounded son, Frank helped the boy into the back seat of the police car, talking calmly to him, reassuring him. Frank closed the door and the car pulled away.

Jack watched on with amazement, the question evident in his eyes.

Frank shook his head, "No, no charges," he said responding to the unasked question. With that he turned and walked away towards the church. The church members turned back with him—none of them looked towards Jack.

"What was that about?" Jack asked Phillips and Watkins.

"Guess you'll find out in the morning," replied Watkins coolly. "Let's get you into your new room. I think we all need some sleep."

"And Jack," said Phillips, "the whole point of this is to keep you alive. It would help if you would stop trying to get yourself killed." His expression told Jack that he wasn't joking. "Please Jack, no more incidents to make yourself stand out. You're supposed to be in hiding, remember?"

The morning sunlight was glowing brightly through Frank's window when Jack knocked on the opened office door. Frank was sitting behind the desk, just staring at his hands which were folded in front of him. He looked up at Jack's knock.

"Come on in. Have a seat, Jack."

Jack closed the door and glanced at the clock. "Well, I'm on time. It's 9 a.m."

Frank shook his head. "Nope, you're late. Around here if you ain't early, you're late."

Jack sat down, and Frank looked him in the eye. "Jack—who or whatever you were is not what you're gonna be here. What you did last night was wrong."

Jack shrugged defensively. "That little thug stole the offering. I don't have to be a missionary's kid to know that's wrong. I caught him, and I gave him something to think about."

Frank frowned. "Yeah, well, 'mister gave him something to think about,' let me give you something to think about. That kid has been comin' to this church for six months. It was a Saturday night. He could have been out doin' coke, but he was here. His father was arrested for armed robbery and is servin' time in Marion State Pen. All that boy knows is the streets, robbin' and thuggin.' "

"So he stole the money," said Jack. "Is that very Christian?"

Frank shook his head angrily. "Boy, you don't get it, do you? You've got to catch a fish before you can clean it. That boy ain't been caught by the net of God yet—and besides, you don't know the progress I've made with him so far."

"Stealin' money is progress?"

"You're alive, ain't you?" Frank replied coolly.

Jack snorted. "What? As if that wannabe was gonna mess *me* up."

Frank's voice became cold. "That's no wannabe, Jack. That kid came here from Hell's Kitchen in New York City. His name is Russell Bowman. They used to call him 'Busta' in Hell's Kitchen 'cause he was the head of the Vice Lords, and when somebody looked at him cross-eyed, he'd bust a cap in their head.

He came down here to stay with his grandma to get away from a death trap being set for him by a rival gang. One night he walks in here with his grandma, and guess what? He likes the music! So he stays. And listens. He stole that money 'cause his grandmother's welfare check didn't come in."

Jack raised his hands. "How am I supposed to know all this?"

"You're not, 'cause you're not the pastor—I am," Frank said, his voice filled with firm authority. "That kid is as bad as you'll ever be. You killed one man by accident. Russell's killed eight on purpose. From now on, you take your cues from me. If you don't see me run, you don't run."

Jack shook his head in disgust. "That kid would've never gotten the best of me."

Frank laughed, almost mockingly. "You're so full of pride and revenge. You not only can't see straight, you can't think straight. Six months ago if you would have chased that kid down that alley, he would have pulled a nine-millimeter and splattered you all over the walls. You wouldn't have gotten within ten feet of him. Did he have a gun?"

"No," Jack said soberly, thinking.

"A knife?"

"No."

Frank shook his head. "Jack, that's called progress. I'll bet he didn't even fight you for the money."

Jack's voice became more reserved, less certain of himself. "No, he threw it over my head."

Frank stood up and walked to the front of the desk. He leaned against it with his hands on the edges, looking down at Jack. His voice was gentler, but firm.

"Before this whole event goes over your head, you need to realize that the only reason you beat that boy down was because you still got a lot of anger in your soul. You're used to solving all your problems with your fists, but it's your fists that got you into this mess. Now, I'm used to dealing with guys like you. I know what makes you tick. And I know what it's going to take to unwind your time bomb. Only God can help me do that." He leaned over and put one hand on Jack's shoulder.

Jack looked up into his eyes.

"You're not here by accident, Jack." Frank continued, his voice certain and soothing. "You were sent here. But you're gonna learn what it really means to be a new creation, truly born again. If you ever see Russell around here...you owe him an apology."

Jack nodded. "OK, I guess I went over the top. But this ain't gonna be easy. It's the only world I know," he said softly.

Frank smiled. "I know that. And it's the only world Russell knows too. I was dealing with two Russells in the alley last night."

"I see what you mean," said Jack. "I need time to think."

"And pray," replied Frank gently. "You can go."

Chapter 10

No Room for Amateurs

Jack left Frank's office with his mind in turmoil. He leaned against a wall for a moment, shoulders slumped, hands in his pockets. He arched his head upward as if looking at the sky, but all he saw were white ceiling tiles pockmarked by a random pattern of holes. He exhaled with a ragged sigh.

"I guess I'm closing in on my goal of making every mistake there is to make in life," he said to himself softly. "My decisions have cost me my parents, my occupation, and my home. I can't even catch a thief without getting in trouble."

Pushing himself off the wall, he walked through a short corridor that led to the backstage door. Stepping through the door, he heard the singing ensemble on stage rehearsing around the church piano. He stopped to listen; the sound of their voices brought back memories he had pushed aside, memories of the mission and the benches by the river, memories of the plain, pleasant native voices singing of their love for God.

The group faltered on an old spiritual; he heard them discussing the words, unsure of the lyrics to the verses.

Jack walked towards them. "I know that song," he said.

The singers looked at him with a mixture of curiosity and surprise on their faces.

Jack smiled. "I know I don't look it, but my parents were missionaries. We used to sing that song at our church when I was little. Sounds like you have the chorus down pretty good. The verse goes like this—give me a C."

The pianist hit the note and Jack began to sing,

"The blood that Jesus shed for me
way back on Calvary;
The blood that gives me strength,
from day to day,
will never lose its power."

His rich voice echoed in the empty church as the words flowed smoothly from his lips. Jack felt the power of the words, remembering the faces near the river and how his parents sang them. With conviction, the words and their meaning came full-force into his heart. As he ended the verse, the ensemble took up the chorus. Jack stepped back to listen—as if for the first time—to words he had known all his life.

"For it reaches to the highest mountain,
and it flows to the lowest valley;
the blood that gives me strength from day to day,
will never lose its power!"

The chorus ended, and everyone stood quietly as the last note fell into silence. The singers started nodding their heads with satisfaction, some clapping Jack on the back, others thanking him.

The rehearsal was over, and the singers left the sanctuary through a side door, leaving Jack alone in the dimly lit space. He moved down the steps of the stage and lay down across the front pew, his hands behind his head. As the door closed, silence descended on the room.

The Prayers of a Righteous Man

Jack lay still for a moment, thinking about the song, the day before, and his life. He started talking softly, whispering an awkward prayer, attempting to start conversation with a God he now intensely desired to understand.

"OK, Big Guy, so what do I do now? I don't preach. I don't teach. I'm not an evangelist. I'm not a missionary, and I already have proven I'm not a good cop. I really want to do something right, something for You, maybe even something my mother would be proud of. If You could just show me You're listening…. I don't care what You ask me to do. I promise I'll do it, and I won't let You down."

Jack stared off into space in the solitude of the makeshift church in the empty warehouse, waiting for an audible answer, but none came.

He didn't hear her enter, but he heard her crying. The sound drifted forward from the rear of the church, the sound of a woman frightened and alone. Jack lifted his head slowly, peering over the back of the pew. In the faint morning light that filtered through the glass front doors, he saw the young woman he'd first noticed at the concert the night before.

She cried softly into her hands, wiping her tears with a tissue. When she lifted her head for a moment, he saw her clearly. Even from across the room he could see she was beautiful, with classically sculptured high cheekbones and full lips that reminded him of a young Katharine Hepburn. Perhaps it was her large, blue eyes, but there was a cuteness about her also, something innocent and girlish. Maybe it was in the sounds she made as she sobbed, like a little girl crying on her daddy's chest because she just fell down.

She was dressed in a simple but colorful pastel blue summer dress. The blue in the dress only made her eyes seem more luminescent. Her hair was a rich, golden brown with blonde streaks that glowed where the light gleamed across it. She could make anybody stop whatever they were doing and just stare. Jack quickly caught himself doing just that, and then ducked his head so she would not notice him.

She rose from the pew, and Jack listened to the tapping of her heels as she walked down the left aisle towards the front of the church. He froze, watching her approach a small wooden box on a stand. She wrote feverishly on a piece of paper. She hesitated for a moment, then signed the paper, folded it, and dropped it through a slot in the box. He watched her compose herself and walk away. When he heard the door close, he got up and quickly moved toward the box.

The sign carved on the lid of the box read "Prayer Requests." Jack looked at the box, his curiosity rising. He pulled out a pocketknife and picked the simple padlock on the box. Hers was the only note inside. He opened it and read it quickly to himself: "Please God, they want to kill me. I don't know what to do. Help me." The signature read,

"Maria." Jack refolded the note and dropped it back in the box, replacing the padlock.

He moved towards the door, breathing another prayer as he went. "Who would want to kill her and why? You know, Lord—if I can call You that now—this sure feels like my territory. I have to check this one out. But if You don't want me to follow her—then You're gonna have to stop me right now. Otherwise…"

He let the thought end as he opened the front door. He looked to the right and saw her walking a half a block away.

Jack smiled to himself. *Well, here's another 180, but this may turn out to be a good day after all.*

He turned to follow her, feeling his spirits rise again along with the warmth of the day.

The walk was not long, and Jack slowed to give her room and to disguise his efforts to follow her. About a half-mile from the church, she walked into one of the tourist theme restaurants at the edge of town. A large neon sign outside flashed "Rock 'n' Roll Heaven," and the building looked every bit the theme. One side was decorated with carvings of electric guitars, pianos, and drums, along with brightly colored paintings of artists from Buddy Holly to Bruce Springsteen.

Well, the music should be good, even if the food isn't, Jack thought to himself.

He casually walked up to the restaurant, pausing to look at the menu as if he were simply interested in ordering a late breakfast. A small, help-wanted sign hung by the door. Out of the corner of his eye, he glanced through the glass door to see Maria at the counter. A waitress handed her an application, and she moved out of his view. He opened the door and went in.

The walls of the restaurant were hung with music memorabilia: records, musical instruments, album covers from the fifties to the present.

Sort of a poor man's Hard Rock Cafe, Jack surmised.

One end of the room opened up to a small karaoke stage, complete with a tiny dance floor and a feeble lighting setup. The staff members were dressed like rock 'n' roll icons. As Jack looked around the room he saw waiters, waitresses, busboys, cashiers, even the maintenance man dressed as anyone from Alice Cooper to Cyndi Lauper. Jack slipped into a booth on the far side of the room where he could watch Maria. She was seated at another booth filling out an application. He ordered an omelet from Jimi Hendrix and sat back to wait.

He ate slowly, watching Maria out of the corner of his eye. First a young man dressed like Elton John looked through huge white glasses as he spoke with her. Then an older man in a Tom Jones outfit approached her. The Tom Jones clone shook her hand and waved to Cyndi Lauper at the cash register, who came over and spoke briefly to Maria.

She got the job, Jack thought, and he realized he was happy for her. *You know,* he said to himself quietly, *I need a job myself.*

He watched as Cyndi went back to the register and another waitress—Madonna in her '80's lace—sat down to talk with Maria.

Jack got up and went to the cash register. Cyndi looked him over and smiled invitingly, and he grinned back. "Hey Cyndi, I've got a question for you."

Cyndi smiled even bigger, and in a mock Brooklyn accent replied, "Is it a one-million-dollar question?"

Jack held up a twenty-dollar bill. "Well, actually it's a twenty-dollar question."

Cyndi glanced over her shoulder at Tom Jones, but he was looking another way. She snatched the bill. "Oh, President Jackson, he's one of my favorites!" She tucked the bill in a shirt pocket. "OK, shoot!"

Jack nodded his head towards Maria. "The new girl—what's her name?"

Cyndi's smile dropped a little, "Oh, you like the new little chicky, do you? Her name is Maria Sparks."

"What hours does she work?"

Cyndi's smile rose back. "Ya know, Mr. Jackson's getting a little lonely in my pocket."

Jack grinned and pulled out another twenty dollar bill.

Cyndi snatched it up just as quick as the first one. She leaned across the counter as if to deliver secret information. "Her working hours are six to eleven, Thursday through Sunday, off on Mondays through Wednesdays—as well as myself. That is, if you're interested in a girl who just wants to have fun."

Jack held up his hands in mock protest. "Just one icon at a time! I need to talk to your manager; who is he?"

Cyndi nodded across the room. "He's Tom Jones over there." She waved to him. "Norman, this little cutie pie," she reached up and pinched Jack's cheek, "is looking for you!"

A somewhat overweight version of Tom Jones walked across to them. He was about fifty, comfortably round, and dressed in ridiculous-looking tight black pants, platform shoes, and an afro wig. Several chains hung around his neck, dangling against a bright white, blousy shirt with a big floppy collar and billowing long sleeves. Jack thought he looked more like a confused pirate than Tom Jones, and fought back an urge to laugh.

The wannabe Tom Jones looked Jack over. "What can I do for you?"

"I'm looking for a job," Jack replied.

Cyndi's eyebrow shot up with interest.

Tom—or Norman—glanced around the restaurant. It was starting to fill up with lunch customers, so he cocked his head towards a back office. "Come on back. I don't think we have anything, but let's take a look."

Norman's office was plastered with Tom Jones posters and souvenirs. He motioned Jack into a chair and sat down behind his desk. "You like Tom Jones?"

Jack was a little surprised by the question. "Well, uh—yeah."

"Greatest singer who ever lived," said Norman with confidence. "I mean next to Elvis. My boy loves Elvis. You like Elvis?"

Jack waved his hands outward in agreement. "Hey man—King of rock and 'n' roll!"

Norman stood up with surprising speed for his size. "That's right—the King of Rock." He shifted his stance, shooting one arm up in the air and ducking his head down. "And the King of Blue-eyed Soul."

Jack stared at him, barely keeping his mouth closed. Norman shook off his moment of euphoria and sat down, which gave Jack time to recover.

"OK, let's see what we got here..." Norman flipped through a schedule book on his desk. "I got a Monday, Tuesday, and Wednesday janitor's job, a Tuesday night three-hour slot for a pizza maker—can you make a pizza?" he asked, looking up at Jack.

"Oh yeah," said Jack, trying to sound confident about it. *How hard can it be?* he thought.

"But I need to work Thursday through Sunday, six to eleven."

Norman looked at the book. "Sorry guy, we're all full. Nothin' I can do there."

A loud bang produced by someone slamming his hand against a table drew their attention through the office door. They could see the cashier's station at the front of the restaurant. A large man was leaning over the counter, glaring at Cyndi.

"What's that?" asked Jack.

"Oh no, he's at it again," said Norman. "His name's Warren Beckem; he owns a gas station outside of town. Every day he comes in here drunk and hassles the waitresses over nothing, chasing away the customers. That moose has cost me more money..."

"Why don't you do something about it? Call the cops?"

145

"We don't have a police department—town's too small. The state troopers will come if there's big trouble, but it has to be huge before they give us the time of day."

Jack could see Warren berating Cyndi. The whole restaurant was staring at the scene. Jack stood up.

"I tried to stop him once," continued Norman fearfully, "but he grabbed my neck and threatened to break my legs and throw me through the window."

Jack moved towards the door. "I'll be right back."

Norman called after him, "Don't get into it with this guy; you'll get your head tore off!"

Jack casually approached the cashier's station as if walking up to pay. He could make out Warren's words as he got closer and the strong smell of whisky surrounded him.

"Listen here, you little whore!" the burly thug yelled at Cyndi. "I gave you a fifty-dollar bill and all you gave me change for was a twenty-dollar bill!"

Cyndi was crying. "Sir, I'm sorry, all you gave me was twenty-dollars…"

Warren roared, "Why, you little trick!" He raised his hand up. "I oughta slap your…"

Suddenly out of nowhere, Jack's foot instinctively slammed a side kick under Warren's raised arm, digging deeply into his side. Warren flew to the side and buckled as he crashed against the wall, sliding down to the floor. The restaurant went silent.

Jack grabbed a fork off the counter and stuck it into Warren's open mouth, prongs up. Jamming the fork against the roof of Warren's mouth, Jack pulled him upwards. Sounds of pain gurgled from Warren's throat.

"Your mouth is way out of control, sir," said Jack calmly, as if he were having a polite conversation about the weather. "Let's go outside and discuss our dining plans for this evening."

Jack tossed the fork on the floor. Blood smeared Warren's lips. Jack could see Maria watching from her booth as he crossed his arms across Warren's chest, grabbing his shirt collar. In the same movement, Jack pulled his fists together, choking Warren with his own shirt. Warren clawed frantically at Jack's arms, but pulling on the crossed arms only tightened the choke. Jack pushed Warren backwards through the doors of the restaurant, ignoring his gasps.

"Where's your car?" Jack asked politely. Warren choked and pointed towards a black pickup truck sitting crookedly in a handicapped parking space. Jack walked him backwards towards the truck, then shoved Warren so that he fell backwards into the driver's door and slid to the ground. Inside the restaurant, customers and employees watched through the window. Jack squatted in front of Warren.

"Now, Warren," he said, his voice turning cold, "listen to me."

"Screw you," Warren gasped back.

Like a piston, Jack's right forearm slammed into Warren's forehead, banging it into the pickup door and buckling the metal.

Faint "Oooos" sounded from the spectators in the restaurant.

"Warren," Jack continued coolly. "Do I now have your undivided attention?"

A cut had opened on Warren's forehead. "Um… yeah," he said weakly.

"Good!" replied Jack, smiling viciously. "Now, you don't know me, and you don't want to know me. But I've got 500 different ways of repeating what I just did to you today. Now I'm keeping an eye on this restaurant from this day forward, and the next time you come around here…well, let's put it this way, you won't see me comin', you won't feel my presence, and you won't hear a sound. You'll just blink your eyes and wake up in intensive care. Now since you don't want to spend the rest of this year using a walker, let's get you in your truck so you can sleep it off. OK tough guy?"

Warren nodded feebly. "Yeah, yeah, OK, OK!"

Jack pulled Warren up by the front of his overalls, opened the truck door, and flopped him across the seat. Warren fell backwards, one foot hanging out of the truck. Jack slammed the door on Warren's foot.

"Oooouuu," Warren cried from inside the truck.

"Wowww," said the people in the restaurant.

Jack grabbed the foot and shoved it in the truck. Closing the door, he leaned in the window. "Warren, that last one was for Cyndi."

Warren moaned.

Jack turned and walked back to the restaurant. He smiled to himself as he saw the watchers scramble back to their tables. Tom Jones stood at the door, a smile as bright as Las Vegas on his face.

"Wow!" Norman cried with delight. "That was beautiful. I wish I had that on video!"

Jack grinned. "Can we talk about that job now?"

"Absolutely!" Excitedly, he led Jack back to his office.

"I want to work Thursday through Sunday, six to eleven," Jack said.

"You got it!" Norman beamed. "By the way, my name is Norman." He shook Jack's hand with obvious gratitude. "And you're...?"

"I'm...Vail 'Toodoo,' " said Jack. "Just call me Vail."

"Well, Vail, you can be Hulk Hogan or James Bond, or whoever you like as long as you're in my restaurant."

"Thanks, but I'll stick with the music theme like everyone else," said Jack with a smile. "Now, I can learn to make pizzas, I can host with Cyndi, or I can just be your bouncer—which is it?"

"Well, you can help us with the pizzas from six to ten every night except Saturdays and Sundays. That's when my son Norman, Jr. makes pizzas—but I can fire him if you want?"

Jack laughed. "That won't be necessary. Keep going..."

Norman nodded. The afro bounced around ridiculously. "Every night between ten and eleven we sell chips, pop, coffee and lattes, and we have karaoke for the customers. You can host that if it's all right with you. Other than that, having you here will just be a joy to us all."

Jack shook his hand again. "It's a deal. See you Thursday."

Jack left the restaurant, feeling every eye watching him—and Maria's most of all. A look of interest was pasted on her face.

I hope Frank doesn't find out about this one, Jack murmured softly. It might even have been a prayer, cause underneath it all, he didn't take Frank lightly.

Chapter 11

The Other End of the Family Chain

The office atop the Tropics Hotel was dimly lit. Through the window, the night sky loomed over Miami, but the dark mood in the room seemed to dim even the city lights below. Johnny Colvack paced back and forth in front of the window checking his watch. His usual persona of control was clearly frayed.

Hal and Mike sat at the marble table, Mike fidgeting, watching Johnny move back and forth.

Hal slouched back in his chair, his face angry and sullen. "How long are we gonna have to wait for this guy?" he growled.

"As long as we have to," Johnny snapped. "Have you checked all our contacts in the FBI?"

"Everybody's keeping their mouths shut about this one," Hal grumbled. "I practically have a mole in every department, but the lid is shut too tight."

Mike rubbed his head as if trying to soothe a headache. "It's like the John Gotti thing. They bust the owner of eight major hotels on a racketeering scheme, especially one surrounding what the press calls 'human cock fighting,' and it's gonna blow sky-high in the media. No one wants to talk to us. If we go down, lots of careers will be made at the bureau."

"We'll find him," Hal swore. "I'll find him if I have to do it myself!"

"Hal!" Johnny stopped pacing, his sharp voice barely controlling his boiling anger. He leaned over the table, staring down his brother. "Don't think ahead of me; don't think alongside me. You only think behind me." Johnny returned to his pacing. "There's only one person I trust to handle this mess."

The door thudded softly three times with a low, precise knock. Johnny rushed to open it, reaching to hug the man waiting outside as if greeting a long-time friend.

The man was short and Joe Pesci-like, but a bit stockier as if he once lifted weights. He was dressed in black from head to toe. He wore a black crepe suit with a black turtleneck. A black leather sport hat with the brim turned up sat on his head. He was older than Johnny, though how much, neither Hal or Mike could tell. The man puffed on a thin cigar, his eyes scanning the room, measuring Hal and Mike with deadly caution. Seeming satisfied, only then did he enter the room with measured, sure steps.

The Fixer

"Boys," Johnny said, sounding less worried, the control returning to his voice, "this is the family fixer. Everything I learned, I learned from him."

The man looked around the room at the expensive furnishings. "Judging by this hotel, you obviously learned a few things from your father too." He spoke in a cold voice, his accent, even more pronounced than Johnny's and obviously Russian. The thick Russian syllables gave his listeners the feeling he could lessen the accent if he wished.

Johnny waved towards the newcomer as if making a presentation. "This is our father's brother, Uncle Zendo."

Hal and Mike stood up suddenly in respect.

"So there really *is* a Zendo," said Mike with awed surprise. "I never thought you were a real person. I thought you were always just a threat."

"Yeah," said Hal. "Like 'step outa line and Uncle Zendo will come get you.' We never thought you was real."

Johnny smiled, a cunning, knowing smile. "Zendo…is very real. He lives in Russia. There are a lot of people here in the States who would pay big money to locate Zendo Colvack. He has…lots of enemies."

"Too many eyes watching me," said Zendo, moving around the room, keeping out of view of the window. He flicked cigar ash onto the marble table. "Johnny, I know what you need. I can find him, but I'll need a lot of information." He pushed the button on the wall to close the curtains. "I need all you got on DeNova, his friends, enemies, men he beat—everything about his parents and their friends." He paused to place the thin cigar back in his lips. He opened his mouth and blew out a thin smoke ring. "DeNova's hobbies, how he relaxes, what he loves, how he loves, what he hates, who hates him…" he continued. "I'll file it down, and at the end of the trail, he'll be there. And I will take him out."

He walked behind Hal and Mike, letting the last sentence linger in silence. He blew another smoke ring that floated between Hal and Mike. "And then…I will go back to the world of shadows…and threats." He placed the cigar between his teeth and smiled, staring at Mike.

"How much?" Johnny asked.

Zendo smiled again. "As much as I need…till I find him." He moved to the door, and looked his nephew in the eye. "And I'll find him. I always do."

The door closed behind him, leaving Johnny, Hal, and Mike standing in a darkened room, alone with the lingering smell of the thin cigar.

Polyester Slacks and the Saturday Night Fever

The days went by in Summerville, and a pleasant level of normalcy found its way into Jack's life. He would work out and spar with Frank in the mornings, help around the church, and work at Rock 'n' Roll Heaven for half of the week. Jack impersonated John Travolta at the restaurant, in a leather jacket and polyester slacks from the *Saturday Night Fever* era. He wanted to keep his presence low key, so he'd opted against the white leisure suit he was instructed to buy. He hated the suit and doubted he could have found one anyway. On Saturdays Norman, Jr.—an overweight version of

Elvis in a spangled white jumpsuit—struggled to teach Jack how to make pizza.

After the single incident with Warren, Jack never had to deal with a difficult customer again, a fact for which he was quietly grateful. Frank had learned about Jack's encounter with Warren, but surprisingly, mentioned very little about it. Frank knew Warren and realized that eventually something like that would happen to slow him down. Nevertheless, Frank cautioned Jack to avoid further fights. In one of their daily counseling sessions Frank told Jack...

"You build a reputation around here as a tough guy and word's gonna spread, possibly to people we don't want lookin' this way. Another incident like that and you could get made. I can only watch you so much, man."

So Jack did his best to stay out of trouble. But that didn't stop him from keeping an eye out for it, particularly where Maria was concerned. She had lightened her hair even a bit more than it had been to take on the character of the old version of Britney Spears wearing a Catholic school girl's uniform. Jack worked to become friends with Maria, to the evident disappointment of Cyndi.

At first she remained cautious and aloof, but it soon became a familiar sight for John Travolta and Britney Spears to host the karaoke nights, laughing with the customers as rock star wannabes mangled their favorite hits. Yet Maria never talked about herself, leaving her life before Summerville as much a mystery to Jack as his was to her.

One Saturday night as the karaoke crowd filtered in, Maria slipped up next to Jack at the counter. He was closing out the register after dinner hours, and she sat down to count receipts. She watched Jack out of the corner of her eye, then glanced at the karaoke set. A mischievous grin crossed her face.

"Vail, you know I can hear you singing along with the customers every night, so I know you can sing a bit. When are you going to get up on karaoke night and do something?" she teased.

Jack smiled at her and leaned over the counter. "Well, I don't know. If it would get me a date with a rock star, I would get up there right now."

Maria smiled innocently. "I'm sure Cyndi Lauper would date you for a song."

Jack laughed. "I'm thinking of someone a little more in this era."

Maria leaned in towards him, mock challenging him. "OK, Rico Suave, a date is a possibility *if* you know my favorite song, *which* I'm sure you don't."

"That's a lot of pressure for one date," Jack said.

"Maybe I don't date much." Maria slid back onto her stool, her tone innocently defensive.

Jack smiled with equal innocence. "Well, maybe I could hook you up on a date with Elvis."

"Well, I don't really go for big…sideburns." She held in a laugh.

Jack grinned again. "OK, what's this favorite song of yours?"

"It's an old one!" Maria teased.

"Well, so am I!" replied Jack. "So what is it?"

"It's a song that has a lot of meaning to me. It's one I used to hear sung a lot when I was little."

Jack nodded slowly. "OK, I feel a challenge. Let me have it."

Maria smiled with confidence. "It's a song called, 'I Don't Know Why I Love You Like I Do.' "

"You've got to be kidding!" Jack said with surprise.

"See, I knew you wouldn't know it," she said smugly.

Jack shook his head. "No, wait! If I pull this one off, I can have a real—away from here, dressed in normal clothes, no rock stars—dinner and a movie date?"

Maria nodded. "If you're good, I may even let you pay."

Jack smiled knowingly. "Start thinking about where you want to eat. I'll be right back." He rushed over to the karaoke stage and began flipping through tapes and CDs. Maria watched him, not quite sure what was happening. Jack pulled out a CD and put it in the player. He grabbed the microphone, hesitated, and ran back to Maria.

"Maria, come here. I want to whisper something in your ear." He leaned towards her, and she lifted her ear close to him. He smiled and whispered, "I don't really have anything to say, I just wanted to stick my face in your hair."

She pulled back, laughing, and shoved him on the shoulder. Jack stood up in mock surprise.

"Sorry, I just needed a little bit of inspiration," he grinned at her.

Turning on the microphone, he stepped back to the stage. He flipped on the karaoke lights, and as the crowd turned towards him, he spoke into the microphone.

"I am very inspired to sing a song tonight for someone *very* special. It's a song she's sure I do not know. And because she is *so* sure, she actually said that if I sang it I would get a date with our own resident queen of pop, Britney Spears!"

The audience laughed and applauded, while Maria suddenly felt a blush rising on her cheeks.

Jack pressed "play" on the stereo. The music intro started, the same familiar tune he had sung to his mother by the Amazon.

"Brit baby!" he cried out, his eyes gleaming with confident delight, "this one's for you!" He joined in with the music, his rich voice filling the room.

"I don't know why I love you like I do;
I don't know why, I just do..."

As he began to sing, Maria's face lit up with surprise. Jack began to dance with the music, moving to the rhythm the same way he had done when he sang to his mother, a movement that came naturally to him. Watching him, Maria gasped as if she saw a memory herself, a ghost she never thought to see again. Her hands went to her face, and when they parted her eyes brimmed with tears.

In the bright lights from over the dance floor, she saw the letters on Jack's knuckles, but this time it clicked in a whole new way: V-A-L-E T-U-D-O. "How could I have missed it?" she whispered.

"I don't know why I love you like I do;
I don't know why,
I don't know why,
I don't know why,
I just do..."

Jack finished and the crowd applauded.

"Sing another one, Johnny T!" someone shouted.

"Yeah, how about a duet with Britney!"

Someone else yelled, "Do 'You're the One That I Want!' "

Jack waved the requests off and stepped towards Maria, smiling like a conquering hero. She grabbed him by the front of his shirt, pulled him close, and said, "I want to talk to you right now!"

The crowd started laughing as she pulled him behind the counter into a hallway leading to the restrooms.

Jack looked at Maria curiously.

"I know who you are!" she whispered urgently.

Jack was surprised, but tried to sound nonchalant. "What do you mean?"

Maria stared in his eyes and said in perfect Portuguese, *"It's been a long time, but now I recognize you. I thought you reminded me of him all along, but now that I hear your voice..."*

Stunned, Jack fell into the Portuguese without thinking. *"You speak Portuguese?"*

Maria smiled, *"Yes, Mister Jack DeNova!"*

Jack snapped his head around, looking to see that no one heard, and pulled her further into the hallway.

"Maria, how do you know my name?" he whispered fiercely.

159

She whispered back, "We need to talk privately, Mister *vah-lay two-doe*."

Suddenly Norman, in full Tom Jones regalia, was at their side. "Vail, that was great!" he cried excitedly. "You know, I bet you do a great Elvis. You need to consider doing some Elvis songs; Norman, Jr. would love it!" He yelled to his son behind the counter. "Hey son! What do you say about Vail doing some Elvis songs?"

Norman, Jr. shouted back—in a laughably bad imitation of Elvis—"I say, 'Yeah baby—thankyouverymuch. Rock and roll forever!' " He snapped his body into the same pose his father had used, right arm stretched into the air, finger pointing, head down. Several customers started snickering.

Jack, his eyes still watching Maria, replied quickly, "OK Norman, I'll work on something for you."

Norman grinned and slapped him on the back, returning to his customers.

Jack turned back to Maria. "And you, after we're done here tonight we'll go to your place and we *will* talk."

She smiled. "We will; I'm sure we *will*."

Chapter 12

Bittersweet Memories

Maria's apartment was small and sparsely furnished, as if she were unwilling to call the place home. The sofa and chairs were thickly padded in an almond yellow fabric that went out of style in the seventies and wasn't likely to make a comeback. Jack could tell they were as much a part of the apartment as the faded green curtains.

The only bit of color in the room was a small bouquet of wildflowers. They were stuck in a glass on a battered end table by the sofa. A portable stereo rested on the opposite end table, next to a stack of CDs. A light blue Bible, its pages well thumbed, lay on the sofa.

Jack stood in the center of the room, eyeing the surroundings and watching Maria as she threw her keys and purse onto a worn recliner.

"All right, who are you, and how do you know who I am?" he demanded.

Maria grinned. "Well, first of all, I'm a bit familiar with Brazil." She grabbed his hands and lifted them to show the knuckles. "And I know what *vale tudo* means." She dropped his hands back to his sides, removed her coat and tossed it also onto the recliner. She looked into his face. "Don't you recognize me? Has it been that long?"

Jack, puzzled, stared at her. "I thought you looked familiar, but I figured most pretty girls do somehow."

She smiled. "Do you remember a little girl who used to defy her parents by attending your no-holds-barred fights? She was the daughter of missionaries and would get spankings because she would scream real loud for you when…"

"Wait a minute…" Jack interrupted her, stunned by the recognition.

"Yes!" she laughed with delight.

Jack said cautiously, "Sarah?"

"Yes!"

"Sarah Wilson?"

"Yes! Yes! Yes!" she cried, "You do remember me!" She jumped into Jack's arms, hugging him. He wrapped his arms around her, lifting her up, spinning her with happiness.

"No way!" he shouted. He set her down, stepping away, holding her arms gently. "Of course I remember. I remember everything. I remember when I was eighteen and you were eleven and you tried to convince me that we were supposed to be dating each other." Jack laughed at the memory.

"What's so funny about that?" she wisecracked.

"I was *eighteen* and you were *eleven*. I could have been arrested!" He laughed again, then said in a mildly mocking tone, "But you were pretty fine-looking—for an eleven year old."

Sarah laughed too. "Do you remember what I gave you?"

Jack smiled. "Yes, of course I do. You were so convinced we were going to be together, you took one of those silver crosses that my father gave to everyone on the opening day of the mission…" He reached into his pocket and pulled out the card with the cross, "…and had it laminated with your picture so I wouldn't forget how cute you were." He flipped the card over, showing a picture of a grinning young girl with very dark brown, almost black, hair.

Sarah's hand jumped to her mouth. "You kept it! All these years…oh my God!"

Jack laughed again, a laugh of happy memories. "You were such a crazy little kid. I gave you the nickname Sparky." He looked at her with realization, "So that's where the name Maria Sparks came from."

Sarah looked down, embarrassed for a moment. "Do you also remember that I invited you…"

"…to be your date at your school dance?" He nodded, smiling. "Oh right! I was eighteen years old, I'd been fighting professionally for two years, and I was going to go to a school dance with an eleven year old? Sparky or no Sparky, I could have gotten sued by your parents and disowned by mine."

"Well, you used to tell me these stories. You had me convinced that you were this great dancer and I believed you." She stepped towards him. "As a matter of fact…" she pushed him in the chest, "you told me a lot of things, like you were John Travolta's cousin, and you taught him how to do all the dances for Saturday Night Fever." She punched him on the arm. "And I *believed* you! All I wanted was for you to show up and dance with me to 'How Deep Is Your Love.?' "

Jack shook his head, laughing at the memory. "That was pretty funny! You were a dopey little eleven year old."

She looked him in the eyes. "Well, I'm not eleven years old any more."

Jack ducked away, embarrassed by the memory of the little girl and the beautiful woman she had become. "I've been observing that for the past couple of weeks." He turned back and looked at her. "These past...twenty years...have done you very well."

She smiled, looking at him. The memories rose up in her mind, and she shook her head in amazement. "Jack, I can't believe it's you. I can't believe you're here."

He raised his hands wide in agreement. "Sarah, *I'm* in total shock."

She looked at him again, cocking her head to the side as if thinking over something. She stepped towards him, deep in thought. "You kept my picture?" she said softly, as much of a question as a statement.

Jack nodded, watching her. "Well, you were cute, and I knew you had potential..." He grinned appreciatively at her. "... but not *this* much potential."

She raised an eyebrow and smiled.

He laughed. "So, do I get the date?"

Sarah nodded slowly and deliberately. "Oh yeah. But you owe me something first," she said adding one last condition to the deal.

Jack looked at her. "And what would that be?" he asked cautiously.

Sarah stepped over to the stereo and slipped in a CD. She turned back to him. "The first thing you owe me is the first thing you denied me."

The music smoothly thumped from the boom box with its lush harmonies and romantic pulsations. Jacks eye's brightened up as he said, "The Bee Gees. My boys!"

Jack laughed as the singing voices filled the room to "How Deep Is Your Love?"

"Jack, you've owed me this dance for twenty years," she said firmly.

"Well, let's see what I remember." He took her hand. But this wasn't the hand of a little girl. It was the hand of a well taken care of woman. The fingernails were painted perfectly. She had the high cheekbones of a fashion model and the long, lithe body of an intoxicatingly beautiful woman. There was nothing eleven years old about this person who stood before him now.

She was smart, intelligent, a real personality plus, and ultra sexy woman, from the way she dressed with her hip hugger jeans and white soft satin top—even to the way she smelled. She filled the room with an enchanting, musky sweetness that was driving him crazy.

Was she trying to do this to him? Or was he just now really taking a healthy look at the specimen of femininity that stood before him? Jack wondered.

How Deep Is Your Memory?

The first few notes of the classic standard began to breathe with a life all their own as they flowed out of two large floor speakers in the apartment. Jack tenderly slipped his arm around her soft waist, and trying to keep his composure, started to bow slightly as if he were asking for permission. Then, to Jack's surprise, she stepped back, and folded her arms.

"Hold on a second," she said, looking at him. "OK, Mr. John Travolta's *cousin,* it's time to see your moves—and they had better be good!"

Jack rolled his eyes, and said "Aw, c'mon, I don't remember any of that stuff. That was ions ago. I barely remember what we're doin' now."

But the smart look in her eye told him she wasn't going to buy it. Somewhere in that moment, Jack lost control of the situation and became her emotional slave. He gave her two points for the power of allure and then gamely started to do his best John Travolta imitation, down to the final finger in the air.

Sarah laughed, applauding the performance. The years had flown away, and Jack and Sparky were sharing a joke together, two kids in a land far from home.

Jack grinned as she stepped towards him again. His heart was completely enraptured by her feminine charms. She was getting to Jack and they both knew it. It was the one arena where Jack was not the king of the jungle.

She was now calling the shots and knew it and liked it so much it bordered on going over the top just a bit. But she wisely pulled it back in and allowed Jack his dignity and sense of control…just to see what he would do with it.

When Jack blurted out, " Did I ever tell you that back in Rio de Janeiro I was…"

Her hands were suddenly on her hips, the cocky eleven year old was taking back control for the moment. She said, "You are so full of it. You were never the Brazilian king of disco!"

Laughing, he reached out for her, pulling her towards him. Instinctively she put both her arms around his neck and fondled the hair on his head. The songs, romance—almost forgotten for years—now began to overwhelm them both as the soft music filled the room.

Inches away from her face he could feel the heat of her passion, and he said softly, "I believe this is my dance?"

She slowly titled her head to the side and gave a yes nod, her eyes wide, but half opened. The look in her eyes said, *How long should I let this moment go on?* So they continued to move slowly with the music.

"How deep is your love? How deep is your love? I really need to learn..."

Almost without noticing it, their steps slowed; they were almost in a standstill, holding each other like they had just survived a plane crash and were the only survivors—the only two people alive in the world.

"I believe in you, you know the door to my very soul..."

He leaned towards her face.

She pulled back, pushing away slightly, and lowering her head.

"What's wrong?" Jack asked, trying to see into her eyes.

She looked up at him, and he could see tears starting to form. "I've been waiting twenty years for this," she whispered, the words almost fearful. "I just can't believe it's actually happening."

"And you may not think I care for you... When you know down inside that I really do..."

Jack smiled, gently pulled her face closer, and softly kissed her lips. She closed her eyes as he did and held onto the moment, as if she was freezing it in a still-frame photograph, branding it in her mind forever. It was just as that moment was over that the damn broke loose and all the pent-up emotion and unqualified romance kept inside for twenty years began to find their expression in the deep and passionate kisses they began to share.

The room disappeared. The music couldn't be heard. They were by rights the only two people in existence. They kissed all through the remaining verse, chorus, and beginning of the second verse. It was as if only a second had elapsed.

"And it's me you need to show...

How deep is your love? How deep is your love? I really need to learn..."

She pulled back gently, her face still tilted towards his, their lips only inches apart. She gave a light laugh, "Well, OK. That's good for one year; what about the next nineteen?"

Jack laughed back. "Well, if it's a debt I owe, then it's a debt I will gladly pay."

She leaned up into his lips and the marathon started all over again.

"Cause we're living in a world of fools, breaking us down,
When they all should let us be,
We belong to you and me..."

Something in the words made Jack pause. He slowly lifted his head away from hers.

"What is it, Jack?" she asked, searching his face with both her hands.

"Wait, hold on a moment," he said, his expression somber. Releasing her, he stepped to the stereo and turned the music down, letting it play softly. He took her hands and guided her to sit on the sofa. She started to protest, but Jack stopped her thought with a question. "When the words came on 'That we're living in a world of fools...' reality just tapped me on the shoulder, Sarah. Why have you changed your name? Why are you hiding here? And who is trying to kill you?"

Startled, Sarah cried out, "How...how do you know someone is trying to kill me?"

"Sarah, I was in the church when you dropped that note in the prayer request box." Her eyes widened in surprise. "I'm sorry, but I picked the lock and read the note," Jack continued. "I've been following you this whole time. I didn't get the job working the same hours as you do by accident. I maneuvered my way in." He looked her in the eyes. "Tell me...what don't I know?"

Sarah dropped her face in her hands and began to sob, "Jack, I saw it; I was there."

"Saw what?" asked Jack, confused.

She looked up, tears trickling down her cheeks. "I was on my way to the family reunion, and I stopped by a 7-11 to get some Cokes and chips for the picnic..."

The story came out in a rush, as if she had needed to tell it.

"It was raining. I was pulling in when two men jumped out of a Mercedes and started shooting into the windows of the car in front of me."

Jack's face went pale.

"Then they looked at me, straight in my face, and began to shoot at me." Sarah stared across the room, seeing the men, the rain, and the guns. "I watched the whole thing. I...I don't even know what it was about. All I know is, they don't know who I am, and they don't know where to find me." She looked at Jack. "I knew I needed to get away and hide until I could figure out what to do. I remembered this place from when we were kids; I drove straight here. I haven't even talked to my parents yet. They probably think I'm still working at my waitress job in Jacksonville. Jack..." She looked up at him, surprised at his movement.

He had stood up without thinking, his mind back on the fight, the prison, the coffins lying in the mission.

"You...saw it..." he said, barely in a whisper. "You saw them kill my parents?"

Sarah's face went white with horror. "Your *parents!* Jack, I didn't know...I heard about an older couple, but...I didn't want to read about it. I didn't want to know." She went to him, clutched his arm, "Jack, that was Art and Julia? Oh my God, I'm so sorry. I'm *so sorry.*"

He took her hand, "I know." He led her back to the sofa, explaining. "They were going to the reunion to stay with your parents," Jack said. "I'm here for the same reason you are. I'm in the witness protection program for the FBI." He looked at her, a thought rising in his mind. "You said you saw two men. Could you for sure identify the two men if you saw them again?"

Sarah nodded quickly. "I could never forget those faces. One was in his late forties, early fifties, a white guy, a real slick dresser. The other man kind of looked like him, but he was younger and bigger—taller than you—about six-four, maybe two-hundred and forty pounds, very muscular."

"Hal and Mike," whispered Jack to himself.

Sarah's eyes widened. "How do you know their names?"

Jack grimaced. "Cause they're the same guys that are trying to kill me. They're the Colvack brothers. I accidentally killed their youngest brother in a no-holds-barred match in Miami at a hotel Johnny Colvack owns."

"The fight. I heard about that on the news…" Sarah said, her hands over her mouth. "That was *you?*"

Jack nodded. "After the fight, the FBI was trying to pressure me to testify against the Colvacks. I didn't want to at first, but when they killed my parents, I agreed to go state's evidence. Now, like you, I'm hiding out waiting for the FBI to call and tell me what's next."

"Jack, I don't know where to go from here?"

Jack looked at the ceiling and stood up again. "Let me think for just a second." He started pacing across the room. "I'm testifying against the whole family in a racketeering charge, and you're an eyewitness to a double homicide." He turned to her, the smile coming back to his face. "We can put these guys away forever!" He glanced towards the window. "But unless I'm very wrong, they are hunting us down even as we speak." He picked up her coat, purse, and keys.

"Jack, where are we going?" Sarah asked.

"We're gonna see a pastor."

Sarah looked at him with surprise.

"It's time to talk to Frank McQue," said Jack. "I've got an idea."

The old wood splintered around the doorlatch, the door crashing inwards, bits of oak and metal skittering across the brick floor. Zendo Colvack stepped into the darkened room, a pistol in his hand. He listened, sniffing the air. The musty smell told him no one had been in this portion of the building for several weeks. The air was almost as warm as the sunlit clearing behind him, muggy and smelling of jungle. It was the middle of the week, and the mission grounds were deserted.

Zendo slipped the 45-automatic back into his shoulder holster and began walking through the old living quarters, pulling apart furniture, dumping out drawers. A photo album tumbled out, and Zendo picked it up. He flipped it open, staring at pictures of Art and Julia and Jack. He whipped out a short, razor-sharp knife and used the edge to lift open the plastic sleeve of one page. A black-gloved hand pulled a photo off the page. Zendo stared closely at it. Two families stared back at him from the faded photo; the faces of a much younger Art and Julia, and a young, sullen-looking teenage Jack, next to another couple, four boys of ages between twelve and sixteen, and a little girl with dark brown hair. A large gateway behind the two families read "Mid-South Amusement Park, Summerville, Florida."

Zendo slipped the photo into his pocket and walked out the door to a waiting jeep. He sped out of the clearing, back down the long dirt road, oblivious to the jungle and the river running beside him.

Two days later, Zendo stepped off a plane into a terminal of the Miami airport. Flipping open a cell phone, he punched a button. There was a buzz, and the sound of Johnny Colvack's voice filtered through the tiny speaker.

"Yeah?"

"It's me," said Zendo. "I think I'm onto something; I've got a hunch. I'll run it down and call you in a few days."

"You think you found him?"

"Ninety-percent chance I've got this one pegged already, but I don't know yet. I'll call you."

"Just get him before he testifies."

Zendo smiled, though Johnny couldn't see it. "Johnny, you're my brother's kid, and I'll take care of it. Now relax." He flipped the phone shut and walked towards customs, with nothing to declare.

Chapter 13

Plans, Dreams, and the Casualties of War

It was Friday afternoon when Jack and Sarah walked into Frank's office.

Frank pointed to a large book sitting on his desk. "You'd think when a former agent calls asking for a mug book, they'd get it to you a little quicker. But that's where the bureau part comes from—as in 'bureaucracy.' " He pushed up a chair for Sarah. "Now, Sarah, just take your time. If you see anyone familiar, you let me know."

She nodded and began to flip through the book. After about thirty minutes passed, Sarah gasped, "Oh my God."

Frank and Jack rushed over to her. Hal and Mike scowled out of black-and-white photos on the page. She pointed to both pictures.

Frank looked her in the eyes. "Sarah, is that them?" he asked, his voice cool and emotionless. "Are those the two guys you saw?"

Sarah nodded, her hands held against her face. "Yes! That's them. I'll never forget those faces."

Frank looked over at Jack. He could see the memory rising up in the fighter's face, the eyes narrowing, the jaw tightening. Jack grabbed his jacket and moved towards the door, but Frank stepped in front of him, grabbing his arm.

"Frank, let me go," Jack snarled. "I'm not playing. Let me go!"

"Jack, I know what you're thinking, and you can't go after them now. The Colvacks won't be satisfied until you're dead."

"I won't be satisfied until they're dead!" Jack roared back.

"Jack, don't go there, " Frank's voice was firm and cool. "Don't go after them. They are the ones the government wants. You go after them like I know you want to and it's murder one for you. Criminals or not, you'll spend the rest of your life behind bars. Jack, you and I both know," looking over at Sarah, "that you have a lot to live for now."

"Jack, please, listen to him," said Sarah, speaking almost too quietly to be heard.

Jack looked towards her and then back to Frank. He felt his anger cooling.

"OK," he said softly. "OK, I won't...I won't go after them."

Frank loosened his grip, stepping back from Jack.

Jack looked him in the eye. "But what if *they* come after *me*?"

"That's different," said Frank calmly. "But you're not the Grim Reaper. Let's play this one by the book, because there's far too much at stake. Look, I'll figure something out. If the FBI knows an eyewitness to the murder exists, the stakes go from racketeering to murder. They will have the Colvacks on a silver platter. Give me some time to work this out. Go back to your jobs, just like normal, same routine...nothing changes. Let me do what I do."

He gently steered Jack to the seat beside Sarah.

"I need to make a few phone calls right now," Frank continued. "Can I leave you two alone and trust that we're not gonna have any surprises?" He eyeballed Jack carefully.

Jack and Sarah nodded, and grasped each other's hand.

Frank accepted their answer. He straightened up his shoulders and walked towards the window and looked out, as if thinking through a plan. "You're supposed to be at work in an hour. You two can sit here, talk, and just calm down. I'll call you as soon as I know something." He left the room, closing the door behind him.

Jack glanced at the open book, at Hal and Mike, and then out the window. "I never thought it would turn out like this," he said, his voice quiet and sad.

Sarah looked at him. "What do you mean?"

He continued to stare out the window. "My life...what I wanted out of life. I'm...not so sure now." He turned to Sarah. "What do you want out of life?"

Sarah smiled faintly. "Well, for the past ten years I've been doing computer work for Mom and Dad, working with the details of travel, organizing their mission trips." She looked out the window too. "It's very rewarding helping those poor people; they're so desperate. I love working with the kids..."

She turned back to Jack.

"But when it's all said and done, I'm really tired of living my life by myself and for myself. I guess I just want my own family, a home, to be loved." She peered into his face. "What about you, Mr. Tudo. What do you want from life?"

He smiled, looking down at his hands. "I fought a tournament in Oahu, Hawaii, back in '97, and since then I've always had this love affair with Hawaii. And believe it or not," he laughed a little, "I know this sounds strange, but I've really come to like making pizzas. I've really thought a lot about this, and my dream would be to open a little pizza place facing a beach in Hawaii. A small, uncomplicated business—no fighting, living the good, simple life, church on Sunday, a family—and I would be perfectly happy."

He looked at Sarah, and she smiled.

"There's a little town next to Kaneohe Bay called Kahalue," he continued. "It has a beautiful view of the Pacific Ocean. I've got a pretty good nestegg put away because of all my years of fighting. I bet the Hawaiians would love pineapple pizza..."

His voice trailed off, his eyes staring at a vision of white beaches, a kitchen, people laughing. He shook his head as if to clear it, looking at his hands again, at the *vale tudo* scrawled there like a brand that marked him for life.

He started talking again, his voice almost bitter. "But it will never happen. My fighting past will haunt me until the day I'm dead and put in the grave. Fighters all over the world will be hunting me down, wanting to beat me just to have my name on their record. I can't do this forever. Sooner or later, the older I get, some young buck will have his day with me. And, most likely, I won't come out alive. I hate the fact that somebody else will choose the way I die. But it's a foregone conclusion."

Sarah looked at Jack. A sad smile filled his face.

"But it is a nice dream..." he sighed.

She nodded, clasping his hand and holding it in silence.

He glanced at the clock on Frank's wall. "Life is so short, and so unfair. I just wonder if anybody ever gets what he really wants? Oh well, I guess we should probably go to work." He sighed again and moved towards the door.

They kept their hands clasped together as they walked out of the room, as if clinging to their dreams like a momentary emotional reprieve, as though they just walked out of a movie theater. Both understood all too well what the real outcome of their lives would be. Jack knew more than Sarah could accept. So they clung to each other and walked off to punch the timeclock and begin their shift.

The karaoke machine was in full swing that night. A trucker borrowed Norman's afro wig for his own version of Stevie Wonder's "Superstition," sung country style. Norman grimaced, shaking his almost-bald head. "Vail, I knew I shouldn't have loaned him my wig," he complained to Jack.

"Why? It doesn't look any worse on him," Jack replied.

"Naw, that ain't it. I wear the wig so I can pull it over my ears and block out noise like what he's making right now!"

Jack howled with laughter. The trucker glared at him.

"Come on, Vail, help my poor ears out here," pleaded Norman.

Jack jumped up to the stage, took the microphone, and began his duties for the night. "I would like to dedicate this next song to two of my very good friends that are here tonight. The King of Rock and Roll behind the pizza counter, Elvis..."

Norman, Jr. snapped into his pose again, to the delight of the crowd.

"And my very favorite waitress, Britney Sparks—I mean Spears."

The audience clapped their approval.

Jack grinned. "By special request from our manager—Tom Jones, this is for you!" He began to croon to the Hawaiian guitar sounds of the classic Elvis tune "Blue Hawaii."

"Night and you
And blue Hawaii
The night is heavenly,
And you are heaven to me..."

Norman threw his hands up in the air. "Finally, somebody's doing an Elvis song!"

Jack looked at Sarah as he sang.

She stopped moving and stood still, watching him and listening. In the song she heard his dreams—and hers. Those dreams seemed very fragile, like the notes of the song itself, which hung in the air for a fleeting moment and then faded away. The melody and vision of the fading song seemed sadly symbolic of their lives together. She wanted to catch the notes and cling to them, to hold them as if to hold the dreams themselves. Her eyes filled with tears, for his past and hers, and for the future she feared they would never have.

"Come with me,
While the moon is on the sea,
The night is young,
And so are we, so are we.
Dreams come true,
In blue Hawaii,
And mine could all come true,
This magic night of nights with you."

Jack stepped towards her as he sang, and the final words found her pressing her tear-streaked face against his chest, while the crowd, who did not see the tears, cheered with delight.

The lights were on late at the old gas station on the edge of town. Warren Beckem lay sprawled on a torn lawn chair outside the office, a half-empty bottle of cheap whiskey sitting on the ground beside him. His snores rose and fell with his chest, a counterpart to the buzzing of the mosquitoes that hovered around him in the sickly yellow light. A late-model, gray, rented sedan pulled into the station next to the dusty pump with "Full Service" printed on it. A pneumatic bell rang, but Warren didn't stir.

A loud blast from the car horn jerked Warren upright. He stood up and lumbered unsteadily over to the car. Leaning on the roof for support and peering through the window, Warren asked groggily, "What'll it be, buddy?"

Zendo Colvack looked out at Warren. He smiled casually. Something about the smile reminded Warren of a frightening dream, but he shook his head to clear it.

"Fill it up," Zendo said.

Warren nodded and stumbled to the gas pump and grabbed the nozzle.

Zendo watched him for a moment, eyeing a small, newly healed scar on his greasy forehead. Zendo lit a thin cigar and waved Warren over. "Hey, let me ask you something."

He pulled out the black-and-white promotional photo of Jack, holding it up for Warren to see.

"You ever seen this guy around? He owes me some money and I'm looking to collect it."

Warren grabbed the photo, holding it up to his face. He looked at Zendo and an evil grin spread over his face.

"Oh yeah, I know this guy real well," Warren said, his speech slightly slurred. "Vail-something. He works at the Rock 'n' Roll Heaven Restaurant down the road about a mile. I think he lives in an apartment underneath a warehouse they turned into a church a few years ago—at least that's what I hear."

His grin turned into a toothy smile, and he leaned his head into the car.

"Maybe I can help you collect. I don't think much of this guy either." Pointing to his forehead he continued, "He gave me this, and I'd love to help you collect."

Zendo smiled again realizing now that he had his man in the crosshairs of his mission. "No thanks," he said, blowing smoke into Warren's face.

Warren coughed and lurched backwards, knocking his head against the roof of Zendo's car.

"I can handle this one on my own."

Either the knock on the head or something in Zendo's manner made Warren step back even more. He rubbed his head and replaced the nozzle in the pump.

Zendo stuck a fifty-dollar bill out of the window. "Keep the change, and thanks for the info."

Warren snatched the bill greedily. "Sure thing, thanks! Stop by on your way out!"

Zendo smiled his chilling smile and drove off, heading down the short road into Summerville.

After eleven o'clock, Jack drove Sarah home. As they passed the church on the way to her apartment, Jack noticed a light shining through the low transom window of his own apartment.

Sarah saw the startled expression on his face. "Jack, is something wrong?"

"I know I turned off the lights!" he replied. He scanned the building out of the corner of his eye as they drove past. He pulled onto a road a block beyond his apartment. The car was shielded from the church by a tall row of bushes. "I'm going to check it out," he whispered to Sarah.

"Jack, be careful!" She grabbed his arm.

"Don't worry," he reassured her. "I'm not going in there."

He left the car and walked towards the church from the back, following the edge of the woods. He saw neither movement around the church nor any sign of a car. As he tiptoed through the grass, he breathed a prayer of thanks that he was wearing the black leather *Saturday Night Fever* jacket.

Staying in the shadows, Jack crept along the edge of the building. He peered down through the transom, looking into the living room of the basement apartment. Everything was as he'd left it. He started to relax—*Maybe I did leave the light on.* Then his glance fell on his television set. The day before he'd placed a small photo of himself and Sarah in their restaurant costumes on the set.

The photo was gone.

Suddenly Jack was aware of everything around him. Adrenaline surged to his muscles. His heart started beating so loudly that he feared others might hear it. Scanning the alley, the street—he saw no one. Yet, his sense of danger was acute and rising. Whoever was waiting or watching had all the advantage, and Jack was wise enough to know it. He slipped back into the darkness and ran back to the car. The Colvacks had found him.

Houston, We've Got a Problem

The pounding on Frank's door echoed through the small house. Frank was up in an instant, alert and aware. He opened a drawer and pulled out a pistol. Instinctively he checked the action, chambering a round. "Who is it?" he called out, making his voice sound sleepy as he moved quietly and quickly towards the door, keeping his line of fire open.

"It's Jack and Sarah," Jack's voice called through the door. "We've got a problem!"

Frank snapped back the bolt and opened the door. Only when he saw Jack and Sarah outside did he lower the pistol, flipping the safety on.

Sarah stared at the gun, but Jack hurried in, ignoring it.

"Frank, I've been made," he said hurriedly. "I went back to my apartment, and somebody's been through it. They took a picture of Sarah and I off my TV set. Whoever it is knows there's a connection between the two of us."

Frank's face showed no emotion. He was taking it all in.

"I can't stay here anymore, Frank," he continued. "I need to leave town immediately, with Sarah. I need to turn her over to the FBI to give testimony, otherwise we're both gonna wind up dead."

"OK, OK, I hear you," Frank replied, his voice was calm and reassuring. "I figured this was gonna happen sooner or later. I've been working on that, and I'll arrange it."

Sarah and Jack sat on the sofa, and Frank slipped into a chair in the corner, angled towards the front door.

Jack glanced at Sarah and turned to Frank. "I have an idea. I have been planning this thing through for a while, and I know what I want to do."

Frank nodded. "All right, tell me, and I'll make it happen if I can."

Jack stood up again and paced a little, tapping his right fingers against the knuckles of his left fist. He took a breath. "OK, I'm going to turn Sarah over to the FBI…in Miami."

Frank sat up sharply.

Sarah looked up in amazement.

"Are you crazy?" Frank asked. "You could be killed—you both could be killed! You'd be walking right into Colvack's kill zone."

Jack shook his head rapidly, "No, no, no—I've got this all figured out. I want the FBI to pick up Sarah Tuesday night in Miami, outside the Tropics Hotel at 10 p.m. sharp."

Sarah stuck up her hand to stop him. "Wait, the Tropics? I thought the Colvacks *owned* that place? Isn't that the place where you fought when all the trouble happened?"

Jack nodded. "Yes, that's it, and that makes it the one place they can't afford a hit in. They know the government is watching their every move. Trust me, you'll be safe."

"I see your point, Jack," said Frank, thinking about it. "It's a popular casino, it's crowded, it's watched—and everything's on video. Anything bad happens there and the Colvacks go down, whether you testify or not."

"Frank, you need to have agents waiting to pick us up," continued Jack. "She needs to give her eyewitness account and murder testimony to the Feds, and I will give written sworn testimony of my involvement with the Colvacks."

Frank's eyes narrowed at the last statement, and he looked at Jack. "And then what? As if I don't know..."

Jack looked Frank in the eyes. "And then I will come back here by myself."

"Jack, you're not coming back here!" cried Sarah, "It's too dangerous! What are you doing?"

Frank stood up and put his hand on Jack's shoulder. "Jack, I know what you're up to, and you're rolling the dice with your life."

"Frank, every time I walked into a steel cage I rolled the dice. It's just another day at the office," Jack replied, his voice calm and matter-of-fact.

"Yeah," said Frank, "but you're not the only one at the office this time." He glanced at Sarah.

Jack gripped Frank's arm. "I'm sure you need to make a phone call or two right about now, don't you? I need to talk to Sarah by myself."

Frank sighed and nodded with resignation, acknowledging Jack's request. There wasn't much he could do with Jack. It was just the nature of the beast. With the young thug who stole the offering, Frank had been able to stop him from carrying a gun, stop him from killing, and actually get out of the gangs. But change was a slow process with these types. Jack's life had changed dramatically too, but he still had a ways to go. Frank patted Sarah's shoulder and walked out of the room.

Jack sat down next to Sarah, holding her hands.

Sarah braced herself for whatever Jack had to say.

"Sarah, Frank is going to give you seven debit cards that represent every financial asset I have..."

She interrupted him, confused. "Why, Jack? What's happening?"

Jack shook his head. "I can't explain right now, but you'll understand soon. Sarah, I don't know what's going to happen

187

to me over the next few days. I may only have a small window of time left to do something right with my life."

"What are you saying, Jack?" A tone of worry rose in Sarah's voice.

"What I'm saying is…" he faltered then reached up to touched her cheek. "I love you."

She reached for his face, touching it gently, ecstatic that she had finally heard the words from him she had waited for all her life.

"I've loved you since you were *eleven*—well, not *while* you were eleven," he stammered.

She laughed, a gentle laugh tinged with sadness. "I understand, Jack. Go on."

He smiled a sad smile at her. "I made a promise to my mother that I'd do something right with my life, something that would make her proud. Being with you would make Julia proud of her only child. So no matter what happens from this point on, just know that I will always be with you."

Then he did something to symbolize his vow. He reached around his neck and pulled off the chain with Julia's wedding ring on it. Gently, lovingly, he slipped it over Sarah's neck.

She caught the ring in her hand.

"I want you to take this as an engagement ring," Jack said softly. "If I live through the next few days, we'll…if not, I promise you'll be taken care of. There's nobody who I'd rather see wear this than you. As long as you wear it, I will always be with you."

Tears came to Sarah's eyes. "OK, Jack, I trust you. I don't understand all of this, but I don't think you want me to understand. So, I'll wait."

She wrapped her arms around him.

"I love you, Jack. Promise me you won't leave me again. Promise me you'll come back to me."

He held her tightly, smelling the sweet, gentle scent of her hair, feeling the warmth of her embrace. "One way or another you'll see me again." Jack well understood the harsh reality of what his words really meant. He whispered, "Pray for me, Sarah. Pray for us both."

They heard Frank approaching and released each other from their embrace.

He walked into the room holding a slip of paper. "OK, guys, everything's set." He handed Jack the piece of paper. "Here's an address of another agent, a really good friend of mine. He's got a place where you can stay before you roll into Miami. He'll call me and let me know you arrived and what time you leave for Miami. But you're gonna have to leave Summerville right now. There's a killer out there, most likely one of Colvack's men under contract looking to take Jack, or maybe both of you, out for good."

Jack reached for the paper.

Frank grunted, looking at their costumes they still had on from work. "You can't walk out of here looking the way you look. Come with me."

Frank at His Best

As he opened a door to a small room with a makeup mirror and dresser, the couple saw hundreds of disguises, wigs, hats, and clothes of all descriptions.

Frank smiled. "I kept a few souvenirs from my days in the bureau. I'm a big hit at costume parties." He pulled some street clothes off the wall and nodded towards a chest. "Sarah, look in there. Most of this stuff ain't your size, but I've got a niece who's sort of taken after her uncle; she left a few things here."

He grinned at Jack. "She wants to work in movies. Waste of talent, I tell her."

Minutes later, Jack and Sarah were dressed in normal street clothes and looking neither like John Travolta and Britney Spears or Jack and Sarah. Jack's skin color was much paler, the wig on his head was curly brown. Glasses and a thick brown mustache also disguised his face.

Sarah's hair was black and straight, her face was ruddy, and her waist was decidedly pregnant.

Frank smiled at his work approvingly. "Well, not perfect, but it'll do. You're definitely not who they're looking for. Now go quickly, and don't stop for anything until you get to the address I gave you. It'll be just outside of Miami in a little town called Biscayne Bay. You'll be safe there."

"Back to Miami," Jack said. "Looks like the 180 thing keeps following me around."

"Let's hope that's all that's following you around," replied Frank.

Zendo Colvack drove slowly through Summerville, the photo of Jack and Sarah beside him in the car. The door to a house opened, catching Zendo's eye. *Who would be leaving home at midnight?* But when he saw a man helping a very pregnant woman into a car, he dismissed the question from his mind and drove on by. The couple's car started and headed in the opposite direction, bound for Miami and Biscayne Bay.

Chapter 14

Lighting the Fuse

On Tuesday evening, Jack and Sarah—once again looking very much like Jack and Sarah—hand in hand casually strolled through the casino floor area of the Tropics Hotel. To most of the casino goers they looked no different than any other young couple on vacation, yet the grip of their hands was tight.

Jack's eyes scanned the room as if looking for someone. A moment later, he spotted his quarry. He leaned over to Sarah and whispered, "Take the ring off the chain, and put it on your finger. Don't ask any questions; just go with everything I say."

Sarah nodded and did as he asked. When she was finished, Jack led her across the room.

Samantha Bentley stood along one side of the casino floor watching the clientele with a practiced eye, measuring each person and classifying them in her mind. *High roller, wannabe, compulsive gambler*—she ticked them off in her head. *Big-time player—get his name for future fight promos; pensioner...* She was suddenly startled as a shockingly contradictory category came straight towards her walking purposefully. *Insane,* she thought.

"Samantha! How are you?" Jack called to her, his face smiling with delight. "I haven't seen you for a long time. How's business?"

A few customers and employees looked her way, and Samantha suddenly felt uncomfortable. She tried to look at Jack and the pretty young woman holding his hand with only casual surprise, or at least without gawking.

"Jack," she said warmly. "I'm surprised to see you!" Her curiosity got the better of her. "I thought you were in jail."

Jack laughed as if the comment was nothing. "Oh, no! I've been out for a while. They couldn't convict me, something to do with how they collected evidence."

He flipped his hand as if to wave the problem away. Then he lowered his voice as if sharing his confidence. "But I'm definitely going to testify against Johnny Colvack—teach him a lesson or two. Don't worry, I'll keep you out of it." Then his voice raised again, as if back to lighter matters.

"Not only that, get a load of this," he gestured to Sarah. "Let me introduce you to my new wife, Helen."

"Helen, this is Samantha Bentley, the promoter."

Samantha was stunned, barely acknowledging Sarah's presence. She leaned towards Jack, "Aren't you concerned that they would be after you?"

Jack laughed again. "Oh, they probably are, but they haven't gotten me yet. We've been hiding out in a place called

Summerville until I testify. It's right next to the Mid-South Amusement Park. We've been working at a restaurant called 'Rock 'n' Roll Heaven.' Can you believe it, me in a restaurant!" He laughed at the idea of it. "But we're leaving tonight. I'm doing my last shift, we're packing up, and then Friday morning the FBI will pick us up and take us to some undisclosed location—so they say." He snorted, as if he doubted it. "It's a part of the whole witness protection program."

Samantha was stunned by Jack's naiveté. Struggling for a response, she searched for another topic of conversation. "So, what are you doing in Miami?" she asked, trying to sound as if her interest were casual. "Are you fighting for someone?"

Jack shook his head, amused. "Oh, no. We just came here for our honeymoon. I wanted to show Helen the sights in Miami before we got relocated."

Samantha tried hard not to gape. *I knew fighters could be thick, but this...* "How nice for you both," she managed to say.

Jack continued, "Well, Samantha, it's been good to see you. I hope this legal stuff doesn't affect business for you."

"Oh no, Jack, not at all," she replied, regaining her composure. "I've got lots of things going on in this town." She smiled her most winning smile. "Where are you going now?"

Jack looked at Sarah, smiling. "We're just gonna stroll down the streets and hit a few of the bigger hotels and night spots," he said, "and find a place to stay."

Sarah looked down as if embarrassed.

"And then we'll leave in the morning."

Samantha nodded. "Well, it's great to see ya Jack, and you, too, Helen. You take care of yourselves and enjoy the evening. Bye-bye!"

Jack and Sarah quickly walked away from her, leaving the casino. Samantha watched them for a moment, and then hurried out of the casino in the opposite direction.

Outside, Jack led Sarah towards a black town car where three FBI agents stood waiting. Sarah leaned towards Jack and whispered, "What was that 'Helen' business?"

Jack shrugged and whispered back, "When you were standing there so quietly, you reminded me of that lady who couldn't talk—remember Helen Keller?"

Sarah punched him on the arm. "If it wasn't for the 'this is my wife' part, I'd beat you up right now."

Another town car pulled in behind the first, and Watkins and Phillips got out. Jack nodded towards them and turned to Sarah. "OK, Sweetheart, this is where we say good-bye."

The sound of the word "good-bye" hung in the air like a doctor announcing his patient's death to the family. In a suspended moment of disbelief, Sarah hugged him tightly.

"Jack, I don't want you to leave—it doesn't feel right. When will I see you again?"

"I don't know, Sarah," he said, his voice unsure, almost sorrowful, "but you've got to go with the FBI agents and testify. They'll keep you safe." He held her face up and looked at her. "I need you to be strong for me. I've got to go along with Watkins and Phillips and do what I gotta do. It's all part of the deal."

Sarah nodded. "I understand that. But why are you going back to Summerville? Tell me the truth, Jack. Will I see you again?"

Tenderly, he looked in her eyes, "Baby, I don't know. Just keep praying," his voice was soft. He leaned into her for a final kiss.

A few moments later, the town cars pulled out of the hotel, each heading a separate direction.

Samantha closed the door to her office near the casino and grabbed the phone, dialing as soon as she picked it up.

"Johnny, it's Samantha. I've found him—I've found Jack DeNova; he was here at the hotel! I know where he's going to be and what time he's gonna be there! Let me spell it out to you…"

In the office upstairs, Hal sat at the marble table listening to a phone, his hand cupped over the mouthpiece. Gently he replaced the handset on the cradle. He looked over at Mike, who leaned against the back of a sofa, kicking the wall, leaving scuffmarks on the paneling.

"Well, guess what, Mike?" Hal said. "Johnny's pretty little toad downstairs may have just caught us a fly."

Mike looked up. "What's Johnny gonna do about it?"

"You already know," said Hal with disgust. "I just heard him tell her he was gonna send Zendo to do *our* job."

Mike jumped up and slammed his hand into the wall. "He can't *do that!* DeNova's *mine.* He killed *my brother!*"

"Mine too, Mike," said Hal coldly. Then he smiled. "But I know where DeNova's gonna be and when. If you wanna finish this job right, we can beat Zendo to the punch and prove we can handle things for ourselves."

Mike smiled back at his brother.

Thursday night at 10:50 p.m., a black Mercedes pulled into the parking lot of Rock 'n' Roll Heaven. The driver and passenger watched the last customers get in their cars and drive away from the restaurant. The doors to the Mercedes opened, and Hal and Mike stepped out.

Hal looked at Mike. "Listen, Mike, Johnny was right about one thing," he said. "We need to just go in there, kill him, and leave."

Mike bristled, "Screw Johnny! Are you gonna tell me that you don't want to see me beat this guy down for Bruce, watch him beg for his life, and then kill him?"

"Mike, I know how you feel and I know what you want to do," replied Hal shaking his head. "But we can't afford to blow it this time, or Johnny will send Zendo after *us.* We just have to go in there, whack this guy, and get this thing over with!"

"Oh, it's gonna be over with!" snarled Mike. "Let's go do this thing!"

Hal nodded, and the two men walked into the restaurant.

Across the street Zendo's sedan slowly approached the restaurant. Zendo saw the black Mercedes and frowned, his eyes scanning the street. Cautiously he backed into a dark side street, stopping the car and turning off the engine. He didn't like surprises; in his business, surprises always meant trouble. And the Mercedes was a surprise.

A sensation like the dull buzz of a distant alarm clock rose in Zendo's mind. He settled back into the shadows to watch the diner, a thin cigar glowing faintly between his lips.

Mike and Hal entered the restaurant as casually as if they were just another set of customers. An older black man in a Rick James outfit was standing by the cash register. He had just hung up the phone.

Jack stood at the kitchen counter wearing his typical white sleeveless tee-shirt and black jeans and kneading pizza dough for the next day's shift. Otherwise, the restaurant was empty.

Rick James looked up at Hal and Mike. "Sorry, man, but we're closed," he said.

Hal pulled out a pistol and locked the door. "You sure are, pal," he said with a sneer.

Jack looked up at Hal and Mike, with no expression of surprise on his face.

Mike stared at Jack, his face filled with hatred and rage. Walking to the center of the restaurant, he sat down and stared at the counter where Jack was standing. He pulled out his pistol and set it on the table beside him. "OK, DeNova, it's time to answer for Bruce!" Mike snarled.

Jack pulled his apron off, wiping the flour off his hands. He picked a roll of white wrapping tape off the counter and started winding it around his wrists, methodically and carefully; his eyes never left Mike. "No, Colvack," he replied coldly. "Tonight you answer for Art and Julia. It's time to visit the Grim Reaper."

"Mike, what are you doing?" yelled Hal. His head snapped nervously around from Mike to Jack to the mock Rick James with his hands up behind the register. Hal's confident swagger was gone. "C'mon, let's waste him right now, Mike, and get out of here!"

"No!" screamed Mike, slamming his hand on a table. "I want to break this fool down myself! We owe it to Bruce!"

Rick James stepped out from behind the register, moving closer to Hal. "Is it OK if I leave now?" he asked calmly.

Jack nodded, "Yeah, Pops, you can go."

"No, it's not!" Hal screamed. He whipped the gun around and pointed it at Jack. "*I'm* giving the orders! He leaves when *I* say he does!"

Suddenly Rick James snapped into a frenzied series of moves, his left hand grabbing Hal's gun hand, forcing the barrel up towards the ceiling. At the same time, his right forearm smashed upwards into Hal's surprised face, driving him against the door with a resounding crash.

Hal crumpled to the floor in a heap, leaving Rick James standing over him holding the pistol and aiming at Mike.

"Give up your other piece, Mike," Frank McQue's voice bellowed from Rick's mouth. "I know you're still strapped."

His eyes on the pistol, Mike slowly reached down and slid a .38 out of an ankle holster. He placed it on the floor and kicked it so it slid to Frank's feet. Frank reached to the table beside the door and picked up the pistol lying there as well. Pocketing it, he did the same with the .38. Then grinning at Jack, he pulled his wig off and peeled back a layer of latex.

"OK, DeNova, you made the invites, it's your party." He flipped the lock and reached down to grab the unconscious Hal with one hand. "Have fun!" he said. Pulling Hal behind him, he left the restaurant.

Outside, Zendo saw a large black man emerge from the restaurant pulling Hal's limp form. He sat up, stubbing out his cigar and reaching for his shoulder holster. Another series of movements caught his eye, and he hesitated—watching as two black town cars pulled up to the restaurant. Zendo froze with caution as four men emerged from the cars, pistols drawn. It was Watkins and Phillips with two backup agents.

"Remember our deal," he heard the large black man yell to the new arrivals. "Nobody goes in until I say so!"

Zendo settled back into his seat, watching. Whatever was going on, it was not going smoothly or according to plan. He now would watch and wait, but Zendo was determined not to leave town until he knew DeNova was dead.

Chapter 15

Someone's "0" Must Go

After Frank left, Jack, still wiping off the flour from his hands, stepped down off the cooking area into the floor section of the restaurant to face Mike.

Carefully, without any explanation, both began slowly moving back the tables and chairs. Each kept a tense eye on the other while clearing off the small dance floor until all the tables and chairs were flush up against the walls.

These two gladiators were creating their own octagon area for their own private fight to the death. Both Jack and Mike were undefeated in their history of no-holds-barred fights. So alongside the number of their victories was an "0" which stood for no losses. But today someone's "0" would go.

Jack's eyes steadied on Mike, his face showing a calm even Jack was surprised he felt, as if something was cooling his anger, controlling it, focusing it. He remembered Marco's teaching, all of it moving and pulsating as if it was engrained in the fabric of his lithe, muscular body.

The fighters were measuring each other, sensing each other's pulse, nervous system, confidence level, looking for signs of weakness or fear. Both realized this fight—win or lose—would be their last.

For a split second, Mike caught a glimpse of Frank through the glass door dragging Hal towards the street. In that instant, his anger was fueled by a sense of entrapment. He heard the cars pull up, the footsteps running about, and he realized the walls of time were closing in on him. His window of opportunity to avenge his brother's death was now. Rage boiled in his brain, his adrenaline pumping like an eight-cylinder race car.

He positioned himself into a firm and confident fighting stance and began to shift towards Jack.

De Nova's eyes were cold and lifeless like a crocodile waiting for a gazelle to get within striking distance. His mind was focused on every nuance of movement made by Mike. He even was counting the timing of Mike's breaths, waiting to feel even the slightest rhythm change in order to prepare a surprise attack. Whatever this predator had in mind was, as of yet, undetectable.

Then, seemingly out of nowhere, with a deep growl Mike lost his cool first and viciously rushed at Jack, throwing out a front push-kick.

Instinctively, Jack moved back, as his reflexes had been faithfully trained to do. But Mike's legs were longer than even a seasoned fighter like Jack could anticipate, and Mike's foot landed into Jack's chest, violently driving him back and slightly off the ground into a pile of chairs.

Jack lost his balance as he crashed into the heap of tangled chair legs, but, in an instant, was back with his feet off the floor scrambling to regain an upright posture.

Both fighters seemed surprised at the impact of the first blow, and Mike paused in shock for a brief second to admire his work.

In that second, Jack regained his fighting stance and recalibrated the whole battle. He was hurt—a sharp pain stung under his heart. He could feel something moving around in his chest—a broken blood vessel, a torn ligament, a cracked rib? This was war, and he had no time to deal with anything until the war was over.

Jack had never sustained such a direct blow. He shifted into a different gear. He could not out-kick or out-punch this opponent. Mike was too big and too strong. He felt his power in that one kick and instinctively readjusted his plan to meet this force before him.

Jack could feel Mike's confidence rising, and he knew he had to level out the battlefield if he was to come out victorious if not just—alive. So he waited until Mike came within a reasonable distance. Jack would have to make some kind of offensive move. But getting past those kicks and punches could be deadly. One well-placed blow could render Jack unconscious, and then Mike would kill him for sure.

Jack shifted forward a step.

Mike took the bait and swung at Jack's head.

Jack ducked, but was still too far away to dive inside and take him down.

Then Mike threw a left jab.

Jack, to his own surprise, caught it with both his hands, yanked it to his chest and in one swift move swung his legs up to wrap around Mike's massive arm. Jack fell backwards and down, shoulders to the floor, almost upside down, firmly grasping Mike's fist with both legs wrapped around Mike's arm.

Mike's body surprisingly stayed erect, but he was bent over with his arm caught in a deadly cookie jar of Jack DeNova's recipe for jiu jitsu. Mike refused to fall over, no matter how hard Jack twisted and turned. But Jack had Mike in an arm lock, and he wasn't about to let go.

Mike swung Jack around in a circle until Jack shifted his pelvis under Mike's elbow and began to crank it.

Jack arched his back and pulled Mike's arm to his chest, while forcing his elbow out with the thrust of his hips.

Mike began to groan and then yell in pain. His arm was being bent back the wrong way by the world's foremost authority on physical pain. Finally, while still standing, arm stuck in Jack's upside-down grip, Mike's elbow gave way with a loud cracking sound. The pain was so great that Mike blacked out for a couple seconds and fell over with Jack still wrapped around his arm.

Jack knew this was a horrendously painful finishing move. He never actually followed through with it on anybody, because his opponents always would tap out as soon as the pain became unbearable.

Mike lay on his side in agony as Jack tumbled over backwards and stood up.

Jack began to walk towards the door to tell Frank to come and get his adversary when a thunderous right hook came crashing into the side of Jack's face from behind. The force threw Jack over across the dance floor, and he slid across the slick hardwood floor for several feet before he came to a stop.

Instinctively, Jack got up to his hands and knees. Blood was pouring from his mouth in a steady stream, his teeth were loose in his jaw. His cheek began to swell up, and as he looked up he could see the figure of Mike Colvack.

"Did you think we was in the gym, DeNova? Did you think an arm bar would make a Colvack tap out? It's your day to die, boy. Say hello to your mommy and daddy for me."

And with that, he picked Jack up by the front of his tee-shirt with his good arm. With his useless, broken arm dangling helplessly at his side, before Jack could regain his senses, he slammed a straight right hand into Jack's chest under his heart.

Mike was trying to kill Jack by breaking his sternum and pushing a bone into his vital organs. But his blow was just slightly off. Nevertheless, the force of it still drove Jack back against the wall.

Jack bounced back and ducked the inevitable follow-up right hand. Then he dove for Mike's legs. Jack grabbed them as a football tackle would, and with an amazing display of brute strength, lifted Mike off his feet and slammed him on his back. Jack quickly scrambled to sit on Mike's chest, raining down blows into his face.

But this wasn't Zakura. Mike took all of Jack's punches and still was trying to throw Jack off his chest.

Jack's hands were sore and bleeding from the blows to Mike's face and head. Jack simply couldn't knock him out. Jack could actually feel a couple of his own fingers break on Mike's head, and he knew this strategy wasn't going to work.

So he went for the other arm, which now was easy to grab hold of cause it was flailing, attempting to block the punches being thrown. Jack repeated the Zakura move. He grabbed the wrist, left leg over the face, right leg over the torso. He dropped to his back with the arm between his legs. He arched up his hips to force the other elbow back the wrong way.

Mike groaned then yelled.

Jack cranked as hard as he could until he heard Mike's other elbow crack and snap back the wrong way like the other one.

Jack rolled off and stood there, looking down at his nemesis. Both arms were broken. Elbows snapped and useless for fighting. Finally, Jack knew he had him. Never before had he inflicted so much punishment on a foe. Even Bruce hadn't experienced this much torture when he was killed.

Now Jack could take a deep breath and assess his wounds. He limped over to a table to get himself upright so he could walk out of the front door with a little dignity.

Suddenly, a size-14 cowboy boot drilled him under his left ribcage with so much force that it threw him up against the countertop, and flipped him over the cash register on his back. More ribs were broken, maybe three this time. Jack could hear them crack like chopsticks as the blow landed. His lungs fought to breathe, and he started coughing up blood and couldn't stop.

He looked up and saw Mike Colvack standing in the center of the restaurant, both arms broken, but in the spirit of a warrior Jack had never before seen.

"It ain't over, DeNova. It ain't over till you die tonight."

Jack was astonished. Never before had he ever encountered anything even in the same galaxy as this guy. Jack knew it was "him or me," so, somehow, despite the pain, he rose to the occasion and charged after Mike.

A kick flew up and Jack got underneath it. When it came down, it rested on Jack's shoulder. It almost looked like Jack was helping Mike stretch out his hamstrings, but that thought ended when Jack used his other leg to sweep Mike's balancing leg out from under him.

Mike fell back hard onto the floor, hitting his back.

Immediately, Jack sat between his legs and took Mike's foot and tucked it under his arm, Then, with both forearms folded under Mike's calf, Jack, using all his might, began to yank back his foot and try to snap Mike's ankle.

Mike fought back furiously.

Finally, after two minutes of yelling, growling, and grunting there was a violent "crack."

Mike's ankle snapped.

Jack fell back as Mike faded in and out of consciousness from the unbearable pain of his injuries.

After a minute or so of moans and groans of his own, Jack finally forced himself to stand upright. Jaw busted, teeth loose, bruised, cut badly, six, maybe seven ribs broken, internal bleeding that wouldn't stop, and welts all over him the size of golf balls—Jack started to limp towards the door, when from behind him he heard a voice.

DeNova, I'm not done with you yet."

Unbelievably, somehow this monster had managed to stand himself up, both broken arms hanging helplessly at his side. Ankle broken, cocked at an angle like a horse with a nail in his hoof, he was balancing all his weight on one leg. And he still wasn't through.

Jack thought to himself, *I gotta hand it to this guy. He's taken more punishment than I've ever given out. Given me more of a beatin' than I've ever gotten in my life, and he still wants to keep fighting?*

Jack's admiration of his opponent melted into resolve. It was getting ridiculous and it had to end.

Strangely, a thought rose up in him, *What would Art and Julia tell me to do in this situation?*

Then it came to him. He walked behind the counter in the kitchen and found the biggest cast-iron skillet he could find, grabbed it, and walked over to where Mike was hopping on one foot on the dance floor.

He said, "It's been a great workout, but it's time to say good night, moron." With that, Jack swung the giant cast-iron frying pan from somewhere down near the floor as though he were going for a home run over center field. The final crack heard was Mike's head, hit so hard it sounded like a baseball bat hitting a flagpole. The force of the blow spun him around twice, and he finally flopped on the ground face first like a fallen redwood in a California forest.

The day was over, and what a day it had been.

Jack stumbled out of the restaurant, his face bloody, the pain in his side growing worse with every step. He leaned against the doorpost staring at the scene outside. Watkins, Phillips, Frank, and the two backup agents—plus two ambulances were there with lights flashing. The paramedics rushed toward him. He caught his reflection in the window; his eye was almost swollen shut and he had cuts and bruises everywhere. He started to laugh, but it made the pain in his side worse.

Frank was the first to reach him. He moved to support Jack, easing him down the steps.

"Is it over?" he asked.

Jack smiled feebly. "I think so."

Frank nodded. "Was it worth it?"

Jack glanced over his shoulder. "If he's still alive, probably not."

Frank and two of the paramedics eased Jack onto the stretcher. Two agents and two other paramedics rushed into the restaurant with another stretcher to retrieve what was left of Mike Colvack.

Jack grabbed Frank's hand. "Please come with me," he coughed in pain, "please."

Frank nodded and followed Jack and the paramedics into the ambulance.

"I might not make it through this one," Jack said weakly as the doors closed behind them.

"Nonsense!" snorted Frank. "You'll be all right."

Jack shook his head, despite the pain. "No. They won't leave until I'm dead. Trust me, it's not over." He squeezed

Frank's hand. "I need you to do something for me; it's very important."

Frank nodded, squeezing back. "Anything. You name it."

Jack smiled. "Look on my ankle."

Frank pulled up Jack's pantleg. An envelope was taped to Jack's ankle.

Carefully, Frank unwrapped the tape, removed the envelope, and handed it to Jack.

"No matter what happens to me," Jack said, "I want you to give the contents of this envelope to Sarah."

Frank nodded.

"One more thing…" Jack continued, "do you have a pen? Can you reach in my back pocket and pull that laminated card out of my wallet?"

Frank nodded again. He found the card with the cross and the picture of Sarah. Pulling a pen out of his own pocket, he handed both to Jack. Jack scribbled on the card and stuck it in the envelope. Weakly, he held the envelope to his lips and sealed it. A small smudge of blood stained the back of the envelope.

"Make sure Sarah gets this, McQue. Now listen close to what I have to tell you now…" Jack's voice trailed off into a whisper.

Frank bent over Jack.

Jack whispered something, and Frank looked sharply up at the paramedic. When he appeared not to have heard, Frank murmured back to Jack, "I'm here." He nodded his head in understanding," I'm here."

In his hidden spot in the shadows, Zendo's eyes narrowed when he saw Jack emerge from the restaurant. He watched as the ambulances were loaded and pulled away. One of the black town cars followed the ambulance carrying Hal and Mike. The other car remained, its passengers in a heated conversation with another agent.

Zendo pulled away unnoticed, following the ambulance that carried Jack. Jack was still his mark—and still a piece of work left unfinished.

Chapter 16

The End of a Job Well Done

Zendo sat in the hospital parking lot, smoking another cigar. His puffs were measured and relaxed, like the ticking of a clock.

It's all a matter of timing, he thought. *First they need to patch him up. That will take about three cigars. Another for them to settle him in his room, and get everything the way they want it.* He flicked ash out of the window onto the asphalt. *Then comes the shift change.* He blew a puff of smoke through the window. *All a matter of timing.*

Jack was wrapped from head to toe in some sort of bandage or brace. Frank stood in the quietness of the hospital room for the longest time just staring at the bed. Maybe he was blaming himself. Maybe he was disappointed in Jack's ability to listen to advice. Maybe it was the FBI side of him trying to figure out the way it should have all gone down, or just maybe it could be that his heart was broken as he looked at his friend laying there, the heart monitor perilously close to going into flat line. It wouldn't be the first time he lost a friend in action. But Jack was a unique character. Only God really knew what was spinning around in Frank's mind as he suddenly turned and stepped out of the room to talk with an FBI agent outside the door.

"Go down to the front of the building and get another man on the back door," Frank said. "Make sure that no one comes in; there's still a killer on the loose. And I'll need three agents at the elevator door."

The agent nodded. "You got it, Frank." He turned and headed down the hall. Frank scanned the hallway, making certain it was clear, and went back into Jack's room.

Zendo Colvack finished his last cigar and stepped through the back door of the hospital. He walked quickly down the corridor, quietly checking doorknobs as he walked along. Suddenly he found a door that opened, and he slipped into a dark office. A few seconds later, Zendo emerged dressed in a doctor's jacket and carrying a clipboard. A hospital ID badge with his picture dangled from his pocket. He walked up to a nurse's station.

"Nurse, what room have they assigned to Vail Tudo?" he asked, pretending to examine his chart.

The nurse glanced up. "Yes, Doctor..." she hesitated.

"Mitzkov," he said smiling, "I'm new."

"Oh." She tapped on a keyboard. "Let's see, Mr. Tudo was just assigned room 501."

"Thank you, nurse." He turned and walked to the elevators, pushing the button. A half-second later, the door opened and an agent stepped out. He hurried to stand by the back door, as Zendo walked past him onto the elevator.

The door to Jack's room swung open and Zendo slipped inside. Frank was not there. *Still getting settled,* Zendo thought. *Nobody thinks I'll be here this soon.* He pulled a pistol from inside his coat, rapidly screwing a silencer onto it. Grabbing a pillow, he doubled it over and stuck the gun inside it. He stepped over to the bed and smiled at the banged-up body. He wanted to take a minute to admire his nephew's handiwork.

"Fight's done, and you're not as tough as you thought you were, Mr. DeNova. I guess the game's over and...you lose."

Zendo pulled the trigger nine times, bullets pumping into the body, riddling the head, and torso. Another win for the Colvacks.

Calmly, Zendo pulled the gun out of the pillowcase. Carefully tilting the pillow over, he tumbled nine spent shell cases into his hand. The cases went into his pocket. He popped the clip out of the gun and inserted another, chambering a round and flipping off the safety. He spun the silencer off the barrel, pocketed it, and slipped his pistol back in his holster. Zendo did everything calmly and methodically, paying no attention to the dead target he'd been hunting down lying motionless and bleeding in the bed.

Leaving the room, Zendo walked straight to the elevator. The door opened and three agents stepped out. Zendo nodded to them.

"I'm glad you're here," he said. "That boy is in bad shape. He's going to need a lot of sleep, so make sure nobody, and I mean nobody, gets up here to visit unless you know specifically who they are. And make sure you check their ID badges." He waved his.

"No problem, Doc. We know our jobs," replied one of the agents.

Zendo gave him an I-sure-hope-you-do look and stepped on the elevator.

Mr. Clean

Walking through the front door of the hospital, Zendo removed the plastic hospital ID. He carefully peeled his photo off the front, slipping it in his pocket. A photo of a much younger man smiled from under where Zendo's had been. Zendo dropped the badge in the parking lot and walked to his car. He tossed the doctor's jacket in the back seat, got in, and started the car. As he pulled out of the parking lot, he flipped open his cell phone and dialed. Johnny's voice sounded in his ear.

"Are we clean?"

"We're clean!" Zendo said. "DeNova's gone, but I've got bad news about your brothers. I'll talk to you when I get the chance. In the meantime, I need to leave the country. Moscow is nice this time of year."

Sarah sat in a conference room with two FBI agents, the U.S. District Attorney for Miami, and the Dade County D.A. A microphone and a video camera recorded her as she testified. In detail, she told the story of the rainy night, the black Mercedes, the guns, and the two men. She was handed a stack of pictures and asked to pick out the men she saw. Without hesitating, she selected photos of Hal and Mike.

The two attorneys looked at each other and nodded. "We have our case," said the U.S. District Attorney with a smile. "The Colvacks are history."

Two FBI agents strode into the penthouse office suites of the Halston Hotel in New York City, with two uniformed police officers in tow, heading for the dark wood doors at the end of the room. Johnny Colvack's secretary stood up, blocking their way.

"I'm sorry, you can't go in there without an appointment," she said rudely.

The first agent stuck a folded document in her face. "Lady," he growled, "I've got a warrant for his arrest; that's all the appointment I need."

The other agent shoved the door open with a bang.

Johnny jumped up from his desk, cold fury in his eyes.

The two officers moved around the desk, pulling Johnny's arms behind him and handcuffing them.

"What are you doing here?" Johnny roared. "What's this about? Get out of here! Do you know who I am?"

"Yeah," the agent replied. "You're Johnny Colvack. And you are under arrest under RICO statutes 891, 895, and 898 for racketeering, illegal gaming, illegal pit fighting, and accessory to murder. You have the right to remain silent. Anything you say can and will be used against you in a court of law."

The police officers grabbed Johnny by the shoulders, shoving him along and out the door.

The agent followed, continuing the familiar drill: "You have the right to an attorney. If you cannot afford one, which I doubt, an attorney will be appointed for you by the court. Do you understand your rights, dirt bag?"

Johnny glared at him, saying nothing, locking his legs to halt his progress towards the elevator. The agent shoved him forward. "Come on, we've got a family reunion waiting for you, not to mention a sweet little lady named Samantha. Name ring a bell, Slick?"

They entered the elevators as a team of searchers rushed into the offices. The last thing Johnny saw as the doors closed was the second agent handing the dumbfounded secretary a search warrant.

I'm Dr. Allen

In the hospital near Summerville, the three FBI agents sat by the elevator, watching the door to room 501. The elevator opened and a doctor stepped onto the floor. The agents stood up, blocking the doctor's path.

"Who are you?" the lead agent asked, his tone firm.

"I'm Doctor Allen," the doctor said, holding out his ID badge. "I'm here to check on Vail Tudo, room 501."

The agent shook his head, eyeing the doctor suspiciously. "The doctor just left, maybe five minutes ago. He said Vail needed rest and not to disturb him."

The doctor's face went white with alarm. "What do you mean another doctor was here? I'm the only doctor assigned to this case. Frank McQue called me from the ambulance. I treated Vail when he arrived in the emergency room…"

"Hold him here," the lead agent yelled to the others while running to room 501. He pushed the door open to see the body, bullet holes, and the bloodstains covering the sheets.

"Oh my God…" he murmured. "They got him." He turned back to the others. "Somebody call Frank!" he yelled. "This is bad!"

Outside the conference room, Frank walked up to Sarah. He took her aside, speaking to her in a low voice.

She cried out suddenly, clutching the ring on the chain around her neck. "Oh no," she sobbed.

Frank wrapped his arms around her, and she buried her head in his chest.

"Oh no…oh no…oh no…"

The funeral was held at the church in Summerville. The body lay in a coffin at the front of the church, surrounded by flowers. Watkins and Phillips sat silently on the front row, the triumph of the case against Colvack overshadowed in their minds by their failure to protect Jack.

Norman and his son sat with the employees of the restaurant. They all looked lost and out of place without their flamboyant costumes.

Frank led Sarah up the aisle to the coffin. She was crying, almost unwilling to look. Finally she stepped forward and looked in.

The fearsome fighter Jack DeNova seemed somehow smaller, diminished, as if when his life left him, all evidence of his former strength left as well. She touched the hands, surprised at how cold and small they seemed now. Looking at the smooth skin, Frank had done a masterful makeup job, the best he could do to hide all the wounds and bruises of Jack's last day on the battlefield.

Sarah looked at Jack in disbelief, finding it just too difficult to reconcile the person in the coffin with the exciting, life-filled warrior that was Jack DeNova. She looked up at Frank and said, "He's not in there anymore, Frank. His spirit is in another location. This is just the shell of what he left behind. If Jack's not here, I don't want to be either. I need to leave. Jack's gone now, and I need to be too."

Frank shook his head. "It's OK, Sarah. I've done the makeup for many a man lying in state. They never look the same. It makes you really understand that when the spirit leaves the body that the person goes with it. You're right, Jack is in another place—a better place. And you need to move on with your life now, too. It's time for that, Sarah.

Sarah allowed Frank to walk her outside to get some fresh air.

There's a couple things that Jack wanted you to have if he didn't make it, and I promised him I would handle it for him. Can you deal with this right now?"

She nodded, and they moved through a side door of the church into the sunshine.

In the warm sun, Sarah turned to Frank. "I know you mean well, Frank." They slowly walked out the back door into the parking lot. Sarah paused one last time to look over her shoulder for one last glance at her white knight.

Frank said nothing, but reached into his coat pocket and pulled out an envelope. It was bulky, and a slight, reddish brown stain streaked the back. He held the envelope out for Sarah.

"Sarah, I need to give you this," Frank said gently. "Jack wanted you to have it. He made me promise that no matter what happened I would give it to you."

Sarah looked down at the envelope, but didn't take it. "What is it, a letter?" she asked. "I...I don't know if I could read it right now."

Frank shook his head. "No, I don't think it's a letter; I can tell by the way it feels."

He pressed the envelope into her hands. "I'm just doing what Jack asked me to do. I think he left something for you—he said you would understand."

Sarah looked up at Frank, her eyes questioning. She took the envelope and stepped towards a car parked near the building. Opening the envelope, she let the contents fall on the car's hood. Six bank cards fell out, along with a driver's license. The driver's license had her picture on it, but she stared at the name. She picked up the cards and read the name on each of them. She looked over at Frank.

"Frank, what does this mean?" she asked, confused. "Everything has my phony name on them like it's a real person. Maria Sparks was just a name I made up, yet this looks like it's a real person." She looked at the debit cards again. "And Jack said he had seven cards, but there's only six here. One is missing. What is going on?"

Frank looked towards the woods behind the church. "I think I know, but I'm not sure. I can only guess. Maybe he needed it to arrange something for you in case things turned out this way. He was working on this for awhile...I do know that." He turned back to Sarah. "Maybe he's wanting you to have a chance to start all over again." He watched her look at the cards in her hand, knowing they were a poor substitute for the man she cherished.

"You know, Sarah," Frank said, as if changing the subject, "funny thing is, after the attack in the restaurant, the feds don't really need your testimony to put away Hal and Mike. Now they've got the guns that match the ballistics on the weapons used in the murder. And the raid on Colvack's offices in New York and Miami netted enough hard evidence to make Jack's testimony just a blip on the radar screen. The Colvacks are finished. Jack wanted me to leave you out of the case if possible, and we were able to. Your name doesn't appear anywhere in connection with this thing. You could disappear or scream your name from the mountaintops, and it wouldn't make any difference.

"Oh, and one more thing..." He reached into his pocket and pulled out the famous little laminated card with her picture on. He flipped it over and handed it back to her. "Jack wrote something on the back of it—said you would know what this means once you read it. I don't have a clue."

On the back of the card next to the cross, Jack had written, "Come with me while the moon is on the sea."

Frank shrugged. "He said you would understand; it doesn't make any sense to me."

Sarah looked at him, at the credit cards. Suddenly she hugged Frank, squeezing him around the neck. "Yes, I know what he did," she whispered. "I think he left me the next best thing to himself. He left me his dream."

She leaned back and Frank looked her in the eyes. "Don't ask me anything else, Sarah." His tone was decisive and firm.

"That's all the information I can give you. Jack said you'd figure out the rest."

She nodded, a faint smile on her face. She reached up and kissed him on the cheek. "Thank you, Frank," she said, fresh tears trickling out of her eyes. "I don't know all you did, but I know you helped Jack in this somehow. I'll love you forever."

Frank smiled. "I guess you've grieved long enough. It's time for you to tap out of this fight and go live again."

Sarah hugged him one last time, then ran to her car. Frank watched with a smile on his face as she pulled onto the road, leaving Summerville. This time…forever.

Chapter 17

Sparky's New Adventure

Sarah drove past fields of sugarcane with the top of her convertible rental car down. The sunlight danced in her hair as it streamed in the wind. To her right she could see the sparkling blue waters of the Pacific Ocean.

A road sign read, "Kahalue—2 mi.," and she slowed down. Spotting a small gas station, she pulled over. Before she could get out of her car, an older native Hawaiian man approached her, his face smiling.

"Aloha, pretty lady! What can I do for you today? Do you want me to fill it up?"

Sarah smiled back. "No, not right now—but I do have an unusual request. Is there any place around here to get a pizza?"

The man laughed. "As a matter of fact, a new place just opened up about two hundred yards down the road, on the left. It's the one…"

"I know, facing the ocean," Sarah finished the sentence, smiling.

The attendant looked surprised, "That's right. How did you know?"

"Just a good guess," she laughed. "Thanks!" she shouted as she drove back onto the road.

A few seconds later she was pulling into a small twelve-shop strip mall. In the center of the mall hung a banner. "Now Open!" it declared. Beneath it, in the windows of a restaurant, was a glowing neon sign: "Sparky's Pizza Parlor." Not knowing whether to laugh or cry, she jumped out of the car and ran into the restaurant.

I Just Do...

Inside, people sat around eating pizza, laughing, and talking. As her eyes adjusted to the room's light, she passed by a table where two Hawaiian natives were flicking pieces of pineapple of a pizza.

"I don't know why they put so much pineapple on these things!" one complained.

The other nodded. "Me neither. I'm sick of pineapple. I wanted extra cheese."

Sarah choked back a laugh and slipped into a nearby table, her eyes scanning the crowded restaurant. In the back of the room, a hand slipped a quarter into the jukebox and pushed the buttons. The Best of Marty Robbins CD plunked down. And the smooth voice of the old country crooner melted out of the speakers like a warm hug from a long lost friend.

She heard music start from a jukebox, and he began to sing.....

I don't know why I love you like I do.

I don't know why I just do...

The song made her head spin around to look at the juke-box. Therefore, she didn't see the waiter walk up to her from the other side.

A rich male voice asked, "Would you like some pizza, ma'am? We have a special; it has extra sauce—not as saucy as you—but it does have Jack cheese."

I don't know why, you thrill me like you do.

I don't know why but you do...

She jumped out of her chair, leaping into the arms of the tall man with a deep tan and thick black hair, knocking them both to the ground.

"Jack!" she shouted, the restaurant turning to stare at them.

On the floor, Jack DeNova grinned at her. "Careful," he said, "my ribs still hurt."

They scrambled back to the table, hugging each other.

"Jack, I thought you were dead," she said weeping tears of joy. "I *believed* you were dead!"

Jack grinned. "I know! Everybody thinks I'm dead! Isn't that great?"

Stunned, Sarah just looked at him.

"So—you like the place?" he asked, waving slightly flour-covered hands around. "That's why I needed the debit card, you know."

Sarah stared at him. "Jack, I can't believe this. I thought you left me the restaurant or something." She hugged him again, then leaned back. "Wait—I saw you in a coffin. If that wasn't you, who was it?"

"Well, I'm not sure," Jack said, remembering. "I don't think anybody knows. I made up this plan with McQue. See, when Frank took me to the hospital, we both knew there was somebody else hired by Johnny Colvack to kill me. And we knew he would not give up until he reported back that I was dead. So we played up the injuries," Jack rubbed his side. "Not that it took much, and Frank called ahead to a buddy of his at the hospital.

While the doctor was patching me up, Frank went down to the morgue, pulled out a John Doe—some poor homeless guy nobody could identify who was about to be cremated—and wheeled him up to my room. I slipped out and caught a taxi to the airport. Frank stayed behind and doctored up the body with bandages and a little makeup to look like me. So when the killer came in and shot up the body, it put a gravestone on Jack "King of the Jungle" DeNova. Frank finished off the job at the funeral home using putty and moldable plastic so no one would notice the difference—not even you."

She shook her head. "But I *did* notice something different. You seemed so much smaller. So that wasn't just my imagination, but I was so distraught that I couldn't think it through. And I didn't want to believe it."

Jack laughed. "Well, Frank got it right more than either of you knew." He showed her his knuckles. The letters were gone; only a faint redness remained. "The first thing I did when I came over to the islands was to go to a doctor and get my tattoos removed." He proudly displayed his hands. "I'm a different man outside and inside as well. God did a miracle in my life."

Sarah looked around the restaurant. "So does McQue know where you are?"

Jack shook his head. "No! He doesn't want to. He doesn't want to have to lie to the FBI about my whereabouts—if it ever comes up at all."

Sarah looked in Jack's eyes. "So, who are we now?"

Jack smiled, a little sheepishly. "Well, we are Jack and Maria Sparks."

Sarah sat back, putting her hands on her hips. "How come you get to keep your name and I have to change mine?"

"Woman, I go through all this and you're still not satisfied!" Jack laughed. "Well the deal is, I get to keep the name, and you—"

He reached behind her, slipping the gold chain off her neck. He undid the clasp and let the ring slide off the chain into his hand.

"You get to keep the ring." Then he slid it onto her finger. "Is it a deal?"

Sarah leaned in and kissed him—a long lingering kiss. "Deal!" she whispered.

Jack smiled, and taking her by the hand, he sighed and looked out the window as if to watch his whole life pass before him in an instant.

Finally, he said, "I think my mom and dad would finally be proud of me. Ya know, this is the first time I've felt at peace with God and in life since I was a kid in Buffalo, New York, thirty years ago.

"Well, Maria, my dear, let's go take a walk on the beach. The winter of our lives is gone, and the summer wind is waiting to embrace us. As long as we're together, we'll have it all. When you walked through that door, I became the richest pizza shop owner who ever lived.

"So, come with me while the moon is on the sea. It's been a long summer."

They embraced, held each other's hands tightly, and Sarah leaned her head on Jack's shoulder as they walked along the beautiful blue waters of the Hawaiian coast.

Personal Reflection Guide

1. Jack De Nova transformed his anger and rejection into fighting. What was the source of that anger and rejection? Is there any "unfinished history" in your life that might lead you to overcompensate negative experiences with other aggressive or passive behavior in your life?

2. Samantha Bentley was a driven woman, who had no heart for the poverty she saw in Brazil. "They meant nothing to her." How does a person get to this point in their own life when they are so focused on their own life that they lose sight of the things that are important?

3. How would you describe Jack's relationship with his parents? How did it get to this point? What did his mom do to help preserve the relationship? What could his parents have done differently to help Jack make the transition and face the challenges created because they were following the call of God? Should kids have any say in the matter when confronted with such a momentous decsion?

4. Why do you think Jack chose fighting as a means of escaping the world he was living in as a child?

5. Describe Jack's relationship with Marco. What role did Marco play in his life? Was it a positive or negative role?

6. What ritual did Jack perform in an attempt to preserve his relationship with his parents? How did this ritual help Jack? What was the source of conflict that existed between Jack and his father?

7. What were the unique passions that drove the Colvack brothers? Johnny? Hal? Bruce? Mike? How would you ever reach these men with the Gospel?

8. Marco taught Jack never to fight in anger. Why? How does anger adversely affect us?

9. How did Jack learn to control his anger? Was this an effective method? How do you control your anger? Does it work? Is repression a good method?

10. When Bruce confronted Jack in the ring, why did his taunting words and attack on Marco create such rage in Jack? Have you ever felt such uncontrollable rage?

11. What drove Bruce to such a foolhardy reaction? Why did he feel that he had something to prove to his older brother? Have you ever done something stupid because you felt like you had to prove something?

12. In the end, how great was Art's love for his son? Why could he not freely manifest that love?

13. It took a tragedy of death to begin a turn in Jack's life. Why does it take such tragedies to force us into making a needed change in our lives?

14. Jack's parents paid a harsh price because of his choices. How do the choices and decisions we make affect other people? Should you be more careful in the decisions you make because of their possible effects on others?

15. How did Jack confront the guilt and shame created by his personal tragedies? How does one escape from the controlling emotions of shame and guilt?

16. Do you think that Jack really got the full closure he needed? When did he get that closure? Are you still dealing with issues in your life for which you've not received closure?

17. How did Frank McQue help direct Jack in a different direction? How important is it to have people in our lives that can help us get a proper perspective on our lives and direct us to solutions for our problems? Is it hard to find these kind of friends?

18. What part did Maria Sparks (Sarah) play in Jack's recovery and restoration?

19. All of us have ideal dreams just like Jack had for his life. How did Jack's past affect his future? How does our past affect our future? Is there a way of dealing with our past so that we can still achieve our dreams? How?

20. What other adventures could you have seen Jack involved in?

The Author

Carman was born in New Jersey where he grew up in an Italian home full of music and laughter. As a boy, Carman played the drums and the guitar, and he began singing in his teenage years. As his career developed, Carman played clubs then went on to Las Vegas. It was after seeing an "Andrae Crouch" concert that Carman gave his life to Jesus Christ and dedicated his talents to the Lord. After five years of ministerial preparation, he began to develop his ministry to reach the world for Christ through the arts.

During the next two decades Carman changed the face of Christian music and evolved contemporary evangelism into what it is today. Carman established "Carman Ministries" and "Carman World Outreach," both non-profit organizations that touch the lives of literally millions of people worldwide. Billboard Magazine recognized Carman's influence in Christian music by naming him their first "Contemporary Christian Artist of the Year". He has since received 15 gold and platinum albums and videos. Even with all this success, the heartbeat of this Champion for Christ continues to beat strong for the souls of people who need Jesus. Carman had more than 50,000 people attend his "Music for Peace" crusade in Johannesburg, South Africa. These numbers topped the charts as his largest concert crusade ever, until more than 71,000 people packed the legendary Texas Stadium, making it the largest Christian concert ever in history.

For over 26 years, Carman has entertained, encouraged and preached the Gospel to millions—crossing denominational, cultural and ethnic lines. During this time, he has never compromised the call to take the Gospel to every person. This vision still remains the hallmark of his life and ministry. Now he is taking his talents into the uncharted waters of mainstream television, movies, and action/adventure novels. When it comes to Carman, all you can expect is the unexpected!

Carman
P.O. Box 3224
Brentwood, TN 37027
website: www.carman.org

WESTERN HISTORICAL THINKING
An Intercultural Debate

Edited by **Jörn Rüsen**

What is history – a question historians have been asking themselves time and again. Does "history" as an academic discipline, as it has evolved in the West over the centuries, represent a specific mode of historical thinking that can be defined in contrast to other forms of historical consciousness?

In this volume, Peter Burke, a prominent "Western" historian, offers ten hypotheses that attempt to constitute specifically "Western Historical Thinking." Scholars from Asia and Africa comment on his position in the light of their own ideas of the sense and meaning of historical thinking. The volume is rounded off by Peter Burke's comments on the questions and issues raised by theauthors and his suggestions for the way forward towards acommon ground for intercultural communication.

Jörn Rüsen was Professor of Modern History at the Universities of Bochum and Bielefeld for many years. From 1994 to 1997 he was the Director of the Center for Interdisciplinary Research (ZiF). Since 1997 he has been President of the Institute for Cultural Studies in Essen.

Hardback ISBN 1-57181-781-6
Paperback ISBN 1-57181-454-X
224 pages, bibliog., index
Making Sense of History

❧ Identities ❧

MAKING SENSE OF HISTORY
Studies in Historical Cultures
General Editor: Jörn Rüsen, in Association with Christian Geulen

Western Historical Thinking: An Intercultural Debate
   Edited by Jörn Rüsen

Identities: Time, Difference, and Boundaries
   Edited by Heidrun Friese

Narration, Identity and Historical Consciousness
   Edited by Jürgen Straub

The Meaning of History
   Edited by Jörn Rüsen and Klaus E. Müller

IDENTITIES

Time, Difference, and Boundaries

Edited by
Heidrun Friese

Berghahn Books
New York • Oxford

Published in 2002 by

Berghahn Books
www.berghahnbooks.com

Library of Congress Cataloguing-in-Publication Data

Identities: time, difference, and boundaries / edited by Heidrun Friese.
   p. cm. -- (Making sense of history ; vol. 2)
   Chiefly written by members of the Forschungsgruppe Historische Sinnbildung, Universität Bielefeld.
   Based in part on Identitäten, ed. by Aleida Assmann and Heidrun Friese. 1998.
   Includes bibliographical references and index.
   Contents: Identity: desire, name, and difference / Heidrun Friese -- Identity and selfhood as a problématique / Peter Wagner -- Personal and collective identity / Jürgen Straub -- Identities of the West : reason, myths, limits of tolerance / Barbara Henry -- The praxis of cognition and the representation of difference / Martin Fuchs -- Constructions of cultural identity and problems of translation / Shingo Shimada -- The performance of hysteria / Elisabeth Bronfen -- The "Jewess Pallas Athena" : horizons of selfconception in the 19th and 20th centuries / Barbara Hahn -- Collective identity as a dual discursive construction / Gerd Baumann -- Historical culture in (post-)colonial context : the genesis of national identification figures in francophone Western Africa / Hans-Jürgen Lüsebrink -- Identity as progress : the longevity of nationalism / Christian Geulen -- Culture and history in comparative fundamentalism / Emanuel Sivan.
   ISBN 1-57181-474-4 (alk. paper) -- ISBN 1-57181-507-4 (pbk.: alk. paper)
   1. Group identity. 2. Identity (Psychology) 3. Ethnicity. 4. Nationalism. 5. History--Philosophy. I. Friese, Heidrun, 1958- II. Assmann, Aleida. III. Universität Bielefeld. Forschungsgruppe Historische Sinnbildung. IV. Identitäten. V. Series.

HM716 .I34 2001
305.8--dc21   2001043052

British Library Cataloguing in Publication Data

A catalogue record for this book is available from the British Library.

Printed in the United States on acid-free paper.

Contents

Acknowledgements

Most of the contributions to this volumes originated from the activities of the research group 'Historical meaning. Interdisciplinary investigations in the structure, logic and function of historical consciousness in intercultural comparison', directed by Jörn Rüsen at the Centre for Interdisciplinary Research (ZIF), University of Bielefeld. The work of the members of the research group was complemented by contributors to conferences and workshops, at which specific issues could be discussed in more depth. The results of the intense and often controversial debates have originally been published in German as a book series on 'Erinnerung, Geschichte, Identität' (Memory, history, identity; Suhrkamp, Frankfurt a.M.).

I would like to thank the contributors to this volume for their willingness to prepare their contributions for publication in this context and for their patience during the editorial process. My thanks go also to Aleida Assmann for the co-operation—which meant more than mere collegiality—in the editing of the volume 'Identitäten' of the above series, which forms the basis for this modified edition. Peter Wagner knows the extent to which he participates in my work and what the adventures of thinking together mean to me. Thanks are also due to Christian Geulen for valuable editorial support. Furthermore, I am indebted to the members of ZIF—and this not only for creating excellent conditions for a co-operation across disciplinary boundaries that still continues after the common work in Bielefeld. I would like to extend a particular word of gratitude, however, to Jörn Rüsen, who created a forum for lively exchange and an institutional setting for multifarious suggestion, but maybe even more importantly an open space for thought experiments and for the elaboration of new ideas. His incomparable personal dedication demonstrates that scholarship can also mean passion and involvement.

Paris,   Heidrun Friese
May 2002

Preface to the Series

Jörn Rüsen

At the turn of the twenty-first century the very term "history" brings extremely ambivalent associations to mind. On the one hand, the last 10–15 years have witnessed numerous declarations of history's end. In referring to the fundamental change of the global political situation around 1989/90, or to postmodernism or to the challenge of Western dominance by decolonization and multiculturalism, "history"—as we know it—has been declared to be dead, outdated, overcome, and at its end. On the other hand, there has been a global wave of intellectual explorations into fields that are "historical" in their very nature: the building of personal and collective identity through "memory", the cultural, social and political use and function of "narrating the past", and the psychological structures of remembering, repressing and recalling. Even the subjects that seemed to call for an "end of history" (globalization, postmodernism, multiculturalism) quickly turned out to be intrinsically "historical" phenomena. Moreover, "history" and "historical memory" have also entered the sphere of popular culture (from history-channels to Hollywood movies). They also have become an ever important ingredient of public debates and political negotiations (e.g., to take the discussions about the aftermath of the wars in the former Yugoslavia, about the European unification or about the various heritages of totalitarian systems). In other words, ever since "history" has been declared to be at its end, "historical matters" seem to have come back with a vengeance.

This paradox calls for a new orientation or at least a new theoretical reflection. Indeed, it calls for a new theory of history. Such a theory should serve neither as a subdiscipline reserved for historians, nor as a systematic collection of definitions, "laws" and rules claiming universal validity. What is needed, is an interdisciplinary and intercultural field of study. For, in the very moment when history was declared to be "over", what in fact did abruptly come to an end was—historical theory. Hayden White's deconstruction of the narrative strategies of the nineteenth century historicist paradigm somehow

Notes for this section can be found on page xiv.

became regarded as historical theory's final word; as if the critique of the discipline's claim for rationality could set an end to the rational self-reflection of that discipline; as if this very critique was not a rational self-reflection in itself. Nevertheless, since the late 1980s the "critical study of historical memory" began to substitute historical theory. However, what has been overlooked in this substitution is the fact that any exploration into the ways of historical memory in different cultural contexts is not only a field of critical studies, but also contains the keystones for a more general theory of history. Each analysis of even a simple instance of historical memory cannot avoid questions of the theory and philosophy of history. And vice versa: the most abstract thoughts of philosophers of history have an intrinsic counterpart in the most profane procedures of memory (for example, when parents narrate past experiences to their children, or when an African community remembers its own colonial subordination and its liberation from it). As long as we fail to acknowledge this intrinsic connection between the most sophisticated historical theory and the procedures of historical memory most deeply imbedded in the culture and the everyday life of people, we remain caught in an ideology of linear progress, which considers cultural forms of memory simply as interesting objects of study instead of recognizing them as examples of "how to make sense of history."

The book-series "Making Sense of History", the first volume of which is at hand, aims at bridging this gap between historical theory and the study of historical memory. It contains contributions from virtually all fields of cultural and social studies, which explore a wide range of phenomena of what can be labeled "making historical sense" (*Historische Sinnbildung*). The series crosses not only the boundaries between academic disciplines but also those between cultural, social, political and historical contexts. Instead of reducing historical memory to just another form of the social or cultural "construction of reality", its contributions deal with concrete phenomena of historical memory: it seeks to interpret them as case studies in the emerging empirical and theoretical field of "making historical sense." Along the same line, the rather theoretical essays intend not only to establish new methods and theories for historical research, but also to provide perspectives for a comparative, interdisciplinary and intercultural understanding of what could be called the "global work of historical memory." This does not mean the exclusion of critical evaluations of the ideological functions of historical memory. But it is not the major aim of the series to find an ideal, politically correct and ideology-free mode or method of how to make sense of history. It rather intends to explore the cultural practices involved in generating historical sense as an extremely important realm of human thought and action, the study of which may contribute to new forms of mutual understanding. In an age of rapid globalization primarily manifesting itself on an economic and political—and, much less so, on a cultural level—finding such forms is an urgent task.

This is why—in contrast to the German version of this series—the English edition, addressing a much broader international audience, sets out with a volume documenting an intercultural debate. This volume questions whether or not the academic discipline of "history"—as developed at Western universities over the course of the last two hundred years—represents a specific mode or type of historical thinking that can be defined and differentiated from other forms and practices of historical consciousness. One of the most notable representatives of the modern historical profession, Peter Burke, delivers an essay outlining ten aspects of the specifically Western way of "making sense of history" that allow us to speak of "Western Historical Thinking" as a discernable type of historical thinking, differing from other ways of dealing with the past practiced in other parts of the globe. The editor then invites scholars from all over the world— from Western countries as well as from Asia, India, and Africa—to critically comment on these theses, to evaluate them in the light of their respective ideas of the sense and meaning of historical thinking, and to reflect on the possibilities of an intercultural communication on these issues. Peter Burke afterwards has the chance to reply to the different comments and criticism, to rethink some of his theses, and to further identify the possible common grounds on which an ongoing debate could be based. Thus this first volume of the series "Making Sense of History" goes to the heart of the matter, and, at the same time, highlights the major conflicts involved in any attempt to reflect forms and functions of historical memory and historical thinking on a global level.

The first volume, therefore, introduces the intercultural dimension of historical theory. The following volumes will represent it as a genuinely interdisciplinary field of research. Historians, anthropologists, philosophers, sociologists, psychologists, literary theorists, as well as specialists in fields such as media and cultural studies, will explore questions such as: What constitutes a specifically historical "sense" and meaning? What are the concepts of "time" underlying different historical cultures? Which specific forms of "perception" inform these concepts and which general problems are connected with them? What are the dominating strategies used to represent historical meaning? Ranging from general overviews and theoretical reflections to case-studies, the essays will cover a wide range of contexts related to the question of "historical sense," including topics such as collective identity, the psychology and psychoanalysis of historical memory, or the intercultural dimension of historical thinking. In general they will indicate that historical memory is not an arbitrary function of the cultural practices used by human beings to orient themselves in the world in which they are born, but that such memory covers special domains in the temporal orientation of human life. These domains demand precisely those mental procedures of connecting past, present and future which became generalized and institutionalized in the West as that specific field of culture we call "history." Among those special areas of human thought, action and suffering that call for a specifically "historical thinking,"

are (1) the construction and perpetuation of collective identity, (2) the reconstruction of patterns of orientation after catastrophes and events of massive destruction, (3) the challenge of given patterns of orientation presented by and through the confrontation with radical otherness, and (4) the general experience of change and contingency.

In accordance with the general aim of the book-series "Making Sense of History" to outline a new field of interdisciplinary research (and to not offer a single theory), the volumes are not designed to establish those general domains and functions of historical remembrance as keystones for a new historiographical approach. Instead they explore them further as subfields of the study of "historical cultures." One focus, for instance, will be on the notion of collective identity. General theoretical aspects and problems of this field will be considered, most importantly the interrelationship between identity, otherness and representation. But case studies on the construction of gender identities (especially of women), on ethnic identities and on different forms and politics of national identity will also be included. The essays on this subject will try to point out that any concept of "identity" as being disconnected from historical change does not only lead to theoretical problems, but also eclipses the fact that most modern forms of collective identity take into account the possibility of their own historical transformation. Thus the essays will suggest to consider identity not as a function of difference, but as a concrete cultural and ongoing "practice" of difference. Therefore they will try to prove the production of "sense" to be both an epistemological starting-point as well as a theoretical and empirical research-field in and of itself.

Another volume will focus on the psychological construction of "time" and "history" analyzing the interrelation between memory, morality, and authenticity, in different forms of historical or biographical narrations. The findings of empirical psychological studies (on the development of temporal and historical consciousness in children, or on the psychological mechanisms of reconstructing past experiences) will be discussed in the light of attempts to outline a psychological concept of historical consciousness around the notions of "narration" and the "narrative structure of historical time." A special volume will be dedicated to specifically psychoanalytical approaches to the study of historical memory. It will reconsider older debates on the relation between psychoanalysis and history as well as introduce more recent research projects. Instead of simply pointing out some psychoanalytical insights that can be adopted and applied in certain areas of historical studies, this volume will aim at combining psychoanalytical and historical perspectives, thus exploring the history of psychoanalysis, itself, as well as the "unconscious" dimensions underlying and informing academic and nonacademic forms of historical memory. Moreover, it will put special emphasis on transgenerational forms of remembrance, on the notion of trauma as a key-concept in this field, and on case-studies that may indicate directions for further research.

Apart from the first volume at hand, there will be another collection of essays dealing explicitly with the intercultural dimension of historical thinking, offering a systematic overview of historical cultures ranging from ancient Egypt to modern Japan. With a view to encouraging comparative research, it will consist of general essays and case-studies written with the intention to provide comparative interpretations of concrete material, as well as possible paradigmatic research-questions for further comparisons. In the light of the ongoing success of ethnocentric world-views, the volume will focus on the question of how cultural and social studies could react to this challenge. It will aim at counteracting ethnocentrism by bridging the current gap between a rapid globalization, manifesting itself in ever increasing economic and political interdependencies of states and continents, and the almost similarly increasing lack of mutual understanding in the realm of culture. The essays will try to point out the necessity of an intercultural communication about the common grounds of the various historical cultures as well as about the differences between them. Such a communication seems not only possible but indeed to be a necessary presupposition for any attempt to negotiate cultural differences on a political level, whether between states, or within the increasingly multicultural societies in which we live.

The special emphasis the series puts on the problem of cultural differences and intercultural communication shows the editors' intentions to aim beyond the realm of only academic interest. For the question of intercultural communication represents a great challenge, as well as a great hope, to a project committed to the general theoretical reflection on the universal phenomenon of "remembering the past." Despite the fact that "cultural difference" has become something like a master phrase of the 1990s, this topic is characterized by a paradox quite similar to that underlying the current fate of the notion of "history."

There has been an intensified political intervention and economic interest of the industrialized states into the political and economic affairs of the rest of the world, as well as an increased (if sometimes peculiar) appropriation of modern economic and political structures in the developing countries, and in the formerly or still officially "communist" states. But this process of mutual rapprochement on the political and economic level is characterized by a remarkable lack of knowledge of, or even interest in, the cultural and historical backgrounds of the respective nations. Thus, the existing official forms of intercultural communication, so often demanded in the public discourse, lack precisely what is "cultural" about them, leaving the themes and problems analyzed in this book-series (identity, memory, cultural practices, history, religion, philosophy, literature) outside of what is explicitly communicated: as if such matters would not strongly affect political as well as economic agendas.

On the other hand, however, the currently dominant approaches of cultural theorists and critical thinkers in the West either claim the general impos-

sibility of an intercultural communication about the common grounds of "cultural identities"—based on the assumption that there are no common grounds (the hypostatization of "difference")—or they politicize cultural differences in such a way that they are relegated to mere material for the construction of cultural subject-positions. Despite their self-understanding as "critique", these intellectual approaches appear to correspond to the exclusion of "culture" on the level of state politics and economic exchange alike. Thus, cultural theory seems to react to the marginalization of culture by way of its own self-marginalization.

The book-series "Making Sense of History" intends to challenge this marginalization by introducing a form of cultural studies that takes the very term "culture" seriously again without dissolving it into either identity-politics, or a hypostatized concept of unbridgeable "difference." At the same time it wants to reintroduce a notion of "historical theory" that no longer disconnects itself from historical memory and remembrance as concrete cultural practices, but seeks to explore those practices, interpreting them as different articulations of the universal (if heterogeneous) effort to "make sense of history." Thus, the book-series "Making Sense of History" relies on the idea that an academic contribution to the problem of intercultural communication should assume the form of a new opening of the academic discourse to its own historicity and cultural background, as well as a new acknowledgement of other cultural, but non-academic, practices of "sense-formation" as being equally important forms of human orientation and self-understanding (in their general function not much different from the efforts of academic thought itself). Such a reinscription of the universal claims of modern academic discourses into the variety of cultural contexts, with the intention to provide new starting-points for an intercultural communication, is an enterprise that cannot be entirely fulfilled or even outlined in a series of a few books. Therefore, the book-series "Making Sense of History" should be regarded as something like a first attempt to circumscribe one possible research-field that might prove to suit those general intentions: the field of "historical cultures."

Most of the contributions to the book-series are based on papers delivered at a series of conferences organized by the research-project "Making Sense of History: Interdisciplinary Studies in the Structure, Logic and Function of Historical Consciousness—An Intercultural Comparison" established at the "Center for Interdisciplinary Studies" (ZiF) in Bielefeld, Germany, in 1994/95. This project was partly supported by the *Kulturwissenschaftliches Institut Essen* (KWI) *im Wissenschaftszentrum Nordrhein-Westfalen* (Institute for Advanced Studies in the Humanities at Essen in the Scientific Center of Northrhine-Westfalia).[1]

As editor I would like to express my deepest gratitude to the staff of the ZiF and the KWI for providing a stimulating atmosphere for the scholars and excellent assistance for their work. I also want to thank the editors and co-

editors of the single volumes of this series for their cooperation. My special thanks go to Christian Geulen, my assistant editor, for his engaged management of this series and to my wife Inge for her intensive support in editing my texts.

Notes

1. In German the following books represent the project: Bodo von Borries, *Imaginierte Geschichte. Die biografische Bedeutung historischer Fiktionen und Phantasien*, Köln, 1996; Klaus E. Müller, Jörn Rüsen eds, *Historische Sinnbildung. Problemstellungen, Zeitkonzepte, Wahrnehmungshorizonte, Darstellungsstrategien*, Reinbek, 1997; Jocelyn Létourneau ed., *Le lieu identitaire de la jeunesse d'aujourd'hui. Études de cas*, Paris/Montreal, 1997; Jörn Stückrath, Jürg Zbinden eds, *Metageschichte. Hayden White und Paul Ricoeur. Dargestellte Wirklichkeit in der europäischen Kultur im Kontext von Husserl, Weber, Auerbach und Gombrich*, Baden-Baden, 1997; Hans G. Kippenberg, *Die Entdeckung der Religionsgeschichte. Religionswissenschaft und die Moderne*, München, 1997; Jürgen Straub ed., *Erzählung, Identität und historisches Bewußtsein. Die psychologische Konstruktion von Zeit und Geschichte. Erinnerung, Geschichte, Identität Bd. 1*, Frankfurt am Main, 1998; Jörn Rüsen, Jürgen Straub eds, *Die dunkle Spur der Vergangenheit. Psychoanalytische Zugänge zur Geschichte. Erinnerung, Geschichte, Identität Bd. 2*, Frankfurt am Main, 1998; Aleida Assmann, Heidrun Friese eds, *Identitäten. Erinnerung, Geschichte, Identität Bd. 3*, Frankfurt am Main, 1998; Jörn Rüsen, Michael Gottlob, Achim Mittag eds, *Die Vielfalt der Kulturen. Erinnerung, Geschichte, Identität Bd. 4*, Frankfurt am Main, 1998; Jörn Rüsen ed., *Westliches Geschichtsdenken. Eine interkulturelle Debatte*, Göttingen, 1999; Jörn Rüsen ed., *Geschichtsbewußtsein. Psychologische Grundlagen, Entwicklungskonzepte, empirische Befunde*, Köln 2000.

Introduction

HEIDRUN FRIESE

The notion 'identity' opens towards a variety of questions. Derived from '*idem*,' the word's semantic field ranges from 'the sameness of a person or thing at all times or in all circumstances; the condition or fact that a person or thing is itself and not something else; individually, personally' to its use in logic and mathematics and asks the question, how something can remain the same despite time and inevitable change. The word addresses at the same time the 'condition' and the 'fact' of remaining the same person throughout the various phases of existence. It underlines the 'continuity of the personality [...], the quality or condition of being the same in substance, composition, nature, properties, or in particular qualities under consideration; absolute or essential sameness; oneness' (*Oxford English Dictionary*, 1989:620-1).

The term 'identity' thus includes a number of quite distinct connotations. It refers first to the structures of things that remain the same, to that which is seen to constitute their 'essence' across all transformations. But it also refers to the relation of the singular human being to him- or herself, to their actions, experiences, wishes, dreams and memories, and thus to the various instances of the 'self'. In this latter form, it entails references to the relations of the singular human being to others. And the term always contains a reference to time. The term thus always already includes a relation to oneself—however it is cast, a relation to others, sociocultural life, and temporality.

Within the social sciences the term is predominantly used in two versions. As 'self-identity' or 'personal identity' it is meant to characterise the consciousness a human being has of him- or herself, of her continuity over time and of her conception of a certain coherence and boundedness of one's own person. Identity in this sense has been used by Erik Erikson in terms of a subjective sense of continuous existence and a coherent memory. The terms 'social identity' or 'collective identity,' in contrast, refer to conceptions of sameness or similarity with others. Such (symbolic) representations of same-

ness within an—imagined—'group' include a notion of being different from others, from those who don't belong.

This phenomenon is currently often addressed in theoretical terms under the—not rarely rather misleading—label 'difference.' It also recurs in the ongoing debates about 'universalism and particularism,' and it becomes practical in the various forms of the politics of social identity that insist on 'otherness.' Both postcolonial and feminist theorising have revived the interest in collective identities, which in general seems often carried by groups that were marginalised or condemned to invisibility in the dominant structure of political hierarchies. Such theories are intricately bound to practices of cultural politics in which identity is connected to articulation, agency and empowerment. Nevertheless, these current debates are marked by a paradox. Within social theory and philosophy, one can observe tendencies to question and ultimately dissolve the concept 'identity,' whereas social practices emerge and increase in significance that persistently thematise, create and strengthen 'identities'—often even with recourse to the sceptical debates in social theory and philosophy.

Even though the term 'collective identity' was not used, the questions of the relation to others and of the idea of sameness with others have long been addressed in the intellectual traditions of philosophy as well as of the emerging social sciences. The concept of 'identity,' however, is of more recent use in this context. It was introduced into psychology during the 1940s and was soon also adopted in other disciplines to refer to both the collective aspects of subjectivity that emerge from the individual's belonging to certain groups, which may define themselves through gender, culture, ethnicity or nation, and the alleged 'identity' of those groups themselves, namely their homogeneity.

'Identity' thus understood, however, is nothing but a new word for an old problem. In earlier periods, the issue was addressed and belaboured through terms such as 'essence,' 'substance,' 'tradition,' 'person,' 'character,' 'civilisation,' 'people.' Gottfried Herder already meant what is now called the problem of collective identity when he spoke of the inalienable 'character' (*Geburtsstamina*) of a people—and similarly Jean-Jacques Rousseau when he emphasised the common political will (*volonté générale*) of a people, a will that connects its members regardless of origin, as well as Friedrich Nietzsche when he took a common heroic will and a limited memory to be responsible for the existence of a nation.

Following up on Herder and relating to motifs in Friedrich W. Schelling— motifs that found their continuation in the theory of archetypes as developedby Carl Gustav Jung and Mircea Eliade—the search was for universal and constant features of culture that found regionally diverse expressions. These concepts have in common that they postulate a universalism in terms of the laws of the human psyche on the one hand, while working with a particularism in terms of the variety of 'identities' of peoples on the other.

The assumption of 'collectively shared' representations also was one of the conceptual pillars of the 'psychology of peoples' (*Völkerpsychologie*) and of the emerging sociology. It was Wilhelm Wundt who provided the most detailed view of psychology and the cultural sciences. His voluminous late writings (1898, 1917) focus on those psychic phenomena that are gain significance for the development of the social life and of the emergence of creations of the collective spirit. The reference to Herder's 'spirit of the people,' which describes the supra-individual features of the members of a people, is as evident as the one to Wilhelm von Humboldt whose comparative linguistic investigations already entailed a comparison of 'peoples's characters.' For Wilhelm Wundt—whose writings were known by Franz Boas and Bronislaw Malinowski, but also by Emile Durkheim—the psychology of peoples was an evolutionary psychology, comparable to the evolutionary thought of Spencer (for a more detailed account, see Vierkandt, 1931). Subsequently, the psyche of this 'primitive man' was in the centre of post-evolutionist psychology of peoples, most strongly connected with the name of Lucien Lévy-Bruhl and with his conception of 'prelogical thought' and of mythic participation, i.e. the community of affect (1910), in 'primitive' peoples (a conception, as needs to be noted, that was not meant to degrade the mental capacities of these peoples, as later interpretations of society of the Durkheim school noted). 'A phenomenon that needs to be subjected to a sociopsychological consideration is given wherever possible values, i.e. novel psychical facts, are created in an isolated individual by the interaction between several such individuals. Such psychical facts are to be found evidently only within the singular human being, but they belong the supraindividual order that stretches beyond the singular being by virtue of their emergence and their context,' as was observed in 1905 by Martin Buber (1972, I:237), whose book series The Society (Die Gesellschaft) aimed at representing 'the living together and the interdependence of human beings.' Even after the decline of evolutionism it was precisely the relations and mutual effects between the 'spiritualmental' processes within singular beings and the 'collective' that were to become the central theme of the various schools of social psychology and sociology.

The question about the relation of a singular human being to the other therefore, is inseparable from the 'most originary questions of modern thinking,' as Michael Theunissen (1972:1) notes. This question and the epistemological issues related to it have thus gained a prominent position in the various trajectories of modern (socio-)philosophical discourse. Edmund Husserl or Martin Heidegger conceptualise the other as 'Fremdich' ('strange-I'), or 'Mitdasein' (Being-therewith), whereas others conceive an of an originary being of the other, which is only encountered in the 'Thou' (Martin Buber), understood as the 'andere Selbst' ('other self '—Karl Jaspers) or as 'alter ego' (Max Scheler).

Three distinct, though interconnected perspectives can be identified in the thinking the other, as Michael Theunissen (1972) has convincingly argued.

Transcendental approaches, first, drawing on Edmund Husserl, focus on the constitution of the other in and through world-projecting subjectivity. Dialogical approaches, second, as in Martin Buber, emphasise the encounter of the other, and the birth of self, in and through the encounter. Approaches, finally, as elaborated by Wilhelm Dilthey, Max Weber or Alfred Schütz, have proposed a hermeneutics of understanding the other and a psychology of empathy.

Whereas transcendental approaches seek the original being of the other in the 'strange-I' and its existential modifications, dialogical thinking encounters the other, originally, only in the Thou as the second person of the pronoun, i.e. the original being of the other reveals itself in addressing the other, in dialogue. Humanistic approaches hope to 'overcome' the 'gap' between self and other by interpretative-hermeneutic means. The constitution of subjectivity is thus always already placed in a particular relation to the other—regardless of whether the other is addressed as Thou, alter ego or being-with *(Mitsein)*. The determination of 'the social' depends on the other: an act, a gesture, a speaking is a social—and thus ethical and political—act, gesture or speaking by turning towards an other. The choice of notions such as strange-I, alter ego etc. therefore, always imply a decision how the 'I', the subject and self, and the other are to be conceptualised, and thus also a decision of the ways in which 'intersubjectivity' and 'identity' can be grounded. A perspective in which the subject—more or less monadically—stood in the centre of reflection required of social thought the conceptualisation of the move from one subject to another one, from the knowing subject to the object to be known, from the 'I' to the 'other' and the 'world.' Thus, the dominant perspective clung for long to a figure of thought which assumed a subject stepping outside of itself to appropriate the other, to sublate otherness and restore unity by stating the sameness of the other with the self. The self-identical subject grandiosely confirmed itself and its unity. The singular human being, however, is hardly a monadic entity, but always already 'part of,' always already constituted by the other and thus, always being altered, 'othered' *(verandert*—Theunisssen, 1972:56). Any firmly established identity of the self is here abandoned without, though, dissolving into the common identity of a 'we.'

Following Benedict Anderson, the common identity of a 'we' has increasingly been conceptualised as 'true imagined communities,' as social and cultural constructions. A critique of discourse that emphasises the variety of forms in which cultural values are produced has replaced the earlier critique of ideology that relied on the assumption of the existence of positive truth and aimed at substituting 'true' for 'false' consciousness. Such critique of discourse is based on the insight that identity is being consolidated through social practices, cultural symbols and discursive formation. The most important strategy to make certain ascriptions and boundaries appear as unalterable is to represent them as 'natural,' objective and inaccessible. Thus, such ascriptions and boundaries are removed from the realm of individual decidability

and political changeability. The thinking of that which is other and that which is one's own is thus always already a part of numerous forms of a—discursive—politics of identity. The other, the stranger—in its alleged collectivity—was to constitute itself through the inversion of the imaginary construction of that which is proper to oneself. Thus, the other had to provide a foundation and affirmation for and of oneself. Such imaginary construction placed the other at an infinite distance and established unambiguous spatial and temporal boundaries. More recently, the thinking of difference has returned to these questions and has made new and different attempts to project the relation to the other. Discourse analysis subjects such essentialist objectivations to a critical procedure that focuses on the institutions and discourses of power and discerns the linguistic and symbolic strategies of power. Poststructuralist theories that no longer place the identification of universalistically-grounded commonalities in the centre of their concern understand 'identities' as the products of exchanges that cross boundaries, and as processes of negotiations that are, as a matter of principle, not subject to any closure. The staging of identity is then considered as a part of social, as well as eminently political, practices and as a cultural text which refers to various significations, employs a variety of historical codes and creates and activates a range of different memories and images.

The problem areas that are critically addressed by the concept 'identity' include the question of biographic personal identity as much as the various representations of collective identity, the latter occurring—in more or less clearly distinct ways—in the forms of gender identity, ethnic identity and national identity. These categories indicate the structure of this volume, which aims at documenting both the problématique and the productivity of the concept of identity in current debate. The contributions demonstrate, on the one hand, how this concept is used and elaborated in various areas, and with various objectives and methodologies, and what heuristic potential it contains. On the other hand, however, they also show which processes of constitution of historical meaning and of work of sociocultural memory are inscribed into it. Thus, these contributions exemplify a part of the task that thinking imposes on the concept of identity: How can 'subjectivity' be grounded and described? How is an other to be thought of who not merely mirrors and repeats one's 'own' identity? How can one think of a relation that recognises difference, on the one hand, without falling into a discourse of incompatibility, on the other?

The *first part* of this volume focuses on the constructions of identity in academic discourse and discusses critically the—implicit or explicit—theoretical assumptions and presuppositions that the use of the concept entails. *Heidrun Friese* reminds us of the origins and contexts of meaning in which the concept has been developed. Identity is connected to desire, name and difference, or, to put it in different words, to questions of consciousness, con-

ceptuality and temporality. The questions are thus raised that the concept insistently poses to thought: the determination of the relations between stability and change, between structure and history, between being and becoming, between unity and difference—questions, obviously, that are also linked to the constitution of the knowing subject, with the certainty of scientific knowledge, the identifying through naming and conceptualising. These are questions that are of lasting relevance for key issues of concept formation in the social sciences. *Peter Wagner* returns to these questions when he discusses some of the elements that have characterised the place of the concept of identity in the social sciences and tries to reopen the debate about this place. In many respects, the concept was tied to normative ideas about the autonomous subject and the subject's capacity to act, furthermore to ideas about the unity and coherence of the social world, and of the beliefs, norms and values human beings hold in this world, as well as to the postulate of the stability and continuity of the social and its structural features. If such presuppositions were to guarantee the reliability of our knowledge, Wagner, in contrast, demands a fundamental reorientation of the ontology of the social. Such an opening requires not merely the farewell to conceptions that incessantly reconfirm the identity of the subject and of society, but it also searches for conceptions that focus both on the historicity of identity and on its projective character, or in different terms, on the becoming of identity and its temporality. In the discussion of the terms personal and collective identity in the social sciences, three theoretical constellations can be distinguished. Identity is linked to meaning and culture in the first place, to agency and modernity, second, and finally to the relation between unity and difference. These lines of discourse and the elaboration of a critical perspective on them will recur in a variety of ways in the subsequent contributions.

Erik Erikson can certainly be considered as the most prominent representative of a theory of identity that has linked the term to agency and modernity. In critical recourse to Erikson, *Jürgen Straub* develops a subject-theoretical foundation of the concept of identity. At the centre of his concern is the structure of the relation of the human being to her/himself and to the world that becomes significant under conditions of modernity, and is based on the experiences of contingency, difference and alterity specific to modernity. Identity is here linked to the agential capacity of singular human beings, which requires coherence and continuity of the person. The latter are never given, though, but need to be persistently created and maintained. Such production of identity, which is continuously demanded of the individual, requires both the safeguarding of differences and the ability to synthesise dissonances and contradictions. Straub takes a critical distance to attempts at transferring a concept elaborated in individual psychology to collectives, which are then endowed with 'identity' of an analogous kind. It thus becomes evident that 'collective identities' are constructions based on common practices and dependent on

some kind of agreement and identification. Such a shared understanding of self and world can be analytically reconstructed, but it can hardly be constructed from the outside and ascribed to a group as a consolidated common characteristic without falling under the suspicion of being an ideological move. Once the term identity is linked to specific historical constellations, on the one hand, and once the mechanisms of the construction of identity are pointed to, on the other, identity can hardly be seen as a fixed phenomenon that is amenable to the external view of the analyst.

Barbara Henry discusses further the relation between 'identity' and 'modernity.' Referring to the 'postmodern' critique of Western universalism, she aims at rehabilitating aspects of the concept—numerical identity, qualitative identity, and group identity—and at demonstrating how the concept in such an understanding is indispensable for understanding contemporary 'multiple' political identities and the ways in which the latter have spelt a crisis for conventional political concepts such as the welfare state and the democratic nation-state. Identities are always also created by means of images, stories and myths. A discussion of the various meanings of myth and of the structural affinity between the old national myths and mythographic experiments of the present day shows how the latter can give political identity significance and vitality. The relation between myth and the identities of the West—and also between individual identity and group and national identity—is thus turned into the philosophical testing ground for a concept of political identity that neither exerts hegemony over other forms of life nor succumbs to irrationalism.

The *second part* of the volume elaborates these questions by discussing the various forms of representation and translation that are used to name and create both selfhood and otherness in the practices of production of knowledge. The relevance of memory for processes of identity-formation has often been pointed to—even before Pierre Nora's path-breaking work. Identities are created in and through individual and collective remembrances that connect the past with the future in the present and mark both continuity and rupture. Identities rely on memory and on the powerful collective practices of political work of remembrance—monuments, memorial days, museums etc.—that aim at creating commonalities across time and thus collective identities.

Such questioning of the academic practices of production of knowledge always requires reflection on the key issues of the social sciences such as the separation of the subject and the object of research, both of which were long considered coherent and homogeneous entities, and the question of the representation of reality in the scholarly text. It is true that anthropology, in particular, has long been posing the question of the translation of the multitude of worldviews into Western academic concepts. The various strategies for establishing the authority of the ethnographic text, however, have only recently been addressed and the idea that literary tropes are inherent in any representa-

tion of social, cultural and historical reality (Hayden White) has entered into disciplinary concerns only a short time ago. In the course of this reflexive move, it is not only the various aspects of the processes of cognition, i.e. the literary procedures of representation, that are problematised, but also, as *Martin Fuchs* convincingly demonstrates, the network of relations between the researcher and the other, that is, the members of different cultures. The relations between academic scholars, the objects of research and the addressees of the research are thus considered—broadly following Michel Foucault—as a part of a powerful 'politics of interpretation' and of 'discursive formations and discursive strategies;' the search for knowledge is reinterpreted as a specific sociohistorical practice of representation. Culture and society are then seen as relational, and their relation—as the example of the Daklit movement shows—can be analysed in terms of mutual translation and inscription of communicative processes between subjects in social interactions and in the power-laden concert of various voices.

Shingo Shimada similarly focuses on the multiple and heterogeneous elements from which cultural identity is constituted. Using Maruyama's work and his reception of Western traditions of thinking, dominated by the dichotomies of community and society as well as of atemporality and historicity, and of tradition and modernity, as an example, Shimada demonstrates how such translations can be constitutive of identity in the Japanese context—and can reenter Western discourse at the next moment as 'the Japanese.' Such 'history of concepts in cultural interdependence' furthermore elucidates the role of basic concepts in the social sciences in processes of cultural translation. Thus, it becomes visible how the West constitutes itself as the West by means of distantiation from the other and thus gains its own self-understanding. The conceptions of selfhood and otherness are therein determined by discourses formed by positions that are opposed to each other but nevertheless share some presuppositions of thinking. Addressing a hermeneutically guided attempt that demands the understanding of the other—and that always presupposes the fixed identities of both the one who understands and the one who is to be understood—Shimada emphasises the insight into the mutual interrelations between cultures, which do not confront each other as self-identical entities, but in which self and other are always already interpenetrated.

The powerful procedures of boundary-setting and exclusion, which are meant to characterise and stabilise that which is characteristic of oneself, and thus of normality, do not only shape the relation to other societies and cultures. In particular ways, they recur within one's 'own' society and in the various historical practices by which 'otherness,' deviancy and thus also 'female' are coded. The contributions to the *third part* of this volume therefore focus on the constitution of female identity and alterity between the end of the eighteenth and the early twentieth century. The contribution by *Elisabeth Bronfen* deals with the staging, the *mise-en-scène* of the female self by the medium of

pictorial representation. From 1870 onwards, Jean Martin Charcot produced in the photographic department of the Parisian hospital *La Salpêtrière* those images of the hysteric woman that were to gain great influence precisely because they visualised the state of hysteria, a state however, in which this illness is produced as much as it is staged. Hysteria as an exemplary female state always depicts the culture that produces it as much as it does the woman who is afflicted with it. In the context of the social encoding of feminity—but especially and precisely in the images of the hysteric woman—this illness appears as the intended transgression and crossing-out of the ideal image of the woman. Largely excluded from any access to the public production of cultural symbols and limited to the sphere of intimacy, sentiment and bodily participation, female identity was meant to constitute itself as the pure inner self and as a form of being resting within its self. Hysteria, thus, is seen as an illness that displays the loss of the core self in compulsive bodily impersonations and stagings, in which the body demonstrates the other of self. Drawing on three further examples, Bronfen illustrates the relation between mediality and staging in terms of the interrelation between hysteria, projective elaboration of selfhood and photography. Any sign language harbours an inherent contradiction. The more the photograph's power, the further away one gets from the security of a fixed identity. The possibility of producing more than one rendering of one's I, a plurality of the self is established, which lets the depicted person as well as the observer doubt the stability of the rendition. The self-portrait, the doubling of the I through the picture, raises a number of questions about the self: does it have a solid identity or is it only created in the staging of the picture? Can the self only be staged as a masquerade and therefore refers to a nothing? The self-portrait turns out to be fundamentally contradictory since one and the same artistic gesture establishes this self and at the same time radically calls it into question. The new medium of photography provided not only means of documentary storage, but also offered itself for the purpose of playful masquerades, hypothetical projections of self as well trauma-related stagings of diffuse and unstable identities in the medium of the female body.

Female identity appears to be tied to the female body. But this body—sign of a commonality—turns into the place of otherness that marks a variety of different identities. In the word 'Jewess,' for instance, it signals both universality and particularity. 'The "Jewess Pallas Athena"': this is how Paul Celan relates different traditions to one another and thus opens a space in which the meanings and ascriptions that constitute the word 'Jewess' can be reflected, as *Barbara Hahn* impressively demonstrates. This word, as becomes evident from the writings of Jewish women, does not merely signal a position within 'German' culture since the period of emancipation nor only pose questions regarding history, tradition and religion, it also points towards the elaboration of a concept or a judgement. Since the onset of emancipation and the begin-

ning acculturation to a bourgeois-Christian world, in which an antagonism had been established between the sexes that could not do without an abstract category of 'woman' as such, female Jews were subjected to two simultaneous exclusionary mechanisms—woman/man; Jew/German. The site of this double exclusion was marked by the concept: 'Jewess.' 'Jewess' meant both unstable identities and twofold strangeness: woman and Jew, woman and author. The literary works of Jewish women show how the concept 'Jewess' and thus the horizons of self-conception shift in the struggle over religion, tradition and modernity during the nineteenth and twentieth centuries—up to the murderous extinction of the female body, the Jewish body, up to the attempt at annihilating the other.

The *fourth part* of this volume, too, focuses on the powerful practices of inclusion and exclusion that, in this case, create ethnic and national conception of belonging and of identification. The production of a we-consciousness that is based on ethnic categories requires the interaction with another social group that is perceived as different from one's own in certain, significant respects. Such criteria of distinction, however, are connected to situations and are determined by the relations of mutual interaction and the various constellations of interest and conflict of those involved. As much as ethnically defined membership in groups is determined by context, as much are the discursive elements that are to distinguish self from other employed and mobilised in variable ways.

On the basis of a study of a multiethnic neighbourhood in suburban London, *Gerd Baumann* shows how powerful official-dominant discourses about identity and ascription are often opposed by counterdiscourses the elements of which are used by human beings in situational contexts by means of a 'dual discursive competence.' Whereas the dominant discourse defines culture mostly in ethnic and quasi-biological categories, thus essentialising ethnos and culture, the identity-constituting discourse used by the members of individual 'communities' is interwoven by a different categorisation that challenges and limits the valididity of the hegemonic discourse. True, the political demands of minority groups are hardly any longer oriented at gaining equal civic rights, at human rights or even at social integration; in contrast, they often now aim at the recognition of a distinct cultural identity. As Baumann shows, however, such identity-constituting boundaries between and within groups are constantly drawn and again removed, as for instance in cases when a 'community' declares differences in religious or class belonging, in regional origin or migratory experience as irrelevant. Cultural identities are constantly reinterpreted and recreated in the various practices in which political alliances are formed or rejected and in which traditional values are newly defined. The discursive constructions of collective identity and their simultaneous rejection are thus part of the historical process of constant renegotiation and redefinition.

Such co- and counterexistence of different discourses in the elaboration of identities is also in the view of *Hans-Jürgen Lüsebrink*, who analyses the constitution of a postcolonial African consciousness of nationhood and history in opposition to the colonial ways of perceiving and representing African history. The thesis of this contribution holds that the national identities of the postcolonial states are an invention of colonial administrators. It is not only the case, as is well known, that the political map of the postcolonial nation-states largely follows the borders of the former sectors of colonial administration; the matrix for the cultural individualisation of certain ethnic groups was also created by the colonial officers. The world exhibitions presented the cultural life of African tribes to the curious European spectator in the perceptive *mises-en-scènes* of colonial exhibitions. These important sources serve to remind us of the fact that national identities are not only created by means of intellectuals' discourses but also through mediating stagings. The phase of colonisation remains constitutive for the self-consciousness of the postcolonial nations in some mediated way, namely by virtue of the fact that separatist counter-discourses were provoked by the colonial situation. The repressed history of the precolonial time was to be validated by reinvention of indigenous tradition and reviving of figures of identification belong to that history.

Constructions of national identity are also at the centre of *Christian Geulen's* contribution, which provides not only an overview of recent approaches to the study of nationalism but also shows that the process of nation-building is conceptualised in highly different ways depending on the choice of history, politics or culture as the *Leitmotif* for the analysis. The central issue in Geulen's analysis is the longevity of nationalism. Following up on an excursus on ethnic nationalism, Geulen discusses the persistence of nationalism, which proves highly flexible and adaptable in the face of the sociopolitical transformations of modernity, in terms of two sociopolitical achievements: first, a form of integration that makes differences of religion, social status, ethnic origin and gender effectively invisible; and second, a safeguarding of identity that is nourished by the permanent mobilisation of a consciousness of imminent dangers and crises.

The last contribution to this section links up to the first one. While the conditions of the emergence, the structure and the self-understanding of ethnic nationalism were at issue in the former, the latter deals with the enclave-like structure of fundamentalist groups. Both these phenomena are products of modernisation and responses to it; in both cases, the therapy of compact constructions of collective identity is applied to a condition of modernity that is diagnosed as a disease—in the one case under secular, in the other under religious auspices. *Emanuel Sivan* analyses fundamentalist movements that either aim at separation from nation-states or at transforming the latter from inside. His comparative study identifies the basic structures of Christian, Islamic and Jewish fundamentalism, all of which can be derived from a draw-

ing in sharp contours the boundary between the inside and the outside. A common consciousness of exile, a sentiment of superiority, clear spatial and temporal orientations, tight relations of solidarity, texts that are considered as absolute, and the existence of charismatic authorities are features that these movements have in common. The boundary to the outside that determines everything else puts the group under a strong egalitarian pressure, a pressure however that is not experienced as constraint, but rather as security-providing—security against the dangers for the soul, the complexity and loss of meaning of an environment that is imagined as malicious and latently invasive into one's own life. The community-creating power of collective identity—the parallel to ethnic nationalism is plainly at hand—depends on the consciousness of a state of crisis and danger that is continuously activated and mobilises a similarly perpetual countermovement.

The objective of this volume is not merely to provide a sense of the variety of constructing identities. By relating the various *problématiques* at stake to each other, it intends to point to some basic structures in these constructions. At the centre of the issue is the question of the boundary and the opposition of inside and outside, here and there, 'I' and you, us and them that accompanies it. Constructions of identity are the more compact—as well as potentially aggressive—the more they erect boundaries against the imagined outside. And they are the more elastic and differentiated, the more they treat those boundaries as themselves an object of reflection that needs to be considered in its temporality, thus in its always open becoming. Once temporality is taken seriously, the concept of identity loses its problematic connotations of homogeneity and totality, of stable substance and timeless essence. Thus understood, identity would no longer be the opposite to alterity, but a persistent practice of difference, which is temporal.

References

Buber, Martin (1972), *Briefwechsel aus sieben Jahrzehnten,* Vol. I-III (ed. Grete Schaeder), Heidelberg.

Oxford English Dictionary (1989) ed. J. A. Simpson/E. S. C. Weiner, Vol. VII, Oxford.

Theunissen, Michael (1972) *Der Andere. Studien zur Sozialontologie der Gegenwart,* Berlin/New York (engl. *The Other: Studies in the Social Ontology of Husserl, Heidegger, Sartre and Buber*, 1984, Cambridge, Mass./London).

Vierkandt, Alfred, (1931) 'Sozialpsychologie' in *Handwörterbuch der Soziologie* (ed. Alfred Vierkandt), Stuttgart, pp. 545-64.

Wundt, Wilhelm (1898) *Grundrisse der Psychologie*, Leipzig.

Wundt, Wilhelm (1917) *Völkerpsychologie. Eine Untersuchung der Entwicklungsprozesse von Sprache, Mythus und Sitte*, Vol. 1-10, Leipzig.

I: Perspectives and Concepts

Chapter 1

Identity

Desire, Name and Difference

HEIDRUN FRIESE

'No name. No memory today of yesterday's name: of today's name tomorrow. If the name is the thing, if a name creates the concept of everything that is situated outside, if without a name there is no concept, and the thing remains blindly, indistinct and undefined within us, very well, then, let men take that name which I once bore and engrave it as an epitaph on the brow of the image of me that they beheld; let them leave it there in peace, and let them not speak of it again. For a name is no more than that, an epitaph. Something befitting the dead. One who has reached a conclusion. Life knows no conclusion. Nor does it know anything of names. This tree, tremulous breathing of new leaves. I am this tree. Tree, cloud; tomorrow, book or breeze; the book I read, the breeze I drink in. Living wholly without, a vagabond.'

Luigi Pirandello, *One, None and A Hundred-Thousand*

'Know thyself !'

A prophecy. Nymph Leiriope, having been raped by the river-god Kephissos, gave birth to a son and a prophet pronounces the threat: 'Narcissus live to a ripe old age provided he never knows himself.' Nymph Echo, who was once punished with the loss of speech, falls in love with the young Narcissus but is rejected like all others who have succumbed to his beauty. Nemesis eventually hears Echo's lament of spurned love and punishes Narcissus with unrequited love for himself. Narcissus, exhausted after the day's hunt and resting by a spring, catches sight of a beautiful young man in the silvery water and tries to kiss him. He soon has to realise that the person in the mirror image is no other than himself—how is he to bear to both possess and not possess his love? Unrequited love drives him to kill himself and the once spurned, the one

---

Notes for this section begin on page 27.

who does not have her speech, mourns the dead man (see Ranke-Graves, 1987:259-61).

A mirror, an image of oneself,[1] recognition and the gain of self-awareness. Knowing: That is me. That is I, my body. That is my will, my desire. Something indivisible. I am the one who I see as I, the one who I recognise as I, the one who I desire as I. But is it even possible to see oneself? Seeing myself as I. Me as I? Do I not lose myself precisely in this glance, and do I not always already see another in an infinite distance beyond reach? Can I only catch sight of myself as I because I *think* myself as an I and *recognise* myself in one leap? 'Oh, I am he! I have felt it, I know now my own image. I burn with love of my own self; I both kindle the flames and suffer them! [...] What I desire I have; [...] Oh, that I might be parted from my own body!' (Ovid, 1977:157). Narcissus and an unredeemable desire: to separate the body from desire and with the same gesture to cut off oneself from thought and self-recognition. But still, what remains is the desire for oneself as the source of knowledge of a self-recognising I and the unresolvable unity of oneself. Desire therefore, as a source of insight into the unity of an I. But for me to be able to refer to myself, does this I have to be an always already given, or does the I only *become* in the course of this process? And why does this knowledge, this grasping of the unity within and as I, end with death? Does life presuppose a plural, a second person, a being which is separated from the first person singular 'I'? Does the establishment of unity—'What I desire I have'—if it is not to result in death, need a second person singular, another 'I' in a 'You' or even in a 'We'? Is the desire for an I always already at the place of another and dependent on it? And astonishingly, a narrative that does not get by without another body, in which Echo is needed as another. Another, though, which only ever repeats the words, a doubling of the own word in the other. A narrative which places Echo, the woman as a further mirror, as a mirrored word. Without a language of her own. Echo and mirror, word and glance, as media of doubling and repetition. Doesn't that mean: I am and I become I as reflection and doubling in the other. Echo, she only has the words of others, she does not have her own words, *she is* the mirror of words. I am the others' words, I am the words of others: 'And she likes herself in these words' (Ovid, 1977:157).

Later one will say: 'In the same way, identity, as self-consciousness, is what distinguishes man from nature, particularly from the brutes which never reach the point of comprehending themselves as 'I', that is, pure self-contained unity' (Hegel, 1970:§ 115; cf. Nancy, 1993:9). Later one will say, I am the one who I have thought, and think, as I. That is what distinguishes me from another. No mirror, no Echo and no desire for the (own-other) body,[2] but rather consciousness which grasps itself as a self. To grasp oneself: thinking which grasps itself as thinking in a unity. Identity as self-awareness, a 'pure undifferentiated' I, which relates to itself and identifies itself as I. Later, this desire

for oneself will be rewritten many times, from body to body and from word to word into: from mind (*Geist*) to mind.

A reply. 'Noman is my name, and Noman they call me, my father and my mother and all my fellows' is the cunning answer to the question for his name while Polyphemos consumes Odysseus' companions (Homer, 1893:145). Where one is foreign, where one neither knows nor recognises, a word is needed, a concept. The unknown needs a name to decide destiny. The right name that demands postponement from death, a password. The characterisation of the one and the possibility of differentiation from another, a characteristic feature of memory. And where the name conventionally fixes and recites a genealogy, or an origin, in this case 'non-being' becomes the guarantor of the salvation in the nameless name—a salvation that cannot do without the determination in the name, but rather determinedly insists on a name: Noman. A delabelling attempt, a vain attempt, which inevitably can only ever end in the name. An extinction that once again calls something into existence and so even fixes the 'Nothing,' identifies even the nonentity with a name, which captures even that, which does not exist, in a word: Nobody, Noman. 'Nothing and no-one.' My name is the name that was given to me, so that I become 'I', distinguished from another. Identifiable. I answer to the name that I have been given. I carry that name, I am addressed by that name, and when someone calls it out I recognise it and turn around. But *am I* in my name? What kind of relationships does this name denote, what constellations—I to me, I to you, and them or I to my actions? Odysseus *becomes* Odysseus through the narrative of his actions and he *is* Odysseus in this name. And if this mythical journey describes the individual self-realisation, as well as the emergence of the Western subject, then this unique subject can obviously not establish itself namelessly, and cannot get by without unambiguous identification in the name. It is a remarkable path on which the individual, who was once subjugated to the Gods and to his intended and inevitable destiny, becomes now responsible for himself and his actions. The continuity of the subject which seeks itself in the past, and recognises itself in its memories and in others' stories, corresponds to the continuity of the actor, who is responsible today for yesterday's actions. The actor's awareness of his own coherent existence is strengthened by the fact that the sequence of his actions forms a chain of action, which constitutes his unique and continuous life (see Vernant/Vidal-Naquet, 1990:49).[3] And this continuous life will be assimilated into the name, into this one name. Where do you come from? Who are you and what is your name? What did you do on behalf of your name? The name, then, fixes a human being's origin, present and future, denotes him in his actions and during the course of events and history. Who are you? That is when a human being is in his name. I am called, I have a name. I am liable with my name. One cannot escape the name. The name will remain. Plato in the 'Symposium,' and, again, a name: 'Even during the period for which any living being is said to live and to retain his identity—

as a man, for example, is called the same man from boyhood to old age—he does not in fact retain the same attributes, although he is called the same person; he is always becoming a new being and undergoing a process of loss and reparation, which affects his hair, his flesh, his bones, his blood, and his whole body. And not only his body, but his soul as well. No man's character, habits, opinions, desires, pleasures, pains, and fears remain always the same; new ones come into existence and old ones disappear. What happens with pieces of knowledge is even more remarkable; it is not merely that some appear and others disappear, so that we no more retain our identity with regard to knowledge than with regard to the other things I have mentioned, but that each individual piece of knowledge is subject to the same process as we are ourselves.'[4]

A providence. 'One cannot step twice into the same river, nor can one grasp any mortal substance in a stable condition, but it scatters and again gathers; it forms and dissolves, and approaches and departs' (Heraclitus, 1979:53). Something remains the same but also changes, we are and we are not. A unity and diversity, being and difference, time and change. The river that changes, and we who change. And do we not think to step into the same river just because we have given it the same unambiguous name? Name and concept. Apart from the name that we have given the river, is there the river that stays the same? We never step into the same water, because there is no stable reality that is the river, but because everything is always in a state of flux, changing constantly, an infinite movement, a becoming which language can never grasp. The words and names of language, which are meant to fix meaning can only ever follow its own rules. Language cannot capture being, there is no being as a stable order that is identical with itself. We can never step into the same river twice, a repetition can never reach the same, because things are not fixed through time and can not be established in a fixed and stable state. Being and substance against time and becoming, identity against difference. Reality, human being, things, the river. Reality? If reality denotes *becoming*, then this becoming is not, as will be said later, the unity of being and not-being. For being is not a continuous self-identical unity. Being *becomes*. The river never stays the same, it changes, it is always already another and never the same. Never stable in a presence, always already scattered and gathered, arriving and leaving, the living can never be captured in a presence. This movement can never be interrupted or halted by a sentence. Language brings this becoming to a halt. But does language not also become? A constant becoming, a coming and a passing? A sentence that replaces another, changes it, extinguishes it and gives birth to another. If the concept itself is not unambiguous, but rather moves in an 'army of metaphors.'[5] And a memory: Is it not the case that the river seems to be the same because we remember a river?

An image, a name and change. Consciousness, concept and time. A warning, an answer, a providence and an old question. Who am 'I'? Who are 'we'? What is 'the thing'? What is language? Identical with itself, or always already

different? Identical with itself through past and present or always already different in a vague present? The notion 'identity' does not just ask for the relationship between stasis and change, between break and continuity, between coherence and dispersion, it also questions language and the names that we give to people and things, it asks about the possibilities of knowledge and the securities of scientific identifications in the concept. How is this unity of things, of the individual or of an 'I' established? How is this unity and its continuity established? And how is this identity secured? Through the body, thought, desire or the name?

While the concept 'identity' had originally no psychological connotations, empiricist philosophy—from John Locke's 'Essay concerning Human Understanding' (1690) to David Hume's 'Treatise on Human Nature' (1739)—called the straightforward 'unity of the self' into question. As long as the Christian idea of a soul remained unchallenged, the self was preserved in this immortal soul and the notion of a unity is indeed unproblematic. With Locke's realisation, however, that identity 'consists in nothing but a participation of the same continued Life, by constantly fleeting Particles of Matter, in succession vitally united to the same organised Body,' precisely this unity becomes problematic (quoted after Glaeson, 1983:911). Pointing beyond empiricism and rationalism, the unity of the self is then reinterpreted, and identity is entrusted—in very different ways—*to thought*, which synthesises the great diversities of sensuousness and contemplation. Kant, with his view that the subject's ideas are always accompanied by the reflective act 'I think' has left the unity and regularity of the scattered apperceptions, the 'identity of the subject' and the 'identity of self-consciousness' precisely to this 'I think' (Kant, 1993:138). Without this competence, so goes the train of thought that changes the Cartesian '*cogito ergo sum*,' it would not be apparent why the subject organises its many ideas, or synthesises them in a unity, neither would it be clear why it can perceive itself over time as identical with itself. 'I am, therefore, conscious of my identical self, in relation to all the variety of representations given to me in an intuition, because I call all of them my representations' (Kant, 1993:138). This argumentation, however, is inadequate in a twofold way: it is neither clear whether the reflecting subject *has* self-consciousness or whether it *is* self-consciousness, nor is it clear how subjectivity thus understood can be unified, and related to diversity at the same time. It is obvious, therefore, that this reflexive competence does not always have to be activated, it merely has to be an *a priori* given possibility. Kant's transcendental deduction and this version of subjectivity nevertheless have to insist on the reflexively secured diversity. Were this not the case, subjectivity itself would become just another variously perceived thing. The mere possibility of synthesis imposes on the subject, having to stay the same, an enduring synthesis and this at the same time obstructs the possibility—and the freedom—to do other than sustain this prescribed unity. And how is

it possible to talk of 'his ideas'? Where does this possessive pronoun come from that blends ownership and cognition and where, 'the meaning of Being and ownership coincide? ('... *das Sein die Bedeutung des Seinen gewinnt,*' Hegel, 1977:185) Why do I think 'my' thoughts?[6] Do 'my' thoughts, 'my' language, make the thoughts that I think 'mine' and establish me as an 'I'? 'I', 'my' possession in 'my' thinking, which in this act owns the things thought by me as 'mine'? 'One can only understand the thing if one owns it?' as already Novalis' Heinrich asks (Novalis, 1982:168). Why do the abstractions and symbolic orders of economic exchange merge, why do the logics of trade and thought merge? Why an 'I', first person singular, that does not *become* through or even *in* the plural of a You or in the We? In contrast to Fichte and his formula of the self-defining I—'to bring oneself into existence and Being, used by the I, is the same thing' ('*sich selbst setzen und Seyn sind, vom ich gebraucht, völlig gleich,*' Fichte, 1965:28)—Hardenberg insists on a conception where the subject becomes only in its revocation in the other. I becomes 'I' not because of the *a priori* competences but rather the fragile I-identity emerges 'as a result of the structures that subjectivity is set into' (Hörisch, 1982:227).[7] Romanticism rewrites Kant's view of the universalistically conceived 'I think, which has to accompany all my ideas,' and turns hermeneutic understanding into a universally valid *condition humaine*, with which man attempts to give meaning and sense to the world, a conception, by which subjectivity is constituted through infinite interpretative acts.[8] Romanticism desires sense at precisely the historical point in time that dissolves it, it invents a sense at precisely the time that it threatens to get lost. Hermeneutics thus understood does not, however, derive from the thinking subject, but rather it enters this subject into the symbolic 'order of exchange, of love and of time which is not available to him but with which it can find the right relation in the course of an interpretation' (Hörisch, 1982:227). As a result, the unattainable distance becomes the trigger that constantly fosters the search for meaning and becomes itself a characteristic of the—lost—meaning. The faculty to think, which substantiates the subject, is substituted not only with the primacy of interpretation and understanding, and not only with the symbolic order of the exchange, but also with the desire, which the subject is always compelled to renounce.

Again is it *desire*, which constitutes an 'I' as 'I' ? Is it a desire for an unattainable other and for an unrealisable sense, which always remains in an infinite distance? This linking of identity and thinking, subject and desire, is not abandoned by thought, even later, and an I is constituted as an I through its desire. 'An autonomous subject is one that knows itself to be justified in concluding: this is indeed true, and: this is indeed my desire,' as Castoriadis notes (1987:187).[9] The identity of a subject that—again—is established through desire? But is it possible that I know my desire and conversely do I have to know about my desire in order to become 'I'? Desire, lust and libido as men-

tal energy of the wish as identity-creating categories? For Freud the notion of identity is of no importance. For him, the term identification denotes the process where the child assimilates external persons and things. But still, the unconscious desires and the will to have these realised—expressed through symbolisation, diverse shifts and compensations—become 'constituents' of the subject. The secret (sexual) desire manifests itself only in the possession of the desired object, or in a symbolic representation, that is in the compensations and stagings of the neurotic symptom, in hysteria, in the dream or in the psychopathologies of every day life—the *faux pas*, the forgotten name, the slip of the tongue or the joke. This desire from early childhood, which, in Freud's topical conception, is settled in the unconscious and belongs to it, moves between the channels of subjectivity, between the Ego, the Super-Ego and the Id, it intervenes in life and rules the subject from afar. This desire, which blends with the original desire, where it has left traces, and whose unconscious content is to be decoded and interpreted as a hidden symbolic form, so that the incomprehensible and nonsensical can at last be transferred to the realm of meaning and sense, so that the border of the unpredictable delusion can be shifted. This desire, which is repeated again and again and unfolds in the space between the desire, its realisation and its repression. This desire, which marks the origin of the different stagings of the female and the masculine (for the possession of the—desired—object is then defined by the fear of losing it). This desire, then—and the varying structures, through which the mechanism of desire works in order to realise itself in different forms—determines the subject. 'I', because I desire? 'I', because I desire another and (therefore) myself? 'I', because I have the desire to kill my father, who obstructs my complete possession of my mother? And the—impossible and obstructed—step from the desire to its realisation in the act, does it end in death and destruction, like it did with Oedipus (and also with Narcissus)?[10] And what does the desire, the wish, look for—the object, lust or something else, an Other? Is the desired object a sign of separation, of loss, is it a signifier? Perhaps it is the case that the unconscious is constituted of a desire, which can exist and last in the subject without the support of a conscious intention. The subject's identity is then always already ruled by itself as another and as an unobtainable, and is established always already in a posterity (*Nachträglichkeit*) and in a discontinuous time frame. But what if the subject's discourse never reaches this other and always stays, as another, unavailable, the other through which the subject is nonetheless established? What if the desire to be aware of the desire, draws from desire itself—and what if the subject determines itself as the subject of its desire because this desire is the desire to become a subject and to allocate meaning to its scattered actions. Then we will have to abandon the concept of the autonomy of the subject. Then the subject becomes and designs itself in the wish and in the desire, in an Other and as another, it designs itself in the past

and in the future, in a sign, in a promise and in a *not-yet*, which as such, however, always marks difference and otherness.

The primary psychical mechanisms as described by Freud are also, however, the functions and the effects of language, of metaphor and metonymy, as effect of the replacement and of the combination of the signified, and the synchronic and diachronic role that they take on in speech. Is 'identity' therefore to be grounded in language, its names and notions? The subject as a unity which opens to the world in the act of representation—or the world which reveals itself to the subject in the act of interpretation and understanding—the subject that imparts this representation in the act of communication. This is the definition of identity that has been dominant in philosophy for some time, proclaiming at the same time the identity between the sign, the object and the (thinking) subject. The validated procedure: to specify being by the determinations of concepts, in order to state that they match splendidly and thereby prove identity and coherence. Thinking as a meaning-giving activity of the subject and reality a thing whose essence, nature or substance are presented. While in classical antiquity the composition of the world was meaning, meaning now becomes the will of the production of meaning and sense. The employed linguistic sign aims to 'lead to meaning or to bring it forward; the signifier has as its aim to present the signified' and to make it present (Nancy, 1987:48). However, language is not suitable as a (mimetical/mnemotical) instrument of adequacy or meaning-giving as it can at best merely approach that which has to be interpreted. 'The teleology of the presentation of meaning is so condemned to the inexpressible. The inexpressible itself has its signifiers, which consequently are nothing other than the signifiers of a distance: this could be science, history, the state, liberty, value, man or meaning itself. It is not surprising that in these signifiers the meaning of the signifier, "God", has found its fulfilment, that is, his death' (Nancy, 1987:48). Modernity and its questioning of language is characterised precisely by the loss of the one-to-one relationship between the signified and the signifier and by the unquestionable identity of *signifié* and *signifiant*, which also frees the word from a strict allocation to meaning and denotation—'an instance of this fundamental moment is the impossibility of identifying either a possible coextensivity or continuity between sign and thing or between signifier and signified' (Benjamin, 1997:3)—and precisely this shift of identity persuaded Hofmannsthal's Lord Chandos around the turn of the century to declare that the 'abstract words, which the tongue naturally has to make use of in order to produce some judgement or other' decompose in the mouth 'like musty mushrooms' (Hofmannsthal, 1979:465).

Once the patterns of identity archived in language and its concepts, patterns that were supposed to fix homogeneity and continuity, once these patterns start to sway they let the signified disappear in an infinite vanishing-line on one hand. On the other hand the unity of the concept and the establishment

of its definitive content is undermined by the insight that the sign is written by the entirety of the other signs and that each element constitutes itself in the traces which the other signs have left in it. This web is the text that emerges both from the transformation of other texts and from chains and systems of traces. 'These chains and systems can only leave a mark in the web of that trace, that mark. The tremendous difference between the one who appears and the appearing [...] is the condition for all differences, all other traces, it is itself already a trace' (Derrida, 1983:13). If one forfeits a transcendental signifier then the field 'of signification' extends 'infinitely' (Derrida, 1978:230). Writing (*écriture*) as a web of traces not only makes it possible that the difference articulates between space and time (Derrida, 1983), but the notion of trace forces to think of a presence that can neither be understood as a completed past nor as a fulfilled presence (Derrida, 1983). The primacy of the trace, which opposes the categories of the logic of identity (see Derrida, 1978)[11] follows from the psychoanalytical insight that presence is hardly a fulfilled presence but rather forms in a *Nachträglichkeit*. This is because the trace refers at the same time to that which is absent and to otherness, which cannot be brought under the power of the concept and restricts the autonomy of the subject. But if the sign is based on what it negates, if the present cannot be thought of as available presence and if the concept, deprived of its former identity with itself, never dominates its subject then these unstable concepts cannot establish, and even less guarantee, either the identity of the present with itself nor the identity of a subject.

It seems that philosophy—following Parmenides' legacy 'for the same is perceiving (thinking) as well as being' –[12] has decided on a legacy of a worldview that defines the unity of identity as an essential feature of Being and that explains Ontos in terms of the concepts of identity and substance. This metaphysics of presence inquires about Being and defines it in terms of continuity, stability and final substance. Once the stable unity of essence is proclaimed, time and becoming are banished from thought. This metaphysics—as Heidegger notes—is determined by an 'oblivion of being' (*Seinsvergessenheit*), i.e. through the forgetting and concealing of the 'difference between Being and being' ('*Differenz zwischen dem Sein und dem Seienden*,' Heidegger, 1990:40), which 'throughout the history of thought remains unquestioned,' and which returns from the 'difference as such, into what gives us thought' (40). In contrast to the 'knowledge that is the suppression of otherness and that celebrates "the identity of the identical with the non-identical" in Hegel's "absolute knowledge"' (Lévinas, 1992:50), being can only be understood in its temporal form, in its finality as well as in its becoming and as that, what it becomes as an 'occurrence,' as the '"happening" of Being' (27). Being cannot be determined by eternity—as in traditional metaphysics –, but has to be thought of in its finiteness and thus with reference to time (Heidegger, 1984). What is requested is to think difference, temporality, finiteness but also becoming. The

task is to think the relation between difference and the different, independent of the forms of representation, through which they are both attributed back to identity. Different approaches to a deconstruction of the 'metaphysics of the presence' have attempted—in quite divergent ways—to question the unquestioned and to think 'that which exists' in its constant becoming and vanishing, in its movement and change. The Cartesian conception, which establishes the subject through the compelling identity with thought is evaded, because Being (*Sein*) is brought into the course of an event and thus becomes an occurrence (Deleuze, 1969). The subject—once liberated from its imperative identity with thought—becomes as an event and within that occurrence as a nonmediated other. It becomes as that which does not exist as converted consciousness or as absolute self-consciousness that embraces all reason. Rather it becomes as finite body, not as representation of the one body, as sign of an 'inside' (mind, creature) or 'outside' (the senses, the sensory, sensuousness), but rather as temporal and therefore a finite singularity that can scarcely be imagined through the construction of a unified sense. That which is *becomes* as finite matter, as weight, surface and extension, as a temporal and historical body, which is exposed and exposes itself (see Nancy, 1993:189-207).[13]

Thinking identity was, for a long time, established via the faculty of *thought* and its operations of synthesising the manifold and the different; it was established via the *desire* of the subject for itself, for the unity of sense and a presence of the absent guaranteed by the presence; it was not at least guaranteed through the proclaimed disambiguity of the relations of *names* and words to that which they should denote. These operations subordinated thinking difference to the thought of unity or synthesis. What the concept 'identity' therefore demands is the work of thinking difference and temporality. Perhaps the *Entwurf* of identity resists an ontology that establishes a unified Being and resists all 'questions of the form "What is"?' (Derrida, 1997:62). This theory of identity, which at the same time gives up the question of identity, must, like any theory, shift the concepts it works with and resist sentences that want to pacify the draft with assertions like 'that is' (43-5). This draft refers to an identity, which scarcely 'is,' which can neither be brought to a standstill in the desire for an ascertainable meaning or a definite sense, nor in the name or the concept. Rather, this draft offers an identity which never gets realised, which will be never fulfilled or realised and thus opens up for that which is to come. As a draft, 'identity' steadily refers to that which is to come and belongs to the dimension of a future. As a draft however, it does not support any—messianistic—hope for an overcoming of the world, some redemption or the mythical arrival of the final meaning. This draft, which resists the one-to-one concept of identity and the subsumation under a definite meaning or content, contradicts the unambiguous uniformity and thus does not get realised in the telos of a meaning. This draft dismisses the synthesis of the different that has its repeal in mind, it *insists* on the opening as a

becoming where that which becomes is always exposed. This draft cannot be presented from afar, from heaven, from the preconceived idea, from history, it does not attempt to include the sequence of single moments into one meaning, nor the mastering, reconciliation or overcoming of the difference in a synthesis, rather it persistently remains in the realm of differences. And: it does not demand a language that is tempted to master that which becomes, but rather a language that moves in the opening, the exposure and the finiteness of that which becomes.

'I' therefore, as desire not for a complete and coherent unity in a conceived synthesis, but rather an 'I' that always moves and is exposed in the realm of the splitting and the otherness as the sphere of identity; 'I' then as boundary and passing, in the intersection of presence, absence and distance; 'I' an I, death before my eyes, constantly becoming and not exhausted in the name; 'I' as the speaking of a language, as the writing of a script, which scarcely attempts to master the differences in one concept and in a definite meaning: 'I' to 'me,' not as confirmation of a fixed, continuous nucleus, a confirmation that always repeats what it takes on and predestines, but rather as an ever open and ambiguous relation, an ever uncertain relation in the sphere of difference. 'I' first person singular to me as another, 'I' and 'I' as an ambiguous relation, as a body and at the same time in the never certain encounter and recognition of a first, second and third person?

Translated by Nadja Rosental

Notes

Translator's note: Translations of German or French texts have been indicated in the references. All other translations are mine.

1. Maybe a glance is always already at the place of the other and the desire actually denotes the split of an 'I'. Then, he look becomes a signifier that marks and uncovers the split, in order to immediately render it vague and illegible in the mirror image. Desire therefore would be a desire for completeness, a desire that is always already disappointed.
2. Nevertheless, the relationship between self-consciousness and desire is not loosened, the former only finding completion through the latter: 'self-consciousness is thus certain of itself only by superseding this other that presents itself to self-consciousness as an independent life; self-consciousness is desire' (Hegel, 1977:§174).
3. For the origin of (auto)biographical writings, which accompany the invention of the *curriculum vitae* and which reached their first pinnacle with Augustine's 'Confessions,' see Misch, 1907.
4. Platon continues: 'When we use the word recollection we imply by using it that knowledge departs from us; forgetting is the departure of knowledge, and recollection, by implanting

a new impression in the place of that which is lost, preserves it, and gives it a spurious appearance of uninterrupted identity. It is in this way that everything mortal is preserved; not by remaining for ever the same, which is the prerogative of divinity, but by undergoing a process in which the losses caused by age are repaired by new acquisitions of a similar kind' (Plato, 1951:207D).

5. Even scientific concepts cannot be separated from the rhetorical and illustrative-metaphorical. For Nietzsche, concepts are metaphors that have undergone 'hardening and rigidification' and truth is a 'mobile army of metaphors' (Nietzsche, 1989:252). The academic endeavour to grasp concepts unambiguously can only rest on everyday language and its fuzziness and on the family-resemblance of expressions which—as Wittgenstein showed—cannot fulfil the demand for clarity and identity (Wittgenstein, 1967). Language is metaphorical and, like thought, necessarily entails metaphors (see Blumenberg, 1960:7-142). Metaphors, however, 'do not establish what 'is,' they do not fall victim to this old idea of a stable reality identical with itself. They do not depict, they produce' (Boehm, 1994:16). They bring out that which (as yet) does not exist and leave the realm of a definite and ascertainable presence. On the immaginative quality of the construction of 'reality,' see Friese, 1996, 1997.

6. See in this context also Nietzsche: '[…] a thought comes when "it" wants, not when "I" want; so that it is a *falsification* of the facts to say: the subject "I" is the condition of the predicate "think". *It* thinks: but that this "it" is precisely that famous old "I" is, to put it mildly, only an assumption, an assertion, above not an "immediate certainty". For even with this "it thinks" one has already gone too far: this "it" already contains an *interpretation* of the event and does not belong to the event itself' (1990, no. 17, p. 47). '[…] ein Gedanke kommt, wenn "er" will, und nicht wenn "ich" will; so daß es eine *Fälschung* des Tatbestandes ist zu sagen: das Subjekt "ich" ist die Bedingung des Prädikats "denke". *Es* denkt: aber daß dies "es" gerade jenes alte berühmte "Ich" sei, ist, milde geredet, nur eine Annahme, eine Behauptung, vor allem keine "unmittelbare Gewißheit". Zuletzt ist schon mit diesem "es denkt" zuviel getan: schon dies "es" enthält eine *Auslegung* des Vorgangs und gehört nicht zum Vorgange selbst' (1980: 580-1).

7. 'Each is on his place only through others,' Hörisch continues, 'this fragment by Novalis appears like an explicit summary of recent interactionist, psychoanalytic and semiological theories of personal identity' (227). Cf. Hardenberg, 1981:104-96.

8. This is the precise moment that the '*Œuvre*' emerges as a writing experience and as a substitute for meaning. Even Nietzsche insisted—against Schleiermacher—that it is a more than useless undertaking to look for meaning in a contingent world. Kittler (1990) understands the hermeneutic method of the Romantic movement not as a presupposition for the reading of texts, but as a—historically underpinned—disciplining of the body, which rests on institutionalised, administrative and educationally substantiated practices. Meaning can therefore not be founded on a universally valid anthropology, but has to be understood as a set of historical technologies. Romantic hermeneutics can not be explained through text-immanent interpretation, but rather as a specific reading and writing technique that has been replaced by Nietzsche and the technologies of the modern age.

9. In contrast to Freud's and Lacan's conception of the autonomy of the subject, see Castoriadis, 1987:104.

10. It is not a coincidence that Freud concludes *Totem and Taboo* (1912-13) with 'in the beginning was the Deed' from Goethe's *Faust* and does not mention the previous lines 'in the beginning was the Word,' 'in the beginning was the Mind,' 'in the beginning was the Force.'

11. See also Derrida, 1978. The insistence on the subsequent—'the living presence has its source in the non-identity with itself and the possibility of the retentional trace' and 'is always trace […], for the primary has to be thought of via the trace and not vice versa'—originates amongst others from the debate with Husserl's investigation into the structure our awareness of time (Derrida, 1975:142-3) and differs from Heidegger's understanding of

being where the delay, the '*différance*' is not directed towards a telos but rather is conceived as an unstable becoming.
12. For a reading of Parmenides, see Heidegger, 1969.
13. For Nietzsche the body, pain and the wound are the '*technique of mnemonics.*' 'A thing must be burnt in so that it stays in the memory. Only something which continues *to hurt* stays in the memory' (1994:41 no. 3/1980:802).

References

Benjamin, Andrew (1997) *Present Hope. Philosophy, Architecture, Judaism,* London.
Blumenberg, Hans (1960) 'Paradigmen zu einer Metaphorologie', *Archiv für Begriffsgeschichte,* 6:7-142.
Boehm, Gottfried (ed.), (1994) *Was ist ein Bild?,* Munich.
Castoriadis, Cornelius (1987) *The Imaginary Institution of Society,* (trans. Kathleen Blamey), Cambridge (orig. *L'institution imaginaire de la société,* 1975, Paris,).
Deleuze, Gilles (1969) *Logique du sens,* Paris.
Derrida, Jacques (1975) *Die Stimme und das Phänomen. Ein Essay über das Problem des Zeichens in der Philosophie Husserls,* Frankfurt/M. (orig. *La voix et le phénomène,* 1967, Paris).
Derrida, Jacques (1978) 'Freud and the scene of writing', in *Writing and Difference,* (trans. Alan Bass), London, pp. 196–231 (orig. *L'écriture et la différence,* 1967, Paris).
Derrida, Jacques (1983) *Grammatologie,* Frankfurt/M., (orig. *De la grammatologie,* 1967, Paris).
Derrida, Jacques (1997) *Einige Statements und Binsenweisheiten über Neologismen, New-Ismen, Post-Ismen, Parasitismen und andere kleine Seismen,* Berlin, (orig., 'Some statements and truisms about neologisms, newisms, postisms, parasitisms, and other small seismisms,' in David Carroll (ed.), *The States of Theory, Art and Critical Discourse,* 1989, New York, pp. 63-94).
Fichte, Johann Gottlieb (1965) 'Über den Begriff der Wissenschaftslehre oder der sogenannten Philosophie', in *Sämmtliche Werke,* Vol. 1, (ed. J. H. Fichte, 1845), Berlin.
Friese, Heidrun (1996) *Lampedusa. Historische Anthropologie einer Insel,* Frankfurt/M.
Friese, Heidrun (1997) 'Bilder der Geschichte', in Klaus E. Müller and Jörn Rüsen (eds) *Historische Sinnbildung—Problemstellungen, Zeitkonzepte, Wahrnehmungshorizonte, Darstellungsstrategien,* Reinbek, pp. 328-52.
Glaeson, Philip (1983) 'Identifying Identity: A Semantic History', *The Journal of American History,* 69:910-31.
Hardenberg, Friedrich von (1981) 'Philosophische Studien der Jahre 1795/96' in *Fichte Studien—Schriften,* Vol. 2, (ed. Richard Samuel in collaboration with Hans-Joachim Mähl and Gerhard Schulz), Stuttgart.

Hegel, Georg Wilhelm Friedrich (1970), *Enzyklopädie der philosophischen Wissenschaften im Grundrisse. Erster Teil, die Wissenschaft der Logik*, in *Werke*, Vol. 8, (ed. Eva Moldenhauer/Karl Markus Michel), Frankfurt/M. (engl. *Hegel's Logic*, trans. William Wallace, 1975, Oxford).

Hegel, Georg Wilhelm Friedrich (1977) *Phenomenology of Spirit*, (trans. A. V. Miller), Oxford (orig. *Phänomenologie des Geistes*, 1973 [1807], Frankfurt/M.).

Heidegger, Martin (1969) *Identity and Difference*, New York (orig. *Identität und Differenz*, 1990⁹ [1957], Pfullingen).

Heidegger, Martin (1984¹⁵ [1927]) *Sein und Zeit*, Tübingen (engl. *Being and Time*, trans. John Macquerrie and Edward Robinson, 1995¹², Oxford/Cambridge).

Heraclitus (1979) 'Fragment' (LI 51), in Charles H. Kahn, *The Art and Thoughts of Heraclitus*, Cambridge/New York.

Hofmannsthal, Hugo von (1979) 'Ein Brief', in *Gesammelte Werke*, Vol. 7, (ed. Bernd Schoeller in collaboration with Rudolf Hirsch), Frankfurt/M.

Hörisch, Jochen (1982) 'Übergang zum Endlichen. Zur Modernität des "Heinrich von Öfterdingen"', in Novalis, *Heinrich von Öfterdingen*, Frankfurt/M., pp. 221-42.

Homer (1893) *Odyssee*, Book IX (trans. S.H. Butcher), London.

Kant, Immanuel (1993) *Critique of Pure Reason*, (trans. S. Meiklejohn), London (orig.: *Kritik der reinen Vernunft*, 1974 [1781], Frankfurt/M.).

Kittler, Friedrich A. (1990) *Discourse Networks 1800/1900* (trans. Michael Metteer, with Chris Cullen, with a foreword by David E. Wellbery), Stanford, (orig. *Aufschreibsysteme 1800/1900*, 1985, Munich).

Lévinas, Emmanuel (1992) *Ethik und Unendliches: Gespräche mit Philippe Nemo/Emmanuel Lévinas*, Vienna, (orig. *Ethique et infini*, 1982, Paris).

Misch, Georg (1907) *Geschichte der Autobiographie*, Vol. 1-5, Leipzig.

Nancy, Jean-Luc (1987) *Das Vergessen der Philosophie*, Wien, (orig. *L'oubli de la philosophie*, 1986, Paris).

Nancy, Jean-Luc (1993) *The Birth to Presence*, Stanford.

Nietzsche, Friedrich (1990) *Beyond Good and Evil*, (trans. R. J. Hollingdale), London (orig. 'Jenseits von Gut und Böse', in *Werke*, Vol. 4, ed. Karl Schlechta, 1980, Munich/Vienna, pp. 567-87).

Nietzsche, Friedrich (1994) *On the Genealogy of Morality*, (ed. Keith Ansell-Pearson, trans. Carol Diethe), Cambridge, (orig. 'Zur Genealogie der Moral. Eine Streitschrift', in *Werke,* Vol. 4, (ed. Karl Schlechta), 1980, Munich/Vienna, pp. 763-900).

Nietzsche, Friedrich (1989) 'On Truth and Lying in an Extra-Moral Sense', in S. L. Gilman, C. Blair and D. J. Parent (eds.) *Friedrich Nietzsche on Rhetoric and Language*, New York (orig. Über Wahrheit und Lüge im außermoralischen Sinn, in *Werke*, ed. K. Schlechta, Vol. V, 1980, Munich/Vienna, pp. 308-22).

Novalis (1982) *Heinrich von Öfterdingen* (ed. Jochen Hörisch), Frankfurt/M.

Ovid (1977) *Metamorphoses. Book III*, (trans. Frank Justus Miller, revised by G. P. Goold), Oxford.

Plato (1951) *The Symposium* (trans. W. Hamilton), Harmondsworth.

Ranke-Graves, Robert (1987) *Griechische Mythologie. Quellen und Deutung*, Reinbek.

Taubes, Jacob (1995²) *Die politische Theologie des Paulus*. Vorträge, gehalten an der Forschungsstätte der evangelischen Studiengemeinschaft in Heidelberg, 23.-27. 2.1987, (ed. A. Assmann and J. Assmann et al.), Munich.

Vernant, Jean-Pierre and Vidal-Naquet, Pierre (1990) *Myth and Tragedy in Ancient Greece*, New York, (orig. *Mythe et Tragedie en Grèce Ancienne*, 1972, Paris).

Wittgenstein, Ludwig (1967) *Philosophical Investigations*, (trans. G. E. M. Anscombe), Oxford/Cambridge. ('Philosophische Untersuchungen', *Werkausgabe,* Vol. I, 1999¹², Frankfurt/M., pp. 231-577).

Chapter 2

Identity and Selfhood as a Problématique

PETER WAGNER

Many formalised discourses of the human sciences—such as law, liberal political philosophy and neo-classical economics—work with a notion of the singular human being as a unit that is characterised by its indivisibility, for those reasons also called the individual. An additional assumption about the guiding orientation or behaviour of these units then needs to be introduced to arrive at ways of conceptualising stable collectivities. In the discourses mentioned above, this assumption is basically one of rationality, with specific variations. In liberal political theory, their capacity for rationality leads the individuals to enter into a social contract for their mutual benefit and to restrict the play of their passions to the private realm. In economics, rationality translates into interest-guided behaviour and the sum of those behaviours into the optimisation of wealth. In legal thinking, the adult individuals can be taken to be responsible for their actions because of their endowment with the faculty of reason. Furthermore, the continuity of such individuals over time needs to be presupposed to allocate responsibility for past actions. Even those sociological and anthropological discourses that were proposed in critical reaction to the presupposition of rationality remained dependent on a prior notion of rationality (as Joas, 1996, has shown). Such limitation of the intellectual space for understanding the singular human being in the human sciences stems at least in part from the fact that those discourses were predominantly developed with a view to addressing the political *problématique*, i.e. the problem of constructing and maintaining a political order (Wagner, 1998).

However, a common view of the history of social life in Europe holds that a 'culture of modernity' spread gradually over the past five centuries. This 'is a culture which is individualist [...]: it prizes autonomy; it gives an important place to self-exploration; and its visions of the good life involve personal com-

Notes for this section begin on page 52.

mitment' (Taylor, 1989:305). Such an emphasis on individuality and individualisation is quite alien to the more formalised discourses of the individual. In European intellectual and cultural history, there is very little connection between these two discourses. Philosophy and social theory proceed predominantly by presupposition and show little interest in actual human beings, who tend to be taken into account only as disturbances the more they enter the public scene. In literature and the arts, in contrast, the experience of modernity is in the centre and, as an experience, it concerns in the first place the singular human being (Berman, 1982). Michel Foucault's lecture 'What is Enlightenment' very succinctly distinguishes between those two readings of modernity. Modernity as an attitude and experience demands the exploration of one's self, the task of separating out, 'from the contingency that has made us what we are, the possibility of no longer being, doing, or thinking what we are, do or think' (Foucault, 1984:46). It is counterposed to modernity as an epoch and a set of institutions, which demands obedience to agreed-upon rules.

Today, one way of discussing this historical separation of discourses is to see it as a long period during which issues of selfhood and personal identity were neglected in the social sciences. A genuine interest in such issues, so the story goes, arose only in the early twentieth century. The ground was prepared outside of what is conventionally recognised as social science, namely by Friedrich Nietzsche, and later by Sigmund Freud. Nietzsche radically rejected the problems of moral and political philosophy and thus liberated the self from the impositions of the rules of the collective life. Freud located the drives toward a fuller realisation of one's self in the human psyche and connected the history of civilisation to the repression of such drives. Against such a 'Nietzschean-Freudian' background (this is Richard Rorty's way of speaking), Georg Simmel and George Herbert Mead could observe the ways in which identities are formed in social interaction and conceptualise variations of self-formation in different social contexts. From then on, a sociology and social psychology of selfhood and identity has developed which is characterised by important advances and insights. It no longer relies on presuppositions about some essence of human nature, and it is at the same time able to connect its findings to both child psychology and phenomenology. It emphasises the socially constructed nature of selfhood, but remains capable, at least in principle, to analyse the specific social contexts of self-formation thus working towards a comparative-historical sociology of selfhood. And without having to presuppose the self-sustained individual of modernity it can demonstrate how autonomous selves develop through social interactions over certain phases of the life-course (Joas, 1998; Straub, in this volume).

This account is in many respects convincing, and it is without doubt true that the understanding of human selfhood in the social sciences has become considerably more complex due to the reflections of Simmel and Mead earlier in the twentieth century. There remains, however, quite some lack of clarity

about what one is actually studying, and what one is interested in, when dealing with selfhood and identity. In recent years, the suspicion that selfhood may be among those 'essentially contested concepts' (Gallie, 1955-6), of which there is a considerable number in philosophy and the social sciences, has been raised again when the notions of the 'decentring of the self' and of the 'post-modern self' have been introduced. The former apparently is a theoretical notion demanding a rethinking of what selfhood is. The latter refers predominantly to the alleged empirical observation that selves are much more transient and fugitive than even sophisticated sociology and social psychology used to allow for. As a consequence of the emergence of these themes, a new separation of discourses can be observed. There seem to be dividing lines of thinking that are almost impossible to cross. In this context, this chapter will head for an exploration of the conceptual field of selfhood not least with a view to identifying some points of passage between those discourses.

Both the ideas of a 'decentring' and of a 'postmodern self' question some major implications of the more standard sociological view of selfhood, namely the existence of the human self as a unit and its persistence as the 'same' self over time. It will need further considerations below to see whether and to what extent such propositions are indeed held. That the assumption is not entirely unjustified, however, can be gathered from the fact that the term 'self' is often—and, it appears, increasingly—used synonymously with the term 'identity.' This latter, though, in most understandings precisely posits existence as an entity and sameness with itself over time. 'Identity' in current social science means 'continuity of selfhood.' These considerations shall start at this point.

1. Selfhood and Identity

'Roughly speaking, to say of two things that they are identical is nonsense, and to say of one thing that it is identical with itself is to say nothing at all' (Wittgenstein, 1984a: par. 5.5303; see also 1984b: par. 215-16). The insight at which the young Wittgenstein arrived seems to be largely forgotten today, at least in the social sciences. Identity is a term that has gained considerable popularity. Wittgenstein's rough remark remains significant, however, as the prevailing confusion in current discussions about identity shows. Should one succumb to the temptation to separate the nonsensical from the void, one easily arrives at the point where any vague hope for a remainder of valid and significant insights threatens to disappear. That, at the latest, would be the time for a halt and for rethinking the rationales of the search. Before aiming at understanding 'identity' and 'selfhood,' it seems wiser to gain an understanding of the ways those terms are used.

Evidently, there is no obligation to share Wittgenstein's scepticism.[1] Regardless of whether one agrees or disagrees with him, however, his state-

ment should convey the need for every reference to 'identity' that there be a 'thing' that is identical with itself or not. (To be precise, there should be two things—the object of consideration and the one with which the former is identical. I will return to this question below). That is why it comes as a surprise that 'identity' occurs without an object in many titles of recent books or articles. The current discussion about identity seems to have liberated itself of this requirement. It has become possible to speak about identity without indicating who or what is identical to itself or to something else. Careless use of language does not seem to be the only or even main reason; uses of language often indicate problems of thought. Let me cast this problem, which will accompany all of the following discussion, initially as follows: The discussion about identity aims at firmly conceptualising something that it avoids to name with any precision in more empirical terms.

A closer look allows the preliminary sorting of some issues. In the social sciences the term 'identity' is used predominantly in two forms. As a shorthand for 'self-identity' or 'personal identity' it refers to a human being's consciousness of the continuity of her existence over time and of a certain coherence of her person, to 'a subjective sense of continuous existence and a coherent memory' (Erikson, 1968:61). The terms 'social' or 'collective identity' expand the idea and refer to a sense of selfhood of a collectivity, or the sense of a human being to belong to a collectivity of like people. 'Identity' then means 'identification' of oneself with others. A consciousness of sameness within a group implies the idea to be different from those who do not belong to this group. This phenomenon is currently discussed under terms such as alterity or strangeness and the setting of boundaries between that which is one's own and that which is of others.

The otherwise useful distinction between self-identity and social or collective identity tends to obscure the relation between the two. Self-identity will usually be 'social' in the sense that a relation to particular other human beings is seen as giving a significant orientation to one's own life. Collective identity, on the other hand, will, it seems, only emerge if and when a multiplicity of singular human beings draw a sense of significance for their self-identities from the same collectivity. More basic clarifications are needed to disentangle the strands of the debate around selfhood and identity. A further step can be taken by trying to discern the cleavage lines between those various strands.

We can start with some illustrations. Erik Erikson's works are a central point of reference in that part of the debate that maybe considered as the mainstream of psychology and social psychology (see Lapsley and Power, 1988; Slygoski and Ginsburg, 1989). Psychological and psychoanalytical analyses from a feminist perspective, in contrast, can often do without a single reference to Erikson, even when they start out from a history of ideas and mention Nietzsche, Freud and Simmel (such as in Weir, 1996). A comparison of modern and post-modern identities is now regularly made in culture, media and

communication studies. Without doubting in any way the plausibility of the findings and the adequacy of the presentations, one has to note that the theoretical references are often very diffuse and haphazard (e.g., Kellner, 1995; Morley and Robbins, 1995). A great variety of orders of reference thus emerges behind the apparent consensus expressed through the term 'identity.' In this light, some doubts can even be cast on the assertion that there is a growth of common interest in 'identity' at all.

In what follows I will try to demonstrate that the debate on selfhood takes place in a semantic space in which the idea of personal identity is variously connected to notions of meaning, of modernity and of difference. The emphasis on continuity and coherence of the self, as mentioned above, will be considered as the modernist position in this debate. It is conditioned by the need to maintain a notion of human autonomy and agentiality as a basic tenet of what *modernity* is about, namely the possibility to shape the world by conscious human action. Such modernism is not strictly tied to the atomist and rationalist individualism of some versions of economic and political thought, most notably neoclassical economics and rational choice theory. It is open towards important qualifications in terms of the corporeality, situatedness and possible nonteleological character of human action (see Joas, 1996, for such a conceptualisation). However, it cannot abandon the link between identity and agentiality and, therefore, needs to insist on some important degree of continuity and coherence of the self.

Objections against such a conceptualisation can go in two different directions. On the one hand, it can be argued that every form of selfhood is dependent on the cultural resources that are at hand to the particular human being when giving shape to her/his important orientations in life. Human beings give *meaning* to their lives by interpreting their situations with the help of moral-cultural languages that precede their own existence and surround them. Cultural determinism is the strong version of such theorising, mostly out of use nowadays, but many current social theories adopt a weaker version of this reasoning which indeed sustains the notion of the continuity of the self but sees this self as embedded in cultural contexts rather than autonomous.

On the other hand, doubts about the presupposition of continuity and coherence of selfhood employ notions of difference and alterity that are not reducible to the idea that selves are formed by relating to others, by intersubjectivity. Such notions rather underline the nonidentitarian character of being by casting the issue of 'the other in me' (see Critchley, 1998, for a most recent account on Lévinas and Blanchot) as a philosophical questioning rather than a straightforward sociological one. While most prominent in the writings of Jacques Derrida, such a view is not at all confined to poststructuralist thought. In another strand of discourse it can be found, for instance, in Hannah Arendt's (1978: esp. 183-7) insistence on the 'two-in-one,' on the relation to oneself as another, as the very precondition for thought.

In the remainder of this chapter I shall first try to demonstrate that, despite some points of intersection, these three discourses pose the problem of selfhood in highly distinct and mutually irreducible ways. An analysis in some detail will show that the first two discourses bear signs of dissolution as a consequence of a recent confrontation of their conceptual terminology with findings of empirical research on current social situations and configurations. The direction of conceptual critique then points towards the third discourse. This discourse, however, has been but little received in the social sciences yet, not least because it raises basic questions as to the possibility and form of theorising in the social sciences.

2. Discourses about Identity

Identity and meaning

In the discourse on meaning, the term 'identity' is evoked to name a form of connection between human beings that is in principle capable of holding together a social order. Even if this is not always apparent, such discourse forms part of the tradition of cultural analysis that reaches back at least to Gottfried Herder. Elements of such thinking have persistently been present in cultural anthropology and in those strands of sociology that emphasise questions of the normative integration of society, such as in Durkheim and in Parsons.

'Culture' refers to shared beliefs, values, norms and forms of behaviour. Cultural theorising thus tends to presuppose that human beings know the cultural features of their own societies, at least to such an extent so as to enact them, even though they may not always be able to explicate them or to assess in how far and with whom those cultural features are shared. In most cases, as cultural theorists tend to argue, human beings have some conception of the community to which they belong. This sense of belonging is their collective identity. In a cultural perspective, the collective identity is the most significant connection between those human beings (for a discussion of recent culturalism see Friese and Wagner, 1999).

Such an understanding of identity appears to have removed the notion of interest from the central position the latter had until about two decades ago in those strands of the social sciences that focused on societal integration. Social life was then described in the language of structures and systems, and human beings were seen as determined by their roles and interests, which in turn could be derived from the position of those human beings within structures. In contrast, in more recent discussions social life is ordered through meaning and values. Human beings live together in cultures, and they no longer recognise the similarity or strangeness of the other through their class position but rather through their identity (see similarly Lamont, 1992:179-80; Lash, 1994:214-5; Griswold, 1994:xiii; Smelser, 1997: chap. 3). Under conditions of the late

twentieth century, however, such return to cultural interpretation could not be effected without modifications.

In the history of cultural thinking, linguistic commonality was the assumption that should lead to the idea of national identity as cultural-linguistic identity. Human beings who share language and values have a primordial commonality that lends itself to the formation of political communities. Such ideas were developed in German at the end of the eighteenth century not least in reaction to the Enlightenment and the French Revolution both of which were reproached for resting on empty abstractions. The Revolution itself founded the political identity of the nation on an idea of membership through political orientation and choice and thus in opposition to language as a criterion of membership that precedes the conscious life of a particular human being.

Such an assumption of cultural and linguistic homogeneity, while always having been contestable, became empirically untenable for contemporary societies. More recent discussions about cultural identity have therefore introduced concepts of 'cultural complexity' (Hannerz, 1992) and the possibility of coexistence of several cultures—including sub- and counter-cultures—on the same territory. Vice versa, it is now also recognised that cultures may expand across large spaces without excluding or dominating other cultures (as it was assumed for national cultures). Jewish culture or the 'culture of science' are evident examples. But even cultures that used to be the traditional object of anthropology, such as the culture of the Samoan islanders, have been analysed as 'multilocal' cultures by underlining both the spatial extension through migration and the simultaneous persistence of ties of belonging (Sahlins, 2000).

Some of those partial identities within a territorially defined society that are currently the focus of attention are implicitly or explicitly analysed in relation to the hegemonic identity group in that society. The term 'ethnic identity,' for instance, is predominantly used for minority groups, such as African-Americans in the US. Similarly, the discussion about gender identity, which was started from a feminist viewpoint (even if it now goes beyond it), is concerned with female identity in a male-dominated society. Identity becomes relevant under conditions of boundary-setting and exclusion, and is accordingly thematised by the marginalised or excluded groups. In turn, one may conclude that identity is not a significant issue for hegemonic groups, who may show an inclination towards universalising reasoning on the terms of which particularity cannot persist.

If all these modifications of the classical concept of culture and cultural identity are taken as an ensemble, they tend to undermine the original quest of the discourse of meaning that resided in the search for identity-constituting commonalities between human beings in their modes of interpreting the world. Such commonalities were seen to precede the concrete human beings and to be genuinely collective. They are constitutive for social life as such. Singular

human beings are of interest in this perspective only in terms of what they have in common with others. The sum of the recent modifications of this discourse, however, amounts to conceptually letting both the commonality and the collectivity disappear. They are replaced by overlapping orders of boundaries and exclusions within and between discursively constituted multiplicities of human beings. Instead of underlining commonality with others, differences towards others are emphasised. The conclusion may be seen in abandoning the cultural form of reasoning about selfhood and identity altogether.

However, abandoning could look easier than it is. Charles Taylor's inquiry into *The Sources of the Self* starts out from the widely familiar argument that the advent of modernity indicates that common frameworks for moral evaluation can no longer be presumed to exist. The key contention in the remainder of the book is then that the ability and inclination to question any existing such framework does not lead into a sustainable position that would hold that no such frameworks are needed at all, a view he calls the 'naturalist supposition' (Taylor, 1989: 30). If such frameworks are what gives human beings identity, allows them to orient themselves in social and moral space, then they are not 'things we invent' and may as well not invent. They need to be seen as 'answers to questions which inescapably preexist for us,' or, in other words, 'they are contestable answers to inescapable questions' (Taylor, 1989:38 and 40). Taylor develops here the contours of a concept of inescapability as part of a moral-social philosophy of selfhood under conditions of modernity.

Identity and modernity

The discourse that connects selfhood to modernity mostly—at least in all its more sophisticated forms—starts out from an assumption of constitutive sociality (or culturality) of the human being as well. Such assumption, however, does here not lead towards the investigation of collective identities in relation to forms of socialisation. Instead the conditions and possibilities of the formation of a self, of personal identity is moved into the centre of interest. Formation of self-identity is here understood as the forming and determining of the durably significant orientations in one's own life. Therefore, this discourse, which often has its roots in (social) psychology, stands in a basic tension to the culturalist concept of identity as sketched above. Whereas commonalities between human beings are of major concern in the latter, the former moves the singular human being into the foreground. No necessary connection is presupposed between identity-formation and individuality; human beings may well form the same or highly similar identities in great numbers. But the identity of the singular human being is in the centre of attention in this discourse, not the group, culture or community.

In such a perspective, identity-formation is sometimes considered to be an anthropological constant of human existence. It is related to the formation of a consciousness of one's own existence and thus biographically to the period

of adolescence. Crises of identity occur accordingly during growing up; more precisely one should speak of life crises during the formation of one's identity.[2] Self-identity once constituted is seen as basically stable further on. Since the very concept of identity is connected to continuity and coherence, stability is turned into a conceptual assumption.[3]

More specifically, however, the creation of such continuity and coherence can also be declared to be a particular *problématique* of selfhood under conditions of modernity. Only the modern human beings, it is then held, know that form of self-consciousness that would allow one to speak of the formation of an identity as well as, by implication, of crises of identity. Such a view may result as a conceptual consequence from a specific understanding of modernity. If modernity is seen to be characterised by the denial of all certainties, by the prevailing of a principled scepticism and of doubt about one's knowledge of the world, then a requirement to question one's own location in the world and the stability of the I follows immediately—and thus also the problem of identity (see, e.g., Giddens, 1991). The view that human beings have to construct their self-identities themselves can similarly be seen as characteristically modern (see Hollis, 1985). Modernity is then precisely defined as a situation in which such a view prevails—rather than considering identity-formation and crises of identity as a consequence of modernity.

This relation between modernity and identity, though, would also need to be conceptualised historically. Significantly, a more specifically social-scientific perspective on the self emerges as late as the early twentieth century. This appears as a considerable 'delay,' compared to virtually all periodisations of modernity—provided that we indeed want to assume a close connection between modernity and identity. This delay merits more attention from sociologists of knowledge and of the sciences than it has hitherto found. It suggests, namely, that the 'classical' sociologists at the turn to the twentieth century (not to speak of their 'predecessors') implicitly pursued a quite elitist approach to society—even beyond those explicit elite theories of society developed by Gaetano Mosca, Vilfredo Pareto and Robert Michels. Up to the early twentieth century, sociologists regarded human beings as basically socially determined. Under that assumption, there always is a relation between the singular human being and the 'social structure' that is not (co-) created by the human being her- or himself. That is why the question of identity did not pose itself. But by implication one would also have to deny the attribute 'modern' to such a social configuration, or at least strongly qualify its reach.

Against this background, it is easier to understand the significance of George Herbert Mead's contribution to the sociology of selfhood and identity. Mead regards the constitution of self as a *problématique* that concerns all human beings and for which there may be a variety of processes which can be generally determined only in their forms but not in their results. As a consequence, it becomes much more difficult to conclude from identities on social

structure and political order. This has often been seen as a 'weakness' of symbolic interactionism, which Mead is said to have inaugurated, as a social theory that allegedly cannot address issues of societal constitution. But by the same move Mead allows for and recognises a plurality of selves that has returned to the centre of discussion today—after the renewal of a regressive synthesis of identity and society in Parsons (to which—what is often overlooked—Erikson contributed as well).

This sociological discussion about identity and modernity has points of reference that differ considerably from philosophical and literary ones. The social upheaval during the second half of the nineteenth century with industrialisation, urbanisation and the phrasing of 'the social question' is often seen as a first 'modern' uprooting of identities, as a first massive process of 'disembedding' (Giddens, 1988). The development towards so-called mass societies during the first half of the twentieth century lets the question of the relation between individuation and growth of the self emerge. This is the first time that the sociological discourses about identity find themselves in synchrony with the societal developments they are about. In such a perspective, totalitarianism can be analysed in terms of an imbalance between imposed individuation and delayed self-formation, the result having been the tendency towards 'escape from freedom' and into stable collective identities (Fromm, 1941; Arendt, 1958). Most recently, the indications of dissolution and dismantling of the rather comprehensive set of social institutions of the interventionist welfare state are one of the reasons to focus sociological debate again on questions of identity.

Some contributions to this recent discussion diagnose the emergence of forms of selfhood that cannot easily be subordinated to conventional concepts of identity. No longer continuity and coherence but transience, instability and inclination to change are said to be marks of the important life orientations of contemporary human beings. Some irritation is caused by the fact that such orientations are called 'identities' despite the counterintuitive etymology of the term, which is counter-acted by adding the adjective 'postmodern' (see Lash and Friedman, 1992). Douglas Kellner, for instance, diagnoses major differences between forms of selfhood that could be found during the 1960s and those of the 1990s. In the earlier period, 'a stable, substantial identity—albeit self-reflexive and freely chosen—was at least a normative goal for the modern self.' In the 1990s, identity 'becomes a freely chosen game, a theatrical presentation of the self, in which one is able to present oneself in a variety of roles, images, and activities, relatively unconcerned about shifts, transformations, and dramatic changes' (Kellner, 1992:157-8; see also 1995:233-47).

If such diagnoses of a historical transformation of identities were correct, they would entail a questioning of the entire modernist concept of identity. If there were a transition to a 'postmodern' condition, in which the prerequisites and/or the necessity for the constitution of stable personal identities in a 'mod-

ern' sense are no longer given, then one would have to speak more generally about historically varying conditions of self-formation. Within a plurality of forms of selfhood, the 'modern' and the 'postmodern' ones would constitute two of the possibilities. Such a statement, however, breaks the conceptual link between identity and modernity that is characteristic of this discourse. 'Post-modernity' remains 'modern' in the sense that there are no certainties about selfhood, but the identities that appear are no longer of the modern form.

Without judging the empirical validity of those observations, an opening of the understanding of selfhood has without doubt occurred that tended to loosen the relation between identity and modernity so that this discourse—like the discourse that links identity to meaning—shows signs of decomposition. The range of questions needs to be widened. Instead of continuing to ask in a straightforward empirical way how personal and collective identities are con-structed, the construction of identity within the discourses of the social sci-ences needs to be moved into focus. The concept identity then inevitably enters into the constitutive relation to its counterconcept, difference, a relation that was always already present in the philosophical discussion.

Identity and difference

A concept of identity is—at least implicitly—of central importance for any philosophy that works with a strong ontology. The basic phenomena are not only existent beyond any doubt and can be defined; they are also stable over time and accordingly traceable through time. Their stable existence makes phenomena also distinguishable. To state the identity of a phenomenon means to note its difference towards other phenomena. After such a step is taken, rela-tions—such as of causality, or of dependence—between the thus identified phenomena can be determined. Difference, however, is then always already preconstituted. One pretends to name a state immediately and positively that is always only created by the act of setting one thing apart from another one with which it is not identical. It is only by thinking identity and difference as part of the same move that the *problématique* becomes visible, which the term identity aims to address.

Such logic of identity, which philosophy and the sciences often employ, turns the stable existence of the observed phenomenon as the one that has been described into a presupposition of the philosophico-scientific operation. How-ever, the status of a possible result of the investigation should be reserved for precisely this assertion of existence. There is a pragmatic justification for such a procedure in terms of the necessary bracketing of aspects that are not part of the specific investigation.[4] But neither is the absence of any reflexive deliber-ation about the status of concepts that are constitutive for theories—such as 'identity'—justifiable nor can the competence for such deliberation conve-niently be restricted to philosophers of the sciences whose discussions will then have little impact on actual research practice.

Stanley Cavell's reflections provide an example for a thinking about self-hood that does not presuppose an idea of identity. Characteristically, it straddles philosophy and social science in what Cavell himself calls an attempt at retrieving Emersonian perfectionism and Wittgenstein's philosophy of culture (Cavell, 1989; 1990). Cautioning against 'any fixed, metaphysical interpretation of the idea of a self' and against the idea of 'a noumenal self as one's "true self"' and of this entity as having desires and requiring expression,' he warns that such an idea would entail 'that the end of all attainable selves is the absence of self, of partiality. Emerson variously denies this possibility.' In contrast, Cavell suggests that the 'idea of the self must be such that it can contain, let us say, an intuition of partial compliance with its idea of itself, hence of distance from itself' or, in other words, he advocates the idea of 'the unattained but attainable self': 'One way or the other a side of the self is in negation' (Cavell, 1990:xxxi, xxxiv and 12).[5] Cavell, drawing on Emerson and indeed also on Wittgenstein and Heidegger, proposes here a relation of the unattained and the attainable as constitutive for the self, that is, he makes the question of attainability a central feature of a theory of selfhood.

For such an elaboration, precisely the concept of identity is crucial—in a twofold way. On the one hand, the concepts of personal and collective identity have become a central element of social theorising, and at the same time a prominent topic of empirical research in the social sciences in a way that, as has been shown, has created new tensions between theorising and research. On the other hand, and partly as a consequence of those tensions, the linguistic constitution of categories and modes of thinking in the social sciences becomes problematic itself, not least the postulate of identity.

The 'deconstruction' of the logic of identity, elaborated in part through observation of the 'discourse of the human sciences' (Derrida, 1978), provides opportunities for critical reflection about social-scientific modes of thinking. This approach has nevertheless only experienced a very reluctant and selective reception in the social sciences yet, more than three decades after the announcement of 'the linguistic turn.' On the one hand, one may well assume that more attention is now devoted to ruptures and inconsistencies in personal 'identities' as well as to asymmetric relations between collective 'identities.' A shift in perception has occurred that becomes visible in the presentation of empirical research. On the other hand, the discourse on difference keeps presenting a problem for the philosophy of the social sciences, the full consequences of which have been little recognised or accepted. Sometimes one even gets the impression that the significance is perceived but repressed and denied at the same time.[6]

Such reluctance—a term that may here be a euphemism—has significant reasons. To take deconstruction seriously would require critical reflection on some basic presuppositions in the theory and methodology of the social sciences. The discussions about identity can serve as an example to demonstrate in

which directions such questioning would have to go. Such demonstration may then also show that the refusal of such a debate is a means to preserve the identity of the modernist social sciences and can possibly itself be interpreted as an 'escape from freedom.' A first step into the direction of such a demonstration is an exploration of the antinomies that are generated by the discourses on identity but can finally not be handled by the established means of the social sciences.

3. Antinomies of Identity

Identity as choice or as destiny

The discussion about identity reproduces the sociological distinction between ascribed and acquired features of the human being and thus also the utterly problematic boundary between the traditional and the modern. Modern human beings allegedly choose actively their personal identities, whereas their traditional predecessors do not even know the *problématique* of identity-formation since they are socially determined. A similar distinction is coined in the discussion about collective identity. Social formations that are characterised by commonality of 'natural' markers of community, such as skin colour or sex, can be distinguished on a modernity scale from others that have been created and are constantly recreated by choice, such as the (political) nation as a daily plebiscite, as Ernest Renan said.

Such distinctions have disappeared neither from social-science discourse nor from political debate. And indeed they refer to an existing *problématique*. At the same time, however, they formulate this *problématique* in such a way that a conceptual dichotomy is constructed that can not be dissolved again by empirical findings of whatever kind. This situation becomes visible as soon as one takes an interactionist position on the constitution of identity, which at first sight looks as a middle ground connecting the other two views, but which indeed opens up broader perspectives. If the understanding of oneself, or of the group to which one feels belonging, is created by turning those images back towards oneself that others provide, then the very question of the ascribed or acquired character of identity becomes mute. Identity cannot be formed without those images; thus it is always the result of social processes. At the same time, it does not emerge without relating to those images whose mere existence is without any significance.

Once formulated, this view seems almost banal. Taken seriously, however, it should allow one to cast some of the empirical questions about identity as well as some political implications of the debate in wider terms. For instance, the answer to the question whether 'natural' characteristics of a person become criteria for this person's identity, i.e. whether these characteristics will be seen as giving significant orientations to one's life, would need to be considered as entirely open. Similarly, there will be no general

way to indicate criteria for the creation of collective identities. The native language or spatial proximity may become relevant for a sense of belonging. If this occurs, however, this will always be a consequence of the experience of the views of others, never by either isolated choice or by predetermination. The mutual constitution of national identities between French and Germans, for instance, has recently been investigated through historical analyses of interactions and exchange, in particular during the eighteenth and nineteenth centuries (Espagne and Werner, 1988; on institutional co-constitution Zimmermann et al., 1999).

Thus, such critical position towards any presupposition about fixed forms or contents of personal and collective identity does not rob itself of the possibility to study the formation of identities in historical and empirical terms. In contrast, such a position brings to light a question that has always been in the background of the discussion about identity, but which has remained largely hidden. This is the question about the human capacity to act. It is about agentiality.

When identity is predominantly related to meaning, the concept always carries the function of guiding action and that, by implication, also means constraining action. Identity then signals the interiorisation of norms or—less strictly—the appropriation of patterns of meaning as a necessary resource and condition for action. The modernist discourse about identity, in contrast, conceptualised the human being as autonomous towards others. Identity, as the perception of the continuity and coherence of one's own person, then becomes a precondition for the capacity to act.

Analogously, collectivities create their existence 'for themselves' through their identity and thus turn into collective subjects and actors. This latter variant of the modernist discourse was a key element of nineteenth- and early twentieth-century debates, but finds only little attention today. Thus, the parallelism between the modernist constructions of personal identity, on the one hand, and collective identity, on the other, are easily overlooked. In some versions of the discourse on difference the illusionary character of this modernist view is emphasised. The elevation of the individual (or the collectivity) from its context is regarded as a discursive construction rather than a description of reality. The theorem of the decentring of the subject consequently leads to the loss of the capacity to act in these discourses.

Summarising the three discourses on identity in such a way, the question—raised at the beginning but then postponed—of the identity of 'identity' reemerges with greater urgency. Does 'identity' refer in these discourses to anything other than the human capacity to act? Or is the concept a stand-in for the position on this point and changes meaning in relation to the discourse of which it is made a part? The conjecture that 'identity' serves as a sign for the question about the (individual or collective) capacity of human beings to act provides the first element in our attempt to position the concept of identity in the social sciences.

Identity as autonomy or as domination

This aspect is most strongly—and affirmatively—emphasised in the modernity-centred discourse about identity. If agentiality is understood in a strong sense as the capacity to give oneself one's own laws, then continuity and coherence, i.e. identity, of the person must be presupposed. The emphasis on this capacity—capacity to autonomy—is at the same time a basic ingredient of the discourse of modernity in philosophy and political theory. Sociohistorical studies of modernity mostly do not step outside such foundations either. At best, they become investigations into the social conditions for identity formation that focus on the diffusion of the precise idea that laws of human life are not externally determined but given by the human beings themselves.

To presuppose autonomy entails the additional assumption of the capacity of human beings, in principle, to separate from the context of socialisation in which identity-formation occurs. Neither internal ('psychical') nor external ('sociohistorical') conditions determine human action entirely (see Castoriadis, e.g., 1991:143-6). A 'modern' understanding of identity, which is oriented towards agentiality, cannot assume any strong 'embeddedness' of individuals in psychical or social contexts. Action in the 'modern' sense would otherwise be unthinkable.

The modernity-centred discourse, however, cannot provide itself the means to safeguard its own validity. The occurrence of 'autonomy' cannot be empirically determined since it can never be excluded that the entirety of contextual factors—could they only be integrated into the analysis—would explain specific human 'actions.' The discourse remains inevitably exposed to the—different—criticisms that emerge from the meaning-centred and the difference-centred discourse. As a consequence, the contours of modern identity get blurred again; it fades into its 'context.'

Furthermore, the 'modern' approach to identity casts a peculiar light onto this 'context' in which the acting human being operates. In a sense, this 'context' is only created by the assumption that an actor, gaining his identity, separates from his environment and then in turn acts upon this environment. The other two discourses aim to counteract the modernity-centred discourse also in this regard. Theories of difference, in particular, underline the will to dominate and the exclusion of otherness from the realm of modernity effected through this operation. Over the past three decades, numerous analyses have gradually created an image of the process through which the identity of modernity was constructed by emphasising differences. 'Modern man' aimed at distancing himself from a variety of forms of alterity—nature, wildness and tradition outside of his own social world, and the lower, dangerous classes, women and the mad inside of it.

In such critical perspective on the emergence of the concept of identity in modernity, relations of domination become visible. The proclaimed conquest of autonomy is then seen as possible only through the marking of (asymmetric)

differences and thus through boundary-setting and the exclusion of the other. That is why postcolonialist, feminist, and other discussions that emphasise relations of domination underline the creation of difference. Initially, the orientation was often towards the construction of counter-identities, but more recently the fundamental *problématique* of the inescapable connection between identity and difference has moved into the centre of concern. Identity-formation is inevitably creating difference. But without any conceptualisation of self and other or self and context, the *problématiques* that are discussed in the modernity-centred discourse under terms such as 'action' and 'freedom' would not be thematisable at all.

Thus, the exploration of the relation of identity and difference under the aspect of autonomy and domination leads to a second element in our attempt at locating the concept of identity in the social sciences. 'Identity' here appears as a discursive sign for the possibility of distancing from a context, and of the separation from the other.

Identity as construction or as reality

Both of the preceding aspects of the discussion about identity refer to a third aspect, the question about the reality of identity. If identity is experienced as fate, then it is seen as part of an objective reality. If identity is conceived of as chosen, then it is just one of several possibilities and as such not (yet) real. If the term identity is taken to express human autonomy, then it is real. If that very discourse of identity as autonomy is conceived itself as constructed, so as to allow for autonomy of the self and for domination over others, then identity is a project and not part of a given world.

At this point, it becomes evident that the social-scientific concept of identity needs to add something to the philosophical understanding of the term (at least outside of modal logic), if the concept is to be maintained at all. There is a close connection to a concept of identity as sameness only in one of the above formulae: If identity is fate, then a singular human being or a group are, and will, remain identical to themselves by virtue of social determinations. Such a narrow social determinism, however, is rarely upheld at all. All other conceptualisations contain the idea that identity needs to refer to the imagination of the sameness of one 'thing' with another one, rather than sameness itself, in the social sciences. The formation of identity has then, always, aspects of a project, guided by orientations and even by theories (Berzinsky, 1988). And the safeguarding of identity entails steady work at the maintenance of continuity and coherence or, in other words, at the interpretation of one's own life, or of the one of the group as a continuous and coherent one. Each identity contains always at least an element of construction. The strong condition that Wittgenstein formulated for identity to exist can then be relaxed. At the same time, however, the openness and ambivalence that are thus admitted need to be fully accepted.

Such acceptance requires, first of all, the insight that the question whether a particular identity is imagined or real can never be fully answered empirically. In each individual life there is a minimum of continuity, most basically of bodily existence, and there are always discontinuities. To pose the question of identity means to consider whether particular changes can be seen within a framework of continuity or as a rupture. A conversion, for instance, may mean for one person a conclusive reinterpretation of her or his own—and 'same'—religiosity and spirituality, for someone else, however, a break with the entire preceding life and identity. Something analogous holds for collective identities. Any observation of 'objective' commonalities between people, were it then possible, would not permit any conclusions about those people's sense of belonging together.

These reflections relate the argument to the discussion about epistemic certainty in the social sciences (see Wagner 2001, ch. 1). There is an inclination in the social sciences to overemphasise both the existence and the coherence of social phenomena, since this is demanded to meet the requirements for epistemic certainty to be obtained. The concept 'identity' has a central role in such an endeavour (and its recent rise to prominence may reflect some awareness of the endeavour being at risk). 'Identity' may often serve less to characterise observable social phenomena, but rather towards providing an interpretation of those phenomena that privileges their persistence and durability over their transience and volatility. 'Identity'—and this is the third element in our effort at determining its location—is thus a sign for the stability of the world and indirectly also for the certainty and reliability of our knowledge about it.

4. Identity and Beyond

Tendencies towards the decomposition of the concept

Reviewing the course of those identity-related discussions in the social sciences over time, a rather clear direction is visible for all three of its aspects. The debate has led from an emphasis on the pregiven, fate-like character of identity towards the possibility of choice; from placing the accent on the objective reality of identity to its constructed nature; and from underlining the acquisition of autonomy as a result of identity-formation to an emphasis on aspects of domination. In all cases, however, some contributions—like this one—do not conclude from the course of both the research and the theoretical debate on the need for shifting the concept into a specific direction, but rather call for dissolving the antinomies. If the shifts in the discussions indeed, as I aimed to demonstrate, expose the concept of identity to a tension that it is unlikely to be able to sustain, does this require that one abandon the concept entirely?

It would not be fruitful to reject studies of identity in the social sciences merely by demonstrating that the explicated understanding of the phenomenon is ridden with contradictions. There is 'something' that is being investigated

even if this phenomenon could not be called 'identity' in any philosophical sense nor even in the understanding of many common definitions in the social sciences. Many people have or develop during their socialisation a sense for the continuity of their person and the connections across their life-story. And many people are able to say to which group or groups they see themselves belonging, what they have in common with other members of that group and what distinguishes their group from other groups. 'Personal identity' and 'collective identity' do occur.

Furthermore, the existing studies do show—despite all objections one may have in conceptual and empirical detail—that that which is referred to as identity can be analysed by empirical sociological means. The findings lead neither to anthropological constants nor to any sharp dividing line between modernity and nonmodernity, but to a variety of possible forms of 'identity.' Identities can be more stable or more changeable, perceived rather as given or as chosen, seen as rooted in a substantive self or oriented towards the realisation of a yet unknown self. Possibly one may even arrive at some propositions about the importance of different sociohistorical configurations for the emergence of specific orientations for people's lives.

But exactly because of this variety, such investigations in their sum also suggest that the concept of identity be cast in wider—and that possibly means: less modernist—terms. It will not be sufficient to define the intellectual space of the social sciences such that approaches that tend to raise issues in the philosophy of the social sciences themselves are taken to fall outside that space. This move, which can be observed, would be equivalent to narrowing the *problématique* and at the same time to denying relevance to many of the more recent findings of empirical research. In contrast, the recent theoretical and empirical attention to identity demands the work at conceptualisations beyond a more narrowly conceived social science and social theory.

With regard to the empirical reach of the concept, the question about the significant orientations in the lives of human beings needs to be uncoupled from any strong presupposition about continuity and coherence. The latter terms would otherwise have to be cast so enormously widely that they were emptied of their contents (when, for example, a radical break with former orientations in life is nevertheless considered in terms of continuity, because it is the 'same' person who performs this rupture). Or, vice versa, the assumption about continuity and coherence would constrain interpretation—in the sense, namely, that significant orientations that do not conform to the idea could not be conceived as parts of identity-formation. If abandoning the connotation with continuity and coherence suggests that the term 'identity' appears inappropriate when analysing the emergence and change of important orientations in human lives, then this conclusion may well be drawn.

More important than a change in terminology, however, is the question: why the analysis of individual and collective orientations in life, and their

social conditions, has been given the label 'identity' in the first place. The concept is borrowed from philosophical debates, but at the same time its former meaning and reach was not maintained but—without explicit discussion—considerably altered. The enigma in the debate about identity lies less in recent research findings but rather in the adoption and current defence of the term. We need to ask about the persistence of the concept in the light of its revealed conceptual insufficiencies.

To pursue this question, it may need repetition that there is a requirement of both an empirical and a philosophical opening in the discussion about identity. Empirical postmodernism is accompanied by a critique of social ontology. The idea of the identity of things with themselves is of central importance in the latter respect. In modernist thought, it is this idea that makes both social science and society possible. Summarising the three elements assembled over the preceding discussion, 'identity,' in both the senses of selfhood and collective identity, represents the capacity of human beings to act, their capacity for critique and the stability of the world. The continuity of selfhood that is implied in all three aspects allows the construction of the 'individual.' The third aspect in particular, but indirectly the former two as well, invites one to assume the possibility of similarly constructing a collective entity 'society.' The existence of this society has often been seen as necessary in both social theory and moral and political philosophy.

The observation that this formula cannot persist in any unquestioned way does not entail any 'end of the subject' or end of sociality or even the end of any intelligibility of the social world. Rather a question as old as philosophy itself has been returned to the agenda and directed to the social sciences: the question of a thoroughgoing deontologisation and deessentialisation of the philosophy of the social sciences. This question can be approached further by looking at the relation between the concepts of the social sciences and the temporality of those social phenomena the concepts are meant to characterise (for the following see also Friese and Wagner, 1999).

Identity and temporality

If propositions about identity as sameness appear either nonsensical or empty of substance at first sight, they gain meaning once one turns from a question of being to one of becoming. As I tried to show above, it is only an opening towards understanding identity at least partly as a project to be realised over time, that can justify the usage of the term in the social sciences at all.

The fundamental *problématique* of identity, both as selfhood and as collective identity, is revealed by considering its reference to time. A reminder of the basic definitions will suffice. The question about the continuity and coherence of a person refers to biography, to the life-course. The same question directed to a collectivity refers to the idea of a common history, a common experience. Identity is constitutively temporal. The implications of

such an observation can be illustrated by briefly discussing the example of collective identity.[7]

A conventional analysis of collective identity would demonstrate the existence of common orientations within a group of people in the present, and would conclude from this observation a cause for present commonality. A historical analysis could confirm the latter, and the collectivity would have been successfully established—as a 'culture' or a 'society.' Such a reasoning, however, would necessarily presuppose a considerable degree of historical constancy and causality or, in other words, it would repress temporality (see Friese, 1991, 1993; Game, 1991:21).

The recourse to common history must remain an insufficient explanation for the existence and solidity of collectively shared orders of belief already on grounds of the impossibility, strictly speaking, of any such 'common history.' Rather than any 'common history,' there is always a variety of experiences, each of which differs from any other. The conjuration of 'common history,' as in theories of national identity, is an operation that is always performed in the respective present—as a specific representation of the past with a view to the creation of commonalities. Such an operation may well 'work' in the sense that an idea of proximity and belonging is created between people in the present. Yet it is not the past in the form of 'common history' that produces this effect, but the present interaction between those who propose to see the past as something shared, and those who let themselves be convinced to accept such representation for their own orientation in the social world.

One may want to object that such a reading ignores the importance of history for sociological analysis and plays into the hands of a presentist empiricism the proponents of which have always doubted the accessibility of the past. Is it not the case that one risks developing an ideology and apology of a present without historical depth and thus also without any understanding of historical possibilities for action and social change (Jameson, 1991)? The intention here, in contrast, is not to reject historicity but rather to come to a more appropriate understanding of temporality and historicity. Such an approach requires to question the status of the present and to reflect about the modes of appropriating history. The social sciences have long assigned only a marginal significance to such reflections.

Most research in the social sciences falls into one of two categories both of which are equally helpless in the face of this issue. Either 'timeless' snapshots are taken of the social world, or history is invoked to deterministically explain the present. In the former case, empirical evidence—such as answers to interviews—are analysed synchronically as present facts without considering their historical constructedness and possibly only limited durability. This is true theoretical presentism, and it comes in characteristically modern guise. In the latter case, in contrast, researchers appropriate the past selectively to explain the present. The identification of continuities between past and present

is a methodological a priori in this procedure. Therefore, it becomes impossible to ascertain whether the coherence of the findings is a result of the selection or indeed the consequence of a causally effective connection between past and present actions (de Certeau, 1988; Friese, 1997).

It may appear that these reflections merely add more problems to social research and social theory and do not indicate any solutions. There is indeed no master approach to the epistemological implications of the temporality of the social world. What was argued in this chapter, however, is by far not the end of the debate. Starting out from identifying the assumption of the continuity of selfhood, both personal and collective, as crucial to current debates about identity, I have tried to demonstrate some basic problems with that assumption and to discern some reasons why it is nevertheless held. Having established the inescapability of a consideration of temporality in social theory, it is from such a consideration that a rethinking of identity should start out, rather from futile discussions about the modern or postmodern, constructed or determined character of identity.

Notes

1. Wittgenstein himself later arrived at the view that, while there may be little more to say about the concept of identity, the *problématiques* that are circumscribed by this term lend themselves indeed to further discussion. The question about criteria of identity is central to the *Philosophical Investigations*. There, however, Wittgenstein no longer provides answers, rather he acknowledges a fundamental problem. The so-called analytical and continental traditions in philosophy share—despite all differences—the insight into the centrality of this problem. To bring some of those reflections back into the social sciences is one of the objectives of this essay.

2. This would be the normal assumption. But major ruptures in later life can also be analysed under the aspect of the attempt of maintaining one's identity or as a crisis of identity in analogy to the equally crisis-prone first formation of identity during adolescence. Migration into a different cultural context or the growing consciousness of a minority position in one's own society, for instance, may fundamentally shatter existing orientations and lead to identity crises.

3. See Cohen, 1994. Furthermore, the concept of personal identity can be connected to role and status; thus, a linkage to societal analysis would be created—such as in some anthropological theories and in Parsons-inspired sociology.

4. This is an observation Anthony Giddens quite rightly makes in the methodological conclusion of his *Constitution of Society* (1984). In his own later work, however, he seems to have reinterpreted such legitimate bracketing as a licence to avoid awkward conceptual and theoretical problems—with the result that the research programme that is entailed in *Constitution of Society* has thus far not been pursued further.

5. Cavell adds that there is a 'companion concept of society' which goes analogously with 'partial compliance with its principles of justice.' This remark could be used analogously for a discussion of collective identity in relation to moral and political philosophy.
6. It is not the ambition of this chapter to continue the debate over deconstruction. That debate keeps being led with fervour and more competence in philosophy. The significance of deconstruction can rather easily be demonstrated even in analytical language (see Wood, 1990).
7. An analogous discussion of temporality for the question of personal identity would have to consider in addition the status of the 'subject,' a subject that, in modernist perspective, functions as the speaker for identity who guarantees sameness over time and becomes both subject and object of continuity and coherence.

References

Arendt, Hannah (1958²) *The Origins of Totalitarianism*, Cleveland.

Arendt, Hannah (1978) *The Life of the Mind, Vol. 1: Thinking,* New York.

Berman, Marshall (1982) *All that is Solid melts into Air. The Experience of Modernity,* New York.

Berzinsky, Michael D. (1988) 'Self-theorists, identity status, and social cognition', in Daniel K. Lapsley, and F. Clark Power (eds), *Self, Ego, and Identity. Integrative Approaches*, New York, pp. 243-62.

Castoriadis, Cornelius (1991) 'Power, politics, autonomy', in *Philosophy, Politics, Autonomy: Essays in Political Philosophy*, Oxford, pp. 143-74.

Cavell, Stanley (1990) *Conditions Handsome and Unhandsome,* Chicago.

Cavell, Stanley (1989) *The New Yet Unapproachable America. Lectures after Emerson after Wittgenstein*, Albuquerque.

Cohen, Anthony P. (1994) *Self-consciousness. An Alternative Anthropology of Identity*, London.

Critchley, Simon (1998) 'The other's decision in me', *European Journal of Social Theory*, 1, 2:259-79.

de Certeau, Michel (1988) *The Writing of History*, New York.

Derrida, Jacques (1978) 'Structure, sign and play in the discourse of the human sciences', in *Writing and Difference* (trans. Alan Bass), London, pp. 280-93 (orig. *L'écriture et la différence*, 1967, Paris).

Erikson, Erik H. (1968) 'Identity, psychosocial', *International Encyclopedia of the Social Sciences*, Vol. 7, London/New York.

Espagne, Michel, and Michael Werner (1988) *Transferts: les relations interculturelles dans l'espace franco-allemand, XVIIIe et XIXe siècle*, Paris.

Foucault, Michel (1984) 'What is Enlightenment?' in *The Foucault Reader* (ed. Paul Rabinow), London, pp. 32-50.

Friese, Heidrun (1991) *Ordnungen der Zeit. Zur sozialen Konstitution von Temporalstrukturen in einem sizilianischen Ort*. Ph.D. thesis University of Amsterdam.

Friese, Heidrun (1993) ' Die Konstruktion von Zeit: Zum prekären Verhältnis von akademischer "Theorie" und lokaler Praxis,' *Zeitschrift für Soziologie*, 22, 5:323-37.

Friese, Heidrun (1997) 'Bilder der Geschichte', in Jörn Rüsen and Klaus Müller (eds), *Historische Sinnbildung. Sinnprobleme und Zeitstrukturen*, Reinbek pp. 328-52.

Friese, Heidrun, and Peter Wagner (1999) 'Modernity and contingency. Not all that is solid melts into air. But what does and what does not?', in Mike Featherstone and Scott Lash (eds), *Spaces of Identity. City—Nation—World*, London, pp. 101-15.

Fromm, Erich (1941) *Escape from Freedom*, New York.

Gallie, W.B. (1955-6) 'Essentially contested concepts', *Proceedings of the Aristotelian Society*, 56:167-98.

Game, Ann (1991) *Undoing the Social. Towards a Deconstructive Sociology*, Milton Keynes.

Giddens, Anthony (1984) *The Constitution of Society*, Cambridge.

Giddens, Anthony (1990) *The Consequences of Modernity*, Cambridge.

Giddens, Anthony (1991) *Modernity and Self-Identity*, Cambridge.

Griswold, Wendy (1994) *Cultures and Societies in a Changing World*, Thousand Oaks.

Hannerz, Ulf (1992) *Cultural Complexity*, New York.

Hollis, Martin (1985) 'Of masks and men', in Michael Carrithers, Steven Collins and Steven Lukes (eds) *The Category of the Person: Anthropology, Philosophy, History*, Cambridge.

Jameson, Fredric (1991) *Postmodernism, or The Cultural Logic of Late Capitalism*, Durham, N.C.

Joas, Hans (1996) *The Creativity of Action*, Cambridge.

Joas, Hans (1998) 'The autonomy of the self. The Meadian heritage and its postmodern challenge', *European Journal of Social Theory*, 1, 1:7-18.

Kellner, Douglas (1992) 'Popular culture and the construction of postmodern identities' in Scott Lash and Jonathan Friedman (eds), *Modernity and Identity*, Oxford.

Kellner, Douglas (1995) *Media Culture, Cultural Studies, Identity and Politics between the Modern and the Postmodern*, London.

Lamont, Michèle (1992) *Money, Morals and Manners. The Culture of the French and American Upper-Middle Class*, Chicago.

Lapsley, Daniel K. and F. Clark Power (eds), (1988) *Self, Ego, and Identity. Integrative Approaches*, New York.

Lash, Scott and Jonathan Friedman (eds), (1992) *Modernity and Identity*, Oxford.

Lash, Scott (1994) 'Expert systems or situated interpretation? Culture and institutions in disorganized capitalism', in Ulrich Beck, Anthony Giddens and Scott Lash, *Reflexive Modernization*, Cambridge.

Morley, David and Kevin Robbins (1995) *Spaces of Identity. Global Media, Electronic Landscapes, and Cultural Boundaries*, London.

Sahlins, Marshall (2000) '"Sentimental pessimism" and ethnographic experience, or, Why culture is not a disappearing "object"', in Lorraine Daston (ed.), *Biographies of Scientific Objects,* Chicago.

Slygoski, B.R. and Ginsburg G.P. (1989) 'Ego identity and explanatory speech', in John Shotter and Kenneth J. Gergen (eds), *Texts of Identity*, London, pp. 36-9.

Smelser, Neil (1997) *Problematics of Sociology*, Berkeley.

Taylor, Charles (1989) *Sources of the Self*, Cambridge/Mass.

Wagner, Peter (1994) *A Sociology of Modernity. Liberty and Discipline*, London.

Wagner, Peter (1998) 'Certainty and order, liberty and contingency; the birth of social science as empirical political philosophy', in Johan Heilbron, Lars Magnusson and Björn Wittrock (eds) *The Rise of the Social Sciences and the Formation of Modernity*, Dordrecht, pp. 241-63.

Wagner, Peter (2001) *Theorising of Modernity. Inescapability and Attainability in Social Theory*, London.

Weir, Allison (1996) *Sacrificial Logics. Feminist Theory and the Critique of Identity*. New York.

Wittgenstein, Ludwig (1984a) *Tractatus logicus-philosophicus*, in Werkausgabe, Vol. 1, Frankfurt/M.

Wittgenstein, Ludwig (1984b), 'Philosophische Untersuchungen' in *Tractatus logico-philosophicus*, Werkausgabe, Vol. 1, Frankfurt/M.

Wood, David (1990) *Philosophy at the Limit*, London.

Zimmermann, Bénédicte, Claude Didry and Peter Wagner (eds), (1999) *Le travail et la nation. Histoire croisée de la France et de l'Allemagne*, Paris.

Personal and Collective Identity
A Conceptual Analysis

JÜRGEN STRAUB

1. Conceptual Notes and Points of Departure

'Identity' has been among the most central concepts in 20th century psychology and sociology. It acquired its significance, which has persisted in all essentials until today, particularly in the context of pragmatist, interactionist and psychoanalytical thought,—even if the term played no role in the work of either Sigmund Freud or William James, but rather only in subsequent attempts to develop their theories of the subject and the self (Straub, 1991, 1994). Of course the remarkable career of 'identity' is due especially to certain works that were still close to the sources of psychoanalysis and pragmatism, even if they were already diverging fundamentally from the teachings of their founding fathers. The decisive influence regarding identity was exercised by the work of Erik H. Erikson. Identity stood at the centre of his *psychoanalytic ego psychology* (see Erikson, 1959a, 1959b). Erikson soon distanced himself from the earlier usage of the term 'ego identity,' which had signalled his affiliation to this special variant of psychoanalytic theory. For theoretical reasons having to do with the relation between 'ego' and 'self' in Hartmann's influential blueprint for a psychoanalytical ego psychology (Henrich, 1979), Erikson afterward spoke simply of 'identity.' He often preceded this term with the adjective *psychosocial*, and his various studies on the relation between identity, biography and historical moment, which not least make him one of the pioneers of psychohistory, demonstrate that his psychological concept of identity is reflected not only *socially*, but also *historically* (see Erikson, 1958, 1974, 1975a).

In a 1970 retrospective on the context of the development of the concept of identity, Erikson attested that this new term had quickly 'secured itself a

Notes for this section begin on page 73.

place of familiarity in the thinking or, at any rate, the vocabulary of a wide range of readers in a number of countries—not to speak of its appearance in cartoons which reflect what is intellectually modish' (Erikson, 1975b:17). He attempts to clarify the *motivational* roots of his conceptual innovation against an autobiographical background. Clearly he had initially used this term to thematise *personal experience*, and to especially generalise the *experience of crisis*. I will return to this point in the next section.

Even this brief suggestion, that the concept of identity that is of interest here would be indefinable without reference to psychological crises, shows that Erikson's concept is primarily *personal, developmental,* and *clinical*. We know that Erikson, the psychoanalyst, made no special effort to define the concept more precisely. Occasionally, he would provide other definitions, sometimes, also, more or less consistent characterisations of 'identity' and 'identity crisis.' So there are common definitional formulations that in my view can be considered definitive—despite a diversity of theoretical approaches—and authoritative. These formal characterisations all tend to conceive (personal) 'identity' as that unity and self-evidence of a person that derives from the active cognitive acts of synthesis and integration, by which persons try to ascertain the continuity and coherence of their life praxis. The assumption here is that continuity and coherence can be constructed in light of diachronic and synchronic experiences of difference, indeed that it is such experiences that bring about these acts of integration. I will also discuss this definition in more detail in the second section.[1]

Erikson's role in popularising the concept of identity can hardly be overestimated. His definition is still fundamentally useful now, in my view irrespective of the many criticisms that have been raised against it, especially in the last few years.[2]

A second line of thought is equally fundamental for the psychological and sociological evolution of the concept of identity, namely the symbolic interactionism of Anselm Strauss and above all Erving Goffmann, who both, insofar as they show affinities with George H. Mead's approach, extend the pragmatist legacy (see Strauss, 1959; Goffmann, 1961, 1963). Of course these writers, as well as others, were attempting, not least, to compensate for a deficit in (American) sociological and social-psychological role theory, which had more or less forgotten that subjects can think and act independently and creatively. The disappearance of the subject in role theory was also a target of those approaches that built on the critical reception of psychoanalytical as well as sociopsychological and psychological identity theories, and—up to the present—propose more or less integrative definitions of the concept of identity. We should mention Krappmann's sociological concept of 'balanced' identity, or the work of Döbert, Habermas, and Nunner-Winkler, who might be assembled, all most aptly, under the aegis of 'communicatively fluid' identity (see Krappmann, 1969; Habermas, 1976a:63–91; 1976b:92–126; Döbert, Habermas and Nunner-Winkler, 1977).

In any case, I do not intend to further describe the career of this interesting concept.[3] However, a few additional clarifications of three particular problems seem in order, which extend through the entire terminological history of, and every debate about, identity theory, and still define or burden the present discussion:

(a) Psychoanalysis, as well as sociology and social psychology, from the outset confused questions of the constitution and structure of personal *identity* with questions of the constitution and structure of personal *individuality*, with little improvement since. These different problem areas have been allowed to overlap to an extraordinarily confusing extent (see Straub, 1991:54). The theory of identity advanced here assumes that 'identity' and 'individuality' stand for two objectively and absolutely different aspects of a theory of human subjectivity. One may consider oneself an irreplaceable individual and yet still have identity problems, and one may consider oneself self-identical, and act independently, yet also appear to oneself to be indistinguishable from others. The predicates of identity do not converge with predicates of individuality. Decades ago Henrich and Tugendhat already called attention to the nebulosity of theories that did not pay attention to this distinction.[4]

We will observe this distinction below by speaking only of identity, but not of the uniqueness of individuals (or collectives), nor of the (culturally specific) *wish* for individuality, nor of the psychological problems that arise when the fulfillment of this wish is denied to a significant number of 'individuals.' It is historically and theoretically less plausible to claim that identity depends on individuality (or vice versa) than to conceive each as the *counterpart* of the other. From this perspective, what is individual appears as what is fundamentally not identifiable, and what can also not be integrated into personal identity. Rather, the individual can be understood as an 'instance' that is not totally assimilable into any system, any structure of rational knowledge, any language, any grammar, any sign system, any hermeneutics, in other words is never completely mediated and can never be completely communicated: *individuum est ineffabile*.[5] Whether or not one likes the Romantic effusions in which the emphatic idea of individuality is like a *basso continuo*: Rudolph's distinction between individuality and identity could hardly be drawn more sharply, nor, for our purposes more usefully. It demonstrates that individuality lacks precisely what is constitutive of identity: unity, continuity, coherence and the self-referentiality of thought and action that underlies it all, through which a person's actions or inactions first attain that transparence that an individual basically never has nor can have not for itself and not for others, insofar as an individual's every act is unique, something unforeseen and unforeseeable, unprecedented and unrepeatable.

(b) The following reflections refuse the simple choice between 'identity' and 'lack of identity.' An empirically more valid, theoretically more appropriate and

finally more persuasive conception of identity from a normative perspective than the currently fashionable and morally coded duality 'identity vs. the non-identical' would be one that attempts 'to still preserve subjectivity as a critical category for understanding interpersonal praxis, without falling victim to fantasies of omnipotence' (Meyer-Drawe, 1990:152). Only thus can the idea of an at least partly autonomous life conduct, inseparable from the concept of identity, be preserved as a regulative ideal, without supporting the rhetoric of 'sovereign lords,' whose ego-strength is only a defence against the nonidentical. And only thus can this idea further provide a standard for criticising social practices that more and more seem determined by autonomous structures, through structures and processes that, ever more completely and yet ever more subtly, make the (supposedly) autonomous subject of the Enlightenment a mere *subjectus*, in the sense of a subordinate and heteronomously determined being. Whoever has abandoned the illusion and the grandiose fantasy of a subject regally constituting its world and itself (and for good reason) need not still take refuge in 'postmodern disillusionment.' Postmodern theoreticians are as often led to exaggerations and distortions as the apologists for the modern subject, whom they criticise, suffer from a doubtless excessive belief in a 'strong subject.' The frequent conclusion that we should simply throw the concept of identity onto the junk heap, and assume that human beings incorporate the nonidentical and nothing else, that the modern subject's striving for identity and similar self-idealisations are mere illusions that ultimately facilitate only inward and outward violence—the present study does not accept this proposal.[6]

The concept of identity that we aim to develop is not concerned with making an 'all or nothing' decision. Autonomy and heteronomy are a dichotomy that, with respect to praxis, and to the personal identity that always orients action, provides always only *accentuating* distinctions. Ultimately the relationship between autonomy and heteronomy can be differently weighed, but one can never have one *or* the other: 'We know that human existence is not only autonomous, nor only heteronomous, and this view is useful to us without necessitating a conclusive determination as to what this existence positively is' (Meyer-Drawe, 1990:11).[7]

The concept of identity in psychological and sociological theories of the subject includes the idea of limited autonomy. As a fragile balance between the different demands of the (material, social, cultural) environment, it is even an essential 'requirement for autonomous action' (Meyer-Drawe, 1990:21) however much penetrated and intersected by heteronomy. The concept of identity draws attention precisely to the latter, showing as it does the unassailable limits and dangers to the construction and maintenance of identity and autonomy of action. Identity is limited, provisional, fragile, and it is all of these things unavoidably.

(c) The concept of identity advanced here is understood as a reflexive concept in the sense of theories of the subject, and accounts for radical differences

from 'traditional,' 'premodern,' or simply 'other' ways in which persons may relate to themselves and their world. If we want to operate with the distinction between modern and premodern identity, we must keep in mind that these two possible ways to relate to the self and the world have to do with two different forms of subjectivity (even if they can be placed into a developmental sequence, which of course is not always easily accomplished). The present study will, in any case, be concerned with one kind of self- and world-relationship, namely that which, as Giddens (1991) has shown, becomes possible only under *circumstances of modernity.*

After the necessary clarifications, in terms of the theory of the subject, of a concept of identity based on specifically modern experiences of contingency, difference, and alterity, the final section will turn briefly to the concept of *collective* identity. Obviously this term is a transposition by analogy of a concept originally adapted to the structure of individual persons' relation to self and world. It is quite evident that this transposition is anything but unproblematic.

2. Personal Identity

Although none of Erikson's writings, as we have already noted, ever provides an unequivocal definition of identity, certain core elements of such a definition are apparent. Among them is the idea that the concept of identity is inevitably connected with a specific *experience of crisis* and its psychological *processing* by the subject of the crisis. When he speaks of identity and identity crises, Erikson is thinking primarily of an experience of destabilization that he regards as normal and characteristic for a certain life period. He describes this experience as *calling into question the orientations* that had given stability and direction to the *actions and the life* of the child or youth. The concept of identity is unavoidably bound up with description of a *crisis of adolescence*, which Erikson had experienced himself and later diagnosed in many young people as the more acute problem of the times.

Erikson considered the experience of crisis, which had already been the focus of his attention as a young adult and whose clinical description and analysis required him to create new terminology, an anthropological phenomenon that occurs in every human being (as we will see, this position is untenable). At the same time, however, Erikson, the psychoanalyst, advances the view that this phenomenon emerged with particular clarity and acuteness in the time and culture to which he belonged, and thus only now attracted such general notice. In Erikson's view, the role that hysteria had played in Freud's time is now, in the second half of the 20th century, assumed *by crises of identity*. Such crises were to Erikson the psychological signature of the epoch, as a psychological manifestation of incipiently epidemic proportions (see Erikson, 1975b, cf. Erikson, 1950).

Of course one can argue about the 'historical moment' in which the symptoms of this acute crisis of development began to become an epidemic syndrome. The *fin de siècle* was richly endowed with 'nervous crises', whose avid descriptions (by essayists, writers, and the 'medical scientists' who were becoming ever more responsible for our common good) resembled Erikson's 'identity crises' to a high degree. Of course, a different point is more important in the present context. This has become particularly evident recently, as Erikson's theory, in my view, has been referred to in order to go beyond it, and in its details has been adapted to the changed circumstances of life in 'late modern' society.

The identity crisis for Erikson is first and foremost an adolescent crisis, yet it is not restricted to this phase of life. In fact its extent is theoretically unlimited. Every youth and every adult is basically always in danger—it suffices for particular psychosocial conditions to converge and disturb the ground of the formation or maintenance of personal identity. Someone who virtually never feels *terra firma* underfoot suffers a chronic crisis, an identity diffusion that Erikson regards as pathological, and which he describes by means of numerous examples from his practice (see Erikson, 1959b).

It is these clinical descriptions of conditions of temporary or persistent identity diffusion that indirectly demarcate the 'positive' horizon of successful identity formation. It is the difficulties and unhappiness typical of individual persons who lack identity that reveal the basic meaning of this term. Whoever is (presently) able to find an orientation in physical, social and moral space, whoever suffers from a diffusion of the physical, biographical, historical sense of time and can therefore no longer act independently; whoever has lost the ability to perform those (sometimes unconscious) 'acts' that create a sense and a consciousness of being the same, identical person despite different circumstances, experiences, and activities, is suffering that lack that Erikson designated an identity crisis. Whoever was never able to learn or has lost the ability to react creatively to such crises, whoever is deprived by other persons or by circumstances of chance to develop this competence, will suffer from a loss of identity. R. D. Laing once spoke in this context of ontological insecurity (1960:39). Ontologically insecure persons have lost the foundations of their being. They suffer symptoms such as a fear of engulfment, feelings of implosion, petrifaction, and depersonalisation, a 'disembodied self,' a temporal and spatial diffusion.

We need to consider the psychological and sociological concept of identity in terms of this phenomenologically rich depiction of a radical loss of identity to understand what Erikson and the philosophers and scientists with affinities to him are basically saying. The normative content of the concept of identity can in my view only be understood in this way. If we fail to consider this, we casually discard the preconditions for *any meaningful* philosophical or sociological discourse about identity. If we ignore it, we abandon, *nolens volens*, the

conditions under which a discussion of 'identity'—in spite of all the undeniable conceptual problems—could express something halfway definite.

Identity problems are *orientation problems*. They therefore require a kind of self-reflection and self-ascertainment through which someone can initially find a particular standpoint in physical-material and corporeal space, in social and moral space as well as in the temporal space of action, or gain (or regain) such a standpoint. Only someone who knows, at least to some extent, his location within the particular framework that defines the sociocultural and individual possibilities for meaningful orientations in action and life, in short: only someone able to *orient* himself can have the sense and the experience of being able to be more or less self-identical (see Straub, 1994/5:54–61, Taylor, 1989).

This point of view is, as one would expect, central to psychological or psychoanalytical approaches. Such researches analyse the preconditions and consequences of the experience described above, in order to specify, in the course of their observations, the theory of personal identity. Terms such as 'identity' or 'loss of identity,' as we have already suggested, thus have more than just clinical or psychopathological significance. They are hardly used only in psychology and psychoanalysis to describe individuals who, in their own words, are suffering massive dislocations of the kind described above. The normative idea that undeniably inheres in the concept of identity still applies at the (at any rate fluid and variable) border between the pathological and the 'normal.' With certain exceptions, modern (Western) psychology *generally* understands one's relationship to the world and to one's self in light of this normatively meaningful concept of identity.

Accordingly no (modern) subject is completely protected against identity diffusion. The loss of identity is a threat against which no one can be completely secure. Furthermore: whoever does not suffer from this kind of insufficiency has to *see to it* that it stays that way. Identity is not something one can possess once and for all, let alone be granted at birth. Theoretically, this term denotes certain features of the personal relationship to one's self which no one simply *has*, but which is everyone's *concern*. It seems an evident fact that 'we' all do so, as a rule. 'Identity work,' as this psychological activity is sometimes called, is entirely natural for us, however it might be socioculturally constituted; it is a culturally and socially specific mode of subjectivity formation, or in other words: it *provides* the self- and world-relation of persons with a specific structure or form. Identity in each case is always just a provisional result of psychological acts in which thought, emotion and volition are inseparably combined, and which for its part is socially constituted or mediated: 'Identity is a social phenomenon, i.e., "sociogenic"' (Assmann, 1992:130).

We need to keep in mind that it is sociocultural conditions of our actions and our lives that first 'create' identity as a specific *form* of subjectivity, that is, require it and at the same time bring it about (cf. Giddens, 1991). Only under the condition of modernity does identity in the sense used here become a prob-

lem, a task that individuals can hardly avoid. The central question in the theoretical discourse about identity of interest here, *what sort of a person one is and what sort of person one wants to be*, has indispensable practical preconditions. One presupposition, in its particular quality and increasing prevalence, is a specifically modern experience, an experience namely, which suggests *that identity is never established, and can never be ascertained once and for all*, that one never know for certain, who someone is, wants to be, could be. The question of identity around which all these theories circle is based on radicalised experiences of contingency, difference, and alterity, on the experience of reality as the temporalised and dynamised space of possibility in which radical *doubt* has become the kernel of a self-reflexive, self-critical thought (see Makropoulos, 1985:esp. 17–26).

The aforementioned kind of experience is the *sine qua non* of the theory of identity thematized here—from its beginnings until today. Theories of identity are, notwithstanding a misunderstanding that is quite common today, diametrically opposed to theories that would understand personal existence in society and culture as a substance, as something that in some way persists once and for all, or is fixed in a stable frame of reference. The concept of identity, and the concepts of *coherence* and *continuity* necessary to explain it, describe only the internal consistency and permanence of a *form* or a *structure*. They do not consider identity as something whose contents and quality could be determined in substance once and for all, or, in other words, as something that could or even should be insulated against change—as though change and becoming were a modern illness from which we must be healed.

Theories of identity do not defend the substantively determinable being of this or that person against contingency and transformations, difference and alterity. Differences and difference now come to our attention continuously, synchronically in representations of the world as well as (diachronically) in representations of both the past and the future. They can appear to those trying to understand what they see around them, what came before them and might come after them, as an opportunity or as a threat, as inspiration or irritation. Differences and divergences from the self are experienced not least as the potential for change in one's relationship to one's self and to the world, in a welcome or unwelcome sense. Theories of identity as they interest us here give no answer as to whether there should or should not be change. Rather, they are trying to conceptualise how, in terms of the theory of the subject, a phenomenologically rich philosophy might look that could 'account for' contingency, difference, and alterity. This means, however, that theories of identity must describe how subjects *could be theorised* so that it remains comprehensible and plausible that they persist as persons capable of *communication, action, and interaction*, when inconstancy and unpredictability are obviously the constituents of human praxis and—in contrast to earlier times and ways of life—are the permanent accompaniment and challenge of life in the modern

world. This identity-theoretical discourse has as little to do with the search for a jargon or experience of authenticity as with a dogmatic and totalitarian transformation of a single and eternal truth that is supposed to serve as the guiding principle of an eternally same conduct of individual and collective life. Identity theories in the psychology and sociology of (late) modernity are all based on the experience of an accelerated, dynamised time, the experience of one's own self, indeed of reality as such, as *a space of possibility*.

The concept of identity has historical and sociocultural preconditions that ground *and at the same time limit* its applicability and validity. The frequent universalisation of the concept of identity, at least in the form in which it is of interest here, is questionable. Given that not all human beings share the modern practices of biographical and historical self-thematisation, identity problems cannot be seen as an anthropological phenomenon. Erikson had already misunderstood the scope of the concept when he investigated 'young man Luther's' identity problems, for example. If we are to be terminologically consistent in our theoretical concept, Luther might have suffered in all kinds of ways, but certainly never under the psychosocial difficulties that we now give the modern designation 'identity problems.' Taylor is correct to write that Luther never suffered crises of meaning or identity as they became typical only for people in the modern, Western world: his 'crisis of faith' never shook precisely the 'meaning of life,' insofar as the 'meaning of life' was all too unquestionable for this Augustinian monk, as it was for his whole age (Taylor, 1989:18).[8] Luther was not concerned with the void or with the loss of orientation in a temporalised and dynamised world out of joint, but rather with radical transgressions against God, damnation, and irremediable exile. Numerous contemporary writers operated in the same way as Erikson. If we ascribe to everyone the same (formally defined) identity, along with identity problems 'as we know them,' then ethnographical naturalisations become unavoidable: one equates what is not equivalent, subsumes the other under the same, and misunderstands where understanding had been its objective.[9]

If we consider more closely what the 'psychological activity' of forming and maintaining personal identity might consist of, and attempt to describe it in *theoretical terms*, the following picture results. When one expresses what sort of person one is and would like to be, one provides qualitative descriptions and articulates ideas that contain 'strong evaluations' (Charles Taylor). In principle one can talk about almost any content in order to characterise one's identity. For personal identity in concrete cases, however, the relevant features of a one's relationship to self and world are those that are not just accidental for one's being, but fundamental. Thus one may characterise oneself as a devout Christian or upright Communist, as a committed scholar or devoted parent, and let one's actions be guided by this self-understanding. The qualitative concept of identity always relates to the framework or horizon that allows one a certain *conduct of one's life*, provides the choices one makes or does not make

with meaning and significance. Thus one's behaviour appears as *oriented action*, as action in accordance with principles and maxims. Only on this level are crises of orientation possible, but not where one is dealing with at best accidental characteristics of a person's mode of being.

Identity formation and maintenance is also concerned with constituting a person as a *unity*, entirely apart from such qualitative or substantive determinations. Only with respect to this activity does the concept of identity acquire theoretical status. Unity, self-sameness, self-evidence: these words mark the basic meaning of the term 'identity'—and nothing else. A more precise definition can be understood as an explanation and specification of these basic meanings, however. Such specifications are indispensable, since the generalisation often does not make clear what it could mean that a person forms a 'unity,' is 'identical to himself': *semper idem*. Two terms current in the debate come into play here. Unity should be conceived as the *coherence of moral and aesthetic systems of maxims*, which in the diachronical context of personal identity means primarily: as *biographical continuity*, thus also as continuity in one's *historical consciousness*, through which one locates oneself in the history of the collective reference relevant to one's identity. Staying the same person then means, in this case: remaining the same even when conditions, and even one's orientations, have, precisely, not remained the same. Identity as a specific *form* of subjectivity is acquired in transition, or in the psychological processing of transitions and transformations, not in static, repetitive situations (see Sommer, 1988).

These two formal terms (coherence, continuity) are concerned finally with the integration of that which is disparate (or that which is different from the subject) into a totally integrated and (measured by particular criteria) *consistent form*. Identity is a (synchronically and diachronically) ordered structure, a 'good *Gestalt*' in the classic terminology of *Gestalt* psychology. Identity as a structural or formal term is the result of a psychological activity of integration which can theoretically be conceived as the *synthesis of the heterogeneous*. Identity, in this theoretical and terminological sense—and every other sense is rather uninteresting for the human sciences—exists as the *unity of its differences*, as Leitner (1990) shows. Identity as a theoretical category—in pragmatism, in the theory of communicative action, and in other approaches—is essentially a *formal* concept. On the theoretical level we are not concerned with the qualitatively defining features of the identity of particular human beings, but with formal features of the specific relations persons have to themselves and to the world, i.e., with a historically and culturally specific form of subjectivity.

Someone who can sense and can express by symbolic means his existence and himself as a coherent and continuous unity from this perspective is, by such acts, not only forming and presenting his identity, but is restituting and stabilising *uno actu* the basis of his communicative, active, and interactive

social competence under modern circumstances of increased contingency, difference, and alterity. The formation of a personal relation to self and world that can meet the requirements of coherence and continuity serves the subject's *autonomy*. Identity is rightly considered the 'conceptual relative' of autonomy. Either term can hardly be adequately defined without the other.

We can therefore conclude that acts of identity-formation are essentially *retrospective*. Not only reflexive, conscious and preconscious synthetic acts of identity formation are retrospective, but also the unconscious process of 'ego synthesis' emphasised by psychology. The realisation that no one simply has an identity, but that identity must be created and maintained in the light of new experiences and expectations by means of restructuring, means not least that a person's identity is a *construct*. The search for identity will not turn up something that is already 'there,' simply hidden somewhere and waiting to be uncovered. Whoever succeeds in the 'search' for identity has made, through creative acts, what he sought. Identity is always just the provisional result of creative, constructive acts; one could even say: it is created for the moment. The medium and the means of expression for such acts are every possible verbal and other behaviour: from description and argumentation through the (very significant) narration of stories to the dreaming and shaping of objects, all need to be considered here.[10]

Identity presupposes the differentiation and maintenance of differences as much as the synthesis or integration of the different. The psychological and sociological theory of identity has to hold on to this insight in different ways. The formal definitions of the concept of identity indicated here suggest how mistaken it would be to connect the discourse about the theory of identity of interest here with a plea for the formation of psychological structures of coercion that would eliminate experiences of contingency, difference, and alterity, along with all plurality and ambiguity. On the contrary, one could even say that the theories of identity that concern us here assume without exception that the acceptance of the difference, diversity, uncontrollability and even ambiguity of our experience is a *necessary precondition* for forming and maintaining identity. On the basis of identity theory, one could even say with John S. Kafka, for example (against the hypothesis of the double bind theory) 'that it is intolerance of ambiguity [...] rather than paradoxical communication, than tends to be pathological' (Kafka, 1989:10). One can at least share Kafka's admiration for the positive, 'therapeutic' aspects of the tolerance for different aspects of reality (1989:31).

'Tolerance of ambiguity' is not in contradiction with, and does not offer a way to criticise the concept of identity (who would do so is perhaps thinking too much of aspects of the logical and epistemological concept of identity, and is ignoring the psychological and sociological concept, which has very little to do with it). Tolerating differences and ambiguities, recognising them as such, and being able to live with them is a necessary component of successful 'iden-

tity work.' All modern identity theories agree on this point; Krappmann's listing of the components, of which he assumes they are necessary for the formation and maintenance of 'balanced identity' offers an exemplary illustration. Of such abilities he writes: 'empathy, role distance, ambiguity tolerance, identity presentation, and verbal ability, which sustains these others' (Krappmann, 1969:210). The kind of psychology that is being advanced here also conceives identity in terms of such basal competences. Krappmann's list need not be taken as definitive. In any case, whatever conclusion we draw here, identity is a construct produced by the symbolically and socioculturally mediated, meaning-structured and meaning-creating *actions* of the person in question. As such a construct, it is permanently *endangered*. Restrictions on competences like those named above restrict personal identity. Dangers to these basic abilities undermine the indispensable foundations of identity. Traumas, for example, embody particularly massive dangers. Illness, too, can threaten a person's identity or the indicated basal competences, not just temporarily but permanently, and even radically destroy it. It should now be clear that all this must be kept in view when we speak of the advantages and disadvantages of identity today. We can remain firmly grounded in the knowledge that identity theories of the type sketched here have nothing to do with regressive invocations of a simple, transparent, and manageable life, or other 'anti-modern' impulses. They can at best 'respect' and 'defend' what is in any case a very fragile thing: a unity that does not offer unassailable certainties and security, but rather provides an orientation in an open and never completely apparent space of possibility, a physical, corporeal, social, moral and temporal space where persons simply must choose, and must act.

3. Collective Identity

Can the concept of identity as it has been developed with respect to personal self- and world-relationships and their symbolic and particularly verbal-reflexive formation through individual subjects be transposed onto collectives? Can collectives form, maintain, articulate, and reshape identities analogous to those of individuals? What does it even mean to speak of 'collective identity'? (see Cerutti, 1996; Giesen, 1991; Taylor, 1992).

The insight into the significance of collectives for the constitution and qualitative determination of personal identity is not seldom confused with the discussion of *collective identity*, which then inadvertently denotes a particular complex of qualitative features that indicate who and what *a collective* is, would like to be or should be. An identity is thereby ascribed to a collective, often as though a 'biophysical unity' like a person were in fact meant—be this collective a group, a gender, an ethnic group or nation, a society or a culture, an alliance of nations or even humanity. It should have become clear from the

second section of the present study that even the formation of *personal* identity can hardly be conceptualised as being tied to the physical existence of a person. References to one's physical being and certainly the acceptance of one's body can, as Erikson has emphasised, be regarded as important moments in the formation and reproduction of identity, and of course the awareness and the sense of one's body may play into the qualitative determination of personal identity. Nevertheless, personal identity as a *formally* defined unity of a self-evident person is always connected to self-referential acts that transcend the material presence of the body. Through these self-referential acts a person seeks, as we have described, to ascertain especially the continuity and coherence of his existence. If we accept this definition, then *no* 'natural evidence of a corporeal substratum' (Assmann, 1992:132) can guarantee personal identity. We can then no longer assume that the formation of personal identity, in the sense of a specific form of subjectivity, is an indispensable and unavoidable concern in the sense of an anthropological constant. The obviously indisputable difference between personal and collective identity, marked by their different kind of physical existence, in no way affects the knowledge that entirely specific, sociocultural, i.e. symbolic forms and practices are *constitutive* for what we are here calling personal identity. The body and the subject's voice that says 'I' to some extent secure that person's numerical identifiability, as Tugendhat would say, who is trying to express who he is and wants to be. Corporeality, however, never completely defines, formally or substantively, how a person answers the so-called question of identity. Without cognition, consciousness and reflection, there can be no identity, writes Assmann categorically at a crucial point, only to add: 'This is true in individual as well as in collective life' (Assmann, 1992:130). What Assmann says about collective identity is certainly true of personal identity: its 'evidence' and intelligibility are subject to 'an exclusively symbolic development' (132). In the case of collective identity this is entirely obvious. Here no 'corporeal substratum' can divert us from this certainty: 'There is no "social body" in the sense of a visible and tangible reality. It is a metaphor, an imaginary quantity, a social construct. As such, however, it is fully a part of reality' (132).

While the concept of personal identity refers to a self-same subject existing as a real biophysical unit, the question about any collective identity is first and foremost a question about the *constitution of that collective itself*: Which persons are 'brought nearer' and 'bound together' by whom and in what way, conceived under particular circumstances as a unit, when certain common characteristics and affiliations are ascribed to them? Whereas in the case of personal identity it is clear, on the basis of the corporeality of personal existence (in the sense of numerical identifiability), when the question of identity is raised, in the case of collective identity the group of relevant persons first needs to be established or determined. The shift in meaning that the concept of identity thereby undergoes is obvious: the (psychological) identity and 'iden-

tity work' of a single person becomes the *unity of many* and its 'substantiation.' A common misgiving arises almost automatically: is it not the case that the adjective 'collective' allows us to misuse a concept from individual psychology, to suggest the existence and unity of 'something' that 'does not even exist'—that in any case never and nowhere 'exists' in the same sense as a person in flesh and blood does?

I would now like to distinguish two ways in which the term 'collective identity' is used. These differ first of all *in the very way they come to speak of collective identity at all*. In this context one could speak of a *normative* and a *reconstructive* type. Whereas the first, with respect to the (putative) members of the collective, (merely) pretends or presents, directs or suggests, or even imposes, common features, a historical continuity and practical coherence 'binding' once and for all, the second type describes the subjects' praxis as well as the self-understanding and world-understanding in order to arrive at a description of the collective identity in terms of a reconstructive and interpretative science of society and culture.[11] Obviously both types are concerned with normative constructs of meaning and significance. Whereas we must call the first a *normative prescription,* the second one can be considered as a *reconstructive transcription* with phenomenological intentions. The first type has been criticised, with good reason, by Kreckel and Niethammer. The second could be related to Assmann's concept of collective (i.e., cultural) identity.

Kreckel draws a clear conclusion from the above objections: 'Only individuals can construct identity. Groups cannot. Societies (or "nations") as well have no proper identity' (Kreckel, 1994:13). Collectives of whatever kind, from smaller informal gatherings to institutions, nations, and societies, can 'certainly appear as collective agents and even—as legal entities—enter into legal relations with natural persons. However, they can possess no proper "collective personality" or "group soul". Whenever a nation is supposed to have its own "identity", we are dealing with ideological language' (14). Every casual transposition of the concept of personal identity onto collectives must thus be rejected, every discourse about concrete 'collective identities' must immediately be subjected to a 'critique of ideology.'

There are sound reasons for Kreckel's skepticism, having to do with the following facts. Ascribing an identity to a collective implies *unifying* some larger number of persons (and thus 'establishing' the collective's facticity). This unification is not seldom undertaken 'from the outside,' perhaps even directed rhetorically or demagogically, potentially without regard for its empirical foundation. Such ascription operates almost inevitably with a questionable characterisation of the collective, supported by the drawing of inward and outward borders. Inclusion and exclusion, integration and distinction, as Assmann calls these sociocultural practices and methods of 'ethnogenesis,' are certainly *general* characteristics of collective identity formation (Assmann,

1992:145). For normativising constructions of collective 'pseudo-identities' it is nevertheless typical that the images of self and other are extremely stereotypical, phenomenologically barren or even empty. Thus the normative codes defining borders between insiders and outsiders, between those who belong and those who do not, between heroes and villains, are detached from any basis in experience, from methodically achieved empirical knowledge especially, and can 'freely' serve purposes of ideological manipulation.

Stereotypical and normativising constructions of collective identity can especially be found when collectives become larger and inaccessible. Anonymous groups such as 'genders,' 'classes' or 'nations' are notorious examples. Such a group inevitably runs the danger of functioning as an 'inauthentic We' (Kreckel, 1994:15). Ideological constructs of this kind often propagate pseudo-identities for pseudocollectives. The characteristics of an 'authentic We' are in such cases simply presumed, invoked, and instrumentalised. Whereas the member of a true We that has evolved through direct communicative relationships and interactions might actually *identify* with the group's traditions and practices, with its orientations and goals, and act accordingly, this identification is often questionable in the case of larger, anonymous groups. Niethammer (1994:378–99) demonstrates how the ambiguous concept of collective identity has been, and is being, functionalised precisely in the above sense (by which it then once again acquires different substantive content). His critique confirms the suspicion that many variants of the talk of 'collective identity' converge in their primarily ideologically manipulative function. What Niethammer especially demonstrates in his historical analyses of German autobiographies on the one hand and the questionable attempts at a national history on the other can certainly, with appropriate modifications, claim a far wider validity: 'Every attempt at synthesising individuals' memories into something more than divergent types of experience and to force them into a meaningful model identity for the national experience of history is doomed to failure or must simply ignore the differences in their experience; between myth and enlightenment there is a huge gap [...] Whoever wants a myth to forge national unity must wait until the differences in our experience become inaudible' (Niethammer 1994:395; see also 1995:25–50).

Niethammer shows that there is a long and diverse tradition of speaking of the 'identity' of collectives, which is deployed to manipulate. Nevertheless 'collective identity' seems to have become a fashionable phrase only after Erikson theorised specific individual crisis experiences as identity crises; with the terminology of this theory of the subject one can now simply reformulate the symptoms of individual crises and pathologies into diagnoses of social pathologies, which require a politics of identity creation. This appeal is particularly popular now, with numerous variations. The longing for the restitution or preservation of 'collective identity' thus has many faces, and many political warning signs need to go up.

One thing is clear: the foregoing manner of speaking of 'collective identity' is scientifically untenable. Hypostasising a collective subject in order to ascribe to it a particular identity, so to speak 'from the outside,' contradicts the requirement that reality be investigated phenomenologically, and (only) then described. The theoretically and empirically unfounded homogenisation of a large number of individuals from an ideologically and strategically motivated perspective creates, as shown, a 'unity' that has practically nothing to do with the concept of personal identity sketched here. Apart from the fact that unity in general has different meanings on the personal and collective levels, the normative discourse about 'collective identity' falsifies a unity that can be completely detached from (more or less unimpeded) communication between persons who come to agree on some commonality. It is not the construction of past, present and future through collectively accepted and shared experiences, expectations, and orientations that here creates a common, socially integrative identity. Collective identity appears in this instance rather as the normativising prescription and suggestion that expects effects without grounding in a consensus reached through communication.

In my view, a concept of collective identity is scientifically useful only in an entirely different sense. Kreckel also implies this alternative, and Assmann makes it explicit, making it, in a more precise form, the basis of his theory of cultural memory. Collective subjects appear in his theory as largely unstable quantities, whose empirical reality and its identity ultimately depend only on *identifications* by the persons who make up this collective. Individuals can be 'constituents' of different collectives as long as they simply identify with certain experiences, expectations, values, rules, and orientations. They can acquire, cancel, or abandon such 'membership' at any time, in principle. In Assmann's definition: 'We understand a *collective* or *We-identity* as the image that a collective constructs of itself, and with which its members identify. Collective identity is a question of *identification* on the part of the participating individuals. It does not exist "in itself", but only to the extent that certain individuals profess it. It is strong or weak insofar as it lives in the thought and action of the group members and can motivate their thoughts and actions' (1992:132).

In the conception advanced here, collective identities are *constructs* that designate nothing else but a *commonality*, which still needs to be specified, in the practical relationship to itself and to the world, as well as in its individual members' relationship to themselves and to the world. Collective identities are expressed in those qualitative descriptions of the self and of the world in which human beings arrive at agreement. They are grounded in such agreements, in self- and world-descriptions capable of consensus, along with common practices. In my view it is not necessary to connect this theoretical conception with the position of methodological individualism, as Assmann does. Empirical methods designed for the study of the *collective negotiation* of such agree-

ments, such as the close observation of group discussions, provide an important argument against methodological individualism in studies of identity in society and culture. One also need not assume that such agreement is merely and in every case 'reflexive' in the sense of 'conscious' or even 'rationally accessible.' It should rather be conceived as often tacit knowledge, latent and everyday, that consistently structures and guides the thoughts, feelings, desires, and actions of the collective's members. This 'knowledge' may be expressed in routinised and conventional forms of behaviour, and it may also, as the psychoanalytical study of society and culture suggests, be repressed in a psychodynamic sense and motivate the collective's behaviour only 'latently.'[12]

Members of a collective share a sociocultural origin and a certain tradition, share certain modes of action and styles of life, orientations and expectations, that not least lead them to expect or dread a certain common future. The term 'collective identity' signifies something that somehow binds certain people together , or in other words: makes of them a collective whose members can at least partly be characterised in a consistent way because they themselves describe themselves in that way, or—as our studies might hypothesise—would do so upon appropriate 'inquiries' and after a potentially more detailed consideration. If such consistent points of reference are not available in the praxis as well as in the self-conception and world-conception of certain people, than one cannot speak of a collective or (in a scholarly context) of collective identity.

Collective identities are communicative constructs; they are *discursive facts* that in the context of scholarship rest on empirical-reconstructive close readings of the relevant aspects of the self-relationship and world-relationship of the persons affected. When they fail to do so, they run the danger of becoming the ideologemes of a praxis and a politics that for manipulative purposes ignores the differences between them, and requires their forced homogenisation. Indeed, scholarly projects do not simply run the danger of undermining their own claims: they would in fact be no better than such ideological and manipulative practices. There is a crucial distinction, and not only on a normative, moral and political view, between speaking about the identity of members of a collective from an *external* perspective or from the *internal* perspective of those very persons, or at least on the basis of a proper understanding of their perspective. This distinction after all defines the distinction between scientific and empirical, i.e. reconstructive perspectives, and ideological-manipulative, i.e. normativising constructions.

Translated by Anthony Nassar

Notes

1. Erikson explains and specifies the highly abstract features of the concept of identity in numerous places, sometimes even collecting them into a sort of glossary, as in 'Identity Crisis from an Autobiographical Perspective' (1975a:20-1); especially important for the theorisation of identity is the aforementioned 'The Problem of Ego Identity' (1959a).

2. I should mention at least the following, in my view, valid objections: (a) Erikson gradually overextended the concept without sufficiently reflecting on the shifts in meaning. This is particularly true of his seamless transition from 'personal' to 'collective' identity; (b) Erikson often combines substantive-qualitative and formal-structural aspects of individuals' relations to the self and the world, and soon also those of collectives of all kinds (from groups to genders as well as societies, nations and cultures all the way to humanity generally), leading to a certain vagueness in the term; (c) the creator of this theoretical concept is rightly accused of connecting the concept, explicitly or tacitly, to an affirmation of features of the American way of life (however he might also criticise it); (d) Erikson is finally famous and infamous for his remarks on 'interior space and female identity,' which tend to naturalise particular socioculturally defined 'female' roles. Some of the aforementioned points are made in Gergen, 1991; Sampson, 1985, 1989; Keupp, 1988. A defense of Erikson's concept of identity against the current objection that it has long been inapplicable to the decentred subjects of our 'postmodern' era can be found in Straub, 1991:61. I consider it particularly inaccurate to accuse Erikson of having conceptualised identity as a sort of prison house for bourgeois subjects, and even to have recommended this supposedly compulsory psychological structure, with a 'totalitarian I' at the center exerting its rigid authority, and tending toward inward and outward violence, as a cosy home. See also the relevant passage where Erikson (1959b:157–8) expressly distances himself from any definition of the concept of identity as a 'totalitarian' structure.

3. With respect to the historical as well as the analytical aspects, I would like to point once more to Henrich's (1990) critical prolegomena to a systematic history of the concept. On the historical and terminological aspects, see de Levita, 1965; Nunner-Winkler, 1983:151–78.

4. Henrich, 1979:136; see also Tugendhat, 1986:254–62. The latter uses the term 'numerical identity' instead of 'individuality.' Some theorists of identity of course separate the different aspects of a subject's identity, and these differentiations can tend in the direction pursued here. This is the case in Assmann (1992:131), when he complicates the simple dichotomy of 'I'—and 'We'-identity by differentiating the 'I' into an 'individual' and a 'personal' identity. This seems to me not to go far enough, since it still understands individuality as an aspect of identity.

5. On the problem of individuality compare for example Frank (1986) as well as the spirited appeal for a rehabilitation of this largely forgotten term in the history of (philosophical) thought: Rudolph (1991). Rudolph defends the individual as 'the true subject of emancipation, missed by the modern concept of the subject or never even aimed at;' he attempts to delineate it as 'actually the counterpart of identity' (8).

6. Noteworthy examples of the 'postmodern' critique of the concept of identity in theories of the subject are Kamper (1980) and Welsch (1990). Welsch writes concisely that 'to be healthy today is truly only possible in the form of schizophrenia—if not polyphrenia' (171). The reference here, quite appropriate in my view, is to Deleuze and Guattari (1977). Welsch's spectacular thesis, however, is incorrect. The present discussion should make it clear that studies such as those cited above oversimplify when they recommend that subjects take 'Identity? No thank you!' as a slogan or even a schizophrenic or polyphrenic way of life as a prescription against modern suffering. Gergen, in *The Saturated Self*, writes of 'multiphrenia,' and there too the resonance of the pathological concept of schizophrenia obscures the important issue: aesthetic play with potential actions and exciting options, a 'sense of expansiveness and adventure' (1991:132).

7. The author is quite emphatic that there certainly exist historically situated exaggerations and fantasies of the strong ego, but the subject, understood properly, 'could never be conceived simply as the spontaneous centre of every act; rather since its beginnings it has been pervaded by a deep ambivalence' (34). Rather than completely eliminating the subject, and celebrating its death which many regard as already fact, it seems more important that we respect and reflect on this ambivalence and contradiction.
8. Identity crises, as crises of orientation and meaning, are seen by many authors as characteristic of modern human beings, who are cut off from *moral resources* as *sources of the self*: 'Personal meaninglessness—[...] feeling that life has nothing worthwhile to offer— becomes a fundamental psychic problem in circumstances of late modernity. We should understand this phenomenon in terms of a repression of moral questions which day-to-day life poses, but which are denied answers. "Existential isolation" is not so much a separation of individuals from others as a separation from the moral resources necessary to live a full and satisfying existence. The reflexive project of the self generates programs of actualisation and mastery' (Giddens, 1991:9).
9. On the methodological aspect of comparisons with and understanding of the other, see Matthes, 1992:75–102; Straub, 1999:esp. Part III.
10. The narration of stories has recently been studied not least for its importance in identity formation. See for example Bruner, 1990; Freeman, 1983; as well as numerous contributions to Sarbin, 1986; Britton and Pellegrini, 1990; Straub, 1998.
11. On the theory, methodology, and methods of reconstructive research, see Bohnsack, 1999.
12. Cf. Alfred Lorenzer's psychoanalytical theory of culture and research practice (1988), which aims at precisely the explication of such latent structures of meaning in collective realities.

References

Assmann, Jan (1992) *Das kulturelle Gedächtnis: Schrift, Erinnerung und politische Identität in frühen Hochkulturen,* Munich.

Bohnsack, Ralf (1999) *Rekonstruktive Sozialforschung: Einführung in Methodologie und Praxis qualitativer Forschung,* Opladen.

Britton, Bruce K. and Pellegrini, Anthony D. (eds), (1990) *Narrative Thought and Narrative Language*, Hillsdale.

Bruner, Jerome S. (1990) *Acts of Meaning,* Cambridge.

Cerutti, Furio (ed.), (1996), *Identità e politica,* Rome.

de Levita, David Joël (1965) *The Concept of Identity,* (trans. Ian Finlay), New York.

Deleuze, Gilles and Guattari, Félix (1977) *Anti-Oedipus: Capitalism and Schizophrenia* (trans. Robert Hurley, Mark Seem, and Helen R. Lane), New York.

Döbert, Rainer, Habermas, Jürgen and Nunner-Winkler, Gertrud (eds), (1977) *Entwicklung des Ichs,* Cologne.

Erikson, Erik E. (1950) *Childhood and Society,* New York.

Erikson, Erik E. (1958) *Young man Luther: A Study in Psychoanalysis and History,* New York.

Erikson, Erik E. (1959a) *Identity and the Life Cycle,* (introduction by David Rapaport), New York.

Erikson, Erik E. (1959b) 'The Problem of Ego-Identity', in *Identity and the Life Cycle,* (introduction by David Rapaport), New York, pp. 101–65.

Erikson, Erik E. (1974) *Dimensions of a New Identity,* New York.

Erikson, Erik (1975a) 'On "Psychohistorical" Evidence", in *Life History and the Historical Moment*, New York, pp. 17–47.

Erikson, Erik (1975b) 'Identity Crisis from an Autobiographical Perspective', in *Life History and the Historical Moment*, New York, pp. 17-47.

Frank, Manfred (1986) *Die Unhintergehbarkeit von Individualität: Reflexionen über Subjekt, Person und Individuum aus Anlaß ihrer 'postmodernen' Toterklärung*, Frankfurt/M.

Freeman, Mark (1983) *Rewriting the Self: History, Memory, Narrative*, London.

Gergen, Kenneth J. (ed.), (1991), *The Saturated Self: Dilemmas of Identity in Contemporary Life*, New York.

Giddens, Anthony (1991) *Modernity and Self-Identity: Self and Society in the Late Modern Age*, Stanford.

Giesen Bernhard (ed.), (1991) *Nationale und kulturelle Identität: Studien zur Entwicklung des kollektiven Bewußtseins in der Neuzeit*, Frankfurt/M.

Goffman, Erving (1961) *Asylums: Essays on the Social Situation of Mental Patients and Other Inmates*, Garden City.

Goffman, Erving (1963) *Stigma: Notes on the Management of Spoiled Identity*, Englewood Cliffs.

Habermas, Jürgen (1976a) 'Moralentwicklung und Ich-Identität', in *Zur Rekonstruktion des historischen Materialismus*, Frankfurt/M., pp. 63–91.

Habermas, Jürgen (1976b) 'Können komplexe Gesellschaften eine vernünftige Identität ausbilden?', in *Zur Rekonstruktion des historischen Materialismus*, Frankfurt/M., pp. 92–126.

Henrich, Dieter (1979) 'Identität—Begriffe, Probleme, Grenzen', in Odo Marquard and Karl-Heinz Stierle (eds), *Identität*, Munich.

Kafka, John S. (1989) *Multiple Realities in Clinical Practice*, New Haven.

Kamper, Dietmar (1980) 'Die Auflösung der Ich-Identität', in Friedrich A. Kittler (ed.), *Austreibung des Geistes aus den Geisteswissenschaften*, Munich, pp. 79-86.

Keupp, Heiner (1988) 'Auf der Suche nach der verlorenen Identität', in *Riskante Chancen: das Subjekt zwischen Psychokultur und Selbstorganisation*, Heidelberg, pp. 131–51.

Krappmann, Lothar (1969) *Soziologische Dimensionen der Identität*, Stuttgart.

Kreckel, Reinhard (1994) 'Soziale Integration und nationale Identität', *Berliner Journal für Soziologie*, 4:13–20.

Laing, Ronald D. (1960) *The Divided Self: An Existential Study in Sanity and Madness*, London.

Leitner, Hartmann (1990) 'Die temporale Logik der Autobiographie', in Walter Sparn (ed.), *Wer schreibt meine Lebensgeschichte: Biographie, Autobiographie, Hagiographie und ihre Entstehungszusammenhänge*, Gütersloh, pp. 315–59.

Lorenzer, Alfred (1988²) *Kultur-Analysen: Psychoanalytische Studien zur Kultur*, Frankfurt/M.

Makropoulos, Michael (1985) 'Kontingenz und Selbstungewißheit: Bemerkungen zu zwei Charakteristika moderner Gesellschaften', in Gesa Dane *et al.*, *Anschlüsse: Versuche nach Michael Foucault*, Tübingen.

Matthes, Joachim (1992) 'The Operation Called "Vergleichen", in *Zwischen den Kulturen? Die Sozialwissenschaften vor dem Problem des Kulturvergleichs*, Göttingen, pp. 75–102.

Meyer-Drawe, Käte (1990) *Illusionen von Autonomie: Diesseits von Ohnmacht und Allmacht des Ich*, (ed. Matthias Fischer), Munich.

Niethammer, Lutz (1994) 'Konjunkturen und Konkurrenzen kollektiver Identität: Ideologie, Infrastruktur und Gedächtnis in der Zeitgeschichte', *Prokla: Zeitschrift für kritische Sozialwissenschaft*, 24:378–99.

Niethammer, Lutz (1995) 'Diesseits des "Floating Gaps": Das kollektive Gedächtnis und die Konstruktion von Identität im wissenschaftlichen Diskurs', in Kristin Platt and Mihran Dabag (eds), *Generation und Gedächtnis: Erinnerungen und kollektive Identitäten*, Opladen, pp. 25–50.

Nunner-Winkler, Gertrud (1983) 'Das Identitätskonzept: Eine Analyse impliziter begrifflicher und empirischer Annahmen in der Konstruktbildung', in *Hochschulexpansion und Arbeitsmarkt: Problemstellungen und Forschungsperspektiven*, Nürnberg: Institut für Arbeitsmarkt- und Berufsforschung der Bundesanstalt für Arbeit, pp. 151–78.

Rudolph, Enno (1991) *Odyssee des Individuums: zur Geschichte eines vergessenen Problems*, Stuttgart.

Sampson, Edward E. (1985), 'The Decentralization of Identity: Towards a Revised Concept of Personal and Social Order', *American Psychologist* 40:1203–11.

Sampson, Edward E. (1989) 'The Deconstruction of the Self', in John Shotter and Kenneth J. Gergen (eds), *Texts of Identity*, New York, pp. 1–19.

Sarbin, Theodore R. (ed.), (1986) *Narrative Psychology: The Storied Nature of Human Conduct*, New York.

Sommer, Manfred (1988) 'Identität im Übergang', in *Identität im Übergang: Kant*, Frankfurt/M., pp. 14–89.

Straub, Jürgen (1991) 'Identitätstheorie im Übergang? Über Identitätsforschung, den Begriff der Identität und die zunehmende Beachtung des Nicht-Identischen in subjekttheoretischen Diskursen', *Sozialwissenschaftliche Literatur Rundschau*, 14:49–71.

Straub, Jürgen (1994-5) 'Identität und Sinnbildung: Ein Beitrag aus der Sicht einer handlungs- und erzähltheoretisch orientierten Sozialpsychologie', in *Jahresbericht ZiF (Zentrum für interdisziplinäre Forschung der Universität Bielefeld)*, pp. 42–90.

Straub, Jürgen (1998) *Erzählung, Identität, und historisches Bewußtsein: Zur psychologischen Konstruktion von Zeit und Geschichte*, Frankfurt/M.

Straub, Jürgen (1999) *Handlung, Interpretation, Kritik: Grundzüge einer interpretativen Handlungs- und Kulturpsychologie*, New York.

Strauss, Anselm (1959) *Mirrors and Masks: The Search for Identity*, London.

Taylor, Charles (1989) *Sources of the Self: The Making of the Modern Identity*, Cambridge/Ma.

Taylor, Charles (1992) *Multiculturalism and 'The Politics of Recognition'*, Princeton.

Tugendhat, Ernst (1986) *Self-Consciousness and Self-Determination*, (trans. Paul Ernst), Cambridge/Mass., pp. 254–62.

Welsch, Wolfgang (1990) 'Identität im Übergang', in *Ästhetisches Denken*, Stuttgart.

Identities of the West
Reason, Myths, Limits of Tolerance

BARBARA HENRY

In recent debates, notions of identity are predominantly seen as coined within the framework of modernity and subsequently criticised by postmodern thought. This chapter will explore the relation of these two modes of thinking with regard to the term identity. Attention will be focused on the controversial question of the relation of myth to the identities of the West (e.g. individual, group and national identity), and the objective will be to explore how this relation can become a philosophical testing ground for a notion of political identity that is far removed from any hegemonic claims over the various *Lebenswelten*, and above all over a-rational concepts; *in primis*, myth.

Subsequently, I will examine the main charges made by postmodern thinkers against Western universalism, and more specifically against the category of 'identity' which sustains the claims advanced by universalism. Although certain objections will be taken into account, I intend to rehabilitate several interpretations of the concept of identity: numerical identity, qualitative identity, and group identity. I will suggest that these concepts are still usable to shape a political identity that can be characterised as 'multiple' and modular (but not polyphrenic!). Furthermore, I will argue that this kind of identity is the only one that can be considered adequate for the present age. Currently the implosion of political forms and consolidated socioeconomic equilibria (democratic nation-state, market economy *and* welfare state) goes hand in hand with the resurgence of allegiances and collective constraints that are no longer aligned with national borders. The emergence of 'new' identities is a phenomenon sustained by mythographic experiments which take shape at the level of collective narration and gradually supplant the older nationalistic myths, *both below and above the nation-state*. The new displaces the old, for-

saking the heroic epic tales of the past, which, at least as far as Europe is concerned, did not erect discriminatory barriers against other collective subjects on a purely ethnic basis. I will then dwell on the characters of structural affinity between the national myths of former times and the ongoing mythographic experiments of the present day (above all in Europe). The task at hand is to infuse significance and vitality into the notion of political identity. To this end I will offer an in-depth analysis of the three meanings of myth that are most significant for the present investigation.

A further objective of this comparative investigation is to assess whether some of the categories traditionally used to describe aspects and problems of individual identities may be helpful in understanding conflicts that arise in the sphere of old and new group identities. I will thus consider links between the concept of *tolerance* and the *numerical* significance of identity. The latter indicates that beyond a certain limit no entity can accept within itself differences or demands that are incompatible with its own true structure and internal balance, under pain of dissolution into the surrounding environment. For *tolerance* (rather than *toleration*) is first and foremost the relative capacity to withstand the impact of an unfavourable external (environmental) factor, and only secondarily an attitude of indulgence towards beliefs and practices different from, or in conflict with, one's own. *Toleration*, on the other hand, implies, among other things, the specific policy of a government which refrains from banning forms of worship or belief that are not officially established or not accredited among the majority of the population.

1. Identity Summoned to Testify

From the 1960s onwards, dire accusations have been raised, within the very heart of the West, against the project of modernity and the principle of rationality that sustains it. The violence of modern reason is claimed to have reached its apex at the very moment in which reason, overcoming all barriers (territorial, cultural, ethical), has extended its own form of order and discipline over all sectors of life, homologating all living phenomena—including human beings—to criteria of efficiency and bioenergetic economy. Thus it would appear that under the motto of emancipation, Western civilisation has in effect produced violence against individuals and masses, bureaucratisation, destruction of material and environmental resources, widespread diffusion of occult power and regimentation of opinions.

The main cause of these developments, it is argued, is the fact that modern reason arose as a means to extend throughout the world the form of subjectivity that constitutes its main characteristic; for subjectivity is none other than a process of integration, carried out under the banner of equality, unity, coherence and homogeneity and driven by a centrifugal power that designs and

implements worldwide actions. A modern subject, so the argument goes, is twofold: power and action, driving principle, and system of order. Since the subject is rooted in the principle of identity, which is the only one capable of endowing the empty shell of self-awareness with ever greater permanence and stability over time and space, the modern subject therefore becomes a centre of irradiation of scientific knowledge accompanied by the resulting technical-manipulative attitude. The latter knows no limits, inasmuch as self-founding subjectivity denies the dimension of externality any right whatsoever (whether such a dimension be called nature, or matter, or life), merely tolerating its sub-sistence instrumentally. I will return later to the meanings of tolerance that are of relevance for identity.

For now, suffice it to say that the predominance of the principle of identity and the colonisation of the living world are considered by many contemporary authors to be conjoint phenomena, since identity is the expression of a logical-functional unity that floods uncontrollably over the multiform, but defenceless, dimensions of life. It is claimed that the abstract principle of equality of self with self, sameness,[1] which constitutes identity, belongs to the sphere of thought, but not to that of concrete existence. Identity is considered to be capa-ble of denaturing all individual phenomena just as soon as it enters into contact with them, since two things are perfectly identical only in the case of logical relations between symbols, or in the abstract form of thinking subjectivity.

The path had already been traced out by representatives of the decon-structivist school, itself owing a debt to Nietzschian reflections concerning the annihilating effects of rationality and logic on life (J. Derrida, J.F. Lyotard, G. Deleuze, F. Guattari). Furthermore, identity had already been challenged by the disciples of Heidegger. Here I will also draw on the exponents of philo-sophical hermeneutics (H.G. Gadamer, P. Ricœur) as well as the authors of the *Theory of Political Judgment* (H. Arendt, E. Vollrath, R. Beiner), who link the final outcome of modernity to the origins of metaphysics and Western logic. Hannah Arendt was scathing in the description of the tyrannical aspects char-acterising the latter two systems. The principle of identity on which they—logic and metaphysics—are constructed has led to politically ruinous effects: by subordinating politics to philosophy, they have given rise to a veritable denaturing of *vita activa*. The origin of the mortal disease of the West lies in the claim of logic to be able to discover *the* one truth for *the* plurality of human beings (Arendt and Jaspers, 1985:195-7, n. 106, 25.12.1950). In Hannah Arendt's eyes, this claim leads to the imperative of freeing the world from dif-ference, multiplicity, the contingency of finite things. The unity of the identity principle does not tolerate plurality, the latter being the phenomenon that lies at the origin of the human condition, in particular, and the condition of the world in general.

Many of the accusations formulated so far may prove to be well-founded, provided we avoid tilting against a false target: that is to say, against the logi-

cal-formal meanings of identity. The situation changes if we take as our perspective the cultural and political past of identity—in other words, if we consider the ways in which the category has historically been described and
socially objectified. From this point of view, identity is not limited to operations on external nature at a cognitive and technical-manipulative level, but
instead it also gradually becomes a model of personal and social behaviour. A
glance at the most representative era confirms this interpretation.[2]

In the pedagogical plans of the mature Enlightenment, identity was called
upon to discipline instincts and inclinations in order to endow the psyche and
individual character with stability, coherence and balance. The model of normality deriving therefrom excluded any tendency to imbalance or excess that
might distract the subject from realisation of his/her own aims, relegating
such deviant inclinations to the sphere of pathological phenomena. A.W.
Schlegel noted that the Enlightenment was guided by the economic principle,
and suggested that since such a principle favours criteria of usability and
applicability, it determines not only the quest for truth but also a moral tension
towards that which is good (Schlegel, 1964:22-85 no. 64, 63). This means distinguishing between virtues according to the degree of their predisposition
toward practical applications, handling of business matters, and respect for
conventions. It is emblematic, in fact, that eighteenth-century theories which
can be regarded as an apology of passions *tout court* (F. Hutcheson, D. Butler,
J. Mandeville) found little support in the overall framework of orthodox
Enlightenment thought.

The trend was reversed only in Rousseau, at the very point which marks
the beginning of the language of authenticity, that which expresses and ex-
pounds the ways in which a subject can remain faithful to himself/herself.
Emotions, sensations, affections, feelings, and passions become the forms in
which (personal) identity is manifested and publicly objectified, constructing
the new words and phrases through which subjects make themselves intelligible and obtain (albeit reluctantly conceded) social recognition (Taylor, 1989,
1991; Pulcini, 1996:133-47). Thus the fact of belonging to the eighteenth century by no means turns Rousseau into an Enlightenment thinker—quite the
contrary. His eccentricity indirectly confirms that the most widely accepted
vision of the self in the period in question was that of a self directed towards
optimisation of individual talents, although always within the framework of
respect for civilised conventions and good manners. It can therefore justifiably
be stated, on account of the cultural and political aspects highlighted here, that
the Enlightenment model of identity and the forms of subjectivity corresponding to this model may not unfairly be considered as forerunners of
instrumental rationality.

A glance at the situation a little further back in time suggests that the eighteenth-century conception of the self, which strove towards saving and investment of one's psychic and physical forces, would not have been possible

without techniques of production, communication, regulation and *social control*. As is known, Foucault (1981:246-54, 1980:39) introduced an additional category to be placed on a par with the aforementioned techniques: the technologies of the self. From the eighteenth century onwards, these technologies underwent various transformations that had an avowedly biopolitical significance, with concern for the individual becoming a duty of the state. This generated interdependence between technologies of domination over others (i.e. social control) and technologies of dominion over one's own interior. Over time, as the disciplines and procedures, both individual and collective, that incorporate these two types of technology have gradually become more consolidated, power has become more and more stably grounded within political systems, not excluding liberal democracies. Foucault criticises the forms of disciplinary regimentation which we, as individuals of Western civilisation, have been led to recognise as society, as part of a nation, and of a state.

As I have tried to show, the strategy adopted so far does not imply a divorce from modern reason, but merely the unmasking of its hegemonic claims over passions and nonrational aspirations. We must therefore exercise extreme caution whenever we wish to involve identity, the principle that informs that rationality, in a critique of modernity (see Heller, 1993: 623-38). Above all, it is essential to avoid the strategy that sees all ills as deriving from the logical meanings of this notion, for such meanings may still prove useful, at least to redefine political identity. Let us now briefly consider these meanings.

2. The Identities of Modernity

2.1. The core of the logical meaning is the following: identity is synonymous with equality of self with self (sameness). The latter, in turn, has two meanings:

a) The first in order of importance is *numerical identity* or *individuality*: this tells us that entities are not fungible, as they remain intact over a given space-time interval without dissolving into the surrounding environment.[3] This meaning is represented in sociology by *personal identity* (E. Goffman). It is an expression that indicates bureaucratic identity. The entry in the registry of births, marriages and deaths, one's passport, driving licence, income tax return, social security number and voter registration—these are all documents attesting to the fact that each of us possesses one specific identity. But sameness also has another meaning.

b) Instead of signifying the nonfungibility of two individuals, it indicates which ones among the aspects that are common to two entities can actually be considered as the same. Let us consider what happens if X and Y have identical uniforms. Then if they are examined from the point of view of what they

are wearing, one may be mistaken for the other, without affecting their individuality. However, numerical identity still remains the logical *minimum* of identity in general, and of qualitative identity in particular.

Nevertheless, it does not follow from the above statements that logical meanings are the source of all ills of modernity. Certainly, one cannot adduce the motive of structural and indissoluble constraints supposedly linking them to metaphysics, for there exist no such links: this was made clear by nominalist solutions, as early as Duns Scotus and Locke. Admittedly, it cannot be denied that identity became burdened with meanings in the ontological and theological sphere, before undergoing further metamorphoses in the field of psychology. Yet there is no evidence to suggest that the various semantic shifts—which will be addressed in detail further on—are the stages of a perverse dialectics that paves the way to the concentration camps. For a more cogent criticism of the undesired outcomes of modernity it is preferable to have recourse to philosophical anthropology, history of the cultural collocations of the *self*, moral and political philosophy, rather than deconstruction of the logical forms of thought.

Even so, many still regard such forms as epitomising, in their transparent perfection, the load-bearing pillars of the political horror of the twentieth century. It is no coincidence that the 'snake's egg' is the image around which unfolds the disturbing film by Bergman on the cultural and technical-scientific premises of Nazism—a choice of symbol that was dictated by the desire to express that which, by exhibiting the form of the archetype, not only epitomises but also reveals a glimpse of its terrifying content, which is the other face of the creative power of knowledge. For the image of the snake evokes both power and science. This symbology offers a powerful model of the insinuating and threatening technological mentality, that is to say the attitude that was at one and the same time both modernist and irrationalist and which was widespread during the Weimar period (see Herf, 1984; Henry, 1993). However, it does not seem to me to represent the 'great collective narrative'[4] capable of reflecting the entire history of the West, in particular of the modern West.

I will now briefly illustrate some of the developmental paths of identity in the framework of the Western semantic universe, introducing along the way the various philosophical, social-psychological and political meanings. The relation between identity and the emotive and myth will be addressed when dealing with the political acceptance of this concept.

2.2. The logical meanings of identity have acquired shape and greater depth through mystical meditations on the condition of creaturehood, influencing the philosophical forms of the constitution of egoity (ipseity, *Selbstheit*). The procedure of identification translates into the first act performed on oneself by the human observer, eccentric with respect to the world and, when reflecting, with respect to one's own body as well. The reflecting nucleus assigns to the exter-

nal world its own appearance, the body, which constitutes an object for this reflecting core (Jervis, 1992:12). From medieval times to the modern age, theological meditations on subjective identity have enriched a stream of thought that was already dominant in continental philosophy, namely that which accentuates the static, nucleic and point-like characters of egoity[5] rather than the process-oriented, constructive and interactive aspects typical of the English philosophical model (Marquardt, 1979:353-7). But it was the latter that would later influence the social sciences.

From Schopenhauer to Kierkegaard right up to the Heidegger of *Sein und Zeit*, the essentialist vision can be summarised as consisting of the claim that the personality is endowed with a substantial and unobjectifiable nucleus, that which we are, which is then overlain by an accidental crust which is dedicated to externality, that which we seem. The sphere of externality gives rise to the dimension of intersubjectivity, which generally bears the negative axiological sign. For Schopenhauer, our 'existing in other people's opinion' is mere seeming, yet, on account of our superficiality, we grant it excessive consideration, despite its being inessential to our happiness. Moreover, for Heidegger, the figure expressed by the impersonal term *Man*, governed by routine and tyrannically ruled by anonymous 'others,' connotes the flight and fall of our authentic *Dasein* into inauthenticity (Schopenhauer, 1976; Heidegger, 1947:41-2, 113-14, 128, 235, 269, 297; Marquardt, 1979:348). In contrast, in the sociopsychological interpretation, to which we will turn shortly, a veritable reversal of positions *vis-à-vis* this point is found. In the meaning deriving from the pragmatist approach, our external image—or, if you will, *all* our images—gradually comes to form our permanent identity. That which we seem comes to shape that which we are.

The sociopsychological acceptation arose within the Anglo-American tradition, which began with William James, continued with George H. Mead and Erik H. Erikson, and eventually developed into the symbolic interactionists. In this tradition the *self* can be said to correspond to subjective identity, which takes on process-oriented and interactive characters. Self-conscious subjectivity is found not at the beginning but rather at the end of the process, since a person constructs the texture of his or her identity through successive syntheses, and this endeavour may actually fail. For one can in fact speak of acquiring or losing identity. James further distinguishes *self* from *social self*. It is the latter concept that expresses the set of recognitions each individual receives from the other members of society. However, as early as James, the innermost portion of the *self* is explained as a chain of progressive appropriations of external situations, which are then internalised and placed in relation with previous situations. Mead offers an in-depth investigation of this second aspect, that is to say, of the idea that the process of edification of the *self* does not occur in a situation of isolation but in a condition of linguistic-symbolic interchange. He does not yet talk of *ego-identity*, as Erikson would do subse-

quently, but nevertheless legitimates the association of this concept with the *self*. It can well be said that for Mead the point of origin of identity is not in the single conscience, just as it was not for James, but rather in the dimension of sociality. Each person internalises the expectations which those social figures who are relevant for him/her—the 'significant others'—display towards him/her. By progressive adjustments all individuals construct an identity for themselves, i.e. a detailed and composite structure of themselves that is adequate to respond to such expectations.

What we are dealing with here is a procedural notion of identity: in other words, we have different, but structured, series of performances. In this model, performances that have an identifying function form a complex of acquired skills, a set of synthetic, communicative and reflective capabilities that allow individuals to unify and endow their own experiences with intelligible meanings. To achieve identification with oneself means to recognise that one has at least a minimum continuity and consistency of attitudes, ways of thinking and modes of behaviour. Memory, and the narrative aspect within it, is predominant, even though instinctual moments are not absent. They are represented by the concept of 'I', as opposed to the 'me' of social interaction. For Mead, the self is composed of both aspects, which must cooperate reciprocally in the integrational synthesis, and although the latter is never definitive, it is nevertheless a whole, consistent and coherent with respect to its own evolutionary phases. The subject can be reflected in the synthesis as in its own self-sameness.

Here affinities emerge with *one* of the logical meanings of identity. It is helpful at this point to touch on the concept of *qualitative* identity, which is the second meaning of sameness. It indicates the common aspects or properties on account of which two or more single entities can be regarded as interchangeable. If we consider the formal procedures of identity construction also to be common aspects, then the *self* is a case of qualitative identity. Furthermore, this version of identity is not restricted to indicating which *model* of psychic normality is held to be the best, but has instead introduced additional and specific substantive elements, for instance the idea that imperfect application of the aforesaid model results in the subject being incapable of acting and reflectively controlling his actions. Indeed the contemporary offensive has been launched not only against the formula of the *self*, but also against its normative precepts: those ideals of normality as well as of social and political integration that until just a few years ago held undisputed sway in Western liberal democracies.

Whatever the metaphor selected—decentralisation of identity, saturated self, patchwork-identity—many scholars agree today that the self, the profile of which has been outlined in the above investigation, is no longer adequate to give a proper account of the average social self as it is found in contemporary societies. The identity they find displayed before them is an identity at risk,

contingent and precarious, polycentric and polyphrenic (Luhmann, 1990:14-30; Gergen, 1991; Straub, 1991). The saturation of the social self is accomplished by means of technologies linked to the communication of images and lifestyles deriving from elsewhere, i.e. from cultures, professions and social milieus that are far removed from the self's own background. Technical means—radio, television, telephone, fax, video-camera, video-recorder, computer, the World Wide Web—all cumulate their effects, multiplying not only the expressive potential but also the obligations and expectations that the *self* must contend with. The individual constantly enters into new contacts and relations, but is also required to satisfy ever new demands arising from expansion of his/her own receptivity towards the world. This excessive burden of commitments produces uncertainty in each individual as to the priority to be assigned to the various duties. 'The daily agenda' must be continually renegotiated with oneself and with others. In the severest cases, individuals lose their capacity to give themselves coherent forms of self-interpretation, and see their own life plan gradually unravel (see Gergen, 1990:48ff., 73ff.).

Some authors regard such a state of affairs as the deplorable outcome of the negative dialectics of identity, held to be incapable of facing the challenges of difference and complexity.[6] Others hail the fragmentation of identity as a liberating event. There are also those who highlight the possibility of refining sensitivity to differences and of learning to tolerate the incommensurable, that is to say, learning to countenance that which cannot be reduced to our commonplace ideals of truth and rational behaviour—for our own customs are just as far from universality as are the products of any other culture. In this perspective, the romantic art of self-persiflage and an ironic attitude towards one's own culture become postmodern virtues. The deconstructivist stream of American philosophy (R. Rorty) finds its own privileged interlocutor in Lyotard (Keupp, 1988:146; Welsch, 1990:171; Rorty, 1984).

However, one can criticise the role played by the self in shaping the model of psychic and moral normality that has so far been dominant in contemporary Western democracies without necessarily having to relinquish identity (Henrich, 1979:136), in particular qualitative identity. The logical term attains in an inescapable way a lot of new specifications. In the terminology of Ernst Tugendhat, qualitative identity resides in the practical consequences each individual draws from his/her answer to two fundamental questions: 'What kind of person am I and what kind of person do I wish to become?' (Tugendhat, 1979:285; Straub, 1991:54-5). The relevant aspect is that individual qualitative identity is translatable into supraindividual identity. It may be called group identity, provided that it has, as its constitutive elements, the shared qualities and procedures through which such qualities are reflectively assimilated by the individual components of the aggregate. In this case one can already speak of qualitative group identity. The question may now be posed as a first person plural query: 'Who are we and what do we wish to become?'

3. Group Identity Versus Political Identity

The step towards supraindividual identity seems to have been achieved without difficulty. However, some precautionary measures are strongly advised in order to avoid falling into the trap of holism. The alternative that needs to be examined here is the one between 'collective identity' and 'group identity.' By using the group as a unit of reference, dangerous misunderstandings can be avoided: those who make reference to the group do so, in the first instance, in order to exclude compact, strong identities that are independent of individuals, unlike the concepts immediately evoked by the notion of 'collective identity' (Berger and Luckmann, 1966; Cerutti, 1993, 1996; Henry, 1996:176). The term group identity, second, invokes the capacity of individuals to reflect and negotiate. Rather than to the collective itself it often refers to the options and preferences such individuals have expressed as members of the aggregation (Henry, 1998).

Identity is the intersection between the subjective and objective aspect of a process of reelaboration of shared experiences, but in order to be maintained over time it needs vessels, symbols. Let us consider as an example a population of men and women, possibly starting from the mere circumstance of finding themselves gathered together by chance, who begin to interpret and express their own collective experience (including any possible conflicts) through the filter of the community, thereby laying the basis for the birth of group identity. Cultural crystallisation occurs, which in the long term is transformed into codes, into typical transmission modes. While the initial contents are modified through the intervention of subsequent generations, patterns of expression and interpretation take shape and persist in each individual cultural concretion—a sort of coinage, as it were, a symbolic seal that characterises the community (Smith, 1986). All those phenomena which, by simply being displayed (artefacts, lifestyles, activities), afford profound insight into the deepest and most characteristic meanings and values of the community are here defined as *symbols*. The forms and genres of artefacts and activities are the models and the *symbolic styles*.

We will now take a further step forward, towards the political dimension with its greater concreteness. Group identity *sub specie* of political identity describes the set of common characters to which we allude when saying 'we the members of this political community.' Political identity is more than a mere vision of the world, for it includes the description of what people think of themselves when they are active in and on behalf of the political group. Political identity includes not only the set of values, options and political features, but also the procedures activated by each individual in order to reflect on such characteristics and fully take possession of them, for as long as they continue to recognise themselves in this shared identity.

Further extending the concepts outlined above, 'political identity' can be taken to mean: a) the set of relations between citizens and institutions, resource allocation criteria and partitioning of costs; b) values, symbols, myths on which collective narration has been built, as well as justifications for the allocation of risks, costs, benefits; c) the reflective combination of these two components.

The second component, i.e. b), refers to phenomena that can be traced both to the realm of popular imagination (epics, stories and legends) and to narrative reelaboration (usually differing from the truth told by the historians) of shared events: flags, monuments, anniversaries, eponymous heroes, typical landscapes, selections from oral history, dramatic or literary reelaboration of historic events, the ritualising of collective traumas and victories. Let us consider for a moment a canonical example of 'political identity': the European (South-American or Asian) political *élites* endeavouring to build their respective national communities. The prototypical stage set is that the ruling classes are convinced it is their duty to teach the rudiments of nationhood to the most disparate territorial and professional groups, the majority of whom live in peripheral and illiterate areas. The first step taken in this direction consists of making nations perceivable, by seeking to breathe life into these abstract communities that extended over far-flung areas, far beyond the local village, and are therefore visible only through the imagination (Anderson, 1991). The second step is to attempt to communicate the principles that underpin the living spirit of these nations, while the third, and most difficult, step is to try to instil into general consciousness the idea that the common belonging to the new political entity implies an act of allegiance toward public institutions. But the symbols of belonging can legitimise this claim for loyalty that the political forces wish to demand from their citizens only if such claims have been filtered through reflection, accepted and reelaborated by the addressees.

Up to now, we have considered the political symbol, casting only dim light on its relationship to myth. We must now turn to an important issue that should not be neglected, namely whether contemporary political identity should or should not resort to the authority of *mythic* reelaborations of the most noble and widely shared features of its past and present. Symbols are indispensable in order to achieve *political identity*, and it can be suggested that myths are a symbolic vehicle within everybody's reach, capable of endowing cold juridical statements with an emotional depth.

With regard to the second component of political identity, we need now inquire whether, and to what extent, dramatic or literary reelaborations of important events and the ritualisation of collective traumas or victories can legitimately be turned into myths. Let us assume that there is a consensus about who and what to mythicise or not to mythicise. Having said this, the more severe the economic, political, or military crisis in which a community

(whatever its extension) finds itself, the greater the danger of a warped use of myths. In such cases of generalised distress, there might arise a desire to suspend critical thinking in order to stress the mythic aspect linked to imagination and emotional fulfilment. If common sense is really, as Vico taught, 'knowledge without reflection' and if this faculty has been predominant throughout the pagan eras of humanity—the most mythopoetic era of history—then a (groundless but) extremely dangerous contrast between myth (useful for life) and reflection (damaging for life) could begin to take shape in Western politics.

In the following sections we will seek to ascertain how this risk can be averted. We will thus enquire into the kind of myth—which would need to have an antiholistic and open character—that could instead be contemplated in support of a political identity. Such an identity, in as far as it corresponds to normative expectations, will not exert hegemony over mythopoetic aspirations, but neither will it be impotent when faced with the dark side of the power of mythic expression and action. From here onwards we will explore the various meanings of the term 'myth'.

4. Myth and Identity: Some Definitions

Without any claim to exhaustiveness in this regard, let us consider three configurations of myth in politics, which will be outlined in this fourth section and examined in reference to the modular notion of political identity in the fifth section.

FIRST DEFINITION. This is a common sense definition: for citizens of the West, myths are imaginary or legendary stories, whose protagonists are heroes and heroines (historical characters, in many cases). These stories release a strong liberating force and often rest on a nucleus of truth. The satisfying effect leads one to believe that the source of these tales is reliable and this increases the belief in the pragmatic 'goodness' of the stories capturing the greatest attention among the public. We will investigate this further later on.

SECOND DEFINITION. This is a theoretical definition, but it is linked to the first one: myths are the main patterns of narration, universal in meaning and following typical models in their structure, which lie at the basis of the imaginary and legendary stories recounted by different peoples and cultures (Eliade, 1978; Frazer, 1978; Coupe, 1997). We may call them mythologems.

THIRD DEFINITION. Myth is the expression of collective emotions and desires; it has two variants: the first has a negative axiological sign, as it has been tainted by the most outrageous manifestations of intolerance and political violence by totalitarian regimes. The second, however, could well contribute to the birth of a political identity compatible with the proposals championed in this paper.

4.1 Myth as a history of heroes and heroines

At present, it is the first meaning that is predominant in the West: myths are imaginary or legendary stories of heroes and heroines bursting with emotional strength and having a liberating effect.

These are myths which, at least in their common representation, have overcome the dialectics between sacred and profane (Altizer, 1966), as the ritual of return into chaos and the primeval celebrations to reconcile the cosmos and society have now 'fallen into disuse.' The myths of Western men and women of today belong to the historical dimension. Even though such tales are studded with unusual or unlikely events and do not exclude cyclical time patterns, common sense myths do not correspond to an archetypal notion of 'mythic narration' that has a value in itself.[7] There is a need for—real or fictitious—human beings who are willing to bear witness to their validity as true examples. Such exemplary nature reduces the common sense myth to its minimum nucleus.

Essentially, myths describe heroic real or imaginary figures that have maintained their persuasive powers over time, as they have represented, above and beyond moral and territorial boundaries, the characteristic features of a given period, of a cultural stage, of a mentality that is felt to have some bearing on modern Europe. The cradle of such myths has been the old continent, from the Renaissance up to the present day. They are not merely figures that can be recognised within a given lapse of time, but also emblematic characters, above all repositories of new certainties and a new sense of disquiet that contrasts with the mythical universe of ancient times and the Middle Ages.

One may object that all modern myths, whether they are tales or characters, are the heritage of the Western world. In fact, almost all of them carry the hallmark of the European symbolic universe. Here are some famous and non-controversial examples: Hamlet, Don Quixote, Don Juan, Dracula, Macbeth and Lady Macbeth, Romeo and Juliet, Faust, Turandot, among the partly or wholly literary myths, and Luther, Cagliostro, Elisabeth I, Mary Stuart, Catherine the Great, Byron, Napoleon, Mozart, among the historical ones. In all cases, even chronologically premodern characters—one need only think of William Tell or Joan of Arc—can be considered as belonging to modernity due to the very extensive transformations they have undergone in numerous media and genres (literature, essays, music, theatre, painting) during a process of readaptation and response to the need for symbolic satisfaction in the modern age. We may return here to an example that is already familiar: massive reelaborations of preexisting storytelling or historical material are but the replicas of heroic epics, made to measure by intellectuals of the Romantic age for the rising nations.

These epic cycles, exploited by individual nations to fulfil their own needs, are not generally considered to contain values that are comparable or could be shared at a European level. But the influence and mutual contact

between myths is not restricted by political or strategic-military boundaries, in spite of attempts made even in modern times to anchor some of them in ethnic-genealogical pedigrees. The contrast between 'particularising' and all-pervasive trends cannot be eliminated. This all-persuasiveness is part of the peculiar nature of the myths of modern Europe, the cradle of industrial society and of print-capitalism, alias the publishing industry and the gradual canonisation of the vernacular languages into more standardised and translatable forms than the various local idioms and *patois* (Anderson, 1991). Luther can be considered as one of the prime figures masterminding this extended change and, as such, one of the European myths: the very fact of translating the Holy Scriptures into the vernacular and spreading the Good News through the printed word became emblematic of a radical change in customs, evaluative attitudes, and the whole political-institutional setup on the European continent, which from that time onwards right up to the First World War was coextensive with the West.

At present, despite geopolitical revolutions and cultural upheavals, we continue to belong to modernity, at least under one aspect: it is not only information, but the myths themselves, whether they be tales or characters, that satisfy our need for perfection and individual fulfilment by the mere fact of circulating through means of communication that are easily accessible to all. They can be used for social and political purposes, as already happened (not only in the West, but on the model of the West) in the classical *nation-building* era, because myths are simultaneously the products and the means of giving birth to a new form of civilisation, whereby imagination becomes a public instrument, a channel to form and inform increasingly extended human groups.

As regards the political role of imagination and the myths it conveys, I am referring here to the ideas of those who have studied the birth of nations as a typically modern phenomenon (Gellner, 1983; Anderson, 1991:9-11). These scholars have highlighted the role played by the nineteenth-century *élites* in institutional and socioeconomic stabilisation of what was, at that time, the newborn nation state. The 'good health' of the nation-state in Europe, South America, and partially Asia depended on the diffusion of literacy, the cultural mobilisation of the masses by means of publishing technology, and capitalist means of production and distribution. At the hands of the publishing industry, whose tentacles stretched in all directions to produce the massive distribution of daily newspapers, homogenous time frameworks were created together with a public space. This development coincided with the birth of nations, but not so much in the sense of concretely perceived communities as, rather, in the form of something that appears familiar to the imagination. Similarly, through uniformed time and public space the sense of alienation and bewilderment produced by the collapse of the traditional types of society and faiths has been overcome. What was accomplished by the most ancient absolute beliefs (of myths and religions), i.e. the relativisation of secular experiences and traumas,

including death, is made possible again by national communities. Through stories and symbols, these incorporate the short and otherwise futile life of the individual into chains of stories and fates of whole communities, of similar exploits and memories, thus rendering individual death tolerable.

The search for the meaning of individual existence and the overall picture of what was once called 'Nature' and 'History' is today, more than ever before, a task for those political communities that are able to maintain over time a firm narrative link between generations: a solid political identity based on the inter-generational link between memories and projects. To date, this task has been performed by political identities grounded on the concepts of a people and national sovereignty—the most typical concepts of modernity. What remains to be seen is whether the mythopoetic experiments undertaken by the *élites* of the past possess links with symbologies and mythologems characterised by broader scope and meaning, notwithstanding the strenuous intentions of the ruling classes who were striving instead to underline the specificity and exclu-sivity of their own nation. For in the prospect of constituting a national politi-cal community, the type of political identity to be devised was at once numerical and qualitative; the declared—or avowed!—nonfungibility of the nation was based on the requirement of qualitative homogeneity, in a histori-cal-cultural sense. A citizen was one who formed part of the people, of the col-lective subject characterised by specific shared properties: origins, territorial links, traditions, language, culture, history. Only rarely did racial purity play a major role, such as in Spain and the Spanish overseas territories, and even in this case it did so on the basis of 'myths of origin' that were constructed and later counterposed to myths of the opposite axiological sign. The *Reconquista* and *Al-Andalus* offer examples of the alternative and allow us to pass on to the second definition of myth.

4.2. Myth as a basic structure of narration (mythologem)

We have seen that the belief in shared mythical stories is one of the reasons why a group endowed with a political identity is ready to take on risks, respon-sibilities and sometimes even heavy costs. Myths connected to a particular land, the tales of its origins and the creation myths of the population inhabit-ing that territory, the stories of ruling kings and eponymous heroes, the stories of wandering populations abandoning their original land that had fallen into decay and their wondrous return to a homeland that is once more rising to glory—these are all examples of stories that strongly captivate our conscious-ness, and they all have a similar narrative structure, despite the different, and at times radically, divergent contents.

Let us now elaborate on the Spanish example, in order to bring to light three elements that are common to two rival myths, *Reconquista* and *Al-Andalus*: their nature as an artefact, their status as instrumental to the ideal of social-political integration (even if axiologically opposed), and their basic narrative structure.

While the ideological aspect is preponderant in any political history, it is nevertheless possible—even in such extreme cases—to trace an outline, albeit somewhat bare, of the essential historical events on the basis of which the two rival myths were forged, at a distance of well over a millennium, the one from the other.

In the year 711, armed units of Arabs and Berbers approached the Rock of Gibraltar and conquered the greater part of the Iberian peninsula. The resident populations put up only the most feeble resistance. Only in a few wild and virtually inaccessible mountainous regions of the North did a few stray groups of 'natives' elude the invading military forces. One hundred and fifty years later, the overall situation had been stabilised; the land once called 'Hispania' by the Romans now bore the new name of *Al-Andalus*. But in the North, new kingdoms had taken shape, characterised by a marked anti-Muslim political identity. From a certain point of time onwards, the Christian kings embarked on a military expansionist policy, which continued for many centuries right up to the conquest of Granada, i.e. the last Arab stronghold in the peninsula, by Isabelle of Castille and Alfonso of Aragon in the fateful year of our Lord of 1492. So far, so good: these are the salient events. Let us now look at the mythographic construction.

The myth of the *Reconquista* arose in the 9th century to justify the Christian kings' southward military expansion, and it achieved immense acclaim in later centuries because it served to construct the political identity of the centralised and unitary state as it now appears to us in the shape of the Spain of modern times. The church devised a very effective translation of the symbolic language of Christianity into a (preexisting) mythic narrative scheme capable of justifying a war against the neighbouring kingdom. The Arab invasion, it was implied, had been an act of divine punishment for man's sins (in particular those committed by the inhabitants of the peninsula); therefore the latter were morally obliged and indeed perfectly justified in fighting vigorously against the Muslims, until the Christians had achieved what would be the final victory for true believers, an outcome that was already preordained in heaven.

If we disregard the aberrations to which this type of justification can lead, one can recognise in the Christianised myth of the *Reconquista,* in which terms such as 'sin,' 'atonement,' 'providence' are embedded in a table of values that is strongly affected by Christian concepts, a much more ancient and all-embracing narrative structure. For if attention is not restricted to merely scanning the phenomena, one perceives a beginning, a development, an end: in other words, an original condition of bliss and virtue, the loss of this condition, and finally its painful reacquisition. The great Christian story is but a variation on a theme whose origins go back much deeper into antiquity. A glance at the mythographic tradition of the West soon uncovers a common structure connecting a heroic name—individual or collective—to a noble, remote and lost

origin, and, in the second instance, to a (grievously distressing) path towards regeneration that must be followed in order to return to that origin.

We will now turn to the rival myth, that of the *Convivencia*, forged and disseminated (over a thousand years later) by the democratic militants in exile, following the victory of Franco's forces in the Spanish civil war. In contrast to the repression of the Jews carried out by the Visigoth kings, the Arabs are depicted as not only tolerating both Jews and Christians, but also allowing active practice of their respective forms of worship, while maintaining the prohibition against proselytising and public ceremonies. A climate of tolerance of this kind, so the story runs, spread its beneficial effects to the lands governed by Christian kings, leading to a special form of cultural coexistence in the Iberian peninsula.

In this latter version, it is startlingly clear that *Al-Andalus* itself represents the original condition of bliss and virtue, and likewise the sociopolitical model towards which aspirations are directed. Furthermore, it is precisely the intolerant and authoritarian regime ushered in by the aggressive policy of the Christian kings, from the 9th to the 15th century and beyond, that constitutes the phase of decadence as compared to the origin, a decadence that reached its peak under the Franco dictatorship.

Thus the *Convivencia* is, in turn, revealed as a form of myth. And in fact, despite the considerable truth of the assertion of peaceful coexistence among the different religious communities, the territory renominated *Al-Andalus* was subjected to a fairly pronounced process of Arabisation, if not also, in some periods, to out-and-out Islamicisation. Arabic became the official language and culture—for the Christians as well! The only subjects who actively sustained *Al-Andalus* economically, because they were obliged to pay the tax levies—were the 'infidels' (i.e. Jews and Christians).[8] Thus, it is evident that no undue pressure was required to persuade many of them to convert. Furthermore, each community had a free hand in judging and persecuting heretics and apostates within its own group, using whatever means they deemed to be most appropriate.

In effect, rather than of tolerance (and toleration) in the modern sense, it would be more plausible to speak of a regime of moderate noninterference among theocracies. What I mean here by *tolerance* is indulgence or even respect for different beliefs, practices or customs that conflict with one's own. 'Toleration,' on the other hand, indicates the specific *policy* of a government that consciously and enduringly avoids placing obstacles to forms of worship and belief that are not officially established or accredited among the majority of the population. This having been said, it can perhaps be suggested that the regime of noninterference among semiautarchic communities may well offer a solution not to be scorned for modern multicultural societies. But this is not the crucial point I wish to dwell on at this point (I will return to it later).

Rather, I particularly emphasise that in both cases it is myth that is acting as the driving force, and that it does so as a function of specific sociopolitical

models, the first being authoritarian and ethnically homogeneous, the second democratic and multicultural. Every time we reread the past according to a mythic construct featuring a structure that is antithetical to some other structure, we irrevocably deliver ourselves up into the grip of the totalising logic of a plot that is both complete in and of itself and refractory to all critique and revision. However, paradoxical though it may seem, the contrary axiological signs of the two myths have no effect whatsoever on the statement that the mythologem, and the justificatory effect, are analogous for both. Furthermore, while the logic of the mythic content is exclusive—all or nothing—that of the mythic narrative structure may leave some room for manoeuvring in the form of reflection and individual action.

The mythologem has a far more wide-reaching scope, and is certainly of extremely ancient origin. It has traversed the Greek, Hellenistic, Stoic-Roman, Christian, Renaissance, and Rosicrucian-Enlightenment civilisations. It is the narration of cyclical regeneration. The narrative schema is not original, but has long since been translated into a Western framework, for it has come down to us in the Roman version of *The Golden Bough* (Frazer, 1978), wherein human action is assigned a decisive role despite the basic cyclical model.

The story recounted in the above work takes place in the Nemi forest, which was sacred to Diana, the goddess of woods and bestower of fruits, and to her consort, Virbius. A rule stated that in the temple consecrated to these divinities any man could become a priest and king of the woods provided that he had previously torn off a bough—the golden bough—from a certain sacred tree and then killed the priest who was his predecessor. The sacred tree is an oak, the bough is mistletoe, which embodies the power of Jupiter, god of the sky and storms, whose power has become condensed in the bough through lightning. He who seeks to become the priest must tear off the bough in order to prove that he has acquired the divine energy necessary to start a new cycle, to bring renewed fertility to the land with the approval of Diana. The king then dies and is reborn, the old sovereign dying to be born again in the new form.

However, there is no certainty that this will always happen, nor that it will happen at the right moment. In the narrative structure of death and regeneration, rebirth is inalienably linked to *periodic* reintegration of the Golden Age. But everything depends on the intervention of a hero, a hero who is uncontaminated precisely because he is 'new' or a foreigner or obscure. He will reestablish order by replacing the king of the age of decadence, in most instances with the ritual sacrifice of the latter. In many cases, the two roles overlap and the 'new' hero, who sacrifices himself to guarantee regeneration, is also the one who is periodically regenerated. This basic narration pattern can be, and has been, adjusted both to the theme of the political redemption of a collective subject linked by lineage to the epic hero, but also to the theme of the rebirth of a civilisation which was once noble but has now declined, which

may face extinction or can rise again by appealing to unsuspected energies hitherto concealed and therefore still full of vigour and health.

Let us search for this pattern in some national mythographic constructions. In the past, the question whether each individual myth was rooted in local traditions or not by no means constituted a discriminating factor, provided that such myths complied with a familiar structure, suitable to the needs of symbolic fulfilment among the population. But with the struggle for national independence, first, and then later with the stabilisation of the nation state, a step forward was taken as compared to previous literary reconstructions of autochthonous myths. Earlier reelaborations and transcriptions of epic poems or narrative cycles, as carried out by European scholars from the Middle Ages onwards, consistently aimed to demonstrate the heroic origins of the nation-peoples, thereby heightening their potential for moral, military and political redemption.[9] Debate on the literary authenticity or folk origin of a story never fails to mention the epic poems or cycles that became the symbol of redemption of the nation and its people in the 14th century. Thus the myth of the Bard Ossian,[10] which was raised to literary and political dignity by Macpherson in the second half of the 18th century, stands at one end of a line of development, at the opposite pole of which stands the highest degree of authenticity of sources (sagas, epics, folksongs).

The Ossianic epics are the most important, but not the only example of manipulations carried out by intellectuals on preexisting folkloristic material. Yet the knowledge of such interventions has not damaged the power to reinforce political identities, either in Scotland or in other countries, of the thus produced stories. On the contrary, a successful poetic artefact that satisfied the need for moral and political renewal in a population eventually generalised the symbolic force of similar operations, which went far beyond the intentions of the 18th- and 19th-century authors and promoters of the heroic heritage of their people. For not only the populations of Celtic origin, such as the Irish, the Scots, the Welsh, but also the peoples of Eastern Europe[11] have reworked the combative, individualistic, and libertarian spirit of the bards and Gaelic warriors, transforming them into a reference point for their own political ideals and future within a nationalistically oriented framework.

However, no nationalistic intellectual seriously thought, or declared publicly, that the real intention was to restore the austere and bloodthirsty ways of national heroes. Rather, such heroes were acclaimed through the printed word as models of excellence and praised for their affinity with the nation. These linkages increased faith in the presence of similar strength, dignity, honour and independent action in the collective subject descending from those ancestors, whatever evidence might be mustered to the contrary. The same mechanism could perhaps be applied to an entire civilisation (the postmodern West?) if the mythologem of the Golden Age were to be rewritten and *above all implemented*, in the highly evocative terms of the *Peaceable Kingdom*.

Indeed, the rich iconographic canvas of the *Peaceable Kingdom* provides an inspiring background—richer in meaning than any textual exegesis of the circumstances surrounding its creation—for exploring several of the political themes discussed here. The 'Kingdom' to which allusion is made is that depicted in the painting of the same name by the Quaker Edward Hicks, created around 1834. It illustrates an event which Hicks believed to have momentous significance, one that would help to usher in the Kingdom of God on earth, in harmony with his own vision. In 1682, a peace treaty was signed in Pennsylvania between Quaker settlers (who were among the few whites to respect the agreements) and Native American tribes, allowing the colonisers to settle in the area. The artist interprets this event in an anagogic sense: it was to mark the beginning of the millennial Kingdom.

In the background, on the left, one notes the representatives of the two communities, standing out against a seascape as they display an attitude that is at once solemn and confident. In the foreground, set on the right against a lush forest, figures that evoke the symbolic context of the psalm of Isaiah rest peacefully side by side: 'The lion lies with the lamb, into the viper's lair the young child puts his hand.' The reign of harmony announced by the Scriptures is already a political reality, yet not through an act of grace by Providence restoring the perfection of Eden, but thanks to the recognition and safeguarding of the equal dignity of the parties involved. This condition, essential for peace, appears to have been brought about by stipulating and implementing what amounts to a genuine 'treaty' among peoples. Thus we are in the realm of the rights of peoples, not of the state. In certain respects, this signals a return to the medieval type of tolerance: can the regime of non-interference among semiautarchic enclaves (even if the latter are intolerant of internal deviancy and differences) offer an honourable solution for modern multicultural societies?

If 'tolerance' (in the second, more common meaning—see the introduction above) is taken to mean at least an attitude of indulgence towards beliefs or practices that differ from our own, or indeed are in conflict with our views; *much more, if the mythographic construction of Al-Andalus is taken for a plausible account of what can really happen*, perhaps we may approach the model of the Muslim millets with some degree of sympathy. But there is one striking distinction to be made: in contrast to such a model, it is imperative not to preclude the possibility—in the name of a supposed excessive tolerance (first meaning) that eventually proves to be self-destructive and obliterates one's own identity—of inducing the *addressees (peoples sharing with us territorium and political framework)* to see things from our own point of view. In the framework of the heritage of the West, this means trying to persuade those who engage in forms of collective life which exclude freedom of conscience, criticism or the individual right to choose, that they should exercise at least toleration as a policy.

Here the link between the concept of tolerance (in the first meaning of the term) and the *numerical* meaning of identity becomes clear, for the latter indicates that beyond a certain limit no entity (in particular, no organic entity) can accept within itself differences or demands that are incompatible with its own structure and internal balance. If it were to do so, it would simply dissolve into the surrounding environment. Thus *tolerance* indicates first and foremost the relative capacity to withstand an unfavourable (external) factor; only in its derivative meaning does it signify indulgence towards beliefs and practices that are different from or in conflict with one's own. The balance between the first and second meaning of tolerance is extremely delicate, and tends to change not only with varying spatial-temporal conditions, but also with variation in social and political circumstances.

It is helpful at this point to again call to mind the characteristics of group identity. There exist no supraindividual barriers between the individual and the aggregates as long as the pitfall of holism can be avoided. Group identity, as is well known, constitutes an identity that a number of individuals reflectively agree to share and hold in common. Shouldering the burden of difference to the bitter end is a virtue—indeed it is one that can be consummately put into effect in the public dimension, where its application may even be enhanced. However, any enquiry as to where one might place the limit of tolerance beyond which a community—or an individual, an organisation—must not stray will necessarily fall within the scope of empirical investigation. Here another virtue, *prudentia*, and another faculty of the mind, wisdom and good judgement, come into play. However, they can at best give indications, never solutions that will be valid once and for all.

Yet these considerations need not be taken as implying unqualified surrender to relativism or the unconstrained dominion of contingency. They do, however, strongly suggest that flights of fancy embodying intransigent universalism should be relinquished in favour of sensitivity to adequacy and a sense of appropriate measure every time it becomes necessary to apply general norms to particular situations (Günther, 1988; Henry, 1992; Loretoni, 1996). A similar suggestion arises from the very fact that the concept of tolerance pertains to the peculiar dimension of experience that stands midway between private and public, whence spring forth emotive demands and instinctual drives which gradually take on a recognisable shape and become experience that can be shared. The same holds true for myth, if understood in its third meaning.

4.3. Myth as an expressive-emotive phenomenon

4.3.1. The definition has two variants: let us begin with the first by which myth is described as 'personified collective desire.' This corresponds to the concept of political myth elaborated by Ernst Cassirer, who made use of this conception to combat totalitarianism. The expression was coined in the first decade of the century by the French scholar Emil Doutté, and extended in the 1940s by Cas-

sirer far beyond the limits of the 'primitive' society within which it had been constrained by anthropological studies. Doutté (1909) restricted himself to claiming that in tribal society all divinities are personifications of the community's desires. Cassirer built on this motif and broadened its scope to encompass it within a far-reaching political perspective. The above-described theogonic process was regarded by Cassirer as embodying a special kind of emotive reaction, typical of a group endangered by an extraordinarily dire threat. Such a reaction results in the invocation of a protective divinity, or else in the abdication of ordinary political power in favour of the extra-ordinary witch-doctor, the magician. The latter is thought to be capable of deciphering the otherwise inscrutable designs of cosmic powers, and, more importantly, he is believed to be capable of acting upon them in order to modify their designs to the benefit of the collective. Rites and those who perform them thus come to assume symbolic meaning, producing a special form of theodicy; fear having thus been endowed with a mediated expression, the deaths and suffering of individuals, which have become necessary or indeed inevitable in order to ensure the life of the collective, are felt to be more tolerable. The part is sacrificed to the demands of the whole and this sacrifice is made tolerable for those who perform it.

The hub of Cassirer's thought is that whenever human communities find themselves in, or returning to, the mythic stage of development of symbolic conscience, they reproduce the political effects of the type of theodicy that is appropriate to the characteristics—whether expressive, pragmatic or holistic—of myth. Furthermore, inasmuch as myth is capable of combining the several wills of a plurality of individuals and directing them towards a common goal, it is collective in totalising terms in that it sacrifices critical skills and the rights of individuals to the superior needs of community. It represents a specific process of establishment of political identity, wherein fusion of the parts with the totality or with whatever entity holds power over totality is predominant. This identification allows no mediations nor does it permit criticism or revision.

Now, if this were the comprehensive and exclusive definition of the notion of myth, then the supporters of unmitigated 'demythicisation' of the political conscience of Europeans would be justified, since such a process would avert the temptation to slide back towards totalitarian formulations of political identity. Well-known examples of such formulations include the myth of the *Reich* and that of the *Führer*. But this is certainly not the kind of common symbology whose absence in the West is so sorely deplored! On the other hand, there is a need to go beyond the idea that it is politically incorrect—for such a prohibition is equally imbued with mythic absolutism—to address the issue of myth. Focusing on this issue does not in itself imply evoking swastikas. Anyway, we must learn to cope with myth.

4.3.2. The point I wish to make is that in addition to its lamentable tendency to trigger the totalising temptation, myth has the precious characteristics of

unveiling symbolic experience in its playful inexhaustibleness, revealing aspects that are fulfilling and liberating in comparison to the oppressive perception of the lack of meaning in individual and collective experience (Ricœur, 1967; Blumenberg, 1979). This consideration introduces the second variant of the third definition, one with a positive axiological sign, according to which myth is an original symbolic function. Myth has a universal and universalisable aspect: it may be pregnant with symbolic meaning.

Since it is an expressive phenomenon, myth fully displays the features attributed by Goethe to the original symbolic phenomenon (as subsequently emphasised by Cassirer). A mythic symbol (similar to a historical-political event) is pregnant with symbolic meaning if it appears and is without residues, if it manifests completely and self-evidently its excess of significance. We might liken it to the hierophany mentioned by Eliade in connection with the original modes of the numinous. Sensitivity to the rich expressiveness of phenomena lies at the root of the human capacity to create symbols and remains a prerequisite of the most abstract and universal forms that such a faculty can assume. Cassirer himself reminded us that myth as a source of expression and creativity cannot be expunged—providentially—from the conscience and cultural heritage of mankind. In certain respects, Blumenberg's criticism of the Enlightenment does not touch Cassirer; on the contrary, it integrates his positions into a broader perspective.

I am referring here to the claim that the Enlightenment failed to achieve its aim of rationalising customs because it naively strove to erase not only individual myths but also the reasons, needs and deep-seated motivations that lead myth, as a phenomenon of absolute significance, to be ceaselessly regenerated at the heart of Western culture. The monstrous totalitarian deviations of the twentieth century, it is argued, arose from this fatal error.

Let us for a moment combine Cassirer with Blumenberg. Even though recent history has shown the dangers of myth, which are manifested when myth is the precursor of totalitarian modes of identification—with the community, or with its chief (Cassirer, 1946)—it is still true that to deny any legitimacy to the expressive and imaginary sources from which mythologems draw their origin, and to the derivations of such narrative patterns, means paving the way for a return of unmediated Myth (Blumenberg, 1979). This being said, and having acknowledged the historical merits of those who support a vision that emphasises the contents of myth (*first definition, 4.1.*), it would be useful to make an in-depth analysis of both the narrative pattern (*second definition, 4.2.*) and the structural notion (*third definition, 4.3.*).

If we interpret myth in the latter meaning of an expressive-emotive phenomenon and take up again our previous comments on the political identities of the modern era, we can conclude that such identities have accomplished the task that was performed by myth and religion in ancient times, namely that of providing an answer to the pressing question about meaning. But the structural

notion of myth has two variants. The first was embodied in its most quintes-
sential form by the totalitarian regimes of the twentieth century. Perhaps there
will be an equal opportunity for the second variant—the one with a positive
sign—to obtain political existence as well.

5. A Meeting Point Between Myth and Identity?

We know that the expression 'identity' can have significance both in the sphere
of psychological conscience and in social and political contexts. Being *idem*
(same) indicates a coherent but dynamic structuring of the qualities one possesses and wishes to possess. Who am I and what do I wish to become? Who
are we and what do we wish to become? This is a process-oriented scheme or
code of reflective elaboration of contents, never a preestablished or stabilised
content. Identity is something that can be acquired or lost—it is a synthesis of
interactive competencies open to the future inasmuch as it is dependent on the
latter for its outcome. Myth, if taken in the sense of an expressive faculty,
appears as no more than one among many demands and aspirations participating in the process of identity construction. It cooperates in forging cognitive
and active aspirations (of individual or collective actors) just as much as it does
in constructing demands that pose resistance to the first set of aspirations, and
it reveals opacity (the consolidated sociopolitical dimension, reality *sui generis*
according to Schütz, Berger and Luckmann). In the former case, that is to say
as an active function in the identity dimension, myth is the direction of conscience oriented to discovery and synthetic elaboration of expressive phenomena; it is sensitivity to the physiognomic characters of phenomena in general,
and cultural phenomena in particular. The activation of sensitivity to expressive
polyphony would be a step in the direction of restoring myth to its role of twin
brother of metaphoric language (Cassirer, Usener, Langer, Ricœur).

In the other dimension, that of nonidentity—opacity, remoteness, resistance to assimilation and social synthesis, but also difference and multiformity—myth represents all those passions, feelings and emotions that 'deviate'
from the norm, once they are no longer relegated to an unformed latent state
but have already passed on to the expressive state, and are therefore active in
the social and political field. Myth as the expression of that which is not identical should be taken seriously, on account of its characteristic lability and
fickleness; it must be elaborated, but this does not mean that it should also be
assimilated without residue whenever it may be desirable for multiformity to
endure. In any case, it must at least be filtered through the mesh of reflection,
and of public discussion. In its most tangible social, cultural and political
effects, myth may act as the source for new and daring forms of coexistence
among manifestations of immutable diversity, but it may also become the focal
point where the collective desire of any agglomeration of individuals takes on

exorbitant and maniacal proportions and spills over into the obsession for identity, seeking to suppress whatever cannot be reduced within the confines of its craving and threatens to thwart its satisfaction. Thus fantasies of omnipotence are generated precisely by the inability to recognise the barriers standing between one's own needs and the satisfaction of such needs. In certain cases—though the pathways may be tortuous—fantasies of omnipotence may take hold in the symbolic universe of the political identity of concrete cultures, historically and spatially rooted in the very heart of the supposedly-civilised West. Those falling victim to this kind of antipluralistic pathology include not only isolated individuals but also whole communities that find themselves in a minority position within a dominant culture, that is to say, communities that are numerically inferior and in an underprivileged position as compared to the overall population or certain sectors of the population, of the society in which they live.[12]

In this perspective, however, it should be pointed out that myth as a mouthpiece for the nonidentical cannot be reduced to a mere factor of public amplification of unbridled and destructive private passions. It may also become an interpretative tool exploited by scholars and political figures, since it provides symbolic access to several modes of reading one and the same event. Suffice it to think of the figurative representations of intolerance: the fantasy of the perfect crime, i.e. of the physical disappearance of the adversary-victim 'viscerally' perceived as unacceptable, is a recurrent motif. Thanks to the twofold link between myth and the emotional sphere, on the one hand, and myth and the historical-social sphere on the other, it is by no means impossible to decipher the hidden significance of such metaphors, even in cases where the ludic or recreational contexts divest verbal and gestual expressions of their most disturbing characteristics. Thus one often hears phrases referring to the elimination or dissolution of the adversary, from the stands of football pitches to many other places where ordinary people congregate and where it is not uncommon to hear rude comments on clandestine immigrants. The negation of the other's numerical identity (fortunately only fantasised and not actually put into practice) is the signal, perceived and communicated individually or socially, that the threshold of tolerance has been reached. Or rather, the saturation level of 'violence' (the metaphor of poison, of a virus), i.e. that specific quota of violence towards oneself that can be incorporated without harm is deemed now to have been reached, both at the individual and social level. This violence, it is argued, has been caused by the acceptance of certain aspects of the other, an attitude of forbearing benevolently put into practice right up to the critical threshold of saturation. The metaphor of the dissolution of the adversary mirrors the extreme danger that is imagined to be looming on the horizon, should one fail be the one to act first.

I do not think there exist any ready-made antidotes to this type of uncontrolled reaction to the (not necessarily well-founded) fear of losing oneself, of

becoming blurred and blended into the surrounding environment as a result of excessive receptiveness (alias tolerance) to external unfavourable factors. Perhaps, cultivating a propensity to a sense of wonder at one's own collective imagination and that of other cultures, activating responsiveness to the infinite expressive and interpretative potential of events would bring a breath of health-giving fresh air into contemporary Western politics. Certainly, it would at least constitute a preventive action.

The risk, instead, is that the opposite scenario may come to pass: an attitude of haughtiness, suggesting that we have no need to elaborate myth (above all as far as the nonidentical is concerned) because we have moved beyond this stage. Without residues? Let us therefore also avoid the myth of the lack of a myth, that is to say absolute faith in the self-sufficiency of reason. For this is a hidden and pernicious temptation of modern thought. This is perhaps the most insidious Faustian temptation, because it creates illusions and leads us to underestimate not only the dangerous nature of myth, but also its irresistible capacity to attract and concentrate meaningfulness and gratification, expressiveness and intemperance, both for individuals and groups. In order to discern, stabilise and soundly maintain the boundaries of this pair of opposing forces, identical and nonidentical (myth is active in both members!), the first requirement is the process of construction of that identity which can embrace them both, a process from which no outcome can be excluded a priori.

Notes

1. Ricœur (1990) suggests that *memête* is the most appropriate term to translate the meaning of *idem*, but not that of *ipse*, which he reserves for the reflecting and agent subject.
2. All this occurred in the era before modern psychology became a scientifically accredited discipline, capable of rendering the nomenclature univocal and clear. It is therefore legitimate to use 'identity' and 'self' as synonyms in this, and similar, contexts.
3. Identification is the operation which declares that a thing is not fungible with another. It is carried out by an observer, who bears witness to the permanence of a thing in time and space. The observer may also be the individual thinking subject who performs the identification of himself, by doubling himself into both an observer and the thing observed.
4. I use this expression in the sense of Létourneau, 1992:775-85.
5. In this respect, the 15th-century *Theologia Deutsch*, by Anonymous from Frankfurt, influenced Schopenhauer.
6. Frequently, those who diagnose the crisis of the *self* in the postmodern era as inevitable and thoroughly deserved still implicitly continue to adopt the *self* as the basic conceptual reference model, using this model as a yardstick against which to evaluate deviation. See for example Lützeler, 1998.
7. It is beyond the scope of this paper to deal with the issue, similar to C. G. Jung's position, concerning the persistence of an archetypal world in the limbo of the human psyche of all times.

According to this hypothesis, archetypes are supposed to be determinate forms that are present always and everywhere, such as, for instance, the impulse towards reintegration and renewal, whose symbol is the woman-mother-destiny. Such forms are claimed to be lurking in the collective unconscious—despite the overlay of bourgeois rationalism—ready to remerge again on the surface in moments of crisis or revolution. See Bonvecchio, 1993:192-4.

8. It should be pointed out that in the period in question the—fairly tolerant—Arabic civilisation was the only light shining in the darkness of Western barbarism. The Christian kingdoms of the North showed unequivocal signs of technical, organisational, economic, and very likely also cultural backwardness. These aspects were intensified by the brutality and intransigence, matched by the ideological coherence, with which the operation of the Christian 'reconquest' of the peninsula was carried out and justified over the centuries, starting from the ninth century and continuing right up to the reign of Philip II—in the second half of the 16th century—and beyond. But any attempt to embark on this road, which justifies the predominance of one civilisation (the Arab civilisation, in this case) over another in the name of a greater degree of progress in technical development, the arts and legal structures, eventually presents the same pitfalls as the path taken by the Enlightenment and modernist thinkers of a later age, and by today's liberals.

9. Let me just mention the Breton legends of King Arthur and the Round Table, the Ulster cycle with the Celtic (Irish) hero Cuchulain, the Finnish Kalevala, the Scottish Ossianic chants.

10. Ossian is a legendary bard and Scottish prince, the son of Fingal, whom the Medieval Gaelic (Irish and Scottish) tradition regarded as the author of a cycle of epic chants, now known to derive from ancient folklore. In 1762-63, James Macpherson published two chants, *Fingal* and *Temora*, and erroneously attributed them to Ossian. They were parts of the Ossianic chants with some interpolations by Macpherson. They achieved great success and marked the beginning of Ossianic fame in Europe.

11. The fervent literary and political activity of Hungarian poet-patriots like Sàndor Petövi (1823-49) and János Arany (1817-82) for example, cannot be understood without taking into account the influence of Irish and Scottish poets and intellectuals.

12. On the fundamental role that the 'collective dimension of difference' plays with respect to the issue of tolerance, see Galeotti, 1994.

References

Altizer, Thomas J. J. (1966) *Mircea Eliade and the Dialectic of the Sacred*, Westport/Conn.

Anderson, Benedict (1991²) *Imagined Communities: Reflections on the Origin and Spread of Nationalism*, London.

Apel, Karl Otto and Kettner Max (1992), (eds), *Zur Anwendung der Diskursethik in Recht, Politik und Wissenschaft*, Frankfurt/M.

Arendt Hannah and Jaspers, Karl (1985) *Briefwechsel 1926-1969*, (ed. L. Köhler, H. Saner), Munich/Zurich.

Armstrong, James (1982) *Nations before Nationalism*, Chapel Hill.

Berger, Peter and Luckmann, Thomas (1966) *The Social Construction of Reality*, Garden City.

Blumenberg, Hans (1979⁶) *Arbeit am Mythos*, Frankfurt/M.

Bonvecchio, Claudio (1993) 'Sangue e aurora', in Raimondo Cubeddu (ed.), *L'ordine eccentrico. Ricerche sul concetto di ordine politico*, Naples, pp. 177-212.

Brague Rémi (1992) *Europe, la voie romaine*, Paris.

Cassirer, Ernst (1946) *The Myth of the State*, New Haven/Conn.

Cerutti, Furio (ed.), (1996) 'Identità e politica', in *Identità e politica*, Rome-Bari, pp. 5-58.

Cerutti, Furio (1993) 'Fra Europa e mondo: i dilemmi di una identità sovranazionale', *Teoria politica*, 9, 3:77-95.

Coupe, Laurence (1997) *Myth*, London.

Cubeddu, Raimondo (1993) *L'ordine eccentrico. Ricerche sul concetto di ordine politico*, Naples.

Doutté, Emil (1909) *Magie et religion dans l'Afrique du Nord*, Alger.

Eliade, Mircea (1978) *The Myth of Eternal Return: Or, Cosmos and History*, Princeton.

Fischer, Martina (ed.), (1998) *Fluchtpunkt Europa—Migration und Multikultur*, Frankfurt/M.

Foucault, Michel (1980) *Power/Knowledge. Selected Interviews and Other Writings 1972-77* (ed. C. Gordon), New York.

Foucault, Michel (1981) *Omnes et Singulatim: Towards a Criticism of "Political Reason"*, in S. M. McMurrin (ed.), *The Tanner Lectures on Human Values*, Vol. 2, Salt Lake City, pp. 246-54.

Frazer, James George (1978) *The Illustrated Golden Bough*, (ed. Sabine Cormack), London.

Galeotti, Anna Elisabetta (1994) *La tolleranza. Una proposta pluralista*, Naples.

Gellner, Ernest (1983) *Nations and Nationalism*, Oxford.

Gergen, Kenneth J. (1991) *The Saturated Self. Dilemmas of Identity in Contemporary Life*, New York.

Günther, Klaus (1988) *Der Sinn für Angemessenheit*, Frankfurt/M.

Heidegger, Martin (1947² [1927]) *Sein und Zeit*, Tübingen.

Heller, Agnes (1993) 'Der Tod des Subjekts—Ein philosophischer Essay', *Deutsche Zeitschrift für Philosophie*, 41, 4:623-38.

Henrich, Dieter (1979) 'Identität—Begriffe, Probleme, Grenzen', in *Identität*, Munich, pp. 133-86.

Henry, Barbara (1992) *Il problema del Giudizio politico fra criticismo ed ermeneutica*, Naples.

Henry, Barbara (1993) 'Filosofie della tecnica e ordine totale: organismo, organizzazione, costruzione organica', in Raimondo Cubeddu (ed.), *L'ordine eccentrico—Ricerche sul concetto di ordine politico*, Naples, pp. 325-83.

Henry, Barbara (1996) 'Fra identità politica e individualità', in Furio Cerutti (ed.), *Identità e politica*, Rome-Bari, pp. 5-58.

Henry, Barbara (1998) 'Le identità del soggetto politico', in Dino Fiorot (ed.), *Il soggetto politico fra identità e differenza*, Milan, pp. 251-67.

Herf, Jeffrey (1984) *Reactionary Modernism. Technology, Culture, and Politics in Weimar and the Third Reich*, New York.

Isaacs, Harold (1975), *The Idols of the Tribe*, New York.

Jervis, Giovanni (1992) *Presenza e identità. L'io e la sua centralità tra conoscenza scientifica, riflessione filosofica e psicologia*, Milan.

Kersting, Wolfang (1992) '*Liberalismus, Kommunitarismus, Republikanismus*', in Karl Otto Apel and Max Kettner (eds), *Zur Anwendung der Diskursethik in Recht, Politik und Wissenschaft*, Frankfurt/M., pp. 127-48.

Keupp, Heiner (1988) 'Auf der Suche nach der verlorenen Identität', in *Riskante Chancen. Das Subjekt zwischen Psychokultur und Selbstorganisation*, Heidelberg.

Kymlicka, William (1989) *Liberalism, Community, and Culture*, Oxford.

Kymlicka, William (1995) *Multicultural Citizenship*, Oxford.

Létourneau, Jocelyn (1992) 'Le "Québec Moderne"'. Un Chapitre du grand récit collectif des Québécois', *Revue Français de Science Politique*, 42, 5:775-85.

Loretoni, Anna (1996) *Pace e progresso in Kant*, Naples.

Luhmann, Niklas (1990) 'Identität—was oder wie?', *Soziologische Aufklärung*, 5. *Konstruktivistische Perspektive*, pp. 14-30.

Lützeler, Paul Michael (1998) 'Nomadentum und Arbeitslosigkeit. Identität in der Postmoderne' in *Post-Moderne. Eine Bilanz*, Sonderheft *Merkur*, 52, 9/10:908-18.

Mammarella, Giuseppe and Cacace, Antonio (1999) *Le sfide dell'Europa. Attualità e prospettive dell'integrazione*, Rome-Bari.

Manzano Moreno, Eduardo (1998) 'Al-Andalus: Austausch und Toleranz der Kulturen? Das Islamische Zeitalter der Iberischen Halbinsel in Ideologie, Mythos und Geschichtsschreibung', in Martina Fischer (ed.), *Fluchtpunkt Europa—Migration und Multikultur*, Frankfurt/M., pp. 93-121.

Marquardt, Odo (1979) 'Schwundtlos und Mini-Essenz—Bemerkungen zur Genealogie einer aktuellen Diskussion', in *Identität*, pp. 347-369.

Musil, Robert (1978) *Die Nation als Ideal und Wirklichkeit*, in Albert Frisé, (ed.), *Gesammelte Werke*, II, Reinbeck, pp. 1042-59.

Pulcini, Elena (1996) 'Tra Prometeo e Narciso. Le ambivalenze dell'identità moderna', in Furio Cerutti (ed.), *Identità e politica*, Rome-Bari, pp. 253-57.

Ricœur, Paul (1967) *The Symbolism of Evil*, Boston.

Ricœur, Paul (1990) *Soi-même comme un autre*, Paris.

Rorty, Richard (1984) 'Habermas and Lyotard on Postmodernity', *Praxis International*, 4, 1:31-44.

Schlegel, August Wilhelm (1964) 'Allgemeine Übersicht des gegenwärtigen Zustandes der deutschen Literatur (1802/03)', in *Kritische Schriften und Briefe*, Vol. 3, (ed. E. Lohner), Stuttgart.

Schopenhauer, Arthur (1976 [1851]) *Aphorismen zur Lebensweisheit*, Frankfurt/M.

Smith, Anthony D. (1986) *The Ethnic Origins of Nations*, Oxford.

Straub, Jürgen (1991) 'Identitätstheorie im Übergang? Über Identitätsforschung, den Begriff der Identität und die zunehmende Beachtung des Nicht-Identischen in subjekttheoretischen Diskursen', *Sozialwissenschaftliche Literatur Rundschau*, 23:49-71.

Taylor, Charles (1989) *Sources of the Self*, Cambridge/Mass.

Taylor, Charles (1991) *The Malaise of Modernity*, Canadian Broadcasting Corporation.

Tugendhat, Ernst (1979) *Selbstbewußtsein und Selbstbestimmung*, Frankfurt/M.

Weiler, Joseph H. H. (1995) 'The state "über alles". Demos, Telos and the German Maastricht Decision', *Harvard Jean Monnet Working Paper*, n. 6.

Welsch, Wolfgang (1990) 'Identität im Übergang', in *Ästhetisches Denken*, Stuttgart, pp. 168-200.

II: Representation and Translation

The Praxis of Cognition and the Representation of Difference

MARTIN FUCHS

Within the field of cultural studies discussions on the relationship between researcher and the subject(s) of research in recent years have mainly been held under the heading of 'representation.' The term, as it has generally been applied, is founded on an epistemological assumption: the notion of knowledge as the mirror of reality. This notion itself is based on a concept of objectivity which introduces a categorical separation between reality and its description or analysis, and thus gets into the problem of the adequacy of representation and its correspondence to the object depicted. The theory of knowledge involved in this conception made social and cultural scientists believe that they were placed *opposite* a world of objects which are to be observed and described and whose mode of functioning is to be explained.

It is not by accident that important impulses for a self-critical reflection of the scientific praxis of representation came from cultural anthropology. Through the process of decolonisation anthropology's own foundations came under scrutiny. Discussions did not only address the social relationships of power in which the production of knowledge is implicated. Critics focussed especially on the means of verifying cultural identities, on the projective character of identifying 'the other' and on the cognitivistic mode of objectification implied in the scientific discourse. For, generally, it was not 'the others' who got a chance to speak; instead the scientists spoke about them or on their behalf, if not in their place.

For a long time the idea of the fieldworker who sets off to appropriate another culture prevailed. All activity in the research originated from him or— only in a limited number of cases at first—from her. The fieldworker had to overcome the others' resistance, who were suspicious of him/her, and had to try to look behind the front stage s/he was confronted with. The polarised

character of the relationship between researcher and subject (object) of knowledge became clearly discernible in the picture used, sometimes frankly, sometimes more discretely, of an expedition or a conquest.

The interaction 'in the field' appeared as the exclusive achievement of the researcher who seemed privileged to grasp the 'inside' perspective of a culture, while feeling able at the same time to also view it from 'outside'—to objectify it, understand it comparatively and 'translate' it. Only the researcher was considered capable of consistently distancing him/herself from a specific social context, whereas the members of the societies taken up for study seemed kept 'suspended in webs of significance' they themselves had spun (Geertz, 1973:5).[1] Statements made were brought down to the information they contained, the individual being taken as an exemplar of his/her culture who could pave the entrance way to the actual subject. What informants said was taken as an expression of the culture concerned, not taken as an expression of people negotiating their cultural reality. For this approach, local people—the 'natives'—had only a notion of *their* own world and not, like the omniscient scientist, a relational or comparatively informed idea of the world (Malinowski, 1953:25). Social actors became vehicles of a culture. Not only their faculties of distanciation and objectification, of reflection and of critique of the meanings and significations they found themselves confronted with, were denied, they also were not acknowledged as actors constantly involved in recreating and interpreting their conditions and their environment.[2] Only the scientist pursuing epistemological interests and making attempts to classify what s/he has observed, received the status of an interpreter. Understanding (*Verstehen*)—became a one-sided affair.[3]

Besides, the holism of classical anthropology created a notion of cultures as individualised objects. Cultural reality appeared divided into discontinuous, discrete entities which are entirely inwardly integrated. The mode of representation long prevailing in the cultural and social sciences was directed at establishing patterns and structures, specific configurations and characteristic features. These were thought to circumscribe a culture or society and to condition the behaviour of its members.[4] The humane world was naturalised. Cultures and societies appeared as independent organic entities developing according to their own particular laws, as objective realities *sui generis* whose existence and mode of functioning seem not to depend on the thought and action of the men and women who inhabit them.

Cultural anthropology thus posits a doublefold distanciation: on the level of research interaction, an epistemological distancing, on the level of representation, a rupture between individual cultures. While, on the one hand, this distanciation can promote respect for difference—the acceptance of distinctive rationalities—and allows to ascribe a formally equal status to cultures, the differences on the other hand obtain an ontological status, fixing the others and making them homogeneous. The possibility of exchanges and intersections between the different entities tends to be cut out. But whereas epistemic dis-

tanciation, for the sake of scientific objectivity, negates the primary coevalness with the subjects of study, a relationship constitutive for anthropological research (Fabian 1983; 1990), on the other hand it also opens up a space for reflexivity, critique and self-critique. For this double reason a metareflexion on the anthropological constitution of its subject (object) seems especially urgent.

The critique of the mode of representation that had prevailed in the field of social and cultural studies for so long meant to raise basic questions about the conditions, as well as the limits, of the possibility of representation of 'others,' of the depiction of difference, and finally questions about the concept of difference itself (see Fuchs and Berg, 1993). The ensuing debate received important impulses from comparative, postcolonial literary studies (Bachmann-Medick, 1996a) and has in the meantime fanned out into several directions. In what follows I will mainly emphasise two lines of discussion and make an attempt to develop them further. First, I will argue that representation has to be discussed in the context of the interaction between researcher and researched, and that changes in the mode of representation will prevail only if they are being accompanied by decisive changes in the mode of interaction and in the (conception of the) relationship of all involved (see Shimada, 1994:253-55). This then would make it necessary to explore the possibilities of changes in the interaction of researcher and researched, in theory as well as in praxis, more meticulously. I will briefly outline which way this may develop (section 1). Furthermore I will hold that the deeply ingrained dichotomy of self and other should be replaced by a discussion on how to deal with the non-identical. This would demand, as a first step, to gain an understanding and recall the process in which identities are being constructed (often with the help of scholars themselves). Connected with this is the task to discern the 'polyphony' of voices 'behind' these constructions, to trace the modalities of interdependence and interference of the different voices, but also to register the latency of meanings which never reach a closure. Culture is not a finished 'text' which is to be read, as Clifford Geertz maintains, rather 'culture' refers to a space within which one does address the world as well as other humans. Taking the Dalit movements of India as example I then want to illustrate aspects of a more refined and controlled cultural and social analytics which no longer makes claims for a transcendental position (section 2). Finally I will plead to continue the debate on the dimensions—possibilities as well as limits—of an approach which builds on a theory of interaction and calls into question the logic of identity (section 3).

1. Consequences of the Critique of Representation: Towards an Interactional Concept of Research

The relationship between scientist or scholars, and her or his counterparts is more and more being recognised as an interpretative and, moreover, interactive

praxis in which the object (subject) of study is not only being unfolded but is actually being constituted. This perspective can be traced back to actual changes in the relationship and at the same time traced to a change of perception which casts this relationship in a new light: a reflective and critical turn. The concept of 'representation,' understood as an act in which one side depicts, and speaks for, the other, had devised the research-'relationship' in a unidirectional and monological manner. The interactional reformulation of the research relationship makes it possible to gradually overcome this bias. Two lines of argument had prepared this step. They supplement each other, but are not fully complementary.[5]

The *first* line of argument starts with an inevitable rupture between social praxis and its hermeneutical and analytical representation. Emphasis is laid upon the basic epistemological as well as social distinction between the experiential mode of a social actor who is seen entangled in a familiar world of appearances, and a scholarly or scientific attitude which is geared at bringing out patterns, rules or codes that structure action (Bourdieu, 1977, 1987). Important aspects of social praxis thus elude scientific objectification or are being reduced to singular functional mechanisms. Since the distance between social praxis and its scientific representation seems impossible to reconcile, the only thing one can do is to bear the stated rupture in mind and address it directly: Pierre Bourdieu calls this 'to objectify objectification' (Bourdieu, 1987:57). In opposition to the 'theory' of praxis which is being implied in the prevalent scientific attitude, a concept of praxis is being conjured up which takes social action as situated, improvised and changeable. Instead of just carving out determining structures, allusion is made to the spectrum of possibilities that inhere in a situation, and to the practical ways in which meanings are handled, with crystallised forms that can be found in institutions, texts or formal modes of operation. Practical ways of handling meaning evade representation, since representation in principle is bound, or so it is assumed, to an outsider's position. Only an indirect approximation of social praxis seems possible. This critique of representation thus still shares the assumption that the researcher is not involved in the praxis s/he deals with in any existential way, or even as participant, but at best transitorily or superficially. This approach continues to allege a permanent distance between researcher or author and the people s/he interacts with. It thus minimises the reflexive competence of actors, but also cements the breaches within the author's own identity—for originally s/he had been interactively linked with the people about whom s/he writes. This mode of discourse does accept, and fix, the *differentia specifica* of science which can only be partially redressed on a secondary level of deconstruction. The problem of representation is taken entirely as a question of *theoretical* reflection—a critique of the social theory and the concept of agent implied. The research relationship is seen as a relation between two understandings of social praxis, one practical, the

other theoretical, which cannot meet. The focus thus is on the constructivist dimension of social research.

The *second* line of argument, in contrast, banks on the belief that the representational relationship is principally revisable and makes demands for new forms of writing and new textual strategies. Here scientific modes of representation are seen as historically conventionalised modes of perceiving and writing. Their genealogy is traced to the hegemony of the visual sense as it arose with early modernity, and they are associated with the literary genres of realism and naturalism which did prevail in the nineteenth and early twentieth centuries. They are perceived as attempts to bring the totality of a culture synchronically before the mind's eye, centred and fixed at an external point.[6] By pluralising the viewpoints, questioning the primacy of the visual, and, finally, through a critique of sociocultural holism and the idea of self-contained cultures, these flat, homogenising constructions of reality are sought to be overcome. Thus research is being embedded in a hermeneutical relationship, honouring not only the *a priori* of interpretation but the interpretative precedence of the interpretations of the social actors: The study of culture is the interpretation of other's interpretations—in the last instance the outcome of a dialogue. The innovative impulse and the claim for a revision of the rhetoric of text, to be redeemed through new modes of writing, is based on this insight.

This line of argument engages the research encounter on a level below, and ahead of, any theoretical construction, and it puts the emphasis on the performative side of representation. In this case the tension which inheres in the research relationship articulates itself differently: Building on a (sometimes idealised) notion of participation, the hope is nurtured that by changing the modality in which the object is constructed and represented not only the theories about the other, but also the actual relationship with the other can be reformed. But even here representation is still being perceived as an individual act, as an individual creative process of designing and textualising. At least, however, this line of argument brings the interpretative and dialogical mediation of the relationship with the other(s) to the fore, which is the ground on which research and the constitution of the object of research proceed, whereas the other position frames the research relationship as inflexible, without alternative options. But both ways of looking at the relationship are still centred on the author or scientist as individual actor. When, instead, research and representation are conceived as part of a (more) comprehensive network of interaction, the continuum of interpretations will stand out.

Both conceptions of the scientific praxis of representation point to the necessity of a strictly interactional restatement of the research relationship, which takes into account the interrelation of all those involved, the charged process of constituting or negotiating the object, the design and the results of research. This requires, on the one hand, to take knowledge (*Erkenntnis*) no longer as monopoly of a few, but as an aspect of social life in general, and on

the other hand, to persistently correlate the interpretations of the members of a society and of the researcher, as well as their respective actions with each other. And this means, before everything else, to avert any idealistic notion of dialogue (as '*herrschaftsfreier Diskurs*,' if not as communion) and to acknowledge the agonistic character of actual relationships, the involvement of all social actors in power relationships of one kind or the other (see Crapanzano, 1990).

All those involved in a research constellation have their own understanding of the situation and pursue their own objectives. They mutually interpret one another, anticipate the actions and interpretations of others and attune their own behaviour. It would be difficult to clearly demarcate in retrospect individual interpretations within this interrelationship. The voices and actions of the others involved become a constituent part of one's own interpretation, either by direct adoption, or as part of one's frame of reference or as a background premise. Moreover, it is not only scholars who entertain representational discourses. For a long time the representations of society given by its members and spokespersons had been regarded as collective belief systems or as reflections of objective conditions, as 'ideologies,' and were not acknowledged as, also, discursive, reflexive statements. For that matter the relationship between the scientific interpreter and these representations—although (or because) they often surreptitiously entered into his/her own interpretation—remained undiscussed.[7]

Apart from the researcher and those with whom s/he directly and most intensely interacts, a whole spectrum of people—individual, collective and institutional actors—have part in the research interaction.[8] Involved are a number of different local and translocal actors with whose (political) activities the work of the researcher intersects and who sometimes directly interfere in the research. Furthermore, other scholars and other intellectuals, themselves members of the globalising scientific community, bring their influence to bear. And the (disciplinary) audience too—which cannot be reduced to a passive recipient of knowledge—codetermines the research design and the bent of interpretation, in a discursive as well as an authoritative manner.

Moreover, individuals involved do not necessarily speak with a single voice. Individuals often operate with different registers, use different 'languages' or move reflexively or ironically between different discourses. This (inner) polyvocality may even include perspectives which 'as such' seem incompatible. Besides participating in normative discourses that give the basic ambience and determine the public face of actors, people often cultivate counterdiscourses which are contextually articulated. Also they regularly evaluate the adequacy of cultural schemata when representing experiences and interpreting social relationships (see Raheja and Gold, 1994:74 ff.; Bakhtin, 1978).

This is only to indicate the flexibility and multidimensional character of research interaction. Not only do the people with whom the researcher interacts pursue their own aims and make strategic 'use' of the researcher's pres-

ence, hold back information or deploy their knowledge offensively, they also represent the researcher her- or himself and her/his context of origin. Scholars and intellectuals of the society concerned express their critique of the representation of 'their' culture given by the researcher and pursue their own discursive strategies. Instead of a simple polar research relationship we have to deal with a close weave of crisscrossing, overlapping interpretations and interventions, commenting upon each other, which makes the constitution of representations an extremely complex and contested act.

The different voices may get stabilised within their respective primary contexts, these being often characterised by a larger degree of inertia and the effort to achieve or retain the sovereignty of definition. The specificity of research interaction lies in the fact that no stable and lasting relationships between the different sides are usually being established. Thus, too, the representation of research undergoes multiple transformations when it moves up from direct personal interaction towards sophisticated textualization. It is at that stage that it achieves the status of consolidated representation, which abides by its own criteria. Ultimately it is this hermeneutic process of detachment and distanciation which allows the formation of more enduring, stabilised discourses that generate the others' 'otherness.'

The demand must be to reintegrate representation within interaction. Although this certainly will encounter resistance, it may open a perspective for a more flexible and refined analysis. I will exemplify this in the following section. But even if that step is taken, the double task remains of extending interaction and establishing a persistent critique of the logic of identity.

2. Interactive Reconstruction of the Concept of Culture

Reflexive anthropology has often been reproached for showing a proneness to solipsism. Preoccupation with one's own doings, the allegation goes, supersedes proper work, that is, creating new knowledge about others. But if one takes a closer look, a strange paradox emerges. Emphasising the researching subject results in her/him being decentred, elucidating the constitution of knowledge results in contextualising epistemological constructivism: it brings the others into the picture.

Research interaction links up with processes of interaction already going on. Correspondingly the view of the epistemic process is coupled to a change in the concept of the object studied, implying an interactive concept of culture. To accept that through research one partakes in the constitution of the object, and, moreover, that oneself is part of the field one is working upon means to draw attention to the generative and performative dimension of culture and society. Culture no longer appears as an integral system of meaning in which the individual would only be an accident(al property), or the vehicle (medium)

of signification. Rather, different actors are involved in the constitution and reconstitution of social relationships and meanings, discourses and representations, and in their 'negotiation.' Creativity and the processes of imagination and institution come clearer into focus. The object loses its solidity, it becomes procedural and 'polyphonic,' heterogeneous and equivocal. Culture is now being understood as the coordination as well as conflict of different and often contending voices, discourses and practices. This also means, that integration or consensus are more than just the articulation of a given, shared horizon of a life-world which cannot be questioned. Integration or consensus appear as contingent achievements of social actors.

This throws new light on the question about the factual status the discourses, patterns of interaction or even 'mentalities' possess. The efficacy and actual power of collective patterns of interpretation and perception can no longer be understood as self-evident and comprehensive. For, implied in this is both the issue of the power of definition which can be ascribed to cultural—and that means cognitive, evaluative and normative—configurations and schemata of meaning, and of the *linkage* of these configurations and schemata with social actions. It has been postulated that a certain inertia inheres in tropes, representations or discourses which even if not giving the world a definite shape, at least mould the way the world is being accessed. The question now would be to what extent and in which way agents in their social praxis make reference to representations and discourses, and how these are being taken up (by them).[9] The struggles for assertion or enforcement of a particular interpretation or a definition of a situation have to be understood against this background.

While, on the one hand, the current debates on culture criticise the essentialist closure of the worlds of meaning in representation and emphasise creation, contingency and polyvalence of social interpretations, it is, on the other hand, exactly the antiessentialist, interactional concept of culture and of research which lets essentialist interpretations and self-constructions stand out as a social fact through which social actors project a world and draft collective schemes (like communitarian ideas of nation, caste, class, religion, or, for that matter, modernity). It is the reflexive approach which most clearly establishes how much culture, in a particular sense, has been identifying, fixing and homogenising, how culture is been substantialised. Essentialisation can now clearly be recognised as the product of interaction and imagination.

Reformulated within an interactional frame culture becomes permeable, being put to diverse understandings and usages. Culture loses its centre which had been invested with the powers of social integration. It thus becomes possible to grasp the miscellaneous character of utterances as well as social actions whose meanings more often than not are contested. Cultural significations are not reflections or a reproduction of the world, rather the world is being opened up and disclosed through interpretation, and new worlds are

imagined. Moreover, discrepant and conflicting interpretations allow for dialogue; one might even say, they constitute dialogue. Exchange across, and mixing of, 'different' cultures, transitional zones and nonrealised potentials, become thinkable and 'visible.'

But what then is 'culture,' what is 'the' one, what 'the' other culture? And is not culture itself, culture in the sense of a circumscribed world of signification, a cultural construction (Kahn, 1995:128) ?[10] With the reflexive turn culture is historicised as a concept and virtualised as a social entity. The conception of the world as a mosaic of discrete cultures becomes discernible as a modern notion, dependent upon a particular time and destined to pass. While this means that we can no longer determine a culture's centre (except in the sense of political usurpation), there are still the social representations asserting a cultural whole, as with ideas of 'community' or 'nation,' or as implied in metanarratives of 'progress' or 'capitalism.'

What, then, is the factual status of 'culture'? Imaginary schemata like those of culture or nation force together what is distinct. They subsume what has been separate, reducing to one point what has traces of something else. They suggest unity even if there are discrepancies and try to assume control over a clear-cut territory. It cannot be denied that such schemata attain a certain degree of social validity, get accepted by many actors and come into 'truth' through action, thus acquiring a social power of definition which seldom gets disputed. This power actually has its foundation in the fact that those schemata are, in a qualified sense, 'not real' and have to be pushed through, have to be brought to reality, to 'life.'[11] To be successful in the long run this endeavour has to be repeated and reaffirmed over and again. In the end these endeavours never fully succeed—a limit set to the logic of identity. This, then, can easily provoke the use of force (to accomplish what does not come on its own). The construction of collective identities is showing again and again dreadful consequences.

The concept of cultural wholes thus is true and false at the same time, it misrepresents reality and is being brought to reality as well. To project closed worlds of signification means to make a certain historical dimension absolute, for cultural homogenisations are the product of a very specific social praxis of interpretation, occurring under specific local and historical conditions.[12] It is the concept of interaction which allows to pull in and bring together the conflicting tendencies of epistemological reflection and social analysis, of a critique of essentialism and endorsement of an essentialist position. After all, this tension articulates the two possibilities which representational-discursive distancing from praxis contains: the possibilities of reification *and* reflection. It also shows that discussions of epistemological and methodological issues and the analysis of social issues cannot be separated.

The tensions between critique and endorsement of essentialism register in the lives of human actors. Social movements, like those of the Dalits in India,

which I will consider here, attest to the struggle against conspicuous confinements. This struggle has itself developed certain essentialistic tendencies and gets tangled up in its own contradictions. This observation holds for the social arena as well as for its academic and journalistic representation.

For a long time, the Dalit issue—the problems of the so-called Ex-'Untouchables'—had been badly neglected by researchers (Fuchs, 1999:ch. 4). This issue had been approached only within the frame of generalistic theories on Indian society. According to these, the situation of the Dalits ensued from the axioms of Hinduism and of the caste system. Their situation was regarded as being inscribed into Hinduism. These axioms were considered as valid although, at least previously, an ethically, metaphysically or socially integrated whole known as 'Hinduism' did not exist (Hindu nationalism today makes strong efforts to create this unity), nor did the 'caste system' mark a unitary object, structured along clear and uniform criteria. The term 'caste,' like the term 'Hinduism,' which is a neologism of the nineteenth century, is a European term. It is true that hierarchical modes of behaviour and of transfer of symbolic, or real, impurities, or the transfer of states of inauspiciousness between social groups can be identified as a widely prevailing practice in India, as can be a strong inclination towards endogamy. But these practices are not bound to a particular social entity, nor are they confined to the relationship between Dalits and non-Dalits. On the contrary, these practices can be found in many interactional relationships, also between members of non-Dalit groups. Above all they do not lay down a definite criterion for a clear demarcation of castes and caste categories which rather is specified in direct situational constellations.

'Untouchability' is a relational term which does not exclusively apply to one social category—individuals of any caste can for some period be in a state of relational 'untouchability.' There exists no uniform definition of untouchability either, even if a state of permanent and hereditary pollution is being ascribed to those groups whose task, *inter alia*, it is to take upon themselves the impurity of others and to carry out physically or ritually despised occupations.[13] Dalits have frequently revolted against this ascription of status and against the stigmatisation, the ostracism and the deprivation of rights connected with this. In many respects Dalits did and do not share the ideas of other representatives of Hinduistic positions. Especially they usually do not share the notion of impurity as permanent and transferable state, the negative reminiscences of certain activities and even some of the substances involved, or the conception of *karman* as justifying their status. The terminus 'Dalit'—like the terms 'Untouchables,' '*Harijan*,' '*Atishudra*,' 'Depressed Classes,' 'Scheduled Castes,' and others which are being used—does not designate a unified social category but a rather roughly contoured group of castes amongst whom one finds many distinctions and who previously did not act as a collective subject. But Dalit, unlike the other terms mentioned, has originally been a concept which people concerned invented for themselves, although it is not being

accepted by all those whom it is meant to designate. It came into prominence in the 1970s as a term of contest. The term was meant to cover all who are oppressed, including women, other lower caste groups as well as the working class. *De facto*, in the social conflicts that ensued, the term became limited to the Ex-Untouchables. 'Dalit' means depressed, broken, torn apart …, it is a substantialization *ex negativo*.

Since the end of the nineteenth century and particularly since the twenties of the twentieth century Dalit movements of resistance have been reported. Their activities often were restricted to a certain region or an individual group (caste), but the members of the different movements were more or less aware of sharing if not a common, at least related situations, and they undertook endeavours for coordination on a transregional and, later, national level. Even the categorisation as 'Untouchables' seems to have appeared in documents for the first time in 1909.[14] Resistance of groups now considered Dalits is not altogether new. There had been, above all, religious forms of opposition which had emphasised the universality of the divine principle, of divine grace, and the universal accessibility of God (for example the *Mahar bhakta Chokhamela* in the fourteenth century). The older forms of resistance and counterdiscourses show at least that a closed Hinduistic or even a homogeneous Indian culture, based on a uniform foundation, had not existed.

Besides, changes in the relationship between oppression and resistance have to be taken into consideration. In the twentieth century alone, the role of the main adversary of the Dalits, or Untouchables, was shared by an often elusive 'Brahmanism' and the regionally dominant peasant castes. Previously, in local contexts an ephemeral ritual reconciliation had often been achieved through institutionalised forms of critique and of personal recognition, intended to make up for everyday stigmatisation and degradation. These now became overlaid or replaced by a new confrontation between comprehensive collective identities on a transregional level. Decontextualized ascriptive features of distinction were brought to the foreground and the arena of action was expanded and became more formalised. Fed back into the local frame this had the effect, in many cases, especially in the countryside, to make immediate interactions more brutal.

Intellectual as well as political perspectives have, before all else, to rid themselves of the dominant holistic schema of interpretation which makes Dalits an accident(al property) of a general principle. Movements of Dalits were, and often still are, seen as merely endeavours for social uplift, as efforts to raise one's status and as forms of emulative behaviour—the emulation of a social model incidentally which actually is marked by its exclusiveness (and thus seems to rule out emulation). Central for this perspective is a concept of adaptation which takes positions as a standard that had been put up by the hegemonic group(s) and are now being considered as generally valid. Other, more important aspects of the struggles the Dalits lead had long been pushed

to the sides: their struggle for recognition, as individuals and as a group, which includes the recognition of their difference and particularity; the appeals contained in Dalit discourses addressed to a larger public; and last but not least, the specific universalist claims of validity which aim at basic changes of patterns of behaviour between different communities, in the structures of authority and in intersubjective relationships.

These messages inhere in socioethical programs (most conspicuous being the reactivation of the socioethical dimension of Buddhist thought) as well as in old and new myths of origin, which, for example, present Dalits as the original, 'pre-Aryan' inhabitants of India or as 'broken men,' men 'fallen' from higher status. These messages also find expression in particularistic, communal religions—like *Ad Dharm* or *SNDP Sangham*—and in songs and certain religious practices. Partly, these go back to the Dalits' own traditions or to older Indian counterdiscourses; partly, prevalent discourses—like universalistic conceptions of God—were appropriated and reinterpreted. Not only Dalits see themselves under compulsion to translate their messages into idioms which are generally understood. This can be the idea of universal 'redemption' or the modern concept of the subject as formulated in civil or constitutional law or in the covenants on human rights. Still, the claim to have a part in these idioms is again and again rejected by many of those to whom it is addressed. On the other hand, certain dimensions of the experiences of Dalits are getting lost in these translations and specific, above all communitarian claims of validity, are being faded out.

This contradiction, the necessity to explicate one's experiences and outlook in a language set by others and the limitations to be encountered when this is undertaken, points already to ambivalences within the discourses of Dalits. The Dalit struggle is caught in a double bind. Dalits either have to confirm the hegemonic ontological code—the endeavour to improve one's status by giving up polluting occupations appears to corroborate the dominant logic of classification and stigmatisation—or they are pinned down to a particularistic position and have to face a renewed essentialisation of social differences. Thus, the turn to Buddhism (or, for that matter, to Christianity, or, also, to *bhakti*- and *sant*-saints who also represent universalistic ideas) is taken, not least by non-Dalits, as reformulation of a caste group's particularist ideology, or as formation of a new, but equally narrow and circumscribed group, as in the case of the 'Neo-Buddhists,' or the 'Dalit Christians' or the Ad Dharmis respectively. The universalistic claims raised by Buddhism and the other religions mentioned are being evaded. But Dalits themselves, in their reactions, repeatedly become partner to this (re)essentialisation of differences. This shows in the modern myth of their pre-Aryan origins and ethnic otherness, in one-sided constructions of 'Brahmanism' against which they are mobilising, or in old as well as new political practices of demarcation amongst the different Dalit groups themselves.

Of even greater importance in this context is the problem that it seems nearly impossible to define an unambiguous and sustainable social identity for the Dalits. If one follows George Herbert Mead, persons try to construct an integral self-image through constantly synthesising the expectations others have of them and anticipating the reactions others make in response to their actions. But this synthesis often does not succeed in the case of the Dalits. The conception of Mead may serve as a grid which can help to sharpen the awareness of the tensions between the different projections the self is being subjected to, or which it is itself providing: being stigmatised and ostracised as a social category by others, such negative identification (negative essentialisation) seems to crush people. But with a totally devaluated self no one can continually live. The individual Dalit groups could take refuge with a positive self-image which derived from the tasks they perform(ed), being crucial in social as well as ritual respects, as well as a certain degree of internal autonomy, which allowed them to sort out many issues amongst themselves or to settle them in direct confrontation with other castes. Moreover they could fall back onto modalities of solidarity within the group, which are one of the foundations of what we usually call a caste position. The social and political movements of the Dalits can then be seen as an endeavour of finding one's self and establishing ways of self-assertion in a transregional context which transcends direct interaction. What makes one despair is that the process of undoing the grip of negative identification makes only slow headway and that it is bound up with a new essentialisation of differences. This not only happens because an anti-Dalit attitude, amongst landlords and peasant castes especially, is gaining ground, becoming more and more aggressive, particularly when the Dalits seem to call their state of dependency into question. Furthermore, the highly paternalistic elements in the relationships between many low and upper caste groups of olden times seem to be largely disappearing. What the Dalits have in common and what unites them, is the stigma. So, in the moment of resistance the negative identity is getting confirmed. A positive centre of Dalitness does not yet exist. Moreover, efforts of resistance and attempts at emancipation hide a conflict: the endeavour to achieve personal recognition in life, to assert the idea of universalist humanism aimed at the resolution (*Aufhebung*) of (communal) difference—at recognition despite difference—is in conflict with the endeavour to gain recognition within difference, through acknowledging difference, as a group of its own with its own way of life. This feeds on the older experiences of solidarity within a caste and represents an attempt to retain elements of one's own 'culture.' Between individual recognition and group identity there is a friction, which perfectly shows in the *Dalit Sahitya*, the literature written by Dalit authors over the last three decades.

It should have become clear that traditional ways of representing the Dalits, or the actions of individual Dalit groups, which authoritatively ascribe a certain image to them and reduce their mode of existence to one particular fac-

tor, are not able to grasp their 'identity.' An interactional analysis, on the other hand, becomes very complex. It would not be sufficient to single out particular Dalit voices or the discourses which address them and place them, in a kind of pluralistic panorama, side by side or in opposition to each other. It also would not be satisfying to state the fact of a 'multiple' identity, since the tensions between the different voices which clash within a subject would in this case be too strong. Rather an interactional analysis would have to include the recipro-cal references and the entanglement of voices, their conflicts and the relations of validity: paradoxes, dead ends, aporias. A particular discourse should not straightforwardly be 'identified' with a particular social position and be repre-sented in a one-to-one relationship. What we have to look for are the ways rep-resentations are being deployed, the way a linkage to certain discourses is being established by social actors. And we have to pursue the question of the validity a representation or a discourse socially has, which range of validity it can claim or gain, and how the claims of validity are being put into practice.

Returning to the epistemological critique with which I have started, this by no means requires to newly take the position of a distanced observer. Rather what I plead for here is a perspective which remains sceptical and hermeneuti-cally open. An analysis of social relationships as indicated here is nothing but one possible attempt of reconstructing interrelations and occurrences, building as it does on the reflexive faculties of the actors we talk about. The impression might have been given that, from a distance, a panorama of all the positions and discourses involved is being drawn and only the author's own position has been excepted. But already the fact that neat representations of the Dalits have been problematised is evidence of an epistemic revision. For now the claims of valid-ity and interpretative linkages made by the actors are centre stage, as well as the discursive interaction which develops when confronted with others and which includes the researcher. Not only have authoritative-hegemonic representations been called into question, but also the unambiguity and homogeneity of a (as it is now often called: subaltern) counterperspective, the presupposition of which does not bear in mind how differentiated the reality of those concerned is and how fractured their perspectives often are. Like many of the actors the inter-preting analyst, too, can barely keep a fixed position within this discursive jum-ble but has to consider various and often ambiguous options.

Technically an ethnographic text of this kind, too, has been strapped off 'its context' (Kahn 1995: xi). But the procedure suggested here also implies to take on the problems and issues of the people concerned, to differentiate them and place them in a wider frame. The context in which actions are seen is broadened, as the actors in the ongoing social process themselves tend to do it. So today the Dalit issue, through actions Dalits themselves have undertaken, has been put on the agenda of global institutions, like the UN, the World Coun-cil of Churches or human rights organisations and conferences, and has entered into new discursive contexts. We, the 'others,' have been involved,

have been addressed and have been made to share in the responsibility. We have to get rid of the idea that a researcher can keep a distance *vis-à-vis* the culture s/he is looking 'into.' On the contrary, interaction and participation, as limited as they may be, are primary, and taking distance is a secondary, reflexive step only, which then happens to be reified as an ontological difference. Every interpreter makes a particular statement within the field researched, thus contributing to the way it is being shaped, and expects the reply of others. 'Culture,' the interpretative dimension of the human relationship with the world, marks an interspace of reflection (Fuchs, 1996: 64-5).

3. Thinking the Non-identical: The Polyvocality of Representation

The plausibility and authority of scientific representations has to prove itself against the background of the relationships of interaction and dialogue from which they emerge. Like others, the scientific interpreters and analysts participate in the social process of interpretation and cannot claim a position or perspective which is *per se* superior. Science's claim to objectivity is not what is decisive, what would be crucial are rather the potentiality of scientific analysis to capture differences, to elucidate processes and develop a critical perspective. It is science's specialisation, building on what must be considered a general competence, to question premises of actions, practices and discourses. At best the *differentia specifica* of science would lie in its strictly systematic approach, its methodological reflexivity, and in the fact that it is specially exposed to critique by third parties, which it is compelled to confront.

When tackling the problem of scientific representation, the question of how to handle difference, two dimensions have to be simultaneously taken into consideration: on the one hand the praxis of cognition, on the other questions of social theory. It should be obvious that the first dimension (the praxis of cognition) is not concerned with the technical problem of bridging the gulf, if it exists, between two or more cultural worlds. If we defined the relationship in this way we would again risk to only identify difference—the discrete other and the distinct self—, that means to determine and to fix it. We have to face the paradoxical task that, while we are under the influence of a logic of identity, we have to make attempts to avoid this logic. An epistemology of difference thwarts formalised modes of procedure, much more than hermeneutic methods do, and makes it even look presumptuous to at all attempt to capture difference.

Difference is not just characteristic of our outside relationships, rather we are already situated within differences and carry differences within ourselves. We are cooperating with and across differences, we practice transfers, we appropriate parts of the other and we are not incarcerated in one identity. 'Difference' thus does not refer to something which should be overcome first of all.

Rather, difference is aimed at mediation. However, it is in constant danger of being hypostatised through rigorous demarcations. How then, if we have to accept that our mode of representation is conditioned by a logic of identity, can we describe social practices and discourses without repeating the errors of (false) identification that were made when the large cultural entities were constructed? Where do we locate the interfaces and the zones of contact of sociocultural difference?

In this final part I can give some of the prospects only. I will at first attempt to examine the 'determination' of difference from various sides, before I try to outline possible strategies of correcting or qualifying (relativising) the representation of difference. All social and cultural sciences are affected when the 'description' of identities, practices and discourses is put into question. Implied in this are not only questions of ethics, or about the 'generosity' we want to extend towards the other(s) whom, or which, we had censored. It above all involves the demand to take the spectrum of 'varieties' of difference into consideration.

The inner copresence of multiple voices, or inner dialogical polyphony, is difficult to represent. The various voices, which are mutually interdependent and determine individual or collective identity, can only be recognised in retrospect and by means of analysis, and therefore require a reflexive mode of representation. The spectrum of discursive interdependence, in which individual and collective identities form up, extends, if one takes recent terminology, from 'creolisation' over 'hybridity' (especially of postcolonial personalities) to 'collage' (see Hannerz, 1992; Bhabha, 1994; Greverus, 1995). All these terms have an artificial ring to them, bound, as they more or less are, to the colonial and postcolonial situation. They have been invented in an attempt to demonstrate and display interdependence, to draw out the separate voices, like threads of yarn, and, as in the logic of identity we are familiar with, to retrace their 'origins.' For the time being these termini mark the limit up to which we can follow up interdiscursive processes and the constitution of multiple identities. But they do not apprehend the actual phenomenon of interference, of either-or, of linkage and fusion in a direct way, they rather refer to it in an oblique way.

Posing the question of interference, or of the coexistence of differences, demands also to pose the question of translation: how to conceive the translation between different voices and how to conceive the social transformations which the process of translation entails? Recently only, discussions have begun which no longer view translation as merely an intertextual relationship (Asad, 1986; Shimada, 1994; Bachmann-Medick, 1997). Conceptions which regard translation as semantic transformation of single texts have used an image of transfer of ideas from one semantic system to another and thus propounded two autonomous worlds of meaning. The picture changes when we conceive translation as a form of action, as part of *social* processes of transfer. Taken as

a form of social praxis, translation no longer is limited to the sphere of semantics, it can be seen as constituting a zone of contact. It does not mediate texts alone, but practices and their respective contexts too. Above all, translation is something which in an existential way affects life's perspective (Fuchs, 1997).

The Dalit movements have shown how an asymmetric social relationship compels actors to couch their message in other idioms, if they want to be heard. On an even larger scale the modern colonial and postcolonial global relationships show how a powerful discourse forces other discourses to switch to the hegemonic idiom. As Sudhir Chandra (1994) writes, if one wanted to gain an understanding for a different intellectual tradition, for divergent ways of constructing the world and for other claims of validity, one had to translate them into the 'language of modern ideas,' that means to trim, reformulate and defamiliarise them.[15] Meaning was only bestowed from one side. A major consequence of this is that not only discourses have been broadened and remolded, but social practices have been changed and specific ways of life extinguished. Translation becomes displacement. Intended to achieve recognition for one's ideas, translation makes certain sides of these disappear. It is here that the asymmetry between contexts and the dislocating effect of differences of meaning shows. Difference is experienced as social change.

The experience of incommensurability and asymmetry, while creating sensibility for questions of difference, suggests to adopt a pessimistic tone: The encounter of the other leads to greater similarity. The dialogue on the recognition of difference comes, it appears, too late. With this in view it seems appropriate, as a first step, to argue for a reflexive mode of representation. It would mean attempting to reconstruct the one-directional mode of translation and its levelling effects, but also to trace marks of what has been lost. This then would have to be countered with a concept of translation which retains a sensibility for heterogeneity and the tentativeness of exchange, as it bears in mind the virtual character of represented meanings. Translations, after all, have to gain recognition, have to be introduced into discourses and made effective.

Translations and representations are being detached from contexts and the circumstances of their own creation: They are abstractions. This makes them, in a specific way, 'nonreal' and *virtual*, even when they retain social links and social relevance. On the one hand, even those representations directly involved in social action are never fully activated, rather it can be said that they are *related to* action. On the other hand, representations in many cases have a projective dimension, they are directed at others, at a larger public; they raise claims of validity, develop a utopia; they possess 'a sense for the future' (*Zukunftsdimension*; Apel, 1993:157). Thus, many representations of society held by ostracised groups contain an appeal for recognition as subjects, for recognition of their individuality, and a bid for mutuality on the basis of 'otherness.' Analytical representation then has to examine the mode of formation of discourses, the interrelation of actions and ideas or projects, the handling of

texts and traditions, of authorities and images. It is not only relevant what is being incorporated, but also what is being left out or is being excluded. The relationship of representation has to be conceived as an open relationship.

Another danger is to level difference when dealing with the performative dimensions of praxis. Scientific and literary representations tend to present ritual or performative practices along the same pattern as systematic discourses. Practical knowledge, skills and actions are frequently taken as forms of propositional knowledge and analysed like symbolic systems since this is the way textual hermeneutics proceeds. This makes us forget that practices often appear to be rather flexible and variable. Woven into (many) practices are forms of discursivity and modes of reflection. Practices can be seen as playing with a broad, open spectrum of connotations, with the different layers and enigmatic character of meanings, and actors may associate with them in diverse ways and divergent directions. Practices refer to a specific situation or a specific event, they build on direct communication. Any conventional textual, or, for that matter, cinematic representation, as circumspect as it may be laid out, suspends and curtails this semantic elasticity. Perhaps there are possibilities to use multimedia techniques, which now are available, to partially put off these inherent limitations and to preserve a sensibility for the nonidentical in every interpretation.[16]

Similarly, a sensibility has to be maintained for the non-identity of those significations that have become socially 'instituted.' Reversing the perspective on the representation of performative processes, it is, in this case, not a matter of averting the closure of meaning but opening horizons and transcending what seemed fixed. Social significations are only the selective actualisation of the potential which inheres in significations. As representations allow to transcend the given state of things in normative, cognitive and aesthetic respects, significations, the way they are culturally deployed, are incomplete. They point to other, latent meanings, surplus significations, which have not been actualised and remain underdetermined. While in the first case a direction of transformation has already been envisaged, the potential of transcendence remains still open and unspecified in the second case (Arnason, 1994). Latency and transcendence cannot be represented. They rather constitute a context which, in the long term, relativises all representational determinations and comes to light in a perceptiveness for new possibilities. What we have to look for are not so much other forms of representation but other ways of dealing with representations.

Therefore, in conclusion, I may sketch just some pragmatic, strategic considerations. If sociality and culture are the place—the interspace—[17] of difference, a field of tension and conflict, but also a field of dialogue and search for interlinkages and commonalities, then science too, commissioned to transmit this, can only be multicentred. Current discussions tend to put the burden of responsibility for 'correct' representation on the individual text and the individ-

ual author. It seems problematic to expect a single author to give a nonhegemonic and balanced representation of discrepant voices and to leave her/his own voice out. At best it seems possible to stage-manage the other voices or to give a reflexive account of processes of interaction and internalisation.

We should not put too much stress on the individual text and the individual author. No representation is final. Instead one should call for careful debates amongst different viewpoints, not to display a panorama of fragmentary representations, but to stimulate mutual reflection and critique. These debates become all the more necessary—to return to the remarks made at the beginning—when our concern is the *recognition* of difference, of the *relationship* of the 'other' with, and inside, the 'self.'

Scholars and intellectuals of those societies which have particularly been affected by asymmetric relationships of representation have begun to prepare the terrain for such a debate. In the field of Indian cultural and social studies for example, diversified attempts are being made to reconstruct the history of Indian confrontation and interaction with western forms of episteme and action under colonial and postcolonial conditions. Not only displacements of the Indian cultural context, but also Western practices of cognition and Western discourses come under critical scrutiny. Self and other seem entangled and partly fused or overlapping. Seen as a move which counters the processes of essentialisation of differences in the political realm, these (self-)reflexive analyses make Western efforts of straightforward identification look more and more preposterous.

If well-worn lines of argument were refracted, and ambivalences, paradoxes, tensions and contradictions acknowledged, an important step for relativising conventional modes of representation would have been done. Additionally it has often been demanded that 'members' of those cultures which had been the preferred object of Western scholarship should do an ethnography and anthropology of Western societies and cultures. Although some research of this kind has been undertaken, it is still only occasionally practised. No strong interest supports such attempts, and opposition against becoming the object of 'the others' is much larger in the case of Western societies. Today there seems to exist at least the possibility to discuss the relationship between different epistemes. Linkages and entanglements of disparate epistemes not only have to become the object of study, but also must be acknowledged within the layout of research itself.

It will be more difficult to change the ground of representation when it comes to those of anthropology's subjects who do not belong to the small group of intellectual spokespersons. It is true that the cracks which have emerged in the great representational structures allow these voices to presently gain a wider attention. These cracks become apparent in editions of oral texts made available by the 'new' ethnography as they are being expressed by a new generation of representatives from amongst the respective groups themselves,

in their media and organisations, or in the form of social action groups and social movements. But still the new attempts at self-representation have to adjust to the prevailing conditions of representation and communication: the frame set by the national state, the modern structures of the public sphere, and the primacy of the visual and realism.

An arena of reciprocal, differential representation(s) would dislodge the authority and monopoly monologic representation enjoyed. But the question is still open if, beyond that, it will be conceivable and feasible, in the long run, to also change the *frame* of representation and communication, the *mode of interaction*, in such a way that it would allow *other* modes of discourse to codetermine the ways of interpretation.

Notes

I would like to thank Heidrun Friese and Antje Linkenbach for their detailed critiques of earlier versions of this paper.

1. See in this context Malinowski, 1953:84. Louis Dumont can be taken as a particularly good example of this position. He never tires to emphasise that what distinguishes the anthropologist from 'ordinary' members of society is that s/he can shift between an insider's and an outsider's perspectives. Not only would this allow the anthropologist to make comparisons, this would also give him/her the ability to discover the implicit premises of social ideas which *principally* remain hidden to those who hold or champion these ideas. That means the anthropologist can principally understand the thoughts of the social actors better than they can themselves (see Fuchs 1988: 314-8, 582-6). The problem of translation has been addressed by Shimada (1994: 224-56); also see his chapter in this volume.

2. The epistemological concept is based on a split of mankind into two categories: those to whom reflexivity and agency are awarded and those to whom they are denied. Even hermeneutical approaches, as taken for instance by Clifford Geertz, at certain points still seem to corroborate this attitude. For a critique of Geertz's approach see Fuchs and Berg (1993:43-63).

3. As it seems, European scholars already possess the necessary inner distance *vis-à-vis* their object, which non-European scholars first of all have to demonstrate (see Das, 1993).

4. If not directly derived from the 'expressivist' (romantic-culturalist) discourse (Charles Taylor) which received its major boost from Herder, it was this discourse's incarnation in the idea of the nation which became the model for the modern concept of society. See *inter alia*, Touraine, 1984:22, 24.

5. The differences between these two lines of argument have not been brought out clearly in the debates on representation. They are often discernible in oblique ways only, or in an occasional polemic (see Bourdieu, 1993; Bourdieu and Wacquant, 1996).

6. For a critique of these approaches, see Fabian, 1983; Webster, 1986; Tyler, 1987.

7. Richard Burghart refers to the role Brahmanical representations played in the anthropology of South Asia. The question which then arises is: 'How does one write the culture of a people which has already been written by its native spokesmen?' (1990:277).

8. The following is built on the assumption that the initiative for research stems from the researcher him/herself (or someone who commissioned her or him for this task).—Ulrich Demmer (1996) presents an exemplary account of a field research which at the same time became a process of getting acquainted with the interactive constitution of the sociality concerned.—Today many anthropologists use the term 'local people,' which also has misleading connotations (see Asad, 1993).

9. Representations, tropes and cultural schemata can be regarded as social specifications and abstractions which—temporarily—fix and close meanings. In relating to representations, social actors are able to revise strategies, intentions, assumptions and perspectives. Likewise, representations can become the object of reflection, they can be processed and can be changed—this because they can be intellectually disconnected from specific actions: they gain a kind of virtual distance from praxis. I have adapted here an idea found in Anthony Giddens: Like those complexes of phenomena which we term 'structures,' representations exist in a state of suspense, in a 'virtual' state, as long as no connection has been established with them, as long as they have not been transposed and 'instantiated' (Giddens, 1984: ch.1). The concept of relating or referring to something—better expressed in German as '*Bezug nehmen, Beziehung herstellen*'—has been introduced here to specify the concepts of link and linkage as found in Ortner (1990) on the one hand and Wagner (1995) on the other. For greater detail see Fuchs (1996, 1999:ch. 5).

10. Kahn applies the idea of culture as a cultural construct to the discourse of intellectual interpreters only, and he is right to see it as a modern phenomenon, but self-conscious institution of culture as 'culture' is not the prerogative of one social stratum only (see Burghart, 1989).

11. This can never be fully achieved. Even the modern medical discourse, as described by Michel Foucault, does not structure praxis *in toto*, it is accompanied by counterdiscourses. Discourses do not completely constitute social praxis, nor do they, in the full sense of the term, unilaterally predetermine actors and modes of action. In most of the cases alternatives of action and interpretation exist. There can be a range of discourses (like alternative models of religion in India), or a particular representation can be dealt with and reinterpreted in different ways.

12. While the history of the construction of collective identities shows that totalising views generated by scholars can influence social imagination, scholarly perspectives conversely can also be conditioned by an assertive social imagination. Robert Thornton (1988) has pointed out the role of holistic imagination in ethnography.

13. These include sweeping and cleaning of latrines, work on cremation grounds, disposal of carcasses (esp. of cattle), consumption of beef and processing of leather. Washing of clothes and cutting of hair and nails have also been considered polluting.

14. The term '*Harijan*' was used (but not invented) by Mahatma Gandhi since 1931/32. In administrative contexts the terms 'Depressed Classes' and, later, 'Scheduled Castes' have been in use. The different terms do not fully coincide and lack uniform criteria of definition. They are, more or less, arbitrary and summary terms, only to a limited extent taken over by those to whom they are supposed to apply.

15. Chandra took this formulation from a text by Tripathi Govardanam.

16. The multidimensional character of cultural praxis has been exemplified in Saskia Kersenboom's analysis (1995) as well as exercise and multimedia presentation of south Indian temple dance (*Bharata Natyam*).

17. The idea of an 'in-between' is found in a number of recent writings. Often it is being understood literally, i.e. in spatial terms: a third space between two existing entities, thus actually reinforcing the aspect of separation. I would prefer an understanding which emphasises that something is being shared or that two sides are interconnected. See Matthes, 1992; Shimada, 1994; Bhabha, 1994; Bachmann-Medick, 1996b; Fuchs, 1997.

References

Apel, Karl-Otto (1993) 'Das Anliegen des anglo-amerikanischen "Kommunitarismus" in der Sicht der Diskursethik. Worin liegen die "kommunitären" Bedingungen der Möglichkeit einer post-konventionellen Identität der Vernunftperson?' in Michael Brumlik and Hauke Brunkhorst (eds), *Gemeinschaft und Gerechtigkeit,* Frankfurt/M., pp. 149-72.

Arnason, Jóhann Páll (1994) 'Reason, Imagination, Interpretation', in Gillian Robinson and John Rundell (eds.), *Rethinking Imagination. Culture and Creativity,* London/New York, pp. 155-170.

Asad, Talal (1986) 'The Concept of Cultural Translation in British Social Anthropology', in James Clifford and George E. Marcus (eds), *Writing Culture. The Poetics and Politics of Ethnography,* Berkeley, pp. 141-64.

Asad, Talal (1993) *Genealogies of Religion. Discipline and Reasons of Power in Christianity and Islam,* Baltimore/London.

Bachmann-Medick, Doris (ed.), (1996a) *Kultur als Text. Die anthropologische Wende der Literaturwissenschaft,* Frankfurt/M.

Bachmann-Medick, Doris, (1996b) 'Multikultur oder kulturelle Differenzen? Neue Konzepte von Weltliteratur und Übersetzung in postkolonialer Perspektive', in Doris Bachmann-Medick (ed.), *Kultur als Text. Die anthropologische Wende der Literaturwissenschaft,* Frankfurt/M., pp. 262-96.

Bachmann-Medick, Doris (ed.), (1997) *Übersetzung als Repräsentation fremder Kulturen,* Berlin.

Bakhtin, Michael (1978) 'Discourse Typology in Prose', in Ladislav Matejka and Krystyna Pomorska (eds) *Readings in Russian Poetics: Formalist and Structuralist Views,* Ann Arbor, pp. 176-96.

Bhabha, Homi K. (1994) *The Location of Culture,* London.

Bourdieu, Pierre (1977) *Outline of a Theory of Practice,* Cambridge.

Bourdieu, Pierre (1987) *Sozialer Sinn. Kritik der theoretischen Vernunft,* Frankfurt/M. (engl. *The Logic of Practice,* 1990, Cambridge).

Bourdieu, Pierre (1993) 'Narzißtische Reflexivität und wissenschaftliche Reflexivität', in Eberhard Berg and Martin Fuchs (eds) *Kultur, soziale Praxis, Text. Die Krise der ethnographischen Repräsentation,* Frankfurt/M., pp. 365-74.

Bourdieu, Pierre/Wacquant, Loïc J. D. (1996) *Reflexive Anthropologie,* Frankfurt/M.

Burghart, Richard (1989) 'Something Lost, Something Gained: Translations of Hinduism', in Günther D. Sontheimer and Hermann Kulke (eds) *Hinduism Reconsidered,* New Delhi, pp. 213-25.

Burghart, Richard (1990) 'Ethnographers and Their Local Counterparts in India', in Richard Fardon (ed.) *Localizing Strategies. Regional Traditions of Ethnographic Writing,* Edinburgh and Washington, pp. 260-79.

Castoriadis, Cornelius (1990) *Gesellschaft als imaginäre Institution. Entwurf einer politischen Philosophie,* Frankfurt/M.

Chandra, Sudhir (1994) ''The Language of Modern Ideas: Reflections on an Ethnological Parable'', in Martin Fuchs, (ed.), *India and Modernity: Decentering Western Perspectives,* Special Issue of *Thesis Eleven,* 39:39-51.

Crapanzano, Vincent (1990) 'On Dialogue', in Tullio Maranhao (ed.), *The Interpretation of Dialogue*, Chicago, pp. 269-91.

Das, Veena (1993) 'Der anthropologische Diskurs über Indien. Die Vernunft und ihr Anderes', in Eberhard Berg and Martin Fuchs (eds.), *Kultur, soziale Praxis, Text. Die Krise der ethnographischen Repräsentation*, Frankfurt/M., pp. 402-25.

Demmer, Ulrich (1996) *Verwandtschaft und Sozialität bei den Jenu Kurumba. Vom Arbeiten, vom Teilen und von (Un)Gleichheit in einer südindischen Sammler- und Jägergesellschaft*, Stuttgart.

Fabian, Johannes (1983) *Time and the Other. How Anthropology Makes its Object*, New York.

Fabian, Johannes (1990) 'Presence and Representation. The Other and Anthropological Writing', *Critical Inquiry*, 16, 4:753-72.

Fuchs, Martin (1988) *Theorie und Verfremdung. Max Weber, Louis Dumont und die Analyse der indischen Gesellschaft*, Frankfurt/M.

Fuchs, Martin (1996) 'Metaphor of Difference: Culture and the Struggle for Recognition', *Anthropological Journal on European Cultures*, 5, 1:63-94.

Fuchs, Martin (1997) 'Übersetzen und Übersetzt-Werden. Plädoyer für eine interaktionsanalytische Reflexion', in Doris Bachmann-Medick (ed.) *Übersetzung als Repräsentation fremder Kulturen*, Berlin, pp. 308-28.

Fuchs, Martin (1999) *Kampf um Differenz. Repräsentation, Subjektivität und soziale Bewegungen—Das Beispiel Indien*. Frankfurt/M.

Fuchs, Martin and Berg, Eberhard (1993) 'Phänomenologie der Differenz. Reflexionsstufen ethnographischer Repräsentation', in Eberhard Berg and Martin Fuchs (eds), *Kultur, soziale Praxis, Text. Die Krise der ethnographischen Repräsentation*, Frankfurt/M., pp. 11-108.

Geertz, Clifford (1973) *The Interpretation of Cultures*, New York.

Giddens, Anthony (1984) *The Constitution of Society. Outline of the Theory of Structuration*, Cambridge.

Greverus, Ina-Maria (1995) *Die Anderen und Ich. Vom Sich Erkennen, Erkannt- und Anerkanntwerden. Kulturanthropologische Texte*, Darmstadt.

Hannerz, Ulf (1992) *Cultural Complexity. Studies in the Social Organization of Meaning*, New York.

Kahn, Joel S. (1995) *Culture, Multiculture, Postculture*, London.

Kersenboom, Saskia (1995) *Word, Sound, Image. The Life of the Tamil Text*, Oxford and Washington.

Malinowski, Bronislaw K. (1953 [1922]) *Argonauts of the Western Pacific. An Account of Native Enterprise and Adventure in the Archipelagoes of Melanesian New Guinea*, London.

Malinowski, Bronislaw (1986) *Schriften zur Anthropologie*, Schriften Bd. 4/2, (ed. Fritz Kramer), Frankfurt/M.

Matthes, Joachim (Hg.) (1992) *Zwischen den Kulturen? Die Sozialwissenschaften vor dem Problem des Kulturvergleichs*, Göttingen.

Ortner, Sherry B. (1990) 'Patterns of History: Cultural Schemas in the Founding of Sherpa Religious Institutions', in Emiko Ohnuki-Tierney (ed.), *Culture Through Time. Anthropological Approaches*, Stanford, pp. 57-93.

Raheja, Gloria Goodwin and Gold, Ann Grodzins (1994) *Listen to the Heron's Words. Re-imagining Gender and Kinship in North India*, Berkeley.

Shimada, Shingo (1994) *Grenzgänge—Fremdgänge. Japan und Europa im Kulturvergleich*, Frankfurt/M.

Stolcke, Verena (1995) 'Talking Culture: New Boundaries, New Rhetorics of Exclusion in Europe', *Current Anthropology* 36, 1:1-24.

Thornton, Robert J. (1988) 'The Rhetoric of Ethnographic Holism', *Cultural Anthropology*, 3, 3: 285-303.

Touraine, Alain (1984) *Le retour de l'acteur. Essai de sociologie*, Paris.

Trawick, Margaret (1988) 'Spirits and Voices in Tamil Songs', *American Ethnologist*, 15, 2:193-215.

Tyler, Stephen (1987) *The Unspeakable. Discourse, Dialogue and Rhetoric in the Postmodern World*, Madison.

Wagner, Peter (1995) 'Sociology and Contingency: Historicizing Epistemology', *Social Science Information*, 34, 2:179-204.

Webster, Steven (1986) 'Realism and Reification in the Ethnographic Genre', *Critique of Anthropology*, 6, 1:39-62.

Constructions of Cultural Identity and Problems of Translation

Shingo Shimada

The revival of interest in cultural identity, now a key issue in world politics and likely to remain so for some time, is an outcome of the end of the so-called Cold War. The Cold War order that had defined world politics and had assumed economic and political bipolarity is no longer dominant. 'Culture' has been rediscovered in an effort to explain obvious differences between states (Huntington, 1993). However, in view of the seemingly endless conflicts in many parts of the world it is increasingly doubtful whether we can justly understand and interpret conflicting realities on the basis of our traditional understanding of the relationship between culture and identity. Scepticism is called for, in particular, towards any essentialist concept of culture. Such view of cultures as universally true and naturally different entities is regularly followed by the political identification of such entities as (nation) states based on categories such as 'the Chinese,' 'the Germans' or 'the Japanese.' The differences between these collective identities are, in turn, related to the prevailing dichotomy between 'the West and the rest' and the goal of world politics is defined as the bridging of the gap between the two poles. The moral appeal, catapulted to the front pages of the media, is to understand and recognise the Others in their Otherness.

As a consequence, the post-Cold War constellation of world politics is putting pressure on hermeneutics, a long-standing and favourite theme in German-speaking countries, as we are no longer concerned merely with understanding foreign cultures as objects to be interpreted but find ourselves struggling to set up principles of understanding which will serve as a platform for intercultural communication (Straub and Shimada, 1999). Translating henceforth acquires a new dimension, the task namely of working within a framework of reciprocity which is the prerequisite for understanding the

---

Notes for this section can be found on page 149.

'Other.' When considering translations—from an objectivist viewpoint—as a reciprocal transmission between two closed language systems, however, the issue is erroneously dealt with on the linguistic level only. Social and cultural relationships between the translator and the text to be translated, as well the relationship between the translator and the recipient up to now have received little attention. It is these very relationships, though, in which prevailing constellations of power are expressed. We will thus assume that the analysis of the social aspects involved in translation processes can provide further elucidation of the background against which conflicts related to the quest for 'cultural identity' arise. In the following I would like to demonstrate how discourses on culture and modernity within a non-Western culture were influenced by the translations of key terms in the social sciences, which then became constitutive elements in shaping an 'own' cultural identity. I thus hope to render the widely accepted polarity between the Occident and the Orient problematic in order to enable us to identify fundamental requirements for understanding the Other.

The analysis will start with the asymmetrical relationship within the translating process: for more than one hundred years now scholarly scientific works, and along with them most of the terminology, have mostly been translated from Western into non-Western languages—a fact that the West has rarely acknowledged—whereas translations from the East have been sporadic and, when they occurred, have only very seldom found widespread attention. To unveil the problem of cultural identity and translation, I focus my analysis on a historical work of social science written in Japanese and considered to be a 'classical' work. I aim to demonstrate how theories and terms that have been translated into Japanese took hold of Japanese thinking and are still holding their ground. In particular, I wish to reveal how the Western way of thinking was received and how it served to draw lines of demarcation between selfhood and otherness. I will start off with a discussion of the ways in which the problem of translation has been conceived in the Western social sciences.

1. Selfhood and Otherness

Who is the Other?

The question of the representation of the Other and of translatability is usually pursued on the presupposition, as described above, of naturally given cultural entities without reflecting on the origins of cultural differences. The concept of translation then seems to reside in the view that social reality consists of a number of distinct societies (Tenbruck, 1989). Although, at first glance, this presupposition could be taken as a description with a certain degree of undeniable validity, it is actually problematic since it entails—and conceals—an asymmetrical relationship. The question of translation has always been approached from one and the same perspective: alien cultures were to be trans-

lated for us so that we can understand them. Claude Lévi-Strauss formulated this relationship paradigmatically:

> 'Whenever we look more closely at a specific religious system—for example totemism—a specific form of social organisation—unilinear clans, bilateral marriage—we are always faced with the same question "What does all this mean?" In order to answer it, we endeavour to *translate* the rules that originally were given in another language into our native one' (Lévi-Strauss, 1992:19).

This apparent reciprocity conceals the asymmetrical relationship, and the question as to who, in such a communicative situation, defines who is the Other and who belongs to us is not even considered. This approach to translation did not become problematic as long as an unequivocal relationship of power prevailed between the anthropologist and the 'native,' a relation which also permitted to postulate the objectivity of social facts. The question that arises, though, is whether this manner of thinking does not presuppose the existence of the stranger as an object and condemn her to silence, since the recognition of the 'Other' as a *subject* is certainly impossible under these premises. Translation always presumes a cultural-linguistic difference, but in doing so the existing difference is often ontologised and naturalised. As a consequence the asymmetry of the relationship disappears from sight. More recently, however, we are becoming aware of the fact that the alleged neutrality and objectivity of the social sciences are always also claims made within the arena of international politics. 'Who is translating whom?' and 'Who wants to understand whom?' are the questions that need to be posed.

The question of 'understanding'

Concurrent discourse on 'understanding' foreign cultures is rooted in certain concepts of 'identity' which developed in the course of European cultural history and were adopted and disseminated by social scientists as well as humanists. These concepts permitted a discipline like anthropology to systematically assess all cultural differences that can be found within humankind. Although we now have access to this systematic assessment of cultural differences, however, the question as to whether we understand other peoples better, thanks to the accumulation of knowledge, is even less resolved than before. To be sure, it is often pointed out that technological innovations will induce diverse cultures to overcome the differences between them, and novel means of communication are, in fact, creating a completely new constellation of time and space. It seems, though, that the homologisation of technological standards is a rather unsettling element with respect to cultural identities. Below the surface of the doctrine that hails technological achievements and their unifying power, doubts are growing concerning the validity of the still prevailing approach to the study of foreign cultures, which is seen more and more as a hindrance to their 'understanding.' At the same time, particularistic movements aiming at self-determination are

growing in various regions around the world along with the global expansion of technology. If the cross-cultural function of 'modernity' has mainly been seen in the elimination of cultural differences, its meaning is now on the way to becoming more and more ambivalent. As technology may have become universal, the universal validity of 'modernity'—paradoxical as it may seem—is more and more cast into doubt. The new dimensions of problematising the Other lie, on the one hand, in a critique of the supposedly universal parameter which has been used to define that which diverse cultures have in common and that which is specific to each one of them and, on the other hand, in the quest for a new universal basis for communication which enables us to recognise the 'Other.'

The calls to defend one's own identity against an invasion of foreign masses in Europe, or in the discourses against the threat of Westernisation in non-European countries, can be interpreted as a reawakening of the dispute over universalism and relativism. For a long time, it was only in the Western social sciences that these questions were discussed. In the meantime, however, they have been taken up in the public discourse in the West as well as in non-Western societies. Starting out from the presupposition of distinct identities of the 'Other' and of the 'self,' an attempt is made to bridge the gap between the two. These discourses rely on such terms as 'ethnic or national identity,' 'understanding,' 'diversity' or 'culture' in order to do justice to this new dimension of understanding the Other. The failure to critically apply these and similar terms, however, threatens to undermine all critical intentions, because the specific hermeneutic (as well as geopolitical) claim that underpins the conceptual instruments remains untouched and keeps functioning as before. Having its origin in the Occident and forming an integral part of the Occident's cultural history, it is only within that realm that the strong claim of the hermeneutic tradition is justified. The very specificity of its origin disqualifies it as an instrument for understanding non-Western 'Others' when applied in a universal perspective. The process of understanding 'Others' is bound to fail if the strangeness of the 'Other' is disregarded even before the process of understanding begins, as the subject endeavouring to understand the object to be understood undertakes to modify, construct and violate it 'according to his very own plan, concept, prejudices and sedimented layers of meaning' (Mall and Hülsmann, 1989:86).

We cannot overcome these difficulties simply by replacing terms inherent in Western vocabulary with terms inherent in the respective culture, since their usage would not only ontologise the difference between self and Other (the viewing subject and the object being viewed) but also reestablish the premises of cultural relativism. On the contrary, the act of 'understanding' should not proceed from existing entities, but the uniqueness that marks cultural encounters, namely the process of translating, should become the focus from which 'understanding' evolves. The image of cultural identities arises only from the interaction of various groups of people in which the relationships between

Other and self are negotiated, defined and agreed. In the interactive situation, translation functions as the constitutive tool in reaching an understanding, first of all, by interpreting what the Other is saying and expressing. In this context, it is also crucially important to determine what 'translation' means in the various cultures. Furthermore, in any such process of translating the presupposed characteristics of one's own culture are reflected, even though the necessity to do so may partly be based on misunderstandings.[1]

If the process of translating is viewed from this perspective, the critical reflection on the rise of the principle of universality , which still dominates the Western way of thinking, gains in importance. For the crisis that the enlightened philosophy of progress and the classical sociological theory of modernisation are going through has shown that a global acceptance of the belief in a completely rationalised society is unlikely to occur. The expectations placed in the creation of a rationally organised world community have obviously not been met, and the claim to close the gap between the cultures by applying hermeneutic methods regains centre place. As I pointed out, however, the applicability of these methods, anchored as they are in their respective cultures, is limited to the cultural boundaries imposed on them. Consequently, anthropological texts can no longer be regarded as valid reconstructions of foreign realities. Rather, they have to be interpreted as narratives, and it is an imperative that the narrative construction of the 'Other' be reflected upon (Fabian, 1983).[2] Even the critical review of the narrative construction of the Other—widespread as it now is—will remain unsatisfactory, though, as long as anthropologists do so merely for the purpose of self-reflection and continue to consciously disregard the *problématique* of cultural differences hidden in those narrative forms. And, of course, anthropological self-restraint, as much as it may be based on insights of earlier errors, will leave unanswered the question concerning communication with the Others. Understanding the Other then is a task for which, at the moment, there seems to be no satisfactory solution.

The translatability of cultures

The problem of cultural translatability has been discussed in the past mainly by British social anthropologists under the aspect of the right way to understand and translate sentences such as 'Twins are birds.' In his classical study of the religion of the Nuer, Edward Evans-Pritchard, one of the founders of social anthropology, came across this statement and tried to understand it by surveying the entire cosmology of the Nuer (Evans-Pritchard, 1957). The attempt at grasping this sentence, first translated into English by Evans-Pritchard himself, demonstrates that a direct word-by-word translation can by no means solve the problem of understanding. The interpretation of the meaning of this sentence sparked a lengthy and heated debate within the discipline of anthropology.

In the quest for the right understanding—an issue that surfaced in the classical phase of social anthropology—the Otherness of the Other was never questioned, and therefore Evans-Pritchard could see the task of the anthropologist in translating 'from one culture into the other' (Evans-Pritchard, 1968:19). The relationship between 'us,' the scientist and the translator, and the 'Others' as objects having to undergo translation was self-evident; and the adequate representation of foreign cultures in the language of the scientist seemed to pose no problems of principle. The difficulty in the act of translating was reduced to the question as to how to transfer a statement in a language 'other' than one's own into a language used in Europe. This procedure overlooks one's own linguistic bonds; the foreign semantic horizons are assimilated into one's own language as 'homogenous entities' and one's own language and system of values is thus not endangered. For a long time this aspect of translating has, as a result of the one-sided approach taken by the social sciences, been largely neglected. It was not until the onset of a critical review of cultural anthropology, instigated by the publication of *Writing Culture. The Poetics and Politics of Ethnography*, edited by James Clifford and George E. Marcus (1984), that the importance to one's own culture of translating procedures was underlined from a non-Western perspective. Talad Asad used Arabic as an example to demonstrate that most of the non-European languages have been changed so much since the second half of the nineteenth century through the translation of European-language texts so that those languages moved closer to the European ones.[3]

To the extent that the classical British social anthropologists, on the one hand, and Asad, on the other, differ in their judgement of the importance of translating procedures, they can serve to demonstrate the asymmetric relationship between the 'Occident' and the 'Orient.' Whereas European humanists understand translation as the assimilation of foreign reality, translation in non-European cultures is understood as a process resulting in fundamental changes of selfhood (see Shimada, 1994). The question of the translatability between European languages has never been posed in a like manner, even though for centuries the questions of interpretability and the possible range of interpretations of classical Greek or Latin terms have been the centre of a discourse which contributed in particular to the development of the self-understanding of the Occident.

Veena Das (1993) elucidates this asymmetrical relationship (expressing constellations of power) between the Occident and other cultures when she interprets the writings of Louis Dumont from an Indian perspective and shows how India was constituted as an object of anthropological research by the construction of a temporal difference between the 'modernity' of the West and the 'traditional' character of India. When Dumont equates Indian culture with traditional vestiges and denies it any legitimacy in the creation of a modern nation, an educated Hindu is expected to transfer his own tradition into the past, as 'orientation along the traditions of one's own society is legitimate only

if traditions are seen as belonging to the past' (405). This line of reasoning produces two significant results: on the one hand, positioning the foreign culture (India) in the past enables Western scientists and readers to view it as an object of study. On the other hand, Indian intellectuals are confronted with the normative proposition to distance themselves from their own culture and to prostitute themselves as research objects. In order to be able to participate in a sociological and anthropological discourse, Indian scientists are encouraged to distance themselves from their own selfhood by identifying themselves with the modern.

One possible counterposition to the Western universalistic stand is taken by the Indian sociologist A. K. Saran. But even his writings remain tied to the premises discussed above, turning out to be little more than their negation. 'Saran succumbs to the view according to which traditional Indian civilisation is the Other (one is inclined to say, an extraterritorial Other) of reason' (421), when he takes a culturalistic stand opposed to universalistic modernity. Once again we are trapped in the dichotomy of universalism and relativism.

This dichotomy results perhaps from a perspective in which Dumont and Saran become representatives of two closed systems, which face each other as the 'Orient' and the 'Occident.' Surely, this counterposition can be read in the context of the postcolonial situation in India in which emancipatory movements have furthered the polarisation between the West and India. However, this opposition of universalism and relativism does not only leave its mark on the East-West confrontation, it is also evolving within cultures and, thanks to its antagonism, forms the very foundation for cultural identities. What I am saying is that the East as well as the West each constitute themselves by means of various discourses, which always relate to one another but also oppose each other.

In the following I will use an analysis of the study *Nihon seiji shisôshi kenkyû* (Studies in the Intellectual History of *Tokugawa* Japan) by Maruyama Masao (1952) to discuss this constitutive process of cultural identity. This study, which has had a lasting effect in Japan as well as in the West, has been used again and again as a starting point for discussions on the characteristics of 'the Japanese.' As I will show below, Maruyama takes a universalistic, modernist standpoint, from which he criticises the state of Japanese society. His stand towards Japanese tradition is similar to Dumont's stand towards Indian society, irrespective of the fact that Maruyama is himself a member of the society he is studying.

3. Translated Terms and Cultural Self-understanding

The Japanese discourse on 'self' and 'other' emerged after the Meiji Restoration in 1868. In the course of debates over what one later called 'modernisation' and 'globalisation,' in which the encountering, and the coming to terms

with, Western civilisation ranks foremost, key terms of the social sciences—like 'society,' 'individual,' 'religion' and 'nation'—along with the major writings from the Western intellectual traditions were translated into Japanese and came to exert a lasting influence on Japanese thought and societal development (Yanabu, 1991). Various forms of translation were developed: major works in the social sciences were usually translated as complete editions; certain theories were partially translated and incorporated in the Japanese author's own publications; and finally a number of archetypal theories were developed using the key translated terms. During this process of transfer some contributions became constitutive of the emerging discourse. One of those works is the study by Maruyama, which together with the new postwar impulses in Japan was to have a decisive and lasting influence on the discourse in the social sciences.

Recently, Maruyama's works have frequently been criticised for their Eurocentrism. This form of criticism propounds the thesis that Japanese society, given its cultural tradition, differs fundamentally from the West. The critique is founded on the cultural-relativistic concept that Japanese culture has undergone a development of its own, one differing from the West, and that consequently the 'negative' representation of the 'self' is not appropriate. Saran, as we have seen, takes an analogous position which sees in one's own culture the 'other of reason.' Whereas Maruyama states that Japanese society needs to be developed along the lines of the Western model, his critics maintain that Japan has to follow other principles of development because it has its own distinct cultural background. Interestingly enough, the very same perspectives that are discussed in Veena Das' essay and portrayed as two poles, one advanced by a Western and the other by an Indian author, can be found within another non-Western society. On the one side are the Western-oriented 'universalists' like Maruyama, on the other the traditionalists oriented towards cultural relativism. However, neither of the two antagonistic standpoints question the foundation of the 'own' society, thus sharing a common starting point from which they develop diverging schools of thought.

Studies in the intellectual history of Tokugawa Japan

Maruyama begins his book, which is divided into three parts, with deliberations on Chinese society.[4] He uses Hegel's philosophy of history as the starting point and emphasises China's ahistoricism, which he attributes to Confucian foundations. From there he moves to Japan and underlines the contrast to the Chinese development: 'In *Tokugawa* Japan, Confucianism disintegrated into completely heterogeneous elements because of developments within its own structure' (Maruyama, 1974:17).

The starting point of his train of thought is obvious: He draws a picture of Japan by comparing Japan with China and Europe without, however, explicitly mentioning Europe. European developments are most significant in this constellation, since we have to refer to Hegel's philosophy of history to truly

understand the importance of the historical stagnation of Chinese society. Maruyama stresses that Japan—in contrast to China—neither got trapped in an ahistorical state—nor did it—like Europe did—produce its own form of modernity. The religious background of Confucianism serves as the platform from which the developmental possibilities towards modernity are investigated. In doing so, Maruyama adopts two approaches from Western social theories. Firstly, a historical model of development serves as a framework in which the three civilisations are embedded; and secondly, the concept that societal development (or nondevelopment) towards modernity is based on distinct religious attitudes is appropriated.

This thinking uses the Western model of an autonomous subject as the basis for its analysis of society. Chinese society is consequently designated as the 'empire of duration' (Hegel) in which 'the subject (the individual) failed to attain his own rights' because of the given societal structure (4). The search for a subject then becomes a leitmotiv for the further studies of Japanese cultural history. The insight emerges that it was not possible during the *Tokugawa*-period (1600-1867) to sow the seeds from which a society based on autonomous subjects would emerge despite the tendency at the time towards a 'rational' approach to the world and despite the separation of the ethics of human action from 'nature.' This philosophy of history creates a bridge between the beginning and the end of the study which finally deals with the prerequisites for creating a nation. As Maruyama sees it, a social unity deserves being called a nation, however, only if it is willed by its subjects (321).

Neo-Confucianism and 'modernity'

The first part of Maruyama's study deals with the first stage of the 'self-disintegration of Confucian thought.' Ogyû Sorai (1666-1728), a court scholar of the Shogunate, thoroughly contested the neo-Confucianism of the *Chu-Hsi* school, which up to then had been accepted as the official state ideology. The presentation is devoted mainly to this inner-Japanese discourse. Nevertheless, at the end of this section the comparison with China becomes obvious as Maruyama explains in clear terms his intention to demonstrate how the seeds of a modern consciousness were sown. By using the term 'modern' he creates a parallel to the European development and shows that thanks to Ogyû Sorai a number of impulses for the further development of modernity can be given (183). Maruyama justifies his search for the origins of modern consciousness in the feudalistic thought of Ogyu Sorai rather than in the countermovement against the ruling classes given that criticism towards the ruling class did by no means lead to radical changes in thinking in the Japanese context. Since the 'bourgeois' forces were not able to develop ('normally') during the *Tokugawa* period, the attempt to find a modern consciousness among the antifeudal forces was fruitless. It was therefore necessary to investigate the process of internal disintegration of Confucianism in the context of feudal social rela-

tions. Once again the premises of the analysis are all too evident: the starting point is the bourgeoisie as the subject of European development, and the lack of such an element in one's own history is ascertained.

'Community' (Gemeinschaft) and 'society' (Gesellschaft)

The second part of the study, which treats the self-disintegration process of Confucianism in the societal context of the *Tokugawa* period, formulates the shift in world view from a system organised on the laws of Nature to one organised by man. And again we encounter the triangular constellation mentioned above. The teachings of the neo-Confucianist Chu-Hsi, which emphasise the natural order, stand for the Chinese culture in which no societal development occurs; in addition, changes in thinking in Europe from the Middle Ages to modern times are depicted; and finally, Ogyû Sorai, who on the basis of the thought of Chu-Hsi produced something different, stands for 'the Japanese' per se.

Community and society is the conceptual couple to which central significance is given. The line of reasoning applied here is again quite clear: The societal conditions during the *Tokugawa*-period, which found ideal support in the thought of Chu-Hsi based on natural order, is called community and the term 'community' is linked at the same time with the term 'religion' (224). Social change upturns the prevailing order, and a need for stabilisation by means of a new legitimisation emerges. Ogyû Sorai, the court philosopher, was faced with this problem and tried to reinterpret Confucian teachings in order to legitimise the claims of the ruling classes. Sorai's theory—according to Maruyama—reflects the development from community to society. Maruyama illustrates this with the terms 'idea' and 'person,' the conceptual order of which had been reversed by Sorai. Up to then, the order of the world was assumed to have been ruled by an idea (Nature). It was Sorai who for the first time placed 'person' at the beginning of the world order and initiated the first step toward 'rationalisation.' Maruyama adopted this approach, as is ever so obvious, from the European interpretation of history which he describes in detail in the chapter on 'The historical significance of the transition from nature to invention.' European history is seen as a means of assessing Japanese history; the result can be measured by the difference between the two despite the analogy in their development:

> 'While the *Chu Hsi* school almost purely and completely embodied the *Gemeinschaft* mode of thought, there are obviously certain historical limitations to a similar accord between the Sorai school and the *Gesellschaft* mode of thought' (231).

The difference Maruyama is referring to lies in the conception of individual:

> 'In a completely modernised *Gesellschaft* mode of thought, the theory that men as agents with free will invent the social order applies to every individual. [...] But

for the Sorai school, the personalities who invent the social order are above all the sages, and then by analogy political rulers in general' (231).

Following up on this comment, Maruyama addresses the question of whether the transformation from the logic of a natural order to a logic of a subjective act lies in the objective necessity through which the subject attained its expression in the 'absolute form' of a sacred. By doing so he refers again to European cultural history which paved the way for the 'actual' course of this transformation. At the end of this section he concludes with the analogy between God in the European Middle Ages and the sacred in the Sorai-teachings and their respective function in the transformation of the way of thinking. Concerning the birth of the subject it was necessary in both cases to do away with the superiority of the 'impersonal idea' thus making it possible to place the 'person' at the beginning of the world order (231-8). As the thought of Chu-Hsi was, in comparison to Christianity, more solidly set in the laws of Nature, Sorai had to place a greater emphasis on the absoluteness of the person, which explains why he restricted the concept of the acting subject to the sovereign and did not expand it to include the individual in general. The limits of Sorai's teachings lie then in equating the feudal sovereigns of the *Tokugawa* dynasty with the person establishing order. Having done so, the prerequisite has been devised which permits us to pose the question of the legitimacy of these sovereigns and to regard the prevailing order as man-made, although—paradoxically—the teachings themselves were originally intended to further the legitimacy of the claims of the ruling classes.

'In effect, the common feature that limited the revolutionary character of the theories of social reform of the later *Tokugawa* period was the fact that all the proposed systems were to be imposed *from above*. The common people were assigned no active role in the implementation of the changes. If we consider the significance of this in relation to my thesis, we see that the theorists discussed here echoed Sorai's call for the reconstruction of institutions, although their proposals of reform are immensely richer in content and even incorporate some modern elements. In this respect they were concrete developments of the theory of invention. But at the same time, they reveal little theoretical progress in that position. The theoretical limit of Sorai's philosophy of invention, the fact that the inventing agent could only be a special personality such as a sage or a *Tokugawa* shogun, still remained. This limitation clung obstinately to all the adherents of the theory of invention whom I have discussed, from Sorai on. In other words, there is no indication that these theorists were inclining toward the concept that it is the people who make institutions (as the social contract theory)' (300).

The process of rationalization within Japanese society remained 'incomplete,' because one failed to achieve what Europe had already practised: '*Entzauberung*' of the sovereign whose legitimacy remained in the sphere of the sacred. Although Sorai's teachings show signs of modern thinking, as the world order is laid in the hands of a person for the first time, the idea of a society

founded on participating subjects was still not able to establish itself. It was not until the Meiji restoration that this situation changed fundamentally, as with the arrival of a specific movement towards democracy (*Jiyû minken undô*):

> 'Furthermore, it was the emergence of the Movement for Freedom and Popular Rights that established the supremacy of the theory of invention in the post-Restoration period. *Here the doctrine of invention was at last able to develop its implications to their conclusion in a clear-cut theory of man-made institutions*' (312).

This does not mean, however, that the model of a world order based on laws of nature was to disappear completely, because a discourse opposing this democratic movement arose which again proclaimed the existence of a natural order.

> 'Apparently on the verge of recapturing his freedom as autonomous personality with respect to the social order, having eliminated the restrictions of the estate system in the Meiji Restoration, man was to be swallowed up again by the new Leviathan, the Meiji state' (312).

Surely, Maruyama's conclusions need to be read in their historical context, since he wrote them between 1940-1944 at a time when the categories of 'the Japanese' and above all the 'Japanese spirit' were of absolute priority. Bearing this in mind, a reading of his analysis of the nation is all the more difficult.

The question of the 'nation'

Maruyama begins the next section of his study, 'The premodern formation of nationalism,' with a short and general description of the concept of nation in which the triangular constellation as a means of comparison is once again applied. The model of the nation that Maruyama presents here is obviously taken from an enlightened-liberal concept:

> 'The objective fact of belonging to a common state entity and sharing common political institutions does not constitute a nation (*kokumin*) in the modern sense. What is obtained in this case is at best a people (*jinmin*) or members of a state (*kokka*), but not a nation. Before a people can become a nation they must actively desire to belong to a common community and participate in common institutions, or at least consider such a situation to be desirable' (323).

Maruyama describes the state of things prior to the building of a nation as follows:

> 'On the other hand, even if a state system encompassing the entire nation exists, this does not automatically and inevitably give rise to an awareness of political unity within the nation. When the internal structure of the system prevents the people from congealing politically into a state, the state system will fail to grasp them from the inside, and the great majority of the people will continue to exist in a natural, impersonal (vegetative) fashion' (325).

In a footnote to this section he refers to the Chinese Empire before the revolution as an example. This constellation is the framework he uses for his comparisons and for his analysis of the Japanese development. With this in mind he then presents a universal theory of the building of a nation: 'At a certain stage in its historical development, a nation is spurred by some external stimulus and more or less consciously transforms itself from simple dependence on the surroundings into a political nation' (326).

Along the lines of this comparison in which the historical necessity of building a nation is described, Maruyama then outlines the development in Japan from the *Tokugawa*-period: 'Despite our long and glorious national tradition, the birth of a national consciousness in the sense described above, and a nationalism built around such a national consciousness, did not occur in Japan until the Meiji Restoration'(327).

How does this comment relate to the one at the end of the second chapter in which he maintains that the new subject was swallowed again by a Leviathan? Did the Meiji Restoration really bring forth a Japanese nation? Finally, Maruyama's remarks in the third chapter reveal that, in spite of the optimistic tone at the beginning, his ultimate answer is negative. Not even in the thinking of the late *Tokugawa*-period can he find any seeds that would have developed into an autonomous subject which would have contributed to the building of a nation.

Nation-building is then seen as nothing more than a change in consciousness of a people that in the course of history has remained homogenous and is categorised under the term 'the Japanese people.' He underlines this perspective when he decides to translate the term 'nationalism' by *kokuminshugi* instead of by *minzokushugi* (*minzoku* is a translation of the term 'people' in the sense of 'ethnic'). The term *minzokushugi* is only appropriate if a minority or a colonised people gained their independence or when a people that lived in several states and set up a state of their own, whereas the term is inappropriate for 'Japan, where racial homogeneity has been preserved from the past and where there have never been any serious racial problems' (324). The homogeneity of the Japanese people is then the incontestable presupposition of thinking in the entire study. The continuity which is constructed here in the narrative form is continuity projected from the position of the 'nation.' The identity bearing the name 'Japan' is seen as a natural presumption which has managed to retain its character throughout the upheavals in history. This identity is seen to stem from the genealogy of its 'citizens,' 'the Japanese people' (*nihon minzoku*). It is now obvious how two concepts of nation can exist side by side: a nation is defined on the one side by the subjective will of its members, and on the other nationality forms the foundation of the Japanese nation. No attention is paid to the fact that the German concept of '*Kulturnation*' was adopted by the political elite during the Meiji period and that the 'Japanese people,' in the sense of attaining equal citizenship status, did not originate until

then. This image of unity of the 'Japanese people' has to be seen as a result of these adoption and translation processes. Maruyama's discourse on the 'racial homogeneity' of the Japanese and the narrative construction of continuity supports this image. As I have mentioned above, this construction of a 'Japanese identity' is grounded in the triangular constellation with China and Europe, and based on a comparison in which one's own identity is repeatedly constructed and confirmed in the Oriental discourse (with respect to China) as well as in the Occidental discourse (with respect to Europe).

Construction of identity through conceptual borrowing

This brief presentation was meant to demonstrate the supportive role key translated terms can play when reflecting one's 'own' society. Maruyama, as a representative of the critical intellectuals, is looking for paths to a society based on a nation-state in which each individual citizen intentionally fulfils his duties. At the same time, his conceptual elaboration relies on an idea of the continuity of the Japanese unity which is founded in the homogeneity of the Japanese people. This is where his concept of nation proves to be inconsistent, as he brings together the liberal and ethnic concept of nation without having formulated their diverging conceptualisations.

The generally accepted starting point of Japanese discourse on its own societal reality is the continuity of Japanese history which has always been lived by one and the same subject, the 'Japanese people.' It is important to bear in mind that even academic scholars like Maruyama, himself a critical thinker oriented towards the social sciences, took this presupposition for granted, a presupposition that dates back to the history of adoption of social-science theories and terminology during the second half of the nineteenth century. In this context, the concept of 'societal history' was also adopted, which marked the onset of the written history of the nation. Once this 'process of historisation' had taken hold, the concept of a subject itself making history was introduced into Japanese society, and the people were constructed as a homogenous nation. With the establishment of the social sciences, which drew their legitimacy, in part, from the parallel establishment of 'society' as an object of study, a perspective was also adopted, of which Maruyama's study provides a good example, namely the perspective that society is to be explained on the basis of its own endogenous development.

The contradictory terminology in Maruyama's study, however, is also a reflection of the historical constellations within Europe. For Maruyama's tacit acceptance of the existence of a Japanese nation corresponds to the idea of a *Kulturnation*, a concept particular to German-speaking countries which developed as a reaction to the universalistic-liberal concept of nation. This Western concept was absorbed but not profoundly reflected in Japan, and this may be the reason why its adoption worked so well in creating a Japanese self-consciousness. Japan experienced industrialisation and rationalisation in the same

manner as German-speaking countries did, namely as an incursion by a 'foreign' civilisation into one's 'own' sphere. It is understandable then that a conceptual model which had only recently been developed in the German-speaking countries would be willingly adopted in its entirety by a different culture and reworked to fit its own interpretation and self-consciousness.

What becomes obvious in this context is that the encounter with a civilisation based on universalistic principles had to pave the way for the development of a concept of selfhood, which possesses a distinct national territory and a distinct endogenous history of social unity. In addition, the particularistic counterconcept, which had developed within the European context as a reaction to the universalistic concept of civilisation prevailing in the Enlightenment, was applied in the course of conceptualising one's proper selfhood.

4. Concluding Remarks

We have seen how a national identity was conceived and at the same time proved to be an incontestable intellectual presupposition in the discourse within the social sciences in Japan. Firstly, key terms played a constitutive role in this process, but secondly, it was the antagonistic perspective within the discourse itself which proved to be the starting point that led to national identity as self-understanding. In this process Maruyama took the stand of a modernist, whereas traditionalists emphasised the cultural uniqueness of Japan; both positions shared a common starting point, namely the adoption of certain concepts from the West. Not only did they share key concepts, they also shared the concept of history and the idea of technological progress which served as the basis for comparing cultures. They were also convinced that religion was a determining factor affecting the social behaviour of a society's members.

I hope I have not only demonstrated the influence of translated terms and theoretical concepts. I also wanted to show that cultural identity can be observed as the result of innumerable translating processes. What is usually regarded as the *natural* foundation of one's own or an alien identity has actually been borrowed from an alien context or is an answer to one. What seems inevitably to happen once a conceptual *self* has been established is that the process of translating is forgotten. The borderline between self and Other has been drawn and given an exact definition, and the elements of Other and self are concealed from view.

A discussion of translation then serves to unearth 'layer by layer' the constitutive moments of self and Other. It is absolutely necessary to keep in mind the prevailing asymmetrical relationship of translating processes. Moreover, the analysis of translating processes may reveal the origins of heterogeneous and pluralistic elements which make up cultural identity. In doing so, the polarisation of cultural identities, which are taken to be homogenous entities, is avoided.

A concept that rests on the principle that self is constituted through a discourse involving disparate positions can surely be transferred to all modern societies. Therefore, it is possible and necessary to move from the Japanese example to Western development, where a similar movement took place which eventually led to the formation of the identity of the West. It was through a continuous reference to foreign cultures and through intrasocietal comparisons that antagonistic positions evolved which although they differed sharply in their views shared the same presuppositions of thinking. And even in the self-understanding of the West the basic terminology of the social sciences played a constitutive role. Regardless of whether we refer to 'society,' of the 'individual' or of 'religion,' each category contains elements of a relationship between self and Other and, moments of exclusion. The latter perspective explains why the West went on to develop *society*, so that the Others should remain in the status of *community*. It was argued that the rise of the individual in Western history was only possible by a process of moving against tradition, and correspondingly the individual was declared the 'key concept of modern society' (Dumont, 1991:27). This construction entails the normative claim that modern societies have to be organised principally on an individualistic basis. And even 'religion' acquired the importance it has today through comparisons (Matthes, 1993). To be sure, the expansion of this term to the so-called 'world religions' helps to counterbalance the universal claim to truth propagated by Christianity, and that again resulted in 'religion' being defined exclusively from a Western perspective. Certain forms of religion as expressed in the terms 'magic,' 'totemism,' 'animism' were excluded. It becomes all the more obvious that fundamental terms in the social sciences contributed to constituting and formulating the self-understanding of the West. This new set of terms, first used within the European discourse, reflects the self and the Other. As we have seen, after having been transferred to alien cultures, they were subsequently used within those cultures themselves. Even the term 'identity' is part of this usually one-sided process of translation, as this term too was adopted by non-Western cultures and was used to construct one's own identity. In this context we can speak of Eurocentrism as a catalyst that generates discourse and defines aspects of the social and human sciences not only in the West but also in non-Western societies.

Even though we may find it extremely difficult to free ourselves of this Eurocentric perspective, raising awareness of the powerful meaning of key concepts of the social sciences and analysing their spread through non-Western societies is an important step in understanding those historical moments that sparked the process of the constitution of 'cultural identity.' A review of these processes can create new prerequisites towards a better understanding of one another. The methodological approach can be termed a 'sociology of knowledge about cultural interactions' through which the interactive constitution of self and Other is examined from a semantic level. We could thus out-

line semantic constructions of cultural differences through which new possibilities arise with respect to the relationship between self and Other. Rather
than fight the 'battle of the cultures,' we could strive for *interactive cultures.*

Notes

1. On the problems of misunderstanding in anthropology see Fabian, 1995.
2. A good example for critical reflection on one's own writing is Geertz, 1988.
3. As Asad (1984:158) points out: 'Take modern Arabic as an example. Since the early nineteenth century there has been a growing volume of materials translated from European languages—especially French and English—into Arabic. [...] And from the nineteenth
   century, Arabic as a language has begun as a result to undergo a transformation (lexical,
   grammatical, semantic) that is far more radical than anything to be identified in European
   languages—a transformation that has pushed it to approximate to the latter more closely
   than in the past.'
4. The three parts of this book have the following titles: 'The Sorai School: its role in the disintegration of Tokugawa Confucianism and its impact on national learning'; 'Nature and
   invention in Tokugawa political thought: contrasting institutional views,' and 'The premodern formation of nationalism.'

References

Asad, Talal (1984) 'The Concept of Cultural Translation in British Social
   Anthropology', in James Clifford and George E. Marcus (eds) *Writing Culture.
   The Poetics and Politics of Ethnography*, Berkeley, pp. 141-64.
Clifford, James and Marcus, George E. (eds), (1984) *Writing Culture. The Poetics
   and Politics of Ethnography*, Berkeley.
Das, Veena (1993) 'Der anthropologische Diskurs über Indien. Die Vernunft und ihr
   Anderes', in Eberhard Berg and Martin Fuchs (eds): *Kultur soziale Praxis, Text.
   Die Krise der ethnographischen Repräsentation*, Frankfurt/M., pp. 402-25.
Dumont, Louis (1991) *Individualismus. Zur Ideologie der Moderne (Essais sur
   l'individualisme. Une perspective anthropologique sur l'idéologie moderne)*,
   Frankfurt/New York.
Evans-Pritchard, Edward E. (1957) *The Nuer Religion,* Oxford.
Evans-Pritchard, Edward E. (1968) *Theorien über primitive Religion*, Frankfurt/M.
Fabian, Johannes (1983) *Time and the Other. How Anthropology Makes its Object*,
   New York.

Fabian, Johannes (1995) 'Ethnographic Misunderstanding and the Perils of Context', *American Anthropologist*, 97, 1:41-50.

Geertz, Clifford (1988) *Works and Lives: the Anthropologist as Author*, Stanford.

Huntington, Samuel (1993) 'A Clash of Civilizations?', *Foreign Affairs*, pp. 22-49.

Lévi-Strauss, Claude (1992) *Strukturale Anthropologie II*, Frankfurt/M.

Mall, Ram Adhar and Hülsmann, Heinz (1989) *Die drei Geburtsorte der Philosophie. China, Indien, Europa*, Bonn.

Maruyama, Masao (1952) *Nihon seiji shisôshi kenkyû*, Tokyo.

Maruyama, Masao (1974) *Studies in the Intellectual History of Tokugawa Japan*, Tokyo/Princeton.

Matthes, Joachim (1993) 'Was ist anders an anderen Religionen? Anmerkungen zur zentristischen Organisation des religionssoziologischen Denkens', in Jörg Bergmann et al. (eds) *Religion und Kultur, Sonderband 33 der Kölner Zeitschrift für Soziologie und Sozialpsychologie*, Opladen, pp. 16-30.

Shimada, Shingo (1994) *Grenzgänge—Fremdgänge. Japan und Europa im Kulturvergleich*, Frankfurt/New York.

Straub Jürgen and Shimada, Shingo (1999): 'Relationale Hermeneutik im Kontext interkulturellen Verstehens. Probleme universalistischer Begriffsbildung in den Sozial- und Kulturwissenschaften, erörtert am Beispiel "Religion"', *Deutsche Zeitschrift für Philosophie*, 3:449-77.

Tenbruck, Friedrich H. (1989) 'Gesellschaftsgeschichte oder Weltgeschichte?', *Kölner Zeitschrift für Soziologie und Sozialpsychologie*, 41, 3:417-39.

Yanabu, Akira (1991) *Die Modernisierung der Sprache*, Munich.

III: Women and Alterity

The Performance of Hysteria

ELISABETH BRONFEN

'*Je est un autre*' ('I is an other') wrote Arthur Rimbaud in 1871, at a time when this statement may still have been understood as a provocation. Ever since the dawn of the postmodern era, however, we are constantly offered new theoretical arguments to persuade us of the plurality and the frailness of the I. It is commonplace nowadays to talk of the individual as a representational construct that is conditioned, manufactured and manipulated by language, images and society, a construct that can even be artificially portrayed. The subject, so the argument runs, emerges precisely because it is *subjected* to the linguistic laws of its culture, just as it has to bow to the prohibitions and desires of its own unconscious. In other words: grafted onto a complex network of significant differences, deferences and dislocations, and marked by a multitude of systems of signs, the postmodern subject is seen as the nexus of the symbolic discourses and of the representations of its cultural context.

These concepts radically question the humanist self-image, which assumes that the individual controls his self to freely use and form it. Perhaps portrait painting has become such a privileged art in Europe since the Renaissance precisely because it serves as evidence that the individual can be captured in the image and that the subject can produce a clear image of itself (Berger, 1972). This insurance of the self, as it were, released for the first time by painting, could then be continued in the nineteenth century by means of the new performing media, like photography and film. For these new media permitted the self to observe itself as multifaceted as it pleased, to recognise and study itself and to be the object of such explorations for others (Chevrier and Sagne, 1984). The soul, man's secret dimension, previously only imaginable, seemed to rise closer and closer to the surface throughout the centuries. At the same time as in medical practice anatomic dissections revealed the inside of

the human body (as Michel Foucault explained in his research about the origin of the modern clinic), work was done on the visualisation of all hidden aspects of the self, at the latest from the middle of the nineteenth century onwards. This is also the time when the police started collecting photographs of criminals and suspects in order to systematise investigative work, and the time when psychiatrists began producing photos of their patients, in the belief that by reading their physiognomies they could build a visual grammar of insanity, pain, suffering and other sensations (Gilman, 1982).

Any sign language, however, harbours an inherent contradiction. The more one gets involved in the photograph's power, the further away one gets from the clear security of an identity. As was already known during the Romantic period, if one can produce more than one rendering of one's I, this plurality of the self lets the affected person, as well as the observer, doubt the stability of the rendition. The doubling of the I through the picture does not only trigger self-assurance, but also fright and confusion. Here, the artistic meets the psychological, because the diversity of the self, made possible through photography, makes visible another, concealed, mark of the I, a psychological frailness, which, as Freud put it in his essay 'The Uncanny,' 'lets you doubt your own I' (1919:246). The artistic multiplicity of the I can tip over worryingly quickly and present a setting where the self rediscovers itself in the midst of a number of familiar and unfamiliar masks.

These duplications at the same time dissolved the borderline between the sexes and reduced the distance between the human and the nonhuman. The photograph turned into a medium that enabled men and women to change gender and to redesign themselves as animals, monsters and machines. This illustrates the fundamental contradiction that the following discussion deals with: because photography offers infinite possibilities of staging, one and the same technology can, on the one hand, depict the facts of the world seemingly objectively, and on the other, become a medium of fantasised projections. What on the one hand can be used to establish an identity—like the use of a passport photo—allows the subjects on the other hand to abandon themselves to the invention of hybrid identities. The individual designs new faces that only emerge in the design, it re-arranges its anatomy, breaks itself up into small pieces and reifies itself, anticipates its death (Barthes, 1981). The staging of the self-portrait introduces a surplus of phantasms into the world, a world that is comfortable in the belief that the identity of the self is determined and that such objective matters of fact cannot be called into question.

The self-portrait then, particularly when it forms a series, as is the case in the examples to be discussed in this article, raises a number of questions about the self: does it have a solid identity, or does it only exist as a masquerade, i.e. is it only created in the staging of the picture? This leads to another problem. If the self can only be staged as a masquerade, the self-portrait refers to a *Nothing*. If the self can only depict itself in varied forms, it triggers discom-

fort, at least in the observer. This is because the observer cannot decide whether there is a consistent subject behind the masquerade, a subject that manipulates and play-acts, in order to prove its artistic power and keep the secret of its identity to itself, or whether perhaps there is nothing behind these masquerades; no hidden subject and no secret, merely shapeless life matter (Zizek, 1994). The self-portrait, at least in the examples of the serial staging of the self, turns out to be fundamentally contradictory. This is because one and the same artistic gesture establishes this self and radically calls it into question at the same time. While playing with the production of self-images immortalises this self—because it makes the images reproducible and therefore conservable—it also extinguishes this self by revealing its transitoriness and mutability. In the following discussion about different series of photographic self-portraits I will try to illuminate this vanishing point between self-staging and *Nothing*, because the discrepancy between self-portrait and identity shines masterly when a self produces a multitude of masquerades.

1. La Divine Comtesse

Comtesse de Castiglione was not the first and not the only great lady in the France of the Second Empire who, abandoning herself to the exhibitionism of photography, had herself depicted in many different ways. It was indeed not uncommon for the celebrities of the royal court of Napoleon III to sell their self-portraits commercially like advertising leaflets. The many photographs of the Comtesse, however, are a good starting point for my discussion, because they show with extraordinary clarity how self staging, apparently a safeguard and immortalisation of the I, is accompanied by the destruction of the self.

Virginia Verasis, *née* Oldoni, Countess of Castiglione, fascinated society not only with her extraordinary beauty, but also with the extravagance with which she sought to make a work of art of her appearance. Gaston Jollivet wrote about her: 'There was at no moment, at least not during my lifetime, another woman, who personified the immortal Venus more perfectly' (cited in: Solomon-Godeau, 1994). She was one of the stars of her time, and Count Robert de Montesquiou, who called himself the king of the transitory, not only collected around 400 of her photos as well as her letters, her jewellery and other personal belongings, he also wrote a book about her where he immortalised her as, significantly, *la divine comtesse*. In 1856 she had come to Paris from Italy with the instruction to convince Napoleon III to support King Victor Emmanuel in the unification of the territories of Piemont, Lombardy-Venice and Sicily under his crown. After having been Napoleon's mistress for a short while, she soon fell out of favour with him. Yet she never ceased to amaze society. She lived a secluded life, only rarely appeared during festive occasions in public, but was at the same time obsessed with her own self-

image. In the course of twenty years she offered herself, driven by a seemingly insatiable narcissistic desire, to the camera of Pierre Louis Pierson, one of the founders of the photographic studio Mayer et Pierson in Paris, who produced more than 600 photos of her. The pictures were produced under her direction, at the interface of the observer's voyeurism, the camera's fetishism and the actress's exhibitionism, apparently exclusively intended for the *Comtesse's* private use.

What is unusual about these self-images is first of all the banal fact that there are so many of them. In addition, these photographs depict the whole range of the portrait, from conventional pictures to narrative scenarios and technically unusual, distorting and dismembering pictures of her body. The *Comtesse* shows herself in her favourite ball gowns, and sometimes she adds remarks about colour and trimming. There are pictures of her in historical costumes (dressed as Judith, for example), or she is dressed up as a nun, a Breton peasant woman, a drunk person, a girl in despair, a mourning widow. The pictures are peculiarly fascinating because, on the one hand, the woman obscured herself, dressed up, changed into different selves, in order not to expose her beautiful face to the imaginary audience, and on the other, she almost shamelessly exposed her legs to the camera so that the photographs could capture the fragments of her body. These photographs of her naked legs and feet are not just particularly unusual because they, unlike the scenic photos, overstep the boundary of what was regarded as the representative norm of photography during the Second Empire. They are also astonishing because the naked legs and feet were staged over and over again, sometimes in a carefully artistic way and at the same time full of suggestiveness, often framed more than once and enlarged, sometimes put together in collages. In the course of this contradictory obsession with her own picture, the *Comtesse* arises out of the tension between a game of hide-and-seek and a cleverly calculated exhibitionism. But at the same time she always withdraws, disappears behind masquerades, which explicitly refer to the transitoriness of this woman's beauty.

Abigail Solomon-Godeau (1994) has worked out precisely which combination of narcissism and fetishism and also which secret agreement with one's own objectivisation can be seen in these self-images. In this choreography of the self, thus, the Countess is incessantly confronted with the difficulty, if not the impossibility, of the self-representation outside the sign-system and the economy of her time. These obsessive self-representations, Solomon-Godeau argues, are not merely the product of an internalisation of the alien and masculine look at the woman, but also the exposure of a radical alienation which abolishes the distinction between subjectivity and objectivity. For 'in the moment the *Comtesse* has her picture taken—a moment where individuality and unique subjectivity merge—she reproduces herself as a work of a carefully coded femininity whose origin is not situated in herself' (1994:103). There is here no clear boundary between self and image. The inner creature and its

depiction are no longer clearly distinguishable, so that, according to Salomon-Godeau, the relationship between the Countess and her photos should be seen as 'a sad parable of femininity,' because subjectivity can now only find expression in so far as it conforms to a culturally pregiven frame.

The statements of the Countess' contemporaries repeatedly refer to the artistic nature of her appearance. De Montesquieu, for example, said: 'This woman's life was nothing other than a great *tableau vivant* that never reaches an end' (1913: 8), or Marshall Conrobert: 'Madame de Castiglione was of incomparable beauty. She resembled at the same time the Virgin of Perugino and Venus; she always, however, remained in a state that resembled a sculpture or a painting, inanimate and lifeless' (quoted in: Solomon-Godeau, 1994:103). I would like to shift the interpretation of these photos somewhat, since they capture precisely this impression of an artificial *desouling* for eternity. My suggestion is to turn the critical eye away from the fact *that* the *Comtesse* turns herself into a reified fetish, into a cult object of her time. By such a move, as Solomon-Godeau suggests, her beauty itself came to represent a kind of mask, a disguise that does not conceal a personality that would not be identical with the masquerade. Instead I would like to focus on the question as to how this strategy of self-staging leads to an ambiguous message about beauty where reification intersects with facticity. Freud defines the fetish as an *Ersatz*-object, as a memorial for a shortcoming that can be denied by means of an elevation of the fetish. Similarly, we could say the following about Comtesse de Castiglione's photos: they capture scenes which put up a memorial to precisely this inability and fallibility, from which the beauty recorded in the picture is to be protected. But this also means a court beauty sets her own memorial, thereby bringing her own death prematurely into the picture, as it were. She constructs a legend—the performance and display of a beautiful woman of the world—and she self-confidently furnishes it with a commentary in her diary at the age of 60: 'The Almighty Father did not realise what he had created when he let her see the light of day. He gave her such a splendid form that his senses vanished when he looked at his work' (quoted in: Loliée, 1954:48).

This objectivisation, the division into self and self-image, illustrated in this diary entry by her use of the third person singular and the reference to herself as a work, is present in the photographs themselves. For the stagings of the *Comtesse* are carried out so consciously that the artificiality of this undertaking finds expression by the same move: disrupting factors are built into the picture, a pane of glass through which one can only see her eye, a picture frame that seems to cut her head off from her body. The *Comtesse* has her pictures taken by Pierson again in old age. Her legs are again one of the objects of the photo sessions, this time from the unusual perspective of looking down onto her feet, which rest on a chair or a cushion. As Solomon-Godeau (1994:108) aptly remarked: 'the deadly white of these limbs, in the context of the black cushion created the impression of a body in a coffin.' The photographs that

emphasise the aging of her body are similarly directed towards disability. There is a picture, for example, where the top of her dress is undone to show off her ample bosom, not covered in fine lace but rather revealing a shabby looking undershirt. There is a nonlocatable grin exhibited in her facial expression. Another picture shows her in her old ball gown. On a piece of paper, under the title '*Série des Roses*,' she lists all the places where she had worn it. Furthermore, she attached pieces of paper to the photo in order to optically reduce her circumference, which results in the macabre impression of there being two creatures, the former slim, like a phantom in the frame, and the woman showing the signs of aging. The *Comtesse* thereby anticipates Roland Barthes's (1981) remarks about photography around one hundred years later: the ability of the picture to freeze time, deaden it, so that the photo offers the subject a portrait of oneself by recognising oneself as an historical object. For the countess, this means the thing that she will have been.

2. Images of Hysteria

The problem of the self-portrait—an insistence on the visualisation of a hidden nucleus of identity, which, by means of duplication and the endless possibility of creative shaping, makes uncertain precisely those notions that it sought to secure, namely that there is a clearly definable self—characteristically appears concomitantly to the reemergence of a mental disorder in which the disclosure of something hidden and about the rendering of the self in a deferred and distorted fashion is also at stake: hysteria. Although it will not be possible here to enter into the complex discourse about hysteria, I would like to give a brief outline of the disorder in so far as it is relevant to the present problem of the self-portrait and the performance of identities.

As is well known, the term hysteria derives from the Greek word for womb—*hystera*. Up to the early twentieth century, it appears in medical papers in order to explain walking disorders, paralyses, breathing difficulties, convulsions, fainting fits and hallucinations in female patients (Veith, 1965; Trillat, 1986; von Braun, 1985). The ancient Greeks thought that the womb, when it dries out, wanders around the body in search of moisture. Ever since, the word hysteria was used to refer to the wanderings of the womb, which is not fixed in the female body, but rather moves around and can be felt sometimes in the neck, or in the appendix, then again in the chest or in the leg. This somatic cause was inferred when a capricious, unstable, vacillating and extremely emotional female person suffered physical pain that could not be attributed to any somatic disorder. Doctors, however, have always also understood hysteria as a disorder that illustrated the problematic relationship between self-identity and self-staging. Not only was it impossible to ascribe hysterical symptoms to physical complaints, but every age seemed to have its

own specific form of hysteria. For those reasons, the Englishman Thomas Sydenham (1679) suggested that hysteria should be understood as an illness of imitation, as it always merely imitates other illnesses without ever taking on fixed characteristics. The hysterical condition, concludes Stavros Mentzos (1980), does indeed take on greatly varying colours and adapts itself to the style, the *modi* of expression and the contents of the different cultures and epochs. Because hysteria is the result of tensions, crises of the mind or conflicts within the culture that surrounds the subjects afflicted with this illness, the symptom that denotes the state of hysteria always depicts the culture that produces it as well.

That is why those famous photos from the photographic department of the Salpêtrière, the psychiatric hospital near Paris where Jean Martin Charcot intensively tried to investigate hysteria and exhibit it from 1870 onwards, are suitable as the next example. Even though many of his theories are rejected today, they had gained great influence precisely because he made use of visualisation. Wishing to establish a five-phase classification of hysteria, he had his female patients hypnotised and then presented them during his notorious *leçons de mardi* to a heterogeneous Paris audience. At the same time he believed that the different aspects of the hysterical fit could be captured in engravings and photographs. These pictures made such an impression on the surrealists that Breton and Aragon printed them in their Surrealist Manifesto of 15 March 1928 and arrived at the insight that hysteria was the greatest literary discovery of the nineteenth century. The iconography created by Charcot was taken up by contemporary artists like Mary Kelly, Annette Messager and Nicole Jolicœur, and it has also gained acceptance in modern day advertising.

Augustine, who is depicted in many photos of *Iconographie photographique de la Salpêtrière* (1876-80), became so famous because she had the ability to confine her hysteric appearances and divide them up into scenes, acts, living pictures and pauses. She was able to appear in the amphitheatre on call and present the realisation of her personal dramas, of her many traumatic woundings in a scene, in front of the camera. But as art historian Georges Didi-Huberman (1982) pointed out, it is a matter of an *invention* of hysteria rather than its discovery, because the bodily claspings and the *attitudes passionelles* that Charcot captured in the picture are imitations themselves, imitations of an already existent cultural repertoire of pictures of possession and demonology. These performances and pictures of the hysterical fit thus combine the pathological and the artistically brilliant. For the hysteric woman who made her appearance in the amphitheatre and who had to keep her pose for many minutes did so only after she had been trained by the doctors of the Salpêtrière. After many hours of conversation she learned how to behave during the course of a fit. She observed the stagings of the other hysterical women and, in order to conform to the demands of the pictures, developed more and more dramatic symptoms.

These photographs illustrate an intermingling of a variety of different factors: (1) the hysterical fit in all its mutability, the way it descends on the patient's body and allows her to express in this conversion her hidden grief; (2) the narcissistic satisfaction that someone like Augustine could set against her traumatic narcissistic wounding because the staging of the hysterical fit gained her the recognition of the doctors; (3) the doctors' desire to make a picture of hysteria, a desire so strong that they were taken in by the mimetic powers of their patients. While Charcot used his performances as well as the medium of photography to visualise this psychosomatic disorder within the framework of clear schemata, the result of his work was at the same time a perpetuating series of his model's self-portrayal. While attempting to derive an objective basis of hysteria from the photographic picture, Charcot has to admit that he always finds himself in the realm of simulation. Augustine does not only simulate real traumata and pain in these portraits, in the sense that she presents the latter as hallucination or delirium and thus in the language of the subconscious. She also simulates these fits in the sense that they are retrievable, directed towards an audience and presented as simulations. Moreover, these simulations form a kind of patchwork, as it were, of pregiven roles in literature, fine art and theatre. One could call Augustine a postmodern subject *avant la lettre,* for she stages herself as an intersection of different discourses. On the one hand, she functions as the medium of cultural iconography, which talks through her; on the other hand, however, she functions as the medium of a message, which announces itself to her from the unconscious (Israël, 1992). Augustine oscillates between the reproduction of scenarios from her own biography and the imitation of heteronomous texts; in this hybrid self-portrayal, she finds expression for the riddles of her own psyche and the sufferings from the traumatic woundings that are a result of the masquerade.

Didi-Huberman, however, was able to locate the sudden shift from picture to actual pain in her biography. Her willingness to assume any pose that Charcot asked of her had repercussions on her mental state. During one period when she was photographed particularly often she developed a peculiar symptom—she could only see in black and white. In the end, the story of Augustine takes an ironic turn, as if the hysteric beat the photographer with his own weapons. She used her ability for masquerade for her own liberation. She disguised herself as a man and one day she calmly left the institution. The rest of her life has not been documented, as if she was only able to exist in the masquerade, where the self becomes a picture. Thus, it appears as if her only possible performances were the strange distortions in two directions—distortion caused by conversion of the hysterical symptoms and distortion caused by passed-on figures of the imagination, namely of the ecstatic, of the seductress, of the imitator of Christ.

During the discussion of the photographic portrayal of hysteria another question emerges: how stable *is* the meaning of these pictures? Although Char-

cot wants to convince us to read Augustine as an example of the five stages of hysteria as invented by him, a contemporary observer may wonder whether the photos do not in fact elucidate something entirely different. For I read a message from these photos that differs from the legends Charcot added to them. The series of photos forms a sequence that documents a woman's pain, and not just in the sense of the hysteric fit that can be permanently produced and reproduced. Rather they give expression to Augustine's mental and physical suffering as something beyond Charcot's framework. It is something that cannot be captured by his nosological system and thereby breaks up and at the same time establishes his entire system of interpretation and cataloguing. For me, the fascination of these pictures does not lie in the imitated pathos, in the interpretations that, in the framework of his stories about passion in hysteria, Charcot attributes to these photographs. Rather, their explosive nature is located in the pain that pervades the picture. No coherent meaning can be attributed to the pain, and so it settles at the picture's vanishing point. For Augustine, the simulation of the pregiven poses was not merely a representational game in the photo studio of the Salpêtrière, for Augustine this pain was also real. It was a pain that changed during the course of her self-portrayals, at times even intensified, and therefore took the liquefaction of the boundary between self and picture quite literally. And ultimately, this pain is tied to the fact that Augustine has only entered into traditional iconography as masquerade. In other words: Augustine's simulated self-portraits tie together four different strands. The director Charcot stages Augustine in order to discover a definable and encodeable language of hysteria. This language turns out to be an invention that makes use of, and copies from, an already existent repertoire of pictures of ecstatic states. Augustine then represents a masquerade, because she stages Charcot's ideas and at the same time imitates pictures of possession by someone else. This interplay is only possible thanks to photography, which offers us self-portraits in which Augustine's drama appears through the masquerade. One could say that this drama illuminates the untidy mesh between, on the one hand, her unconscious whose messages report back, converted, as hysterical symptoms, and, on the other hand, Charcot's imaginary picture presentations, which she also stages on her body.

3. Claude Cahun

What the patients of the Salpêtrière took as the result of their examination and exhibition by the psychiatrist Charcot the surrealists developed as their poetic program: the outwardly driven language of the unconscious, the plurality of the self, the frailness of categories of being. The case of photographer and author Claude Cahun, born in 1894 in Nantes under the name of Lucy Schwob, suggests itself as the next example from the same milieu. First she

was known as Claude Coulis, from 1917 as Cahun, later as Daniel Douglas and then, during the war, as the 'Unnamed Soldier' and 'Silent in the Melée.' Daughter of Maurice Schwob, proprietor and editor of one of the largest regional newspapers, *Le Phare de la Loire*, niece of the author Marcel Schwob and grandniece of the orientalist and curator of the Mazarine library in Paris, Léon Cahun, Claude Cahun studied at the Sorbonne, briefly at Oxford, and began in the twenties to publish her papers in established magazines, and partly also in the surrealists' milieu. In 1930 her first book *Aveux non avenus* (Confessions not allowed) appeared. It is a collection of papers, dream reports, poems, aphorisms, philosophical dialogues and photomontages, which she produced together with her partner Suzanne Malherbe-Morre. The book records how she uses her own female body as a surface for phantasmatic designs. All themes that run through her entire work are interwoven in this book: the dialectic of mask and mirror, androgyny and ambivalence of identity, design as monster, dandyism, aestheticism, metaphysical illusionism, historic pessimism, cynical provocation and instructive utopianism. For a long time, Cahun was only known to a handful of connoisseurs, in particular because of her pamphlet *Les Paris sont ouvert* (1934) and her signature on a number of surrealist manifestos in the thirties. Her name alone started legends and rumours. Many thought she was a man. This uncertainty concerning her identity was of course supported by Cahun, who liked hiding behind masks and mirrors. For the deletion of the self as opposed to the sign that represents it was her declared artistic project. It is to the merit of the photographer François Leperlier (1992; 1995) that Cahun is now experiencing a revival.

The works of Claude Cahun are particularly interesting for our present discussion of the presentation of the self in the photographic picture. Until the late forties she presented herself in different masquerades—as someone else and yet so explicitly changed that these portrayals give more emphasis to the cultural encoding of the body than the body itself; costumes, masks and theatrical make up are prominent. These photos, unlike those of the *Comtesse* de Castiglione, are not expression of a shifted self-glorification, but rather, they serve to break up social identities and to undermine the security of mental identifications. Cahun's repeated change of her name illustrates the general theme that runs through all her work, dressing up and revelation. For this artist, all creation makes the action visible that the subject effects on itself. Transformations, during the course of which the subject turns into its own object, are elevated to the highest objective.

A self-portrait from 1928 shows Cahun in a harlequin jacket in front of a mirror. However, as David Bate (1994) explains, although the picture makes use of a traditional iconographic motif—the *vanitas* picture, which takes female narcissism as its theme, the dialogue between the ideal I and the self—it contains an intrinsic decoding. The woman does not, as might be expected, look at herself in a state of self-contemplation and self-sufficiency. Rather, the

strangely metallic head whose gender it is difficult to classify looks straight at the observer. This double portrait thus emphasises the huge gap between self and mirror image; the two representations are alienated from one another, a narcissistic identification is touched upon and at the same time made impossible. This divide raises the question 'Who is this I?' and leaves it hovering like a phantom between masked figure and mirror image.

Cahun's staged pictures deliberately and radically take up the language of hysteria, not the tragic passion of Charcot's hysterics, but rather the multiple otherness of the self. As early as 1902 Jules de Gaultier talked about '*Bovarisme*' with respect to Flaubert's novel, to describe the phenomenon of someone introducing herself as someone other than she is in order to become what she is. The definition of hysteria that I want to take up once more is taken from Stavros Mentzos' book. For him, this psychosomatic disorder is not so much the expression of a so-called female dissatisfaction, but rather a question of self-fashioning. 'The hysteric,' according to Mentzos (1980:75), 'puts himself in a position, inwardly according to experience and outwardly according to appearance, where he experiences himself, and where the environment sees him other than he is. He puts himself in a position where his own bodily and/or mental functions and/or characteristics are being experienced and appear in such a way that the result is a (supposedly) other, a changed self-representation.' The hysteric tendency to present oneself different from how one is and to experience oneself differently is characterised by theatrical behaviour, emotional instability, extreme excitability and seductive gestures. Mentzos renders the definition more precise by explaining that expressive behaviour and heightened emotionality can only be understood as hysterical if the self-stagings 'are not the natural expression of what is being experienced at that moment.' Rather 'a certain behaviour becomes activated and a certain scene is staged, as if such an experience and such a dramatic situation was in fact the case' (1980:92). In her pamphlet *Les Paris sont ouvert* Cahun describes the search for authenticity of the self as self-creation in this very sense, as metamorphosis of the self: 'The unforeseeable day when poetry will have no more specific purpose, when it will cease to exist, because poetry will have turned human.' Cahun thus uses photography to express an existential and profoundly introverted attitude of mind. She used photography to visualise an exceedingly complex mental theatre in which it was important to experience and examine oneself in relation to signs. Such turning outward of the private theatre—as Anna O., Breuer's first hysteric, called her fantasy scenarios—was supposed to be evidence for the imaginary life, for existence is meaningful only in view of the power of the artefact, in view of the omnipotence of the pictures. For Cahun, all representation had to be embedded in a hallucinatory setting.

The diverse stagings of the 'I' that Cahun designed allow her to oscillate between female and male body, between boy, doll and female beauty; they allow her to hide behind an overly made-up face, say, or behind covered up

glasses. Chameleonlike she puts herself as an object into a cabinet or portrays herself as a beheaded glass reflection. I would like to go back to hysteria as an illness of the imagination, for this picture language makes use of the masquerades in order to express a self, thereby referring to the absent agreement between self-portrait and a so-called real self. Any attempt to read these pictures into the autobiography of Lucy Schwob/Claude Cahun is bound to fail, for there is no authentic, original self, only a staging.

Cahun's portraits are a simulation which stage the performative characteristic of gender, or subjectivity in general. This is to be understood in the same vein in which Judith Butler uses speech act theory to talk about gender as masquerade. In philosophy of language, the term 'performative' denotes a statement that constitutes an action, in particular the action that is described by the verb ('promise,' 'testify,' 'bless'). To detect a performance of the subject, as Butler suggests, means for the subject to adopt a certain gender position only within a given cultural realm, which causes the subject to be discursively fashioned. 'The position articulated by the subject' says Butler, 'is always in a certain form constituted of that which has to be shifted in order for the position to withstand [...] through a number of procedures of exclusion and selection' (1993:39). The I, then, is not simply situated in an identity, it is neither autonomous nor is it its own starting point. Rather it is constituted through the discursive position that it chooses, in order to define itself, just like the given social relations that cause the formation of this I.

As Leperlier points out, Cahun's point was always to disguise herself or to reduce her body to minimal attributes, to find ever new roles for herself, several identities, whose aim it was to drive the sexual indeterminacy to its extreme boundary, to fulfil the dream of a third gender. And indeed, her pictures demonstrate how much she strove for a gender transfiguration. Because of this radical nonbelonging she has no definite place. She could thus only ever be established on her own side, that is to say, always on the other side, and thereby follows the same deconstructivist attitude as Judith Butler. She is a representative of the excluded, of that which is shifted to the other side of the boundary, whenever definite identities are to be established. For Cahun's self-staging, as well as for the language of hysteria where the self renders itself other than it is, this means that the act of self-portrayal is the verb of public staging. The many masquerades impart the message: 'I am a performance, I am only as a performance, as the knotting together of many different fantasy pictures and characters of my cultural repertoire which have determined me.'

Cahun thus emerges as her own creator *and* her own executioner, the subject of investigation *and* the investigating scientist. She says about herself: 'The happiest moments of my life? When I dream. When I imagine I am someone else. When I play my favourite role.' This self-fashioning means discarding useless parts—she writes: 'There is too much of everything [...] I have my head shaved, my teeth pulled out, my breasts removed—everything that dis-

turbs and annoys my eye—stomach, ovaries, the conscious, encapsulated brain.' It also means adding new parts, or, in her own words: 'to elevate the imaginative powers of the propman to the greatest good.' Cahun celebrates the body, its abnormalities, discrepancies, inconsistencies and indecisions. She sounds out precisely those borders which the imaginary force takes back into its possession, which can be left to metamorphosis. At the end of the project there is a self-conquest and self-subjugation wherein the subject becomes the imaginary trigger of the self: '*moi seul enfin. La hâte nue,*' 'me myself finally alone. The naked hurry' (cited in: Leperlier, 1992:15).

4. Zelig

At this point it would be appropriate to move to Cindy Sherman's self-por-trayals—indeed some critics see Cahun and her self-portraits as one of the pre-decessors of this American photographer. Here, however, I will only briefly discuss the problem of Sherman's *Untitled Film Stills*. As these photographs are postpositions of film scenes for which there are no originals they do not just depict the simulacrum in a virtuoso manner. They also force the observer to ask whether there is an essential figure behind the many masquerades of the depicted heroine, or whether identity always in the end disperses in the self-referentiality of the picture. These pictures, as well as all the others, are about an oscillation between the picture's surface, which has no point of referential-ity, and its depth, which, as a concrete point that apparently keeps everything together, is inaccessible. The pictures of the series *Film Stills* have a slightly eerie feel to them because the depicted self does not just disperse in the picture but engrains itself in film scenarios, which look real, even though they are merely imitations of imitations.

In order to pursue this problem of high import for postmodernism, I have instead chosen a different example: Woody Allen's 1983 film *Zelig*. This film is about a human chameleon whose transference love for the analyst Eudora Fletcher cures him. His mental disorders are such that he always changes into the other person, for fear of not belonging. He only exists as a conglomeration of the masquerades that he continually carries out on his body, while the core of his own identity seems to be effaced, a nothing. Woody Allen emphasises these masquerades on the cinematic level, for his film is as chameleonlike as his protagonist. With *Zelig* Woody Allen imitates the documentary: he mixes historical film material from the twenties and thirties with fictitious comments by actual people, his experts (amongst others Susan Sontag, Saul Bellow, Irv-ing Howe), who keep repeating how strange this story really is. In addition, there are interviews, played by actors and amateurs, who are questioned as wit-nesses to the events. There are scenes with the protagonist Zelig that look as though they were actual historical footage. Similarly, while the film *Zelig* pre-

tends to be a documentary about somebody who constantly changes into the other person and pretends to be like the others but is really nothing, so is the film as documentary really nothing, for its subject has never existed. This extinction of a reference point outside the alleged documentary is even more emphasised by the fact that Woody Allen artificially reconstructed a major part of the footage that looked as though it was historical. Allen, playing *Zelig,* was actually put into original film material in three places in the film. The whole film then depicts a hysteric masquerade.

Without going into the course of the treatment presented in the film I would like to select the scene that leads to Zelig's arrest, his admission into the clinic and his treatment by Dr. Eudora Fletcher. For here we can see the two self-portraits that Zelig prefers to any others. The only clues for his identity the police find in his apartment in Greenwich Village are two photos. One of them shows Zelig standing next to Eugene O'Neill, dressed like him. Zelig, O'Neill and the child in front of them all look somewhat wistfully at the camera. The other photo shows Zelig as Pagliacci, obese, wearing a clown's costume, sitting on a big drum ready to beat it, and smiling at the camera.

These two photos next to each other—this is what I propose as my concluding thesis—stage a nothing, a traumatic wounding around which Zelig's chameleon-like masquerade of the self revolves. What is moving about these photographs is their deathly silence, which is diametrically opposed to the scenes before and after, where Zelig displays his transformations into the other person (McCann, 1990). These two photos together trouble the viewer in an uncanny way, for the texture of the image creates the impression that a phantom has returned from the past in order to deanimate his model in the present. Unlike the many other self-portrayals as scenarios that Zelig/Allen presents in the film, these two photos stage the fugitive subject by completely obscuring the boundary between actor and character as well as between historical past, the presence of the viewers and the scenario of the fictitious rendition.

Given that these are the only self-portraits Zelig has kept, we can read them as quasi-other self-portraits that this chameleonlike hero identifies with. These, notably, perform two fantasy scenarios about the identification with the artistic process. On the one side of the double portrait we have the melancholy situation of the writer (O'Neill) and on the other we have the clown (Pagliacci) who puts on the mask of a mask. For Pagliacci is already dressed to perform the last scene in Leoncavallo's opera, in which the jealous actor Canio appears to sing the aria '*No, Pagliaccio non son,*' ready to kill on stage the wife who betrays him in reality (the narrative level of the opera plot). By choosing this masquerade (Canio as Pagliacci) Zelig also imitates the actor's suffering, when reality and fiction coincide. In his refusal to continue to wear the mask of Pagliacci, Canio insists on the nonidentity between himself and his comic role. Canio wants to pull off his unfaithful wife's, as well as his own, disguise but realises that he is inevitably wrapped up in the staging. Even though he

switches from comedy to tragedy, the fatality that he eventually performs is merely the imitation of another operatic plot, just as Charcot's hysterics inevitably perform an already existent iconography of obsession.

The following pattern emerges from the two photographs at another look. Zelig finds himself caught between the author producing fictions and the clown consciously performing them. We as viewers, however, cannot be sure whether the double portrait is not also a self-portrayal of Woody Allen, the author of the simulated documentary *Zelig*, who himself oscillates between the role of director who puts together the various parts of the film, and the clown Zelig whose masquerade indicates a demand for love. Although the explicit mirroring of author and protagonist is a dramatic convention, there is something about these two photos which goes beyond mere convention. For they disappear at their vanishing point, both the protagonist Zelig, who presents himself in his two favourite roles, and the author Woody Allen who plays his chameleonlike hero. Both figures are immersed in a vortex of representations whose referentiality has become entirely indeterminate.

While the Pagliacci photo can be located as a purely fictional scene, the fact that Woody Allen is engrained into the frame with Eugene O'Neill points to a historical moment turned uncanny by the presence of a foreign body. Depending on one's semantic viewpoint the picture either negates the reality of history (the authentic status of the documentary photograph is radically called into question by this engrainment), or the picture allows the reality of history to penetrate the quasi-security of the self-portrayal with a worrying truth. Not only does the protagonist Zelig fade away before the role of the author that he imitates, but Woody Allen, too, the film's author, fades away at the very moment when he finds himself in the same frame as the other, dead, author. As Roland Barthes aptly noted, the essence of the photographic image resides in the reference point's stubbornness always to be there. Something remains in the image although it is in the past; therein lies an unsalvageable nothing that can only be pinned down as a performing trace. Thus each photograph contains, as its final signifier, the nothing of mortality.

As creator and creation meet in this truly bizarre double self-portrayal— and with them the facticity of a historical past and the protective fiction of the present—the nothing of the representation and the representation of the nothing constantly change places. If the message that the photo with Eugene O'Neill proclaims is: 'I will not have existed because I present myself as someone who is already dead,' then the picture of Allen as Pagliacci says: 'I have never existed except as a masquerade.' Tied together, however, these two pictures also declare: 'I exist, but not as the self that I represent in each individual picture. I exist as the vulnerable point of convergence between historical facticity of the self and the self's protective fiction of the masquerade,' just like Charcot's patient Augustine, who could only perform her truth, her identity, between her own traumatic story and the representational masquerades

dictated by Charcot. At the navel of his second birth, which takes place in Manhattan Hospital over a period of time, under the guidance of Eudora Fletcher, and from which the hero Zelig will emerge stabilised in his masquerade, we also find the indeterminacy of identity mirrored in the indeterminacy of two self-portrayals. Oscillating between imitating Eugene O'Neill and disguising as Pagliacci, Zelig/Allen only fits the frame as a foreign body thus throwing this cinematic moment out of the fictional story but also out of every historical referentiality. As with the other examples I dealt with, this performance of hysteria holds the message that the knotted-split subject finds expression in the opposition of symbolic self-staging and a real traumatic knowledge about the nothing, on which these performances are founded.

Translated by Nadja Rosental

Notes

Translators note: all translations from non-English sources are mine.

References

Barthes, Roland (1981) *La Chambre Claire*, Paris.
Bate, David (1944) 'The Mise en Scène of Desire', in *Mise en Scène. Claude Cahun, Tacita Dean, Virginia Nimarkoh,* Exhibition Catalogue Institute of Contemporary Arts, London.
Berger, John (1972) *Ways of Seeing*, Harmondsworth.
Björgman, Stig (1994) *Woody Allen on Woody Allen*, London.
Bourneville, Désiré M., and Régnard, Paul (1876-1898) *Iconographie photographique de la Salpêtrière* (Service de M. Charcot), Paris.
Braun, Christina von (1985) *Nicht Ich*, Frankfurt/M.
Butler, Judith (1993) 'Kontingente Grundlagen: Der Feminismus und die Frage der "Postmoderne"', in Sheyla Benhabib et al. (eds) *Der Streit um Differenz*, Frankfurt/M.
Chevrier, Jean-François and Sagne, Jean (1984) 'Essai sur l'identité l'exotisme et les excés photographique', *Photographies*, 4:47-81.
Didi-Huberman, Georges (1982) *Invention de l'hystérie. Charcot et l'iconographie de la Salpêtrière,* Paris.
Foucault, Michel (1963) *Naissance de la Clinique*, Paris.
Freud, Sigmund (1986[6] [1919]): 'Das Unheimliche", in *Gesammelte Werke*, Vol. 12, Frankfurt/M.

Freud, Sigmund (1986⁵ [1927]) 'Fetischismus", in *Gesammelte Werke*, Vol. 14, Frankfurt/M.

Gilman, Sander (1982) *Seeing the Insane*, New York.

Israël, Lucien (1992) *L'hystérique, le sexe et le médecin*, Paris.

Leperlier, François (1992) *Claude Cahun. L'écart et la métamorphose*, Paris.

Leperlier, François (1995) *Claude Cahun Photographe*, Paris.

Lolieé, Frédéric (1954) *Les femmes du second empire*, Paris.

Lyon, Elisabeth (1990) 'Unspeakable Images, Unspeakable Bodies', *Camera Obscura*, 24:168-93.

McCann, Graham (1990) *Woody Allen*, London.

Mentzos, Stavros (1980) *Hysterie. Zur Psychodynamik unbewußter Inszenierungen*, Munich.

Montesquiou, Robert de (1913) *La divine comtesse. Étude d'après Mme de Castiglione*, Paris.

Solomon-Godeau, Abigail (1994) 'Die Beine der Gräfin', in Liliane Weissberg, (ed.), *Weiblichkeit als Maskerade*, Frankfurt/M., pp. 90-147.

Sydenham, Thomas (1679) 'Epistolary Dissertation to Dr. Cole', in *The Works of Thomas Sydenham*, London.

Trillat, Étienne (1986) *Histoire de l'hystérie*, Paris.

Veith, Ilza (1965) *Hysteria. The History of a Disease*, Chicago.

Žižek, Slavoj (1994) *Metastases of Enjoyment. Six Essays on Women and Causality*, London.

The 'Jewess Pallas Athena'
Horizons of Selfconception in the 19th and 20th Centuries

BARBARA HAHN*

When all had been destroyed, demolished and obliterated, a voice began to speak: 'Mother Rahel / weeps no longer. Hauled over / all the weeped things'—a poem of Paul Celan's from the cycle *Fadensonnen* of 1968 (1990:202). Rahel weeps no longer; no one is there who could mourn as Rahel mourned her children. 'No longer'—a dominant temporal dimension in Celan's poetry, an uncanny time, without relation to the present moment. It is past, unalterable, and related to a site that also no longer exists. '*Rübergetragen / alles Geweinte*'—'Hauled over / all the weeped things'—to another place, a space inaccessible from the present. *Rübergetragen*, in the original, recalling *übertragen*, to translate. Paul Celan—a translator, from German into German, from a German that was exterminated along with the people who spoke it, into the German of those responsible for this extermination. A translator, who in Hebrew names recollects a history that has disappeared into this 'no longer': Rahel and Esther, Sulamith with her ashen hair, and at length a figure who has no name. A figure in whom languages, cultures, traditions clash with one another.

A song in three languages, a song in dialogue with a You, overlaid with a He, a nameless instance that destroys the dialogue. Thus two triangles, one formed from I, You and He and the other from three languages: German, the basic language of the poem, Hebrew and French, present in a word that in itself already recalls another language and another land: Allemande—a German dance. Just as the start of poem dances and twirlingly repeats itself: 'If I know not, know not, without you, without you.' But the song that begins here is soon broken off. It collides with a 'word without sense,' '*Aschrej*'—a word like a

---

WENN ICH NICHT WEISS; NICHT WEISS, ohne dich, ohne dich, ohne Du,	If I know not, know not, without you, without you, without a You,
kommen sie alle, die Freigeköpften, die zeitlos hirnlos den Stamm der Du-losen besangen:	they all come, the Bareheaded ones, who lifelong brainless the tribe of the You-less have sung:
Aschrej,	Aschrej,
ein Wort ohne Sinn, transtibetanisch, der Jüdin	a word without sense, transtibetan, into the Jewess
Pallas Athene in die behelmten Ovarien gespritzt,	Pallas Athena into her helmeted ovaries squirted,
und wenn er,	and when he,
er,	he,
foetal,	fetal,
karpatisches Nichtnicht beharft,	harps carpathian nono
dann spitzenklöppeln die	then made lacework the
Allemande	Allemande
das sich übergebende un- sterbliche Lied.	handing itself down, the im- mortal song.

(Celan, 1990:154-5)

cry, a word from Hebrew. Luther translates it with 'blessed are they' or 'happiness to them.' One can also translate it with a single German word: '*Heil*,' '*Hail*.' For it is a 'word without sense.' The murderers took it up, '*Heil Hitler*,' and transformed it into a death sentence (see Beyerdörfer, 1977:42-54). A word from the language of the You-less, who sang a different song, a song without translation and therefore past. You-less, monolingual, constructed from words without sense. The tribe of the You-less injects its words, instead of giving them to a You, instead of permitting in their address a You. It injects them into the helmeted ovaries of 'the Jewess Pallas Athena.'

In Greek mythology Pallas Athena with her double name wears a helmet upon her head and a shield across her breast. Ovaries, however, she does not

have. She was not born of a mother and cannot become one. She is the daughter of her father Zeus, from whose head she sprang; or which she split according to another version, so that in thunder and lightning she could come into the world. When her mother is mentioned, it is only as someone who has been killed. Father Zeus had swallowed her, thus robbing her of the possibility of childbirth.

Pallas Athena, daughter without a mother, interrupts every female genealogy and founds no tradition. Pallas Athena, the warrior, the thinking woman, whose symbol is the owl, marks a singularity. A point without history, without before and after. The 'Jewess' is something quite different. For decades, the word bore in German a strange erotic or sometimes a sexual connotation. It signalled a danger for the German man and symbolised a 'corruption of German culture;' it stood for the foreign, the threatening, the other. Celan's poem shatters this context. Ovaries are not erotically stimulating. Ovaries designate the fruitfulness of women, and women were implicated in the National Socialist genocide because they could be mothers. They were sterilised—squirted in the ovaries—so that they could no longer hand on life. And they were murdered, so that never again would a Mother Rahel weep for her children.

The 'Jewess Pallas Athena.' This shocking phrase demolishes a pillar of National Socialist ideology: the contradiction between 'Semitic' and 'Indogermanic'—in other languages one speaks of 'Indo-European.' Beyond this opposition a commonality is asserted that encompasses both the culture of ancient Greece and the Jewish tradition. What appear to be entirely contrary meanings can suddenly be thought together, meanings that had been lost in the clichéd images of the 'Jewess.' Two traditions come together, and to monotheistic Judaism is joined a culture that understood Wisdom, Knowledge, Art and Memory as feminine substantives. *Sophia* and *Mnemosyne*, the Muses and *Theoria*. A culture in which female words and figures bear memories just as the Hebrew names of Rahel, Esther and Sulamith, which Celan identified with the Jewish people.

This history of a commonality is destroyed by the tribe of the You-less, and with that a culture disappeared that had been constructed as much from Judaism as from Greek antiquity. It becomes a dead, a vanished culture, that can no longer hand anything down. Yet Celan's poem, published in 1968, hands down a song, an immortal song, that also bears the memory of two writing women whose names are not mentioned. It can be read as a Kaddish for one who also wrote her transtibetan songs and embroidered or spun Tibetan carpets with a carpeted Tibet: Else Lasker-Schüler.[1] As a Kaddish as well for one who wrote as if the Jewess Pallas Athena could write: of a culture of 'the West,' composed from the three elements of Greek antiquity, Judaism and Christendom, of the culture of 'Europe,' an 'extremely masculine culture,' riven by the battle of the sexes, torn between man and woman: Margarete Susman.[2]

The Jewess Pallas Athena: a cultural and a historical provocation. It questions and alienates the word 'Jewess,' and opens a space for reflection on the

meanings and attributions that constitute this word. In a series of books and articles written by Jewish women during the short century of acculturation, the 'Israelite woman' and the 'Jewess' appear as categories that determine a position in 'German' culture. These attempts reach entirely different conclusions, but at the same time they exhibit similarities: The Jewess seems to be the answer to a question posed to History, Tradition, and Religion. Therefore, the word itself does not represent a question, but rather a concept or a judgement. Up until the last text from 1937, where the end of German-Jewish history is described. Concluded—long before its catastrophic end.

When with the 'gates of the ghetto' the traditional Jewish world collapsed, Jewish men and women were confronted with different problems. A tradition that linked mothers to daughters down through the generations put little emphasis on the abstract category of 'woman' as such. In the bourgeois-Christian world, by contrast, an antagonism had been established between the sexes that could not do without this very category. Once the traditional world of mothers and daughters was ruptured female Jews were subjected to two simultaneous exclusionary mechanisms—woman/man; Jew/German—whose site was marked by a new concept: 'Jewess.' As acculturation started, Jewish women tried largely to avoid the word. Rahel Levin, for instance, defines it in her correspondence with David Veit either as an exclusionary signal or as the challenge to legitimacy. It occurs only rarely in her correspondence with the female Jewish friends of her youth. No unhappy love affair with a Gentile, no insult, no illness is explained by the fact that it befell a 'Jewess.' Nor is the concept at work in her letters to Christian friends, male or female. It is a protected word, and it wanders only between men and women. Sara and Marianne Meyer, as well as Esther Gad, point with the word toward a cultural context that they have abandoned, about which they write because it has already become history. The addressees of these reflections, Goethe and Jean Paul, do not take up this theme.[3] On this point, the women conduct monologues without echo. Jewess—a word of transgression. The genre for reflections on these painful and conflict-ridden processes was the letter; later, autobiographical texts appeared as well. At the beginning of the 19th century, women who were not baptised almost never published. Writing and conversion on the one side, remaining Jewish and relinquishing any voice in the written tradition on the other: these options belong together.

Only in the middle of the nineteenth century did unconverted women begin to publish. In 1847, for instance, Johanna Goldschmidt anonymously published *Rebekka and Amalie. Letters between an Israelite woman and a noblewoman on public and personal questions* (Goldschmidt, 1847). As in the eighteenth century, the two fictive correspondents, the Jew Rebekka Meier of Hamburg and the noblewoman Amalia von Felseck of Berlin, have met at the baths. Not, however, in the Bohemian spas, but in Doberan on the Baltic Sea. But unlike in the eighteenth century, the difference between Jewess and noble-

woman has become the exclusive theme. Rebekka speaks with the voice of the oppressed, who along with all 'European pariahs' (203) struggle together for freedom and equality: 'I, the poor oppressed Jewess, I belong among those who raise a free word for a right withheld' (134). She accuses the Prussian king, accuses all rulers who tolerate discrimination. She is teacher and source, reflecting and explaining; she knows the history of the Jewish people. For her, the 'most tormenting aspect of our situation is that we are constantly thrown back and forth between pride and humility' (27). In her addressee Amalia, who still resides in the social and political world of the eighteenth Century, and who longs to break out of the 'static circle of marionettes that surround us in society' (11), Rebekka has found a representative of the 'common sense of the German people,' who 'will soon fight for our rights' (51). But in the book, Rebekka's charge becomes ever more a monologue without an echo, whereby the collapse of dialogue is staged, but never explicitly reflected upon.

At the start of the book Amalia reports from her world, in which a Jewish friend ruffles feathers. The mention of her name causes a scandal in her parents' salon: 'Good Lord! simpered Baroness Z. beside her, that sounds positively Old Testamental' (11). In her letters, this exclusion is tendentiously transformed into a gesture of respect for the friend: 'Your firm, bright spirit drew me on like mountain air, and I felt immediately that this mighty *Weltanschauung* in such a youthful breast could only be invoked by the resolute posture of an Israelite woman' (15). In the course of the correspondence, this debate is overlaid with love stories and anticipated marriages. In the end, Amalie weds the man—a bourgeois—whom Rebekka had herself refused, because he was Christian.

Jewishness is Rebekka's theme. Baptism and the deficient educational opportunities for children are discussed, mixed marriages and the idiosyncrasies of Jewish families. Since the problematic of being Jewish is no longer motivated by the dialogue, external and cultural markers ossify into clichés and stereotypes: 'For the baptismal water has neither the power to wash away an oriental physiognomy, nor so change the speech of the baptised that it no longer betray her ancestry' (de Linge, 1924:87). And later, the Oriental itself is transformed into a moment of self-characterisation: 'You will understand me, dear friend! when, as befits my oriental heritage, I often and gladly speak to you in images' (Goldschmidt, 1847:122).

The fictional dialogue between the two women is thus traversed by rigid internal boundaries. It ends in the manner of a trivial romance novel—with the marriage of one of the two heroines, as if what followed were no longer worth the telling. Bourgeois happiness, an end without end.

Such a dialogue between Jew and Christian could be imagined only for a short time. Between Jewish and Christian women, to speak more precisely, for the texts shuttle between two women who write and are aimed at a female public. In 1883 Clementine von Rothschild's book *Letters to a Christian Woman*

Friend on the Basic Truths of Judaism was posthumously published.[4] Here no dialogue is staged, and the object of the discussion is rigidly restricted: A Jewish woman writes to a Christian woman on the difference between the two religions, granting a superiority to the Jewish faith. The addressee of the letters from an 'Israelite' (Rothschild, 1883:62) is a friend named Ellen, the letters are signed by Esther Izates—a foreign name. Her contemporary situation appears only to the extent that the people of Israel, after centuries-long oppression, now live in relative freedom. 'And now in this new, better time, since the heavens have cleared, since the dark clouds of our misfortune and persecution have dispersed and the glorious sun of happiness and freedom shines so warmly upon us, the Israelites ought to turn to their Father in Heaven all the more sincerely, call to him all the more passionately than in past centuries, for we owe Him so much that our souls should continually overflow with gratitude!' (83) Jewishness is conceived here not only as a category spanning the centuries; it appears simultaneously as the future of all peoples, as a religion unifying all others, 'for one day will come, when through it all nations together will reach the true God' (2). Islam and Christianity are nuncios and forerunners of monotheism for all the 'heathen.' The end and goal of this path is Judaism. Esther Izates, representative of the 'paternal Religion,' does not discuss current conflicts: neither the relation of German to Jew, nor of woman to man is reflected upon.

This, too, can be read as evidence of the book having missed its moment. For in the meantime, forms of writing had been developed implying other debates and other female addressees. *The Jewish Woman or The Modern Jewess or Jewesses*—titles of the books we will consider below—were written by Jewish women explicitly addressing a female Jewish public. The word 'Jewess' now signals a problem that was discussed not among women, but among Jewish women.[5]

Except for the oldest author, Nahida Remy, who would later marry Moritz Lazarus and publish under the name of Nahida Ruth Lazarus, all these writers enjoyed an academic education, but could not, for tellingly revealing reasons, make scholarly work their occupation. And for all of these women—with the exception of Bertha Badt-Strauss and Nahida Remy—the book on Jewesses has no context in their larger oeuvres. It forms a heteroclite block in the midst of diverse publicist or literary activity that has nothing to do with the theme of that book.

Nahida Remy began as an actor, went on to write plays and theatre criticism, later novels as well, until in 1891 she published her first theoretical book, entitled *The Jewish Woman*. It quickly enjoyed several printings; a later edition from 1895 includes a foreword from the author. It begins: 'When I wrote this book, I was a Christian. Today I am a Jewess; I had to become a Jewess once I had recognised through my researches and understood in my cultural studies on Judaism just what the Jewish religion truly means. The attitude that dictated

this work has therefore not remained the same, but has been strengthened—
and sealed' (1922:iii).[6]

In two senses Nahida Remy's study is a book of transgression. In addition
to its autobiographical conversion narrative it has another story to tell, for which
it seems to find no form. Nahida Remy writes her apologia of Judaism as a
repetitive transcription of a book already available, Meyer Kaiserling's study,
The Jewish Women in History, Literature, and Art. The construction and the
analyses resemble each other significantly, but their judgements differ exten-
sively. While Kaiserling indeed writes of women in the plural, and posits no ultimate identity behind them, Nahida Remy reduces all of these to variants of the
Jewish woman she identifies with the essence of the Jewish religion. While
Kaiserling wends his way through history, literature and art in the traditional
manner of '*Geistesgeschichte*' and limiting himself to the women whose names
have been preserved by the historical record, Nahida Remy considers individual
women as being successful or unsuccessful versions of the Jewish woman.
While Kaiserling refers to a given and vital tradition, Nahida Remy constructs
a tradition foreign to her as a bulwark against modernisation at the close of the
19th century. It serves to compensate for the loss of values and orientation, particularly for someone such as the author, active in so many divergent professional fields and ways of life. Thus, the 'Jewish Woman' becomes a synonym for
an adaptable history appropriate to a wide variety of problems and situations.
The 'Jewish Women' therefore is—the Mother, though in a sense quite different
from the role she plays in the contemporary women's movement. For never is
the Mother aligned with Nature, set in polar opposition to Man, to culture. 'Jewish woman' symbolises rather tradition itself; she is a sign for the fact that the
threatening present can be bound to a continuous past. Thus a history without
breaks or caesuras becomes thinkable. Jewish woman—this is the image of a
nonviolent, human world, in which woman is granted a singular place of honour
and respect. An image in contrast to all other ancient cultures, where 'woman is
conceived as not much more than a powerless and will-less domestic creature or
at best in public service as a luxury and pleasure object' (Remy, 1922:22). After
an investigation of marriage, maternity, and the rules governing divorce in the
Bible and Talmud, Nahida Remy concludes that 'Hebrew laws are not only more
philanthropic and psychologically sophisticated, but their unwritten customs
testify as well to tenderness and consideration' (30).

Only with the attempted acculturation around 1800 was this continuum
shattered. Its representatives therefore are seen as traitors. 'Henriette Herz, this
beloved, almost worshipped woman, what could she not have accomplished as
a good Jewess in the most varied circles! She, a magician, the master of all
hearts; the noble, thoughtful Dorothea; the scintillating, genial, energetic
Rahel, what immeasurable influence could these three women not have exercised for religious tolerance, for the combating of medieval prejudice, the
preparation for their co-religionists of the eagerly desired and long expected

equality with the proponents of the religion of "general philanthropy"! But Rahel, Henriette, Dorothea—they wanted nothing to do with this' (147). In writing the last chapter, finally, which has the theme 'the contemporary Jewess,' the author feels 'for the first time a discomfort that I know all too well how to interpret' (192). For in the present, the boundaries that support her book are dissolving: 'Today the Jewess imitates the Christian. Unfortunately in much, as well, that is not worthy of imitation' (196), she complains and hopes for a 'return [of these women] to the virtues of their mothers' (198), and so to 'the doctrine and the love of their Judaism.' (198)

In the figure of Paula Winkler, who published novels and story-cycles under the name 'Georg Munk,' and who was married to Martin Buber, one can find a different attempt.[7] Her conversion is depicted not as a return to the past, but as a turn to the future. In 1901 she published two essays in *Die Welt. Zentralorgan der zionistischen Bewegung.* The first bears the title 'Observations of a Philozionistic Woman,' the other 'The Jewish Woman.' In the first, a largely autobiographical text, we read, 'I am so happy to have stood since childhood on a different footing with Judaism than is granted to most of us. My mother had lived as a young girl in the vicinity of a small Jewish settlement, and from its way of life she received peculiarly strong and persistent impressions. She was immature, fantastic and internally isolated the way almost all young women were, and so her volatile spirit seemed for a while to find refuge on this small island in the ocean of her everydayness.' Here Paula Winkler sketches her relation to Judaism as an indirect, transposed experience. Her remembrance of her mother, who 'knew how to tell stories wonderfully,' coalesces into the following static image: 'A quaint village appears before me, tidy houses, bright windows, colourful summer gardens, much light and cleanliness, a modest abundance and a great deal of love everywhere and toward everything, well-tended children and comfortable, benevolent matrons.' (127) Her mother's stories mediate the memory of a home that never existed. A promise, a dream of belonging and an ordered world.

Another experience, this time her own, while studying German literature in Zurich, opens the way to a new understanding of Judaism. It is a tale of exclusion, and from this Paula Winkler learns 'the peculiar place the Jews have among us.' (96) Children are playing in front of her window. Suddenly a quarrel breaks out. A 'little tousle-headed child' wants to take a toy from a 'cute, black-eyed lad.' He defends himself, and is then mocked by the others as a 'Jew-boy.' 'Before I could intervene, the victim's sister, perhaps eight years old, appears, and, standing before the child, returns the taunts with such skill that one could recognise that she had daily practise in this self-defence. The child's pretty face twisted, her eyes grew penetrating, and in despairing anger she lashed out all around her.' (99)

This experience, upon which the text does not further comment, apparently reveals its significance only against another story. This time it is a man

who is the centre of the scene, neither mother nor little girl. And only now does the meaning of the preceding episodes unfold. They are placed in a context that operates less through an explanation than through the power of an intuition. At the Zionist Congress in Basel, Paula meets a man, unnamed in the text, but easily recognisable as Martin Buber. 'There it happened that a human tongue spoke to me with wonderful force. At times in the manner of a shy child, hesitating, tender, anxious that it would find no echo. Now and then the bashful blush of an innocent soul spread over the face of this person. It was as if my heart stood still, touching and holy.' (74)

All the figures who have moved through the text up to this point now find their places in the constellation formed by this couple: The man speaks like a child, as if the tormented little boy were now taking his own defence in hand. He speaks as if to a mother, for he is understood, always and without limit. The little girl who listened to the stories of her mother has now become an 'I', who devotes herself with 'royal richness, youth, strength, and munificence' to Zionism and to the man who tells of it. 'It overwhelmed me the way all great things in life and life itself do—it came and took me with it.' (36) And so *The Observations of a Philozionist* culminate in a hymn that merges the beloved man with the Jewish people, who now are transformed into a *persona dramatis*, into a love object: 'How I love thee, People of Suffering! How strong is thy heart and how young it has remained! No, thou shalt not change, thou shalt not descend into the confusion of foreign nationalities. In distinguishing lies all thy beauty, all thy happiness and all the joy of the earth … How I love thee! … How I love thee, you people of all peoples, how I bless thee!' (Winkler, 1901a:13ff.).

Paula Winkler falls in love simultaneously with the man she will marry and with the Zionism he works for. And so she falls in love with the Jewish people. For: 'Every Jew is a Zionist. This is true—not every Jew knows this, not every Jew admits this' (17). But what position is left here for a woman? In her next essay, Paula Winkler ventures a definition of the 'Jewish woman,' which allows her to present herself so, inasmuch as she speaks to Jewish women about their mission. The autobiographical speech of her first essay is now replaced by a form of writing that mixes literary techniques with prophetic passages: 'A child escapes from the garden of a noble house, reaches the street, and trades her precious pearls for the glittering bits of glass with which it saw another child playing. That is the Jewish woman' (Winkler, 1901b:2).

Since her emergence from the ghetto, runs the commentary on this passage, 'the Jewish woman of the last decades has been earnestly engaged in becoming a "good European", and has succeeded, as best she could. Nothing good has come of it' (3). Above all, nothing good has come from a mixing of Jewish and German, whereby Paula Winkler assumes a fundamental difference between the two peoples and their cultures. Until now, the Jewish woman

has mediated between these poles, as in early nineteenth century salons. Now, however, she writes, another type of mediation is called for, one that has also been laid upon the Jewish woman as a task. For she, 'the great Understander, the great Stimulant,' should initiate for her people a Jewish art, a Jewish poetry, so that they can mirror themselves in it 'as in a pure crystal!' Woman is responsible for 'a resurrection unlike any experienced by a people. It will be comparable to a force of nature, and faithful hearts will see a miracle' (3). This resurgent people would seek a home outside of Germany. Paula Winkler saw art and children's education as the decisive components in the construction of a Jewish national feeling, a sense that could not be compared to the nationalism of other peoples. 'Let every mother understand: Judaism has but one salvation, there is for the Jew but one redemption, but one vital possibility in joy and beauty: National feeling.' And so she ends with an appeal to all Jewish women: 'The Jewish woman has much to do. And much is asked of her by her people' (7).

Paula Winkler herself, however, could not take up the tasks she here outlines. Her correspondence with Martin Buber displays a division of labour, leading her into other paths. On 18 October 1901 she writes to her husband: 'I must tell you, I have a new mission, that I didn't have before: I would like to be active with you for Zionism; no, I will be' (Buber, 1972:167). Buber's answer directs her however to a different site and assigns her a different task. He writes on 25 October: 'Your letters are most wonderful and unusual [*das Allereinzigste*]. Perhaps the only more wonderful and unusual thing is the idea that a mother is in you, my belief in that. Now I know: I have always and everywhere been searching for my mother' (169).

These two desires are difficult to reconcile. In any case, there are no subsequent publications in which Paula Winkler, on her own or with her husband, battles for Zionism. Instead of this, in 1906 Martin Buber's famous book *The Stories of Rabbi Nachman* appeared, which we know today he wrote together with Paula Winkler.[8] The book, corresponding exactly to the definition of 'Jewish literature' proffered by Paula Winkler's essay, bears only a masculine author's name. As does *The Legends of Baalschem*,[9] published two years later and also written by the two of them. Can Jewish art only be authorised by men? Can only men fight for Zionism? What task is left to the mother Martin Buber had always searched for in his wife? Woman as Mother is apparently a storyteller, who, like Paula Winkler's nameless mother, transmits history in narrative forms. And so, pushed onto a literary terrain, Paula Winkler, under the pseudonym Georg Munk, begins to publish novels and stories. Georg Munk, however, signs no 'Jewish art.' He tells stories from Catholic South Germany. The two factors identified by Paula Winkler's sketch of the 'Jewish woman' are thus both allied with Martin Buber: After 1901, the production of Jewish art as well as the theoretical and conceptual writing on behalf of Zionism are his affairs. For a woman, there remains literary writing under an

assumed name, and a maternal existence—for husband and children. The Jewish woman, for whom Paula Winkler attempted to speak, is rendered silent—someone else, a man, speaks for her.

In 1913 a book appeared that set *The Modern Jewess*—so its title—in a wholly new context. The author was Else Croner.[10] She, too, both before and after this study, wrote other books that do not reflect upon Judaism. Her first book was devoted to female characters in Fontane's novels, then she published *The Diary of a Doctora Philosophica*, the account of a failed academic career. This was followed by a book of etiquette for young girls, and another for older women, as well as an entire stream of novels and stories (see Croner, 1906; [1908?]; 1928). And among all these books, disconnected and singular, her discussion of the modern Jewess. Though Else Croner wrote about many aspects of women, the 'modern Jewess' appears as an isolated phenomenon, featureless, nameless, ageless, and without a history, as if she came from a different time and lived in a different world from the women about whom the author wrote in her other books. And only the book on the modern Jewess begins with a message to its readers: 'This book has been written, now, in a time of fusion and general levelling, in order to preserve in a few quick strokes a type of woman, before this type is irretrievably swallowed up by the great contemporary current 'Assimilation,' uprooted by the tempest of internationalism, consumed in the fires of hatred, or—what would be by far the worst—lost and obliterated in the tepid atmosphere of indifference' (Croner, 1913:14).

Here, too, it is a matter of a distinction affixed to the word 'Jewess,' but Else Croner defines it differently from Paula Winkler. She claims that the Jewess 'among all the women on Earth, whatever their nationality, constitutes a particular type, marked by race and tradition' (13). But as the title of her book already suggests, this commonality is riven by an internal difference: 'the modern Jewess' is clearly something quite other than the Jewess of other times and lands. 'The concept "modern Jewess",' the Foreword states, 'seems to be a self-contradiction, for the Jewess is no modern, rather the oldest and most conservative type of woman' (7). But, supported by a 'liberal view of life [*Lebensanschauung*],' with which she resists a 'Jewish-conservative world view [*Weltanschauung*],' the modern Jewess is the forerunner of and guide toward a new era. She has 'brought a concept into the world that was not there before: the concept of modernity, which would not exist without the Jewesses, for it is they themselves who have, even if unintentionally, created it' (10).

The site of this creation is Berlin, Else Croner writes, and more specifically, Berlin's Western part, where in the elegant salons of the great residences a culture was nourished in which the modern and the traditional came together, and whereby men represented tradition, and women embodied progress. Women mastered the art of acculturation, while the men remained parvenus much longer. At the same time, Else Croner claims that Jewish women managed in this acculturation to preserve their particularity, their mode of thinking,

speaking, and feeling far better than did the men. '[The Jewess] never disappears entirely into Germanness, the way many Jewish men today do, whether intentionally or not' (87-8).

Why then does the Foreword speak of the danger that the Jewess will disappear? According to Else Croner, it is faulty remembrance and deficient self-confidence that threaten this amalgam of tradition and modernity. The modern Jewess, she writes, imitates the Christian women and forgets thereby that she belongs to the oldest cultural nation in the world, 'who already had a high culture long behind them when the Germans were lounging on bearskins' (84). To escape this contradiction, Else Croner sketches a mode of integration that seems to be possible only for women. 'That sort of Jewess, more precisely, the full-blooded oriental with the Asiatic-Jewish cultural background, who is now in a position to bring over into her ancient culture the whole of the Christian-Germanic culture, stands above all other women on Earth' (148). Harmony, reconciliation, unity shine forth as the goals of this integration. Or to put it another way—a vague end to modernity: 'The Jewess of today is the most complicated, most thoroughly spiritualised [*durchgeistigste*], but at the same time most discordant type of woman. May the Jewess of the future become the most harmonic' (148).

To read Bertha Badt-Strauss' book *Jewesses* of 1937, is to see this hope in no way fulfilled. Neither integration nor harmony, and least of all in Berlin. By 1937 not only Berlin, but Germany itself has long since ceased to be representative of Jewish acculturation. *Jewesses*, the last book she published in Germany two years before her emigration to the United States, is almost a resume of all her earlier efforts.[11] This book, which picks up the structure of Meyer Kayserling's study without mentioning Nahida Remy's, is constructed around very few central notions: duality and conflict. The Jewish woman, so the foreword tells us, is a sign of 'this strange duality, that renders her both preserver and destroyer of the ancient Jewish values' (Badt-Strauss, 1937: 31). A glance into history—the author continues—shows 'Jewesses as the most loyal protectors and preservers of the popular heritage [...] and on the other hand Jewesses as the most rapid apostates of the old ways and the ancient doctrines.' (35)

In a series of biographical portraits of women from the ancients to her contemporaries, Bertha Badt-Strauss goes on to develop a spectrum of varying types and individuals, comprehensible only as Jewesses, as an irreducible plurality. But the duality and conflict of which the foreword spoke appears only with respect to German Jewish women. This is all the more surprising, in that Germany, as a site of Jewish culture, occupies only a small part of the book. Of twelve chapters, only four take German Jewish Women as their subjects, and these women all lived at the turn of the nineteenth century, with the exception of Bertha Pappenhein, who appears briefly at the end of the fourth chapter. The corresponding sections have the titles: 'Women of the Age of

Mendelssohn,' 'The Daughter of the Philosopher,' as well as 'Rahel Levin and her Contemporaries.' 'We Jews of today cannot think of those much celebrated Jewesses in the Romantic era without a certain bitterness; it is as the shepherdess said in the Song of Songs—they did not tend their vineyard.' So begins the sketch of the philosopher's daughter, 'Brendel by name; she later called herself Dorothea, once she had traded the tent of Sem for the settlement of Japhet' (Badt-Strauss, 1937:69). It is indeed an embittered portrait of Dorothea, whose later name Schlegel does not once appear in the chapter. Rather less embittered, though, is the portrait of Rahel Levin. She, as opposed to Dorothea, apparently achieved enough to appear in Bertha Badt-Strauss's book with her Jewish name. She represents the prototype 'of that strange duality of nineteenth century Jewesses. Limitless sensitivity let her be a home for others. Unshakeable integrity led her to pose questions that even a century later we cannot solve. But in her innermost heart, she knew that her home, the home of her heart, had been lost to her, and that if it fell to her to pose the questions, it was not given her to answer them. This makes the Jewess of those decades a deeply tragic figure' (79).

The change in perspective of this passage marks the exact point in Bertha Badt-Strauss' book where the biographical strategy collapses. All other Jewish women from these decades, mentioned by name and introduced to us, whether Esther Gad-Bernard or Sara Levy, are presented without this duality. In fact, only Rahel Levin represents this type. Is she then a type, or an individual with many particular characteristics? Why can she alone stand for what the foreword already identified as a feature of all Jewish women?

Perhaps one sees here the trace of an autobiographical rupture. For all the subsequent chapters are written as if her bags were already packed, still in German and still in Germany, but already with a glance at other lands and other languages in which a life might be possible that, in the Germany of the 1930s, had become irretrievably historical. The confrontation with the National Socialist definition of Jew and non-Jew, as set forth in the Nuremberg Laws, forces a self-definition that leaves duality and conflict behind in order to resist this force.

All the subsequent portraits sketch women who, in the most varied times and places, were unmistakably Jewish. Whether Poland or Galicia, two regions that did not appear in the books of Kayserling and Remy, from whence two nineteenth century East European Jewish women are introduced as representatives of living Jewish culture. Or with regard to the countries to which so many Jews emigrated, the United States and *Erez Israel*. Jewish life in Germany appears as a small segment of a long path that has already ended. The German language, too, is left behind, when, in the final chapters, more and more Hebrew words are used. The last sections can only be properly understood by a reader who is familiar with that language. The author tells us twice that she is learning Hebrew, and Rachel Bluwstein, who moved to *Erez Israel* from Russia and there began to write Hebrew poetry, is presented as a supreme model.

And yet, Bertha Badt-Strauss, who emigrated in 1939 to the United States, did not write a book of farewell. For Germany disappears without mourning, without any pain. Germany has already become the past. Something new emerges, of which the Foreword tells us: 'The Temple in Jerusalem was destroyed through the fault of women, says the Midrash. But through the pleas of Mother Rahel, bewailing her children, will Israel be redeemed' (6).

This day of redemption does not seem distant. From the ancient world, the world of Pallas Athena, to the return to Israel, a circle has come round. From one world to another. What conclusion was in the offing Bertha Badt-Strauss could not imagine. Only a few years later, and once again in German, someone would write: 'Mother Rahel / Weeps no longer.'

Translated by James McFarland

Notes

* A first version of this article appeared under the title: "Die Jüdin Pallas Athene. Ortsbe-stimmung im 19. und 20. Jahrhundert, in: Von *einer Welt in die andere. Jüdinnen im 19. und 20. Jahrhundert,* editor (with Jutta Dick). Wien: Brandstätter Verlag, 1993. In 2002, I published a book length study with Berlin-Verlag, Berlin, based on this article: *Die Jüdin Pallas Athene. Auch eine Theorie der Moderne.*

1. See Else Lasker-Schüler's poem 'An old Tibetan carpet,' where she writes: 'Your soul, that loves mine,/ Is entwined with it in carpet Tibet' (1959:164).

2. On this theorising of the West or of Europe, see Susman, 1954:160-77; 1992:209-23.

3. See my study Hahn, 1991:47-70. In correspondences with female Jews, only one contemporary was explicitly concerned about this problem: Charles de Ligne. He addresses his 1801 treatise on Jews to Sara Meyer. See de Linge, 1924:187-99.

4. The book was written between 1861 and 1864, as the dates on the individual letters and the foreword reveal. Clementine von Rothschild, a granddaughter of Clara Hertz, an unconverted childhood friend of Rahel Levin, was born on 14 June 1845 in Frankfurt and died there on 18 October 1865.

5. Meyer Kayserling addressed a female Jewish readership with his study in culture and history: 'The desire to promote the education and ennobling of the female sex led me to write this text, which should not be understood as an apology for Jewish women. [...] The images of women presented in this book are intended to awaken the self-consciousness, to enflame and strengthen their love of faith. For the future of every religion depends to a much greater extent than in masculine religiosity on the religious education and devotion of the female sex' (1879:255).

6. The book was published first in Leipzig in 1891. A second edition appeared in 1892, the third in 1895. I quote from the fourth edition of 1922, in which the forewords of the earlier editions are reprinted. Nahida Remy's *Culturstudien über das Judenthum* had been published in Berlin in 1893. Nahida Remy was born in Berlin on 3 February 1849, and died on 12 January 1928 in Meran.

7. Paula Winkler was born in Munich on 14 June 1877 and died in Venice on 11 August 1958. A bibliography of her writings can be found in Hahn, 1991:143.

8. In her introduction to Buber's correspondence, Grete Schaeder discusses this connection: 'Letters from these months [November and December 1906] prove that a part of the legend [of Baalschem] was composed from the raw material not by Buber, but by his wife.' Compare her preface to Martin Buber's *Correspondence from Seven Decades* (24-40, here 38). Paula Buber's task in this collective production is described by Buber as follows: 'Perhaps it truly does fall to you to renew the story' (250), and shortly thereafter: 'I am genuinely nervous about your judgement, but you must not protect me if indeed there is nothing to the story' (252). Grete Schaeder supposes that the Story of Rabbi Nachman, published in 1906, also was composed in this way. See in this regard, Hahn, 1991:92-102.

9. A letter of Buber's of 1 December 1906 from Berlin begins, for example, 'my dear Maugli, now it is a matter of getting you here as quickly as possible. For that, the legends must be finished right away […]. I'm working away on one of them. But I want to ask you, too, to make a couple over the next few days' (249).

10. Else Croner was born in Beuthen in 1878 and died in 1940; where has not been determined.

11. Bertha Badt-Strauss was born in Breslau on 7 December 1885 and died on 20 February 1970 in Chapel Hill, North Carolina. She is among the first women to achieve a doctorate in Prussia. She defended her dissertation on *Annette von Droste-Hülshoff in her relation to English Literature* in Breslau in 1908. She then turned, as did many women who completed their higher education, to freelance writing. Over the next few years, Bertha Badt-Strauss published an anthology of Süskind von Trimberg and two variously complete editions of the letters of Rahel Levin; later there followed editions of Annette von Droste-Hülshoff and finally Moses Mendelssohn. Among these are also source editions such as, for instance, in her 1932 essay 'Elise Reimarus und Moses Mendelssohn.' I am grateful to Birgit Bosold for this reference. See also Badt-Strauss, 1912, 1920, undated (1928), 1929.

References

Badt-Strauss, Bertha (1912) *Rahel und ihre Zeit. Briefe und Zeugnisse,* Munich.

Badt-Strauss, Bertha (1920) *Die Lieder des Süßkind von Trimberg*, Berlin.

Badt-Strauss, Bertha (undated, [1928]) *Rahel Varnhagen. Menschen untereinander*, (ed. Bertha Badt-Strauss), Berlin.

Badt-Strauss, Bertha (1929) *Moses Mendelssohn, der Mensch und das Werk*, Berlin.

Badt-Strauss, Bertha (1932) 'Elise Reimarus und Moses Mendelssohn (Nach ungedruckten Quellen)', *Zeitschrift für die Geschichte der Juden in Deutschland*, IV:384-400.

Badt-Strauss, Bertha (1937) *Jüdinnen*, Berlin.

Beyerdörfer, Peter (1977) 'Poetischer Sarcasmus. Fadensonnen und die Wende zum Spätwerk', *Text und Kritik*, 53/54:42-54.

Buber, Martin (1972) *Briefwechsel aus sieben Jahrzehnten,* Vol. 1 (ed. Grete Schaeder), Heidelberg.

Celan, Paul (1990[9]) *Gedichte in zwei Bänden*, Vol. 2, Frankfurt/M.

Croner, Else (1906) *Fontanes Frauengestalten*, Berlin.

Croner, Else (undated -1908?) *Tagebuch eines Fräulein Doktors*, Berlin.

Croner, Else (1913) *Die moderne Jüdin*, Berlin.

Croner, Else (1928) *Die Frauenseele in den Übergangsjahren*, Berlin.

de Ligne, Charles (1924) *Der Fürst von Ligne. Neue Briefe*, (trans. and ed. Victor Klarwill), Vienna, pp. 187-99.

(Goldschmidt, Johanna), (1847) *Rebekka und Amalie. Briefwechsel zwischen einer Israelitin und einer Adeligen über Zeit- und Lebensfragen*, Leipzig.

Hahn, Barbara (1991) *Unter falschem Namen. Von der schwierigen Autorschaft der Frauen*, Frankfurt/M.

Lasker-Schüler, Else (1959) *Gesammelte Werke, Gedichte 1902-1943*, Vol. 1, (ed. Friedhelm Kemp), Munich.

Meyer Kayserling (1879) *Die jüdischen Frauen in der Geschichte, Literatur und Kunst*, Leipzig.

Remy, Nahida (1922[4] [1891]) *Das jüdische Weib*, (Foreword to the third edition), Berlin.

Rothschild, Clementine von (1883) *Briefe an eine christliche Freundin über die Grundwahrheiten des Judenthums*, Leipzig.

Susman, Margarete (1954 [1933]) 'Wandlungen der Frau', *Die Neue Rundschau* 1933, 44, 1:105-124 (reprinted in M. Susman, *Gestalten und Kreise*, Stuttgart/Konstanz 1954, pp. 160-77).

Susman, Margarete (1992 [1933]) 'Der jüdische Geist', *Blätter des jüdischen Frauenbundes* IX, 1933, 11/12 (reprinted in M. Susman, *Das Nah- und Fernsein des Fremden. Essays und Briefe*, ed. Ingeborg Nordmann), Frankfurt/M., pp. 209-23.

Winkler, Paula (1901a) 'Betrachtungen einer Philozionistin', *Die Welt. Zentralorgan der zionistischen Bewegung*, 36, 6. September.

Winkler, Paula (1901b) 'Die jüdische Frau', *Die Welt. Zentralorgan der zionistischen Bewegung*, 45 and 46, 8. and 15. November.

IV: BOUNDARIES AND ETHNICITY

Collective Identity as a Dual Discursive Construction
Dominant v. Demotic Discourses of Culture and the Negotiation of Historical Memory

GERD BAUMANN

There is consensus among historians and social scientists that collective identities can undergo thorough and sometimes radical processes of redefinition. Such changes of self-definition have been observed most clearly among populations that have located themselves in new historical contexts by long-distance migration and diasporic settlement. So much is clear, yet this consensus raises a tricky theoretical question. How is it possible that the same social agents can reaffirm putatively ancient ethnic or cultural cleavages in some situations, but can construct new identities and alternative or hybrid cultural forms in others? The answer I shall propose understands cultural identities as discursive constructs, and it posits that there are two different discourses of identity that diasporic populations are able, and often obliged, to use. One of these I have called the dominant discourse, the other the demotic. As I have argued previously (Baumann, 1996, 1997), their key difference lies in their understanding of culture; what I wish to add to the argument here is an emphasis on the role of historical reinterpretation and the social negotiation of memory. My propositions have arisen from seven years' resident research in Southall, a multiethnic suburb of London.[1]

The West London suburb of Southall numbers some 60,000 people of, internally deeply heterogeneous, South Asian, Afro-Caribbean, Irish, English, and several other backgrounds. In most general contexts, Southallians used a rough-and-ready taxonomy of five 'communities' characterised by their different 'cultures': Sikhs, Hindus, Muslims, Caribbeans and Whites. Yet what

struck me most forcefully over the first few years of research was the multitude of intersecting sociocultural boundaries. Following religious cleavages, Southall was a town of Sikh, Hindu, Muslim, and various Christian communities. Following linguistic cleavages, the town's population divided itself into native speakers of Punjabi, Gujarati, Urdu, or several English-language sociolects. Following the cleavages of their migratory histories, Southallians of different religions and languages, national and regional categories could yet again form different communities, such as an East African-Asian as opposed to a subcontinental-Asian component, an Asian-Caribbean as opposed to an Afro-Caribbean one, an Irish-Catholic as opposed to an English-Catholic one. The proliferation of crosscutting cleavages rendered Southall a palpably pluralist society, and to do justice to this pluralism meant ranging across the categorical divides of seemingly autonomous communities defined by a reified culture.

Most importantly, it was Southallians themselves who could be seen to distance themselves, in a variety of contexts, from the dominant paradigm of equating culture, community, and ethnic identity. The more one listened, the more voices one heard that identified different cultures within the same quasi-ethnic community, while recognising or postulating the same culture across different communities as well. The equation between ethnic identity and culture, dominant as it is in much public discourse about ethnic minorities, disintegrated the more I got to know local people. As I have indicated, Southallians indeed replicated the hegemonic equation between one or the other 'community' and what was called 'its culture' in a number of normative contexts. Yet in other contexts, the same people could dissolve the dominant discourse of reification by a demotic discourse which saw culture, community, and identity as dynamic social processes, rather than predetermined social facts.[2]

The data thus showed two different discourses of identity being engaged by Southallians themselves. I need not here recapitulate in detail the features of the dominant discourse, that is, the discourse of reification, as it has been widely critiqued in both the ethnographic and the theoretical literature.[3] Nor do I need to rehearse the mechanisms that can turn a reificatory discourse into a dominant one.[4] What should be stressed, however, is that the two discourses do not spell a choice between 'reificatory = wrong-headed' and 'demotic = right-minded.' There are very good reasons why people should reify the cultural identities that in other contexts they are aware of remaking and reshaping, reformulating and reforming. For one, the reification of cultural identities can be a political necessity in the pursuit of equal rights: precisely because the reificatory discourse is the dominant one in the politics of representation, both political and mediatic, it is a useful resource in challenging established inequalities. Secondly, the dominant discourse answers to some crucial common sense of historical continuity. Culture-making, after all, is not an *ex tempore* improvisation, but entails a project of social cohesion, often called 'community,'[5] placed within, and contending with, the historical dynamics of

social change. Both observations make it quite plausible that, even when Southallians explicitly engage the demotic discourse, the faultiness of the dominant one is effective and, more than that, empirically visible. Thus, the patterns by which, say, Sikh or Afro-Caribbean Southallians, local whites or local Muslims remap the cultures, communities and identities they perceive have remained distinctive to an observable degree. Taking at face value the most general division that most Southallians apply to themselves and each other, let me emphasise the role of renegotiating history and historical memory in their respective projects of articulating collective identities.

Among Southall's Sikhs, the most important process was one of differentiating new communities within the same 'Sikh culture.' In order to understand this process, one has to cast a brief glance at the local history of migration which differed between Sikhs of the *Jat* or farmers' caste and Sikhs of the crafts castes such as the *Tharkan* or carpenters, *Lohar* or blacksmiths, and *Raj* or bricklayers. Most of the *Jat* Sikhs had migrated, between the 1950s and 1970s, from the rural Punjab, and had in England been largely confined to a working-class niche of unskilled labourers. Most of the Sikhs from the crafts castes, by contrast, had arrived rather later, during the 1970s, when they were expelled from East Africa. For the three or four preceding generations, they had formed an 'African-Asian' middle class placed between the British colonisers and the African working and peasant classes. Following their resettlement in Britain, they used their middle-class aspirations, as well as their traditional disdain for *Jat* Sikhs and their claim to caste superiority, to organise themselves as an independent community. The cultural as well as the economic capital which they could draw upon from their East African past is analysed in detail by Morris (1968). The new communal identity which they succeeded in establishing in Britain is described, and in some ways reinforced, by Bhachu (1985). As East-African Sikhs renegotiated their historical memories in the new British environment, two aspects in particular underwent shifts of emphasis. Firstly, East-African Asians in Britain had no place in their view of the past for the centuries-old subcontinental traditions of caste hierarchy and inequality. Rather than remembering a life as landless 'village serfs' (Rose, 1911-19) who were dependent on the patronage of landed *Jat*-Sikh families, they tended to reconstruct a view of their forebears as independent craftsmen, superior even then to the landed, but professionally unqualified *Jat*. In reconstructing their pasts in East Africa, Ramgarhia Sikhs tended to stress their long history of upward mobility and educational success, as well as the prosperity and prestige that they had gained in colonial and postcolonial Africa. Most tangibly, it was commonplace in such recollections to dwell on the number of servants and domestics one had been able to employ. Memories of their forebears' position on the subcontinent were thus largely erased from consciousness, and memories of middle-class experience from East Africa were brought to the fore. A revalidation of their colo-

nial past could thus help to neutralise the precolonial history of caste inferiority on the Indian subcontinent.

Among Hindus, the dominant equation between culture and community was dissolved, not so much in order to argue for internal differentiation, which was conspicuously absent, as to argue for the inclusion of others. In understanding this process, it appears appropriate to borrow Louis Dumont's (1980) idea of encompassment, developed in his analysis of the caste system. Dumont uses the word to describe the hierarchical subsumption of an opposite under a superordinate whole. In its shortest form, this claim stated that 'Sikhs are Hindus,' and that the Sikh community formed an integral part of Hindu culture. Not surprisingly, this argument had to rely on a highly selective validation of Sikh history, and it tended to focus on the founder of the Sikh tradition, Guru Nanak, whose sixteenth-century movement could indeed, in some ways, be seen as a Hindu reform movement of ecumenical aspirations. This meant, however, that almost four hundred years of subsequent Sikh history had to be pushed aside as a series of aberrations which violated the axiomatic participation of Sikhs in 'Hindu culture.' It was sometimes put down to 'Muslim oppression' and 'Moghul rule' that subsequent Gurus of the Sikh faith had defined and enforced the autonomy of Sikhism as a religion, and that Maharaja Ranjit Singh had succeeded, before his defeat by the British, in establishing a Sikh state in the Punjab. This very partial reading of perfectly well-known historical knowledge could fulfil additional political functions in the 1980s, when Sikh separatists fought an armed campaign for an independent Sikh state of Khalistan. The historical construction of Sikhs as Hindus could then serve to neutralise a long history of intercommunal tensions, and the Khalistan conflict could be portrayed as a historically misguided deviation from a shared historical origin and a continuing unity of cultural substance.

Both Sikhs and Hindus in Southall tended to regard the local Muslim community as a marginal category, and although there were as many Muslims in town as there were Hindus, Muslims were indeed positioned outside the circles of political power, economic influence, and cultural self-representation. In rationalising this marginalisation, two historical references tended to overshadow all others. One was to blame Muslims for the 'oppressive' regime of Moghul rule in India, by which they had placed themselves outside the pale of fellow Indians; the other was, not surprisingly, the partition of India and the Punjab, brought about, it was said, by Muslim insistence on an independent Pakistan.

In disengaging the dominant equation between community and culture, historical arguments were of some importance also among Afro-Caribbean Southallians. Here, however, the equation lacked the intuitive credibility which the South Asian 'communities of culture' could grant it when they chose to. Looking back upon a history of cultural as well as economic and political oppression, many Afro-Caribbeans were adamant that 'our community doesn't have a culture yet,' and that the new Afro-Caribbean or African-Caribbean cul-

ture was still to be 'made,' 'created,' or 'found.' Among the approaches consciously aimed at creating such a new cultural identity, three perspectives came to the fore consistently: a religious one which emphasised Rastafarian beliefs, a political one which favoured pan-Africanist ideas, and an expressive-musical one which validated oppositional creativity. Across these approaches, however, one could discern one crucial historical revalidation. It consisted in a new emphasis on the historical unity of all people of African descent. Rastafarianism, pan-Africanism, and the aesthetic discovery of continental African music all entailed a conscious rejection of the national or ethnic boundaries constructed between different Caribbean islands, and indeed the ethnic boundaries constructed between Africans from Africa and Africans from elsewhere. Both Rastafarians and secular pan-Africanists saw themselves as 'Africans, whatever the country you come from,' and Africa was apostrophised, in the words of many informants, as 'our spiritual home,' 'our common cultural identity,' and 'the country where our true culture lies.' This new African identity constructs, not only a global history, but a new and global cultural identity, as an informant from Southall expressed it to my fellow ethnographer Hazel Yabsley:

> 'Through slavery, Africans were scattered all over the globe. Their culture was destroyed, they had no link with Africa. The aim of unity is to join African-Caribbean people—people of African descent and African people. They were forbidden to know about the mother-land, Africa. Coming to England united those who had been separated for 300, 400 years. They can go to France and meet Africans from Senegal, to Holland and meet Africans from Surinam. They go to Africa and are accepted (he claims in objection to my statement otherwise.) [...] Blacks in the American situation identify with Africa' (Yabsley, 1990:113-4).

An explicitly political pan-Africanist position, nonetheless, was not endorsed by many Afro-Caribbean Southallians. It required considerable rhetorical skills to deny the observable tensions between Africans from the continent and Africans from the Caribbean or other diasporas; and while the invocation of common origins was plausible, the intervening centuries of historical and cultural differentiation were hard to ignore. Nonetheless, the pan-Africanist rereading of cultural identity could mobilise public support when it relied on creative transformation, rather than verbal adumbration. Thus, at the Marcus Garvey Centennial celebrations, Southallians enthusiastically applauded two groups of Afro-Caribbean Londoners performing African-derived music and a 'Zulu War Dance,' and the dissemination of contemporary African music through the 1980s marketing of 'World Music' found delighted listeners among young Afro-Caribbean Southallians who saw in it a validation of their 'African roots.' As these examples may indicate, Southallians of diverse 'communities of culture' were thus able, and motivated in chosen contexts, to disengage the dominant equation between culture, community, and collective identity, and this demotic discursive practice made explicit use of historical reinterpretations and the renegotiation of memory.

This does not mean, however, that the dominant discourse of identity is thereby revoked altogether. Southallians continue to engage it, depending upon their judgements of context and purpose. The demotic discourse, which allows Southallians to create new communities, as well as subdivide or fuse existing ones, is not an autonomous opposite, or an independent alternative, to the dominant one. It is used to undermine the dominant one whenever Southallians, pursuing their aims as they see them, judge it useful in any one context. Yet it does not make the dominant discourse lose its salience: it would hardly be dominant, after all, if Southallians could, as it were, switch it off altogether. What the data show, however, is a dual discursive competence. This dual competence turns the ideas of culture, community, and collective identity into objects of questioning, redefinition, and sometimes contestation. I have described a number of these contestations elsewhere (Baumann, 1996). In order, however, to highlight the role of history and memory in the construction of new collective identities, it may be useful to reexamine a process of fundamental cultural and identificatory change, namely the conception, especially among young Southallians, of a comprehensively Asian identity.

One of the most convincing, because unexpected, signs that the younger cohort of South Asian Southallians had begun to construct a comprehensively 'Asian identity' with its own 'Asian culture' arose in discussions about 'arranged' and caste-endogamous marriages (Ballard, C., 1979; Ballard, R., 1972). It was remarkable how many young Southallians saw 'arranged marriages' and the strictures of caste as a part of an 'Asian culture,' rather than their specifically Hindu, Muslim or Sikh heritages. This newly-shared way of speaking about very different strictures of custom enabled South Asian Southallians to discuss their views as 'young Asians' together, and it thus contributed to their discovery of a shared 'Asian identity.' This commitment to a comprehensively 'Asian culture' marked a new point of convergence. This novel discourse of culture and community came to include a secular, cross-religious, cross-caste, and sometimes political, discourse of a comprehensively Asian identification.

To speak of an Asian culture in the dominant sense of a unified heritage defining a unitary community is, of course, implausible, as every child in Southall knows. To do so would require blindness to the enormous diversity and the momentous contention that have long characterised the subcontinent. The term Asian to signify a shared culture, marks a departure which is consciously innovative, although one should be wary here of playing a sociological 'generation game,' as if the forging of a postimmigration Asian culture were the preserve of youngsters alone. Mannheim (1982) has shown up the spuriousness of treating generation as a sociological category. There is, however, an articulate awareness, among young South Asian Southallians, that being young and British involves them in the conscious creation of a new collective identity.

To characterise this evolving 'Asian culture,' four elements sprang to teenagers' minds. The first concerned classification as 'Asians' by others, both white and Afro-Caribbean Southallians; the second entailed an aspiration, 'like the Caribbeans' as it was often said, to achieve a new solidarity within that imposed classification; the third was an aesthetic desire: a wish, 'like the other cultures,' symbolically to express this unity, especially through the music of a newly-created pan-Asian genre called *Bhangra* or 'The Southall Beat': a crossover of Punjabi folk music and Disco styles (Banerji and Baumann, 1990; Baumann, 1990). The fourth element, and one of particular interest here, concerned a symbolic but momentous rewriting of history. The culture-making project of unifying an 'Asian cultural community' must overcome a history of divisions between hitherto exclusivist religious, caste, and regional 'community' heritages. Southall's South Asian communities may fuse what was distinct on the subcontinent, or differentiate what seemed unitary there. To render visible a shared heritage behind these old or recent divisions requires also an alternative writing of history. A telling example may be seen in reviving the memory of a pan-Asian anticolonial hero.

Most heroes of anticolonialism and the struggle for independence are, of course, identified with Pakistani or Indian nationalism, or with Muslim, Sikh or Hindu heritages. One remarkable exception, however, entered young Southallians' purview in the late 1980s. A Punjabi man named Uddam Singh had survived the infamous Amritsar massacre of 1919, in which some 350 unarmed civilians were killed by British troops under the command of General, later even Sir, Michael O'Dwyer. Recasting his name as Ram Mohammed Singh Azaad to reflect the joint Hindu, Muslim and Sikh aspiration toward freedom (*azaad*), Uddam determined to alert the British public to the injustice of British rule by assassinating O'Dwyer. He resolved, remarkably, not to do so in a secret ambush, but at a public election meeting in Westminster, so that his own public trial and his execution, in July 1940, would fuel and inspire the cause. Uddam Singh thus provides a symbolic beacon by which the aspirations toward building an Asian community can mobilise a legitimacy of the past. This traditional legitimacy of the anticolonial cause can now strengthen and complement the widely accepted future legitimacy of an 'Asian community' united by a hitherto latent 'Asian culture.'

Such renegotiations of memory appear as historical necessities because the construction of any 'community of culture,' be it an old one or a new one, requires two legitimations to be used concurrently. One is phrased in the language of a future legitimacy of purpose: Asians must unite to resist their continued oppression by racism and discrimination. The other, however, must be phrased as a legitimacy of the past. Even the newest 'community' needs to appeal to a historical heritage older than its present-day members' efforts if it wants to claim traditional legitimacy. In cases where such appeals might lack immediate plausibility, the historical heritage of the new community must be

portrayed as having been dormant, latent, or unjustly neglected. New identities will thus claim to fulfil potentials that have been extant for long. The two legitimacies must be balanced consistently, so that appeal can be made at once to the legitimacy of future purpose and the legitimacy of tradition. This tradition, however, is always today's recognition of yesterday's heritage as the means to reshape a collective tomorrow.

Yet no such renegotiation of history can overtake historical time, as it were, on the wrong side. It is evident that the new identity of a shared 'Asian culture' is, in social practice, an aspiration rather than an accomplished fact. Southall youth tend, to an overwhelming degree, to marry within their own 'communities' of religion and indeed of caste: the few who do not tend to leave Southall. The dominant discourse of three self-evident Asian communities of a Sikh, Hindu and Muslim 'culture' is subverted in some contexts, but retains its power in many others. What matters, however, is the social fact of a dual discursive competence. It is through the choices and switches between the dominant and the demotic discourses of identity that Southallians perform the postmigration culture which, in this sense, they share across the categorical boundaries of the dominant discourse. This performance questions boundaries of inclusion and exclusion and renders culture, history, and identity subject to deliberate renegotiation and contextual argument. In observing these renegotiations, the researcher cannot but take leave of essentialist assumptions, be they related to the 'given facts' of ethnicity, history, or cultural boundaries. The researcher may certainly encounter them in the field, and often encounter them in reified forms; but they form part of the phenomena to be analysed, rather than the analysis itself.

In examining what happens across, rather than within, the categorical identity boundaries reified by the dominant discourse, the data have pointed to a dialectic that works right across the board, no matter which 'community' or 'identity' is taken at face value. The dialectic is played out by people in their daily lives who negotiate between culture as a reified entity and culture performed as a process of negotiation within, across, and indeed about, putatively collective identities. To approach minorities, or for that matter majorities, as self-evident collectives defined by a reified culture, amounts to an implicit denial of the culture-making processes themselves, and it can make little sense of contending identifications or of contending readings of history and memory. If we wish to document and understand the historical processes of constructing and contesting collective identities, then a rethinking of the concept of culture is part of the task. I have suggested that there are two concepts of culture at work, and that they can be located in two different discourses. The dominant discourse, reificatory though it is, forms part of the social and cultural realities. Yet so does the demotic discourse of culture and collective identity which people engage in at the same time. To delegitimise the dominant discourse would be presumptuous: if informants engage in it,

then it deserves to be documented without censure and needs to be analysed in its historical context. Yet by the same token, to ignore the salience of the demotic discourse would be a wilful denial of the culture-making process, that is, the historical processes of redefining collective identities through a renegotiation of history and historical memory.

Notes

1. In addition to seven years' part-time resident research (1986-93), this comprised a period of fifteen months' full time fieldwork made possible by a grant from the Leverhulme Trust, London, in conjunction with the generous professional and intellectual support of Adam Kuper, Brunel University of West London. Some paragraphs of this text, namely those concerning the summary of the dominant discourse, have been prepublished in Werbner and Modood (1997); the main part, exploring the focus on history and memory in collective identifications, is new, and I thank Klaus E. Müller and the Centre for Interdisciplinary Research, Bielefeld, for spurring me on to work them out.

2. In defining a discourse as reificatory, I follow the classic definition of Berger and Luckmann (1967): 'Reification is the apprehension of human phenomena as if they were things, that is [...] as if they were something other than human products—such as facts of nature. [...Yet] even while apprehending the world in reified terms, [human agents] continue to produce it' (1967:106-7). For a discourse to assume a status of dominance, one would expect it to satisfy five conditions that are, in practice, interdependent: its conceptual make up should be economical, not to say simple; its communicative resources border on monopoly. It should be flexible of application, and should allow for the greatest ideological plasticity. Finally, it should lend itself to established institutional purposes.

3. The first author to draw attention to the reification of 'minority' cultures in Britain was Avtar Brah (1987) who critiqued the representation of women of South Asian backgrounds: 'Many of the contemporary *academic, political and popular* discourses [...] operate within a totally reified concept of culture as some kind of baggage to be carried around instead of a dynamic [...] force which stands in a complex relationship with the material conditions of society' (Brah, 1987:44, emphasis mine). Ann Phoenix (1988) drove this home in her critique of academic studies of 'black' teenage motherhood and analysed how 'narrow definitions of culture' are but translations of an ideology of 'race' into a discourse of reified culture (1988: 153-9; see also Gilroy 1992). Such ethnographic insights have transformed anthropological theories of culture into a consensus against essentialist approaches (Barth, 1994; Keesing, 1994; Sahlins, 1994; Vayda, 1994). Keesing (1994) suggests that this 'conception of culture [which] almost irresistibly leads us into reification and essentialism' (1994:302) is based on an ethnocentric construction of 'radical alterity—a culturally constructed Other radically different from Us' (1994:301). He seems to forget, however, that people may reify their 'own' culture as readily as they reify 'others.' Van der Veer (1994) indeed traces Indian communalist conflicts to 'the basic [...] fallacy of *both* sociological *and* [non-academic] communalist versions [... in that they both] portray Muslim and Hindu values as [two] reified systems' (1994:29).

4. Rothschild defines ethnopolitics as a project of 'mobilising ethnicity from a psychological or cultural or social datum into political leverage for the purpose of altering *or reinforcing*

[…] systems of structured inequality between and among ethnic categories. [… In this process, ethnopolitics] stresses, ideologises, reifies, modifies, and sometimes virtually recreates the putatively distinctive and unique cultural heritages of the ethnic groups that it mobilises […]' (Rothschild, 1981:2-3, emphasis mine). Kapferer (1988) described such processes of 'the reification of culture, the production of culture as an object in itself' (1988: 7) and showed how selected patterns and traits can be '*systematically* removed from their embeddedness in the flow of daily life, fashioned into symbolic things, and placed in a stable, dominant, and determinate relation to action' (1988:210, emphasis mine). Gilroy noted the elaboration of 'new forms of racism [… which] are distinguished by the extent to which they identify race with the terms "culture" and "identity" [and thus converge on …] a belief in the absolute nature of ethnic categories […] (1992:50-3). Vertovec (1995) rightly stresses the dimension of political contest when he describes how 'culture' can be 'made an object in itself so as to articulate a shared ethnic identity in the face of potentially intensified patterns of […] resource competition' (1995:150).

5. To trace the semantic intricacies of the notion of community, one might usefully start with the German sociologist Tönnies (1887) who tried to use it as an analytical abstraction in an essentially evolutionist account. Hillery (1955) researched a grand total of ninety-four different meanings attributed to the term by sociologists, and the word appears quite clearly as a common-sense cipher devoid of any analytic potential. Macfarlane (1977) has forcefully advocated that it be abandoned altogether. More recently, the anthropologist Anthony Cohen (1985) has, in one brilliant short treatise, stripped away whatever substantive meaning one might have attributed to the word, and shown 'community' to be a contextually contingent 'symbolic construction.' This does not, of course, detract from its potential in political contestation and indeed confrontation, as Ignatieff (1992) observed in connection with the Rushdie Affair: 'the only thing on which anti-Islamic liberals and their fundamentalist opposite numbers agreed was that there was such a thing as a "Muslim community". "It" was either a threat to liberal civilisation as we know it, or "it" was a resurgent faith on the march. At the height of the affair, Muslims in Britain could be forgiven for wishing no one had ever thought them a community at all' (Ignatieff, 1992). The word remains attractive, however, not least to the bashers of 'ethnic' minorities, because it appears to recognise people as members of a special collective. What is thought special about this collective, most readily in the case of 'ethnic' minorities, is that they are presumed to share a 'culture' in its reified form.

References

Ballard, Catherine (1979) 'Conflict, Continuity and Change: Second-generation South Asians,' in Saifullah Khan, Verity (ed.) *Minority Families in Britain. Support and Stress*, London, pp. 109-29.

Ballard, Roger (1972) 'Family Organisation among the Sikhs in Britain', *New Community*, 2, 1:12-33.

Banerji, Sabita and Baumann, Gerd (1990) 'Bhangra in Britain: Fusion and professionalization in a genre of South Asian dance music', in Oliver, Paul (ed.) *Black Music in Britain*, Milton Keynes, pp. 137-52.

Barth, Fredrik (1994) 'A Personal View of Present Tasks and Priorities in Cultural and Social Anthropology', in Robert Borofsky, (ed.) *Assessing Cultural Anthropology*, New York, pp. 349-61.

Baumann, Gerd (1990) 'The Re-Invention of *Bhangra*: Social Change and Aesthetic Shifts in a Punjabi Music in Britain', *The World of Music*, 2:81-98.

Baumann, Gerd (1992) 'Ritual implicates "Others": Rereading Durkheim in a Plural Society', in Daniel de Coppet, (ed.) *Understanding Rituals*, London, pp. 97-116.

Baumann, Gerd (1996) *Contesting Culture. Discourses of Identity in Multi-Ethnic London*, Cambridge.

Baumann, Gerd (1997) 'Dominant and Demotic Discourses of Culture: Their Relevance to Multi-Ethnic Alliances', in Pnina Werbner and Tariq Modood (eds) *Debating Cultural Hybridity: Multicultural Identities and the Politics of Racism*, London, pp. 209-25.

Berger, Peter and Luckmann, Thomas (1967) *The Social Construction of Reality. A Treatise in the Sociology of Knowledge*, Harmondswoth.

Brah, Avtar (1987) 'Women of South Asian Origin in Britain: Issues and Concerns', *South Asia Research*, pp. 39-54.

Cohen, Anthony (1985) *The Symbolic Construction of Community*, Manchester.

Dumont, Louis (1980) *Homo Hierarchicus. The Caste System and its Implications*, Chicago.

Gillespie, Marie (1995) *Television, Ethnicity, and Cultural Change*, London.

Gilroy, Paul (1992) 'The End of Antiracism', in J. Donald and A. Rattansi (eds) *'Race', Culture and Difference*, London.

Hillery, G. A. Jr. (1955) 'Definitions of community: Areas of Agreement', *Rural Sociology*, 20.

Ignatieff, Michael (1992) 'Why "Community" is a Dishonest Word', *The Observer*, 3 May 1992, editorial page.

Kapferer, Bruce (1988) *Legends of People, Myths of State: Violence, Intolerance and Political Culture in Sri Lanka and Australia*, Washington.

Keesing, Roger (1994) 'Theories of Culture Revisited', in Robert Borofsky (ed.) *Assessing Cultural Anthropology*, New York, pp. 301-10.

Macfarlane, Alan (1977) 'History, Anthropology and the Study of Communities', *Social History*, V, May, 631-52.

Mannheim, Karl (1982) 'The Problem of Generations', in Chris Jenks (ed.) *The Sociology of Childhood. Essential Readings*, London, pp. 256-69.

Morris, H. S. (1968) *The Indians in Uganda*, London.

Phoenix, Ann (1988) 'Narrow Definitions of Culture: the Case of Early Motherhood', in S. Westwood and P. Bhachu (eds.) *Enterprising Women. Ethnicity, Economy, and Gender Relations*, London, pp. 153-79.

Pryce, Ken (1979) *Endless Pressure. A Study of West Indian Life- Styles in Bristol*, Bristol.

Rose, H. A. (1911-19) *A Glossary of the Tribes and Castes of the Punjab and North-West Frontier Province*, Lahore.

Rothschild, Joseph (1981) *Ethnopolitics: A Conceptual Framework*, New York.

Sahlins, Marshall (1994) 'Goodbye to Tristes Tropes: Ethnography in the Context of Modern World History', in Robert Borofsky (ed.) *Assessing Cultural Anthropology*, New York, pp. 377-94.

Tylor, Edward Burnett (1958 [1871]) *Primitive Culture*, New York.

van der Veer, Peter (1994) 'The Foreign Hand: Orientalist Discourse in Sociology and Communalism', in Carol Breckenridge and Peter van der Veer (eds) *Orientalism and the Postcolonial Predicament*, Philadelphia, pp. 23- 44.

Vayda, Andrew (1994) 'Actions, Variations and Change: The Emerging Anti-Essentialist View in Anthropology', in Robert Borofsky (ed.) *Assessing Cultural Anthropology*, New York, pp. 320-29.

Vertovec, Steven (1992) 'Community and Congregation in London Hindu Temples: Divergent Trends', *New Community*, 18, 2:251-64.

Vertovec, Steven (1995) 'Hindus in Trinidad and Britain: Ethnic Religion, Reification, and the Politics of Public Space', in Peter van der Veer (ed.) *Nation and Migration: The Politics of Space in the South Asian Diaspora*, Philadelphia, pp. 132-56.

Werbner, Pnina and Tariq Modood (eds.), (1997) *Debating Cultural Hybridity: Multicultural Identities and the Politics of Racism*, London.

Yabsley, Hazel (1990) *Proximity. Processes of Ethnicity and Community Explored in Southall*, B.Sc. dissertation in Sociology and Social Anthropology, 4 vols. Brunel: The University of West London.

Historical Culture
in (Post-)Colonial Context
The Genesis of National Identification Figures in Francophone Western Africa

HANS-JÜRGEN LÜSEBRINK

1. Basic Questions

In the Western cultural and social sciences, one usually considers the existence of a nation from three main angles: 1) that of the existence of a national state, 2) of a community living within some well-defined borders, and 3) through national awareness, in which national history can play a central role. In the case of African history and historiography, it is necessary though to reconsider the question with the help of criteria which differ from those used to study its European counterpart:

1. To start with, postcolonial African nations, in contrast to a whole series of European nations such as Italy or Germany, do not draw upon a commonly circulating past-relevant conception of cultural identity. Rather, they base their existence on governmental structures and national borders, which, without exception, all date back to the beginnings of African colonisation, and especially to the Berlin Congress of 1884 when most of the borders were established (only partly modified in the Versailles treaty of 1918).

Within the larger colonial ensembles of *Afrique Occidentale Française* (AOF), French Western Africa and *Afrique Équatoriale Française* (AEF), French Equatorial Africa, the administrative units established between 1884 and 1910 have determined the borders of the African states—with the exception of Mali and Tchad, which underwent some border modifications—that,

---

for the most part, became independent between 1958 and 1960. On the African continent, state- and nation-building did not rely on linguistic, cultural or—however else they may be defined—ethnic criteria or perspectives, but rather on colonial administrative borders and infrastructures of institutions (such as administrative and judicial instances, divisions of districts, etc.) and means of communication.

2. Emerging from the process of decolonisation since the 1940s, the concept of nation in Africa is characterised by two main elements that distinguish it from its European counterpart:

First, the concept of 'ethnicity' in the world of African social representations refers to a 'linguistic community' with fluctuating boundaries and no specific territorial attachment. The colonial discourse—most of all, that of the ethnologists, anthropologists and administrators—over the course of time has filled the concept of 'ethnicity' (or tribe) with ethnic, cultural and psychological meaning and has turned it into a classifying concept (Chrétien and Prunier, 1989; Amselle, 1988). Denominations such as Bambara, Wolof, Tutsi, Hutu, Agni, Igbo etc. were then used to indicate cultural communities with specific mentalities and ways of living, whose study and analysis formed one of the most important aims of colonial administration. Through the use of those names the administration hoped to keep colonised populations more efficiently under control and make better use of all human resources, be it for military or for economic purposes. Only in the case of nomadic societies, such as the Tuareg or the Somalis, however, can one indeed observe an overlap between the protonational concept of 'ethnic unit,' as developed in the colonial discourse, and the sociocultural reality (common language, common sociability, autonomous political organisation).

Second, state forms with autocratic structures, which resemble the European conception of 'monarchy,' can be found in some parts of precolonial Africa, especially in the Sahel region. Kingdoms such as Zululand in Central Africa and the kingdoms of Mali, Ghana and Dahomey in Western Africa owed their emergence on the one hand to the Islamic conquest of Africa (which from the thirteenth century onwards led to the dissolution of traditional clans or tribal societies, replacing them with newly constituted states), and on the other to the reaction to European colonisation in the nineteenth century. The European conquest provoked military resistance and the creation of autocratic states, whose leading figures (as those of Samory Touré and El Hadji Omar) progressively turned into role models and figures of identification in the historical consciousness of postcolonial African states.

Since independence, all African states have, for the sake of their own legitimisation, aimed at the nationalisation of the collective consciousness of their citizens through the use of various media and institutions. This process can be observed in academic institutions, in which a drastic change of canons

took place in the fields of literature, culture and history, at the end of the 1960s, but also in policies of national symbols (toponymy, national holidays, flags, etc.) or in collective forms of mass nationalisation such as in football. In the following, I would like to draw attention to three structures underlying the genesis of national awareness during the time of colonisation, and do so from the very perspective of a growing historical consciousness. The approach is based on the assumption that collective and conscious forms of national iden-tity and concepts of national history do not trace their origin back to collective identities of precolonial times, nor to the nationalisation strategies of post-colonial African societies—which were beyond any doubt extremely effec-tive—but rather to colonial culture itself, its sociocultural dynamic and its inherent contradictions.

2. The Display of Collective Identities in Colonial Exhibitions

French colonial exhibitions, just like other European colonial exhibitions, aimed at the display of non-European populations and their cultural identity. Within the context of colonial expansionism and a period marked by a spirit of conquest, these exhibitions turned the image of foreign populations into highly stylised and stereotyped representations and shaped the mental attitudes and collective consciousness of the time. The colonial sections which since 1851 accompanied the world exhibitions—like those in London, Berlin, Paris and Tervueren near Brussels—attracted a very large public, reaching sometimes thirty to forty million visitors (such as in Paris in 1931). Social strata were attracted which were not accustomed to reading books or to paying attention to ethnological travel accounts about foreign peoples. In Imperial Germany those exhibitions were called 'A Look at Peoples' ('*Völkerschauen*,' see Gold-mann, 1985),[1] and at the same time in France organisers and reporters rather spoke of '*Expositions Coloniales*,' 'Colonial expositions,' trying to conceptu-ally grasp the non-European world by using a metaphor inspired by the arts. The newspaper *Strassburger Neueste Nachrichten* described the colonial exhi-bition taking place in the city of Strasbourg from July to October 1924 as 'an initial contact with the whole of the French Empire,' an event which consider-ably 'attracted the Alsatian population' ([Anon.], 1924:5). As such, French colonial exhibitions were not only exhibitions of a foreign colonial world but a display of national '*grandeur*' as well—especially after the humiliating defeat against Prussia in 1870/71—and a testimony to the evident 'civilising mission' of the French Third Republic. In the catalogue to the Marseilles colo-nial exhibition of 1924, the organisers wrote that the exhibition was to show that France was not a country of average size, but rather a global nation com-prising a territory of 10.8 million square kilometres and a population of nearly 100 million (Commissariat Général de l'esposition, 1922:23). In his catalogue

to the 1931 Paris Exhibition, André Demaison, one of the most famous French colonial authors between the two world wars, insisted on the fact that '*la grande collectivité humaine France*' ('the grand human collectivity called France') was being displayed there—a national community which had already reached 100 million people (Demaison, 1931:3). Considering the demographic decline in France, especially after World War I, the overseas territories seemed to offer an alternative source of energy and human potential, resources which were clearly on display in the colonial exhibitions. In the catalogue of the Marseilles colonial exhibition of 1922 one could read:

'France can nowadays not be thought without its colonies, and the *French bloc* represents a lively reality. [...] This renaissance will constitute the logical coronation and the human nobilisation of the old civilising concept of our country which always held to the idea of our indigenous subjects being the future citizens of the grandest France.'

'La France, d'ores et déjà ne peut être considérée en dehors de ses colonies, et le *bloc français* représente une vivante réalité. [...] Cette renaissance constituera, au reste, le couronnement logique et noblement humain de la vieille conception civilisatrice de notre pays, laquelle a toujours tendu à considérer nos sujets indigènes comme les futurs citoyens de la plus grande France' (Commissariat Général de l'esposition, 1922: 15-6).

The concept of the '*plus grande France*,' the grandest France was used in the official catalogue in an obvious manner in order to counterbalance the representation of a country that was diminished culturally, politically and economically after the war and had to descend to a national status of lesser importance:

'Open the latest edition (1922) of your books of geography which have been given into the hands of our children. You might read there, like I have done, signed by a professor of history and geography, a doctor of history and geography, by a master of literature phrases like the following "Our country is middle–sized, not really big and not really small. Its surface is about 550.000 square kilometres and the French nation counts about 41 million inhabitants."

Well! If we thought we had to do the National Colonial Exposition at Marseilles after the War, because there was a real imperial necessity for all those who knew to tell those who didn't know—be they geographers or doctors of literature—that France is not a country that should be considered as middle-sized, but as large, a very large country, the surface of which is not 550.000 but 10.800.00 square kilometres and which counts not 41 millions but more than 96 millions inhabitants.'

'Ouvrez vos cahiers de géographie de la plus récente édition (1922) mis entre les mains de nos enfants. Vous y lirez peut-être, comme je les ai lues moi-même, sous la signature d'un agrégé d'histoire et de géographie, docteur d'histoire et de géographie, docteur dès lettres, des phrases de ce genre: "Notre pays est d'étendue moyenne, ni très grand, ni très petit. Sa surface est de 550 000 kilomètres carrés, et la nation française compte environ 41 millions d'habitants."

Eh bien! si nous avons tenu à réaliser, au lendemain même de la Guerre, l'Exposition Nationale Coloniale de Marseille, c'est d'abord parce qu'il y avait réellement une nécessité impérieuse pour ceux qui savaient, à montrer à tous ceux qui

ne savaient pas, fussent-ils agrégés de géographie et docteurs dès lettres, que la France est non pas un pays d'étendue moyenne, mais un grand, un très grand pays, qui a une surface non pas de 550 000, mais bien de 10 800 000 kilomètres carrés, et qui compte non pas 41 millions, mais plus de 96 millions d'habitants' (Commissariat Général de l'exposition, 1922:231).

All French colonial exhibitions insisted upon the mission of civilisation carried out by France in its colonies and turned it into a tangible, visual and material reality for all visitors.

A new concept of history developed as a correlate to the concept of the *'plus grande Nation.'* Teleologically constructed, it showed—from a historical perspective linked to the idea of progress—colonial conquests as the decisive turning point. In July 1913, the members of the Marseilles Chamber of Commerce, for example, saw the aim of the colonial exhibition they were preparing (it was to take place in 1916, but it was postponed to 1922 because of the war) in the display of the colonies' progress and especially the progress of their inhabitants. 'Croyez bien,' 'I am sure' said Artaud, the president of the Chamber of Commerce, in his speech,

'that the colonists, the governors, the indigenous of all parts of the world will be more than happy to come every decade to renew and strengthen the relations with all forces of this metropolitan France to exhibit their progress to our peoples, to the ministers, to all of France.'

'que les colons, les gouverneurs, les indigènes de toutes les parties du monde seraient fort heureux d'y revenir, tous les dix ans, renouer les relations toujours plus solides avec toutes les forces de la métropole, y montrer leur progrès à nos populations, à nos ministres, à toute la France' (Chambre de Commerce de Marseille, 1913:14).

The tension between the exotic display of foreign colonial worlds, set up to meet the sensationalist expectations of a wide public, and the political will to show one's own *'grandeur'* was already plainly visible in the organisation of the *'parcours'* that was offered to the visitors. In the Marseilles exhibition of 1922 main attraction was the section on *Afrique Occidentale Française*, next to the one on Indochina. It was made up of a palace built in Moorish-Sudanese style which imitated the town gates of Djenné (in current Mali), of a *Rue Soudanaise*, a Sudanese street with various handicraft shops and a native's village (*Village indigène*), which represented the largest ethnic groups of French Western Africa (Wolof, Bambara, Dioula, Toucouleur, etc.) according to the organisers' image of these peoples.

In contrast to Senegal, Dahomey, the Ivory Coast and French Guinea, which from a French point of view were considered the most developed colonies, French Sudan was not allocated any specific space at the exhibition in 1922 (although it was present in Paris in 1931 and 1937), but was represented through artistic artefacts, jewellery as well as handicraft shops. In 1922, two

photo exhibitions completed the main colonial exhibition. Their aim was to show the ethnic customs and landscapes of French Western Africa and the achievements of the French colonial administration; as such, they displayed pictures of schools, road construction sites, administrative buildings, hospitals, etc.

In the *parcours* of the 1931 Paris colonial exhibition, which attracted almost 40 million visitors and prepared the ground for the establishment of the *Musée des colonies* (after 1945 *Musée de la France d'Outre-Mer* and today *Musée des Arts Africains et Océaniens*), the visitor was to start at the *Cité des Informations*, a kiosk of colonial propaganda, before entering the pavilion for exotic woods and attending the other sections of the exhibition. French Western Africa, including the section on French Sudan, was the sixteenth of the forty sections on the site. It was the first large section on a continental colony, after the visitor had strolled through the sections on the French Caribbean and the colonies of the Indian and Pacific Oceans. The section on *Afrique Occidentale Française*, French Western Africa, which occupied the third largest site in the Paris exhibition of 1931, after French North Africa and Indochina, was placed in the immediate vicinity of the much more modest section on French Central Africa and of the one on the *Forces d'Outre-Mer*, the armed forces, which was dedicated to French soldiers serving in overseas colonies (particularly those in Africa and Indochina). In contrast to earlier exhibitions, the 1931 Paris exhibition organised a section on French Sudan (as on the other seven colonies of French Western Africa), set up with very specific architectonic traits. As in the 1907 and 1922 Marseilles exhibitions, the pavilion for French Western Africa was modelled on the so-called Moorish-Sudanese style of the old cities of Timbuktu and Djenné and even had a sort of *Tata*, a city wall in red bricks. The native village, the second largest attraction of the section on French Western Africa, after the *Village fétichiste*, the village of fetishes with cult artefacts from Dahomey, was equally built in Moorish-Sudanese style and imitated the old city as well as the mosque of Djenné.

As one can see, the aim of the organisers was clearly not to replicate a folkloric image of Africa fit for a museum or a representation of a virgin continent before it was ever submitted to European influence. According to André Charton, general inspector of education in French Western Africa, Africa was not to be shown as it had been, nor as it sees itself, but rather as a developing region under French influence:

'By limiting the exhibition to the indigenous life and to handicrafts one gets the impression that the civilising efforts which are the essential basis of our colonisation aiming at a transformation, an improvement of the indigenous life has not been taken into account.'

'En limitant la présentation à la vie indigène et à l'artisanat, il semble qu'il ne sera pas rendu compte à l'exposition de l'effort de civilisation qui est une des bases essentielles de notre action coloniale et qui vise précisément à transformer, à améliorer la vie indigène' (Charton, 1936:1).

The impression of exotic otherness, created by the architecture as well as by the pictures of the 1931 exhibition's catalogue about French Western and Central Africa, proved to be a bait for the public, a way of transmitting colonial policies and their pragmatic economic objectives. Even the spectacular *Village fétichiste*, which, with its 200 African inhabitants, attracted the largest public at the 1931 Paris colonial exhibition, was clearly used for national political propaganda. It showed, as André Demaison pointed out, the cultural diversity of French African colonies which were not all shaped by Islamic fate: 'which Islam has not shaped by its uniformity' ('que l'Islam n'a pas marqués de son uniformité'). 'Que la jeunesse,' 'may the youth,' Demaison continues pathetically in the concluding chapter of the 1931 exhibition's catalogue about French Western Africa,

> 'remember all those names of peoples and countries the resonance of which he might consider as odd today. Within ten, twenty or thirty years, when these 14 millions in motion will be united by the railway to our provinces in Northern Africa, when air-traffic will play its full role, these denominations will be more familiar to our ears than the names of Provence or Gascogne to the inhabitants of Paris of the seventeenth century. Africa and its masses, united for the reasons of defence and well-being, will then be a magnificent and direct extension of our French fatherland.'

> 'retienne tous ces noms d'hommes et de pays dont la résonance lui paraît aujourd'hui bizarre. Dans dix, vingt ou trente ans, lorsque ces 14 millions d'hommes en marche seront unis par le rail à nos provinces d'Afrique du Nord, lorsque l'aviation jouera son plein rôle, ces appellations seront plus familières à nos oreilles que les noms provençaux ou gascons à celles des Parisiens du XVIIe siècle. Alors, notre Afrique, aux masses étroitement alliées pour la défense et la prospérité, sera un prolongement magnifique et direct de notre patrie française' (Demaison, 1931:35).

The numerous reports about French colonial exhibitions, whether they stem from the official side of the government or from journalists and writers of the most various political orientations, seem to agree with Demaison. In his account about *Les Enseignements de l'exposition coloniale de Marseille de 1907*, 'the lessons of the colonial exhibition,' Paul Girbal underlines the fact that colonial exhibitions not only show how much France can use and benefit from its colonies, but illustrate as well the French colonial policies and their aim of improving the living conditions of African natives.[2] In 1931 *Le Monde Colonial illustré* also insists on the civilising mission carried out by France in its African colonies and sees in the Paris colonial exhibition the evidence for accomplished progress in French Western Africa:

> 'A lesson in humanity finally, because our moral and social efforts to elevate the natives' lives every day on the ranking of human beings, to improve their well-being, to protect them from illness after having them given peace, this lesson is not of minor importance compared to our effort at valorisation.

When we arrived in our colonies, most of them in Africa as well as in Indochina were exhausted. The long periods of warfare, of massacres, of slavery, the millenial exactions had decimated and impoverished the indigenous peoples; the epidemic and endemic diseases had caused remarkable losses, elevated child mortality was rampant. An enormous and beneficent work lay before us.'

'Leçon d'humanité enfin, car notre effort moral et social pour élever l'indigène chaque jour davantage dans l'échelle des êtres humains, pour améliorer son bien-être, pour le protéger contre la maladie après lui avoir donné la paix, n'est pas moindre que notre effort de mise en valeur.

Quand nous sommes arrivés dans la plupart de nos colonies, en Afrique aussi bien qu'en Indochine, le pays était profondément épuisé. De longues périodes de guerre, des massacres, la traite, des exactions séculaires avaient décimé et appauvri les populations indigènes; les maladies épidémiques et endémiques causaient parmi elles des vides effroyables, une mortalité infantile prodigieuse sévissait. Une œuvre immense et bienfaisante s'offrait à notre effort' (Lebrun, 1931:109).

Following colonial ideology, the most drastic and severe cultural and political changes that were inflicted upon the various African populations following the conquest of the continent were described as the ultimate liberation from oppression, anarchy and slavery—a strategy of legitimisation which took a visual, material and tangible form in the colonial exhibitions.

3. Affirmation of Identity: the 'Objects' Talk Back

Displayed as 'living inventory,' Africans played a central role at the colonial exhibitions. First they were exhibited as the inhabitants of the *Villages indigènes*, to which was added the *Village soudanais* from 1906 onwards. Then they were shown as handicraft workers in the various shops displayed (which could be seen in Marseilles in 1906 and 1922 on the so-called *Rue de Djenné*). Finally, they played their role as groups of visitors and official delegations, which consisted of officials, high-ranking members of society and of the old ruling families (*Chefs indigènes*) and were invited in large numbers after World War I.

Those representations—which were welcomed with considerable curiosity and satisfaction not just on the part of the politicians but by the French public as well—met decisive opposition on the African side for the first time in the 1930s. It was not the display of colonies as such, or the display of their history and their inhabitants that were considered disturbing, but rather the inadequate form of representation that became the ferment for a discourse of resistance and opposition. Some press reports written by Western African intellectuals went even further in their criticism. In an article entitled *L'Afrique aux attractions*, which was published in the newspaper *Paris-Dakar* in August 1937, the author 'Mani' (a pseudonym) goes as far as to attack—still with obvious irony and satire—the whole concept of colonial world displays at the 1937 exhibition:

'Here is therefore the Africa which is so dear to the curious onlooker—the traditional Africa of which the cousins of Romorantin and the oncles of Pézenas will not fail to keep their lively memory. The fake Africa that does not really interest them and which they even find less amusing is that of the Ile des Cygnes I can assure you ! There just some rather peaceful artisans are to be found which silently work their wood, ivory, or clay. There is no obscene dancing, and no British missionary in the pot over fire. There are no cannibals or bloodstained sorcerers behind the door, not even the dance of death or a Negro king dancing on sculls.'

'Voici donc enfin l'Afrique chère aux badauds/—l'Afrique traditionnelle dont les cousins de Romorantin et les oncles de Pézenas ne manqueront point d'emporter le souvenir vivace. L'Afrique truquée, celle qui ne les intéresse qu'à demi et les amuse encore moins, c'est celle de l'Ile des Cygnes, parbleu! ils ne trouvent là que de forts paisibles artisans, travaillant avec une application silencieuse qui le bois, qui l'ivoire, qui la glaise. Pas de danse obscène, ni de missionnaire anglais dans la marmite. Pas d'anthropophages ou de sorcier sanguinaire derrière les grilles, pas de danse de la mort ou de roi Nègre trônant sur des crânes' ([Mani] 1937:2).

Fily-Dabo Sissoko, who was born in Horo Koto, near Bafoulabé, in 1900 and first served the French as a school master before becoming Bafoulabé's *Chef de canton* in the mid-1920s, took an even stronger antiassimilation stand in his speech at the *Congrès international de l'Evolution culturelle des Peuples coloniaux*, 'International Congress on the Cultural Evolution of the Colonised Peoples,' which took place on the occasion of the 1937 Paris exhibition. Entitled *Les Noirs et la culture*, 'Blacks and Culture', his speech first addressed the fundamental question of equality between African and European cultures. In the second part, *Les Croquis soudanais*, he developed caricatures of assimilated Africans who adopt the French language, culture and way of life without any reserve or criticism. 'Africans should remain Africans and preserve their way of life,' he writes in his strikingly critical conclusion, filled with footnotes and references particularly to Islamic scriptures and the various kingdoms of the Sahel region.[3]

Sissoko's declarations were considered controversial, not so much because of the sometimes daring geographical and cultural relations he constructed—he declared that the three geographical zones in Africa, the desert, the savannah and the rainforest corresponded with three different types of cultures and cosmologies. Rather, they shocked because of his refutation of the central ideological features of the colonial exhibitions. He decisively attacked the theory of progress, the belief in European (and in particular French) superiority, the domination of civilisation over African cultures, and the doctrine of the necessary assimilation as the only way of accessing a higher level of civilisation. Sissoko's contribution was perceived as scandalous also because for the first time an African Theatre group, actors from the *École William-Ponty* directed by Charles Béart, performed in front of a French audience during the 1937 Paris exhibition. Their performance—which was in the French language but based on traditional African narratives—offered, according to the unanimous commentary of the time, compelling evidence of African cultures' abil-

ity to evolve and could be considered an anticipation of a *Culture franco-africaine*, a 'French-African culture 'to come (Béart, 1936:3), a view Sissoko questioned fundamentally.

Sissoko's position was not only opposed to French public opinion and to the views of the African high-ranking representatives, who attended the exhibition in large delegations, but stood as well against the opinion of most African intellectuals during the 1930s with regard to French colonial policy. In a serious polemic documented in the daily *Paris-Dakar*, Sissoko accuses the Senegalese author Ousmane Socé, who had become famous through the publication in 1935 of his novel *Karim*, of betraying African values and traditions. It is certainly not a coincidence if this polemic referred to the Paris exhibition and the Congress on the cultural development of colonial populations, at which African intellectuals like Sissoko and Amadou Mapaté Diagne from Sénégal participated for the first time.

The 1937 exhibition was to be the last one on French soil. The historical development of the following decades, from World War II to the Algerian War, as well as the uncompromising positions of someone like Fily-Dabo Sissoko from French Sudan, deprived the theatrical display of colonial worlds of its fascination, its innocence and most of all, of its legitimation.

4. The Emergence of 'Protonational' Identities

On three levels, the colonial exhibitions have had long-lasting mental and cultural effects. First, the exhibitions very efficiently displayed exotic representations of overseas colonies which have remained, at least as reminiscences, in the social discourse for over a hundred years. They have strongly influenced the minds of the French population by emphasising colonial history, on the one hand, while completely ignoring and negating all precolonial history, on the other. Secondly, and as a result of a definite refusal of any colonial display of one's own identity, the exhibitions led to construction of counterdiscourses which were articulated by African intellectuals for the first time after the 1937 Paris exhibition. A third effect is that the colonial exhibitions—paradoxically—displayed forms of collective identity which have strongly influenced the construction of protonational awareness in the new African countries.

To start with, the basic organisation of French colonial policies furthered a process of identification with one's colony. Newspapers such as *Le Phare du Dahomey* and *La Voix du Dahomey*, published accounts of Dahomey's section at the Paris colonial exhibitions of 1931 and 1937, whereas other parts of French Western Africa were not mentioned with a similar emphasis. The journalists of *La Voix du Dahomey* actually reported in the edition of May-June 1933 that they had received a distinction (*diplôme d'honneur*) for their reports, which advertised the Dahomey section at the 1933 Paris exhibition. In fact, they

used this opportunity to explain their participation at the exhibition, underlining their role as representatives and speakers for their country, Dahomey:

> 'Participating at the huge colonial exhibition of 1931, we have just this ambition: to let our voices be heard as possible to the centre and to bring friendly greetings to the great national press and to bring in our views for the greatest benefit of our remote homelands.
>
> The reward that has recently been given to us shows well that we have been noticed and that the Mother-Fatherland has well understood the nobleness of our thought and the greatness of our action. We do express here our gratitude as from child to mother. Dahomey which we proudly represent is happy that its voice has been heard.'

> 'En prenant part à la grande manifestation coloniale de 1931, nous n'avions que cette ambition: nous faire entendre de plus près de la Métropole, porter un salut cordial à la grande Presse nationale et mêler nos accents pour le plus grande bien des terres lointaines.
>
> La récompense qui vient de nous être décernée montre bien que nous avons été remarqués et que la Mère-Patrie a compris la noblesse de notre pensée, la grandeur de notre action. Nous lui exprimons ici toute notre filiale gratitude.
>
> Le Dahomey dont nous sommes fiers d'être le porte-parole se réjouit que sa voix ait été entendue' ([Anon], 1933:2; see also [Anon], 1931a).

Critical accounts of the representation of Senegal at the 1937 colonial exhibition concerned just the Senegalese section and they were made in the name of the population of the Senegalese colony (*Colonie du Sénégal*). In 1937, the daily *L'Eveil du Cameroun* reported proudly about the decision of the colonial section's organisers, at the Paris exhibition, to grant the Protectorate of Cameroun a separate pavilion, between those of Algeria and French Western Africa, instead of integrating it to the *Afrique Equatoriale Française*.[4] Even in the exhibition's catalogue, the various French colonies were individualised and presented with separate cultural identities—a good example is the section entitled *Personnalité et valeur de l'Ile de la Réunion*, 'the personality and worth of the *l'Ile de la Réunion,* in the 1931 Paris exhibition catalogue ([Anon.], 1931:1-12). Algeria, which since the colonial exhibitions of the 1920s and 1930s was represented as an integral part of French territory—in such a way that even its place within the colonial section was being put into question—was described in 1931 as a '*pays de vieille civilisation,*' a country with an old civilisation. Its important position and its significance among Mediterranean countries should not be diminished by the French colonisation (Bertrand, 1931: 825).

Foires-Expositions, 'Fairs-exhibitions' which since the beginning of the century had been staged in African colonies—in Senegal (Dakar, Saint-Louis, Kaolack), Dahomey (Porto-Novo), Cameron (Dioula) and the Ivory Coast (Abidjan, Bobo-Dioulasso)—as well as the founding of ethnographic and historical museums in the mid-1930s served to reinforce the models of cultural identity already present in French colonial exhibitions. Contrary to French

colonial exhibitions though, which played a considerable political and cultural role, it was rather the display of local colonial products, that is, the economical aspect of the *Foires*, that counted in these events. Reports on African exhibitions in the regional press and official speeches nevertheless tended to indicate that, besides their economical function, they also played an important role in the construction of national identities.

It is possible to identify similar models of identity in numerous other African *Foires-Expositions*. One significant example is an article published around 1935 in the newspaper *Paris-Dakar* (Abidjan), which insists more on the developing possibilities and economical potential of the country than on the colonial status of the region: 'La Côte d'Ivoire a pu se ressaisir, si elle a pu reprendre le cours de son développement' ([Anon.], 1935:6); [Anon.], 1934:3). During the 1939 *Foire-Exposition* of Bobo-Dioulasso, which attracted more than 120 000 visitors, the press reported under the heading *Côte d'Ivoire 39* (Ivory Coast 39) that Castelli, the Colonial Inspector for Agriculture and Farming had declared in a very important speech how decisive the role of the farmers had been in the development of the Ivory Coast: 'He concluded,' says the article in *L'A.O.F. Echo de la Côte Occidentale d'Afrique* (Dakar), 'with an homage to all inhabitants of the colony which have made the Ivory Coast and its richness' ('pour conclure, un hommage ému à tous les paysans de la colonie, qui ont créé la Côte d'Ivoire et qui en ont fait la richesse' [Anon.], 1939:1).

Even official declarations thus seem to have partly distanced themselves from any colonial ideology, which during French Colonial exhibitions summoned the unity of the 'plus grand France,' its hundred million inhabitants and its various regions. Such unity of *l'Afrique Française* was not conceived as being constituted by models of autonomous development and identities. The latter were rather characterised as forms of 'local folklore'—'the style and local colour which characterise each of its colonies will be faithfully reproduced', 'le style et la couleur locale qui caractérisent chacune de ses colonies seront fidèlement reproduits' ([Anon.], 1930:359)—which according to many colonial politicians are unavoidably destined to disappear. Together with the local press and the administrative and intellectual institutions of each colony such as the *Ecole William-Ponty* or the *Ecole de Bingerville*, colonial exhibitions functioned as generators for the construction of a collective identity. They communicated the consciousness of a political, cultural and economical connection, which had already brought forth protonational forms in the discourse on French colonial exhibitions and in the African *Foires-expositions* between the two World Wars.

5. Anticolonial Replies and Historical Consciousness

The constitution of a postcolonial African historical consciousness followed and developed as a reply to colonial representations and perceptions of African

history. The character of the counterdiscourses of African writers, publicists, intellectuals, and historians in the later phase of colonialism, as a reply to the colonial discourses, is clearly evident in the following quotation by the Ivory Coast author and politician Bernard Dadié. The quotation is part of a prison diary written in 1949-50 while the author was interned at the colonial prison of Grand-Bassam because of 'anticolonial activities.' In his pathetic defence, addressed to the head of the court and the public attorneys, Dadié presented role models which form an integral part of colonial historiography (like Vercingétorix, Jeanne d'Arc and Binger, the conqueror). But he referred to the heroes of his own history—like Queen Aoura Pokou and Amadou Bamba, a religious leader and symbolic figure of resistance against French colonisation—as well:

'Yes, Mr. President, gentlemen of the court, Perrault's fables enchanted us, but the ruse of the hare and the spider provide us with enthusiasm. That is why we want to come to France on our own background. After having spoken about Vercingétorix, we intend to speak about all the Amadou Bamba who have let themselves blown up in their besieged fortresses.

After having spoken about Jeanne d'Arc we want to speak about our heroines, all our amazons, of that queen Aoura Pokou who threw her only child into the Bandama for the liberty of her people.

After having spoken about Binger, we want to speak about that queen of the Bobo, Makoura Ouattara who received him in peace.

Everywhere, though, we encounter nothing but obstacles, nothing but barriers. It seems one wants to suffocate our genies to then better subject us.'

'Oui, Monsieur le Président, Messieurs de la Cour, les Contes de Perrault nous enchantent, mais les ruses du lièvre et de l'araignée nous enthousiasment. C'est pourquoi nous voulons venir à l'Union Française avec notre fond proposé. Nous entendons, après avoir parlé de Vercingétorix, parler de tous les Amadou Bamba, qui se sont fait sauter dans leurs citadelles assiégées.

Nous voulons, après avoir parlé de Jeanne d'Arc, parler de toutes nos héroïnes, de toutes nos amazones, de cette reine Aoura Pokou qui, pour la liberté de son peuple, jette dans le Bandama son unique enfant.

Nous voulons, après avoir parlé de Binger, parler de cette reine des Bobo, Makoura Ouattara qui le reçut pacifiquement.

Mais partout, nous ne rencontrons que des obstacles, des entraves. L'on semble vouloir étouffer notre génie afin de mieux nous asservir' (Dadié, 1981:207).

Dadié's militant declaration seems to prove the absolute repression of African precolonial history in the media and institutions of colonial culture, a fact which proved to be evident already in the representations of identity created by the colonial exhibitions. Looking at the situation more closely however, it becomes obvious that the dividing lines of the debate are not constituted by thematisation and repression, but rather concern the status, the role and, most of all, the interpretation of African precolonial history within the colonial context.

The first writings that were published in French Western Africa by Africans, namely *De Faidherbe à Coppolani* by the Senegalese elementary school teacher Amadou Duguay-Clédor, address specific episodes of precolonial history, which were considered as being merely 'folklore' or 'folktales' by official historical discourse. Since 1918 a number of African intellectuals and authors have published in journals such as the *Bulletin de l'Enseignement de l'AOF*. Many of those papers discuss African precolonial history, even though the titles very often mislead the reader about the ambivalent, if not outright anticolonial positions of the authors. The works of Duguay-Clédor reveal this indirect strategy. In *La bataille de Guîlé*, 'the battle of *Guîlé*' published in 1912,[5] the author erected a 'literary monument' (Glinga, 1990: 434) to the memory of one protagonist of colonial resistance. He did so not by narrating the history of the encounter between the invading French led by Faidherbe and the Senegalese kingdom, but rather by concentrating on one episode. The battle of Guîlé, a battle between the antagonistic princes Damal Samba Lawbe Fall and Albouri, recalls the conflicts between the precolonial feudal States in the Northern region of today's Senegal.

Duguay-Clédor's second historiographical work, *De Faidherbe à Coppolani. Les Gandiols—Gandiols au service de la France*—[6] a title which has but little to do with the book's content—uses the same indirect form of idealising the actions and personal qualities of ruling figures from the precolonial age. The title names two French officers and the inhabitants of the Gandiol in the South of Senegal, who, in contrast to other ethnic groups in the Northern part of the country, supported French colonisation. Thus, it creates the expectation that the following study concentrates on the conquest of Africa from a French point of view. Even though Duguay-Clédor uses ideological notions such as '*la plus grande France*' (in his words, the union of the Metropolis and the colonies) and refers to the French soldiers as well as their native allies as 'our troops,' the main subject of his study is the 'anticolonial resistance of some of the nations' leaders and that of the marabouts' (Glinga, 1990: 435). As Glinga remarks, the '*assimilé*,' the assimilated Duguay-Clédor definitely writes at two different levels, a colonial and an anti-colonial one.

> 'To avoid any collision between both perspectives, he tells the story of anti-colonial resistance with the pathos of heroic legends, without offending the colonial nature of its French enemies, and uses the same amount of enthusiasm to describe French military campaigns, without defining the position of the African opponents' (Glinga, 1990:435).

Forms of representation such as those used by Duguay-Clédor, which were quite symptomatic of early colonial times, show on the one hand the ambivalent sociocultural position of the '*assimilé*,' the assimilated, those Africans who have experienced colonial culture and its institutions and have made it up the French social ladder. On the other hand, they achieve the the-

matisation of precolonial African history in colonial printed media. In the same way, intellectuals and authors of the second generation, such as Abdoulaye Sadji and Léopold Sédar Senghor, express through various forms of counterdiscourses the mechanisms behind their partial repression or marginalisation in the public sphere.

In 1936, Abdoulaye Sadji, who can be considered—together with Léopold Sédar Senghor—the most acknowledged Senegalese author, published a series of short stories entitled *Ce que dit la musique africaine* in the most important journal for colonial education and cultural policies, the *Bulletin de l'Enseignement de l'AOF* (1913-1960). The stories focus on the leading figures of Western African kingdoms during the eighteenth and nineteenth century, such as Soundiata, Samory and Samba Guéladjegi. As Glinga has shown in detail, those short stories take after oral epics, which, until the colonial time and partly until today, have been memorised and adapted by the *Griots*, professional storytellers. Two aspects, presented in the introduction to the collection of the short stories, are of major importance for the cultural status and the mnemonic devices of precolonial history.

First, Sadji's refers to the category of 'Contes' and 'Légendes' (fables and fairytales) as oral forms of historical consciousness: 'It is wrong to count among the African fables,' he writes, 'the story of Soundiata, Samba Guéladjegi and many others. These people have really existed.' 'On a tort de chasser parmi les contes africains,' écrit-il, 'l'histoire de Soundiata, de Samba Guéladjegi et de tant d'autres. Ces personnages ont réellement existé' (Sadji, 1985:9).

Secondly, Sadji insists on the fluidity of the orally transmitted historical tradition, which does not offer an access to historical truth but reveals collective psychological dispositions: 'éclairer la vérité psychologique de l'âme nègre, c'est plutôt l'action mystique de cette âme sur le canevas offert par la vie des héros' (119) ('to illuminate the psychological truth of the Negro's soul, is most of all the mystical action of this soul on the canvas which is offered by the life of the heroes'). In a highly provocative and decisive way, Sadji demonstrates that oral songs or narratives, dismissed and labelled as 'folklore,' 'tale' or 'legend' by the colonial discourse, actually display a powerful and effective form of collective historical consciousness (119).[7]

Léopold Sédar Senghor's poem *Hosties Noires* (1938-45), just as Sadji's works, uses the written text to transmit oral tradition, to defolklorise figures of identification in African history and to assign them a central role in the colonial public space. The rhetoric gestures of his poems *Poème liminaire* ('Liminal Poem') and *Aux tirailleurs* ('For the scirmishers') adopt in their rhetoric form the oral genre of praise and the poet explicitly assumes the role of the traditional *griot*. In both poems, the author sharply distances himself from the folklorising and repressive colonial discourse—by mentioning the *Banania* advertisements (a publicity campaign for a popular cocoa drink which displayed an African soldier with a good-natured, intense and naive

smile), by calling the paternalist speeches of ministers and generals '*louanges de mépris*' ('disdainful praise') or by mentioning the racist German campaign against the settling of Black African soldiers in the Rhineland after World War I—a situation he refers to as 'a Black disgrace.' And last but not least, at the end of his poem he replaces the title *Aux tirailleurs sénégalais morts pour la France* ('To the senegalese scirmishers who gave their lives for France')—which recalls the inscriptions on the monuments to dead soldiers—with the verse 'MORTS POUR LA REPUBLIQUE,' leaving it deliberately unclear whether the word 'Republic' refers to France or the Senegal (Senghor, 1964:53-4).[8]

Senghor's *Hosties Noires* enable the author to reappraise his own repressed history by taking over—as the lyrical 'I' shows—the role of the *griot* and his function as the narrator in the oral tradition. Through the vocative structure of the text—calls such as 'Ecoutez. ....,' 'Listen ...'—the *Tirailleurs sénégalais* (the *Senegalese scirmishers*) become national figures of identification, the memory of whom is reinforced, assured and consecrated through the parareligious concept of the '*blanches hosties*' ('white sacrifices').

6. Canonised Figures of Identification in National and Political Discourse

Within the context of colonial culture, its media and institutions, these counterdiscourses and historiographical texts—which, as we have seen, predominantly adopt literary genres—show the genesis of national figures of identification from the early 1930s onwards. In this context, the modern concept of 'national' refers, on the one hand, to the regional cultures and, on the other, to the pan-African dimension. Since the end of the 1960s, the *Tirailleurs sénégalais* and the *Ceddo* (a cast of warriors in the North of Senegal), who have both embodied the spirit of resistance against Islamic and European conquerors, as well as famous precolonial leading figures such as Samory, El Hadj Omar, Ahmadou Bamba, Almamy Albouri, Samba Guéladjegi and Soundiata, found their way into European printed culture through literary versions of traditional oral epics.[9] A series of curricular reforms for school teaching further enabled them to gain not just institutional legitimation but to become key elements of postcolonial African social historical memory.

Besides phenomena of 'nationalisation' and national adoption of figures of identification, historical role of which cannot be reduced to the territorial limits of independent states, the appearance of radically different models of historical interpretation takes a capital importance in this context. The *Ceddo* cast of warriors, which in official Islamic Senegalese historiography has mostly been negatively depicted as brutal and digressive, becomes the embodiment of precolonial values of courage, freedom, and resistance in the movie *Ceddo*,

produced by Ousmane Sembène in 1977 and censured the same year in Senegal. The *Ceddo* 'defends the people against the old corrupt aristocracy and the new power thirsty marabouts' (Glinga, 1990: 239). The Lycée Faidherbe in Saint-Louis, also provided a strong example of a radical symbolic act as it changed its name in 1972 into *Lycée El Hadj Omar* and made the Toucouleur prince, who fought and won against Faidherbe (he actually forced the former French conqueror of Northern Senegal into exile in 1882), its role model.

With regard to the evolution of historical meaning, as well to the genesis of 'national' role models and precolonial historical material in an African context, four major conclusions are to be drawn:

The concept of 'nation,' along with the concept of national identity, rests upon various forms of historical memory, which refer either to regions (this is one of the levels of signification, as in *les langues nationales du Sénégal, les littératures nationales*, the national languages of Senegal, the national literatures) or reach far beyond the territorial limits of postcolonial states. The process of constructing a national identity tends to become rather functional and instrumental, absorbing elements from geographical territories extending beyond the natural borders into historical memory; a phenomenon reflected in various national media and institutions. Examples are the *Musée historique de Dakar*, the historical museum of Dakar which was created in 1956, during the colonial era, and was modified at the end of the 1960s, or the *Histoire de l'Afrique et du Sénégal* (History of Africa and of Senegal) published for the first time in 1972, in which El Hadj Omar and Amadou Bamba appear as models of Senegalese national identification.

Second, in order to analyse the genesis of national figures of identification, it is necessary to distinguish between oral and written forms of historical memory, which are each tied to specific nets of mnemonic practices and rituals. The written forms have developed since the beginning of the colonial time and have been used in the media and other institutions such as politics, publicity, the press, monuments and their inscriptions, all explicitly referred to by Senghor in his poem.

Thirdly, the productivity of colonial culture challenges us to rethink the representations connected to the phenomenon of colonialism. Rather than exclusively focusing on controlled and forced acculturation and on the repression of original and different thinking the dynamic between acculturation and the potential to resist needs to be taken in view.

Finally, contemporary literary and historiographical texts have since the end of the 1960s renewed and transformed historiographical forms and have— beyond the controversial interpretation of isolated events (such as '*Ceddo*')— led to the emergence of a kind of counterhistoriography within the cultural context of the new African independent states, questioning the historiographical models and discourses developed during the colonial time. Examples are the novels of Yambo Ouologem from Mali (*Le devoir de la violence*, The duty

of violence, 1968) and Boubacar Boris Diop from Sénégal (*Les tambours de la mémoire*, The Tambours of Memory, 1987), which sweep away the distinction between fact and fiction. In his novel *Les tambours de la mémoire*, for example, Boubacar Boris Diop tries to deconstruct national mnemonic forms in Senegal and inserts officially repressed episodes of Senegalese history (the example of Casamance) in his work. *Le devoir de la violence*, a historical novel by Ouologuem, is based on a reinterpretation of Arab chronicles and oral epics of Western African tradition (thirteenth to twentieth century). It touches in a very provocative way two taboo subjects of the anticolonial historiography (1930s to 1960s). First, Islam appears here as an ideological conqueror and ruler. Second Diop establishes a correlation between the authoritarian power structures in precolonial African kingdoms and in postcolonial dictatorships, which in his view show the continuation of old power practices on the side of the rulers and on the side of mental dispositions of the people to be ruled.

Translated by Hélène Destrempes

Notes

1. On the question of the exotic representation of non-European societies and cultures in European and American colonial exhibitions, see Leprun (1986); Baxandall (1990); Hodeir, Leprun and Pierre (1993).

2. 'After having shown the great material interests that our colonies provide and the real progress that has been made in their valorisation, the exhibition has proved that our work in the countries which are under our authority wanted to promote civilisation in an eminent way. Nowhere was a tendency towards a brutal or deceitful exploitation of the indigenous peoples manifest, but in contrast one could see everywhere the concern of the administrators to improve the conditions of our subjects or of our protégés, and the colonisers on their part tried to peacefully live together with the natives and to obtain their collaboration in order to use the exploitable resources in the best way.'

   'Après avoir montré les grands intérêts matériels que nos colonies représentent et les réels progrès qu'a réalisés leur mise en valeur, l'Exposition a prouvé que notre œuvre dans les pays soumis à notre autorité voulait être éminemment civilisatrice. Nulle part ne se manifestait la tendance à l'exploitation brutale ou sournoise des indigènes, partout on voyait, de la part des administrations, le souci d'améliorer la condition de nos sujets ou de nos protégés, et de la part des colons, la préoccupation de vivre en bons termes avec les premiers habitants du pays, d'obtenir leur collaboration pour mieux utiliser toutes les ressources exploitables' (Girbal, 1907:37).

3. 'We just add what we have said in 1926: Blacks have to stay Blacks and that holds for their way of life as well as for their development' ('Nous ajouterons seulement, ce que nous avons dit en 1926: *Le Noir doit rester Noir, de vie et d'évolution.*' [Sissoko (1938:122)]. Sissoko refers here to his article 'Le Soudan Français,' the 'French Sudan' (1926) which was published in the journal *Europe*.

4. 'With pleasure we understand that Cameron will be represented with dignity at the exhibition in Paris, and in the picturesque context of the l'Ile des Cygnes. The section devoted to Cameron is situated opposite to that of Passy, between Algeria and French Western Africa.'

   'Nous apprenons avec plaisir que le Cameroun sera dignement représenté à l'Exposition de Paris, dans le cadre pittoresque de l'Ile des Cygnes. La section consacrée au Cameroun est située face à Passy, entre celle de l'Algérie et celle de l'A.O.F.' ([Anon.], 1937:6).

5. The book first published in 1913 is a critical new edition. See Duguay-Clédor, 1985.

6. Both works were published together in Saint-Louis: Imprimerie du Gouvernement du Sénégal.

7. 'To consider these histories as legends or as fables unworthy of attention and credibility means to overlook some elements that are essential for the profound knowledge of the Negro's soul. [...] That is why after having collected the most important legends and having assembled them under the title 'what African music tells,' I will engage in codifying those songs and monotonous chants, which are rich in sentiments and in philosophical truth with regard to the soul of the Negro'

   'Considérer ces histoires comme des légendes ou comme des contes indignes d'attention et de créance, c'est laisser dans l'ombre quelques-uns des éléments essentiels à la connaissance profonde de l'âme nègre.[...]. C'est pourquoi, après avoir recueilli ces légendes, qui sont les principales, pour former un tout intitulé: 'Ce que dit la musique africaine,' je vais entreprendre de codifier chansons et mélopées, plus riches en sentiments et en vérités philosophiques, relatives à l'âme nègre' (Sadji, 1985:119).

8. See 'Poème liminaire' (april 1940:61-3) and 'Aux Tirailleurs sénégalais morts pour la France' (1938).

9. See the systematic study by Glinga as well as the critical edition of orally transmitted epos by Correra (1992).

References

Amselle, Jean- Loup (1988) *Au coeur de l'ethnie*, Paris.

[Anon.] (1924) 'Die Strassburger Kolonial-Ausstellung wird sich zu einem wunderbaren Schauspiele gestalten', *Strassburger Neueste Nachrichten*, n° 182, 2.7.1924, p. 5.

[Anon.] (1930) 'Afrique Occidentale Française', *L'Afrique Française*, n° 6, juin 1930, pp. 359-60.

[Anon.] (1931) *Exposition Coloniale Internationale de Paris, Commissariat général: Ile de la Réunion, Côte Française des Somalis, Etablissements Français dans l'Inde.* Paris: Société d'Editions Géographiques, Maritimes et Coloniales.

[Anon.] (1931a) 'Le départ des Représentants du Dahomey à l'Exposition Coloniale est ajourné', *La Voix du Dahomey*, n° 53, 1er-15 avril 1931, p. 2.

[Anon] (1933) 'Une Déclaration de La Voix du Dahomey', *La Voix du Dahomey. Journal politique et économique*, n° 76-77, mai-juin 1933, p. 2.

[Anon.] (1934) 'La Foire d'Exposition d'Abidjan', *Paris-Dakar*, n° 55, 21 février 1934, p. 3.

[Anon.] (1935) 'La IIe Foire-Exposition d'Abidjan', *Paris-Dakar*, n° 105, 5 février 1935, p. 6.

[Anon.] (1937) 'Le Cameroun à l'Exposition', *L'Eveil du Cameroun*, n° 255, 15 février 1937, p. 6.

[Anon.] (1939) ''Côte d'Ivoire 39.' Foire-Exposition de Bobo-Dioulasso', *L'A.O.F. Echo de la Côte Occidentale d'Afrique*, n° 2013, 4 mars 1939, p. 1.

Baxandall, Michael (1990) 'Exhibiting Intention: Some Preconditions of the Visual Display of Culturally Purposeful Objects' in Ivan Karp and Steven D. Lavine (eds) *The Poetics and Politics of Museum Display*. Washington and London: Smithsonian Institution Press, pp. 33-41.

Béart, Charles (1936) 'Le Théâtre africain et la culture franco-africaine', *Bulletin de l'Enseignement de l'A.O.F.*, n° 96, p. 3.

Bertrand, Louis (1931) 'A travers les sections de l'Exposition Coloniale. L'Algérie', *Revue des deux Mondes*, 15 juin 1931, pp. 825-37.

Chambre de Commerce de Marseille (1913) *L'Exposition Coloniale de 1916. Réunion tenue le jeudi 27 février 1913 à 9 heures du soir*, Marseille.

Charton, André (1936) *Rapports de M. l'Inspecteur Général, rapport 520/E. Exposition 1937, 10 mars 1936*. Manuscript of the *Archives du Sénégal*, Dakar, Série O, dossier 183.

Chrétien, J.-P. and Prunier, G. (eds) (1989) *Les ethnies ont une histoire*, Paris.

Commissariat Général de l'exposition (1922) *L'Exposition Nationale Coloniale de Marseille décrite par ses Auteurs. Quarante-trois articles, quatre aquarelles, huit cent onze illustrations en noir et blanc et douze plans*, Marseille, Commissariat Général de l'exposition.

Correra, Issagha (1992) *Samba Guéladio. Epopée peule du Fuuta Tooro. Texte pulaar par Amadou Kamara. Transcrit et traduit par Issagha Correra*, Dakar.

Dadié, Bernard B. (1981) *Carnet de prison*, Abidjan.

Demaison, André (1931) *Exposition coloniale internationale. Paris en 1931. Texte de A. Demaison*, Paris.

Duguay-Clédor, Amadou (1985) *La Bataille de Guîlé. Introduction de Mbaye Guèye. Nouvelle édition,* Dakar/Paris.

Girbal, Paul (1907) 'Les enseignements de l'exposition coloniale de Marseille', *Revue Pédagogique*, 15 janvier 1907, pp. 29-39.

Glinga, Werner (1990) *Literatur in Senegal. Geschichte, Mythos und gesellschaftliches Ideal in der oralen und schriftlichen Literatur*, Berlin.

Goldmann, Stefan (1985) 'Wilde in Europa. Aspekte und Orte ihrer Zurschaustellung' in Thomas Theye (ed.) *Wir und die Wilden*, Reinbek, pp. 243-69.

Hodeir, Catherine, Leprun, Sylviane and Pierre, Michel (1993) 'Les Expositions coloniales' in *Images et Colonies. Iconographie et propagande coloniale sur l'Afrique française de 1880 à 1962*, Paris, pp. 129-39.

Lebrun, Albert (1931) 'L'Exposition Coloniale ouvre ses portes', *Le Monde Colonial Illustré*, n° 93, mai 1931, p. 109.

Leprun, Sylviane (1986) *Le théâtre des colonies. Scénographie, acteurs et discours de l'imaginaire dans les expositions, 1855-1937*, Paris.

[Mani] (1937) "L'Afrique" aux attractions', *Paris-Dakar*, n° 481, 28 août 1937, p. 1-2.

Sadji, Abdoulaye (1985[1935]) *Ce que dit la musique africaine*, Paris.

Sadji, Abdoulaye (1936) 'Ce que dit la musique africaine', *Bulletin de l'Enseignement de l'A.O.F.*, n° 94, avril-juin 1936, pp. 119-20.

Senghor, Léopold Sédar (1964) *Poèmes*, Paris.

Sissoko, Fily-Dabo (1938) 'Les Noirs et la Culture (Extrait)', *Congrès international de l'évolution culturelle des peuples coloniaux, 26-27-28 septembre 1937. Rapports et compte rendu*, Paris, pp. 116-22.

Identity as Progress –
The Longevity of Nationalism

CHRISTIAN GEULEN

It has become almost obligatory in recent work on the history of nationalism to insist that this very history has not and, for the time being, will not come to an end. History continues in the conflicts in Eastern Europe, in the Western revival of the nation as an acknowledged cultural category, and also in the ethnic conflicts of postcolonial societies. Such observations presuppose that nationalism exists as such and that it possesses one single history, despite all evident differences. In contradistinction to phenomena such as Imperialism, Communism or National Socialism, which appear to be fixed in time and space, nationalism seems to be a recidivist phenomenon. It can reemerge or reoccur and fails to die, in short: it is an integral part of the general danger of modernity. This longevity, an aspect recent research focuses on, indicates a preexisting relationship between nationalism and its historical manifestations, between nation and history.

This paper will address different forms of relationship between history and the nation. It poses the question of the consequences for modern historical research on nationalism given the fact that history in all its dimensions—as past, memory, tradition, change or temporal consciousness—is a constitutive part of the 'national.' Three hypotheses can be stated at the outset:

1. Attempts to explain the longevity of nationalism, using the traditional definitions and models of modern historiography, run the risk of uncritically reproducing the functional link between nation and history.
2. A critical analysis of that link calls for a new reflection on 'historical meaning' and the ways it is produced in order to perceive the historical diversity of nations, nationalisms and national identity as the very condition of the longevity of nationalism.

Notes for this section can be found on page 238.

3. Instead of presupposing that longevity is an ahistorical fact, we should analyse the immanent historicity of nationalism. By focusing on the historical differences between nationalisms we can also acknowledge and reconsider the question of cultural differences which has been at the political core of the nation all along.

The following remarks point out some basic problems concerning the relationship between nation and history. The solution of these problems might yield a specifically historical access to the question of modern collective identities and their political meaning. The first part analyses some influential concepts and models taken from the German historiography of nationalism. The second part considers alternative approaches by focusing on some specific aspects in the relationship between nation, history and race during the turn of the nineteenth/twentieth century Germany.

1. Nationalism and German Historiography: Recent Debates

Historical research on nationalism is on the rise. Within the enormous amount of literature that is produced in Germany on the subject, some major approaches and models structuring the field of research are discernable. Dieter Langewiesche (1995) has provided the most recent overview on the topic, critically presenting almost every important approach. Beginning with the well-known 'Janus-face' of the nation shifting between the promise of participation and the will to violence, Langewiesche convincingly demonstrates that, whereas the older German historiography turned the ambivalence of the nation into a theory of its development, younger historians—in the light of nationalism's most recent revivals—perceive its Janus-face to be a persistently recurring structure of the nation itself. Despite the heterogeneity of models and theories that are in use today, this change has surely been the most important 'turn' in the research during the last fifteen years. Confronted with an apparent longevity of the nation as a site for the production of political, ideological, social and cultural meaning and power, modern research has abandoned theories of development and turned to questions concerning the temporally overarching structures and contents of nation, nationalism and, above all, national identity.

Most of these works share two common aspects: On the one hand they stress the fact that it is impossible (or more precisely: improper) to define nations by relying on presumably objective and 'real' differences between groups of people. On the other hand they emphasise certain (although variable) aspects on which the nation as a mental construct is based, through which it is defined and from which it receives its content. Nations do not have an objective core that could define membership and belonging, rather they are imagined,

invented, constructed patterns of particular exclusions and inclusions. While this epistemological presupposition is widely acknowledged, despite different terminologies, the issue of what transforms those constructed unities into nations and why they differ significantly from other forms of collective particularism in terms of their historical importance proves highly controversial.

To some degree, a dilemma has returned that was already addressed at the end of the nineteenth century by Ernest Renan: How can the phenomenon be causally explained without recourse to 'objective' factors such as ethnicity, language, religion or geography? Renan attempted to understand the nation as a general 'will' that constitutes and reconstitutes itself on a daily basis, thereby providing a daily guarantee for the existence of the nation: 'A large aggregate of men, healthy in mind and warm of heart, creates the kind of moral consciousness which we call a nation. So long as this moral consciousness gives proof of its strength by the sacrifices which demand the abdication of the individual to the advantage of the community, it is legitimate and has the right to exist' (Renan, 1990:20).

The morality of this consciousness lies in the fact that it is devoid of any concrete criterion which differentiates human beings from each other. In Renan's eyes, the nation is a particularism without a particular.

Despite Renan's belief that nations are a 'daily plebiscite' and therefore would soon be exchanged for something else, they have turned out to be quite resistant. The fact that nations obviously take some time to vanish, makes it all the more important for more recent historical approaches to find a solution to the problem first posed by Renan. With the beginning of modern research on nationalism the general supposition that nations do not have an objective core led to the question of the mechanisms that nevertheless made them the most important political structures in modern history.

The functionalist approach of the 1960s and 1970s regarded the nation primarily as a vehicle of integration and intrasocial stabilisation. Thus the unity of a nation was seen as a result of external social interests and functional relations. This explicitly critical approach can be regarded as the beginning of contemporary research on nationalism. Besides its causal analyses, it opened the possibility of reconstructing the general lines of nationalism's development by pointing out the most effective main functions of nationalist ideology in a given period (see Langewiesche, 1964:198-205; Lemberg,1964; Deutsch, 1972; Schieder, 1992; Winkler, 1979a:13-80; 1979b:36-51; Wehler, 1995:144-58). The drawback of the functionalist approach however, was a structural blindness to the internal dynamics of nation-building. The more historians stressed social and political group interests as the real motives behind national interests, the more nationalism itself moved out of sight. Problems such as the social and cultural dissemination of national ideology, the secret of the nation's success in creating collective meaning, the reproduction of national stereotypes and symbols or the mechanisms of inclusion and exclusion were simply

outside the view of functionalist interest theory. By overemphasising external factors, by taking the hasty step from the 'constructed nation' to the nation as 'economy's puppet,' functionalist approaches threatened to obscure the issue of nationalism even before it became properly visible.[1] One alternative to functionalism, which owes a great deal to its tradition but challenges it at crucial points, can be called the political approach. Its advocates regard the nation as the product of a certain modern form of politics centred around the idea of state-building. In the words of John Breuilly, the most important representative of this approach:

> 'Nationalism cannot be linked to any particular type of cultural attribute or social arrangement; or to any particular structure of communications; or to any particular class interest, or to any particular economic relationship; or to any particular psychological state or need; or to any particular social function or objective. It is therefore impossible to construct any acceptable theory of nationalism upon such bases. Nationalism is a form of politics' (Breuilly, 1993:35-6).

In this view the world's different nationalisms—separatist, reformist, anticolonial etc.—can be described and explained exclusively by an analysis of political strategies, decision processes and institutional structures. All other cultural or social dimensions are to be analysed simply as aspects of such politics, i.e. by describing their instrumentalisation as a community on its way to becoming a modern nation-state. Thereby, the principle that nations lack an objective core becomes radicalised to the point that nationalism appears as a pure political strategy—a nationalism without nations (382). Thus advocates of the political approach move from the analysis of a general characteristic of nationalism directly to the analysis of origins. They simply cut the historical lines of connection between beliefs, feelings, or political identifications and the nation, then point to what is left over: a form of politics. The continuity of nationalism is thus explained almost mechanically by the well-known structures and developments of the modern state, which itself, of course, has nothing to do with apparently irrational identities or cultural differences. Although it is important to stress the effects of the political rationality undoubtedly inherent in nationalism, one should not overlook that which lies outside of that rationality.

Another common approach to nationalism is based on typologies. Here, specific differences and identities are not neglected, but rather assigned to certain types of nationalism which can then be compared. M. Rainer Lepsius (1993:193-215) for example, regards the nation as a '*gedachte Ordnung*' (imagined order) defined by three main criterions of belonging: First the '*Volksnation*' (ethnic nation), second the '*Kulturnation*' (cultural nation) and third the '*Staatsnation*' (political nation) or '*Staatsbürgernation*' (civic or democratic nation), which is constituted through the rights and duties of political participation. As in the political approach, which had to employ developmental models of the modern state in order to explain nationalism's history,

typologies, too, need to be supplemented with models of development and modernisation if they are used by historians of nationalism. That becomes quite clear in Lepsius, who understands the nation as a fundamentally modern phenomenon which gains special importance 'when state power is legitimated by the principle of a sovereign people and the participants of that legitimisation have to be defined' (196). On that basis the development of different types of nations is structured by an underlying modernisation process characterised by democratisation, rationalisation and individualisation. The extension of belonging, up to the point at which it can be claimed by virtually everybody, is one aspect of that model of modernisation. The other is the individualisation of belonging up to the point at which it can be claimed only by single individuals.[2]

Where they imply such modernisation theories, typologies are in danger of modelling the historical reality and turning it into a subject of teleological principles. This becomes especially obvious in the case of the '*Staatsnation*': it defines the structure and direction of the modernisation process, thereby deploying an artificial historicity of nationalism. According to Lepsius' typology nations cannot exist beyond the '*Staatsnation*.' In the '*Staatsnation*' the history of nations and nationalism comes to an end. The problem of national identity is (dis)solved within a system of individual participation and universal equality. But at this point the typological criteria which were originally used to describe a certain type of nation are now effectively replacing it. From the perspective of a victory of a rational society over the irrationality of community, progress and regress become the only possible forms of the history of nations and nationalism.

Gaining distance from functionalist, typological and political approaches, a number of new works have emphasised the importance of culture.[3] They, too, start out with the assumption that nations are constructed. By taking this idea much more seriously, however, these new works try to analyse the cultural practices such as symbols, languages, ideas, memories, traditions, myths, metaphors, monuments, in short: the internal world of the nation as an imagined collectivity. They claim that 'culture' is not only a reservoir of symbols that can be politically instrumentalised, but also the very medium in which the imagined community of a nation is constituted and reproduced. Although these works do not represent a homogeneous approach or theory, one can analyse the implicit assumptions about the relation between nation and history. What is it that connects culture, consisting of contingent symbols and signs, to the continuity of nationalism? Which kind of a history of nationalism becomes visible by looking at the cultural representations of political inclusion and exclusion? Or, to use Droysen's phrase: When and where does the everyday business of culture turn into the history of nationalism?

An important theoretical problem is hidden in such questions: if one looks at the nation as a cultural construct then there are two possible ways in which

culture and nation relate to each other. Either the cultural symbols and signs are instrumental means deployed to nationalist ends, or the nation is indissolvably wrapped up in the medium of culture so that a 'history of the nation' is no longer possible. Cultural approaches, which reject functionalism and its models, are therefore bound to conceptualise an alternative temporality of the nation. In order to avoid the double danger of teleologically simplifying cultural identification or reinforcing the power of existing national cultures, some of those recent works try to explain the effects of national symbols and imaginations by referring to certain anthropological structures of human behaviour. These basic structures guarantee the continuity of nationalism, but still allow for various specific manifestations. However, nationalism's diversity and continuity remain disconnected. The temporality of the nation resulting from this concept is a continuity that assumes various shapes; the actual process of change remains invisible.

Influential works on the national cult of memory and national stereotypes reveal this tendency. Pierre Nora, for instance, describes national places of memory (*lieux de memoire*) as 'Russian dolls' that take on a new 'coat' of national meaning with every single act of remembering, but still continue to reproduce the original event to be remembered (1990:11-33, esp. 28). The idea of connecting history and memory can indeed contribute to the analysis of national forms of memory in myths, monuments and symbols. But there is no way of interpreting the function of collective memory for the nation as the historicity at work in the nation. For that would lead to a simple continuity of constantly reproduced traditions that might reveal new aspects in the history of memory, without saying anything about the relation between history and the nation. A similar problem can be identified in recent works on national stereotypes. For instance, the idea of a continuity in various guises lies also at the core of Michael Jeismann's convincing thesis that the French/German stereotypes and enemy-concepts originating during the Napoleonic wars became revitalised first during the wars preceding the unification of Germany in 1871 and then, again, during the First World War (Jeismann, 1992). What guarantees the continuity of the stereotypes analysed by Jeismann is not their historical development, but the transtemporal continuity of the friend/foe-difference presented as a basic law of political group formation. With this concept it is indeed possible to reconstruct and interpret the revitalisation of certain images of the self and the other in times of crisis and war, but for that very reason it becomes impossible to consider the reproduction, dissemination and historical change of stereotypes.

Approaches that concentrate on the culture of nationalism usually regard this culture as a stabiliser that activates emotional needs and codes of self and other so as to uphold the nation as the centre of every possible identification. This view tends to forget the historicity of culture itself and, moreover, is constantly in danger of transferring this rigidity onto the nation. The temporality

of the nation, implicit in such a concept of culture, appears as a tradition that continues because it is remembered, returned to, and reactivated again and again. The presupposition of such a continuity, however, makes it impossible to perceive it as a historical process. The more static the concept of culture used in attempts to localise the invention and construction of national myths, the more difficult it becomes to avoid the danger of reproducing nationalism's greatest myth: its self-image as an atemporal continuum. Thus the question arises, whether or not there are alternatives for a 'new cultural history' of nationalism which might consider not only the spatial but also the temporal dynamics of the nation.

2. Longevity and Transformation

In the recent research on nationalism two trends can be identified which show an obvious relationship to the present political situation. On the one hand, historians, in contrast to previous decades, now consider the concrete phenomena of collective identity and seek to explain their continuity in, and resistance to, modernity. On the other hand, the origin of this continuity is not located in the history of those concrete forms of collective identity, but rather in ahistorical principles and codes which transform identities into nations. Whether referring to mentalities or to cultural patterns of behaviour, to typologies or political strategies, in every case the different manifestations of national identity are bound together in a general concept of the nation and the continuity of nationalism is explained by recourse to other continuities.

What holds these two trends together is a concept of the nation as something invented. No other keyword expresses this more clearly than Eric Hobsbawm's concept of 'invented tradition' (Hobsbawm, 1992). In this view the nation is a tradition, insofar as it signifies an identity-producing heritage; at the same time the nation is also an 'invention,' insofar as such a tradition actually cannot (or should not) exist in modern times. By integrating the modern category of cultural or social 'construction' and concepts of the 'nonmodern' such as tradition or community, historians of nationalism try to bring the ambivalence of the nation under control, and neutralise the precarious relationship of the nation to universalism and particularism, society and community, modernity and tradition.[4]

What Ernest Renan in 1882 called the 'will to the nation' today returns as its 'invention.' However, there remains a difference: whereas today's historians seek the key to understanding nationalism in the external interests and the need to invent a nation, Renan identified this motivation in the national will itself. The latter does not envision the nation arising out of nothing, but by reference to the particularity of an already-existing group, a collective sharing common memories, 'healthy in mind and warm of heart' (1990:20). Thus, in Renan's

view, the nation does not really extend beyond concrete and ever-changing differences and identities, rather it amalgamates them into a superior particularity, which, as a result of that process, loses its relation to those differences. Seen in this perspective, the 'national will' signifies not the invention of a new particularity, but a bundling of existing heterogeneous and diverse identities. They do not dissolve, but become transcended and homogenised, which gives to the resulting 'nation' the flexibility of a daily 'will.'

In contrast to Renan, the approaches discussed above hypostasise the fact that the nation cannot be reduced to single differences of physiology or language, and therefore are bound to claim that the nation is, by nature, disconnected from those differences, following its own logic and principle. This view, however, is related to its subject—'nations'—in exactly the same way in which the nation is related to other collective identities: this view tries to transcend the concrete appearances of nations and nationalism in a general concept charged with explaining nationalism's longevity.

The criticism presented here does not counsel abandoning the search for a general explanation of that longevity, nor does it promote something like a *'micro-histoire'* of national, ethnic or other cultural identifications. Instead it tries to call into question the common assumption that the nation is a political super-identity that reproduces itself independently of the concrete historical, cultural, ethnic or social diversity within human relations. If the nation, as most of the research suggests, is in fact a genuinely modern phenomenon, then it does not make sense to explain its continuity by pointing to other continuities. Something which is able to survive the structural conditions of modernity and to settle within it must adapt to those conditions through flexibility and immanent change. But these aspects tend to be forgotten whenever historians look at the result of that flexibility, i.e. at the national as a continuous danger spanning time and space, instead of the processes that produced this very image in the first place.

The alternative to be outlined here puts the relationship between the nation and other forms of collective identity into the centre of historical research. Instead of excluding this relationship by reducing the continuity of the nation to the continuity of class interests, structures or cultural patterns, the discontinuity of nationalism—its transformation through time and its intersection with heterogeneous competing identities—should be reconstructed as the historical process causing its apparent continuity. This historicity of nation and nationalism, however, becomes visible only if historians acknowledge the political and historical effects of ethnic, religious, gender, and other identities. For after all, the refusal to acknowledge cultural diversity, its dissolution into a homogeneous superstructure and its autocratic instrumentalisation, is a crucial aspect of nationalist ideology itself. Thus the explanation of the longevity of nationalism should start with the heterogeneity of identities, not with the presupposition that all the differences and identities

have always already been repressed by the nation. The concept of the nation as a constructed, imagined and invented order might lead to an analysis of nationalism's discontinuity as a symptom of its permanent transformation, and to an acknowledgement of what the nation tries to homogenise again and again: the contingency of collective identification.

Using the example of the process in which the nation became charged with racial connotations at the end of the nineteenth century, I will show in what follows that a focus on the diversity of national and other constructions of identity can indeed provide an alternative explanation for the longevity of nationalism.

3. The Language of 'Race' and the Instability of the Nation

In 1916, in the midst of World War I, the German-Jewish philologist Eduard Engel published a book entitled: 'Speak German!' Outraged by the increasing use of foreign and especially French words in the German language, which he pejoratively called '*Welscherei*,' Engel wrote:

> 'Language is *Volk* and *Volk* is language; and with the soiling and shambling of the German language, as it is now common all over Germany, the continuity of that wonderful piece of art, called German *Volk*, is in the most extreme and deadliest danger. […] The World War over Germany's existence has indeed shown […] that we can do many things better than other nations, but also that, even in this life-or-death struggle for the preservation of the German nationness we do not manage to accomplish what even the lowest of our multicoloured enemies achieved: the unshakeable preservation of the most stable basis of all nationness: the undistorted and unsoiled mother tongue. […] It is wrong […] to imagine the *Welscherei* as a penetration of many single words. No, they turn up in large tribes. They come in herds and hordes, they breed, as all pests do, from one day to the next in loads and masses. They lodge in all the warmest lively parts of the German language, the German thought, the German emotion, and they suck the living blood out of the word arteries of the native children of the German mother tongue. […] They spread proliferously like a rotten sponge, like a cancerous ulcer all over the living cells of the body of the German language. The essence of the German language is an unlimited vitality; there is no other language that is comparable with the German language in its creative power to produce new meanings. But the root of this flushing vitality is now the victim of the deadly axe of the *Welscherei*' (1916:6, 8, 20; transl. mine).

The language Engel used to describe the cultural power of language, in general, over the life of a nation is obviously the language of racism. The result is a kind of nationalism that manifests itself not only beyond the difference between a racial and cultural nationalism, but also beyond a system of signs and symbols expressing a general particularism. Engel's text is, in fact, about this very generality of particularist inclusion and exclusion. Engel does not talk about the specific German particularity as opposed to some other, but about particularity as a general principle, as a nation's vital elixir. What the lit-

erature on nationalism often presupposes, as a general anthropological need for group formation and exclusion, appears in Engel's nationalism as a universal law of the natural history of nations. Moreover, this law does not function as a simple legitimation for a specific national project—to stabilise the nation or to beat an enemy—but it is the project itself. The war—the inclusion and exclusion, the purification and differentiation, the preservation and vitality—are not parts of the mythical construction of the nation's originality, but its task, its mission, the nation's 'realisation' of an ongoing perfection.

A closer look at the contexts of the specific kind of nationalism represented by Engel reveal some of the problems discussed above as primarily theoretical problems. Engel's text can be seen as a typical example of the nationalist discourse before and during World War I. However, it contains no special ideology that can be identified or isolated. Engel's text is not marked by a specific ideological reification or a discernible stereotype. Instead, it is characterised by a very incoherent mixture of various elements of nationalist thought. One example is the ambivalent relationship between the representation of the nation as a necessarily eternal order and the equally important stress on its change and history.

Engel attempted to describe something like the linguistic colonisation of the German culture, a process of endangering a current cultural identity by the penetration of a foreign culture through 'linguistic miscegenation.' To represent this process he used a system of racist and imperialist metaphors and images of the pathological other, which informed the entire text. The attempt to analyse the ways in which foreign words undermine the purity of German and Germanness necessarily opened up a gap between a given cultural identity and its potential for historical transformation. It is the well-known gap between the identification with something real and its representation within language, between culture and its discontents (see Henrich, 1979; Hall, 1994:180-222; Auernheimer, 1988). As soon as Engel sees the need to protect his culture against the influences of foreign words, his ideal of cultural purity is already infected from within, so to speak; his ideal of an essential identity and its purity dissolves into nothing but language. If a cultural identity can possibly be threatened by foreign words, then there is obviously no objective core that could possibly define and constitute the identity and essence of this culture above and beyond language—be it race, blood, or character. This contradiction within Engel's argument uncovers the theory of a nation's natural life, expressed in the countless biological metaphors that try to cover up the gap between nature and culture, between nation and history. It becomes clear that the so-called 'racialisation' of the national during the imperial era cannot be understood as the simple victory of a materialist ideology that reified the nation and reduced collectivity to timeless bodyshapes. Rather, Engel's racism, which simultaneously invoked and neglected racial purity, reveals the very ambivalence Benedict Anderson (1992:173) identified in nationalism in gen-

eral: A racist nationalism, too, projects the nation onto the space between historical temporality and the natural timelessness of heredity.

Still, what does this ambivalence have to do with the question of the longevity of nationalism? Stuart Hall writes about the influence of racism on other ideologies:

> Racism is especially powerful and its effect on the every-day consciousness particularly strong, because it discovers in racial features such as skin-colour, ethnic origin, geographical position etc. something, which other ideologies have to create in the first place: an obviously natural or universal basis within nature itself. Despite these natural legitimations through biological facts, however, racism—as an ideology appearing outside of history—affects other ideological formations within the same society, and its appearance alters the entire ideological field, in which it became effective' (1992: 275).

Racism can appeal to a certain order of things already existing in reality and described by scientists. Based on this order or structure everything which is not nature—history, politics, economy, culture in a wide sense—becomes the raw material used by racists to build their ideological arguments, which are always arguments about the natural order of things, independent of the subject they describe. This is the basis of racism's immense social power: culture (not nature) is the playground of racist ideology, on which it can transform any difference and any similarity into a universal law of nature. Racism empirically transcends the demarcations, established by historians of racism, between ethnic, political, cultural and economic motivations of racist ideology. The semantic mixture of social spheres, the transference between them, has always already taken place when racists talk about the reality of life.

This difference between racism and other ideologies reflects the theoretical difference between a classic ideology and a discourse. Since the concept of 'discourse' signifies a realm beyond the differentiation between thought and action, between language and practice, it ultimately problematises the difference between true and false statements. Discourses never consist of a single statement, but always of a plurality of statements that constitute the network of a discursive formation. This formation does not apply a true or false knowledge in a correct or incorrect way, but produces in various texts, contexts and actions, in discursive practices, a certain knowledge in the first place (see Hall, 1992; Foucault, 1992; Jelavich, 1995). The concept of discourse, which replaces the emphasis on function with an analysis of ideology focussing on production, provides an alternative access to the question of how the racialisation of the national relates to nationalism's longevity.

The complex process in which the national and the racial coincided in late nineteenth century German culture was not only another step in the development of nationalist ideology; it also stands in close connection to a general discourse of cultural or social differences and collective identity. From the social reform

movements to early feminism to the new cultural sciences it was evident that collective identity itself became the central subject of academic disciplines, political parties and a wide range of social organisations. In fact, one of the many riddles in the history of nationalism is the question of why nationalism became the most successful identity industry exactly during a time in which all sorts of alternative ethnic, social or gender identities started to gain access to the public and political spheres. Why was it the national idea that proved to be most successful in integrating, dissolving or repressing all other forms of particularity?

A classic way to approach this problem would be to ask for that one special element that provided nationalism with a greater power of convincing people. This might be the social status and political power of its promoters, or the ability to provide clear-cut definitions of the collective that were easy to internalise. In contrast to such views, the discourse-analytical approach concentrates on the relationship between the national and other ideas of collective identity and cultural difference. The apparent repression of those other identities would then have to be understood as a specific historical action or process, as a production of a certain hierarchical knowledge. That the intersection of race and nation around 1900 can be analysed as such a production and reproduction of differences, which supported nationalism more effectively than processes of repression, becomes clear by looking at three special aspects: at the production of collective identity, at national stereotypes and at the integration of the two in what can be called the historical consciousness of nationalism.

Despite its appearance at the turn of the century as a category of hard science, the concept of 'race' is indeed characterised by a strong ambivalence. Similar to other criteria of social grouping such as class or gender, race (like ethnicity) has generally a double meaning: It is an externally defined category of description, implying a whole range of additional criteria (skin colour, physiognomy, gene pool, behaviour etc.), but it also implies the direct and internal belonging to a social group. Thus a collective identity based on the idea of 'race' owes its stability and strength much less to the restriction of belonging to a single distinctive feature than to the possibility of giving an objective name to what is experienced as a subjective belonging. This naming can be repeated as well as changed again and again without revealing itself as what it is: a constantly ongoing transformation of identity (Jenkins, 1994). The category of race and the drama of 'race struggle' made it possible to transfer the general inconsistencies of an 'I/We-identity' into a realm beyond the 'I/We-experience' in a way that guaranteed the stability of the collective self-awareness. Thus the imperial myth of an ongoing struggle and war between the races, sexes, and cultures was splendidly performed at fairs and colonial exhibits, in the colonial literature and popular magazines without ever calling into question the eternal continuity of the national self (see Gilman, 1985; Goldmann, 1984; Rydell, 1984; Sieferle, 1989:129-203; see Lüsebrink in this volume).

The racialisation of national stereotypes reveals a similar dynamic differentiating the collective perception rather than restricting it to single elements. Thus the well-known transformation of the 'stranger outside' into the 'inner enemy' taking place in Germany in the decades before 1914 gained, with the racial discourse, immense semantic power (see Jeismann, 1992:349-63; Wehler, 1995:144-58; Pick, 1989). For here too the category of race, which could identify practically anything as an expression of nature, provided a highly flexible instrument of differentiating whenever necessary between true and false, right and wrong, genuine and artificial, pure and impure forms of identity and belonging. The very difference between belonging and not-belonging could be articulated in the biological language of disease and infection, along the line of the normal and the pathological. As Canguilhem, Foucault and others have shown, the social effect of this medical logic was not a totalisation of the difference between members and nonmembers of the healthy community, but the reduction of this difference to the very unstable distinction between two conditions determined by the same biological rules (Canguilhem, 1974). The enemy was not simply within the community; he could moreover reproduce and proliferate there. Thus sexuality, for instance, became a crucial arena for the struggle over German identity, precisely because it constitutes the site where friends as well as enemies of the nation literally can be born.[5] Moreover, the racist's play with differences and various identities was not restricted to the perception of the other within the self, but could also determine the perception of the strangers outside: in the years before and during World War I, nothing irritated German nationalists more than the fact that the '*Erbfeind*' France did not appear on the battle ground as the 'pure' Frenchman, but rather made German troops fight against 'multi-coloured' soldiers of 'lower races.'[6] Through the 'splitting of the "I", as well as of the world, into good and bad objects, the bad "I" becomes distanced and identified with the imagined representation of the bad object;' a process performing the political power of stereotypes less along a distinctive borderline between inclusion and exclusion than rather in a creation of ever new-differences (Gilman, 1985:17).

These heterogeneous and multiple effects of the intersection of race and nation indicate that the racial or *völkisch* concept of the nation does not necessarily imply a traditional idea of its history as an eternal continuity. Rather, the opposite seems to be the case, and the question that arises is which aspects of the nationalist's own concept of history corresponds to the ambivalent play with identity and difference.

One of the most important ideological aspects of the racial nationalism before 1914 was a simplified version of Charles Darwin's theory of evolution. Although most historians regard what they call 'Social Darwinism' (Kelly, 1981; Wehler, 1979:281-9; Sieferle, 1989; Weindling, 1989:11-48) as something like a background religion for nationalism, especially in the German

Empire, only few of them have asked how it was possible that a scientific theory promoting the historical change of races over time could provide the ideological basis for an immortal Reich. Darwin's version of natural evolution represented a gigantic anthropomorphism, which discovered as parts of a natural will some of the most important elements of human history: power, suppression, competition, hierarchy, sex roles, conflict, struggle, selection, exclusion, etc. As a centre piece of intellectual history in the late nineteenth century, Darwin's 'temporalisation of nature' (Lepenies, 1976; Blumenberg, 1988:267-90) provided a double explanation of the natural basis of humanity: its origin in an evolutionary nature and its genesis through the internal mechanisms of this very evolution. Origin and genesis, beginning and continuity coincided within the Darwinian model where they were amalgamated into the ambivalent idea of evolutionary differentiation. Placing humanity's origin in its development declared this development at the same time to be a continuous repetition of the origin. Thus an ontology of timely change was born which made it possible to conceive of 'origin' as both a given natural basis and a contingent historical beginning. In an evolutionary view, exclusion as well as inclusion, selection as well as assimilation are always perpetuations of the origin as the basis of continuity.

When nationalists gained access to this scientific religion via the categories of race and ethnicity, they could represent the invented construct of an ever-existing and eternal German '*Volk*' in a very modern outlook. For in the evolutionary discourse of the nation, historical change and the timelessness of heredity conjoin. Whatever discontinuities, gaps and moments of dissolution the factual history of the nation might show (and which Renan and other historians and critics of the nation have constantly pointed out)—an evolutionary nationalism could declare those deformations in the nation's history to be heroic moments in the struggle for survival, which proved the progress of the nation all the more powerfully the more they endangered its very existence. This discourse was more than just another way of inventing a national past. It was less a nationalist rewriting of history than a historicisation of nationalism.

In the intersection of racial differences and their evolutionary interpretation, the nation became temporalised: the factual ethnic mixture turned into a mere step in the process of purification, the gaps within the nation's history turned into heroic leaps forward in the nation's natural development, and the experienced change of the nation became its expected renewal.[7] Instability—the idea of crisis—was thus not only one of the external causes of nationalism, but an internal mechanism that did not hinder but actually drove forward and perpetuated the national project as a process of 'survival.' Nationalism's continuity turned from a continuity-despite-crises into a continuity-through-crises. In the very moment when nationalism started to promote the purifying improvement of the nation, imagining the end of the nation could reassure its longevity.

Therefore, pointing to the contradiction between the factual historical changes of the nation and the nationalists' claims of biological timelessness misses the point. Above all, it misses the core of a new nationalism which developed, by virtue of 'race' and 'ethnicity,' an immanent historicity in the first place. As the apparently illogical crossovers between blood, belonging and language in Engel's nationalism revealed, it was the contradictions within racial stereotypes themselves that made it possible to represent the nation as an always endangered community, always in need of active protection. The necessity of purifying the nation was all the more convincing the more drastically its actual hybridity was pointed out. A strong racial nationalism needs a factually 'weak' nation.

By instrumentalising a Darwinian temporalised 'nature' for national stereotyping, actual contextual aspects such as concrete danger, historical crisis, possible defeat or survival became the basis of the nation's continuity, of its eternal nature. Thus it was the racial ideology that helped transform the instability and ambivalence of the nation, pointed out by critics as proof of its mythical character, into a national tradition. A lack of confidence in the nation's existence, the acknowledgement of the inconcreteness of its substantial essence, paradoxically reinforced the idea of the nation as a natural necessity. As a community based on racial heredity, the nation could exist only as a process of perfection driven forward by one national crisis after the other (Chamberlain and Gilman, 1985; Koselleck, 1980; Harvey, 1989; Bauman, 1992:1-36; Young, 1995:29-54).

What in July and August 1914 became acclaimed by large parts of the German people as the 'final fight for Germany's existence' and the 'great battle of humankind,' was in fact the recognition of an absolute crisis as that which had all along signified the very essence of the nation. Thus the outbreak of the war was related to a cultural discourse that for decades had inscribed national responsibility into the nature of the nation's members in form of a potential danger. The public debates over miscegenation, protection of mothers and the biological causes of social inequality, over youth-protection, hygiene, environmentalism and physical education, over the diseases of the national body and the pollution of the German language and culture, as well as the collective memory of moments of deepest national danger in monuments and memorials, all of this, despite the construction of social discipline and the imagination of the national community, had the additional effect of envisioning national regress, crisis, destruction and dissolution. What was new in the nationalism of the early twentieth century, in relation to its earlier forms, can be described not only in terms of the social history of nationalism, but also as a discursive shift within national ideology. By way of integrating racial differences and cultural hybridity the new national discourse was able to traditionalise as 'evolution' even what represented the most concrete threat to the nation's claim to be eternal: contingency. In the Germany of the 1920s, racial nationalism lived on

untouched by the national catastrophe of World War I, and revealed its ability to imagine the nation's continuity not beyond historical change, but within a very modern concept of history as progress and perfection.

4. Conclusion

To draw some conclusions: The nation as a racial hereditarian community represents neither an archaic premodern romanticism nor a hardening of the nation into an eternal natural order. Rather, many aspects indicate that the racialisation of the national in the late nineteenth and early twentieth centuries represents something like a historicisation or perhaps even a modernisation of the national discourse, which facilitated the instrumentalisation of history not only as 'past' or 'tradition' but also as historical progress. By virtue of the new self-image of the nation as a community, which envisioned its survival as a 'survival of the fittest' and immortalised itself in a process of perfection, nationalism gained an immanent transformability. The racial turn of nationalism was a turn from experiencing the nation's great past and present into expecting its future progress. The ever-new production of ethnic, racial, cultural, political or linguistic definitions of the nation as performed by a complex discourse integrating all possible differences between human beings, had the effect of representing change and chance as continuity and fate. Thus the often mentioned capacity of nationalism to adapt to certain circumstances is not only a matter of social spaces but also one of nationalism's historical change, providing continuity through progress.

A critique of progress, Walter Benjamin wrote in 1940, has to begin with a critique of progression in general. Following Benjamin, Benedict Anderson regards the instrumentalisation of the homogeneous empty time of progression as one of the most effective strategies of nationalism (Benjamin, 1991:701; Anderson, 1992:155-62, 204-6). Accordingly, one might say in this context, the historical explanation of nationalism's longevity would have to begin by abandoning this very longevity as a fact. In order to understand the effectiveness of nationalism, one should not uncritically reproduce its appearance and self-image as a homogeneous ever-existing danger caused by some kind of 'empty' continuity. Instead, one should deconstruct nationalism's active transformation of cultural differences into its specific homogeneous and empty temporality. One should analyse the points at which nationalism tries to bring the history of collective differences to an end so as to appear itself endless. The advantages of such an approach would have to be tested—as done only briefly here—with regard to processes such as the late nineteenth century racialisation of nationalism, or better: the nationalisation of race. However, reconstructing such turns in nationalism's history implies the acknowledgement of ethnic, racial and other collective identities, which are so often represented as the

antiuniversal malignant powers behind it. Their hybridity and contingency is what has to be saved. For it is not the eternal return of irrational collective identities and traditions that allows nationalism to live on, but rather nationalism's ability to make them disappear.

Notes

1. See Langewiesche (1995) and also the criticism presented by Jeismann, 1993.
2. This modernisation model is a central pattern of thought that not only informs typological approaches of historical research but also the general ways in which the problems of nation and nationalism are debated in the German public. For its presuppositions in terms of the history of nationalism see Rüsen, 1995:333-43. See also the debate over multiculturalism between Jürgen Habermas and Charles Taylor (Taylor, 1992).
3. See among others François, 1995; Koselleck and Jeismann, 1994; Dörner, 1995; Hardtwig, 1994; Link and Wülfing, 1991; Assmann and Hälscher, 1988.
4. On the political implications of the notion of 'invented traditions,' see Palti, 1993:109-26.
5. An interesting example is the journal '*Mutterschutz*' edited by the social reformer Helene Stöcker between the 1890s and 1914. In hundreds of articles, authors discussed the national meaning of a 'new sexual morality' and the 'new woman.' However, the explication of women's interests in terms of their contribution to the nation had the antifeminist effect of resolving the problem of gender and equality within a nationalist paradigm. See also Weindling, 1989:48-79; Foucault, 1999.
6. See Jeismann, 1992: 299-338; similar examples can be found in the German colonial newspaper '*Kolonie und Heimat*' or in the debates of the '*Reichstag*' over the French Foreign Legion. See also Young, 1995:159-82.
7. This ideological notion of the transformation of national catastrophe into national power can also be found in the writings of Julius Langbehn, Paul de Lagarde or Max Nordau. They represent not so much a traditionalist mysticism, but rather a kind of progressive belief in the idea of renewal through survival as it became also expressed later in Ernst Jünger's notion of 'war as emotional experience.' Thus, neither Jünger nor the nationalist prophets of the 1890s are appropriately described by the prominent concept of cultural pessimism.

References

Anderson, Benedict (1992) *Imagined Communities*, Princeton.

Assmann, Jan and Hölscher, Tonio (eds.), (1988) *Kultur und Gedächtnis*, Frankfurt/M.

Auernheimer, Georg (1988) *Der sogenannte Kulturkonflikt*, Frankfurt/M.

Bauman, Zygmunt (1992) 'Survival as a Social Construct', *Theory, Culture & Society*, 9:1-36.

Benjamin, Walter (1991 [1939/40]) 'Über den Begriff der Geschichte', in *Gesammelte Schriften*, Vol. I 2., (ed. Rolf Tiedemann and Hermann Schweppenhäuser), Frankfurt/M., pp. 691-704.

Blumenberg, Hans (1988) *Lebenszeit und Weltzeit*, Frankfurt/M.

Breuilly, John (1993²) *Nationalism and the State*, Manchester.

Canguilhem, George (1974) *Das Normale und das Pathologische*, Munich.

Chamberlain, J.-E. and Gilman, Sander L. (eds), (1985) *Degeneration: The Dark Side of Progress*, New York.

Deutsch, Karl W. (1972) *Der Nationalismus und seine Alternativen*, Munich.

Dörner, Andreas (1995) *Politischer Mythos und symbolische Politik: Sinnstiftung durch symbolische Formen am Beispiel des Herrmannsmythos*, Opladen.

Engel, Eduard (1916) *Sprich Deutsch! Ein Buch zur Entwelschung*, Leipzig.

Foucault, Michel (1994) *The Order of Things*, New York.

Foucault, Michel (1999) *In Verteidigung der Gesellschaft: Vorlesungen am Collége de France*, Frankfurt/M.

François, Etienne (ed.), (1995) *Nation und Emotion: Nationale Mythen, Symbole, Rituale*, Göttingen.

Gilman, Sander L. (1985) *Difference and Pathology: Stereotypes of Sexuality, Race and Madness*, Ithaca.

Goldmann, Stefan (1984) Wilde in Europa: Aspekte und Orte ihrer Zurschaustellung, in: Thomas Theye (ed.), *Wir und die Wilden: Einblicke in eine kannibalische Beziehung*, Hamburg.

Hall, Stuart (1992) 'The West and the Rest', in Stuart Hall and Brem Gieben (eds), *Formations of Modernity*, Milton Keynes, pp. 275-320.

Hall, Stuart (1992) 'The Question of Cultural Identity', in Stuart Hall, David Held and Tony McGrew (eds) *Modernity and its Futures*, Milton Keynes, pp. 273-316.

Hall, Stuart (1994) *Rassismus und kulturelle Identität: Ausgewählte Schriften 2*, Hamburg.

Hardtwig, Wolfgang (1994) *Nationalismus und Bürgerkultur in Deutschland 1500-1914*, Göttingen.

Harvey, David (1989) *The Condition of Postmodernity: An Enquiry into the Origins of Cultural Change*, Oxford.

Henrich, Dieter (1979) *Identität: Begriffe, Probleme, Grenzen*, Munich.

Hobsbawm, Eric J. and Ranger, Terence R. (1992), *The Invention of Tradition*, Cambridge.

Jeismann, Michael (1992) *Das Vaterland der Feinde: Studien zum nationalen Feindbegriff und Selbstverständnis in Deutschland und Frankreich 1792-1918*, Stuttgart.

Jeismann, Michael (1993) 'Alter und Neuer Nationalismus', in Michael Jeismann and Henning Ritter (eds), *Grenzfälle: Über neuen und alten Nationalismus*, Leipzig, pp. 9-26.

Jelavich, Peter (1995) 'Poststrukturalismus und Sozialgeschichte', *Geschichte und Gesellschaft*, 21:259-89.

Jenkins, Richard (1994) 'Rethinking Etnicity: Identity, Categorization and Power', *Ethnic and Racial Studies*, 17:197-223.

Kelly, Alfred (1981) *The Descent of Darwin: The Popularization of Darwinism in Germany 1860-1914*, Chapel Hill.

Koselleck, Reinhart (1980) '"Fortschritt" und "Niedergang"—Nachtrag zur Geschichte zweier Begriffe', in *Niedergang: Studien zu einem geschichtlichen Thema*, Stuttgart.

Koselleck, Reinhart and Jeismann, Michael (eds), (1994) *Der politische Totenkult: Kriegerdenkmäler in der Moderne*, Munich.

Langewiesche, Dieter (1995) 'Nation, Nationalismus, Nationalstaat: Forschungsstand und Forschungsperspektiven', *Neue Politische Literatur*, 40:190-236.

Lemberg, Eugen (1964) *Nationalismus*, 2 vols., Reinbeck.

Lepenies, Wolfgang (1976) *Das Ende der Naturgeschichte*, Munich.

Lepsius, Rainer (1993) 'Nation und Nationalismus in Deutschland', in Michael Jeismann and Henning Ritter (eds), *Grenzfälle: Über neuen und alten Nationalismus*, Leipzig, pp. 193-215.

Link, Jürgen and Wülfing, Wulf (eds), (1991) *Nationale Mythen und Symbole in der zweiten Hälfte des 19. Jahrhunderts: Strukturen und Funktionen von Konzepten nationaler Identität*, Stuttgart.

Nora, Pierre (1990) *Zwischen Geschichte und Gedächtnis*, Berlin.

Palti, E. J. (1993) 'Liberalism vs. Nationalism: Hobsbawm's Dilemma', *Telos*, 95:109-26.

Pick, Daniel (1989) *Faces of Degeneration: A European Disorder*, Cambridge.

Renan, Ernest (1990) 'Qu'est-ce qu'une nation?', Lecture of March 12, 1882, (translated by Martin Thom) in Homi Bhabha (ed.), *Nation and Narration*, London/New York, pp. 8-22.

Rüsen, Jörn (1995) 'Identität und Konflikt im Prozeß der Modernisierung: Überlegungen zur kulturhistorischen Dimension von Fremdenfeindlichkeit heute', in Gangolf Hübinger (ed.) *Universalgeschichte und Nationalgeschichten*, Düsseldorf, pp. 333-43.

Rydell, Robert W. (1984) *All the World's a Fair: Visions of Empire at American International Expositions 1876-1916*, Chicago.

Schieder, Theodor (1992) *Nationalismus und Nationalstaat*, (ed. Otto Dann and Hans-Ulrich Wehler), Göttingen.

Sieferle, Rolf Peter (1989) *Die Krise der menschlichen Natur: Zur Geschichte eines Konzepts*, Frankfurt/M., pp. 129-203.

Taylor, Charles (1992) *Multiculturalism and 'The Politics of Recognition'*, Princeton.

Wehler, Hans Ulrich (1995) 'Nationalismus als fremdenfeindliche Integrationsideologie', in *Die Gegenwart als Geschichte*, Munich, pp. 144-58.

Wehler, Hans-Ulrich (1979) 'Sozialdarwinismus im expandierenden Industriestaat', in *Krisenherde des Kaiserreichs*, Göttingen, pp. 281-9.

Weindling, Peter (1989) *Health, Race and Politics between National Unification and Nazism 1870-1945*, Cambridge.

Winkler, Heinrich August (1979a) 'Liberalismus und Nationalismus', in *Liberalismus und Antiliberalismus*, Göttingen, pp. 13-80.

Winkler, Heinrich August (1979b) 'Vom linken zum rechten Nationalismus', in *Liberalismus und Antiliberalismus*, Göttingen, pp. 36-51.

Young, Robert (1995) *Colonial Desire: Hybridity in Theory, Culture and Race*, London.

Culture and History in Comparative Fundamentalism

EMANUEL SIVAN

Over the last two decades or so, a thriving cottage industry has developed dealing with the origins and genesis of fundamentalist movements around the globe. Yet the scholars, policy analysts and intelligence experts involved in this huge effort had precious little to say about why such movements survive, and even flourish at times. After all, the odds are pretty much against them, as evidenced by the fact that the membership turnover rate is high. The stringent behavioural requirements, typical of fundamentalist groups, stand in stark contrast to the anything-goes, hedonistic, open society around them. One can just pick up one's things and quit the religious group and join the tempting, easygoing life teeming so close to it. The group rarely has any coercive powers to retain members and many resort only to moral pressure (the exceptions are, of course, terrorist groups, e.g. the Islamic *jama'at* which may execute collaborators and defectors). Neither do fundamentalists, who pride themselves on their austerity and asceticism, possess the material means to reward the members of their groups. Moreover, in the Third World countries, the latter may even suffer persecution by the authorities or harassment by rival sects and end up in hospital, prison or on the scaffold. It is here that the Cultural Theory developed by the anthropologist Mary Douglas sheds some new light (cf. Douglas, 1984, 1986, 1996).

One could argue that while these movements secure many a recruit due to social conditions and crisis (i.e. unemployment of university graduates, rural migration from town to city, foreign conquest etc.), they succeed in retaining enough of these recruits over the long haul thanks to something which is of their own making; name, a way-of-life, or culture, combining cosmology, organisation and mode of behaviour in a close and rather cohesive fit.

This culture tends to fit the mould of the *enclave*, or low grid/high group, positioned by Mary Douglas as the one which satisfies best the need of moral dissenters (who are, by definition, a minority). To survive, such a group must see to it that, most of the time, most of its members will conform to its enclave-like mould. This does not mean that variations in the mould, both over time and between groups adhering to the same religious tradition may not exist, or that there may be combinations of enclave with elements of other moulds, usually hierarchy, or high grid/high group.

1. Dissent and Exile

The root of the rise of all fundamentalist groups, be it in Christianity, Judaism or Islam, lies in the marginalisation of the major religious traditions in industrialised and developing societies. The self-styled defenders of the faith perceive this process and realise that the tradition must be reshaped in order to withstand the challenge of slow and sweet death, of being sucked into the vortex of modernity, and thus deserting religion—knowingly or tacitly—as the backbone of their way-of-life. And whereas more often than not the majority still professes the tradition, while in fact deserting it, the defenders of the faith see no way to stop the leakage than to dissent in public and organise themselves outside the realm of the decaying tradition.

Ultra-Orthodox Jews, in Germany and Hungary, thus left the allegedly Orthodox, (not Reform or Conservative) communities in the third quarter of the nineteenth century. Those who held on to Protestant 'Fundamentals' against the 'modernists' (and gave us the term Fundamentalism) quit the major denominating churches in the U.S., and set up their own during the second and third decades of the twentieth century. In the American south they took over most churches. In roughly the same period, the Muslim Brethren of Egypt established their own communities outside the sway of what they saw as a lax and derelict Islam establishment.

This sense of marginality and alienation is best rendered by metaphors of exile which remain the hallmark of their cosmology to this very day. The *Haredis* (ultra-Orthodox) speak of their condition as of being 'in exile among Jews;' the majority of so-called Jews having ceased to observe the *mitzvot* (precepts) and being indifferent to divine Providence. This predicament is worse where Jews are particularly successful in socioeconomic terms (as in the contemporary U.S.) or are the hegemonic majority (in Israel).

Radical preachers, such as those of the Islamic Salvation Front (FIS) in Algeria, speak of the 'exile of Islam in the Modern Age,' when Muslims stick to just a few rituals and neglect the laws. This situation is claimed to be reminiscent of the straits the Prophet Muhammad had found himself in Mecca in the seventh century, and was hence forced to migrate to the town of Medina so

as to allow for his community of faithful to thrive. The followers of these preachers (in Algeria and elsewhere in the Muslim world) are told to glory in the fact that they are *ghuraba* (exiles), for it is them who will inherit the earth.

In Protestant America doubts were raised already a century ago as to the solidity of the Bible-believing block, which was seen as being taken over by church modernists, devoted to progress-oriented social gospel, and to accommodation with the discoveries of science. Half a century later the danger seemed to come from an external force, which also had many allies within the Faith. The ideology of 'secular humanism' was predicated upon the twin doctrines of atheism and evolution as well as upon an amoral, bestial way of life. The true believers were, hence, outsiders. In the words of the popular revivalist hymn, 'I am a stranger here, within a foreign land.' Some theologians would even speak of a 'new Babylonian captivity' of the Church.

The combination of loss of hegemony and mass defection represents, in Protestant parlance, 'the worst danger to the Church since Luther.' *Haredi* rabbis (Jewish ultra-Orthodox) consider it the worst calamity in two millennia of life in exile. *Shiite* clerics, in Iran and Lebanon, like to compare themselves to the tiny host of Imam Hussein, encircled (and later massacred) by the army of the allegedly-Muslim Caliph (in 680 A. D.). What makes the danger all the graver is its lure and insidiousness.

The alternative secular way of life is alluring—for it appeals to the instincts, promising instant gratification, better material conditions as well as 'marrying one's own times' (in science and technology). How easy it is, and how common, to become addicted to it. Religious tradition is likely to be shed lightheartedly, often unwittingly. No wonder Jewish zealots speak of 'assimilation mania' as the major peril, while their Islamic counterparts dub it westoxication. Protestant (and Catholic) theologians have resorted to an imagery of sexual obsession, especially to the metaphor of AIDS—which they have depicted as an insidious malady contracted due to promiscuous behaviour. The modern way-of-life thus represents, for Christiandom, a syndrome of pleasurable self-destruction.

The insidiousness of the peril proceeds from its operating on not only the overt, intellectual level but even more so by appeals to the subconscious, to imitative action, and that in every walk of life. It subverts norms of behaviour well before consciousness follows suit, shaping social and ritual practice even among people who still consider themselves true believers. The end result is a state of limbo, the blurring of distinctions, confusion and disorientation.

'The number of defectors is on the rise, while the distinction upheld in the past between Apostates and the Faithful has gotten blurred.' This diagnosis, though taken from a commentary on the state of pre-Holocaust East European Jewry, can easily be borrowed by present-day *Haredim* or, for that matter, by the proponents of Islamic and protestant Fundamentalism. The prescription to the malady is to establish an enclave-like community of moral dissenters. Yet

the outer boundary of this very enclave is bound to be leaky due to the social and material temptations of the hegemonic, secular, way of life.

2. The Elect

What is to be done? All the enclave can offer are moral rewards, relying on persuasion. Cultural theory posits that the enclave must stress the voluntary character of the membership who are specially chosen. As we deal here with religious enclaves, moral suasion indeed relies heavily upon the notion of being elected to salvation by God. The community is, hence, said to be beholden to their commitment to the 'holy cause.' The value of each member is highlighted and distinctions (and least overt and formal ones) between them tend to be minimised as much as possible if not rejected out of hand. The egalitarian, low-grid, strategy shapes the nature of the enclave's authority, as we shall see below. Yet in the present context, what is important is that the notion of the 'elect' tends to create an impermeable boundary (high group) between an oppressive and morally defiled outside society and the community of virtuous insiders. A sort of 'wall of virtue' is thereby constructed, separating the saved, equal and morally superior enclave from the hitherto-tempting hegemonic community.

The wall in question may be at times physical, as in the case of the fence surrounding Bob Jones University in South Carolina. But even then its significance is primarily moral; a significance most obviously transmitted through the short-hand terms used within fundamentalist group (e.g. in everyday conversation in order to designate fellow members: Believers, Christians is unmistakable: they are the true-blue, full-fledged proponents of the given tradition. All the rest are cut from an inferior cloth, or worse, outright rejects—apostates and disbelievers.

The tradition, as could be expected, is presented as shrunken and under siege, nay even persecuted. The faithful are the 'Believing Remnant' (in the Protestant U.S.), the 'Remnant of Israel' (for *Haredis* as well as for Marcel Lefevre's Catholic disciples), 'the Block of the Faithful' (*Gush Emunim*). Shiite zealots in Lebanon are self-styled 'oppressed,' and present-day Iran is the 'Liberated Part of the Abode of Islam.' The virtuous significance of adherence, against all odds, to the Remnant, is highlighted by such terms as 'saved' (in Christian lingo), the 'righteous' (*salihun*, in Islam), 'redeemed' (the land of Israel, for *Gush Emunim*).

In order to preserve their virtue, it behoves upon the insiders to separate themselves from the defiled outside and to fight it in order to save souls or to win over to obedience to the Divine Law. The outside indeed casts a heavy shadow upon the dissidents inside, for it is not merely polluted but contagious and dangerous. It is all the more harmful since it may look as if it partakes of the same tradition as the inside, while being in essence its very negation.

The perception of ever-lurking risk goes some way towards accounting for the prevalence of conspiracy theories in fundamentalist thinking. They see everywhere the infiltration of some Fifth Column. The enemy—i.e. modernity—may be a sheep in wolf's clothing. Imperialist plots preoccupy Islamic militants. Catholic zealots fight the 'liberal satanic plot' against Church and Papacy, launched at the Second Vatican Council.

3. Black – White – Grey

The more tangible and defined the enemy, the easier it is to maintain the boundary and dissuade members from defection. The enemy's hallmark is modernity, which is man-centred, and assumes human autonomy as an end. The latent significance of this phenomenon is man's revolt against God. Imperialism (*isti'-mar*), the enemy of the Iranian Revolution, is tantamount to arrogance (*Istikbar*)—an often-used pun, directed above all against the U.S., its culture and government. *Hamas* militants see Israel both as a proud oppressor and as a tempting material civilisation. Yet such cases of totally dark, distinct enemy are few and far between, vis-à-vis infidels (see also the *mujahidin* in Afghanistan, Rabbi Kahane's Kach in Israel, perhaps the Pentecostal Christians in India), blatantly aggressive atheists and agnostics of one's own society (the leftist *Meretz* party in Israel, Hugh Hefner and Gloria Steinem in the U.S.). More commonly, the case of the 'outside' is made up of coreligionists who are de facto agnostics (unwittingly and by default), or are committed to modern idols (be they consumerism or nationalism) without openly relinquishing their religious affiliation and maintaining some eclectic vestiges of practice ('out of respect for tradition') but with their heart, and belief, not in it anymore.

So in fact enclaves deal and are entangled with shades of black and grey. There is no one clear-cut boundary, but rather a number of gradations. Fundamentalists spend a lot of energy on fine-tuning these shades of grey. Most Muslim radicals, for instance, do not accuse the society as a whole of being apostate (*murtadd*)—an epithet as bad as infidel (*Kafir*). Apostates are the intellectual elites, who spread the narcotic of the Enlightenment, and who, when political, knowingly institute man-made laws to replace the *Shari'a* (Islamic law). The bulk of society drifts away from the Faith, of hedonistic allure, the victim of brainwashing from above. Ever here, in the realm of shallow belief and lax practice, grades calling for different modes of action can be distinguished, ranging from admonishment to vigilantism in order to enforce religious precepts. Total separation from the lukewarm believers is rarely suggested. In fact, one is responsible for their salvation as members of the *Umma* (the Universal community of the believers), as they are still judged redeemable.

This state of affairs has its advantages drawing little by little some members of that slack majority into the enclave. Yet drawbacks and dangers are

equally prominent. Contact with parts of this many-shaded 'outside' may constitute an avenue for pollution to slip inside by sheer osmosis. This inherent dialectic grows particularly acute when the enclave is successful in its efforts to impose its norms on the 'outside.' Fundamentalists lobbying in the Egyptian or Israeli Parliament may establish such a cosy, and effective working relationship with secularist MPs that some of the norms of the latter rub off on them. Preaching to growingly receptive outsiders, one also learns their consumption habits, brings inside their audiocassettes, starts to listen to 'their' radio stations.

To resolve this contradiction, the leadership has from time to time run ferocious campaigns, besmirching all outsiders as evil, be they just lukewarm coreligionists, and imposing stringent rules of separation. Yet only for a while. Economic realities (these enclaves are rarely self-sufficient) as well as the various degrees of receptivity of the 'outside' to the enclave message, soon reestablish a chequered state of affairs characterised by shades of black and grey. Cohesion of the white (though not always lily-white) 'inside' is not easy to maintain in a free-floating modern society.

4. Space and Norms

Marginalization of religion is the diagnosis of the malady. Separation is the cure. But how to separate?

It cannot be done by mere formal, doctrinal boundary-making. As we deal here with religion as a way of life, it behoves, in the lingo of American fundamentalists, not just to believe in the Bible but to live it. And if this is true of Christianity where Orthodoxy is supposed to have precedence over Orthopraxis, it is even more so in Judaism and Islam where praxis as codified by *Halacha* (law) and *Shari'a*-reigns supreme. A viable enclave wields efficient group constraints and has its members conform to homogenous public norms. It follows that the most immediate product is a separate space.

Space is, to begin with, symbolic, as evidenced, first, in the self-referential terms used by fundamentalists. On a broader canvas, it is present in the vocabulary one has recourse to, suffused as it is in the King James' Bible in the Schofield commentary, the Talmud and its Rabbinical exegesis, the Koran and *Hadith* (oral tradition of the Prophet Muhammad). Language, in turn, is reinforced by the audial space created by the enclave which tends to prefer a particular kind of music: nineteenth-century Evangelical hymnals, Koranic psalmodies, Hassidic chants. Body language, dress (by gender), hairstyle, names given to offspring—all contribute their share to the creation of a distinct symbolic space.

Space requires, then, strict and rather homogeneous norms of behaviour. Strictness is predicated upon the need for clarity in an age of ambiguity and confusion. It is made possible by the fact that so much traditional (i.e. local)

practice has been lost by migration and other demographic dislocations. The set of rules imposed in these communities is hence, in part, a new creation geared to fight the laxity of the hegemonic culture. While obsession with innovation, typical of modern society, is flatly rejected, some innovation—not merely in adopting elements of technology (from tapecassettes to machine guns)—but even in religion– is condoned, provided it is hypernomian. 'Stricter than thou' is made the object of competition among members, especially with regard to ritual but at times also in austerity of lifestyle (e.g. in consumption).

5. Claims on Time/Space

The imposition of such norms makes for the strong claim of the fundamentalist community upon individual members' 'optional time,' as a group (not individual) resource. There is no distinction between sacred and profane, workbound and free. Note the way that the religious calendar regiments and punctuates the cadence of members' lives.

The place of ritual (church, mosque, synagogue) becomes the focus of social life. And 'operational space' becomes, thus, like time, a group resource, an object of the enclave's claims.

Welded by time/space, the enclave becomes an arena of sociability. Individual members find that most of their social interaction is with fellow members. Human warmth, generated within the group, compensates for the strict norms and tight time schedules dictated by the group. It follows that enclave solidarity is both confrontational (against the black/grey outside) and uniting, both negative and positive.

Yet the burden of claims (on time, space, behaviour) may be too heavy. How is it possible to keep the standards without condemning the community to be a minuscule sect? After all, fundamentalism aspires to ensure that as many as possible will persist in the faith, perhaps even create an alternative society.

The solution often adopted is to divide the community into concentric circles: an inner one of ascetic 'religious virtuosi' who observe, in a rather hypernomian manner, a maximum number of norms; and one or several outer circles wherein a lesser number of precepts are observed with the same stringency, and where less time and effort is invested in other precepts. Among the *Haredim*, for instance, the inner circle is made of yeshiva students (and their rabbis), dedicated to the study of Talmud 'for its own sake' and living off scholarships. The purity of their monastic-like effort is supposed to radiate upon, and set a role model for the bulk of the lay people of the community. The latter are gainfully employed, but are expected to observe 'fundamentals' of law and ritual and to engage daily in some evening study.

The core/periphery mode of organisation is not easy to maintain, particularly because slackness tends to creep the periphery due to both its closer

interaction with the Outside and its temptations. Controlling the periphery is a constant preoccupation of the leadership. When it does succeed in doing so, this mode enables the community to maintain an equality of effort (and status) at each level, while enlarging the scope. Equality is crucial, for in an enclave the grid has to be minimal in order to preserve its voluntary character. Furthermore, the periphery mediates between the core and the hegemonic society and allows the movement of moral dissent to operate within society—and even recruit members from it—without polluting the core, in belief or in action.

6. Cosmology

Cultural theory posits that for a type of rationality to survive in its social context it requires cognitive anchors—notions about historical space and time, physical and human nature, knowledge—i.e., a cosmology. The latter sustains and moulds the culture of the enclave, its mode of behaviour, authority and organisation.

Historical time is the most salient cosmological factor, whereas it relates directly to the primal impulse—the diagnosis—that Fundamentalism feeds upon. The community's time-perspective tends to be shrunken, collapsed and condensed. The past is reduced to a few key areas, closely related to the movement's notion as to what accounts for the glory and the decline of the tradition. The future perspective is short, pessimistic, even doomladen. The past explains the dismal present, the future is projected there from.

The specific content, the vocabulary, of the time perspective is determined, of course, by the tradition in question, by which we mean the living tradition and not some marginal past component such as a heresy. Fundamentalism is the product of the mainstream of the tradition, not a case of a medieval heresy rising from the ashes of the Inquisition. Here lies its strength and its attraction for the believers.

Islamic *Suni* radicalism was born out of the antiaccommodative attitude towards political power which had always existed within this tradition as a vigilante-type, legitimate, albeit secondary strand. Its most consistent and powerful paragon over the last seven centuries was the neo-Hanibalite school of Islamic law. When modern Sunni radicals looked in the 1920's and 1960's for a tradition to build upon, they turned quite naturally, like their predecessors in the late eighteenth century (the founders of Saudi Arabia), to neo-Hanibalism.

It is from such a living tradition that fundamentalists draw a time frame in which they are located towards the end of a historical era. American Protestants see it as a later stage in the Church Age (which began with Christ's resurrection), a stage when apostasy and heresy threaten Christian civilisation with collapse. Some would even suggest a parallel between themselves and the underground Church of the first century. Note the analogy with the Islamic notion of modern exile reminiscent of Muhammad's. The Age ends as it began.

Such a cyclical notion is, however, secondary to the linear perception of time: in crucial respects the present danger is unheard of, worse than anything that has happened since the combative early days of the tradition.

This pessimistic outlook is best expressed in the binary (before/after) formulations that enclaves are obsessed with. The watershed for fundamentalists is the historical moment when decay set in: middle (or late) nineteenth century (for Protestants and Jews), post-World War I (for Muslims); the second Vatican Council (for Catholics).

An imminent danger of decline seems to concentrate the mind, to condense the past. Relevant are only those periods which account for the present menace and/or which may provide an ideal to strive for, a model to be reconstituted (allowing for some adaptation to economic/technological realities). Sunni Muslims, for example, are fixated upon the Golden Age of Muhammad and the first four caliphs (622-661) taken to be the era when divine normative injunctions were effectively applied by the state and voluntary obedience was the rule in civil society. Thus the golden age serves a foundation myth—an explanation of origins, as well as a yardstick to measure the present.

The past has its counterpart in the future, for history, as American fundamentalists put it, is 'purposeful,' governed as it is by an omniscient Providence. The intersection of the past and the future grants the believer a secret road map, enabling him to comprehend whence he comes and where he is heading— a 'plan of salvation' in Protestant lingo. 'Whence he comes' encompasses not merely the 'foundation myth' but also the Decline, which consists of the spread of man-made, progress-oriented cosmologies. Major landmarks of this process, such as the abolition of the Ottoman Caliphate (1924) are intensely highlighted.

'Purposeful' as history is, it must comprise miracle, the breaking of patterns by an omnipotent deity, in order to further the plan. This goes not only for the formative periods, as depicted by the Scriptures, but also for the later periods, not excluding the recent past. *Gush Emunim* interprets the Six Day War in a like vein. Muslim militants attach miraculous qualities to the demise of Nasser (1967-1970).

Perceptions of the future are as binary as those of the past and are likewise permeated by the symbolic capital of the given tradition. One should stress, however, that this is no mere perception but also a call for action, having definite behavioural consequences. The dominant strand in American Fundamentalism is premillennial and pretribulationist (a tradition imported from Ireland in the mid-nineteenth century). Its message of messianic Redemption following an imminent catastrophe (wherefrom only 'saved' Christians would escape) sat well with the beleaguered mood in the independent Baptist Churches in the early twentieth century. It seemed to be confirmed by the carnage of World War I which dealt a heavy blow to the 'illusions of progress.'

Premillenialism is indeed a strong incentive for an effort towards personal salvation, with the independent church serving as the support group. It sets

limits to sallies into the Outside, which are geared to recruit new members (who may be among the saved), and to improve the Christian quality of life in the immediate vicinity of the enclave, a sort of protective perimeter. Transforming the entire society is usually viewed as an impossibility in this day and age. It can only come after the Tribulation is over; but there is no telling when this will be, even though this is definitely the last stage of the Church Age. Both the Rapture (the miraculous saving) and the subsequent seven years of tribulation are expected to take place at some indeterminate date.

Possessing the secret road map for the future is likely to empower the enclave member, fill him with a sense of orientation, enable him to 'decipher' oncoming events. One can identify players on the world (or national scene) by their biblical codes: Russia, for the pessimistic American messianists described above, is the Kingdom of the South (or Magog). Code names are pointers to the ultimate behaviour and fate of the players. Deciphering them is evidently helpful for decisionmaking in conditions of uncertainty, i.e. in moulding risk perception and risk management strategies. As risk is a cultural construct, moral commitments do enter in its evaluation and in the lessons drawn therefrom.

The fundamentalist enclave tends to see itself as inherently fragile, given the ever-lurking Outside. Its future is expected to be different from the present, most probably—in the short run, at least—for the worse (or for the worse preceding change for the better). The enclave must, hence, fear irreversible, involuntary and hidden changes; changes about which there is imperfect knowledge and little or no control. A fundamentalist group rarely discounts a piece of bad news about future events. This explains, to repeat, its propensity to indulge in conspiracy theories, as well as the shrill tone of its press and preachers in reporting current events.

It is indeed risk obsession which underlies the *Haredi* view that Jews in the Exilic Age are eternally persecuted by hateful 'goyish' nations, 'a lamb surrounded by seventy wolves,' harassed (at times oppressed) by obtuse if not hostile 'apostate' Jews. Both evil forces are powerful and have already brought catastrophes upon the Faithful (Holocaust, assimilation) and may perpetrate worse. The strategy, therefore, must consist of risk avoidance (or risk minimisation): as little confrontation as possible (limiting, at times, the scope of the 'sallies'); no provocation of the type which had cost Jews the destruction of the Second Temple and the loss of sovereignty, ushering in the Exilic Age. This concept ('The Three Oaths') makes the *Haredi* parties adopt, on the whole, dovish attitudes to the Arab-Israeli conflict. Their prominent rabbis severely condemned their own hotheads, yeshiva students who (in the early 1950s) dynamited and set fire to shops and restaurants that broke the Shabbat, sold pork etc. This is not a recent attitude. The concept of the 'Three Oaths' is embedded in Talmudic literature (treatise *Ketuboth*) and represents a major strand of Jewish thought and action all through the medieval and modern periods. It underlies

the rejection of Zionism by Hassidic rabbis in the interwar era as a movement which breaks the commitment not to 'take off the yoke of exile.'

The Lubavitcher Hassidim are the exception to this *Haredi* pattern. Most *Haredim* do not renounce the hope that the Messiah may come 'soon,' but that is in principle only. The Lubavitchers had intimations of this imminent arrival, during the very life of the Rabbi. The process of Redemption had already begun. Their future perspective was not just shorter, it was optimistic. Risks were, hence, of small magnitude or are to be more than compensated for by redemption which is just around the corner. Risk-taking was justified. 'Goyish' threats were discounted. The Lubavitcher Rebbe was rigidly hawkish in terms of holding on to Judea and Samaria, the sacred arena of redemption (and that although he recognised the State of Israel only de facto).

So much for cosmological time. What about cosmological space? By that we mean space as learned—not as directly experienced (the latter being dubbed 'operational'). In such a context, physical realities, so crucial for operational space (for example, a contiguous area around the mosque/synagogue/church creating a 'sacred environment') lose much of their value. Areas physically far away may be perceived as structurally near. Children in afternoon classes held in a Cairo mosque declared to me that the Philippines and Burma are 'lands close to our heart' because of Muslim minorities persecuted there. Other than that they knew nothing about these countries, not even what their majority religion was. *Haredi* school children in Bnai Brak easily tackled Poland and the Soviet Union on a globe, pinpointing towns in which major Hassidic sects originated. But they were otherwise quite ignorant as to the geography of these states. Jerrry Falwell's moral (or imaginary) space refers above all to the 200-odd churches whose pastors are graduates of Liberty University—the saved enclave in pagan America.

Cosmological space is not linear. One may not actually care for 'apostate' neighbours, yet feel intense affinity with members of like-minded enclaves. The common model is that of concentric circles in diminishing status of spatial importance. 'Egypt for me is this [*al-Nur*] mosque with its afternoon and evening school, its preschool and outpatient facilities,' says a radical sheik in northern Cairo. 'This working-class area [*al-Abbasiyya*] where most of our members live is our immediate buffer. Beyond, I look at Egypt as a map studded by those *ahli* mosques engaged in the same sacred work of changing Egyptian society from within. And beyond that? I do care for our long suffering brethren in Palestine and in the Sudan. and beyond that, well, the whole *Dar al-Islam* [Abode of Islam, countries where Islam is the majority religion] at least in as much as it is populated by Muslims enraged by apostasy and resolved to combat it.'

What is striking in this interview is that despite the sheik's repugnance for the nation-state ideology of Sadat and Mubarak (a 'polytheistic idolatry'), Egypt is the outer circle he cares for most. Transforming Egyptian society (not

Dar al-Islam in general) is the maximum he can hope for. The division of *Dar al-Islam* into territorial states is deplored but accepted as a *fait accompli*. These radicals are not obtuse, neither are they indifferent to geopolitical realities.

Finally, what about the human agent operating within the confines of time and space? The *Hafetz Hayyim*, founder of Jewish ultra-Orthodoxy, seems to have said it all for his Christian and Muslim counterparts: 'The whole world is topsy-turvy, our religion suffers persecutions, is vilified by infidels, ridiculed by apostates—let alone that each and everyone of us suffers from his own evil will.' Human nature is bad—though perfectible—and subject to constant infiltration of outside impurity. The advice to the faithful is clear: always be on your guard, strive to the faithful defences against temptations, clean up your act by meditation and strict behaviour. Any visitor listening to tapes played by taxi drivers in Cairo and Jerusalem is likely to hear Sheik Abd al-Hamid Kishk or Rabbi Nissim Yagen dispensing such counsel.

The underlying assumption is always one and the same: there is a strong correlation—set and controlled by Divine Providence—between Macro and Micro, the state of physical nature and human nature, society and morality. Social disorder is but a symptom of the individual's moral transgressions on the Inside as well as on the Outside (e.g., the decline of the traditional family in the U.S., the spread of homosexuality and abortion, higher criminality, AIDS, lower economic performance and lesser clout in world politics). 'Our problems are neither economic nor political, our problems are moral,' chanted the Islamic demonstrators in Algeria during the 'couscous riots' (fall 1988). Their firebrand preacher, Ali Belhadj, claimed later that the consecutive droughts in recent years are the result of sexual permissiveness, mixed education, soccer fever and the video craze.

Yet human nature is capable of improvement. Both *Haredis* and independent Baptists point as a guideline to the proverbs verse: 'He who spares the rod spoils the child,' acting upon this at home. By extension, they seek to impose stringent regulations on behaviour in school, streets, swimming beaches and malls subject to municipalities they control, as did mayors associated with the *Front Islamique du Salut* (1990/91). Particular attention is given to the norms related to women, that 'weak-by-nature' agency through which Evil insinuates its way. This has to do not merely with sex-related issues—'women are a constant temptation to men'—say the Islamicists—but also to consumption. Female obsession with material acquisitions is said to nudge their husbands towards individualistic (market oriented, i.e. low-group/low-grid) efforts which threaten from within the equality and austerity of the enclave. It may lead to competitive shopping, conspicuous consumption, limiting fertility (to three or four children) etc. This is why, though in principle fundamentalists think women should be given lesser education than men, for their task lies at home in accordance with their nurturing calling, they do in fact invest a lot in continuing education for women, during their entire lifespan.

It is through education that some harmony between nature and society, society and the individual may be restored, provided that the rotten inside is purged, outside influence barred, boundaries reimposed.

7. Governance and Empowerment

Authority is the murkiest, most vulnerable aspect of an enclave, posits culture theory. This is indeed the case with regard to fundamentalist communities. These communities are predicated upon voluntary membership and upon the equality of the virtuous insiders. Such characteristics, combined together, produce an unintended consequence: they hamper decisionmaking and render authority ambiguous. This is all the more acute as formal ranking and differentiated remuneration tend to be shunned (or minimised) for fear of defection. Who is, then, to constrain whom? How will virtue be maintained and strife avoided?

The solution to this quandary lies, in part, in the doctrine of the inerrancy of the authoritative text (and its approved commentaries) which takes pride of place in all the religious enclaves discussed in this essay: the Scofield Bible; papal encyclicals and Church council resolutions; the Talmud (and the codes based upon it, notably the *Shulhan 'Arukh*); *Qur'an*, *Hadith* (oral tradition) and *Shari'a*. So central are these texts, even to everyday life, that enclave members resort to 'bringing out the word,' i.e., a random selection of a page in order to deduce instructions or omens for mundane choices and actions. The term is Protestant but the custom appears in Jewish and Muslim enclaves as well. Of course, the major use of the texts is as a sort of objective, impersonal tool to set boundaries between virtue/vice, Inside/Outside. Yet to function properly they require some flesh-and-blood authority, preferably alive, to interpret them. For without interpretation—whether literal, allegorical or otherwise—how can the text be applied to rapidly changing realities of our time? Still, this has to be done in a manner which will not introduce institutional hierarchy into the enclave and thus disrupt that cherished asset, the intrinsic equality of the insiders.

In no area is the modern nature of the enclave more evident than in that of authority, fashioned as it is in quite a novel way. Authority is usually vested there in a small number of individuals (preferably one, at least for each local community of the enclave). Scholarship and formal training may play a role in the selection of the leader(s), but the crucial factor is charisma: that special heavenly grace which sets one man—it's virtually never a woman—apart from the rest of the enclave members, combining virtue, decisionmaking ability and mastery of the tradition.

Khomeini, despite his long career as scholar and teacher on a *Qom madrasa*, was never considered to possess towering intellectual acumen before he entered the political arena in 1962/63. His most popular book, *Islamic Gov-*

ernment, is actually based upon lectures to theology students and retains a conversational style. His most effective medium, before and after the Revolution, were sermons and talks (distributed on tape cassettes, later on TV), delivered in a homespun style—reminiscent of the fables which Hafetz Hayyim was famous for—and utilising an old fashioned rural-provincial vocabulary.

Other examples abound: The Hassidic rabbis of the *Haredim*, and even more telling—the Yeshiva heads, promoted by intellectual achievement but surrounded by a virtual Hassidic adulation, the televangelical preachers in the U.S., Luigi Guissani, the mentor of North Italian students, who founded the *Communione e Liberazione* movement, anti-Vatican II Catholic traditionalism (at least until the death of Archbishop Lefebvre).

Charismatic authority was upgraded to the level of full-fledged (and new) doctrine in *Haredi* and *Shi'ite* circules. Faced with the decline of the authority of the local community's rabbi throughout the nineteenth century, the *Haredis* developed, especially during the second quarter of the twentieth century, the concept of *Da'at Torah*: the authority of the great Torah scholar. The Torah scholar gained this authority by virtue of his total immersion in the scriptural-exegetical tradition as well as his model lifestyle and character, and was thus qualified to issue binding rulings, not just on purely Halakhic matters but likewise in mundane issues of the day, including politics. Each autonomous *Haredi* grouping—constituted around a major *yeshiva* or Hassidic court—has such a *gadol* at its head. The structure of the Haredi world, which leaves sufficient leeway for the various 'circles,' is, in consequence, a sort of loose confederation of enclaves—not entirely unlike a network of independent Baptist churches (those grouped around the Convention; Operation Rescue, Christian Voice, the Religious Round Table; churches shepherded by graduates of Liberty University) or Sunni groups (*jama'at*) subscribing more or less to the same ideological variant (e.g., *Tanzim al-Jihad*).

The *yeshiva* heads, as men who control the core ascetic groups and who serve as models for the whole *chug* (group), have transferred into their own hands decisionmaking powers (on matters political, economic, etc.) which since the Middle Ages had been in the hands of the prominent laity. The charismatic dimension of their power is best encapsulated in the doctrine of *emunat hakhamim*—belief in the sages without daring to question their rulings.

This doctrine was crystallised in these far-reaching terms in response to the Holocaust, which raised tough questions as to the vision of the *gedolim* in prewar eastern Europe, who had resisted migration (especially to Palestine), and many of whom had escaped during the war (thanks to affidavits sent by American disciples), leaving their local communities behind. And no wonder. For charismatic leadership finds it more arduous than any other type to weather a crisis of confidence.

The *Shi'ites* have the advantage over the *Haredis* (and the Sunnis), in having developed by the mid-nineteenth century a hierarchy. It was not, however,

a Catholic-type hierarchy, for it was constituted of *ulama* (mullahs), graded by scholarly achievement. At the pinnacle of the hierarchy were located the 'models of emulation' (*Maja' al-taglid*, plural *maraji'*). The *maraji'* possessed the authority to operate the *ijtihad* and overrule the lower levels. In principle, but not always in practice, they should be headed by a 'supreme model' (*marja' a'la*); since 1962, for instance, this post is unoccupied.

The authority wielded by this hierarchy—including the higher ranks (from *mujtahid* to *marja'*)—extended solely to legal affairs. In matters political, they could at most advise and admonish the ruler, which in fact they did quite often as they were less dependent economically than their Sunni counterparts upon the government: they enjoyed a steady income from tithes donated by the believers (as a sort of material acknowledgement of their holiness and from lands held in mortmain.

Khomeini's revolutionary contribution to *Shi'ite* thought consisted in the doctrine of *wilayat al-faqih* (Persian *velayet—e faqih*). He claimed that in the absence of the Twelfth Imam (said to be 'in occultation' since 941 A.D.) governing powers lie in the hands of the mullahs who are inheritors of this descendent of Ali; inheritors, that is to his political and legal—but not spiritual—authority. In a situation where it is possible to reach some understanding with the ruler, the task of the mullahs is to castigate his aberrations so as to return him to the right path. Yet when the aberrations reach such proportions that accommodation is no longer possible—as was the case, said Khomeini, under the Pahlavi dynasty—the mullahs must take the reins of government into their own hands. This duty befalls in particular upon *mujtahidun* (authorities in matters of jurisprudence) and the *maraji.'* One of the latter, the Virtuous Jurist (*faqih*), would serve as apex: in him would be vested not merely religious authority but also political rule (*wilaya*). The ulama were thus supposed to be led by the *mujtahidun* (*ayatollahs*), with the Virtuous *Faqih* at their head. The *faqih* mantle devolved upon Khomeini's shoulders almost as a matter of course, although he was just one of six *maraj'i*: first, because he conceived the whole doctrine, and, second, his disciples (mostly mullahs who has been his students in Qom, or later in Najaf, his place of exile) formed a sort of 'circle' or nebula which was to constitute the revolutionary cadre (later, the Islamic Revolutionary party, the IRP).

In 1979 Khomeini was elected *Faqih* by the council of Experts, set up by the new Iranian Constitution, and placed above the President of the Republic. In effect, much like the *Haredi* sages, his was not a hands-on government. He would intervene in matters deemed crucial (certain appointments and demotions, the decree against Rushdie) or in order to break the stalemate within the *ayatollah*-dominated political elite (on nationalisation of land, right to strike, cease-fire with Iraq).

Among *Haredim*'s decisionmaking is heavily influenced by chug or party organisers (*'asqanim*) who may not have any formal position but carry weight

either as wealthy *ba'ale batim* or as shrewd manipulators and mediators with the outside. Because the *gadol* depends on the organiser for his information as well as upon his uncanny assessment of the 'world,' the latter's input may be crucial. The *gadol* is shielded, in part, by the fact that his is no hands-on government. He tries to intervene selectively and rarely.

It follows that in actual fact, both in the *Haredi* and *Shi'ite* cases, and in American Protestantism (e.g. the Jerry Falwell network, the southern Baptist Convention)—we have a dosage of hierarchical (high grid/high group) and enclavist modes of organisation, due to the fact that they control substantial resources. A bureaucracy has oversight in such a 'confederation' (producing educational material, negotiating with the state, channelling funds, training future teachers and local religious leaders etc.). Yet this bureaucracy is kept with as few grades/grids as possible (a 'small hierarchy' in cultural theory terms); it is headed by a charismatic authority which can cut through layers of the bureaucracy and act directly, and substantial autonomy is devolved upon local pastors, mullahs and rabbis.

This seemingly brilliant innovation is not immune to contradictions and pressures. First, and foremost, it depends (even in the case of 'small' hierarchies) upon force of personality and rhetorical skills. The demise of the leader (whether at the top or at the local level) may throw the whole delicate equilibrium into turmoil. Thus the death of Khomeini dealt a heavy blow to the charismatic facet of the *Faqih* institution, due to the paler personality of his successor, Ali Khamene'i (who can likewise be faulted for his scholarly record).

The catholic anti-Vatican II movement has still not recovered from the death of Archbishop Lefebvre who was replaced by a Church bureaucrat. The Lubavitcher awaited with trepidation the disappearance of the Rebbe and this is why they underwent a messianic crisis. As the Rebbe had no offspring, and thus could not have dynastic succession in the manner common to Hassidic courts, the only solution seemed to be, again, a 'flight forward,' upping the ante. The Rebbe was declared, by some disciples, to be the Messiah and called upon to reveal himself in public as such. One possibility would be the move from 'normal' history into the miraculous End of Days, when Jews are ruled forever by the Rebbe-Messiah.

Secondly, splits in a fundamentalist enclave result more often from a personal challenge to the leadership than from an ideological controversy. In a way, splits are the staple of enclave life. Addicted as it is to homogeneity and to equality-in-purity, a 'loyal opposition' has no place there. Any opposition is bound to be accused of treachery and become the object of witch hunts, ostracism, liable ultimately to be 'exorcised' (the latter term, borrowed from the King James Bible. is a Protestant usage, but has analogues among the Sunnis, *Shi'ites* and *Haredis*). The sequels of splits, whether recent or long-standing, are the vituperation between 'confederations' (disciples of Haredi Rabbi Schach against Lubavitchers, *Takfir* against *jama'at*). These consume a lot of energy, generate much heat and are sometimes more poisonous than invectives directed at secularists.

Yet even without internal squabbles over authority life inside the enclave is not all sweetness and light, as its denizens would like the outside to believe. Grumbling, bickering and envious calumny are the price one pays for the idea of equality-in-virtue, as they serve too as means for enforcing conformity and for nipping in the bud any formal distinctions. It is not in vain that the *Hafetz Hayyim,* fully aware of the claustrophobic, hothouse atmosphere of the enclave, and influenced by the late nineteenth century *Mussar* (ethics) movement, dedicated a major essay to slanderous gossip, tagged as an insidious vice of the *kehilla.* That this essay has been, and still is, a best-seller and provides the topic for many a sermon or adult education class, indicates its relevance. The same concern is evident when talking to members of the *jama'at,* pursuing their press and listening to tapes of preachers.

An air of conflict and ambiguity envelops relations of authority within the enclave. But this is compensated to some extent by the empowerment of its members. Members possess a secret road map with regard to past and future, they know where they are located in space (operational and cosmological), they hold firm answers to questions related to nature (human and physical). Their behaviour is regulated but in an equitable manner with other enclave members; and not just for the benefit of other human beings (as happens, they claim, in other forms of organisation), all this rather for a higher entity. Within the face-to-face structures that form the hub of enclave life, members are thus kept virtuous, on a par with other insiders, superior to all outsiders. They have no human master except for one (at most several) guru-like figure, whose unique, virtually out-of-this-world qualities, legitimate his position.

One may hasard a guess that this may account for the particular appeal such movements have for isolates. By this term we refer to people who find themselves in a social context which is, structurally, the very opposite of an enclave-atomised subordination (high grid/low group). Individuals living in such a context are severely constrained, in an inegalitarian manner, as to how they behave, usually in terms of the category (or rank) they are assigned to; yet they do not enjoy the protection and privileges of group membership. They are manipulated, peripheral to all decisions, which may determine their destiny and have a limited scope for forming alliances. Consequently they are isolated, passive and conformists. Such people are not perhaps blatantly oppressed or deprived, but certainly alienated. Examples abound: American suburbanite commuters who feel stuck at mid-level in large corporate organisations; recent migrants (from small town to urban sprawl in the American south, from villages to the shantytowns of Teheran or Cairo, from the Italian South to Milan or Turin; Holocaust survivors and Moroccan immigrants in Israel, whose old reference groups have been disrupted; students in huge, anonymous, congested and understuffed universities in Italy, Algeria, Iran and Egypt who on top of their atomised predicament suffer anxietey as to the likely future awaiting them—as members of the *Lumpenproletariat* of diploma holders. What

they also have in common is that they figure prominently among recruits to the enclaves discussed in this essay.

The reason may be that a major strategy for extricating oneself from the manipulated/alienated context is to move into one diametrically opposed along the 'negative diagonal.' You shed your worst constraint—isolation and subordination to a large and impersonal structure—and you gain what you lacked most, group identity and insertion in a sociability network.

When U.S. fundamentalists fulminate against the bankrupcy of the federally controlled welfare state; or when the *Communione e Liberazione* decry the inept government bureaucracy, captive to political clientelism and big business vested interest; when *jama'at* decry the alliance of the all-intrusive state and the economic opening profiteers linked to multinationals—their message falls upon ready ears. Ears are particularly attentive among the multitude of people trapped within the lower ranks of huge, impersonal modern institutions (or dependent upon the benefits thereof). The ideal of *communione*, fellowship, *khavruta* or *jama' a* may mean here not just human warmth, face-to-face interaction and equality-in-virtue; it may signify the lessening of outside constraints and a measure of self-determination, Human solidarity, or *communione*, becomes, as in the C & L vision, both the social ideal one hopes to implement one day for the society-at-large, but also a mode of life actually achieved within a group (or countersociety); a mode which satisfies intrinsic needs of the members.

The antistate, anti big structures message gains in credibility to the extent that there is a growing consciousness in the society-at-large that these institutions function badly. Yet the message, couched as it is in lingo and concepts building upon a certain monotheistic tradition, require that their target populations be somewhat familiar with this tradition. This sets no significant limits in Muslim countries where in-depth secularisation (and the resulting profanisation) is still rather circumscribed. In other traditions this would mean that among people trapped in the atomised social context, prime targets would be U.S. evangelicals, catholic traditionalists in France and Germany, the Israeli national religious milieu, recent transplants from the Italian South and so on. Would it be justified to speak of 'black diaper babies'?

While the enclave recruits also among hierarchists and individualists, it has a special interest in the isolates, those excluded from the benefits of modern life. As Mary Douglas argues, they come to it less burdened, more malleable. For they do not carry the imprint of market competitiveness or bureaucratic manipulativeness—these prime facets of modernity.

8. Shifting Patterns

A culture is in process of constant negotiation, between its members and between them and the outside. The enclave should not be viewed as a type of

equilibrium but rather as a shifting pattern which *tends*, if successful, towards low constraints of group imposed upon members' behaviour and perceptions. But as it is shifting, almost never static, both grid and group are in danger of moving each in the opposite direction (high and low, respectively).

The *group* dimension risks to be lowered due to the difficulty of maintaining the boundary in the grey area discussed above. Separating oneself from a blatant secularist, be he atheist or agnostic, is relatively easy. Much more arduous is it to distinguish oneself from the lukewarm traditionalist. All the more so as many enclave members have relatives, neighbours and friends among the latter, behavioural requirements may be useful (avoiding eating and praying with nonrigorist family members, visiting them, playing with their children).

A hostile hegemonic society facilitates separation, yet when that society turns more accommodating, when religion becomes 'in' (as happened in Israel from the late sixties), the boundary is harder to maintain. An outside which goes out of its way to establish a dialogue, to be considerate, suffocates you with kindness. Dependence upon Federal and State subsidies made fundamentalist schools in the U.S. more amenable to pressure, but also more mindful (and understanding) of the concerns of the authorities. Total refusal of any subsidy, as practised by Bob Jones University, may be the only way out, but not one easily taken. Persecution is a better guarantee of purity (though not of size). It is however, barely existent in the West, while in the 'Third World' it may be lethal, leading to physical elimination of enclave (as happened to the Syrian Muslim Bethren during the 1982 massacre at Hama and to Shiite militants in Iraq in 1980, 1991).

The nature of the modern, open market society complicates matters. Unlike premodern groups, such as the Amish, these enclaves are located in urban surroundings or in suburban sprawls and are thus rarely self-sufficient. They get hold sometimes of certain economic niches which facilitate group cohesion (the New York diamond trade, electronics retail), but more often than not many members (usually male) work in various sectors and locations. Not only may they be easily 'tempted,' given human nature, as posited by the enclave, but behavioural requirements are harder to keep to and are less subject to social control. Outside norms (in consumption, entertainment) creep in casually. Distinction in clothing may help, but just up to a point. Even residential separation can be difficult to keep. The guards on the 'wall of virtue' are lowered and so does the group dimension,

The grid dimension is likewise the hostage of the material success of the enclave. Economic achievements imperil the austerity and genteel poverty which the enclave prides itself. Furthermore, it creates grids or ranks by wealth and positions in the society-at-large which might eclipse the equality the groups aspires to. Wealthy lay people may get some sway over the pastor.

As contacts with a more benevolent Outside develop, members of the enclave more conversant with outside discourse acquire a special rank as

mediators (Egyptian Islamic bankers or members of Parliament, for instance). The enclave as such gets richer, as it relies less upon moral suasion than upon manipulating members' dependency through material rewards (scholarship to *yeshiva* students), which the community gets from rich benefactors or from the state. The community thus moves downgrid. It may slide further along this track when getting richer, in group resources, and/or more successful in retaining members. Sizeable membership requires a more differentiated governance body, i.e. a hierarchy. One solution to block such development was discussed above, decentralised a network of enclaves, co-ordinated by a bureaucracy at the top (of which there may be a charismatic figure, as in the *Haredi* or in Jerry Falwell's worlds, or there may not, as in the Southern Baptist convention). Yet this a fragile compromise, already introducing a hierarchical mode. However much one can try to keep it down to size, the danger of the bureaucracy taking over, always lurks; especially when it controls resources and social rewards.

Depending upon a charismatic authority is, as we have seen, a tricky proposition. A leader may die and be replaced by a pallid bureaucrat or may be eclipsed by a powerful bureaucracy. Opposition to such a leader may bring about splits and the subsequent investment of energy in fights with other enclaves. the rise of entrepreneurial competitive market-type success within the enclave, might confer upon rising individualists (who are, by definition, low grid) a measure of authority.

An enclave subject to either, or both, of these developments—downgroup and upgrid—is likely to lose its religious specificity, be less of an enclave, decline end even die out. It may introduce outside norms and perceptions accommodating the hegemonic society (some *Haredis* becoming a-Zionist rather than anti-Zionist; Muslim *Brethren* diluting their opposition to the Jordanian 'secularist-minded' state as they are sucked into its political process; corruption and conspicuous consumption may spread through Islamic or *Haredi* banks and enterprises). Or it may lose members; they may drift into an outside society as separation landmarks get blurred; or they may defect as former isolates are disappointed by not finding in the enclave that absence of grid controls, and/or group solidarity, they hankered after.

As Algerian preacher Ali Belhadj—now imprisoned but whose audiocassettes are still enormously popular—never tired of repeating: maintaining the cohesion and purity of the *jama'a* (enclave) is an arduous and everyday task. or, in his Islamic lingo, before setting upon the 'small *Jihad*' against society-at-large, one must engage in a 'great *Jihad*' to cleanse one's own heart and group. *Jahad*, comments Belhadjy, means effort, or struggle, and a constant one at that. It is a full-time job.

References

Douglas, Mary (1984) *Purity and Danger: an Analysis of the Concepts of Pollution and Taboo,* London.
Douglas, Mary (1986) *How Institutions Think*, Syracuse.
Douglas, Mary (1996) *Natural Symbols: Exploration in Cosmology*, London.

Notes on Contributors

Gerd Baumann studied ethnology and social anthropology at the universities of Cologne and Belfast before taking up a Junior Research Fellowship at Wolfson College, Oxford. His first anthropological fieldwork formed the basis for his first monograph: *National Integration and Local Integrity: The Miri of the Nuba Mountains in the Sudan* (1986). In 1986, he began a second period of some six years' fieldwork in Southall, London's most densely settled postmigration area, which resulted in the monograph: *Contesting Culture: Discourses of Identity in Multi-Ethnic London* (1996). Among his other publications are, with Thijl Sunier: *Post-Migration Ethnicity: Cohesion, Commitments, Comparison* (1996) and, most recently, his textbook: *The Multicultural Riddle: Re-Thinking National, Ethnic and Religious Identities* (1999). Baumann is currently attached to the Research Centre Religion and Society, University of Amsterdam, and the Amsterdam School of Social Science Research.

Elisabeth Bronfen is Professor of English and American Studies at the University of Zurich. She has been guest professor at Columbia University, Princeton University, Sheffield Hallam University, the University of Copenhagen and the University of Aarhus. She has widely published on nineteenth and twentieth century literature, gender studies, psychoanalysis, film, cultural theory and art. Her recent book publications include *Over Her Dead Body. Death, Femininity and the Aesthetic* (1992), a collection of essays *Death and Representation* (coedited with Sarah W. Goodwin, 1993), *The Knotted Subject. Hysteria and its Discontents* (1998), *Sylvia Plath* (1998), *Critical Nostalgia. Construction of Home in Hollywood Cinema* as well as *The Consequences of Feminist Theory* (coedited with Misha Kavka) are forthcoming. Her current research projects include a cultural history of the night and a cultural reconsideration of the fifties.

Heidrun Friese, Berlin and Florence, received her Ph. D. from the University of Amsterdam. She was Fellow at the Maison des Sciences de l'Homme, Paris; the Institute for Interdisciplinary Studies (ZiF), Bielefeld; the Centre for Stud-

ies in Higher Education, University of California at Berkeley; Kulturwissenschaftliches Institut, Essen; and the École des Hautes Etudes en Sciences Sociales, Paris. She has published widely on the social constructions of time and the images of history, the anthropology of the sciences and on social imagination. Her book publications include *Der Raum des Gelehrten. Eine Topographie akademischer Praxis* (with Peter Wagner, 1993), *Lampedusa. Historische Anthropologie einer Insel* (1996), *Identitäten* (coedited with Aleida Assmann, 1998), *The Moment Time and Rupture in Modern Thought* (edited, 2001). Her current research interests are in 'concepts of happiness' and in 'German/Jewish Identities'.

Martin Fuchs, anthropologist and sociologist, is a research scholar at the South Asia Institute, University of Heidelberg. He received his M.A. from the University of Heidelberg and his Ph.D. from the University of Frankfurt/M., and did his Habilitation at the Free University Berlin. Martin Fuchs has taught at several universities in Germany and Switzerland. His main publications are: *Theorie und Verfremdung. Max Weber, Louis Dumont und die Analyse der indischen Gesellschaft* (1988), *Kultur, soziale Praxis, Text. Die Krise der ethnographischen Repräsentation* (co-edited with Eberhard Berg, 1995), *India and Modernity: Decentering Western Perspectives*, (special issue of 'Thesis Eleven', 1994), *Kampf um Differenz. Repräsentation, Subjektivität und soziale Bewegungen – Das Beispiel Indien* (1999).

Christian Geulen studied history and social sciences at the University of Bielefeld, and at Johns Hopkins University. He is currently finishing his dissertation on '*Wahlverwandtschaften: Studien zur Biologisierung nationaler Zugehörigkeit im 19. Jahrhundert*'. Since 1998 he is research assistant at the Kulturwissenschaftliches Institut in Essen. His publications include articles on the history of nationalism and scientific racism, on multiculturalism and on the discourse of nature in nineteenth century Germany.

Barbara Hahn is Professor of German Literature at Princeton University. She published widely on German-Jewish culture from 1800 through 1933 and on feminist and gender theory. She is currently working on 'Sites of Knowledge. Salons and Universities' and on Forms of Writing between Literature and Theory. Her book publications include *'Antworten Sie mir!' Rahel Levin Varnhagens Briefwechsel* (1990), *Unter falschem Namen. Von der schwierigen Autorschaft der Frauen* (1991), *Frauen in den Kulturwissenschaften. Von Lou Andreas-Salomé bis Hannah Arendt* (edited, 1994), *Pauline Wiesels Liebesgeschichten* (1998), *Die Jüdin Pallas Athene. Auch eine Theorie der Moderne* (2002).

Barbara Henry is Associate Professor of Political Philosophy at the Scuola Superiore di Studi Universitari e di Perfezionamento S. Anna in Pisa and is one of the coordinators of the Interuniversitary Seminar of Political Philosophy. She did research at the Universities of Bochum, Erlangen-Nürnberg, and lectured at the University of Frankfurt/M. The main issues of her inquires are: German classical philosophy, neokantianism, political judgement, German philosophies of technics and modern political myths, multiculturalism, political identity. She has widely published on Ernst Cassirer, Hannah Arendt, Martin Heidegger and Ernst Jünger. Her main publications are *Il problema del giudizio politico fra criticismo ed ermeneutica* (1992) and *Mito eidentita. Contesti di tolleranza* (2000). She edited *Mondi globali* (2000).

Hans-Jürgen Lüsebrink is Professor at the department of Romance Cultural Studies and Intercultural Communication at the University of Saarbrücken. He was guest professor in France, Canada, the US, Austria, Denmark, Senegal and Burkina Faso. He is convenor of the joint program of the 'Etudes transfrontalières franco-allemandes' of the Universities of Metz and Saarbrücken. His main research interests are French literature and cultural studies of the French-speaking countries, theory and history of intercultural relations.

Shingo Shimada is currently Research Fellow at the Research Centre for Social Sciences of the University Erlangen-Nürnberg. His main research fields are sociology of culture, sociology of religion, and problems of cross-cultural comparisons. His publications include *Grenzgänge – Fremdgänge. Japan und Europa im Kulturvergleich* (1994).

Emmanuel Sivan is Professor for History at the Hebrew University, Jerusalem. His book publications include *L'Islam et les Croisades* (1968); *Communisme et Nationalisme en Algerie* (1976), *Radical Islam* (1985, 1990), *Interpretations of Islam* (1985), *Mythes politiques arabes* (1995), *The 1948 Generation* (1991, in Hebrew), *War & Remembrance* (with J. Winter, 1998)

Jürgen Straub is Professor of Psychology at the University of Erlangen-Nürnberg, the Private University of Witten-Herdecke and the University of Chemnitz. He is fellow at the Kulturwissenschaftliches Institut Essen, where he was research director from 1999-2001. His work focuses on identity, memory, biographical and historical consciousness, theory of action, (cross-)cultural and narrative psychology, violence in modern societies, hermeneutics and qualitative research methods. He is coeditor of several interdisciplinary journals. His recent books include *Handlung, Interpretation, Kritik. Grundzüge einer textwissenschaftlichen Handlungs- und Kulturpsychologie* (1999), *Verstehen, Kritik, Anerkennung. Das Eigene und das Fremde in den interpretativen Wissenschaften* (1999), *Erzählung, Identität und historisches Bewußtsein. Die*

psychologische Konstruktion von Zeit und Geschichte (edited, 1998; English edition *Narration, Identitity and Historical Consciousness. The Psychological Construction of Time and History,* coedited with Jörn Rüsen, forthcoming, 2002), *Die dunkle Spur der Vergangenheit. Psychoanalytische Zugänge zum kulturellen Gedächtnis* (1998), *Unverlierbare Zeit. Langfristige psychosoziale Folgen des Nationalsozialismus bei Nachkommen von Opfern und Tätern* (coedited with Kurt Günberg 2001), *Übersetzung als Medium des Kulturverstehens und der sozialen Integration* (coedited with Joachim Renn and Shingo Shimada, 2002), *Pursuit of Meaning. Advances in Cultural and Cross-Cultural Psychology* (coedited with Carlos Kölbl, Doris Weidemann and Barbara Zielke, forthcoming, 2003).

Peter Wagner is Professor of Sociology at the European University Institute, Florence and the University of Warwick. He works on issues of a sociology and history of modernity in terms of both social and political institutions and intellectual discourses. His recent book publications include *A Sociology of Modernity* (1994), *Le travail et la nation* (coedited, 1999), *Theorising Modernity. Inescapability and Attainability in Social Theory* (2000), as well as *Not all that is Solid melts into Air. A History and Theory of the Social Sciences* (2001).

Index